The Bygone Wars:
Book 1

Songs of Space
and Time

by
Scott J. Robinson

ISBN: 978-0-9943355-2-4

For more information visit
www.tengama.com

This book is
dedicated to

Kelly

Like everything else.

Songs of Space and Time

-oOo-

"THE GIANT STATUES ON EASTER ISLAND? You know the ones?"

Kim pulled her thoughts away from the aliens and nodded. "Yeah, of course. In general."

"Well, they're called 'moai'."

"Tuki's people are called moai, right?"

Dongoske nodded. "But wait, there's more. My people, the Hopi Indians, who were based to the southeast of here, have legends about our ancestors arriving from other worlds by climbing up through holes in the ground. Our traditional religion is based around that idea with most ceremonies carried out in an underground chamber called a Kiva."

"Kiva is the name of Tuki's world," Meledrin said.

"Correct. So, suddenly, ancient legends take on a whole new light. Here we are, within a few meters of an underground gateway to a world called Kiva."

"But the Indian cultures aren't that old, are they?"

"They're a few thousand years old, but no, nowhere near the kind of timespans we're talking about here. We aren't saying that the Hopi really crossed from another world, but their legends had to start somewhere, and the coincidences are starting to build up. The predecessors of the Hopi were called the Anasazi, a word that means 'ancient ones' or 'lost ones' depending on who you ask."

"What about Roswell? That's around here somewhere, isn't it?"

Dongoske laughed. "Roswell is in New Mexico, not that close to here, but still within the Hopi and Anasazi regions. But, a spaceship did *not* crash there in 1954. A weather balloon crashed." He smiled at the look of disappointment on Kim's face. "However, when the Air Force went to investigate the claims of a spaceship crashing, they did come across something."

"A spaceship?"

Dongoske smiled some more.

Elsewhen

Elsewhere

SCREE OPENED HIS PACK and pulled forth his crappy bone flute. He doubted it would ever play a proper note in its life, but the sounds it made were still recognizably music and had to help. Scree knew it would make *him* feel better anyway. He had no idea how Ping would react.

And she didn't reacted at all.

Scree danced merry tunes all through the night, hardly stopping between. Ping was still awake and watching when the sun peeked over the horizon and he finally lowered his flute and took a deep breath. "It's strange, you knows, but I've never really needed help. I mean, yeah, sure, there were times whens a bit of help made things easier, but I didn't *needs* it. Because the only helps I've ever been offered was with things I cans already do myself." Except the monk. There was always the monk.

Scree examined the valley to see if any of the bats had come back during the night. A few kilometers away, settled into a tight group, were half a dozen of the creatures.

"You knows, other trolls came along and helped me bash things and break things and kill things. But, really, I could've dones all that on me own. You see what I means?"

Ping still didn't react.

"Being big was never a problems before. Being big was always a good thing."

Ping watched silently.

"Burning kittens, woman, how was I supposed to know I was going to need your help?"

IN KIM'S EXPERIENCE, strange mornings invariably turned into even stranger afternoons, but almost running over a geriatric Robin Hood before lunch could never have prepared her for how the day was going to turn out.

She hit the brakes and the crappy old car slid to a halt with a crunch of gravel and clatter of engine. She took a deep, calming breath as she examined the old man in front of her car. He came complete with the unlikely tights, hat and floppy feather. The spectacles were a nice touch though. She wound down the window and poked her head out into the cool. "Sorry. Are you all right?"

Robin waved away her apology and almost upset his hat. "I'm fine," he said. "It was my fault; I should look for traffic before stepping onto the road. I'm not as spry as I used to be."

That was obvious enough. As well as getting on in years, this Robin had spent far too much time drinking ale and not enough time running from the sheriff. Kim pushed hair away from her face. "Well, as long as we're all okay."

"Don't worry, I'm fine."

With a small nod to Robin, she got the car moving again.

The parking lot was packed and, after making her way up and down a few of the lanes, Kim started to wonder why she'd agreed to come here. She finally found a spot in the back corner where the roots of a large oak had broken the road surface, forcing the more careful drivers to leave a gap between cars. Kim really didn't care and ignored the metallic complaints as the car bumped and scraped over the roots; she was just about ready to hock the car to some other poor, unsuspecting backpacker and give up her wandering ways.

After a final clatter and hiss, the car fell silent. Kim sat and enjoyed the peace for a moment then climbed out, stretching her legs and back. Starting to feel normal again, she leaned in the back window and pulled her mobile phone from the pocket on the side of her pack. One message. She listened as Nina explained, in a French accent that probably drove guys crazy, that she wouldn't make it to Nottinghamshire until late in the afternoon.

"Shit."

1: Festival

Kim looked at the people around her. Some were heading towards the *Sherwood Forest Visitor Centre*. Most were following a gravel path towards the wonder and merriment of the *Robin Hood Festival.* Knowing she was going to regret it, she pocketed her phone, locked the car, and followed this second group.

Beyond the plywood-castle gate the festivities were in full swing. Kim strolled along, watching the strange array of characters who'd made the journey to Sherwood Forest to celebrate Robin's birthday. Robin himself was popular, of course. He ranged from babies in prams to men older than the one she'd almost run down earlier. Friar Tuck was popular as well — shaven scalp and all. Little John look-alikes were congregating around a tent selling cans of 'ye olde ale'. For the women, the three main choices seemed to be Maid Marion, witches, or fairy princesses. About half the people were dressed normally.

Kim nudged her way among the stalls, past a silversmith and a weaver, a potter and a dressmaker. There was carved timber, weaponry, wrought iron, and all sorts of things for sale. Historical societies had tents and camps where they could tell people about their little piece of the past. She followed the crowd, dodging past lacy wings, capes, drooping feathers, and curly-toed shoes. On any other day Kim could have happily wandered around taking it all in, but she was sore, and tired from driving, and pissed off that Nina had abandoned her, if only for a few hours.

She stopped to buy a hotdog and spent a moment wondering what such a delicacy might have been made of in the thirteenth century. Probably about the same as it was made from these days. A couple of minutes later she bought a salad sandwich and a drink for the second course. Making her way along the edge of the forest, she spotted a rare vacant seat at a picnic table and sat down with a grateful sigh.

Nearby, a young boy fired a blunt arrow at his sister and received a half-hearted smack from his father. A troubador got down on one knee to serenade an embarrassed looking Goth girl. A knight, helm under his arm, clanked and rattled through the crowd, smiling and bowing to almost any woman who looked his way. When he spotted Kim he paused.

Kim knew that look. She sighed as the knight jammed his helm onto his head and started in her direction. His armor gleamed. The faceplate of his helm was lowered, offering only a small slit through which he could look.

When he was standing in front of Kim, he bowed with a rattle and a screech of metal that made him sound a lot like her car.

"My lady," he said.

"You know, I'm really too tired to put up with this shit." Kim shifted slightly on the hard wooden bench and examined her sandwich. "I just want to eat my lunch in peace."

"Oh, I see." But he stayed where he was.

"You see?" She was trying to be polite, but it was hard. "That's surprising with that stupid bloody helmet."

He quickly reached up to remove the offending object and seemed to think he'd found an opening. "I apologize for my rudeness in hiding my face, but once I saw you I could think of nothing as trivial as my helm." As if he hadn't put it on just a moment before. But, give a man a suit of armor and a classic phallic symbol like a sword, and he seemed to think he could do anything. "My name is Sir Douglas."

Kim shook her head. "For Christ's sake, Doug, take a hint and piss off, would you."

"Right." He looked around, perhaps searching for witnesses he'd have to eliminate. "Right." And he did as he was asked.

Kim turned her attention back to her sandwich. It tasted better than it looked, which was something.

As she chewed, a haggard old witch zeroed in on the vacated seat next to her. The woman carried a twiggy broom in her arthritic hands and used it to clear a path. She sat down with a sigh of relief and spent a moment getting arranged. She leaned her broom against the tilting picnic table and set her pointed hat down carefully before turning to gaze around the fairground.

Kim looked as well, as if something might have changed in the last few minutes. It was a quaint setting. Picturesque. But, in her current mood, she could only take so much quaint and picturesque. She wondered how much worse her mood would have been if she'd been sitting in some dirty old city.

Several minutes later, when Kim was almost over the whole idea of sitting, the old woman spoke.

"I'll get you my pretty," she said in a convincing Wicked-Witch-of-the-West voice. She added a cackle for good measure.

Kim thought about that for a moment, wondering if she was being offered a line for the second time that day and suddenly wishing she'd chosen bachelor number one. "Pardon."

"I'll get you my pretty," the woman said once more, this time in a normal voice. She shrugged apologetically. "I'd have gone for something out of Macbeth but I can never remember much more than 'When shall we three meet again', and, well, there are only two of us. My memory isn't what it used to be."

Kim dismissed a couple of very lame jokes before saying, "Macbeth probably would've been more suitable to our surroundings. The Wicked Witch of the West is a bit far from home." Or perhaps a fantasy wasn't out of place at all.

"I know. A bit of a shame really. Old Westie is a lot more interesting than anyone dreamed up for Robin Hood."

"Yeah. At least you admit Robin Hood is a fantasy. Nobody else here seems to realize."

The old woman fixed Kim with a surprisingly penetrative gaze. "You shouldn't be that cynical until you get to my age. I think most of these people know Robin was a fabrication, or a conglomeration at best. But they just want to have some fun on Robin's birthday. Look at the clothes they're wearing." She gestured with a knobbly hand. "More of them are in fantasy costumes than traditional medieval ones. They're just having some fun and there's nothing wrong with that."

"Fun is great. Idiots, not so great. If a fifty ton dragon turned up now, half these knights would draw their swords and run to fight it instead of running away and calling in some professionals."

"Professional dragon hunters?"

"You know what I mean."

"Perhaps. But maybe idiocy suits their disposition today. I know being the funny old grandma suits mine."

"You're here with your grandkids?"

"My granddaughter." The witch looked around. "That's her there, by the singer."

"The fairy?" Kim asked, looking at a little girl with curly blonde hair and pink wings. She was smiling and laughing at the contorted faces made by the singer. "Cute. Shouldn't you be with her?"

"No. That's my daughter just behind her."

"Oh, that's all right then."

"Yes, it is." The old woman cackled her Wicked Witch cackle again as she collected her hat and broom. "They seem to have lost me. I'd better go, I suppose." She smiled and pushed a lock of stringy grey hair away from her face. When she brought her hand away, a few strands were clinging to her fingers. She showed them to Kim with a look of mock horror on her face. "I'm moulting," she wailed, then shuffled away through the crowd with a wave and a smile.

"Okey dokey, then." Kim shook her head. "She's probably been waiting all day to do that joke."

Eventually, Kim got to her feet and headed into the crowd once more. She examined some of the stalls and chatted to a woman about the origins of her very Scottish surname.

Just before 2 o'clock, the rhythm of the crowd changed. Kim joined a growing surge of people and jostled her way past several street performers as she crossed the main green. All the performers wore suitable medieval raiment, but one of the acts involved a monocycle called the 'one wheeled chariot of doom'. The two monks who owned the chariot, Brother Phil and Brother Terry, were soon lost from sight as the current moved Kim on. On the far side of the green the throng reached a bottleneck between two rows of stalls and the pace slowed but it wasn't long before Kim and everyone else broke into the clear and crossed a dirt road.

"Come to see the battle, have you?"

"What?" Kim turned and discovered she was once more looking at the Wicked Witch of the West. Or, at least, at the top of her pointy hat. The press of people was still too tight to make eye contact an easy task. Her daughter was hovering by her shoulder carrying the little girl with the pink wings.

"The battle," the witch repeated.

"Which battle?"

"No, the usual kind. Not a single witch involved." She cackled.

"Oh, har-de-har-har."

The witch craned her neck. "This is the tourney field, otherwise know as the cricket ground. They have mock battles and such here. Can be interesting. On the other hand, if you don't find this sort of thing interesting, it can be boring."

They turned a corner and shuffled along with the crowd. The makeshift grandstand up ahead seemed to be filling fast, so Kim found a likely vantage point on the grassy bank that ran along the edge of the field. The old woman managed to sit down as well, with a grunt of effort and a wince of pain.

"This is my daughter, Karen," she said, settling as comfortably as possible. "And *that*, is Jessie."

Kim nodded. "Hi, Karen. And hello, Jessie. How are you?"

"Good, thank you," the little girl said, cuddling up to her mother.

"That's good. Are you having fun?"

Jessie nodded. "I rode a horse and talked to a princess."

"Really? Wow. I might have to go see if I can go find the horses later."

Jessie laughed.

"They're only ponies, aren't they honey," Karen said, straightening her daughter's wings.

"You're too big," Jessie agreed.

"Oh well."

"You're Australian?" Karen asked after a moment of silence.

Kim nodded. "Either that or American, whichever will get me through the door."

"Oh."

"Long story involving elopement, unimpressed grandparents, and the CIA."

Normally a line like that got people interested, but Jessie asked a question and her mother was sidetracked. Kim was happy enough — she'd told the story too many times since hitting the road a couple of years earlier. She turned to look out over the field.

A dozen tents were clustered near the edge of the forest to the right. Weapons of all shapes and sizes were standing in racks nearby, most of them looking impressively real from a distance. Dozens of warriors, archers, and camp followers were milling around, but none of them seemed to be ready for action just yet.

The crowd continued to grow and eventually a group of eastern European soldiers from the early renaissance rolled three cannons out onto the field. Introductions and speeches were made over a loud speaker before the battle was declared open with a wadded-paper, three-gun salute. Parents opened their mouths wide in mock shock, children screamed with delight. Most other people seemed to prepare themselves for the real action.

Two teams filed onto the field as the announcer told the crowd a little about each group and the period and regions they represented. Then challenges were called and tributes offered to various damsels and princesses. It was all very awkward and overdone. When the battle finally got underway, it was much the same. There were rules and obvious safety issues that kept it all very sterile and theatrical.

"So, is this as interesting as it gets?" Kim had spent eight years in the army and been involved in real military action, much to her mother's eternal mortification. So, while she had a slight appreciation for the fake battles as a form of art, she could not put much stock in them as a type of instruction.

"Oh, goodness, no. There is no limit to the excitement around here. There are archery displays later and jousting. And more battles of course." The witch pulled a sheet of paper from inside her robe. "I have a map and itinerary."

"Oh boy."

The witch wrinkled her nose for a moment then pointed to a spot on her map. "Here, this is the Major Oak where Robin kept a stash of food in case of emergencies."

Jessie leaned over to have a look. "Can we go there later, gran?"

"We were there earlier, honey. That's the big tree with the hole in it."

"Oh."

The witch continued the inspection of the map. "The stream where Robin fought Little John is..." She turned it over as if something else might be on the back. The only thing there was a picture of the 'Sherwood Forest Country Park Visitor Centre'. "Well, I don't know where the stream is but it's around here somewhere, I'm sure."

"All of this," Kim said, glancing at the girl and wondering if she was about to give away a secret, "despite the fact he never existed. I suppose he's going to arrive later and hand out gifts?"

"He's busy stealing them from the rich at this very moment."

Kim smiled and looked at the map. "Robin must have been very skilled. He lived in an area not really large enough to hide a group of somber men, let alone a group of merry men."

"The forest is quite a bit smaller now than it was, but Robin *was* very skilled. He'll be at the archery display later if you need proof."

After the second battle Kim decided she'd had enough. "This is wonderful," she said to her companion, "but night is coming and I must get to grandmother's place before dark."

"Really? I know a short cut."

Kim smiled again. "Thanks," she said. "You're the nicest evil witch I've ever met."

"I'm not sure if that's a compliment or not."

"It is." She smiled at the little girl. "And you're the best fairy."

"You really think so?"

"Oh, of course."

With that she rose to her feet and sidled away though the crowd, back towards the main green. Amongst the stalls again she passed a man playing folk songs on a violin, an instrument that wouldn't be invented until a few hundred years after Robin Hood's time. For a while she watched a group of women working on a tapestry then moved on to a wood carver.

Soon, she'd gone up and down a few rows of stalls and stopped to listen to the shouts, cheers, and screams from the latest battle. Shaking her head, she started following a path northwards into the forest. A long line of people were strung out in front of her like beads on a child's necklace, though most were heading in the opposite direction. She continued forward with no clue as to where she might eventually end up. Perhaps she should have paid better attention to the old lady's map.

It was more than fifteen minutes before she arrived at her destination. The Major Oak, standing near the edge of a wide clearing, was about as exciting as one might expect for a tree. It was quite large, Kim had to admit, and quite hollow, with a high, narrow, curving split giving access to the dark interior. Some of the larger branches were propped up with metal braces.

Kim leaned on the fence that surrounded the tree. Monica loved James, apparently. And, according to another message carved into the moss-covered trunk, Nick had been here about ten years ago. When the excitement became too much, she made her way to a log seat. She sat down with a sigh and closed her eye. Everyone else seemed to have wandered away leaving the clearing strangely quiet. Sounds still came from the festival, a football riot heard from outside the ground.

Just when she was about to nod off to sleep, sitting on the uncomfortable bench, Kim heard a voice. At first she thought she *was* asleep, and dreaming. But the voice came again, deep and rough, in a language she couldn't understand.

"[The tree is huge, you must be able to get in further than that.]"

2: Wilder Parts

MELEDRIN HAD NOT VENTURED into the wilder parts of the forest for many years and, as she strode along the game trail, she suddenly wondered why that was. In recent years, hardly any elves went beyond the quiet dells and leafy dales surrounding Grovely. It was only the young men who wished to live the way they once had, if only as a way of avoiding their responsibilities. As a child, Meledrin had listened to her grandmother tell stories of weeks spent in solitude, wandering through the forest for the pure joy of it. What stories would *she* pass on to the younger generations?

Whatever used the trail that Meledrin followed was nowhere to be seen. She had carried her bow, strung and with an arrow nocked, for several hours without coming across anything larger than the robins and warblers that sang from the high branches or hopped amongst the undergrowth. She was unconcerned by this lack of game. There was food in her pack and she was enjoying the verdant crispness of her surroundings too much to bother with serious stalking.

Grovely was a distant memory, Palsamon a warm glow in her consciousness.

She had fought with Palsamon the night before her departure — he had spoken yet again of having children — but out here, amongst the trees, everything seemed different. The two of them had shared a cabin for 23 years, something almost unheard of. Usually elf women selected a new man to share their bed every week or even every night. They chose new, younger men all the time as if any hint of age might pass on to them. Yet they tended to the Ohoga tree almost as if it were a religion because its great age gave it an aura that could not be ignored. For Meledrin, it was the same with Palsamon. He was ten years her senior and could offer so much more than a night of entertainment.

Though Meledrin's friends would never admit to it, she sometimes felt they avoided her because of her loyalty to Palsamon. Takande often suggested she find a new man to raise, if only for a short time, above the ranks of the saveigni. She spoke of Halbaden in one breath and Suldon the next as if each was the answer to the same prayer. They could not read or recite poetry, but they could be used for physical pleasure and sent on their way afterwards.

Whispering a *Lesser Changing*, Meledrin pushed her long auburn hair away from her face, tying it back with a bright green ribbon as she continued to walk.

Despite the fact they sometimes fought, Meledrin knew she would not turn Palsamon out. When she had spoken of her need to spend time alone in the forest, he had understood — more than Takande or anyone else. He understood that she needed time to think and knew not to push for an answer on the spot.

Four days later she was still unsure if she was ready to have children, but it was an idea she no longer dreaded.

Her spirits were lifting with each step.

Some time after the sun had passed the zenith and started its long journey toward the horizon, Meledrin broke free of the tree cover for the first time that day and found herself in a clearing barely twenty meters across. The grass was lush, reaching almost to her waist. She looked up at the clear blue of the sky, shading her eyes to watch a brown eagle drifting in lazy circles. The sight of the bird's effortless grace lifted her spirits further.

Meledrin whispered another *Lesser Changing*, shadows to light. "Olin saso mo'koo."

So accustomed was she to weaving her day around the ceremonies, the ceremonies around her day, that she hardly noticed. *Ending, Lesser Questioning, Greater Action*. Those, and a score of other minor rituals, divided each day into controlled, manageable sections. Some of the elder elves needed to say the words and weave the patterns both, but like many others, Meledrin felt that the one or the other was enough. When her hands were occupied, she spoke the words. When her mouth was busy, she danced her hands.

Wading away from the protection of the trees, she hardly left a trail at all. She crossed almost to the other side, grass whispering around her, before coming across a three-meter circle of grass that had been completely flattened. In the middle of the circle, surrounded by chunks of wood and shavings, was... Something.

At first she thought it was simply a log, for stringy bark still clung to the outside, but upon closer inspection she discovered it was actually a chest. It had been carved from a single piece of wood, with a hinged lid and short, bulbous legs. She flipped open the top to find the inside hollow, though incomplete. The sides were rough, and the bottom was littered with long yellow curls of timber shavings.

Why would someone carve a chest in the forest? Meledrin wondered, shading her eyes and looking about. *And if they felt the need to begin, why would they leave the task unfinished?*

There was no evidence of a camp in the area, other than a small pile of food scraps. The condition of the wood and leftovers suggested the area had been vacated two or three days previously.

The trail the retreating wood carver left was a wide swath of flattened grass. Arrow nocked, *Beginning* on her tongue, Meledrin strode forward, too curious to let the stranger slip away so easily. She followed the trail for the remainder of the afternoon, occasionally stooping low to examine the ground, but generally walking purposefully, with the dappled sunlight on her cheek and a breeze coming in over her shoulder.

With the coming of night she stopped by a stream and ate fruit from her pack, content to sit under the stars. The chatter of the stream kept her company.

Two hours after rising the next day, Meledrin stepped into another clearing, this one at the top of a low, rocky hill, and pulled up short. A lush carpet of small, blue flowers mirrored the sky and on a flat stone near the middle of the clearing, was a chair.

Meledrin quickly examined her surroundings. Nobody was evident, so she continued forward slowly. She held her bow half drawn, but no threat emerged.

The chair she stalked was a sturdy looking affair, made from a slice from the end of a log, four straight sticks as legs and three slats for the backrest. But beside it on the stone were scattered the pieces of another chair and what might have been part of a table. It was as if a dining setting had come to the clearing to die. Or perhaps the chairs, the males of the species, had come to do battle for the remains of a loved one. There were no food scraps to be seen this time, but the scraps of industry were much more numerous. Again, it all seemed to be a couple of days old.

Meledrin took to the trail again with a *Lesser Beginning* and followed as it swung to the west, back towards the river and Grovely. The township was no more than twenty kilometers distant. She quickened her pace. As the day wore on and the trail failed to veer away, she started to run.

The carpenter led her home. On the way she passed a half finished mallet lying in the path and another pile of timber, stripped of bark but not yet starting to take shape. Meledrin did not slow. She raced along the path, lungs burning, legs aching, mind aswirl with possibilities. The stranger may well ben harmless, but she would rather be prepared just in case

She ran into the village late in the afternoon, exhausted and wondering what she might find. But all seemed to be as it had been when she left. Other residents went about their business as if nothing was amiss. The quiet life of Grovely went on. She jogged among the cabins, following the main trail — a ribbon of brown on the velvet of the lawns. Eventually, she collapsed under a tree on the edge of the common lawn that fronted the Ceremonial Hall. Without the breath to speak an *Ending*, she danced her hands in a lazy, perfunctory manner. A moment later, Delfrana tottered through the rune carved Ancestors' Door and onto the porch of the Hall.

"Meledrin," the old woman said. "Meledrin, you look as though you have seen a spirit of the dead." She came down a couple of steps. "It is not seemly for a Warder to perspire in that manner. Get you where you cannot be seen."

"Delfrana, High Warder, someone is here." Meledrin tried to catch her breath. "I have followed a trail from out in the forest. It led directly here."

"We are aware of the stranger." Delfrana waved her walking stick. "Now go, before a saveigni sees you."

"You know?"

"Yes. Two nights past, while we were sleeping, someone completed the restoration of the dock. Last night the fence around the sheep enclosure was renovated as well." The old woman waved her stick again. "Go and wash, Meledrin. Quickly. We shall speak about the stranger later."

Meledrin nodded and climbed slowly to her feet. Her legs were aching. Her shirt and breeches were clinging to her skin.

"Oh, if a man should see you now," Delfrana hissed. She spun about and returned to the Hall. Meledrin plucked at her clothes to stop them from clinging and hurried away.

In her cabin, Palsamon was waiting.

"I heard you had returned," he said, offering her a flask of cool water. "Larawin passed by not long ago. She informed me that she saw you running towards the Ceremonial Hall." There was more water in a cauldron over the fire, and Palsamon added more, even as Meledrin drank. He went outside to the well for one more bucketful then maneuvered the bathing tub into the middle of the room. "The water will be a good while yet. Why don't you rinse off first, while I prepare some food."

Meledrin nodded; her lover knew everything she needed. *How could I return him to the cabins of the saveigni?*

When the shutters were closed tight, she stripped off her odorous clothes and crossed to the cauldron.

"What do you know of the stranger?" Meledrin asked. Like all elves, she was tall and thin with slightly angular features, large eyes, and pale skin. She did not think she was particularly beautiful with only her unusual, copper colored hair setting her apart, but Palsamon was watching her avidly. Dipping a cloth into the water, she started to wipe away the grime of the forest.

The man shrugged, not taking his eyes off her though he was slicing fruit. "He is a large man. Or woman I suppose, though the latter is unlikely."

"Why and why?" Water sluiced down over her body and disappeared between the floorboards.

"Why is he large? Because of the size of the tracks his boots left. Bigger than anyone I know." Palsamon mixed fruit in a bowl as he continued to watch. "Why is he a man? Because he was able to repair the dock on his own in a single night. The quartet of us who started the task expected to be working for another day. There was much heavy lifting involved."

"So, we have a large man wandering around Grovely mending things at random? In the forest he was making things. At least, he started to. Nothing seemed to be completed, however." Discarding the cloth, she collected a brush to remove the tangles from her hair.

"Making things?"

"Indeed." She enjoyed the way he looked at her but was pleased to know he was listening as well. "A chest, a table and chairs, a mallet. All half complete."

"How good were these items?"

"The quality of workmanship appeared first rate. The craftsman merely possessed no perseverance, apparently. What is being done?"

"Not a great deal. He does not seem dangerous."

"I would still like to be certain."

Palsamon shrugged. "You might want to get dressed before you take it up with Delfrana. I believe I'll just stay here and watch your dinner and your bath water." With the fruit salad finished, he sat down by the table. "Of course, if we are going to all this effort of making you a bath, we could get you really sweaty to make sure it is worth while."

"Palsamon!" Meledrin gaped at him for a moment before remembering herself.

"Yes?" he asked innocently. "I was merely thinking that we require more fire wood. I am sure you are aware of the location of the axe."

Why is it that he can play the child and I cannot? Is it a thing of men? Or of age? Or something else entirely? Meledrin was not certain, but she tried to join in the spirit. In a moment of audaciousness, she crossed the room to take a seat on Palsamon's lap.

He kissed her softly, running a hand along her thigh, over her hip, and up to her breast. Though the sun was still visible outside, Meledrin returned the kiss.

-oOo-

Meledrin awoke to the sound of banging. Dawn had just started to spill through the window at the far end of the room, painting vivid stripes across Palsamon's muscled chest. She disentangled herself from his arms and sat up. The sound continued — a slow, rhythmic knocking.

"Wake up." She nudged his shoulder. "Wake up."

His eyes slowly opened and he smiled as he looked at her body. "Not again. I am exhausted."

"Listen, you fool." Meledrin climbed over Palsamon and slipped into a long white dress that emphasized her hair. Then she quickly pulled on a pair of soft shoes and tied her hair back with a ribbon — it really needed to be brushed, but she did not have the time. She had her bow and was out the door while Palsamon was still lacing his boots. The sound was coming from the old smoking shed, out near where Faldorin's Path began. Meledrin quickly made her way in that direction.

There was nobody ahead of her, but she was pleased to see that others were stirring in the buildings behind.

A few moments later she saw a man kneeling in front of the shed. He was extremely short, but broader than any elf, and solid. He wore only stained, cloth breeches and large, heavy, leather boots. He worked methodically, hammering a long nail into a loose board on the wall. His broad, bare back was to her, muscles flexing with each powerful, precise stroke.

Bang. Bang. Bang.

"Hello," Meledrin said softly.

The hammer paused, then descended one final time. The man turned to look at her. A beard, curly and unkempt, covered his face. Sweat plastered down his short dark hair, on both his chest and head. He was younger than she had first thought — he had seen perhaps 25 summers — but his dark, brown eyes seemed like those of a child. A strange contraption of gears and metal had been strapped to his arm in place of his left hand.

The stranger stared for a moment, looking Meledrin up and down. Four nails were clenched between his teeth. "Whistler," he mumbled, "you're the tallest dwarf I've ever seen." Then, "Sorry, did I wake you?" He smiled crookedly.

"Yes. I believe you have woken everyone." Meledrin glanced over her shoulder and saw a dozen more elves almost upon them. "Pardon? Dwarf?" She turned back to the stranger and lowered her bow. She had suspected he was a dwarf, but she had never seen one up close and would never have assumed. But he thought *she* was a dwarf?

"Work starts at dawn. That's the rule. Every dwarf knows that. And you dwives should know it too, if you're going to help."

"I'm sure. Perhaps you might have thought of some quieter work?" Meledrin thought it strange, chatting with a dwarf while the sun was still struggling to lift its weight above the horizon, but what else was she to do?

The ugly little man shrugged. "This is what needed doing. Winter's coming and if we can't dry meat properly we might have problems."

"Undoubtedly." The residents of Grovely had eaten mainly fruit and vegetables in recent years. The men trekked to the human markets and traded elfish craft products for whatever else they required. The smoking shed had not been used for a long time.

But the dwarf nodded as if pleased she could see the sense of it. "Keeble's the name. Pleased to meet you. I asked to be reassigned to your work gang. You don't have a center punch, do you? These nails just don't look right."

She examined the nails, considering what might be the correct aesthetic for such things — Palsamon would know — before shaking her head. "My name is Meledrin." She wondered what else she might say. Manners dictated that she talked to him, but she really wanted to be somewhere else. She could smell the sweat on him. And Keeble was obviously having problems she could not comprehend.

Others finally started to arrive, all with arrows nocked and ready.

"What is happening?" Takande asked as she came to a halt beside Meledrin. Her long blonde hair was loose and she wore only a sleeping robe that failed to cover her knees, but her bow was ready.

"They breed dwarves to look like trees out here, do they? Or is it just the dwives?"

Meledrin gestured vaguely. "Takande, Keeble is repairing the smoking shed."

"So I see. He is a dwarf, is he not?"

"Yes."

Takande nodded as if that explained everything. Meledrin decided that quite possibly it did. She did not know much about dwarves, only what had been passed down from older women.

"Why is he repairing the smoking shed?" someone asked. It was a young man, and he was not looking at the dwarf, but rather at Takande's legs.

"It is what dwarves do," Delfrana explained, moving towards the front of the group. "Go and get dressed, Takande. That is not decent." She poked the younger elf with the stick as she continued forward. Without the support she wavered dangerously and a Warder rushed forward to steady her. "Lacking work and community, dwarves go batty and eventually die. They pine away. It is a documented fact. From what this individual did out in the forest, and from the way he is acting now, I would say he is well on the way."

"What did he do?"

"He started projects that he failed to complete."

The dwarf rose to his feet, his face set. It appeared he would say something, but his eyes glazed over and he turned instead to examine his handiwork. "Done," he said eventually, with a small, teeth-clenching smile. "No smoke will get out of there." He turned back for another look. Whatever had been troubling him a moment before was forgotten. "If we had some mud, we could do some daub to really make sure."

"No. That will not be necessary."

"Well, I guess I'll get started on one of the other buildings then. I saw some loose shutters earlier. Hanging terrible, they were."

"No. That will not be necessary either."

"Oh."

Delfrana hobbled forward to get a better look at the dwarf with her bad eyes. The old woman wrinkled her nose in concentration. Or maybe she had noticed his stench as well and was unable to hide her disgust. Meledrin felt several women tense, ready to leap to the High Warder's protection.

"What crime did you commit?"

"What? None." Keeble fiddled with some of the wheels on his mechanical hand, winding the two pronged forks closer together then further apart.

"Oh, do not take me for a fool, boy. You are a Wanderer, are you not? You are being shunned. No other dwarf would leave the mountains of his own accord. What did you do?"

The dwarf hesitated. He examined the nails in his hand.

"What?"

"I failed the Singing Test. But I'm not a Wanderer. They gave me a choice. Change gangs or leave."

"Oh, I see." Delfrana grunted, relenting slightly. "Why did you try if you were unable to do it? That is the thing that always confuses me."

"I could do it, though."

Delfrana grunted again. "Obviously."

Meledrin was confused. Dwarves valued singing so highly they would cast out one of their own who could not do it? That did not seem right. It did not fit with the little she knew of the uncouth, uncivilized people.

"So, what would you like me to do then?" Keeble asked. "If you don't want me to fix the shutters? If you have a center punch I could finish this job properly."

"I think, actually, that you should leave."

"Leave?"

"We cannot have you waking up decent people at all hours of the night with your hammering. Go home, lad. Die with your family."

"But they will not take me back." He scratched at the turf with his boot. "I was assigned to this work gang."

"It is not possible for you to stay here."

Meledrin did not like Keeble with his dark, messy hair and heavy lidded eyes but if his only crime was an inability to sing, it seemed uncivilized to send him away to his death. She knew something of being on the edges of a community. "Delfrana," she said, almost taking a step back when the old woman rounded on her. "If all he needs is community and work, we can offer both, surely."

"Do you like rising before dawn, Meledrin? Do you wish to do that every day?"

"Perhaps we can find him some quiet work for the mornings." There was always plenty of work to be done.

"And for a dwarf, being near people is not enough. He will need almost constant interaction. Talking, talking, talking, every hour of the day. Probably talks in his sleep. He will say more in an hour than you will say in an entire day. In two days. Elves like to talk, Meledrin, but all our talk has a purpose. A dwarf will make inane chatter all day while he thinks of something he *really* wants to say."

Meledrin dreaded the thought of listening to Keeble's rough, deep voice all day but could not condemn him to death on that basis alone. "It cannot be that bad, surely."

There was muttering from among the group.

"Are you questioning me?"

"No, High Warder, but surely you cannot wish for him to die."

"I do not wish for him to die, Meledrin, but whatever he is to do, I wish for him to do it in some other location. Elves and dwarves have been avoiding each other for centuries for a reason. Our cultures are incompatible. He will have no respect for any of our laws or our traditions. He will challenge everything we stand for."

Meledrin wanted to say more, drew a breath to do it, but forestalled.

Delfrana noticed and gave her a solid poke with her walking stick. "Very well, Warder, the dwarf can stay." She smiled coldly. "But he is your responsibility, every moment of every day."

Meledrin gasped and tried to order her thoughts. "I am to be with him all the time, or I am to be held accountable?"

"You are to be accountable. You may let him do whatever he wishes, but if he does something I do not like, you will pay the same price as he." Delfrana's smile grew. "Either that, or we send him on his way."

Meledrin chewed on her bottom lip as she thought. She did not want the dwarf dead, but she hardly wanted to be his nursemaid either when he may well be completely insane. He certainly did not look complete, standing bemused but smiling while his future was decided. And she did not want to spend her days in his company. Meledrin almost told Delfrana to send him on his way — how would she get any reading done if he were constantly talking — but she felt a hand grip hers. She did not have to look to know that it belonged to Palsamon. She would know his hand anywhere: the strong fingers, the callous on the heel of his thumb. His hand squeezed hers slightly, and she knew, suddenly, that she could not back down. Delfrana would never forget her small rebellion either way, but the others would only forget if Meledrin was proven to be correct. And for her to be correct, the dwarf had to stay.

"Very well, Delfrana. I shall be the dwarf's mother." The child she was not sure she wanted to have.

Delfrana laughed at that and shook her head, but Meledrin saw the sneer that crossed her face first. "Very well, Meledrin, Warder of dwarves, but I shall be watching."

"I am sure you will," Meledrin muttered when the old woman had turned away.

"Takande," Delfrana said as she started to make her slow way back to her home, "I thought I instructed you to get dressed." She thumped the younger elf with her stick. "Do not come complaining to me when some dirty saveigni touches you."

"Was that wise?" Palsamon asked quietly, when the others had walked away.

Meledrin sighed and turned to look at the dwarf. "You told me to do it."

Palsamon laughed. "Did I? Well, yes, perhaps I did, but only right at the end. You came to that end by yourself."

"Wise or not, it is done and cannot be undone."

"You don't have a center punch, do you?" Keeble asked.

"Do you think I was correct?"

Palsamon turned her to face him. "Of course I do, but perhaps we are a little bit different from everyone else."

Meledrin looked at the retreating elves and took a deep breath. "Perhaps we are."

"These nails just don't look right. Where do you dwarves keep all your tools? I'll see if I can find a center punch." Keeble started to stride away towards the houses and Meledrin was forced to rush to catch up. Palsamon stayed by her side.

"Do you think he would bathe if we suggested it?" Meledrin asked.

KEEBLE PUT DOWN HIS BORROWED HAMMER and rose to his feet. Normally he wouldn't have laid a hammer on the grass, but the tool was already terribly rusted. In the two days he'd been in Grovely, none of the other dwarves had shown any concern about the state of their equipment.

"A bit more rust won't even be noticed."

Turning around, he strained his senses as he fiddled nervously with the gears on his mechanical hand.

"What is it, Keeble?"

Keeble had almost forgotten Meledrin was there. It felt as if he were talking to himself half of the time. She'd done some archery earlier but for most of the morning she had been reading, leaning back against a tree, long legs stretched out on the grass before her. He thought it strange that a dwarf would sit all day when there was work to be done, but he didn't mind. It just meant there was more for him. There was also a nagging thought about women.

"Shhh. Can't you hear it?" He scratched his chin with his fake hand. The gears caught in his beard, horribly short though it was, and he winced as he freed himself.

"Hear what?"

'Hear' wasn't exactly the right term. He turned to the east, peering through the trees as if he might be able to see what he couldn't exactly hear. But for all of his looking and listening, Keeble couldn't decide the origin of the feeling that had gripped him. "Don't know where it's coming from," he said.

He realized, standing in the shade as the sun dipped down towards the horizon, that the sensation had been present for a long time. "Been there for a while. Don't know how long, but I finally realized what it is." Or what it almost was. Or what it might be. He grunted in disgust. "Should've worked it out ages ago."

"Am I able to hear what?" Meledrin repeated. Rising to her feet and waving her hands in one of her silly little ceremonies, she followed his gaze through the trees.

"Singing," Keeble said. He looked around. "Where's my multi-tool." He'd found it in a shed and claimed it as his own but was forever forgetting where he put it. With an axe on one side and a sledgehammer on the other, it was extremely useful. When he saw it lying on the ground nearby he stooped to collect it then took a few steps forward. He thought perhaps he should finish the gate before he left. He turned

3: Builder

back to look at the gate that kept the three sheep in the pen. The fence had obviously been repaired recently as well. "Timber's such a horrible medium," he said. "Who'd want to make anything from timber?" He shrugged. "It's only a gate."

"Singing?" Meledrin asked.

"I don't like singing much," Keeble said. "You dwarves sing way too much. Must be all the timber, I reckon."

"You said you were able to hear singing."

He cocked his head to listen. "You're right," he said, once he'd caught the faint tickle of it in his mind. He was surprised Meledrin had noticed. "It sounds almost like the magical part of Rock Singing, but not quite." He couldn't hear the magic, of course, but he could feel the power of it, the rhythms and melodies waltzing in his mind.

"I hear nothing."

"But you just said..." Keeble grunted in disgust. Looking around for the source of the Singing, he discovered that someone had left a gate half repaired. He shook his head. "Very lazy." He would've finished the job himself but he didn't have time. Making a guess, he strode away through the trees. Meledrin, muttering under her breath, collected her book and bow, and hurried after him, covering the ground one step to his two.

After several minutes of walking Keeble stopped to look. He turned a full circle. "This way," he said, picking a new direction and starting forward again. The feeling was growing within him, flowing into the cracks and fissures of his mind.

The next time he stopped he was in the center of a wide clearing. The main green of Grovely was to the west, several hundred meters away, not visible through the dark columns of the trees.

"Where are we going?" Meledrin stopped by his side, bow held negligently. She pushed her fiery hair back from her face with long pale fingers as she gazed down at him. Not for the first time, the hidden depths of her green eyes unsettled Keeble. He had a vague thought that the whole idea of her was unsettling, but he couldn't grasp the idea fully. When he hurried on again she stayed where she was. He could feel her watching him like he could feel the Singing. It was as if she knew all about him, or was about to find out.

"What is that?" she said a moment later.

"I told you, I don't know, but it's this way." He flung the words back over his shoulder, silently cursing her loose tongue while he tried to concentrate.

"No," Meledrin said. "What is *that?*"

Keeble stopped and looked back at the dwife, annoyed that she continued to try to distract him when important matters were afoot. She pointed skywards and he turned to look.

"It's a bird." He turned to continue on.

"Yes. But it is extremely large, is it not?"

He turned for a moment to look, as if he, cave dweller that he was, would know more about the subject than she. "It's still a bird." He started to walk, picking up the threads of the magic rhythm in his mind again. Over to one side of the clearing he saw a building that was hardly distinguishable from the natural surroundings. "Ingenious."

"There's another."

Keeble looked again. There were a lot of birds. A lot of *big* birds. But birds were birds, and the Singing was etching its rhythms onto his bones. "I once saw an eagle with a wingspan of about three meters," he said. The birds they were looking at seemed to be much larger than that, but the Song filled his mind. "I'm not sure if they are birds," he said, having another look. "Whoever called them that is crazy. They're bats." Being a cave dweller, he *did* know a bit about bats.

He turned and walked quickly into the trees, not really caring if Meledrin followed. He stopped twice more, senses straining, before he was finally sure of his bearings. "This way," he said. With the direction of the Singing set in his mind, he picked up the pace until he was almost running. Dwarves and dwives were all about, clustered in groups and staring off at nothing. They seemed to be ignoring him for a change. Keeble ignored them back as he wove through the trees. He had more important things in his mind.

"I once saw a bat," he said, "almost a meter from the tip of one wing to the tip of the other." The bats flying over the forest were quite a bit bigger than that. He didn't know if Meledrin was following him.

As the pulsing of the Song grew in his mind Keeble decided that it wasn't really much of a Song at all. "The rhythm is much too complex to follow. If there's a rhythm at all."

But as he walked forward some more, he decided that there *was* a rhythm and it danced syncopations across his nerves. He felt the flow of his steps changing to match. "There *is* a rhythm." Or, more accurately, dozens of rhythms. He counted at least fifteen layers to the Song. "It's like a bar full of Singers all Singing at once, bringing their magic to bear on one place."

And that place was a tree.

Keeble stopped at the edge of a clearing and examined the monstrosity before him. "Whistler's Mother," he swore. 'Tree' was hardly a fit description. The tree, of a species he didn't recognize, was enormous. The clearing was more than two hundred meters across and the tree seemed to shade half of that area. "Seventy meters high," he said, though he knew it was not *exactly* right. For a moment he was horrified by the thought that he wasn't exactly right. He should be *exactly* right. "And the trunk has ten meter diameter." Close enough. He nodded to himself as he continued to examine the arboreal giant. Smooth, red-tinged bark. Leaves slightly larger than his good hand. And the symphony, the Song, dancing its impossible rhythms in his head.

Three tall, slim dwives were tending the tree. One was high up, sawing slowly at a dead branch. Another was collecting seeds from the ground, seeming to say a prayer over each before placing it carefully in a woven basket. The third, standing on a tall ladder, was reaching up to check the lowest leaves.

"Bugs, probably." Though Keeble found it hard to believe that any number of bugs could kill such a tree. He hefted his multi-tool and examined the edge of the axe blade. "A blunt spot." He sniffed his distaste. "Would you look at that." He turned to show Meledrin, but she wasn't there. He shrugged and started the hike to the base of the tree anyway. He stopped when he heard a shout of fear and shock from behind.

Keeble spun about and peered back the way he'd come. Meledrin *was* there now, not twenty meters behind, but she wasn't the one who'd shouted. She stood, bow at the ready, looking back as well. Another shout rang out and a burst of flame seemed to erupt out of nothing. Keeble walked back to stand by Meledrin's side.

"Dragons," the woman said, her emotions held in check like a flock of sheep behind the flimsy gate he'd seen earlier.

"No." He licked his lips. "Explosives."

"What?"

"That isn't natural." He sniffed the air. "There's cordite, sulfur, potassium nitrate, and some other things I don't recognize. Very dangerous mix. Unless one of those ingredients I don't know is the control agent, I suppose."

"We must go back and assist."

He turned his glance skywards for a moment. There were lots of big bats circling overhead. "I don't think we'd be much help."

The dwives who'd been working on the tree seemed to have other ideas. The three of them ran past, long ceremonial dresses not slowing them, hair streaming behind. They each had an arrow nocked.

Keeble shrugged and turned back to the tree. The others would have to fend for themselves. He had more important things to do. He didn't think anything could be done anyway. "I don't have any explosives and no time to make any." And there was no stout war party to take up the defense, just dwives and their bows and dwarves with light swords. He shook his head in disgust. He hadn't seen a war-axe or war-hammer since arriving.

"The tree can save us, anyway," Keeble said. "I'm not exactly sure how, but there's too much power for it to be otherwise."

The tree was calling to him like a steam whistle starting a work shift. If only this backward place had whistles and shifts. Bats were just bats, even if they could shit fire, as appeared to be happening. But the Song was astounding.

He didn't look up at the tree in case it distracted him. Adjusting his mechanical hand, he strode to the base of the tree and set to work, chopping with strong, economical strokes. He was going to sing a chopping song but none came to mind.

"Stop."

Keeble did stop, but only for a moment. He glanced over his shoulder and saw Meledrin staring at him in horror. She still held her bow, but it was forgotten. He turned back to his work. A nagging thought about women. "Bloody women."

Another explosion shook seeds from the tree, bringing them down like hail. Keeble took one from the top of his head and examined it for a moment, spinning it in his fingers, before tossing it away. He set to work again, a smile on his face. Explosions came more regularly. And they came closer. He could almost chop with the rhythm of the explosions.

It was only a dozen strokes before Keeble made a breakthrough. He jarred his good hand badly and almost bent his mechanical one when a thin wall of wood fell apart. It showed empty space beyond. At almost the same time Meledrin grabbed his shoulder and pulled him back from the tree. The woman was stronger than she looked, but he twisted free and glared at her.

"What do you think you are doing, Keeble?" Her voice was shaking with rage. "How dare you touch the Ohoga tree! You profane this sacred place just by being here."

"Do you really think that matters now?" He gestured to the sky, and there were still dozens of the huge bats there. Each had an assembly of shining metallic cylinders strapped to its belly, and they all wheeled about as if looking for somewhere to land. The clearing where the huge tree was located was an obvious choice.

The first of the creatures shook the trees with its enormous wings and settled to the ground even as Keeble and Meledrin watched.

Keeble had a vague feeling he should be afraid, but he wasn't. "The Song gives me strength," he said. Or perhaps it just distracted him.

Fires were sending thick blankets of smoke through the forest. People were shouting, screaming.

"Perhaps it isn't a bat," he said, cocking his head to one side as he looked. "It isn't quite a bat and isn't quite a bird." Either term would probably do.

For a tree, the tree was huge, but the bat-bird would've crushed it had it tried to find a perch. It flared its leathery wings for a moment to get its balance, and it was like a storm cloud had passed across the sun.

"Forty meters across," Keeble said. "It has to weigh a few ton. Something like that shouldn't be able to get off the ground. Especially with those cylinders."

But the Song was still echoing around the corners of his mind, and he'd broken through to a hollow section of the giant tree, so he didn't want to spend time working out size to weight ratios. He turned and started chopping again.

Another explosion shook the ground, and Keeble almost lost his rhythm. The Song kept him working steadily though, kept his mind focused.

"Stop." Meledrin's face was even paler than usual.

"The tree is hollow, woman." He took a great chunk of the tree away and crouched down to look into the hole. There was nothing to see.

"Keeble."

The dwarf turned. Meledrin had backed away a few steps and was pointing her bow at him. An arrow was drawn back to her cheek. He looked into her green eyes and shivered at what he saw there.

"Guess you'll just have to kill me. The tree is *hollow*. Don't you think that's strange? And there's a huge bat behind you with cylinders strapped to its belly." What they did to flight dynamics was unthinkable. Dwarves had been working on flight for a few years. "If anyone had come up with something like that bat they'd have been laughed out of the mountain. And quite possibly the forest as well, though who knows with you strange dwarves."

The bat had crouched and brightly armored figures were emerging from the two outermost canisters. The first such person was almost as tall as Meledrin and wore a chunky, riveted suit of armor with flaking green and purple paint. The second was the same. They were only thirty meters away.

"There's a huge bat behind you that seems to be a vehicle for people." His subconscious calculations of flight dynamics were thrown into the forge, and he began to recast them. "Can those people move about in the canisters, do you think? Or are they strapped in? What are they strapped to? What are those suits made from? They could use a gas that's lighter than air." He nodded in satisfaction. That idea had been doing the rounds recently in Tab Cavern. "Has to be it."

"What?" Meledrin still had her bow drawn. Thankfully it was pointing the other way. It was pointed at the first colorful figure but Keeble didn't think it would have much effect.

The ground was moving in a nonstop dance now. Keeble was having trouble staying on his feet, and he could hardly even hear himself speak over the hum of giant wings, the crackle of fire, and the clamor of battle.

"A gas that's lighter than air — hydrogen for instance. That could alleviate some of the weight problems. Though probably not enough, really." He started his calculations again, working on the presumption that the canisters were filled with hydrogen and the people inside either breathed the hydrogen — would that make them lighter than they appeared as well? — or carried oxygen tanks somewhere in their brightly colored armor.

He turned and continued to cut while he thought. He swung his multi-tool with calm urgency, taking out great chunks of wood with each powerful blow.

A fire erupted nearby.

After a flurry of strokes Keeble finally opened up a hole large enough to crawl through. He turned once more to look at Meledrin and was just in time to see her loose her first arrow.

The long shaft hit one of the strangers on the base of the neck and bounced away harmlessly. A second shaft hit the same place a moment later. And a third.

Keeble liked the idea but didn't think it'd work. "I don't think you'll weaken the armor like that," he said.

All she'd managed to do was draw the strangers' attention, which Keeble *didn't* think was such a good idea. Three of the figures swiveled slowly in their direction. The armor screeched in protest.

For a moment Keeble wondered what to do. Explosions were toppling trees all around Grovely with casual efficiency. *Attacking from above: what an advantage.*

"Shoot the bat," he shouted to Meledrin. He was about to say 'shoot the bird' as well, in case she was confused by the changing names. But, she shifted targets almost instantly, letting fly with deadly accuracy towards the huge bat's head. She hit an eye once, twice, eliciting screams from the wounded creature, then aimed lower, at it's exposed neck. The first shaft bounced away, but the second bit deeply.

Keeble grunted. "Huh. Just might work." It wouldn't work if she weren't given more time. With another grunt and a shake of his head, he raced towards the nearest of the armored figures.

"Stupid bloody dwarf." He dropped his shoulder and barged through the first of the figures. It fell to the ground and squirmed like an overturned tortoise.

Keeble might well have used the same tactics for the next target, but his shoulder was numbed from the collision. "That armor is bloody heavy. It explains why they're so slow," he said, as he swung his axe one-handed. The tool almost shuddered from his grasp when he made contact with an armored chest. "But it also makes them hard to hurt." And it affected the calculations that were running through his mind. The Song was still dancing around in his skull and he fitted his new sums in with it.

"I wonder if there are more armored people in that middle cylinder." It was impossible to tell.

For the next swing he reversed the tool in his hand and attacked a knee with the sledge. There was a loud crack and a hiss of air, but apparently no other result. Help for his victim was arriving, though at a slow, plodding rate. Keeble looked around and noticed that most of the armored figures, all painted the same colors, were pointing bulbous arms in his direction.

"Weapons." He darted to the side and gasped. The hair on his arm stood on end as an almost-visible beam of power passed close by. "Whistler's Mother. That felt like electricity."

More of the bats were nearing the clearing, presumably coming to drop off their passengers.

"Get into the tree, Meledrin," Keeble shouted. The woman had run out of arrows and stood silently watching. "Typical woman. Being able to fire arrows doesn't help if you have no head for battle."

"I cannot hide," she said after a moment. "I cannot run away."

"Forget it. What you can't do is *win*." Keeble moved quickly back to his most recent target and struck at the side of the already damaged knee. The figure tumbled to the ground, and Keeble whooped in delight.

Then he took a parting swing at someone else and ran. "Get in the tree, stupid dwife. That or die." He ran harder. The distance to the tree seemed to have grown. "You can't help anyone if you're dead, Meledrin."

"It is not possible that the hollow in the tree is large enough to hide us, Keeble."

Keeble ran. "I don't know. But it will. It has to." The Song was beautiful and powerful and had taken a hold of his soul. "The Song is calling me to the tree." It wouldn't let him die.

Finally the woman turned and crossed to the tree. A sizzling beam of energy passed through the spot where she'd been standing.

"Definitely electricity." Dwarves had known about electricity for twenty-two years, but nothing like that.

He looked back over his shoulder. A dozen arms were zeroing in on him, but seemed to move in slow motion. But he was even slower than they were. Loath as he was to do it, he dropped his tool. It wasn't good to leave tools lying around, but he was able to run quicker.

When Keeble reached the tree Meledrin had only just entered the hole. As he scrambled in himself he felt a sizzle of energy melt the soles of his boots and send a spasm through his legs.

"For Whistler's sake, woman, move. Move." He pushed at her, poking with his mechanical hand. "The tree is huge, you must be able to get in further than that." He didn't know why he'd thought the tree would save them, but the Song still filled his mind and he could not doubt.

When he looked back, he saw the armored figures closing in.

SCREE WATCHED AS THE NIGHT and storm retreated, slinking away like a pair of half-drowned cats to leave the morning fresh and cool. Two of Kiva's three brother moons rode the cloudbank westwards.

Sitting on a rock, Scree looked out across the valley and scratched a three-day-old cut on his bare chest. The hills on the far side, a couple of kilometers distant, were rugged thrusts of landscape, higher and steeper than anything near where he sat. But most of the slopes over there were covered with trees and were less stark. There could've been some magical line running along the valley floor, following the curves of a road. Life and greenery on the far side, mud and stone on this. The village that sat in the center was neither here nor there. The people lived on the divide between life and death and didn't even realize.

Scree smiled and licked his teeth.

The previous night, when the storm had been at its fiercest, he'd known there were people about but he'd been too tired to know where, and too tired to find out. Now he knew and intended to take advantage. He flexed the muscles in his shoulders and back. He wiped a slick of dew from his bald scalp.

"Yo, Scree," Gravel called.

Scree turned to look at the other troll who was poking through a pack as if he might find some long-lost morsel of food hidden in a seam.

"What we gunna do today?"

Scree sneered. "What do you think?" he replied. "We's going to run." They'd been running non-stop for more than a month. It wasn't likely to change any time soon.

Most of the Redworm pack was stirring. Grumbling and scratching, they put hands to weapons before they'd even risen to their feet.

"We gunna mangle that village first?"

"Course."

"Yeah, but..."

Scree didn't hear what the other troll had to say. His attention was fixed on the dozen, pointy roofed buildings half a kilometer to the east, clustered like flies around the muddy scar of the road. There was a small stone chapel to the south with a stable

4: Books

beside it. And a tavern hunched like a beggar beside the road leading north. Between those two outposts rough timber houses huddled together, butting shoulders despite all the vacant space.

Scree made his way back to the camp. Everyone was awake, sitting in silence mostly. Flint and Shale had just finished rutting. They ignored the clinging mud as they quickly pulled on their clothes. Lichen was neatly repacking her pack after changing out of her running boots.

"You lots ready?" Scree asked, rubbing himself. He grabbed his backpack from the ground and slung it over his shoulder.

With business at hand the trolls started placing bets and boasting before the deeds of the day were done. Some scrambled to their feet to demolish the rain soaked scenery with maces, flails and clubs. They scattered the brittle white bones of the bushes and cracked stone skulls.

"Come ons."

Flint was still donning her shirt, tying leather laces over her big tits, but Scree led the way down the hill. He followed a well-worn trail that wound a random course through the waist high trees and small stone cairns.

The village was stirring when he strode between the first of the houses. A man, hair like a sun-browned tussock of grass, stepped out onto a gap-toothed porch and stretched, arms above his head, mouth gaping in a yawn. Gravel sent the human's brains in a glistening arc across the wall of his home. The body collapsed almost gently as a scream erupted from inside. The sound stopped a moment after Gravel went through the door.

Scree stopped in front of a ramshackle blacksmith's workshop. Smoke poured from the chimney and a horseshoe glowed on a much-battered anvil, but there was nobody in sight. All was quiet. The other trolls had already disappeared and the village's residents were either cowering behind barred doors or running across the fields towards the hills.

Scree smiled and strode up onto a lopsided porch to attack the door. The first blow of his club split the warped timber. Two more and he stepped through. An old woman sat in the corner, shocked and silent, holding a broom as if for protection. But she didn't even scream when he left a muddy footprint on her face.

It was hardly worth the effort. The only food she had was a couple of leathery strips of bacon and brown onions. Scree grunted in disgust as he ate. He gave the old woman another kick. "Bitch."

Outside, Scree wondered where to go next. Just as he was about to find another house to search, he saw movement. A pale, human face peered from a narrow slot between two buildings. A moment later, the woman broke from cover. She ran, wild and screaming, along the street. Her night-robe flapped about her legs. Waist-length hair flew out behind her. Scree licked onion juice from his fingers and set off in pursuit.

The woman turned down beside a building. She was quick, fear lending her speed, but Scree was enjoying the hunt.

A fence beside the house slowed the human for a moment. She struggled between two loose palings, kicking desperately like a grounded fish, gasping for air and groaning with fear before making it through. Scree barely broke stride as he vaulted into the yard. He caught his prey as she tried to go over the fence at the rear.

"You not going nowheres," Scree said as he grabbed her around the waist. The woman screamed some more, whipping her head back and forth, kicking and swinging her arms. She barely came to his chest. All her struggles did nothing and it wasn't long before her screaming and fighting slowed.

"No," she said, barely raising her voice above a whisper.

Scree laughed and licked her ear.

"Let me go. Help."

No help would've come even if she'd been shouting. The other villagers had problems of their own. But *someone* had come.

"Yo, Scree. What's you got there?"

Scree was furious at being interrupted. Furious he'd let someone surprised him. He looked up, but the curse died on his lips. Mica was there, leaning on her club and smiling.

The trollop wore a pair of soft linen breeches that didn't even cover her thighs and a shirt that barely contained her tits.

"What you gots there?" Mica repeated.

Scree shrugged. "Nothin' much."

"Looks alright to me. If you don't want her..."

Suddenly, Scree didn't want her. He wanted Mica. The trollop had resisted his advances since joining the pack— he had a lump on the back of his head and the wound on his chest as proof of that.

Scree looked back at the human he held then threw her to the ground. Before Mica could react, he crossed the small space to the trollop and pushed her back against the wall of the house.

He tore at her clothing, throwing away her shirt like he'd thrown away the unwanted human. When he started to push at her breeches, he felt a line of pain across his throat.

Mica smiled at him as she ran the blade of her knife along his skin. "Are ya feeling lucky?"

Scree kissed her and she bit his lip. He kept her pressed against the wall with the weight of his body, working at her breeches with one hand and his own with the other.

She could have killed him, but didn't.

When he eventually finished, Scree was sweating and weak at the knees.

"That was good," Mica said after long moments, breathing as heavy as he. "But if ya done it again I *will* kills ya. Understand?"

Scree knew an invitation when he heard one. He licked blood from his lips and smiled. "Yeah. I understands."

"Good." Mica nodded as she stashed her knife.

"Finds anything interesting inside?" Scree asked, motioning to the house with his chin as he started to fasten his breeches. His breathing was still ragged.

"Nah."

Scree looked up from the rise and fall of her tits and saw her smiling as she dressed.

"It's just a kind of... watcha call it..? Book place?"

"A library?" He wiped a warm dribble of blood from his neck.

"Yeah, that's it. A library. Lots a books and not much else." The trollop gave up on her shirt— it was torn and useless. She threw it back on the ground and collected her club.

"Whats the hell is a farmer living in the middle of nowheres doing with a library?" Scree asked, more of himself than Mica.

"Don't knows that he was a farmer. Just a crazy old guy. I went in there and he was mumbling something and waving at me."

"What'd you do?"

Mica shrugged. "Smacked him." She thumped her club into the palm of her hand.

Scree was still looking at her tits. "Did you takes anything?"

"Nah. Like I said, just books in there. Down stairs at any rate. Didn't go up."

"Right." Scree had once spent a couple of months stuck in a human monastery recovering from two broken legs. A daft old monk had taught him to hate religion and to read. The first lesson had proven useful plenty of times already; the second was bound to sooner or later.

When Scree brought his attention back to the present, Mica was gone. He looked around— clothes hanging on the line, a small pile of wilted parsley, the whimpering woman, a bucket leaking water into the dust— then hurried into the building.

He had to duck to avoid knocking himself out on the ceiling beams as he strode down a dark passage. Bare walls crowded close beside his shoulders. To the left, a small kitchen. To the right, a room filled with boxes, as if somebody was still moving in. At the front, right near the door, he found the library.

A wooden desk dominated the room. Overflowing bookshelves lined one wall. Volumes, teetering dangerously, were stacked on the floor and the corners of the desk.

"They only needs one more shelf," Scree said, shaking his head in disgust. "How's they supposed to find anything whens it's so disorganized?"

A small book lay in a clear space on the desk. Its pages were stained with age, the curling letters faded almost to invisibility. A big ball, painted blue and green and brown sat on a stand. The human, head caved in on one side, chest bloody, lay on the floor under the desk.

Scree ran his eyes along the top row of books on the shelf and struggled to make out the letters. He sounded out each word as he'd been taught, but it didn't seem to help.

"Who is there?"

Scree jumped and upset a pile of books. He gripped his club tighter and prepared to do some damage.

But it was the man on the floor who'd spoken. He should've been dead.

"Who is it?" The human was holding onto his life like a troll with his last shank of meat. "Is that you, Akawi?"

Scree said nothing but stepped closer.

When he was a meter from the stranger, he stopped. A soft voice seemed to whisper in his mind, picking at the edges of his consciousness like a vulture working at a carcass. He didn't go any closer— he knew magic when he felt it.

"Akawi, you must take the books and flee. You must. I know these men who attack us are just trolls and will not stop to steal two books, but they may burn them." The man coughed a dollop of blood onto the polished timber floor. One of his legs shook violently, drumming a ragged rhythm on the tasseled edge of a rug. "You must take the books." He coughed again. "We are so close. I know it. Continue the search for the portals."

Scree didn't move, hardly dared to breathe, and the dying man grew more urgent.

"Take the books and go. Flee."

The troll could feel the man's desperation pushing at him even as the whisper of magic started to fade. "Where's the books?" Scree asked softly. "Where?"

"They are where they have always been, Akawi. Where my precious books have always been."

"Where's that?"

"In the..." He struggled to sit up, though he should've been dead as dead. "Who are you? You are not Akawi. You..." But the man couldn't say any more. He stared for a moment before slumping to the floor and remaining still.

"Gutted cats." Scree stood up and kicked the finally-dead human. "Where's they at?" Akawi, who ever he was, would know.

"So," Scree asked the dead man. "Does I finds Akawi? Or does I finds something more useful, like food?" Food did sound good— he hadn't had a half-decent meal in days— but a dying man's last thoughts were for some books, not himself!

As if to decide the issue, a skinny, bony young man crept into the room, peering back over his shoulder. He looked as nervous as a cat in a room full of hobnailed boots.

Smile on his face, Scree grabbed the man around the neck before he could react.

"Akawi," he said, "how is ya?"

He got a gurgle in response.

"Your friends here was talking abouts some books." He gestured towards a stockinged foot, the only part of the dead man visible from the doorway. "Where's them books at?"

Akawi, if that was who it was, shook his head and sniffed like a girl through his long, pointed nose. Scree decided he might save himself some trouble by first finding out if he was talking to the right man.

"You *is* Akawi, ain't ya? Keeping in minds that if you ain't, thens I mightn't have any more use for you."

The man nodded, eyes widening with fear as if he'd expected to live before that.

"Good, so hows about we makes a deal? You tells me where them books is hid, and I'll let you lives." Scree smiled. "Sounds like a fair deals to me."

Akawi nodded again and Scree loosened his grip on his neck.

"The secret compartment is behind those books there."

"Let's go have a looks then, eh." Scree dragged his captive across to the bookshelf and thrust him toward it.

Akawi stumbled, righted himself on the corner of the desk then crouched down. He folded a section of the shelf out of the way to reveal a small stack of books.

"You said you'd let me go," Akawi said, sidling towards the door.

Scree looked at the man, at the books, and back at the man. He rubbed at his head. He didn't make many deals, but the ones he made he kept— the daft monk was proof of that.

Akawi would live another day, Scree decided, but not until he helped some more. He shoved the man down into the corner furthest from the door.

"Sits there and don't move."

All the hidden books looked much the same to Scree but seeing he could read, sort of, he had an advantage no human would suspect. He worked out the first title as quickly as he could, then held the volume up for Akawi to see. "What's this called?" He could read them all himself but that would give him a headache.

Akawi cleared his throat. "*The Valley of Mist.*"

He was lying. Scree held up the second without attempting to read it. When they'd gone all of the way through the pile Scree moved to crouch down in front of the human.

"Let's try agains," he said. "And for every lie you gives, I'll break a limbs. Don't know what I'lls do once we gets to number five. We'll just haves to wait and see." He sucked some blood from his finger and smiled.

The new list of titles mostly involved the word magic or something close. Only two didn't. *The Gates of Hakahei* and *The Second Opening*— two volumes of not much more than a dozen pages each. That meant that those two books were probably the valuable ones the dead man had wanted to protect— he'd mentioned searching for portals, not doing magic. The other five books would probably be worth *something* though.

"Goods. See ya." Scree collected his books and put them carefully in his pack, arranging them in order of size. His canteen was in a pocket on one side, his flint striker on the other. As he exited the room a moment later, he looked back over his shoulder and saw the human sitting in stunned disbelief. The look on Akawi's face made the whole incident worthwhile, even if the books proved worthless. Scree liked to shock people.

He paused for a moment. "You really should tidy up in here. It's disgusting."

And then he left.

The street was deserted. Scree figured the rest of the pack were still at their rutting. Or eating, if they were really lucky. And all he had to show for the morning's work were some books.

Scree grunted and scratched himself.

He was about to find himself a lonely human woman when movement caught his attention. There was a large group of men to the north of the village. They were moving quickly.

Screeching kittens. Scree was impressed. The humans had been on their trail for a week or more but must've run through the night to catch up.

He started backing down the street. He could waste some time warning his companions but sooner or later they'd all be caught. Or he could leave on his own.

I cans hide if I'm alone. And maybe if they killed the rest of the pack in the village they wouldn't continue the search.

With a shrug, Scree decided to split the difference. Shouldering his backpack he shouted, "Soldiers," at the top of his voice. Then before he saw any of his companions he fled, past the church and stable, onto the highway and southward. Reaching the ragged fringes of a forest he turned aside, angling eastward, following a game trail as it rose and dipped and twisted, snaking through the trees and sodden undergrowth.

The stolen books were a comfortable weight in his pack as he continued to run. There were more companions to be had, but only if he stayed alive to find them.

5: Tree and Sky

KIM OPENED HER EYES, but the owner of the rough, gravely voice was nowhere to be seen. She glanced around, dark eyes narrowing in concentration. Though she couldn't understand what was being said, the urgency was palpable.

Kim rose from the bench and scanned the shadows at the edge of the forest. She couldn't see anything and jumped slightly when the voice returned. It was closer than she thought.

"[Keep going, for Whistler's sake. For my sake.]"

It was a strange language, like nothing Kim had ever heard before.

"[I am not a mule, Keeble. All that prodding will not make me move faster.]"

This second voice was soft and calm. A woman's voice like a dollop of golden honey compared to the rasping landslide of the man. Kim still couldn't understand anything more than the tone. The man was seriously stressed. The woman seemed unconcerned.

Kim squinted towards the dark mouth of the Major Oak, sure she spied movement. She walked warily back to the fence that penned the tree in but obviously had little effect in keeping people out.

"[Wait,]" the man said in a harsh whisper. "[Can you smell that?]"

"[Smell what?]"

"[You're a forest dweller and you can't smell the difference?]"

"[I noticed the difference, Keeble, but was unsure if you were referring to something more specific. I was unsure if you would notice.]"

"[Well I did.]" He grunted. "[I seem to be thinking clearer than I have for ages.]"

"Hello?" Kim said. People had commented on her stupidity on numerous occasions; she never knew when it was best to give curiosity the finger and head on her way. She felt this was going to be one of those occasions. "Hello. I don't think you're supposed to be in there, you know?" That was obvious, really, but she couldn't think of anything else to say.

The woman stepped into view inside the tree.

Kim gasped, on the edge of bolting, before getting control. "Whoever's lighting this film should be paid more," she said softly.

Shadows covered half the stranger's face, leaving her looking mysterious and slightly ominous. She stood perfectly still for a long moment, green eyes unreadable. Then she turned sideways and carefully climbed through the sinuous slot in the tree and out into the open.

"Very dramatic," Kim said. "How long have you been hiding in there, waiting to surprise someone?"

"[Hello.]" As she spoke, the woman wove her fingers in something that may have been sign language. She was tall and lithe with pale skin and sharp features. Her long green dress worked well with her auburn hair. It looked as if she had just stepped out of a beauty salon, not a tree. She appeared calm enough, but glanced back over her shoulder as if worried she'd forgotten to lock her car.

After the graceful, beautiful woman, the man who emerged from the shadows was hardly what Kim expected, though his voice should have given him away. He declined to be dramatic, immediately squeezing out of the confines of the tree with lots of grunting and cursing. He wasn't very tall at all and had a broad, swarthy face and unkempt beard. He wore ragged, dirty pants and a linen shirt.

He sniffed the air. "[Told you. If this is your forest then I'll sit on my hands and do nothing for the rest of the day.]"

A mechanical contraption of medieval appearance had been fitted in place of his missing left hand. He wound some gears that adjusted the hand before stumping across to the fence and hauling himself over.

Kim stared for a moment longer.

"[Where are we, dwife?]" the man asked in the impossible language.

The woman added something equally unintelligible, and they stared at each other.

"Great costumes," Kim said eventually. They were the best she'd seen. "A dwarf and an elf, right?" She still didn't know why people insisted on coming to a medieval festival dressed as fantasy creatures. And she didn't know why they'd go to the bother of inventing a language. Though the woman looked slightly Nordic, so perhaps they were speaking something Nordic?

The man asked his question again, sounding out each word as if Kim might understand the gobbledygook any better.

"I," Kim replied. "Don't," she added. "Understand."

It appeared he'd speak once more, but the woman forestalled him with a quiet word and another wave of her long fingers. She climbed the fence with much more grace than the man had managed and, after demurely smoothing her dress, pointed to herself. "Meledrin," she said, slowly and clearly. She then pointed to her companion. "Keeble."

Kim thought for a moment. There were two possibilities here. One: these two really didn't speak English. Or two: they were just having some fun at Robin Hood's birthday party. Kim remembered the words of the witch and decided to play along. She pointed to herself as the other woman had and stated her name. Then she waved and said, "Hello."

The man grunted but Meledrin bowed slightly in response before waving and also saying, "Hello." Then, crouching down, she laid a hand on the ground and looked up with a question in her eyes.

Now what? Did she want to know grass? Or ground? Or England? Or Nottinghamshire? Or Sherwood Forest? Kim was saved the trouble of figuring it out when a sound intruded. There was a clatter and a screech of metal as another figure stepped into sight beyond the split in the tree. This one was about the same size as Meledrin but wore some kind of colorful, full-length armor and had no hope of getting out into the open. It stood, silent and watching.

Elves and dwarves were easy enough to recognize, but the newcomer was beyond belief. Maybe it was a supposed to be a robot, which was stretching things even for Robin Hood's fans. The thick, chunky armor, with huge rivets holding together the seams, must've been taken through the slot piecemeal and assembled inside. The head swiveled one way, then the next, as if it might find some alternate escape route.

"Hello," Kim said, waving slightly. "How many more people have you got in there?"

The robot stopped his inspection of the tree. Kim had the feeling he was staring straight at her but couldn't be sure.

After an interminable moment in which nobody moved, the robot took a slight step to the side and started to raise his arm.

"[Look out.]"

Keeble grabbed Kim and pulled her a few meters to the side.

"Hey, buddy, watch it."

"[That thing'll fry you where you stand.]"

"What?"

In the tree, the robot was having difficulties. Apparently there was enough room in there for three people, but not enough room to raise his arm. The bulbous appendage hit against the wood three times before he gave up.

"[Isn't that a shame?]" Keeble said. He flung himself back over the fence and strode purposefully to the tree. He looked as if he wanted to attack either the tree or its occupant, but the first was pointless and the second impossible to do through the crack. So Keeble stood talking animatedly to the armored figure instead. The tone was more apparent than ever, and Kim thought she could pick the profanity from amongst the clutter.

Perhaps the robot stared back defiantly. It was impossible to tell. It did try to raise its arm again, as if reality might've ducked out the back for a coffee and let things slip out of control. Kim knew how he was feeling.

"Hello, Kim," Meledrin said.

Kim snapped her attention to the tall, thin woman while Keeble continued to rant.

"What's going on?" she asked. Finally, the figure in the tree turned laboriously and disappeared.

Meledrin spoke, but Kim hardly took any notice. She squinted into the tree, trying to see where the robot guy might be hiding.

"Meledrin," Meledrin said again, pointing at herself. Then she pointed to the ground and said a single word in the strange language. "[Where?]"

"Can't help you." Kim turned and quickly made her way back towards the festival, wondering where she could report what she'd just seen. Wondering exactly what she intended to say.

Ten minutes later, Kim had started to calm down and think clearly. Back amongst the stalls she slowed down and breathed deeply. *It was street theatre.* She wasn't convinced but she was *not* going to report that an elf and dwarf were setting up house in the Major Oak.

She took another deep breath and stopped to look around.

Nearby, traditional Scottish dancers were leaping their way through a number to the accompaniment of pipes and drums. An old man was regaling people with stories of dragons and damsels in distress. And, further down the aisle between the tents, the two monks were just pulling out the 'one wheeled chariot of doom' for another session.

Street theatre, Kim thought again.

She checked her watch and pulled out her phone to see if Nina had called again. Of course not. She was stuck here for a while longer yet. "Damn." She walked to the cricket field, looking for something to occupy her mind, and discovered she was in time for the archery demonstration the wicked witch had mentioned earlier. A group of archers were checking over their equipment just outside the roped off area of the camp. About fifty meters away, down past the grandstand, some squires, or something similar, were erecting targets.

There was still a bit of crowd left over from the tourney, and fifteen minutes later more people started to arrive. Kim caught sight of Meledrin and Keeble as the mismatched pair crossed purposefully to where she sat halfway along the range. Meledrin joined her on the grassy bank and the man stood stock sill at the base of the slope.

"Why you..." Meledrin gestured, wiggling her fingers in the air as if attempting to entice forth the elusive word. "Why you go?"

"Oh, so suddenly you speak English? How surprising. I went because I didn't want to sit in the forest playing games."

"I no understand much. Games?"

"Yes, games."

"I know not this."

Kim sighed.

"Think you I speak English?"

"Obviously you do."

"Now, yes. Before, no."

"Yeah, right. Go play with someone else." Kim turned to look out over the field as a trumpeter, bright blue feather in his floppy hat, blew a fanfare.

"Play?" Meledrin said. "[These people talk in circles. And backwards and forwards.]" At the bottom of the slope, Keeble grunted and shrugged, paying more attention to the arriving spectators than the conversation. Kim tried to ignore everyone. "[It will take forever to understand them.]"

"[I can barely understand *you* half the time.]" Keeble fiddled with the gears on his mechanical hand.

"I no speak English before. Learn. Listen, follow. Much speak." She gestured at the growing crowd around them. "Elves have language knowledge. Learn quick."

As more people started to arrive Keeble moved to sit beside his friend. Kim considered returning to her car.

"I no speak English. When enter from..." Meledrin stopped and pointed at a tree.

"Tree."

She shrugged. "Tree? When enter from tree I knowing words you say. Elf and dwarf you say. What?"

"[What's all this talk of elves?]" Keeble asked.

Kim ignored Keeble's gibberish, answering Meledrin. "Because that's obviously what you're supposed to be."

"[You haven't seen elves around here, have you, Meledrin?]"

"Supposed? What 'supposed'?"

"[I don't like elves. All that singing and poetry.]"

"Meant. That's what you want people to think."

"Ah. If we supposed elf and dwarf, why not?"

"[Poetry won't get you through the winter. It won't make life easier.]"

Kim was ignoring Keeble because she had no idea what he was saying. Meledrin seemed to consciously avoid looking his way.

Kim tried to gather her thoughts. "You aren't an elf because this isn't Midkemia or Middle Earth. It's just plain old Earth." Kim thought that maybe the man really was a dwarf. Under a meter and a half, wasn't it? She didn't know. He had to be close but she was pretty sure that wasn't what Meledrin meant.

"Why think?"

"Because he's short and squat and hairy. And you're tall and thin and pale."

"If that description elf, why I not?"

"Because they don't exist."

"Don't exist?"

"Aren't real."

"Ahh. I sorry hear. How say? Other elves knowing will not be please not existing, I think."

"I'm sure."

"What make elf else?"

Like a large portion of the world Kim had read *Lord of the Rings* and seen the movies, but it had been a while ago. "Pointy ears. They all have pointy ears. And an affinity with trees and forests. Skill at archery."

"Pointy ears?"

Kim made a triangle with her fingers and held it up to her ear. "Pointy ears." She didn't know why she was bothering. Just trying to be polite again.

"Ah." Meledrin pushed her hair away from her own ear. It wouldn't be used for impaling fruit, but it was pointy.

"Huh." Kim said. "The makeup guy needs an Oscar as well." It looked very real.

Meledrin was moving on though. "What affinity? And what archery?"

"Affinity is a close connection. A link."

"Connection? Link?"

"And archery is that." Kim pointed out onto the cricket field where three of the archers were lining up facing the targets that were down in front of the grand stand. They seemed to be using handmade recreations of traditional weapons.

"Archery? Ah." Meledrin climbed to her feet and stepped lightly through the crowd. "[An opportunity to order my thoughts, if nothing else.]"

"Where's she going?" Kim decided the woman was quite possibly insane and should be stopped. She jumped to her feet and followed, though not nearly as gracefully.

"Sorry. Coming through. Sorry."

A string of muttered curses and surly oaths followed her path, and the sound swelled as Keeble barged along behind. She stumbled down to the fine leg boundary and hurried towards the archers.

Meledrin, calm and assured, was talking to the first of the men when Kim arrived.

"...use archery?"

"Pardon?"

"Will let me use..." she seemed to realize that she hadn't used the word 'archery' correctly and simply gestured to the bow.

"You want to use my bow?"

"Your bow? Yes."

"Sorry, love, can't let you do that. I put a lot of time and effort into this bow. Almost eighteen months. I can't afford to get it damaged. We'll be showing people how to use bows later though. Come back then."

"I not damage bow. I skilled, but friend Kim not..."

"Believe," Kim suggested, sighing and shaking her head. "Think it's true."

"Not believe." Meledrin nodded her thanks. "I use once? If not believe, give back."

The next archer in line cleared his throat. "Let her have a go, Bill. What harm can she do with you standing there watching?"

"You let her use yours then."

"Sure. Okay." The next man held out his bow for Meledrin to take, eying her slim form appreciatively as he did so. Ulterior motives abounded. "Here, Ma'am. Try mine."

Kim sighed and shook her head again.

Meledrin bowed her thanks, a graceful maneuver that left the receiver gaping, then stepped lightly forward. Before she took the weapon she pulled her hair back into a thick ponytail and tied it with a green ribbon pulled from her sleeve.

"Fine bow," she said in a hushed voice. She wove her hand in another of the strange, intricate patterns then finally took the bow. She plucked an arrow from the man's quiver, muttering under her breath, and nocked it as she tested the tension of the string. Kim watched silently. She knew almost nothing about archery, but the other woman seemed sure and confident.

"Where?" Meledrin gestured vaguely.

For a moment Kim wasn't sure what she meant. "The targets?" She looked to the right. "The targets are just there."

"There?" Meledrin laughed. "But they *there*."

The man who had loaned her his bow shook his head. "What did you expect?"

"I not use that close target since child."

The first archer laughed. "Show us then, love."

Keeble looked bored, standing and shuffling his feet at all the talk he apparently couldn't understand. He was muttering something under his breath.

Meledrin raised the bow, drawing the arrow back to her cheek. "A fine bow," she said again. "But wrong weight slightly." With that she let fly and, a moment later, the arrow struck the target, dead center.

The crowd surrounding the field, growing restless with the wait, clapped loudly. Some cheered and whistled. Kim looked from Meledrin to Keeble and back again.

A couple of the archers still waiting their turn whistled appreciatively.

The owner of the bow cleared his throat. "The weight *isn't* out, actually," he said. "I'm left-handed."

"Left-handed?"

"Yeah." The man mimed using the bow left-handed.

"Oh, yes. Should known." Meledrin plucked another arrow from the quiver and, using the bow left handed, put the second arrow into the target, right beside the first. She nodded in satisfaction. "That much better. Fine bow."

There was more cheering from the crowd and more gaping from the archers.

"I not prove tree affinity, Kim, so would like I do else?" With a muttered phrase, the woman took another arrow and turned to look towards the other end of the cricket field. "What is that?" she asked, gesturing.

"What?" The breeze was chasing a plastic bag across the outfield on the other side of the pitch. It was about a hundred and fifty meters away. "That's just a bag. Rubbish."

"Rubbish? Not important?"

"That's right."

Meledrin raised the bow, drew and fired in one smooth motion. She hardly seemed to aim at all. A couple of seconds later, the arrowed pinned the bag to the outfield.

The owner of the bow was impressed. "Wow."

Kim was impressed.

Meledrin didn't seem to think anything of it. "Need help, Kim. My people killed now."

"What?"

"Think you that perhaps these warriors assist, if spoke you with them?"

"Which warriors?"

Meledrin gesture at the archers and then some of the armored figures who'd taken part in the earlier mock battles.

"They aren't warriors. They're just people in costumes."

"What costumes?"

"A costume is... What am I saying? You're in a costume, you daft woman."

"You still not believe?"

"No."

Meledrin took Kim by the arm in a firm but gentle grip and started to lead her away, back towards the main green and the Major Oak beyond.

"Wait a minute. What's going on here?" Kim said, twisting free. Meledrin reacted, but an instant too late, and she could do nothing. As Kim dropped instinctively into a fighting crouch, Meledrin looked shocked. Keeble was smiling slightly.

One of the warriors standing nearby, a big man with shining armor and a long sword, stepped forward to assist. It was Sir Douglas, from earlier, seeing another opportunity, Kim supposed. He was about fifty centimeters taller than Keeble, but he stood in front of Douglas and didn't back down. Apparently the little man's amusement only went so far when it came to violence.

Kim tried to divide her glance between Keeble and Meledrin, not sure who she should be worried about. Meledrin was obviously in charge, but the time had come for action.

"Please, Kim. Come, I show. You believe." Meledrin bowed her head slightly and waved her fingers.

"This is just crazy."

"Perhaps, Kim. But there perhaps be more —"

"[Forget it, Meledrin,]" Keeble said. "[She can't help us now.]"

Kim turned to look at the little man, but he was staring out at nothing and not really offering any clue as to what he was saying. Sir Douglas was looking mighty annoyed at being ignored.

"[Of course she can. All we need is —]"

"[No, look.]"

He pointed, and Kim realized he *wasn't* looking at nothing. But she didn't understand why it was so fascinating. It was just a bird.

Kim blinked. She licked her lips and blinked again, narrowing her eyes against the afternoon sun. The bird was further away than she had first thought but it was huge, as big as a jumbo jet and even less likely to fly. "Jesus."

But it wasn't really a bird. It was a bit like a bat, with huge, leathery, strangely jointed wings. And, even stranger, there were three metal cylinders strapped beneath it.

Kim looked at Keeble, then Meledrin, then back out at the *thing*.

"[I think we should take cover.]"

The thing kept coming, whatever it was, and a minute later it was over the cricket field, only thirty meters off the ground. Kim thought she could hear the thrumming of its wings. There was no other sound. The crowd had fallen silent. Everyone was watching.

A huge, winged shadow skittered across the cricket pitch as the creature straightened, steadied.

"I don't like the look of that." Kim instinctively took a step back. And just as she did, a pair of square, shining canisters dropped from the middle of the three cylinders strapped to the creature. Her heart rate skyrocketed.

"[Get down,]" Keeble yelled.

Kim stared at him stupidly. She couldn't exactly understand the words, but she knew what he meant and still she didn't move. Keeble grabbed her arm and pulled her to the ground. He and Meledrin both covered their heads, but Kim looked at the crowd and the two packages — she couldn't help but think of them as bombs — falling towards the grandstand. Time seemed to slow, stretch, contort. She could hear the rushing of blood in her ears.

People were scattering in all directions, but not quickly enough.

THE EXPLOSIONS CAME IN QUICK SUCCESSION. The ground shook and a huge gout of flame shot into the air. Shrapnel whizzed past, thudding into trees, people, and armor, ripping holes in tents. A wave of heat followed. Something heavy hit the ground a few meters away, and Kim, in a daze, turned to look. A fallen branch had crushed a tent at the edge of the forest. A rain of leaves drifted down as well. It was beautiful. Mesmerizing. Until the sounds of the screams hit her like a Mohammed Ali jab. She snapped her attention to the crowd. Or what was left of it.

The grandstand had collapsed. The timber seats were burning, the metal frame twisting in the heat. People were still running, but not many. Most were lying on the ground. Some writhed in pain, but for the most part they were still, burnt black in a moment. In a dozen places small fires burned where something like napalm had set people and clothes and grass alight.

"Shit." Kim got to her knees and stared. "Shit, shit, shit." She wanted to run and help, but she stayed rooted to the spot like the Major Oak. Her feet stood still while her mind ran in circles.

Closer, more people had been injured. One woman bled from a head wound and Sir Douglas, teeth gritted, was plucking a shard of metal from his arm. Another piece was lodged in his breastplate. While Kim watched, the knight tore a strip off his clothing to bandage his wound then went to help someone else. And still Kim couldn't move. She knelt and stared while people wailed and screamed around her. She tried to swallow, but her mouth was so dry.

"Hey."

A little boy was crying nearby. He was bleeding from a wound on his leg.

"Hey. Help me with this, will you."

Kim turned and saw one of the 'German' cannoneers — a short, balding man on the wrong side of fifty. He had picked up one of the ropes used to pull a cannon into position and was trying to get it out of the camp and into the open.

The cannoneer turned away from a stunned and staring archer and saw Kim. He turned his attention to her. "Help me with this," he said in his English accent. "There's another one of the damn birds."

6: Weapons of War

Kim followed his pointing finger.

"Just grab the rope and pull."

Kim was trained to follow orders in battle. She did as she was told and Keeble came to help as well.

"[This had better be a cannon,]" he said as he pushed at the back. "[It looks a bit flimsy.]"

Kim had no idea what he said, but she pulled on the rope and tried to keep up; the little man was surprisingly strong and his low center of gravity gave him good leverage.

The cannoneer stopped pulling for a moment to shout at five of his friends. "Sonneberg Artillery. Don't just stand there. Gets those cannon moving." He let go of the rope completely and went to shout from closer range. The other men hadn't moved.

"Are you crazy, Johnno?" said someone from inside a tent. It wasn't the best place to seek protection from bombs.

Keeble kept pushing, so Kim kept working as well. It seemed better than thinking about the people in the crowd. Or about any of the other things she might think about. She pulled on the rope and tried not to think.

"Are we artillery men or are we just playing with our toy guns?" Johnno shouted.

He pushed someone towards a second cannon and glared at another man until he went to help. Soon all three cannons were heading for the open ground. Another four men were getting a large chest from beside a tent. They pushed through the onlookers, straining with their burden.

"[This is the worst bunch of soldiers I've ever seen,]" Keeble said as he took a quick look over his shoulder. "[Pathetic.]"

Johnno encouraged his men one moment and abused them the next and soon had all the cannons lined up about five meters apart.

"Harry, what's the range at maximum elevation?"

"Christ, Johnno, I don't know," a big man replied, barely keeping the quaver out of his voice. "We've never fired them at maximum elevation."

"We've got no chance of hitting a moving target," said one of the men lugging the chest. "Can we load shrapnel of some kind? Cutlery maybe?"

Johnno pointed at the bat. "We don't have time."

Kim looked again. "Shit." She took a couple of steps back and looked over her shoulder to see just how far away the forest was. Her heart was racing.

"Come on boys, let's do this." Johnno strode along behind the three cannon, checking to see the alignment of each, as if they could possibly know what they were going to need. "We've fired these things hundreds of times. Easy as pie."

One of the men looked at him and shook his head. "Who're you kidding, John?" A couple of the others looked at him as if he were crazy.

"Where's Boydie?"

"Here." He'd been helping with the chest and was now pulling a key from a chain around his neck. He was a thin man with a long nose and hollow cheeks. His costume seemed about two sizes too big, as if he was expected to grow into it. Now was his chance.

Johnno jumped. Up until then he had been as calm as a seasoned campaigner but his tension finally came through for a moment. He took a deep breath, trying to calm himself, with mixed results. "Good. Excellent. Let's load up then." His leg was shaking. He grabbed it with his hand to get it under control. Kim wished it were all that easy as she wiped sweat from her own hands.

The bat was coming in over the trees.

Two men adjusted the cannon's muzzle height while Boydie supervised the loading.

Kim watched as Johnno took a packet of matches from his pocket. She wiped sweat from her face, licked her lips and examined the bat. Two minutes at most. Did they have time? Did they have any choice? She looked back at the remains of the crowd. A couple of hundred injured people and bodies littered the edge of the cricket field. They were a writhing, moaning mass. About the same number had come from the forest. Some were helping while many just stood and stared.

She swallowed and watched the cannoneers working. The bat seemed to come so quickly; the men seemed to work so slowly. *Christ. What the hell are they doing?*

They were waving their sword at the dragon and not waiting for the experts, that was what they were doing.

When the first cannon was loaded, the men moved on to the next, and someone came forward to fill the fuse hole with gunpowder.

Kim looked around, as if hoping someone sensible would turn up to tell her what was really happening. Her heart pounded. She suddenly needed to go to the toilet. Smoke drifted across the field. The sounds of death and pain came with it. And the smell. Burned flesh. Fire. Explosives. Fear.

"We ready?"

Kim looked back at Johnno in his costume. Panic clawed at his eyes, trying to get out. But he held a match in his hand, and it was as steady as a rock. The bat was still a long way out; surely the cannon couldn't fire that far.

"Beware," Johnno yelled.

Everyone nearby turned to look at him, even those in the important loading detail.

"Fire in the hole."

Everyone covered their ears, and Kim thought it might be a good idea if she did the same. Keeble seemed to work out what was going on just in time. He covered his ears just as Johnno lit the match and touched it to the fuse.

The explosion was much louder close up. Kim's ears were ringing as she watched the cannonball sail majestically across the field. It cleared the pitch square, cleared the field, and crashed into the trees on the far side. A couple of hundred meters.

She stared through the drifts of smoke for a long time after the ball had landed. It was crazy. The first shot had fallen well short of the bat — Johnno obviously didn't know much about the capabilities of his cannons — but possibly had some use as a range finder. Stupid bloody Englishmen, trying to hit a moving target with a cannon that had never been fired in anger.

The bat was still coming.

"Don't just stand there," Johnno bellowed. "Finish loading those cannon."

Boydie and his assistants got back to work. Keeble rushed over to watch them, chattering constantly in his strange language. Meledrin had reappeared and stood watching. After a few moments she said something to Keeble and he fell silent, though he didn't look happy about it.

The next cannon was loaded, and Boydie moved to the third.

"What do you think, Harry?" Johnno asked.

"Not yet," the big man replied, suddenly an expert after his earlier protestations. He seemed much calmer, too. "A few more seconds."

"Range was good on that first one," Johnno said proudly. Then he shook his head. "The height is what'll screw us."

Harry gave a bark of humorless laughter. "That's confidence for you. I reckon there's about a dozen things that are gunna screw us."

Kim couldn't believe what she was hearing. "This is crazy," she said. "What the hell are you doing?" She looked into the woods and wondered if it was too late to run. It probably wasn't, but she stayed where she was.

Johnno shrugged. "Some jobs have got to be done," he said. "And some times the right person isn't available, so the *only* person has to do it."

"Christ." Wiping her hand on her jeans, Kim turned to look at the sky. The bat was coming. It was almost there.

Johnno got out his matches again as he shouted at some of his men to get the second cannon repositioned.

"We ready?" Johnno shouted. He answered his own question. "Looks good to me. Beware." And a couple of seconds later, "Fire in the hole."

But that couple of seconds was too long. Kim knew it as soon as she saw the ball's flight path. It was going to cross behind the bat.

Kim uncovered her ears in time to hear Johnno swear. He moved to the next cannon and shouted as his companions to adjust it.

The bat was only a hundred meters from the remains of the crowd. It was almost skimming along the ground, moving fast and sure.

"Beware." Johnno came forward, and Kim jumped back out of the way. "Fire in the hole."

It was going to be close. Maybe.

Kim shaded her eyes to watch. She willed the cannonball on. Her heart skipped a beat. "Shit." She leaned to the right. She leaned further, hoping to upset the tilt of the world. Hoping to affect the spin of the universe for just one moment. She was aware of others doing the same. "Shit."

The bat kept coming, bearing down on the injured people as if they were still a threat. As if they'd ever been a threat.

Boydie was already back at work on the first cannon, stuffing gunpowder down the muzzle. He would be too late, though. There was no doubt about that. Way too late.

The bat was almost there. Kim thought of closing her eyes. She sucked in a deep breath, wiped at her face. She didn't want to watch but couldn't look away. Her heart still pounded, a million beats a minute.

The bat dipped lower. Time seemed to stop. For just a moment.

Breathe.

Then, out of nowhere, a jet streaked across the sky.

"Harrier," Kim shouted. She felt like jumping for joy but kept her feet on the ground. The plane looked the worse for wear, but it was still a sight for smoke-stung eyes. Kim relaxed slightly, wiped at her face again, started to breathe without conscious thought.

The experts.

She watched a long line of tracers pummel the bat from the side, seemed to feel each impact. The creature fell from the sky like a lead balloon. It screeched and writhed, tossing its head with the pain. Then the canisters strapped to its belly exploded. Long arms of flame reached for the crowd. Almost got them. Shrapnel did. Kim ducked instinctively as new screams joined the ones from earlier.

More injuries. It wasn't good, but better than it could've been.

Then the jet was gone, out of sight behind the trees, and the sound washed over them like a tsunami.

Kim turned to look for Johnno, to tell him that, sometimes, the right people were available. But Johnno was dead. Gagging, Kim locked her knees to keep herself upright. He'd been right there, a nice old guy who probably had a wife who cooked him bacon and eggs for breakfast and ironed his cannoneer uniform every week. Now he was lying on the ground with a piece of metal the size of a CD embedded in his skull.

He could have run. It would have been the sensible thing to do. If Kim had been able to get her legs moving at the right time, *she* would've run. But now? Now it was too late. The bat thing was dead. Johnno was dead. Half the crowd were dead.

Kim fell to her knees and cried. The sound of it was lost amongst the chorus.

Half the crowd were dead. The half that weren't were either injured or trying to help. Sir Douglas was nearby, crouched over a boy in a page's costume. The knight had a fresh gash on his forehead, and the metal was still lodged in his breastplate, but he didn't seem to notice. An old woman, dressed in the lace and frills of a lady, was looking at someone else. They probably weren't the right people for the job, but they, and others like them, were the only people.

Kim climbed slowly to her feet. She was probably more right than most. She'd been in the army. She had training, even if it was a couple of years out of date. She should be helping, not standing around like some stunned tourist. She'd felt nothing but disdain for Douglas earlier, but he was doing his best to prove her wrong.

"Shit." Kim didn't like being proven wrong. Deep breath. There were injured people scattered amongst the tents behind her, but relatively few. Most were already being seen to. She glanced at Johnno wondering when someone would come to help him. Swallowing, she set off across the field and tried to order her thoughts. There would be burns. There would be panicking friends and relatives. There would be people with good intentions who should not be left in charge of a Band-Aid and a box of aspirin. She dragged up memories from the army that she hadn't used for years.

But Kim was only halfway to the edge of the field when somebody tugged on her sleeve. She turned to see Keeble and Meledrin.

"Will help us now?" Meledrin asked. "These creature attack my people as well."

"What?"

"[I don't think we're going anywhere yet, woman.]"

Keeble was pointing again. Kim followed his finger out to where another bat was heading towards them.

"Damn it." Kim almost fell to her knees again. She'd thought the main danger was past. She looked in the direction the jet had gone. It was probably halfway to London by now. For a moment she was caught. She'd been on a mission to help the injured and was suddenly loath to abort that plan. But if nobody did anything about the bat then the help would be short-lived and possibly painful.

So, she would wave her sword at the dragons. She would tilt at the windmills. "Damn it." Kim raced back the way she'd come. She was crying once more.

"Boydie?" she called. It came out as hardly more than a squeak. She cleared her throat. "Boydie, get those cannon loaded." The skinny man was sitting on the ground tying a makeshift bandage around his leg.

"What?" But he saw for himself. "We don't have time."

He was probably right but Kim pointed at the mass of injured people on the other side of the field. "They're the ones who don't have time."

"But..."

Kim crouched down and finished tying the bandage. Her hands were shaking. "Come on. Get moving." She looked around. "Cannoneers," she shouted, "let's go."

Keeble had already opened the chest and was poking amongst the contents. Kim wasn't sure if that was a great idea but let him keep going. It proved to be the right decision. Boydie saw what was going on and scrambled to his feet.

"Get out of there," he said, shooing the little man away.

"If you aren't going to do it," Kim said with a smile, "then someone has to."

Boydie sighed and, in a surprisingly loud voice, called to his companions. He set to work straight away while the others gathered about him, shuffling their feet and watching the sky nervously. It seemed they would stand there all day or, at least, right up to the time when they got a bomb dropped on their heads.

"Harry, don't just stand there," Kim said. She had to clear her throat again.

The big man looked at her as if to say, *Well, what else am I supposed to do?*

"We need the cannons adjusted." Kim said it as if she knew what she was doing. The second bat was coming in from a different angle, slightly higher. "We need them spun to the right."

Harry kept standing for a moment, watching the bat, then shrugged and looked around. "You heard the lady, lads." He and another man went to the cannon next to Boydie and started to heave on the ropes while Kim sighted along the barrel.

"That'll do it." Highly technical stuff. An exact science. Kim wondered if she was going crazy. Her mouth was so dry she could hardly swallow.

Two more men had already started shifting the next cannon. Kim followed Harry to the one that had just been loaded. Less than a minute and the bat would be upon them. Kim had to make some real decisions. She stood behind the cannon, Harry nearby with a box of matches in hand. It was surreal. Thick, bitter smoke drifted around them one moment, and the next it was clear. Sound came and went. Moans and shouts filled her consciousness, leaving no room for other thoughts, and then she could think all too clearly.

Kim took a deep breath and tried to calm her racing heart. That was a futile exercise.

"What do you think?" Harry shook his head. "Bloody hell, we're being attacked by giant space-bats."

"Space-bats?" Kim said. "You think they're from space?"

"Can you think of a better idea?"

"Well..."

"Beware," Harry bellowed and stepped forward.

7: Open Doors

"NOT YET," KIM SAID, A HAND ON HIS ARM. She tried to gauge the bat's speed and imagined the flight of the previous cannon balls. The idea of space-bats kept getting in the way and she shook her head to clear it. "Not yet." She used her shoulder to wipe sweat from her forehead. When she looked up again, the bat was skimming over the trees just beyond the far side of the field. "Fire," she said softly.

"Fire in the hole."

Kim covered her ears. She felt the explosion hit her in the chest, smelled the cordite , watched the ball sailing across the field.

No good. No good. She could tell almost immediately. While the others continued to stand and stare, she hurried to the next cannon, checked the aim, then started to push on the back corner. Keeble came to help a moment later.

"[Who are these soldiers? They just don't understand how battle works, do they?]"

Kim ignored him. What else was she supposed to do? "Harry." And Harry ignored *her*. "Harry."

She stepped back then pulled Keeble away a moment later.

"Harry. Quick"

Harry shook himself, turned, and went to the second cannon.

"Fire the damn thing."

"Fire in the hole."

The thump in the chest. Ringing ears. Kim held her breath. "Come on. Come *on*." The ball sailed though the sky, a black spot against the blue.

Kim leaned to the left. She held her breath.

She almost thought she heard the impact of the ball hitting the bat. That wasn't possible. But it *did* hit. She turned to look at Harry for a moment, saw the same look of stunned disbelief that she knew must be on her own face.

"Huh."

They'd hit it.

There was a screech that cut through all other sound and Kim turned quickly back. The huge creature was leaning dangerously to one side, tried to correct, went the other way. After a couple of seconds of struggle a wing clipped the ground. It came down in a rush, plowing a long furrow in the outfield and sending up a storm of dust. Sounds of pain came from the cloud, but if Kim knew anything at all about giant space bats, and she didn't, she didn't think that one was going anywhere in a hurry.

"What now?" Boydie asked after what seemed like an hour.

Smiling, Kim continued to watch the results of their handiwork. "We should go see who we can help." She had almost forgotten about all the injured people.

"What about those cylinders though?" Harry asked.

"What?"

"Those cylinders that were strapped under the bat-thing."

"Well..."

"I don't imagine the bats made them."

Kim wiped sweat from her face and looked at the cloud of dust, as if she could see the creature inside. She chewed her lip for a moment as she thought. "Your point?"

"My point," Harry said, turning to look at her, "is where are the people who did do the making?"

"As far as points go," Kim said, "that's a pretty good one." If she hadn't still been feeling the rush of shooting the thing down she might've had the same thought.

"*I* thought so."

Bats from outer space were bad enough. Bats from outer space that were nothing more than vehicles for other things were even worse.

Boydie cleared his throat. When Kim turned to look at him she had the distinct impression he'd been a couple of steps further forward a moment ago.

"Perhaps we can ask them," he said.

The dust cloud was starting to disperse and figures were now clearly visible around the still writhing form of the bat.

Kim swore.

They all wore colorful, clanking, hissing armor, like the strange figure who'd been standing in the Major Oak. Kim turned to Meledrin. "What the hell is going on here?"

"I told already. Monsters attacking here have already attacked my people."

"Yes, but..." Kim watched as more and more armored figures became visible. There were more than a dozen of them, moving with a sense of slow implacability.

Keeble said something then crossed quickly to a display of weapons outside a nearby tent. He selected a sword, swung it awkwardly, threw it aside and took an axe instead.

"Keeble says creature weapons fire... Not know word. I believe it like lightning."

"They shoot lightning?"

"As I said, not certain."

"Shit." Kim looked around as if inspiration might strike her. It was better than anything else that might strike her. "Boydie, you might want to get those two cannons loaded."

But Boydie was gone. He was disappearing into the trees at a sprint. There were still a few cannoneers around.

Kim took a deep breath. "Cannoneers, load up."

None of the men moved.

"I just gave an order. Why aren't you moving?" They weren't real soldiers, but they started to move. One of the men who'd been assisting Boydie took charge. There was one cannon already loaded so Kim took Harry by the arm and dragged him over to it.

"Shouldn't we wait to see if they attack us?" Harry asked, match held in his trembling fingers. It was finally getting the better of him, and Kim used that thought to gather courage.

"Do you think these things were prisoners of the bat?"

"No."

"Right."

But at that moment a knight, just a couple of meters away, started to scream. He shuddered and convulsed, caught on the end of a long beam of crackling, distorted air. Smoke streamed from the joints of his armor after he'd fallen to the ground.

"Don't stop," Kim shouted to the men loading the cannons. She swallowed bile and rushed to lower the muzzle of the one that was already loaded. Harry pulled her away after a moment.

"Beware." He dropped his match, quickly regathered and lit it with shaking fingers. "Fire in the hole."

The cannonball crashed into one of the armored creatures and took out another behind.

"We'll get the bastards." Harry said in a shaking voice as he moved to another cannon.

But there were fresh screams coming from the main crowd. People were scattering again.

Kim wanted to help but didn't know what to do. She stayed where she was, dividing her glance between the monsters and the crowd.

"Beware. Fire in the hole."

Kim remembered to cover her ears. And again a minute later. More of the creatures fell, but not nearly enough. The rest continued their slow advance. They were three quarters of the way to the main crowd now.

Men came to load the cannon in front of her.

"This will be our last shot," Harry said.

"What? Why?"

"Today was the last day of the festival. We never bother lugging spare powder around. Hell, the balls are just for show. You're lucky we had any at all."

Kim wasn't feeling lucky. "Damn it."

She looked around for inspiration once more. Keeble was by the weapons' rack, lazily swinging his newly acquired axe in his one good hand. There were more than twenty other 'warriors' standing around as well. Sir Douglas was one of them, blood seeping through the bandage on his arm.

"Doug." The big man didn't answer. "Douglas."

He spun to look at her.

"Get your sword."

"What?" No knightly affectations at all.

"Get your sword, buddy." Kim headed for the nearest rack to find her own weapon, wondering with each step if her legs would support her. She made it all the way and, looking at the choices, decided on a solid, spiked mace. She didn't know if she'd be able to do any damage with a sword even if the creatures didn't have the armor.

"Are you crazy?" Douglas asked.

"The way I see it, standing around isn't an option. Either run or fight."

Douglas glanced at the creatures then back at Kim. He gave a small nod and picked up a sword from near his feet.

"Get some weapons," Kim called to nobody in particular. She cleared her throat to try again, but the men heard. They turned to look at her though none did as she suggested. "So all this is just a game?" She gestured around at the tents and the weapons. "You're just like little boys playing cowboys and Indians in the back yard? Get some God damned weapons and help those people."

Finally, they started to move.

"Beware. Fire in the hole."

Kim almost hit herself in the head with the mace as she covered her ears. "Come on."

One of the armored figures, blue and green with rusting rivets, was heading towards the cannons, plodding along as if it had all the time in the world. Kim headed for it, shoulders hunched as she ran, angling across in front of it as it started to raise its weapon.

"Slow as hell," she muttered to herself.

"What?" Douglas was just behind her, rattling along like a shopping trolley full of empty cans.

"These bastards are slow."

Her arm was already starting to ache from the weight of the mace, but as she got closer she stood up straight and raised the weapon. Her target was swiveling slowly to meet her but wouldn't be quick enough. Its arm bucked slightly as it fired an experimental shot in her direction. It missed, but Kim still felt the hairs on her arm stand on end. He mouth was instantly dry again.

"Electricity," Douglas said before she had the chance.

She thought he sounded very calm for a man dressed as a human lightning rod.

Kim swung her mace with all her might, aiming for a seam in the center of the chest. Her hand shuddered so hard she almost dropped the weapon.

Momentum carried her past as Douglas hit the same area a moment later. Keeble, just a second behind, swung his huge axe at the back of their enemy's knee. Kim spun, trying to ignore everything else. She had enough problems. It felt as if her hand was still shaking. Her arms felt like they were going to drop off. She heaved the mace up and swung. The armored figure was trying to turn to face them, and the mace crashed into the faceplate. She heard a crack, pulled the weapon free and swung again. A moment later, as she tried to get the mace up off the ground once more, Douglas pushed past and rammed his sword into the hole she'd created.

The armor stopped moving.

"Is it dead?" Kim gasped. She went to have a look through the hole as Douglas reefed his sword free. "Shit. Shit, shit, shit." Whatever was in there wasn't human. Its face was a mess of exposed flesh, thick, dark red blood, and splinters of bone, but there was no way anyone could ever think it was a human face.

Kim almost threw up.

"What is it?" Douglas asked.

She wiped her face. "I have no idea." And it wasn't the time to be worrying about it. Kim tried to put it from her mind and looked around. She knew that if she thought about it she'd be no use to anyone.

Keeble had already moved on and was working at the knee and shoulder of one of the creatures like a madman, swinging his axe as if he could do it all day. Kim hefted her mace with a grunt and went to help.

Warriors swarmed around her, mainly carrying a mixture of swords and maces. One man had a huge war hammer, and there were two others with flails. Suddenly in a real battle, the men fought with none of the melodrama of earlier in the day. They swung their weapons with grim, wide-eyed determination or a half-wild frenzy. They died in a number of realistic ways.

Kim gritted her teeth and tried to ignore what was happening around her. The men probably would've lived if she hadn't insulted them. They would have run into the trees to hide like sensible people. But others would have died — women, children, damsels. She stopped thinking about it and concentrated on the one creature in front of her, with its slow movements and deadly arm. Just one creature. Just one alien. She almost laughed at the absurdity of it.

As she rushed in, Keeble shifted his attack to the creature's faceplate. He swung with a grunt of effort then quickly moved out of the way so Kim could attack the same place. Her mace broke through and Keeble was already swinging again, finishing the creature off.

"[We can't win,]" he said, leaning his axe against his side for a moment while he wiped sweat from his face.

"What?"

He shrugged, picked up his weapon again, and moved quickly towards the edge of the field where the crowd had once been. Kim followed at a slower pace. The little man looked like he had the energy of a four year old, but Kim was struggling. She didn't know if she'd be any help at all.

As she approached the remains of the grandstand, Kim saw the wicked witch's granddaughter, Jessie, standing next to the fallen figure of her mother. Her fairy wings were hanging crookedly, and her curly hair was black with soot. She was wailing and sobbing as she stood and looked around for someone to help. Anyone.

Kim studied the crowd as she ran, looking for the witch. There, under the trees. Kim spied the old woman at almost the same moment she spotted her granddaughter. A look of horror crossed her face and she headed out into the open as fast as she could, which was barely above walking speed.

There was an alien not ten meters from the girl. It finished off a man who, face bloody, was struggling to get to his feet. Then it started to turn. Kim headed towards it. She wasn't going to make it though. Her legs were aching. She was almost dragging the mace behind her as she leapt fallen people.

She watched in horror as the creature brought its bulging arm to bear on the girl. It paused, adjusted aim.

The witch was there, hobbling terribly, wheezing from exertion and smoke. She grabbed the girl and crouched, putting herself between her and the weapon.

And the creature paused. It was completely still for one second, two seconds, then it started to move again, swinging its weapon around as it tracked a small man in a monk's habit. Summoning up the last of her energy, Kim swung her mace just as the monk let out a scream of pain and fell to the ground. Tears blurred her vision but she swung again and again, yelling with frustration, with fear and anger.

The creature died where it stood. Kim swung two more times before she took control of herself. Even then, she might have kept going had not a noise impinged on her consciousness. It took her a moment to work out what it was and a moment more to realize it was a good thing. Heaving smoke filled breaths into her lungs, wiping the tears from her face, she turned and examined the sky. Three helicopters, barely audible over the sounds of battle, were dipping down towards the far side of the cricket field.

Before they had even settled, men were streaming out. Soldiers. Red Berets. They assessed the situation quickly and set to work with spectacular results.

Gunshots rang out, adding to the general clamor. Suits of armor started to explode. Kim crouched down, leaning on her mace, and watched. Breathing was still hard, and her chest was tight with tension, but she gave a small smile. Some of the knights gave a ragged cheer. Kim saw Sir Douglas turn to look for a moment. He glanced at Kim, too, and she gave him a nod. But he'd already moved on to blunt his sword on the face of an alien who was still trudging among the bodies.

It was too late for some, and there would be more deaths before the battle was over, but now the professionals were here. The experts.

"Kim?"

Nearby, the old woman was leading Jessie away from her mother's body, gently tugging her hand and saying something. It wasn't a happy ending. It probably wasn't really an ending at all. Just the beginning of something much stranger.

"Kim?"

Kim turned to see Meledrin stepping carefully across the field behind her. The woman's red hair was still immaculate. Her dress was marked with soot and grime, but, with her calm assurance, it hardly seemed to matter.

"What do you want now?"

"Can assist me now? Can assist my people?"

"What?"

Meledrin sighed, the first real sign of any emotion Kim had seen from her. "My people being attacked by these same creatures. Need help."

Kim looked around. British soldiers were advancing across the field. Some were already setting up defensive positions as more bats circled overhead. If the strange creatures really were aliens, then they seemed to be paying a lot of attention to an insignificant place like Sherwood Forest. Unless it was actually an important location. Unless.

Kim couldn't dismiss what Meledrin was saying out of hand. The armored alien had been in the tree long before any of the others had turned up. Meledrin had asked for help before they had turned up. How could Kim question anything without checking the facts when she had just finished killing aliens with a mace?

"Okay. All right."

There was a group of soldiers not far away checking on injured people while they continued to scan their surroundings. One of them was an officer.

"Captain," Kim called.

The man turned to look.

"Can I have a lend of ten men?"

"What? No."

"Are you in charge?"

"No."

"Then who is?"

He looked around. "The major is busy at the moment."

A group of men on the other side of the field were setting up a mortar.

"Kim, we do not have time," Meledrin said.

"How about one guy? He can come back in a couple of minutes and tell you I'm an idiot, or he can come back and get help."

"Help?"

"There may be more aliens in the forest."

"Aliens? Who says their aliens?"

"Have you seen them?"

"Nothing has landed in there." But the captain chewed on his lip for a moment. "Manning, go see what the hell she's talking about."

A private rose quickly to his feet and followed Kim as she, in turn, followed Meledrin.

"[Wait for me, woman.]" Keeble was racing across the field, short legs pumping.

"What's this all about?" Manning asked as they hurried along the path. He was watching the woods, rifle held ready.

Kim shook her head, and then decided to answer. "These two claim to be an elf and a dwarf. They claim they didn't speak English an hour ago." She shrugged. "All I know is they seemed to appear in the Major Oak as if by magic, and one of the armored alien guys was following them. And this was well before the bats arrived."

"And that means?"

Kim shrugged again. "Beats me. But I think we should find out."

Meledrin was leaning against the fence when they started across the clearing towards the Major Oak.

"Us wait for Keeble." Meledrin said when Kim had joined her. "My people know defend selves, Kim, but not warlike. Can get more warriors? Might be needed, still."

"I can't get anyone else but Manning can if he thinks it necessary."

Meledrin glanced at the soldier, dismissed him. "He just a man. You Warder. Have authority. "

"A Warder?" Kim couldn't think straight. It seemed to be contagious. "I'm not a Warder. I don't even know what one is."

"You only person when we arrived. You tending to tree."

"I wasn't tending to anything. I was resting. Tending to be bored, maybe."

"Yes, but..."

Keeble came across the clearing, muttering all the way. He reached the fence and clambered over. Meledrin followed.

"Are you come? Time is..." Meledrin searched for a word, then shrugged. "[Short.]"

Of course it was. People were dying. Strange creatures and even stranger creatures were attacking Sherwood Forest. "Sure it is." Kim climbed over the fence, but only went half of the distance to the tree. She could see inside more clearly now.

Keeble had entered a moment ago, struggling through the gap, but was nowhere to be seen.

Manning stood beside her and looked nervous for the first time. "Ah, where is he?"

Meledrin looked over her shoulder. "Keeble to Grovely. Come, we must go low."

"Crawl?"

"Yes. Crawl, I think. Go hands and..." She tapped at her knee.

"Knees."

"Yes." The tall woman made her way into the hollow tree, hitched up her dress, lowered herself to her hands and knees, and crawled out of sight.

Kim tried to see where she was, squinting into the darkness, leaning forward to see if there was anything to see.

"All right," Manning said, "what the hell is going on?"

When the woman stepped into the light once more Kim jumped, and the soldier's rifle snapped around to point at her.

"Are you come?"

Kim shook her head. Manning licked his lips.

"Not danger now, I think. Warriors from sky moved on." The woman's voice was calm, but Kim could see the tension in her jaw and neck. She saw a flash of horror in her eyes, but an instant later that was gone as well. "Come. There is no longer need to crawl. The hole has been enlarged."

And then she was gone. One moment the woman had been there, tall and striking like nobody Kim had ever seen, and the next she was gone. And this time Kim knew she really had *vanished*, not just stepped into the darkness.

"What the hell is going on here?"

Kim stayed where she was. Away through the trees she could still hear battle. The sun was dipping down behind the trees. Finally, she moved the rest of the way to the tree and peered inside. As expected, there was nothing there to see.

And isn't it strange that I expected to see nothing? "Are you coming?" Kim swallowed and climbed through the gap into the tree.

Manning came behind.

Inside, darkness was almost complete, so she felt around.

At first she felt wood, rough and old and dry, and felt like a fool. Then her hand slipped into nothing where there should've been something. She walked forward slowly.

After less than a meter she stepped out into a clearing that most definitely hadn't been on the far side of the Major Oak.

She was beneath the largest tree she'd ever seen but huge branches, as big as normal trees, had recently broken off, creating gaps overhead. Two moons were visible. Huge black bats were circling. Fires blazed in numerous areas, and the smell of low-grade explosives permeated the air.

Closer by, a scatter of bodies lay amongst the wreckage of the tree. Most appeared very similar to Meledrin, tall and thin, but there were also some in the armor.

Kim quickly went back the way she'd come pushing past Private Manning as he stood and stared. Outside the Oak, she climbed back over the fence and sank to the ground, leaning back against a rough timber pole and staring out at the forest. She was shaking all over. She couldn't stop.

For a long time, Kim stayed that way, legs stretched out before her, until she heard sounds coming from inside the tree once more.

Manning was there a moment later. He vaulted over the fence, slung his rifle over his back and ran. "Be careful," he shouted over his shoulder, "the aliens are still there."

A couple of minutes later, Kim heard noises behind her and scrambled to her feet, looking for a place to hide. After a second she recognized Meledrin's voice and turned to look.

"[Careful with him, Keeble. His head is not as hard as yours.]"

"[If he lives with you, it'd have to be.]"

Keeble was slowly emerging from inside the tree, dragging an unconscious 'elf' out into the open. Meledrin did what she could to help from inside, but the gap was too narrow to make the task easy.

"Who's this?" Kim asked. She shook her head in disbelief. Here she was, looking at someone in serious trouble, and she was worried about his name.

"This is Palsamon." Meledrin waved her fingers around.

The stranger had an ugly gash across his leg that was bleeding heavily, and his arm was broken. Burns marked his chest and neck. A lump the size of an egg lifted the waves of his silvery hair near his left ear. Biting her lip, Kim tried to think. She quickly removed her jumper. It was a woolen affair that would be no good as a bandage. Then she removed her T-shirt and tied it tightly around the man's injured leg.

"[What do you think you're doing? That's the most disgusting display of...]"

"What?" Kim looked up to see both Keeble and Meledrin staring at her with expressions of shock stamped on their faces.

"What you do?" Meledrin gestured. "It is not proper."

"What?" Kim was wearing jeans and a bra. It wasn't as if she'd stripped naked. And it wasn't as if she'd done it for fun. Reminded of her T-shirt, she took a moment to make sure it was doing its new job successfully. It seemed to be, so she returned her attention to the elf and dwarf. "What?"

Meledrin turned away in disgust and Keeble shook his head.

"[Have you no sense of decency?]" he asked.

Not sure what he'd asked, Kim shrugged, and that just seemed to upset the little man more. She looked back to Palsamon and tried to arrange his own burned shirt into some type of sling for his arm.

As she was finishing, a poor attempt and probably not much help at all, Kim heard a noise. She turned to see Manning leading a dozen soldiers into the clearing.

"Are you all right?" he asked.

"Yes, fine, but he isn't."

A sergeant climbed the fence and looked at Palsamon. "We have medics here. See if you can get him to Captain Thorpe back at the fair."

"Okay."

The soldiers got Palsamon over the fence then made their way into the tree one at a time. Kim watched them disappear and still couldn't believe it. To distract herself she grabbed Palsamon's legs. "Come on."

But Keeble was holding out her jumper with the obvious intention that she put it on. And it probably wasn't a bad idea. Sighing, she put down her burden, put on the jumper, and got ready again.

It seemed to take forever to return to the cricket field, but when they arrived, the battle was still going at full tilt. More bats had landed and disgorged aliens. The SAS were outnumbered, but holding their own. Kim could see more helicopters in the distance. Even if the battle ended soon, there were dozens of injured people and soldiers would probably get first priority.

"They could be going for a while," Kim said, glancing at Palsamon. He was pale and breathing shallowly. "We need to get him to a hospital."

"Hospital?" Meledrin asked.

"Yes. A place of healing." She rubbed at her aching arms.

"Is near?"

"Christ, I don't know."

"Where must we go?"

Mansfield is probably closest, Kim thought. She said as much.

"Where?"

"Come on." She grabbed Palsamon's legs again and headed for the car park. Doing something would help. It would stop her from thinking.

TUKI FAZED OUT OF THE TRANCE, letting it slowly slip away. Sounds and scents, colors and sensations followed one after the other like sand draining through his fingers, but the trailing edges of the vision clung to his consciousness like never before. For a moment, it was hard to separate the here from the *there*, to separate the now from the *then*. He drew in a deep breath, trying to calm his swirling thoughts. He felt a terrible sense of foreboding. When he opened his eyes, even that was gone, leaving him naked in the heat of the desert with just the memories. He blinked rapidly.

The warm wind touched his dark skin. Sand set it to tingling.

The day had drifted on, farther than he imagined. The shadow in which he sat had pushed its ragged edge several meters closer to the shattered, sand-choked well in the center of the square.

"I have travelled far," Tuki said to the glass ewer as he took it up in his hand. He knew he should not judge, but he would never have thought that such a plain item, made by humans, would be able to take him so far. When he had first found the ewer, buried beneath the sand in the corner of a desert-drowned house, he had thought it would hold no life within its flawed form. But life it had contained, and what a life!

He wondered what long-dead human had possessed enough skill to produce such a wonderful Eye. And he wondered what journey he had made. Obviously it was a journey of many kilometers, for no such hills were in the desert, and he had never heard of anything like the strange snaking creature he had seen. But had he also travelled in time? Had he witnessed what was, or what will be? Or had he watched the meteor's destruction of the silver trail as it happened? And what of the other creatures — the three legged ones and those with the hard, colorful shells who rode the strange bats? There were too many questions to be answered by one young male, alone in the desert.

Pursing his full, thick lips in concentration, Tuki turned the ewer over. It was a small item for him, sitting comfortably on the palm of his broad moai hand, but for a human it would have been quite large. The glass was green, cracked, with a single, simple geometric pattern that offered no real attraction. Finishing his examination, Tuki found no physical qualities to match the spiritual one he had already witnessed.

8: Shifting Sands

He placed the ewer carefully onto his naked thighs. Closing his eyes, he once more pushed his consciousness into the glass. This time however, he did not join completely with it, instead just touching at its edges so that he could ask questions of it.

The breath of the desert caressed his chest as he twisted his thoughts through the silicates, touching at the reflections they offered. The wind brushed gently across his thighs and stomach. It kissed his face and fingers as he chanted softly. It ruffled his dark, curly hair.

But the ewer, thousands of years in the desert, held nothing beyond what it had already given. It provided hints of the journey he had already taken, but could not tell of its home.

When Tuki fazed into the real world once again, letting himself down gently, the shadow of the wall had stretched its fingers all the way to the well, poking at the crumbling stones, the first tentacles of night groping across the landscape.

He carefully set the ewer down in a protective hollow of sand, rose to his feet, and stretched, arching his back and standing up to his full two hundred and fifteen centimeters. When he was done, he looked to each of the compass points in turn and bowed to the remains of the day, thanking Poti, the Mother Blower, for the gifts She had given.

To the south, he could see nothing except the rise and fall of the desert, going on forever as far as anyone knew. "Thank you for the Desert," Tuki said.

To the east, a hill thrust up above the dunes, a rocky knob in the waves of sand. "Thank you for life."

Northward, out of sight over the horizon, was Dry River, snaking its way from the moai homelands into the world of man. "Thank you for what you have given."

And westward, where the Mother Blower was sinking down behind a long ridge. "Thank you for Glass: the present, the past, the future, light in darkness."

Tuki left the ewer where it was and explored the rest of the village in the gathering gloom. Only three buildings of the dozen in evidence still had more than one wall standing. Most had long ago given in to the creep of time and sand. He searched until the Mother Blower was long gone and the Skeleton constellation was high above the horizon, but he could not sense any more glass that might let him unravel some of the mysteries he felt he had uncovered.

When he finally started to run north, Tuki's mind was alive with questions that would probably never be answered.

The heat of day dispersed quickly as Tuki continued to run. He flowed through the night like the cool wind, not rousing the creatures of the desert from their nocturnal activities, his broad feet hardly marking the desert. He counted each step as the landscape slipped by. Each kilometer much like the one before, each hour much like the one before, with just the dunes and occasional islands of stone, and the numbers in his head. Counting.

The air was cool, the sounds of the night a gentle chorus.

Near midnight, Tuki stopped for the first time, resting on the crest of a tall dune, the desert stretched out around him in all directions. He wriggled his large toes in the sand, stooped and let the fine grains sift through his fingers. He lifted a handful and threw it into the air, watching as the silicates caught the moonlight and flared like a thousand new stars for a moment, before raining down around him. Tuki closed his eyes then, breathed in the crisp presence of the desert, letting it fill his being.

As he stood, silent on the dune, Tuki felt something change, as if the drift of the world had slowed. He looked at the night and the desert. The desert remained as still as ever, but the sky was ablaze with the light of a new moon. Except it wasn't a moon. It moved like a meteor, flashing across the darkness for three heartbeats, four. It seemed to look into him as the desert had earlier. But it was not like the attention of the desert. It was not like a friend or mother.

Then suddenly, unspeakably, the meteor changed direction, zagging back across the sky like an errant firefly.

Tuki stared. He shivered, suddenly cold and fearful, and wished he had some clothing to cover his nakedness. But he had nothing, no way he could hide from the penetrating gaze above him.

As suddenly as it had come, the comet was gone, hiding behind the glare of a real moon, revealing the stars once more, all exactly where they should be — a few days short of their Midsummer Night's position. For a long time Tuki stood staring at the sky, waiting for something to happen. But nothing did happen, and he started to run again. The beauty of everything around him was forgotten, the joy washed away by a residue of fear.

-oOo-

Millennia earlier, a dozen moai communities had dotted a five hundred kilometer length of Dry River. The furthest east had been just twenty kilometers from human lands. The furthest west had been located at the point where the snaking gully of Dry River met the feet of the Fargo Hills and curved to the south. Now, only one village remained.

Danyon Ford, halfway between those two outposts, had always been the largest village and was the natural congregation point for survivors when populations started to dwindle. A hundred moai had once resided within Danyon Ford, but that number had swollen to more than five hundred several centuries earlier. Now the population stayed at a worrying, almost constant level. Danyon Ford was home to one hundred and twenty seven moai: all that remained on Kiva as far as anyone knew.

Tuki could not see the village from his vantage point atop the dune, but three wisps of smoke from the first of the breakfast fires were drifting up out of the trees four kilometers from where he stood. With a deep breath he started to jog down the long slope, angling slightly westwards, toward the place he left his clothes five days earlier. He did not realize how tense the sighting of the comet had made him, but it was unusual to be so far off course after such a short run. And with home in sight he felt as if a great weight had been lifted from his shoulders.

As soon as he reached his robe and sandals Tuki snatched them up and scrambled down the bank of Dry River and into the welcoming shade of the trees. He did not stop to thank Poti, as was proper, nor did he wait until he was dressed. Instead, he struggled into his sandals as he hurried along the winding, hard packed path, then arranged his short toga over his right shoulder and tied the rope belt about his waist. He was still adjusting the folds of material when he came upon the first of the other villagers. A go'shin, wearing his toga wrapped about his waist to show his married status, was clearing clumps of weeds from a narrow irrigation channel that took water from a well to the vegetable gardens. Tuki wanted to relate his tale to a mo'shi as soon as possible, but he was forced to stop when the other man rose to his feet.

"Tuki," the go'shin said as he wiped his mud caked hands on his toga. His name was Ulani, and he was a few months younger than Tuki. "You were not expected back until tomorrow."

"I know, go'shin." Tuki examined the ground as he spoke and continued to toy with his clothing. "I completed my pilgrimage, but have run non-stop to return."

"Where did you go, Tuki? Did you find anything?"

"Yes, go'shin, I found a village fifty kilometers beyond the Konane Line, and there was something there." Tuki shifted from foot to foot. He looked up briefly and saw that the go'shin already had the first Shin tattoos on the right side of his upper body.

"Really? An uncharted village? Are you sure?" Ulani's wife, Ko'uka, had drawn four symbols on the dark skin of his right pectoral.

"Yes, go'shin, I am sure. I may only be a go'gan, but I know the location of all the human villages."

"Of course, Tuki." Ulani held up a placating hand. "I was not questioning your knowledge. I was merely surprised. No new villages have been found for centuries."

"I apologize, go'shin."

"No need to apologize. You have a right to defend your honor."

"Thank you, go'shin." He glanced up to look along the path towards the village.

The married man laughed slightly. "You look as if you want to be somewhere else, go'gan."

"Yes. As I said, I did discover something, and I wish to speak with a mo'shi as soon as possible."

"Oh? You really did discover something? Other than the village?"

"Yes, go'shin."

"Well, come with me. Ko'uka may only have married me a week ago, but she is a mo'shi. She is in the weaving hut at the moment."

"Thank you, go'shin."

"We used to be friends, Tuki," Ulani said, "you can call me by my name if you wish."

"Thank you, go'shin, but it would not be proper."

Ulani shrugged and, wiping his hands some more, led the way towards the village — his back was still bare, but would not remain so for long. Tuki hurried along behind, ducking under low hanging branches without thought, trying to calm himself before meeting a mo'shi.

He examined his own tattoos, as if that might help. All it really did was remind him that he had seen nineteen summers and still had no markings on his right hand side. He did not yet have a wife to mark his skin.

On his left pectoral was a triangle, sides curving inwards. On his shoulder and dipping down his arm, were leaves from the Tree of Life. The leaves seemed to be chained in place just below his shoulder by the six Links of Creation. And on his forearm were hundreds of tiny ants, crawling across his dark skin.

He still had a small spot on the back of his hand to fill before he would stop. After that, it would be up to the Goddess to decide if any other parts of his body were to be marked as well.

He would be able to do his own face, if he undertook important duties for Poti, though it was unusual for that to happen to any man. The rest of his body? Tuki sighed and thought of Keala for a moment before shaking his head and turning his thoughts out to the real world.

The center of Danyon Ford was only fifty meters from the northern bank of Dry River. The half dozen buildings to the south of the plaza were the dormitories for the go'gan. The structures, built from carved logs and thick thatch, were supposed to house more than one hundred people. Now, most of them were silent apart from the thatching whispering to the breeze. With day still coloring the sky, the unmarried men were all working and the narrow alleys between the buildings were still and lifeless as well.

The unmarried women, the mo'by, were working in the plaza, talking quietly as they did. Some were grinding meal between smooth glass stones; others were preparing fruits to be preserved. Keala was there, her thick braid a stripe of black across her tattooed shoulder and pale wrap. Tuki watched her, noting the play of light across her cheek, before catching himself and returning his attention to Ulani's broad back. He heard a snatch of laughter from Keala's friends and his face warmed with embarrassment.

On the far side of the plaza were the houses of the mo'shi. Tuki and the other unmarried males were not permitted beyond the shin-high stone wall that marked the boundary, so he was forced to wait in the shade of a haver tree beside the ceremonial gateway while Ulani continued forward to find his wife. He did not have to wait long. He counted only 52 green haver nuts before she arrived.

Ko'uka was a small, slim woman, not even two meters tall. Her hair was piled in a grand bun on the top of her head, marking her as married. A sunrise was tattooed on her chest, a tree skink on her left shoulder, and the Skeleton constellation on her right. Around them all swirled the whorls of the Life Mist. She would have marriage tattoos as well, though none but Ulani would ever see them. Her face already carried the calm certainty of her position. Tuki watched as she stepped up to the fence and nodded slightly.

"Thank you, Mother, for coming to see me." Tuki risked a glance up from the ground. Though she had not held the title of mo'shi for very long, the change in Ko'uka was noticeable. The playful glint Tuki had known well had disappeared from her eyes.

"Why would I not, Tuki?" she asked.

"I don't know, Mother. I am sure you are busy."

"What is it that you want? Did you complete your pilgrimage?"

"Yes, mo'shi. But while I was in the desert, something happened that I wish to speak of." Tuki had a quick look about for Ulani, but the other man had already returned to his work.

"Yes?"

Tuki was very uncomfortable. He could not remember a time when he had been alone in the presence of women. There were not even any girls about. "I saw a meteor, Mother," he said softly, eyes once more focused on the ground at the mo'shi's bare feet. He bit his bottom lip as he tried to control his twitching hands.

"A meteor?"

Tuki glanced up and the glint had returned to Ko'uka's eyes, though it was more like the glint of steel than the warmer flash of sunlight off glass that he remembered.

"You saw a meteor, Tuki?" The woman laughed. "Don't be ridiculous. The mo'min has said nothing of a meteor."

Perhaps it hadn't been a meteor, but he had seen *something*.

"A meteor! Would you like me to tell the mo'min what you have said?"

Tuki continued to examine his feet.

"And what else would you like me to tell her? Perhaps I could let her know that the Poti will rise in the west tomorrow?"

"No, mo'shi."

Ko'uka cocked her head to one side. "You want to say more?"

"The meteor, it changed direction."

"The mo'min has said nothing of a meteor, Tuki. And the rest..."

When Tuki looked up, Ko'uka had gone. He turned about himself, and quickly made his way towards the dormitory that was his home. 15, 20, 24 Mo'by in the plaza. That was all of them. Every one. They were watching him as he hurried away.

Tuki climbed the stairs onto the dormitory's front porch and sat down against a wall, head in his shaking hands. He would be lucky if he ever married now. Why would Keala want anything to do with him? Why would any of them? And he had not even told the mo'shi about his vision.

9: Sharp Bits

SCREE SAT UP IN THE DARKNESS and leaned against the wall of the cave, dragging his pack closer. He was feeling rested for the first time in weeks and decided to read one of the stolen books.

He'd pulled a particular volume out so many times since fleeing the village two days earlier that he knew the title by heart, could tell by touch alone that it was the one he was after. But he'd never gone as far as opening the cover. He sat with it in his hands in the darkness, wondering if he dared open it, and wondering why he wanted to.

"The Gates of Hakahei," he said, running his callused fingers over the letters stamped into the leather cover. He still thought this was one of the books the wizard had been trying to protect, but didn't know why. He figured he'd never know if he didn't read at least a little.

So he concentrated inwardly for a moment, focusing on a certain spot hidden in the back of his mind, until the darkness started to slide away. Soon his night-eyes were painting everything in shades of red and black. Taking a deep breath and closing his eyes, as if that could save him from any magical protection, he flipped to the first page of the book. Nothing happened. Scree opened one eye. The page was blank. He opened his other eye.

"All that," he said, "and the damn things is empty. Rotten cats. Stinking, rotten cats." He cursed loudly, throwing out showers of obscenities. When he turned another page, almost tearing it in frustration, he saw the title printed in dark, curving letters. The page after that was covered in writing— tiny writing that he struggled to read even with his night-eyes. He squinted at the letters and allowed himself a small smile.

"'The seven worlds of Hakahei are unique in all the known universes of Tengama.'" Scree read the sentence a second time, just to be sure he had everything right, though if he didn't get it right the first time, it was unlikely he ever would. He moved on. "'They are not amazing in themselves, beyond the way in which any world might be amazing. Atlantis has the Tashbar Falls and Amar River, while Tiandi lays claim to the Wixen Harsh and Sherindel to the giant secowa trees. But any of these things could have occurred on a thousand different worlds given a slightly different tilt of the table during the Big Bang throw of the dice. What makes the seven worlds of Hakahei unique, what makes them stand out, are the Ohoga Gates. Imagine stepping from one world to another, instantly, as if you are stepping through your front door.'"

Scree thought his head might explode if he read any more, so he carefully put the book back in his pack and sorted through the words, rearranging them this way and that as if that might help him understand.

Seven worlds? Gutted cats! For years he'd thought one world was more than large enough. He'd spent most of his thirty-three years wandering and not yet come back to the start, but... Other worlds? Maybe there were worlds without humans. Maybe there were worlds were trolls lived on their own. He picked at a slowly healing scab on his arm as he thought.

As a troll he'd always imagined that he'd die violently, surrounded by humans and battling to the end. But, if there was a world *without* humans...

Scree laughed. If there was a world without humans, the trolls would probably just get around to killing each other a whole lot quicker. But still, it would be amazing...

He heard something beneath his laughter and fell silent. For a moment he thought he'd imagined it but the sounds came again— voices echoing down the passages, punctuated by the tread of heavy boots worn by a group of tired men.

"Shredded kittens." He gathered his pack close, sitting for a moment in the night-eyes-painted darkness.

The soldiers had found him.

He thought of staying where he was and letting the humans drift past, but they wouldn't have entered the cave without torches and he'd run too far to sit like a startled rabbit now. He pushed himself to his feet, spat on the floor and edged his way to the entrance of his short passage.

The glow of torches reflecting around a bend stung his night-eyes. He turned and hurried further into the side of the hill, choosing tunnels at random. He had no plan but wasn't worried about finding his way out. He struggled to remember letters, but like all trolls he could read the world better than any human could hope to.

With his mind refreshed from sleep, Scree noticed that the walls and floor of the passages were polished smooth. He ran the tips of his fingers along the stone. As a boy he'd heard heaps of stories about the 'Builders', the midgets who lived underground, carving huge cities into the mountains. Once, the tales had sounded like a load of crap, but with the book in his pack describing other worlds, the smooth stone under his fingertips made him wonder.

At the next junction he turned, and again at the one after that. Eventually, Scree found himself in a big chamber, ten meters across, twenty deep, with the ceiling out of sight above. The walls were all still polished, but now there were designs carved into the surface. Stone-relief humans lined the walls, staring forward. Each figure held an object. One had a slender, two-leafed branch, another a ball, like the one in the magician's study. Others held pikes or swords or strange stuff Scree didn't recognize. At the end of these two lines of people were tall ribbed columns, one in either corner, with a blank wall between.

Scree was about to retreat and find a hiding spot where he could wait the humans out, but he stopped for one more look around. When he finally turned to leave, a shadow caught his eye.

Between the columns at the far end of the room, sunk almost to the hilt in the wall, was a sword. He didn't know if the weapon was whole, or if only a stub of the blade was left. Either way, he'd lost his club the night before and anything was better than nothing. It was years since he'd used a sword, but it wasn't that hard. Hit the enemy with the sharp bits and don't get hit yourself. Nothing to it.

With a quick look behind to be sure the humans weren't too close, Scree moved forward.

Up close he could see the sword wasn't thrust into the bare stone like he'd first thought. There was a crack running from above his head down to the floor, so straight it couldn't be natural.

With a shrug, Scree spat again and wrapped his hand around the hilt. He pulled, grunting with the effort, thick cords of muscle straining. He added the strength of his other arm to the task and set his foot against the wall. His arms quivered. For long moments it looked like nothing was going to happen. Then the weapon slowly started to slide free with a loud metallic shriek of protest. The blade kept coming and coming until Scree started to wonder if it was ever going to end.

When it did finally slip all the way free he was left holding a weapon as tall as he was, almost a hundred and ninety five centimeters. It was plain. There was rust on the first twenty centimeters of blade, but closer to the point it was still shining like the owner had just been polishing it and put it aside while he went to kick his dog.

Noises.

A soft rumbling, like thunder, and voices as well. He spun about to see if the humans were already there. The light of their torches was visible, dancing on the walls.

The rumbling continued, coming from behind him. He spun again and saw two large sections of stone swinging towards him like massive doors opening. He stepped backwards, turning to flee.

But the humans were coming.

Standing in the middle of the room, sword gripped in his hand, Scree spun from one threat to another. He didn't know how many humans were coming, but it sounded like a lot— too many to fight at once. Especially when he knew nothing at all about what was going to step into the room at his back.

The thick stone doors were still swinging open, silently now. Inexorably. The light from the humans' torches painted the walls out in the corridor.

Scree dropped into a fighting crouch, searching for a way to escape. He'd fight if he had to, but he'd rather live. He thought he saw what he needed. Above the door through which he'd entered was a rectangular patch of deeper darkness, going all the way from one wall to the next

He threw his new sword up there sideways. It disappeared, clattering against stone, and didn't come back down.

With a grunt he threw his pack after it and dashed across the room. With the help of the stone humans, he scrambled upwards. He used a carved knee, then a belt buckle, and then a shoulder, his strong fingers finding hand holds in the background designs. Then he was as high as he could climb. Turning to look, he could see a room above the door with a low rail protecting it. With two sets of sounds pressing in on him, Scree tensed his muscles and threw himself upwards and outwards.

As he thumped against the stone his hands clutched at the rail. He grunted when he hit, struggling for breath, then hauled himself upwards. His feet slipped over the edge and he lay still.

A voice from below roused him moments later. He couldn't understand anything that was being said.

"[We're through, sir, and still alive.]"

It was a weird language, like nothing he'd ever heard before.

"[What can you see, Sergeant? The cameras aren't working.]" This second voice came from further away, sounding hollow and thin. It was gibberish too. The two men kept talking while Scree stayed perfectly still behind the protection of the rail.

"[Sir. We're standing between two columns. The walls are covered in carvings of people. There's about twenty people, each holding a different item. There are swords and helms plus a heap of other stuff.]"

"[We can get some experts in later.]" There was a pause. "[The silver sheen still fills the doorway; we can't see you at all, though obviously we can hear you just fine. None of our electronic equipment is penetrating the barrier. Report on the conditions.]"

Another pause.

"[Air: normal, if a bit stale. Radiation: normal. The room is definitely empty. Whatever was making the noise earlier is gone. Looks like another room above this one— a balcony or something. We'd need more light to be certain.]"

Scree could hear the humans coming. They must have taken a wrong turn earlier, but they were on the right track now and heading for the room he'd just left. The voices continued from the room below, but the tone had changed, as if they'd heard as well.

"[I hear something, General. Footsteps.]"

A third voice joined the discussion. "[And there's light. Fire-light by the looks of it, sir.]"

"[Do you want to pull back, Sergeant?]"

"[I'd love to, sir, but I don't think it's an option. If we go back through that door we might never get through it again.]"

"[Very well, hold your position. I have reinforcements ready, but I'll keep them back for now. Try to do this diplomatically.]"

"[Of course, sir. What would you expect of me.]"

"[You're a highly trained killing machine who's spent the last few years guarding a locked door— do you really want me to answer that?]"

There was a bark of laughter from below.

Scree carefully crept closer to the rail as the humans got closer. At last they clattered into the room. They sounded like inept troddlers, intent on getting themselves killed. They certainly made enough noise to attract the attention of any watchers.

So, Scree gritted his teeth and stuck his head up to have a look around.

SCREE SAW FIVE MEN, humans by the look of them, standing in front of what was now an open doorway. The one at the point of the small triangle was down on one knee, holding something out in front of his face. The others were on their feet, larger black items nestled into their shoulders. Scree knew those things were weapons, but they were like nothing he'd ever seen before. Below him, in the sights of the weapons, were the other humans, the ones that had been chasing him.

"[Throw down your weapons,]" the leader of the strangers shouted. "[Drop them.]"

For a long while nothing happened. Finally the leader of the pursuers stepped forward slightly, sword drawn, and sank into a crouched guard position.

"[Do you understand English?]"

It was obviously a question, but it was all still gibberish.

Another of the five men spoke, then another, and it seemed to Scree they were trying different languages. The fourth man cleared his throat.

"Can you understand me?"

Some of the words were strange, but the meaning was clear enough.

The leader of Scree's pursuers nodded. "Yes."

"Who are you?"

"I am Keyman Talgayni. And I want the troll."

"[He says he wants the... I'm not sure what he wants exactly, sir. I couldn't understand the word. Something to do with a *kachina*, maybe. It's a spirit of some kind, normally. It's not easy, sir. A lot of Shonsone words don't translate to English, and he uses other words again...]" And then to Talgayni: "You are a soldier?"

"No, I wear this uniform because it is the height of fashion." Talgayni hardly moved in his crouch. "As I said, I am Talgayni, Keyman in the Popago Plains United Guard."

"I'm Ben Dongoske of the United States Air Force Ravens. My rank is Senior Airman." The strangers hardly moved either.

"Well, Senior Airman Ben Dongoske, as I said: all I want is the troll. We lost him, but there are clear signs out in the passage. There is nowhere else he could have gone."

"I'm sorry, sir, but I can't help you. I don't know what a troll is, but we've only just entered this room and it was empty when we arrived."

"Then he must have gone beyond you. We shall follow."

"No, sir, he didn't go past us. You can't follow."

Scree wanted to laugh at Talgayni. Couldn't he see that these strangers held weapons? He mightn't get to kill any humans himself, but he had a feeling he was going to get to watch. Anyone could tell what a sword was, and what it did, so the Ravens could be in no doubt. But those black things...

Smiling around his clenched teeth, Scree glanced through the door behind the strangers. A transparent silver sheen covered it, and like the stranger had said, he couldn't see through.

Talgayni laughed. "Five against twelve? Do you really think you can stop us?"

"We can, sir, if you intend to use *swords*."

"These? Oh, we intend to use them all right."

Scree watched as Keyman Talgayni leapt forward, sword descending before he'd crossed half the space to the strangers. Most of his men followed.

Thunder barked out, deafeningly sharp. Scree covered his ears, and watched as Talgayni stumbled and fell to the ground. None of the strangers had gone anywhere near him. They'd hardly even moved. Talgayni was still alive, clutching at his stomach and writhing in agony, groaning and screaming all at once. The air shattered again and more Popago Plainsmen fell as they rushed forward. Sprays of blood erupted from legs. One man was flung backwards, spinning about and cracking his head against the wall.

In a moment there was silence again, or something like it. Scree's ears rang.

Mixed with the moans of injured men, he could hear something else fluttering at the edge of his attention. Someone had escaped. Scree wanted nothing more than to be gone as well, but he stayed still, holding his breath so he could hear better.

Two men had escaped. One was near to death, wheezing pathetically, half carried by his friend. He found it hard to believe the strangers couldn't hear them as well. Scree wanted to take another look over the rail before he fled himself, but he didn't dare.

"[We need medics in here, General,]" someone shouted. "[I don't want to be the first man responsible for killing an alien.]"

"[Is the area clear?]"

"[There is nil threat here.]"

"[Very well. Stand by, Sergeant.]"

Scree scanned his hiding place and saw a door in the rear wall. Crawling backwards he carried his pack in one hand and the huge sword in the other— the sword that had wedged shut the door in the room below. He continued slowly, until he reached the entrance to his small balcony, then rose to his feet and went down the stairs he found there.

Picking up the pace, he leapt awkwardly down the last four stairs, stumbled and twisted his ankle. He cursed softly and limped forward as fast as he could.

Around the next corner Scree almost ran into the two fleeing soldiers. One was healthy enough, but the other was clutching a hand to his stomach, as if that would stop the flow of blood. His legs were painted scarlet. His pale face was slack with shock. Scree wondered if he was in shock himself. He couldn't seem to think straight and paused to lean against the wall and flex his aching ankle.

"Leave hims," he said to the other man, hardly more than a boy, really. "He's dead. If you keeps moving at this speed you'll get dead too."

Scree got himself upright and shoved past.

"I can't leave him to those butchers." The soldier's face was bleeding from a gash and the look in his eyes suggested he was only just holding himself together.

Scree laughed. "Butchers? Ways I saw it, your good old Keyman attacked first. And after he was givens a warning plain as anything."

"Yes but..."

"Ain't no buts about it. I weren't in the room behinds them Ravens, and theys was defending their patch. You dumb cats deserves what you got."

"And you'll deserve what you get, too, troll."

Scree looked around the tunnel and wondered what he was doing, standing there talking to a man who'd kill him if given the chance. "You's right," he said with a smile. "And whats I'm getting is out of heres."

Before he'd gone two steps the human shouted at him. "Don't leave us. Please. I don't want to die."

"Dump the corpse, kid, or nothing I can do would helps you anyway. And shuts up that cat screech of yours."

"Help me. I can't leave him." He wiped his nose on the sleeve of his uniform.

"You gots food? You knows anything about this place?"

"No," the young man said. "I don't have enough to spare. And I know nothing."

"Suits yourself." Scree shrugged and turned to start jogging again.

"Very well." The soldier lowered his friend to the ground. "If you promise to help I'll share all the food that I have."

"What sort of foods?"

"Does it matter?"

Scree could have just taken the food, but decided he wanted someone to talk to after days on his own. A young human would be better than nothing. With a grunt at what the world was coming to, he hurried back and picked up the wounded man.

"What's your name?"

"Nemucca."

"Well, hurry up then."

They moved deeper into the maze of tunnels. Scree tried not to leave a trail.

-oOo-

Scree looked at the dead man speculatively.

"You are *not* going to eat him," Nemucca said. The young soldier was weak, but on the mend. He'd lost a lot of blood from a wound to his leg and his face would carry a long, wide scar. But he'd survive.

"I don't eats people, you fool."

"Then why are you looking at him like that? It's not likely he'll be carrying anything you want."

"He isn't nows. But he did haves a good knife earlier."

"You took his knife?"

"Yeah." Scree took the weapon out to show the boy. It only had a short blade, but was well made. "What? He won'ts be needing it any more."

"But... He's dead."

"Noticed. He complained enough abouts it before it happened." Scree had smothered him during the night just so he could get some sleep.

"But you can't steal from the dead."

"That's right. They's dead, they don't owns anything."

"No. What I—"

"Just shut up, Nemucca. If you thinks he should have his knife back then you come and gets it. Or he can."

The soldier kept his mouth shut, but watched Scree edgily.

"'Bout time I changed my policy on bloody deals," Scree muttered. "Fetid cats guts." He sniffed.

"What?"

"Shut up." He waved the knife.

"You won't kill me."

"Why's that?"

Scree continued to look at the dead man. He'd told the truth: he didn't eat people. The thought disgusted him. But he did have other uses for bodies. He ran his fingers along the handle of the knife while he examined one of the corpse's pallid legs. Nemucca wasn't likely to like what he was really thinking any more than what had already been discussed, but Scree didn't give a shit what the human thought. He'd been stuck in the cave for two days, sharing one man's already meager field rations, listening to one man die and another one complain constantly. He needed something to ease his tension.

"Don't do anythings stupid," he said to Nemucca as he crawled across to the body. "I ain't going to eats anything."

"What are you..?"

Scree used the knife to start cutting through the corpse's leg near the knee. Nemucca shouted angrily and surged forward. Scree turned to glare at him.

"Please, no. Don't."

Scree continued to saw at the hardening flesh. Behind him, he heard the human gag.

"You never seens a man get cuts up?" There was no reply, so he kept working.

After a minute, Scree gave the leg a violent twist and it came away with a loud crack. He pulled his prize away and held it up in triumph.

A shaft of sunlight angled down through a crack in the ceiling and he moved slightly so he could examine the end of the bone more closely. It was thinner than he normally liked, but would do. He started stripping the meat away, leaving a small pile at his feet. Nemucca wasn't watching any more.

"I can't stay here now that you've done that," the human said, motioning wildly over his shoulder.

"You was going to be staying here with the stinking corpse? Damn, I shoulds have taken the boot offs first." He slit the low leather boot and struggled to pull it free so he could keep exposing the bone.

When he reached the ankle joint, Scree separated the foot from the leg and tossed it back down with the rest of the body. What was left was a strong bone covered with small amounts of gristle and blood. He tore away a section of the dead man's clothing to remove the latter and then started to work with the knife with a little more care. Another ten minutes passed before he was satisfied.

"You did all of that for a club?" Nemucca asked.

"What?" Scree grunted as he used another section of shirt to wipe his hands. "No. Why would I hits someone with a bone when I gots that bloody great sword?"

"What is it then?"

"There's two things I have really haven't gotten enough ofs in the last couple of weeks, Nemucca: music and sex."

"Sex?"

"Yeah. You nots—"

"No." The young man held up his hand and backed himself into a corner. "No, I'm not interested. Even if you were human. Even if I hadn't just seen you cut off someone's leg. Even if... There's no way I would be interested."

Scree shrugged. "Didn't thinks you would, but there's no harm in asking. I'm ain't much into thats myself, but there's only so many times you can polish the sword before you gots to use it in battle."

The boy grunted in disgust.

"Know what?" Scree kept working on the bone, slowly sawing through the ends. "I think those Raven guys came from another world." He'd been thinking about it for a while.

"Another world? That's just crazy. There are no other worlds."

"That's what I thought. But I gots this book, you see, and it says there are other worlds, and they's joined to this one by these doorways called Ohoga Gates."

"You have a book?"

"Yeah, so I gots a book."

"And you can read it?"

"Yeah, I can reads it. And likes I said, it says there are—"

"Yes, I heard you. Lots of worlds joined by doors."

A week ago Scree would have killed a human for talking to him like that. He probably would have killed this one before he'd even opened his mouth, but the youngster would be more use alive than dead. He just gave Nemucca a cold look and continued working. "There's lots a worlds, yes, but only seven of thems is joined by the Ohoga Gates. Those weapons them Ravens had, they ain't nothing I've ever seen before."

"I'll give you that. And they did have a strange language. And clothes."

"That's right."

"So why did they only just appear then? They could have been wiping us out long ago."

"I thinks the sword was jamming the doors shut."

"The sword? And you pulled it out?"

"Well, how was I s'posed to knows. It was just stuck ins the rock." Scree didn't really care anyway. Like he'd told Nemucca— the strangers had done nothing more than defend themselves.

"Sure."

Scree gave the human another glare and the lad hurried on.

"So, what else does it say in this book of your's?"

Scree shrugged. "Don't know. Been kinda too busy to reads lately."

"Where is it?" Nemucca crawled across the smooth, polished stone of the floor to where Scree's pack sat. He pulled it open and tumbled the books out onto the floor.

"Careful." Scree wanted to tidy up the mess but his hands weren't really all that clean. He glared for a moment until Nemucca started to go through the pile. "Pack that away properly when you're done."

Along with Scree's flask and flint, there was also a hard, dry bread roll, a silver chain and amulet, and a silver ring, all of which had belonged to the man who was now missing a leg.

"You stole his things."

"I thoughts we already had this conversation."

There was a long pause. Scree watched the emotions chasing across the lad's face; anger, fear, disgust. He smiled.

"Which book is it?"

"*The Gates of the Hakahei* is the ones I was reading. *The Second Opening* mights have something in it as well though. A wizard types guy was willing to die to protects them two books."

"And I suppose he *did* die?"

"Course. But I hads nothing to do with it." Scree got back to work.

"And I'm supposed to believe that?"

"You think I yearns for your good opinion?"

Nemucca gave half a bark of uncomfortable laughter. The *Hakahei* book was the first one he found. "Not much of a book," he said. "It will only take ten minutes to read it. He opened it up to the first page and settled back against the wall to read. After several minutes, he raised his head.

"You think this is true? All these worlds?"

Scree shrugged. "The wizard guy who owned the books seemed to takes it serious enough. He reckoned he was close to finding the portals and wasn't all that far from here."

"How far did you read?"

"First page was about it."

"Well, it says there are thousands of worlds, but only seven are linked by these magical gates."

"That's what I said."

"And people used to sail to the other ones in huge flying ships."

"Sailed to other worlds in ships?"

Nemucca nodded.

"That's stupid. How do you gets them off the ground?"

"It says something about 'blasting' them into the sky. Putting a fire under them and—"

"Yeah, right. I tried something likes that once. The ship just burned and alls of the humans jumped off. Which was kinda what I wanted."

Scree finally finished with the bone. He held it up in the shaft of sunlight and examined his handiwork. It looked good. Well better than he'd expected anyway. It was clean and white and the ends were both lying on the ground beside the foot. The holes were drilled. All that was left was getting the marrow out of the centre. Normally he would've used water, but that wasn't an option; water was running low as it was. He sighed, put the bone to his mouth and blew.

Nemucca turned away in disgust. "What are you doing?"

Scree spat the taste from his mouth.

"Why did you do that?"

In answer, Scree put the bone to his mouth again. This time he blew more gently and got a slightly raw, off key, note.

"It's a flute!" Nemucca said. "You play the flute?"

"Yeah, I plays the flute. By the look on your face anyone'd thinks I sprouted wings and flown aways."

"Well, it's just..."

"Yeah, I'm a savage bloody troll. Knows all about it."

"Why doesn't anyone know about this. I've never heard anybody speak of trolls playing music."

"Because most humans who see trolls ends up dead." Scree smiled wickedly and worked at the flute for a moment. It didn't improve the sound. "Nots very good," he said. "The bone is supposed to be treated and dried and stuffs first."

He played for several minutes, dancing the almost-notes around in the still air like dust in the shaft of sunlight. Nemucca continued to read, but cocked his head now and then to listen.

"So," Scree said at the end of the tune, "what's the names of this world ours is linked with?"

"We're actually linked with three worlds. There's a map thing in here." The young soldier held the book up for Scree to have a look.

"Which ones are we on?"

"This one." Nemucca pointed to one of the worlds, a circle drawn on the map.

"How does you know?"

"Because our world is called Kiva, and that's what that says."

"You sures?"

"Yes."

"Then wheres are that other lot from?"

"That's what I don't know, yet. But it's sure to say somewhere."

"Yeah, sure. Somewheres in that book, it's going to say wheres the 'humans with the loud weapons and the strange accents' is from. Am I rights?" Scree started another tune while Nemucca went back to studying the book.

Scree knew they should get going, but now that he had music, no matter how bad it sounded, he couldn't force himself to move for a long time. He sat, leaning against the wall, eyes closed, and played. The music calmed him like nothing else could. The strangers were out there somewhere, but for a while that didn't matter. After several tunes he lowered the flute and looked at Nemucca.

"Other days, how'd you finds me?"

"I didn't. You found me, remember?"

"No, I means how'd you knows I was in the cave in the first place?"

"Oh. We didn't. Keyman Talgayni..." Nemucca paused there, as if thinking about his leader's death. "Keyman Talgayni had given up. We found the ruins in the valley and thought we might be able to find shelter from the storm. We found the cave. When we got inside, someone thought they heard laughter and we followed the sound."

"Right then. You knows the name of the city out there?"

"The ruins? No, but the valley is called Salisha, I think. Why?"

"Well I was just thinkings, seeing this Ohoga Gate things is here, you'd reckons the city would be mentioned somewheres in the book. Knows what I mean? But if you don't know the name..."

Nemucca smiled. "Wait, Salisha was mentioned, I think. Or a word something like it." The soldier flipped through pages. "You trolls aren't as dumb as everyone says."

Scree stared at Nemucca. "You keeps pushing your luck, boy."

Nemucca looked up for just a moment before quickly turning back to the book. While the human read, Scree repacked his pack, arranging everything so they'd be easy to find if needed.

"Atlantis," Nemucca said eventually. "The gate from here leads to a world called Atlantis."

Scree grunted. That didn't really tell them anything at all.

11: Rivers

KIM CHECKED WITH THE DOCTOR again then assured Meledrin that Palsamon was going to be all right. When they'd arrived the previous evening it hadn't been obvious.

The elf didn't show any signs of caring. "Thank you." She gave a slight nod. "I will make my way outside to check that Keeble has remained as we requested. I will be surprised if he has not left in search of something of interest."

Kim pursed her lips and gave a nod as well. "Okay. But if you've finished here then I guess I have as well." The hospital had her mobile number and there wasn't a lot more she could do. "Are you sure you don't want to stay?"

"Palsamon must remain at this location for some days yet. Unfortunately, if I am to summon help for the remainder of my people, we must depart soon."

"Come on then." She couldn't believe the elf. Kim was more worried than Meledrin, apparently. She couldn't stand the thought of leaving. She felt responsible now. "So how long have you known him?"

"I have known Palsamon since my tenth summer. He was assigned to work in the same glade as I when I first began my training. He assisted with the movement of some heavy branches when I was unable to complete the task on my own."

Barely a flicker of emotion.

"Right."

Out in the car park Kim glanced up at the sky. The war continued. Both planes and bats were visible, but trying to work out what was going on was like trying to watch a game of football from two suburbs away. The TV hadn't been a whole lot more enlightening.

Keeble wasn't by the door. He was down in the car park, trying to talk to a doctor but not having much luck. The dwarf was getting frustrated and the doctor was getting angry.

"[How does it work?]" Keeble said.

"If you don't get away from my car now I'll call the police."

"He doesn't speak English," Kim said as she grabbed the dwarf's arm and pulled him away.

The doctor shook his head, muttered under his breath and got into his car.

"[Keeble, I requested that you remain in the vicinity of the door,]" Meledrin said.

"[I've never met a dwarf like you,]" he replied, watching as the doctor drove away. "[Even Ari had more interest in the world than you, and she was just a regular dwife.]" He scuffed at the ground. "[How am I to learn anything if I don't go and look?]"

Kim was ready to go, but it looked like the two of them were going to talk all day.

"[You may depart at any time, of course.]"

"[I know I can.]"

"[You are not leaving?]" Meledrin raised a long, slim eyebrow.

"[No. I want to find out about their flying machines. Has Kim said anything to you about the flying machines?]"

Kim didn't know what the dwarf was saying, but he was very excited about it.

"[I am unaware. I have not inquired.]" Meledrin's response seemed to stamp all over Keeble's excitement and took him back to frustration.

"Let's get going," Kim said, heading for her own car.

"[Come, Keeble, we are departing,]" Meledrin said.

"[Where are we going?]"

"[To speak with the leaders of this world and gain assistance for our battle.]"

Keeble climbed in the front seat before Meledrin had the chance. He looked very excited by the prospect of riding in a car again, but Kim couldn't even get it started. The engine whined and spluttered and made all sorts of strange sounds, all to little effect.

"Damn it." She thumped the steering wheel. "Damn it."

His excitement stomped on again, Keeble looked as if someone had stolen his brand new bike. His shoulders slumped and he furiously wound the gears on his hand. He stared at the steering wheel as if it was the culprit.

Kim sighed. There were bigger problems in the world at the moment, but this was one more little thing she really didn't need.

"Wait here." Slamming the door behind her, she went back inside and made her way to reception. "I need to get to London in a hurry," she told the harried woman behind the counter.

"Try the trains," she said.

"The trains are running? Trust you Brits to just get on with things."

"I think they only started up again a couple of hours ago."

"So, where's the station?"

Kim got directions and went back to the car. Keeble was lying on the ground looking at the engine. Meledrin was looking on disapprovingly.

"Come on. They've got the trains running again. It's a few miles walk."

"[What's happening?]" Keeble asked.

Meledrin started to follow Kim back towards the gates. "[Apparently there are some things called trains and, according to Kim, they are running once more.]"

Kim watched Meledrin and Keeble as they walked. The elf didn't seem to notice anything at all, walking along as if she were strolling along a street she'd known all her life. The dwarf, on the other hand, tried to see everything at once. He squinted up at the street lights though they weren't even on, then raced over to try to talk to a man with a lawn mower. He examined cars as they went past and poked at a public phone with his mechanical hand. He ran ahead then fell behind, talking the whole while, shooting questions at Meledrin that the elf ignored more often than not.

After a mile, the road they were on ended at a T-intersection.

"It's amazing, isn't it?" A tall, gangly man said, shading his eyes to watch the planes and bats passing high overhead, cutting through the columns of smoke that seemed to be everywhere, like weeds in an overgrown garden. "The greatest event in human history, and this is the most we get to see. They don't even show much on the news. We should be thankful, I suppose."

Turn right, then a short walk to an overpass and down some stairs to the station.

"[I'm hungry,]" Keeble said, as Kim made her way to the ticket window.

"Keeble has questioned me about food. I am feeling hungry myself."

"We can get some in a minute. It'll only be chips or something from a vending machine, though." She motioned through onto the platform. But there was already a train waiting.

Kim got the tickets, almost emptying her account, and hurried her companions onto the train.

"[Where are we?]" Keeble asked as he sat down in a window seat.

"[This is known as a *train*,]" Meledrin replied.

"[What's it do?]"

"[It is a vehicle of some description. Apparently it locomotes on metal rails.]"

"[A train? I know what a train is.]" He looked around. "[They must clean the soot off every day.]"

A few minutes later he was bored again, fidgeting in his seat. Kim just wanted to sleep, but the dwarf was ready to go for another week. "[What happened to our food?]"

"Keeble has once more inquired about food."

"We don't have time. I might have some lollies in my pack."

"[I'm near starving.]" The dwarf watched Kim as she began a search. "[Gotta have some food. And ale. Whistler, do I need some ale. You two couldn't organize an explosion in a fireworks factory.]"

The doors of the train slid shut and Keeble was distracted, which was good because the only edible thing Kim could find was half a Mars Bar with fluff coating the end.

"[Hear that?]" he said. "[Hydraulics. That's what that was.]" He leaned over to get a better look at the door. "[Know what hydraulics are? No, course you don't.]" And he was off, telling Meledrin something she obviously had absolutely no interest in. The dwarf kept going anyway, through the next station and beyond.

He finally stopped, falling silent for about a minute. He swung his legs until Kim thought she'd go crazy from the squeaking of the chair.

"[Where are we going?]" Keeble asked when the silence stretched on.

"[A city called London.]"

"[What's there?]"

"[The leaders of this nation.]"

Apparently that was all the inactivity Keeble could stand. He fidgeted and squirmed for a few seconds more then got to his feet and pushed out into the aisle.

"Where are you going?" Kim asked him.

Meledrin asked something as well, probably the same thing.

"[Walking.]"

"[Where?]"

"[I don't know. Do you really think I can get lost?]"

"[Perhaps.]" The elf turned to Kim. "He wishes to go for a walk."

Kim didn't bother trying to stop him. Keeble didn't seem like the kind of guy who would change his mind just because someone asked nicely. Instead she pushed the train ticket into his hand.

"Take this." She showed her own ticket then slipped it back into her pocket. "Keep it with you. Okay. Tell him, Mel."

The elf said something as Keeble started to walk away. He waved over his shoulder as he went.

-o◯o-

Kim flopped down into a seat. "I shouldn't have let him go," she said, not taking her eyes from the scenery flashing by outside.

Meledrin arranged herself opposite. "He did not become lost, Kim. He deliberately left us, I am sure."

"Why? He's got no idea where he is or where he should be. He can't speak the language. He's got no idea about anything."

"That may be so, but I am unsurprised by his sudden departure."

"You're not?"

"No, Kim. For two reasons. Firstly, he is a dwarf."

That was a bit confusing. "Right."

"He is a dwarf," Meledrin repeated, "I am an elf. Our peoples have cohabitated on Sherindel for millennia, virtually next door in worldly terms, and yet we all but never speak. We avoid each other as much as possible. Elves are a high culture, and the little men are arrogant and elitist, despite being the basest of men. I am surprised he stayed as long as he did."

Kim thought that maybe Meledrin was right, but if the woman was indicative of her own 'high' culture, then the elves were no better. "I don't believe this story about elves and dwarves," she muttered. "What's the second reason then?"

"Keeble is not in complete control of his faculties."

"He isn't?" He had seemed a bit distracted at times, but it was a bit hard to tell in different languages.

"No. It is known that without community and organization dwarves quickly become ill and die."

"They die of loneliness?"

"That is correct. And Keeble failed some type of test set by his superiors and was shunned by all in his community. He spent quite some time wondering alone in the forest. I personally saw evidence of his having commenced tasks that he left incomplete. For a dwarf that indicates a grave sickness."

"You're kidding?"

"I do not kid."

"Bloody hell." Kim shook her head. *Elves and dwarves.* It was ridiculous.

But back at the hospital she'd watched the reports of the alien attacks. She hadn't dreamed them. So, if there could be aliens attacking earth on the backs of giant bats, then why couldn't elves and dwarves cross from another world through the 'magic faraway tree'?

And, sitting next to an 'elf', she took a deep breath.

"The earth is being attacked by aliens," she said softly. Like everyone else, she was going about her business as if the world hadn't recently gone though the greatest moment in recorded history. Admittedly, it was unusual business, but she was sitting on a train chatting amiably as if she would wake up tomorrow, or next week, and everything would be the same as it had always been.

"What's your world like, Meledrin?"

"Pardon."

"Your world, what's it like?"

"Very much like this one. There are trees and rocks," she waved her hands towards the window, "mountains and streams."

"Obviously," Kim said. "It has to be a lot like Earth or you'd be dead. Carbon based life, oxygen, photosynthesis, minerals, gases. You could probably drop me somewhere on Sherindel, and I wouldn't be able to tell for sure I wasn't on Earth."

Meledrin nodded. "I could inform you that there are mountains that touch white tipped fingers to the sky, lakes that so perfectly mirror the sky that you can shoot birds just by watching the reflections. There are trees that sing the breeze in perfect choruses and fields of crowded sun worshipping flowers in a thousand colors. I could tell you these things, Kim, but the things of simple beauty in this carriage would have more meaning."

"The things of beauty in this carriage?" Kim looked around, not sure what things the elf was talking about.

"You do see not the beauty here?" Meledrin asked, with one perfect eyebrow raised. "How terrible your life must be."

"Terrible?" Kim looked around again in the flickering fluorescent light. "Point this beauty out for me then."

Meledrin looked around the carriage. "The face of the child." She gestured towards a little girl sitting on the other side of the aisle a few rows back. "Her smile, the concentration so apparent in her eyes, the line of her jaw, the way her hair outlines the delicate curve of her ear." Meledrin looked around again.

"And the old lady over there. Her shawl. The colors are perfect -- slashes and swirls against the plain, straight lines of the seat. That young couple over there. Their clothes could not be more different, their features could not be more different, but look at the expressions they wear. That is beauty, Kim: a smile, a look, a simple, unexpected pleasure."

Kim knew what the elf was saying but couldn't truly see it. When she turned to Meledrin to say so, she wondered if the elf really *could* see it. Meledrin knew that beauty was there, perhaps, but she looked with the eyes of an art critic, not an art lover or an artist. She was so emotionless that she could not possibly see it any other way.

Kim closed her eyes. She wondered where Keeble was. The dwarf didn't like Meledrin, and she was starting to agree with him. Meledrin had seen her people slaughtered and crossed between worlds. She left a man, a good friend at the very least, in critical condition, in the company of strangers, and was separated from another companion. She had generally been thrown in over her head and hadn't shown one visible human emotion, or even an elfish one for that matter. She'd kept a couple of emotions hidden, but that was not the same.

The trees continued to stream past the window. Farmhouses were stars in the darkness of space. Towns were galaxies.

"Why do you think they're here, Mel?"

"Who?"

Kim sighed. "Who do you think?"

"I do not believe that 'why' is important. It does not change what is."

"'Why?' is very important. They travelled a gazillion or so kilometers to attack Earth. All the space between here and there means they have a very good reason for doing it." She remembered the alien that had spared the witch and her granddaughter at Sherwood Forest. It had seen them, aimed, then changed its mind. "We need to talk to them, Mel," she said. "We need to find out what the hell is going on, because they aren't monsters. I know they aren't."

"Perhaps not, but I still do not see how that changes what is."

"Of course you don't. But maybe we can sort all this out peacefully. Maybe we don't have to kill them."

"Why should we not kill them? They come and attack our worlds, and you wish to make friends with them?"

"Of course I do. I *left* the army, remember?"

"People are dying. People are dead. I do not feel the need to make friends with the killers."

"Well, then maybe *everyone* will end up dead."

"No. You humans on Earth will survive."

Kim turned to look at the Meledrin, to see if she was at all bitter. But as usual, the elf showed nothing. "Just because the aliens aren't having any success at the moment, doesn't mean they won't in the future."

"They are obviously no match for your flying warriors. Their bombs are pitiful, they damage hardly anything, and the damage is quickly controlled."

Kim didn't agree with the elf's definition of 'hardly anything', but she let that slide. "You're talking about something you know absolutely nothing about. All the aliens need to do is find one half-decent sized rock to throw at us."

"A rock? You are worried that they might start throwing stones?"

"A big rock, the size of a office block, thrown from space."

It was obvious Meledrin still didn't understand but Kim didn't care. She turned to look out the window. The English countryside continued to flash by. London couldn't arrive soon enough.

-oOo-

"Is the other side of the river really so important that all these bridges are truly required?" Meledrin asked.

Such questions convinced Kim that Meledrin was for real. No human, even acting as some weird alien, would ever think of asking the point of television soap operas. They may ask what they were, but never why. They'd never ask about the spiritual importance of pop music, especially English pop music, with a straight face. And they'd never ask if the other side of the river was really that important.

"Yes, it's important," Kim replied. "For humans, the other side of the river is about the most important thing there is." She wasn't sure if the elf was aware of symbolism or metaphor, but she wasn't about to explain them in the back of a cab travelling to Parliament House.

"Where is this place to which we go?"

"Not far. So what, exactly, do we do when we get there?" Kim asked, leaning across to close Meledrin's window against the heavy rain.

"What is it that you mean? We go and tell them what is happening on my world, of course."

"They already know what's happening, Mel. Their army is fighting a war on Sherindel."

"There must be understanding between our peoples. We must forge an alliance against these attackers."

"Well, we won't get close enough to anyone to say a damn thing. We won't even get in the door."

Meledrin began to say something, but Kim continued, cutting her off.

"I *wasn't* guarding the tree. I was just standing there. Nobody was guarding the tree."

Meledrin looked out the window, lost in thought. "Are the Lords meeting today?"

Kim leaned forward and tapped on the partition that divided them from the driver. The man opened a flap. "Yes, Ma'am."

"Is parliament sitting today?" She probably should have checked that earlier.

"I don't think so, Ma'am."

"Thank you."

"That's fine. Probably be another five minutes."

"Do they have offices in there?"

"Some do, Ma'am, but I don't know if they'll be there."

"Why's that?"

"Big target like that?"

"Obviously. Thanks."

The flap thudded closed again.

"They're not meeting."

"Yes, I heard."

"Good."

"Then we will just go and see what happens. Some may be there in any case; surely they have duties they must attend to."

"Fine. There are worse ways to waste a day, I suppose." Though she'd already visited all the famous London tourist attractions.

Kim turned away, watching the rain spatter against the window. She was glad Meledrin didn't speak for the rest of the journey.

12: Absent Lords

MELEDRIN WONDERED HOW THE LORDS could be so negligent to their duties. There was a war, how could they not be meeting? She listened as Kim got the information, again, out of a recalcitrant guard at the main gate.

"So, are there *any* Lords in there?" Kim asked. "Are they Lording, or whatever it is that they do?"

"Maybe, miss."

"What about MP's?"

The man shrugged.

Meledrin could not remain silent. The guard could not be trusted, saveigni that he was. "Would we be allowed to go and converse with one of them?"

"Sorry, Ma'am. State of emergency and all. No unauthorized people in or out."

Kim smiled at the man as if she had found the solution to their dilemma. "Well, if you say we're allowed, surely we'd be authorized."

"Sorry."

"We have information about the aliens."

"Doesn't everyone?"

Meledrin wished to help but did not interrupt again.

"Not like this. We know what's happening in Nottinghamshire."

"Well, try going to your local member."

"From my accent, would you think my local member might be somewhere nearby?"

"Sorry, Miss."

"Okay. Just checking."

Meledrin finally opened her mouth to speak but Kim took her by the arm and drew her away before she had the opportunity.

Meledrin whispered a *Lesser Changing* as she stepped back out into the rain.

She followed as quickly as dignity would allow as Kim, running with her head down, pack bouncing on her back, led the way back towards the river. Vehicles moved along the streets, throwing out arcs of spray, but the roads seemed to be carrying far less than their full capacity. Pedestrians either hurried by or stood in the rain, staring up at the sky. There were small stalls near the end of a long, stone bridge, but they were closed.

Meledrin was not far behind when Kim dashed across the street and took shelter under the arched concrete portico opposite. The woman sat at a small table and stared at a huge, motionless wheel with gondolas suspended from it. When a servant came, she ordered a drink, not speaking until she had taken her first sip several minutes later.

"What do you want to try now?"

Was that not obvious? "We find these Lords of yours and make them help."

"They aren't *my* Lords."

"What is it that you mean?"

"I'm not English. I'm Australian, mainly. I don't have any right to ask anything of a British politician. And neither do you."

Meledrin suppressed a sigh. "Then let us go and ask for assistance from one of *your* politicians."

"Huh. That'd be like asking a school yard bully to fight Asian crime gangs."

"Pardon?" Meledrin said. Even if she understood every word of English, she doubted she would always understand.

"If we got to talk to an Australian politician, they'd talk big and say 'yes, of course we'll do something'. But as soon as you turn your back they'll go back to doing what they do best."

"Then who is likely to listen?"

"Americans." Then she shook her head, as if arguing with herself. "Maybe."

"And why will they listen when others will not?"

"Three reasons. One, they're the most powerful nation on Earth and didn't get there by sitting on their hands. Two, like everyone they like to be popular and the good thing about this war is that *everyone* on Earth will be on their side, for once. And three, according to the reports, they're copping more from the aliens than anyone else."

"Then let us go to America." Meledrin rose to her feet and waited for Kim to lead the way.

Kim stood and made her way to the edge of the street. "We can't go to America —"

"Why not?"

She sighed. "You don't have a passport. You don't have anything. You don't exist. But if you hadn't interrupted me, I would have said, we can't go to America, but we don't have to."

"I apologize for interrupting." It had been rude, but she was having trouble controling her emotions. She could feel fear bubbling beneath the surface and was unsure how long she could keep it hidden.

"That's okay. But now we have to find a cab."

"To go to which location?"

"The American Embassy. But just remember, like I said before, they may not listen."

"Why would they not listen? We have important information."

Kim gave a grunt of laughter. "The world is being attacked by aliens. I know it might be a bit hard to tell, standing here, chatting as we are, but pilots are flying around above us risking their lives, possibly, and shooting big, black space-bats." Kim shook her head and muttered, "Ed Wood's about to rush onto the set and yell 'cut'."

"Who is this Ed Wood? Is he an American Lord?" *And what is he wishing to cut?*

"The point is, the people in charge don't have time to listen to every crackpot that comes knocking on their door with conspiracy theories and tales of magical gateways."

"But it is the truth."

"The truth doesn't always matter, unfortunately."

"Many people are dying. Surely they want every piece of information that might help."

Kim laughed again. "You obviously don't know humans all that well. Sometimes not knowing is preferable. The existence of aliens has already upset a large proportion of the world, but at the moment it's still just a war. One that we seem to be winning. Mention magical gateways and you'll open up a whole new can of extremely smelly worms." Kim paused, chewed on her lip. "You'd think the aliens would learn, wouldn't you?"

"Your meaning?"

"Well, hundreds of thousands of people, maybe millions, have died, and more are dying every hour but, in the grand scheme of things, it isn't really that many at all. They keep sending the bats and we keep shooting them, apparently without a whole heap of trouble. Since the first few surprise hits, firebombs have hit a couple of places, but that's about it. There's more chance of being injured when you're hit on the head by a bullet-riddled corpse."

"Perhaps they are slow to learn."

"Perhaps they're stubborn. Perhaps they have so many bats they can afford to just keep sending them."

"I do not understand." Meledrin paused as a strange look passed across Kim's face. "What is the matter?"

It was a moment before the woman replied. "Well, this planet of yours, Sherindel, is nowhere near ours. We know that. So what are the odds that these aliens coincidentally attacked our two worlds at the same time?"

"I do not understand what it is that you are saying, Kim."

"The aliens know that Earth and Sherindel are linked in some way. That suggests they know more about us than we think. It also proves that this isn't just some random attack by evil alien hordes."

"I do not think that you can make judgements like that with the limited information available."

"Look, something's going on, and we have to tell someone. And soon."

"I was under the impression that is what we have been attempting to do."

"Yes, I know. Come on, we need a cab."

They waited by the side of the road for several minutes before Kim waved at a passing vehicle. It pulled over and Kim climbed into the back. Meledrin followed a moment later muttering the words of *Action*. Kim's words had finally sunk in. An enemy without end. But according to the woman that piece of news paled into insignificance against the realization that the aliens knew about the gateway in the Ohoga tree.

She rolled down the glass window. The rain was slackening. It was enough to be an annoyance, but the cool breeze helped. She worried about her people. She worried about Palsamon.

She took a deep breath, belatedly hoping that Kim wouldn't notice. "What is love, Kim?" she asked, schooling her face to calmness and watching row after row of buildings file past. She had heard humans everywhere talk of love but was not sure she understood.

"Love? It's... Well, depends on the type of love, and who's defining it."

"You are defining it. You are defining all types."

"Well, love, I suppose, is intense positive feelings one living creature has for another living creature."

"That is it?"

"Yes. Basically."

"Intense positive feelings?" Meledrin shook her head. It had to be more than that. The concept seemed to dominate the lives of humans.

"Yes. I mean, that's the general definition." Kim sighed. "Look, Mel, tell me what brought this question on and I might be able to do a better job of explaining."

She wished Kim would stop calling her 'Mel'. It was not dignified. "It does not matter. I was merely wondering." She did not know, and Kim obviously could not explain. She gave it no more thought.

Meledrin climbed out of the cab when it eventually pulled over to the side of the street. *Lesser Changing.*

"So, where are we going?" Kim asked the vehicle's driver as she handed over paper money.

"Down there."

"Where the crowd is?"

Meledrin turned to look as well. A large group of people were gathered in front of a building. Many of them appeared to be men. That was another thing she could not understand.

"That's it, miss."

The driver smiled and chatted with Kim as if they were equals. He showed no deference at all. It was all Meledrin could do to hold her tongue. Instead, she tilted her head back so the rain could massage her face. They didn't really have rain on

Sherindel. Not like here. There, it was never much more than a mist. The difference pleased Meledrin, but she was unsure how long that feeling would last.

"Come on."

Meledrin allowed herself to be drawn to a small dry area in the doorway of a building.

"You'll catch a chill standing there like that, you idiot."

"A what?"

"A chill. A cold? You know running nose, sneezing, that kind of thing."

"We do not have such things on Sherindel."

"Well, this is England, Mel. I reckon you'll find out what a cold is."

Meledrin shrugged and sighed. Shrugging was hardly dignified either, but humans used the action often, and it did convey quite a lot. "Now, what action do we take?" Meledrin leaned back against the cold bricks of the wall while Kim looked about. The young human seemed at a loss as to what to do. "Are we not going to see the Lords?"

"Yes, but..."

"But what? The operator of the vehicle indicated that we must go in this direction." She pointed down the street. The crowd was quite large.

"All right, let's go then."

Meledrin watched as Kim dashed from the protection of the doorway and ran down the footpath as if all the dwarves in the world were after her. Meledrin waved *Lesser Action* and followed at her usual pace. Her long strides kept her close. The rain was an inconvenience, perhaps, but not worth losing one's dignity over. Though by the time she caught the young woman, standing in another doorway, Meledrin was starting to wonder. Her dress was clinging to her body, revealing her breasts almost as if she were naked. Indeed, even as she joined her companion she noticed a man ogling her from a window nearby. She stared at him until he looked away.

Kim continued to dash from scant cover to scant cover while Meledrin followed not far behind and worried about what she might say to the Lords of the United States. She had never met any humans before Kim, and she was discovering that reading about them could not prepare her for what she needed to do. They were so unpredictable. They did not seem to have any guiding tenets as a race, with each one viewing situations from a totally individual perspective. So, with no real grasp of what drove humans, she had no point from which to start. Did she appeal to their greed or their compassion? The riches of the world they would have access to, or the riches of elfish culture? She decided that, in either case, she would not mention the dwarves. The little men would be of no attraction to anyone, either in the way they lived their lives or the way they destroyed the land.

Meledrin followed Kim into the crowd of people. *Lesser Changing.* Many of them had little boxes held up to their eyes or were talking into strange objects. Kim pushed her way through and Meledrin followed, slipping through the crowd. She tried, without much success, to avoid brushing against the men. When the way became too congested, even for Kim's outrageous shoving, they were forced almost to a standstill.

The building they were trying to reach, the center of all the attention, faced out over road and a small park. A huge sculpture of an eagle soared five floors above the door. The stone facade, covered in a metal grillwork, gave the impression of impregnable strength without clashing with the surrounding architecture.

Meledrin was impressed. Other buildings in London were much the same — if not in design, then in size and spirit — but she hadn't really stopped to look. Now, she slipped laterally through the crowd, crossing to one of the stone columns that lined the front of the building. She hesitantly touched the cool surface. Kim followed close behind, apologizing as she went, but being ignored for the most part.

"I have never known that stone could be so alive," Meledrin said, pushing wet hair away from her face. "It has always been mere stone in the past."

"I thought dwarves were supposed to be the best stone masons anywhere," Kim said.

"You learned this in your tales of 'fantasy'."

"Well, yeah." She sounded slightly embarrassed.

"No, you are quite correct. They are supposed to be stone masons without equal." Meledrin broke away from the stone and moved closer to their destination. She moved to another column, touching at its surface. The rain was lessening, the cloud cover breaking up. *Such a strange world where conditions can change so quickly.*

"'Supposed to be the best masons?'"

"Well, I have never witnessed any of their work."

"So, let me get this right. You hate dwarves? Can't stand them? And yet you have never even seen the one thing that defines them as a race?"

"Masonry does not define dwarves." Meledrin sighed and continued to examine the column, running her fingers along the perfect ribs, feeling at the joints. "Their love of work does. Their need to be *doing*. Their superior physical skills come from that, not the other way around."

"Okay, but you have never seen the dwarfish homelands, or whatever they call it?"

"No, I have not."

"How many dwarves have you met in your entire life?"

Meledrin thought for a moment. "Only Keeble."

"Only Keeble?"

Meledrin stopped and turned to face Kim. "I see where you are leading with this, Kim. You are going to ask, 'How can I judge a race of people by just one of their number?' That is what you are going to ask, is it not?" She smiled. Kim was young and naïve and would not understand, even when it was explained to her.

"Yes, that's my question."

"Well, I do not judge them. I let people that I trust judge them. My ancestors. My friends." She could name her mothers all the way back to the turn of the millennium, and none of them liked dwarves.

"And how many dwarves have your friends seen? And your ancestors? How long since a group of elves visited the dwarves, or the other way around."

"It has been many years. The dwarves always end up making trouble and leaving. They are unrefined, loud, and have not a thought towards custom."

They finally reached a low wooden barricade with a serious looking saveigni in a green uniform on the other side. A whole line of them, stiff and staring, guarded the barricade.

"You mean they have no thought for *your* customs. Have you considered that they have customs of their own, dating back as long as yours, that say you should show your hosts that you're having a good time?"

Meledrin turned away from her inspection of the guards. "What is it that you mean?" She knew Kim was going to come up with a ridiculous example, but it was only polite to ask.

"Well burping, for instance."

"I beg your pardon. I do not know the word."

"Belching. Expelling air from your stomach out through your mouth."

"Ah, yes. I understand."

"Well, in my culture belching is considered, well, not rude but uncouth."

"As it is in mine." Meledrin thought of pointing out that elves and humans had much in common, but Kim was speaking again.

"Right, but there's at least one culture on Earth where belching after a meal is thought to show your enjoyment of the meal."

"I do not believe you." Meledrin said with a sniff. *Belching a display of contentment!*

Kim turned to the nearest guard. "I'm not lying, am I?"

For long moments the man did not reply. When he did, his eyes continued to rove, scanning the crowd. "Ma'am, I'm pretty sure the Chinese have a custom like that."

Meledrin sniffed again. Of course the humans would stick together.

"See," Kim said. "But if a Chinese person went to someone's house in my land, they might offend when they were trying to please. All through a misunderstanding."

"Well these misunderstandings have been going on for longer than anyone can remember."

"And they'll continue to, as long as nobody hangs around long enough to talk."

Meledrin shook her head. "It is not that easy, Kim."

"I'm sure it isn't."

Meledrin shook her head and sighed. Kim would never understand. She turned to the guard. "Please allow us through, saveigni."

"I'm sorry, ma'am, unless you're a citizen of the United States, you can't pass."

"Well, as a matter of fact..." Kim removed her pack and searched through one of the pockets. After a moment she pulled free a little book and held it out to be examined.

The saveigni glanced at it. "That's an Australian passport, Miss."

"What? Oh, shit. Wrong one." Kim searched again.

The guard raised an eyebrow. "You have two passports?"

"It's a long story. It involves elopement, unimpressed grandparents, and several official enquiries."

"Right." He turned his attention back to the crowd while Kim continued to go through her pack.

"Anyway," Kim continued, "surely we aren't in the U.S. until we've passed through the doors. There's still a little bit of England behind you there. Have you gotten permission to keep English citizens off English soil?"

Meledrin sighed. Kim seemed to enjoy annoying people.

"I couldn't say for sure, ma'am. Not sure if we're allowed to stop Australians, either, come to think of it." He said it with what appeared to be a friendly smile, as if he was enjoying himself as well. "Why don't you go and ask the Prime Minister?"

"Tried to ask the British Prime Minister. Didn't work. "

"Well then, maybe your own Prime Minister?"

"I could. Ah-huh." She pulled a little book, similar to the first, triumphantly from the pack. She smiled. "But today, I'm American."

The saveigni took the book and opened it up. "Well, Miss McLean, you are free to enter, but unless your friend here also has an American passport, she'll have to wait out here."

Meledrin had had enough — being forced to stand in the rain and talk to a *man*.

"Kim and I have information regarding the alien attacks," she said. "Kim suggested that the United States might be the nation that could best make use of the information."

"It's all right, Mel. I'll go in and get someone."

Meledrin ignored her. "Immediately inform your lord that we seek an audience."

"My *lord?*" the saveigni said.

"Yes, go and get her now."

Kim put a hand on Meledrin's shoulder and pulled her back slightly. "Please excuse Meledrin. She's not from around here. She isn't aware of how things work."

"Not from around here? What planet is she from, exactly?"

"My world is called Sherindel," Meledrin said. She realized too late that it might have been a rhetorical and sarcastic question all in one.

The man was no longer enjoying himself. "Look, we've had all sorts of crackpots turning up here over the last few days. None of them got in, and you aren't going to get in either." He looked at Kim. "I'm starting to have my doubts about you as well."

Meledrin opened her mouth to speak, but Kim got in first.

"Look, it's all under control. Meledrin will stay out here while I go in and tell your boss about the magical gate in Nottinghamshire." Kim turned to look at the elf. "It may take a while, though. I'll have to start at the bottom and work my way up to someone who knows something. All right?"

"There's a magical gateway in Nottinghamshire?"

When the savegini said the words, Meledrin suddenly realized how ridiculous they sounded. The look on Kim's face suggested that she was thinking the same thing.

But the woman continued anyway. "Actually, your superiors might already know about it. The English army knew a couple of days ago."

"A gateway?" The soldier looked at his nearest companion. When he turned back, it was clear that the conversation had almost reached its conclusion. Before he could say anything, though, a tall, aging man stepped into view from the Embassy.

The crowd waiting outside the barrier launched into a cacophony of sound. They all seemed to shout a dozen questions at the newcomer, but he ignored them all and moved quickly to where Meledrin and Kim waited.

Meledrin waved a *Beginning*.

The man was not dressed in a uniform, but his bearing was much the same as that of the guards. Straight-backed and proud. "Ladies, my name is Mathew Gainis. If you'll just come with me, please." Instead of leading them back inside, he led them through the crowd and to the street. As they arrived, a large black car with dark windows met them. "Nottinghamshire, you say? Helicopter will be quicker."

"You know something about this gate, don't you?" Kim asked as she ducked into the car.

Meledrin glared at the stranger as he put his hand on her waist to usher her inside as well. She did not move.

"No. Not this gate." The man saw Meledrin's expression and removed his hand with a slight bow of apology. "The English authorities have not been kind enough to let us know though we have had our suspicions that something was going on."

"There's another? Were you kind enough to let the English government know about your one?" Kim smiled as if something was extremely funny.

The man did not reply, merely hurrying around the far side of the car and climbing into the front seat.

The car took them to a helicopter and that machine took them back to Sherwood Forest. It was much quicker than the train journey had been, but the ensuing conversation between the American and the local soldiers seemed to last forever. Eventually Mr. Gainis passed through the tree to Sherindel. When he returned, he immediately headed for the helicopter.

"You, Meledrin, come from Sherindel?" Mr. Gainis asked when they were back in the air a couple of minutes later.

Meledrin wondered how many times she would be asked, and by a man at that. She had answered the same question several times already. If it was taking this long for this man to be satisfied, she could not imagine the type of questions a Warder or a Lord would ask and how long the process would take. She sighed. At least it allowed her to concentrate on something other than the motion of the helicopter and the alarming distance to the ground.

"You haven't informed the Brits of your presence here?"

"They would not speak with us, though the soldiers spoke with me when I arrived. Have you found my companion?"

"Yes, Palsamon was in the hospital where you left him. He's on his way to London right now. He'll be taken to a private hospital." The man checked some papers in a folder on the seat beside him. It had not been there when they exited the helicopter previously. "Kim, how did you get involved in this. A pilot with the Australian army?"

"Not for a long time, years, as I am sure your records show."

He flipped through some pages. "Usual, everyday stuff since. A few times to America?"

"My father's family still lives there. They don't like my mother much, but they're willing to provide me with free accommodation."

"And your father was in the diplomatic corps?"

Kim laughed. "Something like that, yes."

As the conversation continued, Meledrin watched as Kim spoke with the man and wondered what she was missing. Kim seemed to think carefully about every answer, as if they were all vitally important, or potentially dangerous.

"So, how did you get involved?"

"I just happened to be there when Meledrin and Keeble came through the gate. I've been backpacking."

"Keeble? There's someone else? And you didn't think to mention this before?"

"Well, you weren't giving me much time to think." Kim shrugged. "I don't know where Keeble is. We lost him on the train."

"Lost him?" Gainis sighed and raised his eyebrows all at once.

"Well, possibly he deliberately ran away. It's hard to know for sure. He and Mel don't like each other too much, you see."

"So there's another elf walking around somewhere?"

Meledrin laughed. *How ridiculous.* "No elves. An elf would not have become separated, either by mistake or on purpose. Keeble is a dwarf."

"A dwarf? Oh, this gets better and better."

"You are suggesting that I am lying?" Meledrin arched an eyebrow. The manners of every human she met left a lot to be desired.

"Of course not; I went to another world."

"Dwarves and elves, right?" Kim said. "You are wondering if you will see hobbits next. Well, get used to it."

"Yes."

He checked his papers again, though what he might find there, Meledrin could not imagine.

"Any ideas where we might start looking for Keeble?"

"No," Kim replied.

"You know nothing that might help us?" He turned for a moment to look at Meledrin.

Meledrin did not know why she had originally risked her reputation and standing in Grovely by deciding to help Keeble. She had regretted the decision almost every moment since. But she also wondered if the changing circumstances gave her the right to ignore the responsibility she had taken on. She looked away for a moment. "He will probably be repairing something."

"Pardon."

"He will be repairing something," Meledrin said again. "It is what dwarves do. They make things and repair things."

"Great. That narrows it down."

Meledrin sniffed and looked around at the interior of the helicopter. Like most of the human vehicles she had seen, it was cold and lifeless. Meledrin wanted to feel the breeze again, and rain. She wanted to be away from the men and their incessant questions. She wanted to be back on Sherindel. She had wanted to stay when they had taken the American to see, but neither he nor the English soldiers would allow it. They were battling the bats on Sherindel, strengthening their position and moving outwards, but had not managed to find many survivors. Some of their own men were missing.

Meledrin sighed. Palsamon and Keeble were both here on Earth. Perhaps her place was here was well, but all she really wanted was to be away from the saveigni and the endless questions.

PING GLANCED AT HER COMPANIONS before closing her eyes and whispering a short, all-encompassing prayer. She crossed her fingers. Perching on the edge of her seat as she waited the final few moments, she crossed her ankles as well.

Twice a day for the last six months, at eleven in the morning and eleven at night, the clock in Elephant Tower had sung the hour right on time. Today was not going to be any different.

Ping held her breath and scrunched her eyes tighter. The zorigami crowded in the square outside, and possibly right across the city, hushed in expectation as well.

"Three..." Mrs Kew said softly, "Two... One..."

And right on time, the clock started its long, melodic chime.

The crowd outside, not visible from where Ping sat, cheered and rumbled into life once more as the Mid-summer Festival neared its noon crescendo.

Ping drew in a deep breath and opened her eyes. She smiled at Mrs Kew.

The old lady, seated by the table, smiled at everyone. She snapped the door on her ornate traveling clock closed and, with trembling hands, slipped it carefully into its hard leather satchel. "I am not sure which is worse," Mrs Kew said, "being in Shark Tower or Elephant Tower on the day of the Noon Chorus."

Ping shook her head, knowing what was to come. Tung would have an opinion and, sure as the Great Clock, he would offer it.

"I've been in both," he said, pausing for four seconds of reflection and a sip of dark, cool wine, "and Shark Tower is much the worse. Imagine, if you can, the tension of waiting on the edge of your seat since midnight."

Lan, Enial and Shen went to pour some wine. Deshi rolled his eyes and made for the safety of the balcony.

Ping rose quietly. She straightened the pleats of her lavender skirt and made her way through the arched door and out onto the balcony as well. Tung remained with Mrs Kew and his own rambling.

The gods were smiling on the Mid-summer Festival again. Deep blue sky— north, south, east and west— with just a lacy frill of clouds on the horizon. A cooling breeze, unexpected rogue from the outlands, kissed at the twelve Cardinal Towers and set their flags to fluttering.

From her position halfway up the side of Elephant Tower— the eleventh tower, between Shark and Tiger— Ping had a grand view of the city. The Great Clock was situated in the centre and twelve broad, tree-lined avenues radiated out from there. The Cardinal Towers sat on the top of the hills, at the heads of the avenues, a crown on the king of cities.

A thousand years earlier, Shadon had started out as a small village nestled at the base of the bowl shaped depression. Since then it had grown considerably, flooding up over the hills and into the plains beyond.

And, on this one day of the year, all the zorigami of the world was focused on the clocks. Or so Ping liked to think.

All the main roads, from the Great Clock to the tops of the hills, seemed to already be at a standstill. The crowd around Elephant Tower had grown unbelievably since Ping had last looked. The Jugglers of Jilin were undoubtedly the reason for that. Like the Emperor, the legendary troupe left the Imperial City on just this one day of the year, so there was always a large audience.

The square was designed like an amphitheatre but the balcony of Elephant Tower was the best vantage point of all, and Ping was there. In a clock makers' club for little more than a year and she was standing in one of the Cardinal Clocks looking down at the Jugglers of Jilin.

Ping remembered previous years when she had stood almost a kilometer from the Jugglers, down the hill and far away, just hoping beyond hope to catch a glimpse of some of the flying colored balls. She had seen nothing, and most people would see nothing today, but tried anyway.

A group of farmers, with sun-browned skin and serious expressions, took up all the shade offered by the oak tree in the corner of the square. They may have been there since the night before. Hawkers had given up trying to move through the crowd. A line of young raven-haired boys, as eager to watch the show as any, had long ago claimed their places along the edge of the stone cistern at the very top of the seating slope.

As Ping stood quietly, one of the boys looked upward. His slanted eyes went wide with wonder. Ping smiled gaily and waved. The boy waved back, beaming. Then he tugged on the arm of his closest companion and pointed, exhorting his friend to look. Soon all of the little group were smiling and waving until Ping blushed.

"It's strange, isn't it?"

Ping turned and saw Enial standing by her side, a mug of wine in one hand and a banny loaf, dripping with butter, in the other.

"What is?"

"Those boys are all exited by the fact that you waved to them."

Ping chewed on her thumbnail as she looked back down at the boys. They were still gazing up at her. "Yes, it's strange."

"But, you might well have acted the same way just a year ago."

"No, I—" But she *had* just had that very thought about the jugglers and wanting to view greatness, however distantly or obliquely.

"How old are you, Ping? Twenty?" Enial leaned back against the rail and took a sip of wine. "I can remember staring up at the Cardinal Towers when I was your age, thinking that gods worked within. And the Great Clock? Well, I was sure that the walls of heaven would be made from the same polished stone... To hear that magical midsummer's day chime..."

"We aren't gods," Ping said defensively when her companion trailed away dreamily.

Enial laughed. "Of course *we* know that, but them down there..." He shrugged. "What evidence do they have either way?"

Ping chewed on her thumbnail some more. She waved to the boys again, and they all stood staring at her, mouths hanging open, toes wriggling in the open air over the edge of the cistern. They had not believed the first miracle but could not refute the second.

"And what's more," Enial said, as if he hadn't stopped, "You are young and beautiful. That in itself is normally more than enough reason for boys to worship girls. Now come inside and have some wine to celebrate."

Ping blushed some more, smoothing down her bobbed brown hair. *Beautiful?* "Celebrate what? We haven't won yet."

Enial sighed and took her by the arm. "Celebrate the fact that you are here, Ping. Those boys would give anything to be in your place, win or not. Your first year in a clock makers' club and you are in the Great Countdown. Something that you have worked on for a year is within an hour of fulfilling its purpose, and tomorrow it will be pulled apart forever."

"But the jugglers?"

"They'll be fifteen minutes yet, at least."

Ping allowed herself to be led back in through the ornate archway, beneath the elephant gargoyle, and into the shadowed interior. She took a cup of wine when it was offered and resumed her seat.

Tung was still talking to Mrs Kew. The judge was nodding slowly, but it was obvious to everyone— except Tung— that she wasn't paying any attention. Everyone was too polite to tell him. When Tung finally paused for a breath and a sip of wine Ping asked Mrs Kew a question and a smile of thanks fluttered like a butterfly across the old woman's crinkled face.

"How long have you been a judge, Mrs Kew?"

"Oh, many years." The old lady counted in her head, looking skyward for heavenly help. "Twenty-seven. Twenty-seven years. But I really don't know why I gave up making clocks. I used to work on the Great Clock you know, now and then."

"You did?"

"Oh, yes. And a finer thing I cannot remember. Your clock is very fine, very fine, but compared to the Great Clock it is nothing."

Ping chewed on her much-abused thumbnail and stared at the old woman, wondering what it must be like to touch the workings of the Great Clock. Only the best of the best even got to *see* the interior of the clock... As she stared, Ping was reminded of the boys outside, and what Enial had said.

"That was a long time ago now, though." Mrs Kew sighed. Then, suddenly business-like, she pushed herself to her feet. "Time for the final inspection," she said. With a clipboard in one hand and a stylus in the other, she tottered across to the steep steps and up to the clock level above. Tung made to follow but thought better of it. Instead, he paced from the foot of the stairs, across to the balcony, and back again.

"You don't think the fifth fly wheel is too loose, do you?" he asked of nobody in particular. "Maybe we should have taken off the sharp corners for safety."

"Maybe we should have made the workings out of timber," Ping said. It was an idea she'd been thinking about for some time, though she didn't mean to mention it.

Tung was in one of his moments of panic. "What? Why?"

Ping licked her lips, suddenly nervous as well. She *had* been thinking about it for a while, but that didn't mean anything. Everyone was looking at her, all those people with many years more experience than her. She licked her lips again. "Well, metal expands and contracts with changes in temperature. Only slightly, but..."

They were all staring at her. Ping looked from one face to the next. "What? It's silly, I know—"

"My girl, that..."

"Everything looks fine up here," Mrs Kew said from the top of the steps. She was marking things off on her clipboard with a shaking hand. "I like what you have done with the counter-weight."

Mrs Kew was almost as bad as Tung at times. She commented on the counter-weight after every inspection.

Enial sidled over to Ping's side while Mrs Kew, round face tense with concentration, slowly descended the stairs.

"Not a word, Ping. *Not a word.*"

Ping nodded.

"The Cog Club was in the Great Countdown the year before last, were you not?" Mrs Kew asked. Having reached level floor once more she struck out for the table.

Tung was still staring at Ping, so Enial answered. "No, Mrs Kew. It was the year before that. In the last two years we were knocked out at the mantle clock stage."

"And this year?"

"Grandfather Clock finals are this afternoon, of course, and we believe we've got a chance of making the Great Countdown again."

"Not joining the festivities this afternoon then?"

Tung, having collected his scattered thoughts, shrugged and smiled. "We will still have a drink or two, I imagine. Our Grandfather Clock is made and will win or not... There is nothing we can do now. The same as the Cardinal, really." Tung looked upwards, and Ping could not tell if he was offering a prayer to the gods or once more wondering if there *was* anything else they could have done.

But of course, the Cardinal Clock had been completed six months ago and had not been touched since, beyond routine maintenance. Any mistakes in its design and construction were long past repairing.

Mrs Kew nodded vaguely as she put her clipboard down on the table and resumed her seat. As Tung started talking again, Ping returned to the balcony.

"Do you realize you may have just changed clock-making forever?" Enial said softly when he joined her at the rail.

Ping blushed. "It is just an idea. Maybe the wood will—"

"Maybe the wood will do a lot of things, but still, one little idea can change everything. Even if we don't use wood, because it can be effected by moisture, but... "

"Let's worry about today," Ping said. She did not want to think about *changing clock making*. "The Great Countdown and the Grandfather Clock finals."

Enial smiled and gripped her arm for a moment. "Yes, let's. Excited?"

Ping was excited about seeing the Jugglers of Jilin without even beginning to think about clock making finals.

"This is the worst time," Enial said. "Between our last chime and the Noon Chorus. Tung is right though— we only have to wait an hour to know the result while Shark Tower has been waiting since midnight. The tension can almost be too much." He motioned to the next tower, about half a kilometer distant, the one directly north of the Great Clock. "Can you imagine trying to sleep? Waking each hour to hear the other clocks ringing and going out to look at your own clock to see if it was keeping time?"

"But if it chimed on time just twelve hours ago..."

"Easy to say, Ping. I saw you praying though you know very well our clock was on time last night." He smiled and took a sip of wine. "Nothing is ever as simple as it seems."

Down in the center of the square, the Jugglers were almost ready. The six members of the troupe, four women and two men, were arranging themselves on a patterned carpet they had carried all the way from the Imperial City. They stood with stars and moons arrayed about their feet. The crowd hushed expectantly. All movement seemed to stop, apart from zorigami craning their necks and standing on their toes to try to get a better view. Even that stopped when people got what they wanted, or realized that they never would.

One of the jugglers, a giant of a woman well over a hundred and fifty five centimeters tall, took up six colored balls and started to juggle. Her dark blue robes, with stars to match the pattern on the carpet, were full and heavy, but did not hinder her. She tossed the balls in ever-higher arcs, graceful and fluid, in ever more complex patterns. A rainbow of color swirled over her head. Then two more jugglers started, perfectly mirroring the first. After another minute, the other three joined in as well and dozens of balls were spinning through the air, catching the light in dazzling splendor.

There were some zorigami who said that the sun was just another star and that the world spun about it in space. They said that other worlds circled the stars of the night sky, impossibly far away. Ping imagined she was looking at such a dance of nature. Worlds spinning about the juggling stars.

Then the patterns changed again. As if the six individuals juggling on their own wasn't amazing enough, the Jugglers of Jilin each took one ball from their group and threw it to one of their companions. Balls were sailing across the intricate patterns of the carpet in impossible rhythms.

Ping was speechless. She gripped the rail tightly, leaning forward as if she might add another couple of centimeters to her height and somehow get a better view. At some stage the rest of Cog Club and Mrs Kew had taken to the balcony. Nobody moved. They stood as the boys had earlier, open mouthed and staring.

Across the other side of the city, a clock started to chime. Ping looked up for a moment. They all did. Mrs Kew pulled out her traveling clock.

"Flywheel club in Giraffe Tower. Fifteen minutes early," the old woman said.

Ping gave a slight sigh. Cog had not come last at least, though they may still run late... It was one thing to get a clock to chime every twelve hours, but quite another to get it to do one distinctive ring a year after you'd started to build it.

When Ping looked back at the Jugglers of Jilin, they had changed their rhythm to match the ringing of the clock, looping the balls high, holding them back just a moment longer.

And then...

Ping watched the center of the formation, where balls flashed past each other from all directions. As she watched those worlds in such startling proximity, the unthinkable happened. A red ball and a blue, coming from opposite directions, collided.

The two balls bounced away from each other, falling to the ground and rolling away into the crowd. For five seconds the hush of the audience changed from one of reverence and wonder, to the silence of shock. Then chaos erupted as zorigami made a mad scramble for the errant balls.

The Jugglers of Jilin, without a mistake in public in the last century, struggled to keep going, ignoring the small riot breaking out behind them. But with two balls gone from the pattern, they lost their rhythm. Struggle though they might, they could not get it back.

Ping was still leaning against the rail, yearning out into space.

Another clock started to chime.

"Pendulum, in Cat." Mrs Kew said absently, quietly. "Ten minutes an thirty two seconds early."

Down in the square, two more worlds collided. Those in the audience who were not scrambling to retrieve balls, gasped, as if they had not believed the first miracle, but could not refute the second.

The jugglers gave up completely then, perhaps in shock themselves, and balls rained to the ground. Some came to rest on the patterned carpet, others bounced away into the crowd and fresh scuffles broke out.

Ping settled back down herself, the heels of her sandals thudding against the ancient planks of the floor. Her hands gripped the rail tightly, thumb twitching, working nervously at a knot in the timber.

The clock in the tower above her head chimed. It started to sing just as Giraffe fell to silence.

"Elephant Tower, eight minutes and twelve seconds early," Mrs Kew offered.

Ping looked up, as if she'd be able to see the face of the clock to make sure it was still running on time. Looked up as if she might be able to stop the ringing. But she could not see the clock and found herself looking at the blue arch of the sky instead.

Tung swore. Lan started to cry.

"Stop," Ping said quietly, though she felt like swearing or crying herself. Louder: "Stop." She was still watching the sky, fear growing within her. "Everyone, look." She pointed a trembling finger and slowly, one by one, her companions followed her gaze. There was a black cloud in the otherwise clear sky.

"What is it?"

"It's... I don't know."

Ping shaded her eyes. "It's like it's falling from the top of the sky. It just keeps coming and coming."

Down in the square, nobody had noticed the thing in the sky. They still battled among themselves.

"It looks like a storm cloud but..."

Minutes later the object was close enough to see clearly with the naked eye. It was not *one* object at all, but a group of birds.

One single bird was out the front, leading the way. Monstrous wings beat steadily and Ping almost thought she could hear the air thrumming.

As the bird came even closer, with the flock behind, it became apparent that it wasn't a bird. Not a normal bird anyway. It was more like a bat and there was something strapped to its belly.

Cylinders? Ping was not sure, it was too far away. But she did see when it dropped a package of some sort. *A bat laying eggs while on high?* But bats didn't lay eggs.

Ping watched as the package fell, momentum sending it in a graceful arc towards the city. It fell and fell, almost too slowly to be real, and hit a low, slate roofed warehouse halfway between Elephant Tower and the Great Clock.

Ping gasped.

The old building exploded in a ball of fire, sending sparks and debris high into the air. A couple of seconds later a blast of heat washed over the square and the tower. Ping instinctively turned her face away. She did not see the second package released.

What she did see was another bat breaking away from its fellows. And more after that, a whole line of them coming to add their fire.

"Oh, no," Tung wailed as another explosion pummeled the valley.

Ping lowered her gaze to look once more at the city.

Smoke was now rising from the warehouse in the valley below, a column to hold up the sky in case the whole world should start to fall apart. And another column was just starting to billow up from the ground.

"Oh, no."

Ping put a hand to her mouth to hold in the wail that was building within her. Her mouth gaped, tears streamed down her face. She remained silent, unable to move, unable to push beyond the fear that had gripped her.

The Great Clock was in flames.

WIPING HER EYES, Ping stared out at the creatures.

They were everywhere. After dropping one volley of fiery eggs the giant bats circled around and came in again, then rose up on columns of smoke and passed out of sight. More of the creatures were swooping down behind the hills.

Fire spread rapidly in some areas. Loud reports could be heard as ancient stone cracked in the heat. Timber buildings erupted in flames. Dolphin Tower, on its own, greeted the afternoon. Even the Great Clock was silent.

Ping broke into a fresh spasm of crying as she surveyed the ruins below.

The focus of the attacks slowly shifted away from the centre of the city, a flood of fire climbing the hills. Buffalo Tower collapsed under the barrage, even as it started to chime. It's song ended with an anguished clatter and the thunder of falling stone.

As the dust from the tower swirled about in the air, mixing with the smoke from a swath of burning buildings, Ping turned to take comfort from the presence of her friends. She wanted to know that all of *her* world was not collapsing though the world outside was. But they were gone. She was standing alone on the balcony. Enial was last in the queue, racing across the room behind, following Tung and Lan toward the stairs and the street below.

With a small cry, Ping rushed after them. She flung open the door and ran down the stairs, following the fearful voices and thump of footsteps. She couldn't think.

Dust rained down all around, shaken from the walls and ceiling.

When she made it out into the square, none of her companions were in sight. Ping found herself amidst a heaving mass of people. She was jostled from all sides. Someone poked her in the stomach with their elbow. Someone else stepped on her toes. Nobody seemed to know where to run.

Each breath was hot in her lungs. The air held the bitter, cloying taste of ash. She needed a drink.

One of the bats raced overhead, huge wings fanning the exploding eggs into crackling life. The three cylinders strapped under its body glowed orange with reflected fire.

14: Djinns of Smoke

For three seconds the surging crowd parted and offered Ping a glimpse of Tung. He'd been splattered by a green gel that burst into flames of its own accord. The people around him were suffering in the same way or simply could not pause a moment to lend a hand. The mass surged again and Tung was lost to sight, his mouth open in an unheard scream. Ping could not get to him through the press. She didn't know if she could force herself to move anyway. She couldn't breathe.

When the bats finally spiraled heavenward, one-eyed monsters, slow and unstoppable, marched up from the outer regions of the city. They had hard, bright carapaces that clanked and hissed as they moved. Whenever they came, death followed.

The monsters walked with their thick, bulbous arms raised and wherever they pointed, zorigami died. Ping watched, stunned, as a screaming woman's skin sizzled. The woman fell to the ground and screamed no more. Others took up the task.

The crowd started to move. They went anticlockwise along Dial Street, away from the main concentration of monsters. Pushed along in the ebb and flow of the throng, Ping stumbled and almost fell. A strong grip on her arm saved her. She looked up to see Enial by her side, tall and lean and grim faced. Then Enial went down himself, trampled in a moment under hundreds of feet. Gone. Ping, sobbing, saw Mrs Kew's traveling clock being carried by a scarred, huffing tinker.

She felt each second like a lifetime.

-o◯o-

Ping didn't truly know what had happened to the rest of her club, but she had not seen them in the screaming, running aftermath of the first attack, nor in the fearful hours that followed. She had run past Deshi's house at three forty five, fleeing another of the monsters. The door was hanging from the frame like a drunken visitor. The walls were blackened by fire, and djinns of smoke peered out through the windows. She had not stopped to investigate further, fearful that if she stayed in one place too long she would be caught.

Night came, or perhaps it was a darkness born of smoke and fear, and she continued to wander aimlessly, stumbling with fatigue, drifting from building to building. She was an insubstantial wraith herself, a djinni of flesh and bone.

At eleven o'clock, or as near as she could make it in her exhaustion-addled mind, Ping paused to listen for the lulling chime of Elephant Tower. But even if all had been right with the world, even if fire and smoke and clanking monsters did not now dominate, all the cardinal clocks would have been dismantled, ready for the new season. She shuddered and ducked into the doorway of a warehouse. Sheathed in shadows, she sat down and leaned back against the hard, bare planks.

In the darkness, she fussed with her skirt and blouse with trembling fingers. She tried to wipe away the grime and straighten the pleats. She combed her fingers through her singed and tangled hair though it would make no difference. Eventually, she clasped her hands in her lap and tried to sit still.

Ping closed her eyes for just a moment and woke with a start, blinking away tears. A monster was standing on the far side of the street. It seemed to stare at her for long minutes before starting to raise its arm.

Ping gasped, drawing in a lungful of poisoned air. Coughing wouldn't help, but she did it anyway while she fumbled with the handle on the door behind her.

Eventually, she slipped through into deeper darkness, across a small office and to a door at the back.

Once there, she paused, not daring to move as she waited for her eyes to adjust. She would have stayed longer, leaning against the jam of the doorway, but the clanking of the monster's steps was audible out in the street. She took a careful step forward but stopped once more when her smarting eyes detected movement.

"Who's there?" she asked in a timid voice. She was ready to flee, though surely no monsters would be skulking in the warehouse.

There was no answer, but muffled sounds reached her from the fug.

"Who's there?" she said again.

"Go away, woman. You'll get us all killed."

"But I..."

"But nothing. Scram or I'll put an arrow in you."

"Put an arrow..."

"Yeah. We have been hiding here for two and a half hours and now you've gone and led one of the bastards right to us."

"I didn't mean to." Ping couldn't think. Was this man really going to kill her? She realized she was probably silhouetted in the doorway, no matter the smoke and bad light, and took a small step to the side. Trembling fingers clutched at the front of her skirt, twisting the material.

"Get out. Go. I *will* kill you."

"Leave her, Cai," another voice interjected. "You can't—"

"I can and I will. If it's a choice between her and me and my wife, I know who I'll chose every time."

There was a momentary pause before the speaker named Cai resumed, as if rebutting another argument from his partner. "There's only one of her and there's seven of us. You do the math, Wen."

"Yeah. Well, no matter which way I do the sums the answer ain't right."

But Ping knew Cai was probably right. They couldn't fight the monster's terrible weapon, so what right did she have to endanger their lives? What right did she have to expect their help? She would have turned and fled then, but her pursuer had already reached the outer door and was clumping toward where she stood. Distressed boards groaned. The whole building seemed to shake. Ping sighed silently and sank to the floor. Tears streamed freely from her smoke-stung eyes. She wept quietly into her hands and waited, ready to feel the heat and sizzle that had been the end of so many zorigami.

Cai and Wen, the unseen wraiths who had condemned her, started to move at the same moment the creature stepped into the room. Despite the conversation, Ping had no idea of how far away the two men had been. All she knew was that she could hear them retreating into the smoke as if they were right in front of her. The monster heard them as well. It did *not* notice her huddling on the floor nearby. With screeching slowness it continued walking, large head swiveling backwards and forwards as it scanned.

A soft shaft of light emerged from the monster's shoulder. By the time it took another step the light was a powerful beam that lit upon bales of wool and rolls of silk. It clumped into the first alley, following the clearly audible sounds of retreat. Ping watched, mouth gaping, before scrambling to her feet. She rushed outside before she was forced to view the aftermath of the hunt.

A building across the street had caught on fire. Flames licked at adjoining structures. Another section of the city would be razed before long. Roiling clouds of smoke advanced like ghostly armies.

Ping was confronted by the problem that had always stumped her. Where to go? Where would she be safe from the armies— those of fire and smoke and those of hard chitinous shells?

Before she had a chance to ponder, a growing rumble drew her attention toward the source of the smoke. A mass of zorigami surged into view, a multi-limbed beast in mad retreat. The men and women were wild eyed but pounded along with grim determination. The quickest members of the group rushed past her, not taking the slightest notice, and the reason for their flight emerged from the grey shroud. Two of the monsters, bulging arms already raised.

Still, Ping could not move. She stood by the warehouse door as the zorigami, her people, raced past. She watched as the now familiar sizzle of energy brought down a straggler. Another fell, and a third. This last man, bare-footed and carrying a shovel, was close to her. He clattered to the ground not three meters distant.

The smell of burned flesh shocked Ping into motion and she staggered away, coughing once more as smoke clouds engulfed her. Wiping at her eyes she stopped in a shallow doorway and turned to watch. She could have run, but she no longer knew if there was any point.

One of the monsters turned in her direction, but didn't seem interested in her death. It continued to follow those still running, shooting them down with casual ease, though they were outpacing it. It went by close to her, clanking noisily. Ping slumped to the ground. If running would get her killed then she would stay right where she was.

I no longer care what happens. But a metallic sound snapped her attention out into the street just a five seconds later.

Smoke and exhaustion muffled everything. To her left were screams, shouts. To the right...

Ping started to breathe again, tasting the bitter air. A copper flowerpot, dented and scratched, was rolling back and forth in a quickly decreasing arc as it came to rest at the bottom of a slight depression in the road. A daphido, in full bloom, twirled prettily.

Ping huddled further into the corner and started to weep. For a long while, she thought that was all she wanted from life. That and to die quickly. She couldn't think and without clear thought it seemed useless to act. Running had gained her no advantages that she could see.

A new sound reached her then, the soft patter of feet. Zorigami feet. A child's feet. The little girl was naked and hanging onto a glass-fronted clock, barely able to stay upright. She hugged it close to her body as if it was all that was left of her family, and quite likely it was.

Ping suddenly knew where she needed to go and wondered why she had not thought of it earlier.

"The Great Clock," she said to the child, who ignored her completely. "I must get to the Great Clock."

The Great Clock was where everyone would gather, if they could. The Council would certainly gather there, and they were the ones who would know what to do. Ping pushed quickly to her feet, wiping her eyes. She looked in one direction, then the other, and dashed from the doorway. Another zorigami emerged from the smoke nearby and was cut down a moment later by a monster in the smoke. Ping didn't stop.

She had no idea where she was or what the time might be. She was completely lost. She ran for the next street hoping to learn where she was, hoping to find a way down to the Great Clock. The street she found was Eight Avenue. And across the way was Sundial Park. She was little more than a kilometer from her destination, though she couldn't work out how she'd ended up so far south.

Eighth Avenue seemed deserted but lazy ghosts of smoke hinted at hidden movement. Indistinct sounds; voices maybe, grunts and scufflings; emerged from Sundial Park. She thought she saw somebody scurrying between buildings to her left, but smoke stung her eyes terribly and she didn't really want to know anyway. She backed into a shadow while she tired to stop her shaking and catch her breath.

Finally, Ping turned to the left and continued towards the Great Clock. She didn't know who would be there, didn't know if that was where she truly wanted to be, but could think of nowhere else.

At the next corner, she stopped to listen. Muted sounds emerged from the smoke, but she could not identify or pinpoint any of them. Everything looked the same; buildings, street, fire-dancing shadows looming from the park. Corpses littered the street. Each shift in the smoke threatened to reveal an enemy, or prove that she was in fact lost and walking in circles. But Sundial Park was on the right, as it should be, and therefore the Great Clock must be ahead.

Ping crossed the street, the sound of her feet on the cobbles seeming loud in her ears. She tried to ignore the dead hands that groped at her ankles, seeking help that they were long past needing. Did she know any of them? Did the blackened husks belong to her friends? Were they locals or were they just visiting for the Mid Summer Festival? Did it make any difference now? She tried not to look. She tried not to think.

Over her footsteps and small sobs of despair, she could hear something else. A screech... A continuous, jolting screech that gripped her by the spine and shook.

In another protective shadow, where a jutting butcher shop butted against a jeweler's store, she paused to examine her surroundings. Nothing seemed to have changed. She couldn't trust her ears and couldn't clearly see beyond the end of her out-stretched arm, but thought the terrible sound was coming from ahead of her, towards the Great Clock. She dared not move.

Three and a half minutes passed by. Each second ticking away in Ping's mind felt like an hour. She counted the seconds. The screech seemed to shift around her. Now coming from the left, now from the right, now right in front of her. She shivered, her elbow drumming out her fear on the rough timber wall at her back. She clenched her fists to make the shaking stop.

Then, from the right, back towards the warehouse, came a naked child. The little girl that she'd seen a lifetime ago, minutes ago. She no longer carried the clock, but dragged it along the street behind her, using an ornately carved figure on top as a handle. The glass front of the clock had been smashed, as had the panel behind. The inner workings were displayed for all the world to see.

Ping stared, suddenly guilty. She'd seen a child, alone and in danger, and had done nothing. She'd left the child on her own and set about saving herself. That was no better than what Cai and Wen had done. Was it? Ping, suddenly knowing what she must do, stepped toward the little girl. The child saw her and stopped to look. But the horrible sound didn't stop. The screeching continued to slice through the smoke with brutal precision. The child remained motionless, unconcerned, as Ping searched with watering eyes.

Emerging from the smoke as slow as the tide of years was one of the monsters. Its colorful shell was scratched and stained. A long gouge had been taken from an arm. It dragged its leg as if the bones had been broken. With each step, it sent up a shower of sparks and the horrible sound. Ping stood, transfixed, as the figure continued to walk, not even slowing as it raised its deadly arm towards the child.

Ping did nothing, though she knew she should. She watched as the child was killed in the street. She opened her mouth to scream. But the little girl died without a sound and Ping's cry died on her lips at the same moment. Tears streamed freely down her cheeks, but she made no sound or movement. Though inside she wailed and shook her fist in the air, in reality she slipped slowly back into the shadows and waited for the murderer to continue his slow, agonizing walk down the street. All the while she was praying that the beating of her heart wouldn't give her away. Once again, she thought only of herself, when she should have done something. She had watched as the girl had been killed and not even tried to help.

Seven minutes later, Ping moved on. She walked as slowly as the murderer had, no longer bothering to hide. No longer thinking about what she might find when she arrived at her destination. One moment she let an innocent child die because she didn't want to risk death herself, and the next moment she might have cried for joy had somebody stepped from the smoke to end her misery.

She wondered if her misery would *ever* end.

The Great Clock had once occupied a lush garden at the point where the twelve avenues met. Flowering shrubs had nuzzled the foundations, while more mature trees waited at a respectful distance. Winding paths; cobbled and graveled, paved and boarded; offered all manner of views. Over by the pond, one could once stand and catch a glimpse of the tower, framed between poplars and spruce. Or, where the drinking fountain offered respite, a single graceful window on the side of the building had been on display.

Most of the trees were gone now. Three still stood, though even they leaned at crazy angles. Craters and mounds of debris dotted the landscape. Paths wandered away into no-man's-land.

The Great Clock itself was also gone. The tower was a long line of rubble, as if the foundations had been removed and it had fallen as a whole. The city's administration building, not far away, still stood in some places, thought the top floor was gone and the lower looked like a sailor's mouth after a tavern brawl. Most of the west wing was teetering precariously on the lip of a huge crater. The east seemed to be in tact, though it burned merrily. The flames crackled noisily and painted the underside of smoke-drifts.

Ping wandered across the ruined ground, stumbling through the rubble, forsaking the remains of the pathways to make straight for the main door of the Great Clock building. There may well have been a dozen figures following her but she didn't pause to look. She didn't care. She hardly even noticed the dead that were all around.

The main door of the building was open. One leaf was hanging crookedly on a twisted hinge, the other was wedged between a toppled column and the remains of a glyph carved bench.

Beyond the door, a dozen stairs led down to the foyer, and across the foyer was the door to the tower. That door hung askew as well, leaving a large triangular hole that showed only darkness beyond. She crossed the singed blue carpet of the foyer, weaving a path around timber and stone and flesh. She averted her eyes from the motionless zorigami, as if that would make them go away, and ducked her head, passing through into the base of the tower without stopping. Moments later she almost stumbled when she came to the top of another two stairs.

Ping stopped, wondering what to do next. Her only thought had been to reach the Great Clock. When she had first set out, she hoped to find the leaders of Shadon gathering to formulate the defense. But she'd known then and knew now that no defense the world of Tiandi could muster would do any good.

Above her was open sky. The second story had been ripped away when the tower fell. A coppery moon was already high, sailing through curling waves of smoke.

The greatest moment of my life, Ping thought. As a child she'd always dreamed of being allowed to enter the tower of the Great Clock. Now she was there, if only on the ground floor, and the clock was no more. Near her feet was a huge gear wheel, twisted and chipped. Part of the Great Clock, lying on the floor like litter. Ping sighed and sat down in a shadowed corner at the top of the stairs, wriggling back beneath a tilting column.

After a moment of silence, she began to cry. She sobbed and sniffed, not caring who heard. She closed her eyes and shuddered as the remains of the day worked upon her mind.

She stayed like that for thirty-nine minutes and may well have stayed like that all night, face buried in her hands, but a noise snapped her back to the present.

A scraping noise. Muffled voices.

She opened her eyes and, leaning forward slightly, could see around the ribbed protection of the column. A moment later two men stepped out of thin air, high above the ground.

There was a grunt, a scream, a thump and a groan, though it took Ping a moment to sort out the order in her mind.

Both strangers seemed to hit the ground awkwardly, but one rolled to his feet to stand perfectly still in the center of the room, crouched, ready. The other stayed where he was, perfectly still as well, though for different reasons.

Ping watched silently, not knowing what to think. It was a strange end to a strange day. She wiped tears from her eyes and silently moved deeper into shadow.

Outside, she could hear the monsters coming.

TUKI WAS READY for the extra duties. It was not punishment, the mo'min would never prescribe such a thing, but more like a way to tune himself back into the well being of the village. He had set off along Dry River that morning, glad to have the opportunity.

Since then, with time to give the matter some thought, he had decided he had been wrong to mention the meteor. If it existed, the mo'min would have seen it in her nightly correspondence with Poti; such a thing did not just appear unexpectedly. And if she had seen, then the mo'min must have had a reason for not speaking about it. Tuki was either mistaken in what he saw or was poking his nose into women's business, a place where it most definitely did not belong.

As he trudged east, Tuki tried to put the whole incident from his mind. That, and the vision shown to him by the green ewer. He still wished to speak with someone about it but doubted he would get close to even a small girl without her breaking into fits of laughter.

Tuki continued to walk steadily for the rest of the morning. He could have run the distance quite easily, but he enjoyed the time alone to think. Unfortunately, time and again, he found his mind returning to the meteor. Its very presence scared him.

But he had already sorted that out in his mind. He *had*.

But if he had imagined the meteor, why had he imagined that it changed direction? Was it a sign of some kind? Was it the Mother Blower telling him to change his ways? Or change his life? And if the meteor were real, and the mo'min had chosen not to mention it, that seemed to be much worse. A meteor that could change direction? A divine message that was too frightening, ambiguous, or secret, to be passed on to all the moai in Danyon Ford?

Reaching the next village, abandoned long ago, Tuki waited a long time near the edge of the trees, squinting out at the remains of the buildings, which were bathed in bright sunlight. Humans ventured down Dry River as seldom as moai entered the realms of man, which was almost never, but still, that was too often for his liking.

Finding no evidence of anything other than animals of a base nature, Tuki made his way between the buildings, stealing with a twinge of guilt between the dormitories of the mo'by. He could not even understand young girls, so he most certainly did not want to pry into the secrets of the unmarried women lest something deeper be revealed. Entering the plaza, he crossed to the low wall on the northern side, which set apart the houses of the married moai. There was nothing stopping him from stepping through the narrow gap that was the gateway, but he stopped nonetheless and glanced about as if a mo'shi might step forth to remonstrate with him.

When he was satisfied that he was still alone, Tuki bowed slightly and, offering a small prayer of protection, passed the wall. Never would he have dreamed of stepping over the wall itself, even on his own in the silent village and with the low wall hardly standing at all.

At the first building Tuki stopped to look inside. What he saw was the tumbled down remains of a wooden bed decades out of use. The bed was large enough to hold two people, and he wondered what huge woman had lived there. With another small bow he hurried on, almost with his eyes closed, as he followed the mo'shi's directions to the Glass Blower's Workshop.

When he finally reached the door to the workshop, Tuki stopped to stare. When he'd been told of his task he had thought it pointless, beyond channeling his thoughts in the proper direction, but now he was not so sure. The door was solid, as was proper in such an important structure, but also a thing of great beauty. Colored glass beads had been set into the surface, mapping out the constellations of Mid-Summer's Night. For as long as he could remember, Tuki had not attended the Mid-Summer Festival. Instead he had drifted away to a quiet place he knew. There, he would lie back and watch the heavens wheel above him. He remembered each point of light like the features of Keala's face, and they were duplicated perfectly on the door. After gazing for several minutes, Tuki carefully, and with a feeling of sacrilege, pried the door away from the frame. With a grunt of effort he hoisted it onto his shoulder and began the long walk home with his ear pressed against a window that showed the sky two nights into the future.

-oOo-

From his position just outside the village, Tuki could just make out the fire in the plaza. The men were in the light while the women waited elsewhere. Perhaps they were in the darkness around the plaza or performing some ceremony of their own; Tuki did not know.

The festivities had continued unabated since dusk. The go'gan, the unmarried men, were dancing, beating out the rhythm of the desert with their hands and feet, naked and chanting. The go'shin sat in a semicircle to the south, clapping and chanting as well, but still wearing their togas about their waists. They were married, and therefore married to the Mother Blower, and it would not be proper for just anyone to look upon them.

Tuki closed his eyes and listened to the rhythms, watching in his mind's eye while his friends danced about the fire. Attendance of the festival was not compulsory, but everyone went. Except Tuki. He sometimes wondered if that were one of the reasons he was not yet married, but it was not his place to ask, so he did what he did and hoped that Poti did not hold it against him. He valued the company of his friends and the good favor of the women, but he also liked to sit in the quiet to think. Especially on Mid-Summer's Night.

He opened his eyes again and pillowed his head on his arms. The sky above was clear, the stars bright with the promise of a new year. For a moment Tuki thought he saw a meteor again, but this time he knew it was his mind playing tricks on him, dreaming up proof of the earlier sighting. He sighed and watched the stars wheel.

When Rapa, largest of the moons, slipped into view between the trees, he knew that the women would be emerging from the darkness to sit to the north of the fire in their long, ceremonial robes. Moments later he heard their keening song, like the wind across the desert, joining the chorus. Even the mo'min would be there, skyglass held protectively in her lap, on view this one time a year for the men to catch a glimpse.

"Tuki? Tuki are you out here?"

Tuki sat bolt upright and held his breath.

"Tuki? Where are you?"

Keala emerged from the trees then, and Tuki knew that staying silent would not help.

"I am here."

"Why didn't you answer me?"

He shrugged in the darkness. "I do not know." He was very uncomfortable, alone with a mo'by like this. It was not proper. "You should not be here," he said. "If they found us, we would be punished."

"They will not find us." She laughed softly, pushing her braid back over her shoulder as she sat down by his side. "None of them would leave the ceremony without instructions written in stars across the sky." She glanced up then, as if to be sure no such instruction were appearing.

Tuki was aghast. "Keala, you cannot say things like that. What if the mo'min found out?"

"Are you going to tell her, Tuki? From what I hear you would not get anywhere near the mo'min right now."

"What have you heard?"

"Oh, so now you suddenly want to talk with me!"

"What?" He tried to shimmy away without her noticing. She was scaring him.

"I have been trying to talk to you for days, but you keep avoiding me."

"I do not." But he did. If she knew he had seen a meteor when there was none to see, she would laugh. Her laugh normally warmed his soul, but it certainly would not if were directed *at* him. "You should not be out here, Keala."

"Yes, I know. But I could not talk to you any other way."

"You can simply send for me."

"No, I cannot." She lowered her gaze.

"The mo'min has said you are not to talk to me? And yet here you are!"

"What happened, Tuki? Why do you have the extra duties? Why are the mo'shi laughing at you?"

"The mo'shi are laughing?" The mo'by were one thing, but to have the mo'shi laughing as well.

"I am sorry."

She placed a hand on his knee, and he flinched. He dared not push it away.

"Tell me what happened. I am worried for you."

"You are?"

She shifted closer so that her whole side was pressed against his. "Of course I am."

"I should not say," Tuki said.

"Just because Ko'uka is a mo'shi, she does not know everything. They are just people like everyone else."

"Keala!" Tuki would have risen to his feet but was afraid he might hurt Keala, or upset her, and he did not want that. "You cannot say things like that. Please."

"If the mo'shi knew everything, they would have let me marry you by now, Tuki. You are the only man I would ever want to marry."

Tuki turned to look at Keala and inadvertently brushed his nose against hers. She was so close to him, leaning in. "You have asked? You have asked for permission to marry me?"

"Of course, Tuki. I ask almost every week, but they keep saying no."

Keala did not let Tuki reply. She leant forward further, crossing the tiny space between them, and pressed her lips to his. She took the words from his mouth along with the breath. He backed away slightly, but she followed, only allowing the contact to break for a moment. After that, he stayed where he was, helpless, as if she were a demon drinking of his soul. But it was a wonderful release, and he soon started to respond. When he did, the mo'by slipped her tongue between his lips and, feeling slightly faint, Tuki laid back on the ground. Keala followed him again, laying a hand against his cheek as her tongue continued to probe.

She tasted of sweet jilaberries.

An eternity, too short by far, passed before Keala pulled away slightly. She ran her fingers up his arms, making it feel as if the tattooed ants had come to life. She used her thumb to trace the edges of the three pointed star on his chest — the gateway to heaven caused by the joining of the three moons. She touched her fingers to his tingling lips. "That is called a kiss. It is a simple thing, a wonderful thing, isn't it?"

She kissed him again, quickly, biting his lip.

Tuki steeled himself and wrapped an arm around her, praying to the Mother Blower that he was doing the right thing.

"The mo'shi show us," she whispered. "They show us all but say we cannot do these things with men until we are married. Not all the rules made by the mo'min and the mo'shi are good ones, Tuki."

"Why? Why would they not let us do such a thing?"

"They show us so many things."

Tuki swallowed, eyes growing wide. "There's more?"

"Oh, yes. There much more."

Tuki swallowed. He didn't dare ask.

Keala kissed him again, running her tongue along the tips of his teeth. "Not now. Next time."

"Next time?"

"Yes, but now I must get back. They may not miss you at the Midnight Ceremony any more, but they will miss me."

"*I* will miss you." He felt embarrassed before he finished uttering the sentence.

"And I, you." She was gone then, running quickly away through the trees.

Tuki watched her go, silent and marvelling.

-oOo-

Tuki carefully wiped the last layer of soil away from the tuber then worked his large fingers down the sides until he could pull it from the ground. He set the vegetable on the cloth with the others before a sound from the trees, a rustle amongst the dry undergrowth, disturbed him. He looked across a narrow irrigation drain, but the sound did not repeat, so he returned his gaze to the ground as he tried to find more food to add to the community's supply.

Tuki had hardly returned to his search when he heard the sound again. He turned quickly, heart racing, to discover Keala leaning against a tree, one foot raised to press against the rough bark behind her.

"Hello, Tuki. How are you?"

Rising to his feet, Tuki wiped his shaking hands on his toga. His heart was still racing, but for other reasons now. Whenever possible, Tuki made an effort to be alone with Keala, or made it possible for her to find him alone. Then they would kiss.

The thought of the promised 'more' kept him awake at night. But so far it had not eventuated.

"Aren't you happy to see me?"

He walked to the edge of the irrigation drain in two long strides, pausing for a moment to gather his breath. He looked about, over his shoulder towards the village, to his left, towards the nearest trail. Nobody was in sight. He took another step, across the drain, and a moment later was kissing her gently on the cheek.

He wondered at his boldness.

"No, Tuki," she said. "Don't."

"What?"

"We cannot do this."

"Nobody will see us."

But she pushed him away slightly. "Stop it." The sound of command was strong in her voice, and he had spent too long doing as women asked not to obey.

Tuki took a step back. "What? Why?"

Keala walked a short distance away. "We may not like the laws that the mo'min has made, Tuki, but they are the laws. I feel guilty about what we have been doing. But at the same time, I love you so and wish to be with you all the time."

"Then what can we do?"

"I don't know, Tuki." Keala pushed a lock of hair away from her face. "But until we are wed, or the law is changed, we cannot kiss again. We just cannot. Please understand."

"Then we must get married." Tuki stepped forward again and gripped Keala's hands. "We must get married."

"Oh, Tuki, you know that I would in an instant, if only they would let us. But they will not let us. We cannot get married without the approval of the council of mo'shi."

"Then we must change the law."

"But, Tuki, only the mo'min can change the law. You know that."

"So you must become the mo'min."

Keala laughed at that. "Tuki, you know very well that the mo'shi choose the mo'min from amongst their number. Unless..." For a long moment Keala looked thoughtful, then shook her head and slumped to the ground.

"What?" Tuki asked. He sat by her side and rested his trembling hand on her arm. "What were you thinking?"

"Nothing. It's just, the mo'min is the mo'min because she is the rightful holder of the skyglass."

"So, you take the skyglass."

"Now you are really thinking with your wishbone, Tuki. I said the *rightful* holder, not the person who happens to have it."

"What are you talking about then, Keala?" Tuki could not resist. He leant forward and kissed her cheek again. She did not complain, so he moved to the corner of her mouth.

"I was just thinking, if I had *another* skyglass I would have as much right to be called mo'min as the current mo'min." She finally responded to his kiss for a moment before turning her head away. "Tuki, there were other mo'min before, long ago. There must be more skyglasses somewhere."

Tuki heard what she was saying but did not really care. "But where will you find one?" he asked absently, knowing that such a question had to be asked.

"One of the younger girls brought me a book, Tuki. An ancient book. She says she found it in a buried box. It explains where one might be found."

"Does it?" What a book might be he could not guess. More women's secrets, like kissing, he supposed.

"Yes. Tuki, if you find that skyglass and give it to me, I can be a mo'min as well, and I can change laws."

"Yes." He kissed her again.

"Tuki," Keala said a moment later, "when I see you I cannot keep my longing at bay, so until you find that skyglass, I don't think we will be able to see much of each other at all."

Tuki groaned. "Of course I will find it, Keala. Where is it? Do you know?"

16: One Good Thing

THE RUINS OF SALISHA stretched for kilometers along the side of the valley. In some places it looked as though the ancient streets had been carved into the slope. Knee high walls drew ragged lines across Scree's night-eyes' view of the world. Scattered rubble and crooked, half-hidden paving stones made the footing treacherous.

The sky was clearing and Scree eyeballed the last of the night's stars. The skeleton constellation danced on a retreating cloudbank. The Hunter stalked it, just peeking over the horizon. "How fars to this place?"

"About four hundred kilometers. I think. I've never been there but Tartila is a major trading port."

Scree grunted. He could manage about forty kilometers a day. Halve that because of Nemucca. Take a bit more off because of the terrain. Down to maybe fifteen kilometers a day. And four hundred kilometers all up... He struggled with the sums in his head.

"A month, maybe," he muttered.

"You can count?" Nemucca asked. Scree turned to glare at him. The lad cleared his throat nervously. "I imagine there was a major road between the two cities as some stage. We'll be able to follow that."

"So we spends a week lookings for this road?" He decided one place was as likely as the next and turned to make his way directly up the slope. They followed a rough once-was-street up over the top of the first ridge. After dipping down into the next slight valley the path died out and they were forced across the slope again to find the next gap in the greenery. They zigzagged into the hills. Nemucca limped along, his injured leg still covered in makeshift bandages. He cursed every awkward, half-seen step, while Scree almost thought he was at home again.

He laughed at that. *Home!* It'd been ten years or more, since he'd spent any more than a couple of days in one spot through choice.

"What's so funny?" Nemucca asked, pausing to flex his leg.

"I was just thinking abouts home."

"What's so funny about that? I think of home all the time."

"What's funny is, I don't really haves a home."

"How can you not have a home?"

"I'm a troll, Nemucca. First twelve years of my life I was running around Mount Cardenze, inside or out. I slept wheres I got tired, ate wheres I found some food. After that I joined a pack and beens on the move since."

"So you've spent about half your life sleeping under trees?" He sounded horrified.

"Something like that. Not trees though— usually farmers around whos glad to share with us." He smiled. "Course, that's better than most trolls get. My mother was near the mountain when I was born so she took me there to be rid of me. Most trolls is running with a pack from the day theys born."

"But that's horrible."

Scree shrugged. "And I suppose you spent all your life walking the sames streets, talking to the same peoples, until you joined the army?" He blew a quick trill of notes on his flute.

"Well, yes, but..."

"But what? I probably seen mores of this world than you ever wills. And I wouldn't change thats for nothin'."

"What about your friends? A group of them were killed not too long ago. Wouldn't you like them back?"

"No. None of thems could help me now." Scree smiled at the lad. "You my new friends now, Nemucca."

He didn't seem too pleased with the idea. "And what happens when I can't help you either?"

"Thens we'll see."

They walked on. Scree played a slow dirge on his flute as Nemucca watched him intensely.

"So, why are we doing this?" the human asked eventually. "Why are we going to look for this gate?"

"Don't knows about you, but I wants to leaves this world. My peoples is running out of places to run, boy. I haven't seen a troll I don't knows for more than five years, and I traveled right across this continent and a couple of others besides."

"So you want a world where you can get rid of your bad image and start as just a man, helping the needy and doing good deeds?"

Scree ignored him, walking for a while in silence. "What about you? You could've left over the last couple of days and I wouldn't have chased you."

He ducked his head and blushed. "I'd like to fly between the stars, like the book says. That would be an amazing thing."

Scree shrugged. "Going through a magical gates will hardly be likes flying to the stars. And a minute ago you weren't even interested in this world."

The lad shrugged. "I know, but..."

They were moving across the slope again. Scree ran his fingers along the top of a crumbling wall, watching as daylight started to bleed into the sky. A roosting bird launched skywards and Nemucca jumped in surprise, stumbling on a half-hidden cobblestone. The lad stopped for a moment to rub his leg and curse.

"If you tells me you twisted your ankle I'll leave you heres," Scree said. "You won't even get to see the top of the next hill." Nemucca *could* help him, but wasn't worth worrying about.

"Do you think they're chasing us? The strangers, I mean."

"Doubts it."

"Why do you say that?"

"They'd be stupid if they was. What theys got to do now is strengthen their position. Nobody on this world is any threat to thems."

"Rubbish. There are better soldiers than Keyman Talgayni. And a lot more of them."

Scree laughed. "Five against twelve and theys slaughtered you withouts even moving. That was just with... personal weapons. Imagine whats their catapult can do, boy? I knows for sure that I wouldn't want to get in the ways." Scree found another clear street leading into the hills and turned to walk with his back to the first stains of the day. "Nope, whats they'll do is spend a few days searching thems caves proper, thens they'll send small parties outside. When theys see what the valley is like they'll occupy it completely then either send out peoples or waits for someone to come to them."

"Emissaries? You don't think they'll attack."

"Nope."

"Why not?"

"You attacked thems, boy. Theys tried to avoid a fight."

Scree started to walk faster. He was pissed to see they'd left the city behind and seemed to be following the road that his companion had predicted. It wasn't a highway, but the path through the bushes mostly ran in straight lines, or swept around long curves. Occasionally it switch-backed up the sides of the steeper hills. The waking day offered the only noise as they continued, climbing steadily higher as the sun climbed the arc of the sky.

The day wore on, and Nemucca's complaints grew louder. When the sun started sinking they'd made barely fifteen kilometers.

"You was in the army," Scree said as he leaned on his sword, waiting for the lad at the top of another long rise.

"So?"

He spat. "So, hows did you survive? We hardly done half a day's walking and you fit to drops. And you never shuts up. Noisy as a cat nailed to a fence you are."

"Well, I'm injured, remember. And we chased you for... I don't know how long."

The lad was trying, which was more than most humans would do, but that didn't help much. "Got some good news for you," he said.

"What? You found one of those starships?"

"Nope. Next best thing..."

Nemucca narrowed his eyes suspiciously. "What?"

"There's a river that looks like it's goin' in the right direction. I can evens see a boat." The owner wouldn't want to give it up, but there were no lights showing in the small ramshackle hut beside the water.

"Tartila is on a river."

Scree smiled. "Well, if this is the right river, we could be there in a couple of days. Come on."

-oOo-

Scree paddled the boat towards the dock. After five weeks of almost constant effort he thought he could feel the muscles in his arms growing by the moment. Four hundred kilometers had turned out to be more than a thousand. A few days ago a farmer, cowering under a table, had pointed them in the right direction. So, they'd spent the best part of two days climbing over a low range of hills to another river and another boat.

Apparently, this was the right place.

"Can you see anything?" Scree asked, searching the shadows on the dock for signs of movement.

Nemucca shook his head nervously. "There doesn't seem to be any of them about. It's hard to tell though."

Fires were raging all along the edge of the river. A dozen timber warehouses were ablaze. Stone buildings were burning as well. Clouds of smoke choked the sky.

When the boat nudged against the dock, Scree leapt up onto a ladder and wished he hadn't. His legs and arms were aching. He wondered if he'd be able to make it to the top. Eventually, he climbed up onto the old wooden planks and crouched painfully behind a pile of large boxes.

Nemucca scrambled up the ladder behind him. His leg had healed during the journey down river and now Scree thought that *he* might be the one struggling to keep up. Not that it was likely the lad would lead the way anywhere.

"Who are they, do you think?" Nemucca said when he caught up. "Where'd they come from? Are they from Atlantis, like those humans?"

Scree didn't bother answering. How was he supposed to know?

From the boat they'd watched as strange creatures, like colorful cockroaches— hard shelled and clattering— moved slowly about the city, killing anyone in their path. They had weapons as powerful as those carried by the human 'Ravens'. The city's residents fought back in some areas, but it never seemed to last.

"Where is this gates going to be?" Scree said.

He received a shrug in reply.

"You ever beens here?"

A shake of the head. "I told you that. We aren't even in the Popago Plains any more." He said it as if it was a bad thing.

"You wanted to fly between the stars a few days ago. Now you don't even want to explore a new city?"

Nemucca turned to look at him for a moment. "There are *monsters* here."

Scree laughed. "There's trolls and humans and those moai within a few thousand kilometers of this place. You think there won't be all sorts of monsters on other worlds?"

Nemucca swallowed loudly and wiped a sweating palm on his breeches.

"Probably ins the church," Scree said. He tried to find a spire amongst the smoke, but there was nothing. He grunted and smiled slightly at the thought of the attacking monsters doing at least one good thing for the world.

Scree rose painfully to his feet and pulled his sword from the straps Nemucca had sewn onto his pack. He headed into the city. The monsters made the venture much safer for Scree than it would otherwise have been.

He crept along a narrow alley between two fire-blackened buildings. The air was thick with smoke and alive with the sounds of destruction. A building collapsed somewhere close by. People screamed and shouted. Metal clashed with metal.

Rounding the first corner, Scree was almost knocked from his feet by a fleeing man. He jumped back and a crackling, distorted stream of air knocked the stranger down. The man screamed but only for a moment. The hair on Scree's arm stood on end. The smell of burned flesh filled the air. The dead man spasmed on the ground.

"Stinking cats." It reminded him of lighting.

Licking his lips, Scree edged along the wall. He listened to the monster's slow, clanking approach then leapt around the corner with a wordless shout. He swung his sword.

The shout was useless and the sword bounced away without even leaving a mark on the creature's hard shell. He attacked again. Each impact shuddered through his body. Except close up, Scree could see it was armor, not a shell. Same difference in the end. Scree's elbows and wrists rang with pain as he kept pounding. It looked like the monster wasn't worried. It swiveled slowly, joints screeching all the while.

Scree knew his opponent's weapon was in the bulging left arm. He also knew he could get in close to stop the monster bringing the weapon to bear.

Swearing and throwing his sword down in disgust, Scree did just that. He bent and wrapped both of his arms around a square, boilerplate leg and heaved upwards. Eventually, the creature toppled backwards.

Trying to catch his breath, Scree collected his sword once more. He rammed it with all of his might into the single, large black window in the front of the helmet.

His first attempt made a crack in the surface, though his hands flared with pain. The second attempt shattered it completely. And beneath was an ugly, misshapen face.

Scree stared for a long time, standing astride the fallen figure, sword embedded in an eye-socket. When he pulled the weapon free and looked up, another monster was close by with its arm raised. Scree threw himself sideways as one of the almost-invisible lightning bolts crackled through the air. He rolled to his feet and scuttled away, down the street and into an alley. Nemucca was close on his heels, wide-eyed and fearful.

At the next corner he turned left, towards the centre of the city. He looked back over his shoulder and saw a small section of wall crackle and pop and let off a thin mist of steam. The monster didn't have a hope of catching them, but Scree continued to run.

All through the city men, women and children were dead or dying. The monsters ambled around, hissing and clanking, dealing out death like a troll in a litter of kittens. Except their sizzling weapons struck down people from fifty meters away. They seemed impervious to smoke, pain and just about everything the locals could think to attack with. Here and there, the humans met with success, but it was always limited and very short lived. They normally didn't live long enough to celebrate.

Scree didn't know if he would be able to win another fight himself. Seeing a bakery, he slipped through a huge hole in the side wall.

"Where are you going? The gate won't be in there," Nemucca said.

On the river, Scree had eaten more than the human— he'd done most of the paddling, after all. They'd stopped at farmhouses to steal food and had snuck through a village at night to find their dinner, but it hadn't been enough. The constant energy-draining effort was starting to catch up with him.

"I need food," Scree said. "I need lots of food real quick." Given that, he'd be able to go for a few more days yet. Without it, he'd go nowhere.

In the bakery, he started to shove things in his mouth, not stopping to see what it was first. Moldy bread and stale cakes. Flat bread and bisca. Nemucca emerged from a back room with a small hamper containing a wizened apple, crumbling cheese and a flask of wine. Scree left the cheese but crunched through the apple and drank half the wine in one long pull. It wasn't the best food, but Scree gorged himself for ten minutes.

"That was interesting," Nemucca said, when Scree finally slowed down. He was sitting on a stool nibbling on the cheese and a piece of flat bread. It appeared as if the relative normality of the situation had calmed him. Scree doubted either the normality or calmness would last.

"Needed energy," Scree said. He was ready to go again. He took the final swallow of wine, rubbed his crotch and headed for the door. "Comes on."

"Can't we stay here for a while? They won't come back, surely."

Scree wasn't sure of anything. He stalked out onto the street stepping around some dead humans on the porch. So much for normality. Nemucca shoved the last piece of his dinner in his mouth and hurried to follow.

Darkness and smoke made hiding relatively easy but hampered progress at the same time. Scree kept to the back streets, always moving towards the centre of the city and always climbing. He hadn't seen a church but it was sure to be in the best position. There was no guarantee the gate would even be in the church, but religions seemed to believe that myths and legends were theirs to claim if they wanted and he had to start somewhere.

17: Wrong Church

EVERY TIME SCREE DARTED across a street, or crouched in a smoke-shrouded doorway, every time he watched colorful monsters stumping about in the smoke, Nemucca was there beside him, like a shadow. Scree laughed at that and the human turned a fearful gaze towards him.

"What's so funny?"

"I was just thinking that it's amazing hows everyone is suddenly your best friend whens there is worse peoples about."

"I don't think you're a troll at all," Nemucca replied petulantly. "Trolls wouldn't hide from an enemy, would they?"

"You don't know nothin', Nemucca. Trolls'll hide from any fight theys don't want and any fight theys can't win. Unlike humans who thinks honor is more important thans living."

With that he was up on his feet and running across to the cover of an alley on the other side of a wide street. Nemucca followed.

It was a long, roundabout, smoke hazed journey, but eventually Scree found what he was after. The church had once been a huge thing of blue-grey bricks and stained glass windows. Now only one small section of wall and a long row of buttresses on one side still stood. The rest lay in ruins, spread across the street and the smoking remains of nearby buildings. A fire was blazing amongst the pews.

"What now?" Nemucca asked quietly.

"We has a look."

One of the monsters was standing on what had once been the church's portico. Scree couldn't work out whether it was a guard, had stopped to rest, or was using the vantage point to pick off the humans who wanted protection from the gods. It didn't matter. What mattered was that it didn't look like it was in a hurry to move on.

Scree handed his sword to Nemucca, shrugged out of his pack and took a deep breath.

"What are you doing?"

He sprang into motion, sprinting towards the armored figure. The monster swiveled slowly, armor protesting and Scree bounded up the stairs, launching into the air. He twisted and struck with both feet. The impact jarred his knees and rattled his teeth. He fell to the ground heavily, winded and aching.

Scree struggled desperately to rise. Once he was on his feet though, breathing hard and favoring his left knee, he saw that it didn't matter. The creature was lying on its back, thrashing uselessly. The metal of the armor was scraping against the stones, leaving long scratches but finding nothing to help.

"Hurt, did it?" He moved aside as the monster tried to aim its weapon. "Probably didn't hurt at all."

The monster stopped moving and said something in a deep voice that sounded as much like coughing as anything else.

"What?" Scree crouched down, but didn't get a reply. He grunted and spat. "So, hows I supposed to kill you, 'zactly?"

Then Nemucca turned up and handed Scree his sword.

Scree smiled. "Yep. That'd be the ways."

Nemucca turned away while he rammed the blade through the tough glass and into the face beneath.

"Let's go."

Scree strode through the remains of the church door. The fire was starting to die down. A few dozen bodies lay amongst the rubble. Did the gate lead directly off the church? From between the buttresses, maybe? Or was it hidden away in a cellar? Or was it in some other place completely? He decided that it must be below ground, otherwise someone else would have found it by now.

And who's to say theys haven't found it, he thought. *Probably some old fart priest sitting on another world right now, safe and secure. Cat piss on him if he is.*

"What're we looking for?" Nemucca asked. The lad didn't look like he wanted to do a lot of looking at all. He slouched on the splintered, upturned remains of a pew, clutching Scree's pack to his chest and trying not to gag on the stench.

"Stairs." He strode across and snatched the pack away. "Stairs down. Or loose pavers ons the floor. Or something. I don't knows."

"Well, that helps." He swallowed loudly and closed his eyes for a moment.

Scree moved to the rear of the church, through a low spot in the rubble that might once have been a door, and into the space beyond. A low wall still stood at the rear, holding up a tumble of stone. A smoldering wooden door was lying on the buckled pavers to the left. Scree tramped over the top of that and found himself in the remains of a small room. The stump of a stairway lead upward, with a pile of rubble beside it. Another body.

He smiled. "Yo, Nemucca, get in heres."

By the time Nemucca arrived Scree had already dumped his pack and sword. He had dragged the charred body out of the way and was beginning to work at the pile.

"What did you find?"

Stopping for a moment to glare at the human, Scree grunted. "Reckon there's stairs down to a cellar under this pile."

"Why?"

"Because."

"Ah."

"You goings to help, or what?"

"There's probably nothing there." But Nemucca set to work as well, grunting with effort as he picked up the first of the stones.

Scree bent to the task again, working quickly and keeping an eye out for trouble. The first moon was drifting lazily down towards the horizon before he stopped to rest.

Sitting on an upturned bureau, sipping water from his flask, he noticed they were being watched. He cursed himself for not looking properly in the first place. A priest cowered behind yet another pile of rubble, dark robes blending with the shadows. The man set off a small landslide as he attempted to peer around his protection. Scree wandered over and leered down at him.

"No, don't hurt me. Please. I'll do anything."

"You can starts by telling us what's in the cellar."

"What?" The old man wiped his face with a shaking hand.

"The cellar. What's in it?"

"Cellar? No. Nothing. There is no cellar."

"What?" Scree grabbed him by the front of his robe and hauled him to his feet. "There ain't a cellar?"

"No." The old man could hardly speak. He shook violently. "No cellar. Not that I know."

"Cat's guts."

"You aren't one of them! You are a troll."

"Don't looks so relieved, old man. I can kills you as quick as thems."

"Yes. Yes, of course."

"There ain't no cellar?"

"No."

"A secret rooms?"

"No. Nothing at all like that." The priest smiled slightly. "You must have the wrong church."

"What?" Scree lifted him into the air this time.

"Ah... The wrong church. You must have... the wrong church."

Scree raised his eyebrows.

"There is another church. A bigger church. The church run by the order of Bengo Ohoga"

"Ohoga?" Scree dropped the old man, who crumbled to the ground with a cry of pain.

"Scree!" Nemucca rushed to the priest's side, flashing a dangerously hostile glance.

"What?" Scree asked. But he was already collecting his pack and sword. "Where's this church?"

The priest was too busy whimpering with pain to answer. At least one of the frail bones in his ageing leg had snapped. Scree didn't have time to waste. He strode to the two humans and looked down at them.

"Where's the church?"

The old man pointed a shaking finger.

"How far?"

"A hundred meters."

Scree nodded in satisfaction. He left quickly, striding between two still-standing buttresses and into the ruined warehouse next door. Nemucca shouted after him, something that involved threats, swearing and his mother. Scree grunted and spun about but the sight of another monster had him ducking for cover instead. He wasn't seen.

In the shadows offered by a leaning chimney, Scree examined his surroundings. The moon had slipped down behind the buildings, but there were enough fires about to make normal sight easy enough. The armored figure continued to move slowly down the street, skirting piles of rubble, head swiveling slowly from side to side.

Scree stayed where he was, picking his nose while he waited. It looked as if the monster was merely patrolling, so he was willing to wait it out.

A moment later he cursed. Nemucca hadn't noticed the monster at all and rose to his feet.

"Go on," the human shouted. "Go to your new world and leave us here to fight."

"Rancid cat guts," Scree said softly, watching as the monster changed course and headed toward the church. "Of all times to grow a spine."

"What are you waiting for?"

What am *I* *waiting for?* But Scree wasn't sure Nemucca had outlived his usefulness. If nothing else, the human would be able to read the books again if they ever found a suitable time and place.

He swore. "If you are comings, Nemucca, you'd better hurrys."

"Why would I be going with you?"

"Because you knows, plain and clear, thats you can't beat these monsters." Scree pointed to the armored figure advancing through the church even then.

"Damn."

Scree smiled as Nemucca snatched up his pack and raced across the broken ground towards him. "Suddenly, that priest ain't such goods company?"

"Just get us out of here."

"I never did like priests." Scree stayed where he was, just to annoy Nemucca.

"Hurry up."

"If you'd shut ups for once we wouldn't have to run anywheres." The monster was nearing the rear of the church, lowering its arm to blast the priest.

"Yes, all right." He glanced back over his shoulder but quickly turned away once he saw what was happening. "Just lead the way."

Scree smiled as he turned to find cover amongst the remains of the warehouse. The church was not far beyond.

They moved carefully, staying behind cover when they could, but Scree thought that the monster had probably already given up.

"Stupid bloody humans," Scree said.

"What have I done now?"

"Not just you. All humans. Easy as drowning a cat to gets away from these monsters, but you humans still fight when you has to realize that you can't win. Death before dishonor and all that cat piss. Like I said before, ain't no honor in death."

"Depends on how you die, Scree."

"Nope. But there's honor in staying alive so you can win some other way. You dead a long time, Nemucca."

"When you find someone whose honor you crave, then you'll change your mind. But now, nobody is more important to you than yourself."

"And there's something wrongs with that?"

"You'll see, one day. Maybe."

Scree grunted but had nothing to say. They'd arrived at the church. A fire had long since burnt out, though smoke still hung heavy.

They collected torches from fallen sconces near the door and climbed a pile of bricks to light them on the blazing wall next door.

At the rear of the church, behind what had once been a thick oak door, Scree found what he was after. He led the way down the stairs and into a long, low room. Unrecognizable piles of timber were letting out small plumes of smoke. At the far end he stopped before an empty doorway.

"Well," Nemucca said quietly. "Are you going through, or what?" He held his torch a little higher, as if the extra few inches might help show more than was already on offer.

Scree squinted through the gap. The columns on either side looked the same as the ones in the cave. They were tall and pointless. He thought there was a silvery sheen in the doorway, but with shifting smoke and the flickering torchlight he couldn't be completely sure. Beyond the door was a short passage, and beyond that a room that was much the same as the one they were in.

"Are *you* goings through?"

"I..." Nemucca shook his head. "You're leading this expedition."

"If I'ms in charge, thens I'm ordering you to go first." Scree glared at him.

"Uh-uh. No way." The lad stepped back a few paces.

Scree sneered as he turned back to the door, but couldn't really blame him. With a deep breath he hefted his sword, closed his eyes, and stepped forward. He remained living and on his feet. For long moments those conditions seemed to continue, so he opened one eye. He was exactly where he thought he should be. He opened his other eye.

"So," he said, turning to look at Nemucca, "Am I ons another world, do you think?" He slung his pack up onto his back and shrugged into the straps.

"I don't know. If you are, then... Well, it just doesn't seem right."

"What?"

"Well, it just seems that something should've happened if you just stepped onto another world."

"Why's that?"

"Just because."

"Well, there weren't no thunder or nothing whens those Raven guys came through the other door."

"Maybe there was on the other side."

"You on the other side now, Nemucca. Did you hear anything?" Scree shook his head. "Now gets rid of that bloody torch."

"But I won't be able to see."

"There's nothing for you to see anyway. I'm the one who's gots to see."

"But—"

"Put the damn thing out or I'll go back there and put it outs on your face." Scree turned away and closed his eyes, waiting for his night-eyes to start working. When he was ready, he took a deep breath. "Thats torch out?"

"Yes."

Opening his eyes, Scree examined his surroundings with the red tinge of his night-eyes. No shadows remained for creatures to hide in. Apart from that, nothing had changed. The stones on this side of the doorway were the same kind, and the same age, as those on the other side where Nemucca stood fretting. The floor was level and stable. The ceiling wasn't going to collapse. All was right with the world, whichever world it was.

In the next room, Scree paused to look around. More columns. More carved people, and to his left...

Scree screamed.

He kept screaming as he fled back the way he'd come. When he reached the place where Nemucca had been waiting the human had already disappeared across the long room and up the stairs beyond.

Scree stopped, somehow managing to hold in his laughter while he listened to Nemucca stumbling his way through the ruined church above. Finally the laughter broke free and Scree leaned against the wall for support. Eventually, the noise above stopped.

"That's not funny," Nemucca shouted, voice higher than it should've been.

"It is from wheres I'm standing. And you better stop shouting." Scree wiped at his eyes. "Now gets back down here. The Ohoga Gate thing is in the next rooms."

He went to stand before it while he waited for the lad to return.

"Scorched kittens, you is a bloody idiots, Nemucca. Puts out the torch." Scree closed his eyes and covered them.

"It's pitch black in here."

"It is not. If it was pitch black, I wouldn't be ables to see either."

"All right, it's just plain dark, then. Either way, I can't see a thing."

"You could sees well enough before whens you was running."

"Well, I was running then and I'm not now."

Scree sighed, concentrating and waiting for his night-eyes to turn off.

When he could see normally, Scree returned to his attention to the magical doorway. It looked like a twin of the one in Salisha, but he had no idea how to get it open. He tried pushing it, but nothing happened. Then he found a place to grip the stonework and started pulling with all his strength.

"Use the sword," Nemucca suggested quietly.

"What for? You's the only person around heres to kill." Scree grunted and continued to pull. He thought he felt some movement, but wasn't sure. "You wants me to kill you?"

"No. Use the sword as a lever."

"You wants me to use a few-thousand-year-old sword to lever open a great-bloody-big stone door?" Scree shook his head.

"How do you know how old it is?"

"Nemucca, that's the only weapons I got. I ain't going to snap it ins half just yet."

"What ever. You might not get the door open though."

"Well, I'd haves more of a chance if you'd either help or shut up and gets out of the way." He grunted and strained.

Nemucca set the torch in a bracket on the wall and dropped his pack on the ground, lending his skinny frame to the effort. Scree wished he hadn't. The human just kept getting in the way. He was about to tell him to go sit in a corner when he *definitely* felt some movement. He pulled harder and both doors started to swing open on their own, as if driven by some long-still magic. Scree and Nemucca jumped back and moved quickly to the other side of the room.

The silvery sheen in the doorway was obvious.

"Can you see anything?"

"Couldn't last time either."

Scree moved away from the wall, creeping across the floor like a cat towards a dog kennel.

"Stinking cats."

He paused once when he thought he heard a sound, but then it was gone, or had never been there at all, and he was moving forward again.

He made it all of the way to the door, but didn't see anything he couldn't see before.

Taking a deep breath, he stuck his head into the sheen of color. He didn't feel anything strange. Trouble was, it was dark on the other side and he couldn't see anything either. He didn't like the idea of leaving his head poking through while he waited for his eyes to adjust. He moved backwards.

"What can you see?"

Scree turned to look back over his shoulder. Nemucca was still crouching in the corner, torch in hand again and held above his head.

"I was just asking," the lad said.

"Well, if you is just going sits over there, you don't gets to ask nothing. Right?"

Nemucca shrugged, but he collected his pack and crossed to the door. "I can't see anything."

Scree grunted.

"Are you going through?"

"Yep. And so are you." Collecting his sword and pack Scree took Nemucca by the arm. "Let's go."

Scree stepped through the door slightly ahead of the human. When his boot passed through the silver sheen he knew instantly that he'd made a mistake— damn Nemucca and his distractions. The ground on the other side wasn't where it should be.

KEEBLE GRUNTED and made his way down the aisle towards the rear of the train. He examined the little, stiff piece of parchment Kim had given him. There were lines of neatly printed writing, but nothing understandable. Through the next hydraulically powered door, he threw the paper onto the floor.

As he walked, Keeble started to sing a Song. Well, it wasn't a Song really, but an attempt to recreate the noise the door between the worlds had made. There were clicks and whistles and buzzes, but no matter what he did, he couldn't get it right. His mind kept pushing the Song in another direction, as if never quite coming to grips with what he was trying to do.

He gave up and continued to walk.

Three carriages later, Keeble was wondering why he'd bothered. One row of seats looked much like the one before, and though the people might have been interesting, he could understand nothing of the conversations.

At the end of the carriage, Keeble discovered he could go no further. With a grunt of disgust he chose a seat and sat himself down. The large black dwarf beside him looked him up and down for a moment.

"[Heading to Nottingham? Or further?]" the stranger asked.

Keeble shrugged and spoke in his own language to demonstrate that conversation was going to be impossible. The other dwarf shrugged as well and returned to staring out the window.

It wasn't long before another dwarf tried talking to him. This one emerged from the locked door. He wore a grey uniform.

"[Tickets, please,]" he said. "[Tickets, please.]" He touched Keeble on the shoulder when he didn't respond. "[Could I see your ticket please, sir?]"

"Can't understand a word you're babbling," Keeble replied. He put on what he hoped was a pleasant smile.

"[Can I see your ticket, please?]" The dwarf in the uniform reached past him and took something from the black dwarf. It was a little slip of paper. He held it up for Keeble to see, then handed it back.

"You want to see my little bit of parchment? What for?" He pointed back the way he'd come. "It's down that way, about two carriages back. You want it, you can go get it yourself."

18: Engineer

"[Do you have a ticket? If you don't, you'll have to buy one or get off at the next station.]"

"Why do you keep talking at me when it's obvious I can't understand a word you're saying?" Keeble smiled again and shrugged.

He watched the stranger pull what appeared to be coinage from a shoulder bag he carried. "[Do you have any money?]" he said, twiddling the silver disk between his fingers.

Keeble thought he knew what the dwarf meant there. He shook his head.

"[Then I'm sorry, sir, but you'll have to disembark at Hucknall Station.]"

Keeble shook his head again. "You really are an idiot, aren't you?"

"[Would you please come with me, sir.]"

The stranger gripped Keeble's arm, but he shook him off angrily.

"[Are you going to leave quietly?]"

Keeble didn't move, and the stranger had a short conversation with one of the talking boxes. A moment later another uniformed dwarf came from the other end of the carriage. This one was larger and younger, and Keeble didn't bother resisting as he was led from the train when it next stopped.

Meledrin wasn't going to be happy. Keeble smiled as another dwarf in uniform escorted him from the station and left him standing beside the road.

"[Just think yourself lucky you haven't been fined.]"

Keeble ignored him, looking one way and then the other. "Maybe I should have taken them to talk to Kim."

But it was too late. And there was too much for him to look at to remain worried for long. He set off after a bicycle that had gears and what looked like a generator on the back wheel to run its own little electric light. The bicycle and its rider soon left him behind and he tried to follow a two-wheeled motorized vehicle instead. When he stopped to rest, Keeble saw a tiny car, hardly more than a foot long, racing along the raised walking area beside the road. He was off again.

Keeble wandered around the city as the afternoon waned, moving from one wonder to the next. Eventually he made his way into a narrow alley to investigate a noise and discovered a fabulous workshop.

Keeble watched from outside the workshop for a long time. Sometimes he leaned with his back against the cool red bricks of the building across the alley. Sometimes he sat on an old wooden box, though it was in a horrid state of disrepair and looked as though it might fall apart at any moment. Sometimes, when the engineer disappeared into another part of the workshop, he even went all of the way across to the doorway to have a look around. There were so many things he wanted to examine. The strange vehicles were everywhere inside with inspection panels opened, parts removed. But he didn't go in. A workshop was a dwarf's life; he'd never invade it without being invited.

When darkness descended and the engineer locked his doors, Keeble stayed where he was. He found a corner and sat himself down. He used a paperboard box as protection against the wind. He was hungry and tired and cold, but he stayed where he was, awake for hours as the strange moon marched shadows around the alley.

In the morning he was awake and standing by the little wooden door when the engineer returned to open up. Keeble played nervously with the gears on his arm as the dwarf looked at him sideways.

"*Hello*," Keeble said. He'd learned at least that much of the language.

The engineer was older than Keeble had first thought. His beard was run through with flecks of grey, and his face was creased with the weight of years. "[Hi, there. How you doin'?]"

Keeble shrugged. He didn't understand but smiled and nodded because he thought that might be a good response. "Can I watch you work?" he asked, motioning into the workshop. He wouldn't go in there without being invited, but surely he could ask to be invited.

"[Not a clue what you're talking about there, buddy.]"

Keeble shrugged once more, then pointed to his eyes, then to the other dwarf, and into the workshop.

"[What? You want to watch me work?]" The engineer paused for a moment, shrugged, then motioned inside.

Keeble took that as his invitation. He walked quickly in and sat on a barrel near the vehicle that appeared to need the most work.

"Me Keeble." With a nod.

"[What?]"

"Keeble." This time he simply pointed.

"[Your name's *Keeble*? Jesus, what were your parents thinking?]"

"Keeble."

"[Yeah, Keeble, how you doin'? Don't understand a goddamned thing, do ya? And you want to watch me work? Oh well, whatever. Just don't touch nothin', you understand? Jesus, course you don't understand. My name is Colin. Colin.]"

Keeble nodded happily. "Colin." Then he had to sit and wait for a couple of minutes while Colin took himself off to another room. When he returned, he was pulling on a one-piece set of clothes that covered his whole body. He already had one arm in a sleeve, and he was using that hand to carry two cups of steaming liquid.

"[That's a weird lookin' arm you got there, Keeble,]" Colin said as he handed over one of the cups. "[Where you get that from?]"

Keeble nodded and smiled as he sniffed suspiciously at the drink. It smelled wonderful.

"[Know much about cars, do you?]" Colin took a mouthful of drink, smacking his lip appreciatively, then collected a hammer from a box full of tools and started to

147

pound on a part of the engine. Keeble watched carefully. The old dwarf didn't seem very enthusiastic, so Keeble jumped down from his perch and wandered across to get a better look.

"That's a bolt," he said. "Why are you hitting a bolt with a hammer?"

The engineer went to strike the offending object again, but Keeble grabbed his hand before he could do so. With a grunt, he took the hammer away, crossed to the tools and selected the appropriate spanner. The bolt was tight but it took him only a moment to work it loose. He handed the spanner to Colin.

"You use a spanner to undo bolts."

"[Strong little bugger, ain't ya.]"

Keeble watched half the morning and Colin didn't even fix one of the vehicles. After a while a dwife came in. She babbled for a while, gave Keeble a strange look, then moved quickly out of sight.

"You allow dwives in your workshop?" Keeble asked. He suddenly understood why the engineer was so slow. If he had to put up with women nattering inanities at him all day he wasn't likely to get *anything* done.

When the strange bell started ringing, Keeble was bored enough to go to investigate.

Down in the back corner of the workshop he found a fading plywood door, and when he pushed it gently, he was offered a view of a small office. The dwife, her floral dress trying to compete with the drab but not having much luck, sat at a desk with a black thing nestled between her shoulder and drooping head. She was speaking into it rapidly and didn't see him watching.

She talked, nodding and punctuating long silences with "Uh huh, uh huh," as if she were holding a conversation with the thing. As she talked, the dwife wrote in a large notebook. *She wrote.* Keeble was sure she was writing. Random squiggles wouldn't be so uniform and neat. But how could they let a dwife learn to write? Finally it was too much for him. Allowing women to work was one thing — Ari had always wanted to work, and he had reluctantly let her — but to let them write? Keeble pushed the door the rest of the way open and marched across the room. It wasn't a very big room, and his short legs covered the ground quickly. The dwife didn't look up until the last moment. When she saw him she surged back, and the thing fell away from her ear.

"[Get away from me.]"

Keeble snatched the stylus from her, fending away a weak blow with his metal arm. "Women aren't allowed to write," he said, as if she'd understand. He was about to find Colin and tell him what had happened when the engineer grabbed him on the shoulder.

"[What's going on here, Mona?]"

"[He barged in here and grabbed my pen. I was talking on the phone and... Oh, God.]" The dwife grabbed the black item off the floor. "[Mister Dennis? Mister Dennis? God, I wouldn't be surprised if he is calling the police right now.]"

Keeble used the stylus to gesture at the book. "She was writing, Colin. I saw her." They ignored him.

"[*Do* we need the police?]"

The dwife shook her head. "[I don't *think* so. He's a bit soft in the head, isn't he? Not all there?]"

"[Can't rightly say. Seems sensible and friendly enough for the most part, except for that gobbligook he speaks.]"

"[Well, sensible and friendly don't mean right in the head.]"

"What?" Keeble asked, pointing at the black thing.

"[That's a telephone, lad. Telephone. Christ, he doesn't even know what a phone is.]" Colin took his arm and led him from the room. "[Come and watch me fix the car.]" Over his shoulder he said, "[Mona, why don't you ring a couple of hospitals, see if they know anything.]"

But Colin didn't work any quicker after that, though he did name each part as he removed it, then again as he put it back in. Sometimes, when Keeble asked, he would try to explain the use of the parts with words and gestures.

By late morning, Keeble hadn't learned much about cars. But he had learned how to make coffee, and he'd learned what a cream biscuit was. Those discoveries were almost worth the morning's frustration. With his latest brew in hand he moved away from the engineer to look around the workshop. There was a wide array of tools, some of which Keeble had never seen, and most of which appeared to have been exactly where they were for a long time. For the most part, Colin seemed to make do with an adjustable spanner, two screwdrivers, and a hammer.

And then, wonder of wonders, he found a book. Normally books didn't excite him much at all, but this one contained pictures of a motor, with all the parts separated as if they'd been dismantled. Sitting in a corner, his coffee forgotten on the oil-stained concrete floor, Keeble searched the pages until he found a picture of a part he knew, then worked out from there. He examined each part, trying to imagine what it might do. The air filter was connected to the carburetor. That was where air was mixed with the fuel. Keeble asked Colin about the name of the next part, and followed the steps until he reached the end. Then he looked at the radiator.

Keeble ate fish and chips for lunch, sitting at a table with Colin and Mona. He drank some more coffee, listening to the two of them speak. He understood little of what they said but wasn't worried. He had the book open by his side and was still reading.

"[Did you find anything out from the hospitals?]"

"[No. They don't seem to know anything. And, with everything else going on, they don't really care.]"

"[Right. Excellent.]" Colin turned in Keeble's direction for a moment, and he took the opportunity to interrupt.

"Excuse," he said. "What?"

Colin looked at the picture he was pointing at, but at that moment the telephone rang in the office.

"[I'll get it, Mona,]" the engineer said. "[You finish your lunch.]" He rushed into the office, leaving Keeble and the dwife alone together.

Mona leaned over the see what he was pointing at. "[That's the clutch plate,]" she said, giving a slight smile. "*Clutch plate.*"

Keeble eyed her suspiciously. "*Clutch plate?*" She was only a dwife, how would she know?

"*That's right.*"

But he didn't trust her. He flipped back through the pages and pointed at another part that Colin had named earlier, covering the name with his thumb so she couldn't read it. "*What?*" he asked.

"*Thermostat.*"

She was right. Keeble turned some more pages and pointed again.

"*Fuel pump.*"

She was right again. Keeble went back to the picture he'd started from. "*Clutch plate?*"

"*Yep.*"

Keeble grunted and gave a slight nod of his head. He said nothing more as he started to work away from the clutch plate. He didn't know what it did, exactly, but he would ask Colin later. He was *not* going to ask Mona.

-oOo-

Keeble watched the ticking hands of the machine on the wall. They'd kept a constant beat all day long. He decided the machine was a timekeeper, one more accurate than any he had ever seen. When the two biggest hands formed a straight line from top to bottom — six hours past noon, he guessed — Colin packed away his spanner, screwdrivers, and hammer and removed his work clothes. He washed up in a sink near the shit box at the back and came out wiping his hands on a dirty towel. Mona had left some time ago and the telephone had rung several times and remained unanswered.

"[Time to go, Keeble.]"

Keeble guessed that meant quitting time but wasn't keen on the idea. The box he'd slept in across the alley didn't seem all that welcoming. He loitered as Colin started to pull the chain that rolled down the big door.

"[You coming?]"

Keeble stayed where he was. He wound the gears on his hand, clutching at nothing.

"[You don't have anywhere to go, do you, lad?]"

Keeble shrugged.

"[Where do you live?]"

He shrugged again.

"[Jesus.]" Colin scratched at his grease stained neck. "[I can't take you home. Shelly'd kill me.]"

Keeble stood where he was and wound his hand in and out. In and out.

"[Jesus. How 'bout you stay here? Can I trust you in here? I can't believe I'm doing this.]"

The engineer led the way back to the office where Mona had spent most of the day. Keeble followed close behind.

"[Once I leave, you'll be stuck for the night, though. Understand?]"

Keeble didn't understand and said so.

"[Jesus. I saw you looking at the clock out there. You know a clock don't you.]" He pointed to one of the timekeepers on the wall.

"*Clock?*"

"*Yes, clock.*" Colin nodded. "[Well, you'll be stuck in here for twelve hours, until the little hand has gone all the way around and come back to the six.]" He drew a big circle in front of the clock and Keeble understood what he meant.

"*In here for...*" He stumbled through half the sentence in the strange language, but didn't need to go any further.

"[Twelve hours. Yeah, that's right. You okay with that?]"

Keeble nodded and smiled.

"[Yeah, I suppose you would be. This couch was always too small for me to sleep on, though I done it often enough. Probably about the right size for you though.]" He led Keeble to a big, soft, shiny chair against one of the walls. "[And there's a bit of food and drink in the fridge. But you know where all that is.]"

Keeble remembered the fridge. It was the box that hummed and rattled and kept things cold.

"[And there's coffee.]"

"*Coffee.*" Keeble liked coffee.

Colin stood where he was and looked around. "[Well...]"

"*Thank you.*"

"[You're welcome, Keeble. I suppose. Just don't touch anything. Understand?]"

Keeble nodded. "*Don't touch.*"

"[That's right. Jesus, what am I doing?]" He sighed. "[Just make sure you turn the lights off before you go to sleep.]" As he went back out into the workshop, Colin paused by the door and flicked a little white switch a few times.

Keeble jumped to his feet as the light in the room came and went with each flick. He rushed over to the switch to try it himself and was still playing when Colin locked the workshop's outer door.

19: Coffee and Cars

KEEBLE TRIED NOT TO TOUCH. He sat at the desk in the office, feet swinging above the cold plastic tiles of the floor, and flipped through another book. He made a coffee, with no milk or sugar to dilute the taste. He opened one of the plastic packets and ate the crunchy potato slices inside. He lasted until the little hand on the clock was pointing to the seven.

The cars were just outside, but he avoided the temptation. Instead he pulled apart the little music maker on the desk. A radio, Mona had called it. There were all sorts of things inside. He started at the power switch, following wires to each component, trying to work out what they might do. After that he pulled apart the computer.

But while we worked, the cars waited, crouching in the dark like dragons. It wasn't long before he screwed the computer back together, made himself some more coffee, and went out into the workshop. He spent a few minutes searching for the light switch for the workshop. He realized, eventually, that it would be by the door. When he could see, Keeble chose the car closest to the bookshelf, so he could read the name on the badge of the car and look at all the books at the same time to see the ones that matched.

Morris Minor. He couldn't read the letters, but found a match and pulled it from the shelf.

"Yes." Five minutes later Keeble had pulled the covers off the ignition. He was examining how the key fitted and what happened after that. He knew where the starter motor was. He knew where the electricity holder was: the battery. He shook his head at the thought and smiled. "A little black box to hold electricity."

In a little diagram near the back of the book, he saw how they were linked and he followed the path on the car.

Then he reverently took the key, closed his eyes, and turned.

Keeble almost panicked when the whole car lurched forward.

He released the key and everything was still again. He got out to make sure nothing had been damaged.

"The motor's still connected to the wheels," he muttered once he was back in the driver's seat. "I need the clutch." He found the appropriate page in the book. He looked at the pictures. He looked at the pictures that connected to those pictures. He *did* need the clutch, a little pedal on the floor that he could hardly reach. He also needed the gears, which were controlled by the lever, by his side. He perched on the edge of the seat and pushed the pedal while he put the gears into the neutral position. He also found the lever that controlled the brakes. He tried the key again.

Keeble listened as the starter motor whined and tried to get the engine started. It rumbled into life but died just a second later. "More fuel," he said. "I need more fuel." But how did he get more fuel into the engine? He remembered seeing a picture that might explain how it was done, but that was a long time ago. He started going through the book. "Another pedal," he said eventually. "Of course."

So he pumped the pedal while turning the key. The engine rumbled into life, speeding up every time he pumped, and continued to go even when he climbed out. Keeble cheered and did a little jig.

But the engine didn't run very smoothly. Not as smoothly as some of the others he'd heard. There was also a scraping sound. He turned the car off again and started to examine the pictures in the book.

The strange Song from the magical door between worlds started to fill his mind with its shifting rhythms and dancing flows. He tried to make the sounds out loud, clicking and humming and Singing. He fitted it around his work.

The 'Morris' caused problems, but when Keeble finished that, two hours after midnight, he moved forward at full steam. He repaired the bit between the wheels of a 'Toyota' in a couple of hours and then started work on a 'Ford'. He was almost done with that, but before he could get the hood reattached, Keeble heard the rattling of keys outside the door and knew Colin had arrived. The song of the magical gate faltered for the first time. He worked faster for a few moments, before returning to his regular, steady pace. He needed about five more minutes and a mad dash now wasn't going to help. He was tightening the first bolt on the last hinge of the hood when the engineer finally came through the door.

"[Keeble, how are you lad?]"

Keeble looked up. Obviously Colin hadn't seen him. He didn't really want to be there when it happened.

"[What the hell? I told you not to touch anything.]" The older dwarf hurried down to the end of the workshop where Keeble was holding the hood in place with his metal hand and his shoulder and tightening the second, and last, bolt with the other.

"[Why are you removing the hood? Lucky I got here when I did.]"

Colin took the spanner from Keeble's hand and quickly finished the job while Keeble watched and held the hood in place. When it was done, he jumped down to the floor and wiped his hand on a towel.

"It's fixed," he said. Colin couldn't understand him, though, so the anger showing on the dwarf's creased face continued to grow as he moved about the workshop looking at various cars.

"[What the hell else have you fiddled with?]"

Keeble decided the only way to halt the dwarf's growing anger was to show him what he'd done. He went quickly to the 'Morris' and climbed in.

"[What do you think you are doing?]"

Making sure the car was out of gear, Keeble pumped the pedal a couple of times as he turned the key.

"[Get out of there.]"

The car rumbled into life and Colin grunted. "[I reckon that thing hasn't sounded so good in twenty years.]"

He reached in and opened the hood. Keeble didn't know why when none of what he'd done was going to be visible. He turned the engine off and climbed out. When he joined Colin, the engineer was staring at the engine and muttering quietly.

"[How did you do this?]" Colin shrugged his shoulders, and Keeble got the message. He pointed to the books on the shelf and received a shake of the head in reply. "[You read a book and fixed it?]"

"*Repair.*" Keeble said in Colin's language. "*Work good.*" He pointed to the other two cars he'd done as well. "*Them.*"

"[What?]"

"*Them. Work good.*"

Colin almost ran from one car to the other, starting the engine of each and sitting for a moment to listen to the smooth growl.

Sitting in the last one he asked: "[You fixed them last night?]"

Keeble looked at him. 'Fix,' he knew, but the rest...

Colin went to the last car in the workshop and beckoned Keeble over with a long crooked finger. "[Can you fix this one? It needs a new gearbox.]" Colin showed him a part sitting near a bench, then pointed back to the car. "[Gearbox in there.]"

Keeble smiled and set to work.

The books remained on the shelf. Keeble saw enough engines during the night for the details to be indelibly inscribed across his consciousness. He worked for two hours and Colin stood close by watching his every move. When he was done, the engineer still didn't move. He stood and stared.

"[That's amazing. Amazing. Bloody hell.]" He wiped his hands on a towel, though the closest he had come to work was handing tools to Keeble when he was asked.

Mona walked in as he muttered.

"*Hi, Colin.*" The dwife nodded to Keeble as well.

"*Mona,*" Colin said in reply, though he hardly knew she was there.

"[What's the matter?]"

"[Keeble fixed them.]"

"[Fixed what?]"

"[The cars. Mister Henry's Morris and Jackie's car and Terry Dale's. And now he fixed this as well.]"

"[What?]"

"[He fixed them.]"

"[When.]"

Finally, Colin turned to look at her. He tugged at his beard. "[When do you think? Last night. This morning.]"

Mona seemed about to say something else. She opened her mouth, gave it some thought, then snapped her teeth back together.

Colin nodded. "[That's what I thought.]"

Keeble wondered if they were done. He turned off the car and climbed out. He stood for a while, looking at them while they stood looking at the car. Eventually he went and made some coffee. He made two at first then thought he would probably make someone angry if he didn't make Mona one as well. So he collected another cup from the cupboard under the sink and carefully measured out the brown powder and the sugar. He took the cups out into the workshop where Colin and Mona were deep in conversation.

"[He saved you about three days work, Colin, you have to give him something.]"

"[I didn't ask him to do anything at all, though. I was doing him a favor, remember. Maybe he was just paying me back.]"

"[He has no home, nothing besides what he has on his back, for all we know. A couple of tenners won't send us bust. Probably a good idea to offer him a job.]"

"[A job?]"

"[Looks like you could sit back with your feet up and watch.]"

Keeble handed them each a mug and sat on an overturned metal bucket. He sipped his coffee, boiling hot and strong, and sighed contentedly. But when he'd finished drinking, Mona and Colin were still talking. Just like a dwife. Stand around doing nothing and stop others from working as well. He shook his head and made his way over to the door.

After spending most of his life in a cave, he discovered that the sight of the sun in the morning was a wonderful experience. Such clarity and color. Out in the alley he looked up between the canyons of the buildings to the piercing blue of the sky. A scatter of clouds raced for the east.

And there, overtaking them all was a flying machine. Keeble smiled, hardly able to stop himself from running after it. Shading his eyes, he watched it go. It was a long way away but still seemed to move so quickly. It banked to the left, smoke streaming out behind, and disappeared behind the brown stone of the workshop. "A flying machine." He rushed back inside. "Colin."

"*Yes.*"

"Flying machines? How do they work? Do you have one?"

"[Sorry?]"

"The flying machines." Keeble stretched his arms out to either side and sailed about the room, banking from side to side, bending his knees and stretching up on his toes. "The flying machines."

"[Planes?]"

"*Planes. Yes...*" He knew the words. "*How work?*"

"[Well, ahhh...]" Colin scratched at his cheek and stared at the ceiling as if searching for inspiration. "[That really depends on the plane, Keeble. There are normal planes, and there are jet planes.]"

Keeble didn't understand much of that at all, and he decided that he'd never learn if he relied on Colin to teach him. He would have to find out for himself. He waved. "*Goodbye.*"

"[What? No, stay. There's no need to rush off.]"

"*I go plane workshop.*" Keeble struggled through the sentence.

"[You just got here. Have another coffee.]"

"*I want see planes.*" He waved again.

Mona started searching through the leather bag she carried over her shoulder. "[At least take this, Keeble.]"

"*What?*"

"[It's money.]" She handed him a small bundle of paper, closing his hand around it tightly.

Keeble didn't know the word. He shrugged his shoulders.

"[It's money,]" Colin said. Then to Mona: "[Show him a coin, he might know one of them.]"

The dwife searched through her bag again and pulled out a small metal disk with a face on one side and another picture on the other. A coin. So, maybe the paper was money. Keeble unfolded one of the pieces of paper and examined it. And the same face was on there. Money it was then.

"[One of those notes there will get you a coffee, love.]" Mona pointed at the note Keeble was examining then pointed to the coffee cup Colin still held.

Keeble smiled and thanked them but his mind was already on the planes. "*Planes?*" he asked.

"[Well, Hucknall Airfield is,]" Colin pointed, "[that way, I guess. I wish you would stay though, Keeble. We'll give you a job and all. So you can earn some more money.]"

"*Planes. Thank you. Goodbye.*" He hurried out into the street.

Out on the main street, Keeble paused to look around. He'd forgotten how many dwarves there were, and cars and things. Everywhere he looked, something was happening.

He could see smoke between two buildings. Away to the northeast, bats swirled through the air like burnt leaves. Planes came and went, stitching the sky. But it all seemed so far away.

Another plane passed silently overhead, snapping Keeble's attention back to his mission. He wound the gears to adjust the angles on his hand.

"How far is it to the plane workshops?" he asked himself. "Which is the best way to go?" He looked one way along the street, then the other. And both ways looked much the same. Tall, rough looking buildings. Abnormally tall dwarves. Cars. He was about to choose a direction at random when a large car with a sign on top pulled up nearby. He'd seen similar ones before. An old dwife climbed gingerly out, struggling with a pair of bags and a walking stick.

Before he could decide where to go, someone put a hand on his shoulder. He turned to see Mona standing by his side.

"[It's only a couple of miles, but you'd just get lost. I'll give you some money for a cab.]" She hurried over to the car with the sign and spoke through the window with the driver. She handed him some money.

"[Come on. Get in.]"

Keeble didn't understand a word of it, but Mona motioned for him to get into the car. "*What? Why?*"

Mona pointed to the sky where a plane was racing across the blue. "*Airport,*" she said. "*Plane.*"

Perhaps the driver was going to take him to where they kept the planes. The airport. "*Thank you,*" he said to Mona as he hurried to climb in the car. He sat on the edge of the seat, straining to see exactly how it was that the driver made the vehicle go, the rhythms that gave the actions life. Mona waved, and he waved vaguely in reply.

Clutch out, fuel down...

He licked his lips and wound the prongs on his hand in and out. The driver started to talk and didn't stop for the entire journey. Keeble liked him.

At the airport, Keeble jumped out almost before the cab came to a halt. He ran across the parking area and stopped at a high fence, fingers gripping the wire mesh tightly. Planes were parked nearby, lined up beside a large shed. Keeble smiled as he looked about for the easiest way in.

"Where's the gate?"

A building filled a break in the fence, allowing access from the car park to the area beyond.

"There we go."

Inside, he found himself in a small, carpeted room. Pictures adorned the walls. One of a plane in flight. One of what must have been the airport from a plane. Another of a dozen men in front of three planes. There were some blue plastic chairs under the photos, and a yellow plant in a large pot in the corner. A counter took up one end of the room.

He tried a glass door that would lead him out to the planes.

"Locked." He sighed. The only other visible door was behind the counter. "I'm probably not allowed back there, though."

He went to the counter and waited. He could barely see over the top, but there didn't appear to be anything worth seeing anyway. He waited some more.

"*Hello?*"

No answer.

There was a sign on the counter with an arrow pointing to a button. Keeble looked at the sign, looked at the button, and looked at the sign again. With a shrug, he reached up and pressed the button. He was rewarded with a wonderful, mechanical buzzing sound from beyond the door. He left his hand near the button, his short fingers gripping the edge of the counter. No response, so he pressed the button again, and once more a few seconds after that. Finally the door opened and someone emerged.

A dwife. Always a dwife. Keeble grunted in disgust.

"[I'm sorry.]" She paused when she saw him. "[I was just on the phone.]"

"*Phone.*" Keeble said in the local language. He smiled, holding his hand up to his ear and nodding.

"[What can I do for you? I'm sorry, but with all that's happening we aren't sending any planes up today. Or anytime soon, probably.]"

"*Plane. Me fix plane. Work good.*"

"[You... Which plane? What are you talking about? I would like to help you, sir, but I don't know what you mean.]"

"*Me...*" Keeble looked at her.

"[Yes, I understand the words you are using, sir, but...]"

"*Fix... plane.*"

"[You're looking for work?]"

"*Yes. Me work plane. Fix.*"

"[I'm sorry sir, we aren't hiring at the moment.]"

Keeble didn't know how to explain to her. She was a dwife, so how was she to understand? He decided he'd sit down on one of the blue chairs and wait until a dwarf came so he could talk to him. Keeble sat down to wait.

"[I am sorry, sir, but I think you should leave. We aren't hiring. There are no positions available.]"

Keeble swung his legs, examining the tip of each boot in turn as it came into view. Scuffed left, shiny right. Scuffed left, shiny right. He wondered how his left boot had gotten into such a terrible condition when his right still looked so good.

"I'll have to fix that first chance I get."

"[If you don't leave, sir, I'll...]"

Left, right. Left, right. Keeble could have waited all day, but he didn't have to wait long at all. The dwife left the room and returned a moment later with a large, bald dwarf. Keeble recognized him from one of the pictures, though he had certainly aged since it had been done. He jumped up and shook the dwarf's hand, smiling.

"[Good morning, sir. I believe Tanya asked you to leave. If you don't leave right away...]"

"*Me fix plane. Work good.*"

"[All our planes already work. Now if you could —]"

Keeble dug in his pocket and pulled out the money Colin and Mona had given him. "*Me fix plane.*" He forced the notes into the dwarf's hand.

"[You want to pay me to let you fix a plane? What, are you kidding?]"

"*Me watch. Learn. Fix plane.*"

"[Look, you'd need to pay me more than twenty three pounds to let you near one of my planes. All right?]" He put the money pack in the Keeble's hand and ushered him towards the door. Keeble thought of resisting for a moment, stating his case again, but he knew it would be useless. He'd have to try something else. Perhaps when they went home.

20: Tourist

KEEBLE WATCHED as James tumbled from his stool and landed in a puddle of ale on the floor. A cheer went up from those still gathered.

"You lot can't hold your ale," Keeble said. Nobody understood him, but he thought they got the general idea. They all cheered again, and Keeble raised his glass to them before draining away the last of his drink.

He'd been drinking the stuff for almost three hours and couldn't feel the effects. All that money, and he might as well have been drinking water. He was just glad he hadn't paid for most of what he'd drunk. His own money had run out before he'd wet his palette, but the locals had taken pity on him, strange foreigner that he was, and kept his wheels lubricated for the rest of the evening. He'd drunk three of them under the table and was looking for a fourth.

Keeble had waited by the airport until night fell and the last cars pulled away from the parking area. Not long after that, just when he was preparing to go over the fence, he spotted a uniformed dwarf, much like the one who threw him from the train. The dwarf wandered lazy, random patrols with a big dog. He rattled doors and shone a light-stick in windows before moving on to do it all again. Keeble had decided it wasn't worth the risk and wandered away, disappointed and wondering what to do.

He'd walked along quiet back streets, turning left then right and left again, until finding a busy road and the bar. Since then he'd attempted to drown his sorrows with little luck.

"If only they could brew a decent ale."

Every tall dwarf he met was hardly a dwarf at all. They couldn't brew ale. They worked slowly, as if there were no more jobs to do when there were always more jobs. And they couldn't explain the simplest piece of technology. Keeble was starting to have his suspicions.

While he waited for someone else to buy him a drink, he turned to watch the television. The little black box sat on a shelf behind the bar, offering up an array of pictures. For most of the night he'd watched dwarves chasing a ball around a rectangular field in a game of '*football*', whatever that meant. Most of the rules eluded him, but those playing the game seemed to enjoy themselves, when they weren't lying on the ground squirming in pain. And the other patrons in the bar shouted themselves hoarse with every bit of action.

That had long since ended, replaced by two people sitting at a bench, apparently talking about other games of football. Or perhaps it was the same game, only in different colors. If they were different games they all looked much the same to Keeble.

Now, there was another dwarf and another desk. He was not talking about games though, Keeble quickly realized. He didn't seem any more serious than those talking about football, but the little short sections of action were all quite different. Some people at the top of a set of stairs, surround by other people. A dwife by a flooded river. A huge room with dozens of people sitting around talking. Keeble suspected that what he was watching was important, but since he couldn't understand much of what was being said, he might as well have been watching the football.

Then there were the big, black bats, shot down out of the sky, and suits of colorful armor split open, revealing what was inside. Except the bodies had already been removed and the suit was too far away to show much detail. Keeble wished the dwarves of this world could speak a *real* language. He tried to follow the voice on the television but gave up in disgust. Where was Meledrin when you needed her?

Keeble was just wondering how he might go about finding Meledrin and Kim when he saw them, up on the television. They were being hustled through a large crowd, away from a big ugly building with an eagle on top, and into a car.

He grabbed the arm of the nearest dwarf and pointed up at the screen.

"*Where?*" he asked.

The dwarf squinted upwards as if that might help clear his ale addled senses.

The barman answered first. "[That's the American Embassy, that is,]" he said as he polished a glass.

"[How do you know that?]" Keeble's barstool neighbor asked.

"[See that big eagle? Dead giveaway. And besides, the reporter just said that it's been unusually busy at the American Embassy today with lots of comings and goings.]"

"[Yeah? Who was coming and who was going?]"

"[Well, Ministers and the like,]" the barman said. "[Plus lots of others that nobody recognizes.]"

Keeble hadn't understood any of what had been said. "*Where?*"

"[American Embassy. Down in London somewhere.]"

"*American Embassy?*"

"[That's right.]"

"*How go?*"

"[How do you get there? Don't know, really.]" The barman got a drink for someone down the other end of the bar. "[Train first, I suppose, then a cab.]"

A train then a cab, perhaps. *"Pay?"*

"[Yeah, course it'll cost you. Don't know how much, though.]" He continued to polish the glass as he watched the television. He added nothing more.

Keeble watched the screen as well, but it was already showing a different picture.

"[So, you want to go to the Embassy, do you?]" The dwarf sitting at the bar beside Keeble turned to look blearily at him. "[Here, I can give you... three pounds.]" He straightened out some of the paper money and carefully placed them on the bar where he flattened them out again. "[Has anyone else got some money so our short friend here can annoy some Americans?]"

"[What? Where's he going?]"

"[The American Embassy.]"

"[He isn't a yank, is he? Doesn't look like one.]" But the stranger pulled out some money as well and added it to the pile.

A third dwarf, one of the few remaining who was still sober, joined them. "[Do you have any idea how much he'll need?"

"[Nope. Where is the American Embassy?]"

"[Mayfair.]"

"[Mayfair? So how much will that cost then?]"

"[I don't know.]"

Keeble tried to follow the flow of the conversation without luck. All he knew was that another couple of men added money to the pile and he now had about ten pounds, if he had all the symbols right.

"[What has he got here?]" The sober fellow picked up the pile and counted. "[Thirteen quid.]" He added some more from his own pocket. "[Eighteen. Phil, put in for Keeble, will ya. He want's to go to the American Embassy.]"

A dwarf over in a corner, holding a glass in one hand and a dart in the other, turned to look. "[What's he a tourist, is he, or what?]"

"[I don't know. He wants to go to the Embassy though.]"

"[That's down in London. That'll cost about fifty pounds to get there.]"

"[Well, we've got eighteen.]"

Phil threw his dart at the board and went to the bar to add his own money to the pile. "[Little bugger's been drinking for free all night, and now we pay for him to get to London as well?]"

Keeble had no idea what was being said, so he sat silently and awaited the outcome. Up on the television, the people behind the desk had gone and another game was being shown. It was not football this time. The ball was a different shape and the players were allowed to use their hands. They were also allowed to stomp on each other's heads, apparently. Keeble couldn't understand the rules of this game either, but it seemed like a lot more fun than football.

The barman told him the game was rugby. Keeble continued to watch while the little pile of money in front of him continued to grow.

-oOo-

Keeble carefully placed the little piece of paper in his pocket with the remains of his money before sitting down. He made himself comfortable beside an old dwarf who looked like he'd been doing hard labor every day of his life. Keeble smiled and nodded. "*Hello.*"

The other dwarf ignored him. Keeble sighed.

Outside the window, James, looking pale and sick in the first light of the morning, waved and gave the thumbs up. Keeble gave a slight nod in reply as the train pulled away from the station. Moments later, both James and the station were gone from sight and the train was rattling along. Then, the city was gone and only occasional islands of buildings sang counter point for the greenery.

Keeble checked the timekeeper on his wrist. The barman had found it in a '*lost property box*' and said he could have it. At the station, when he was buying the ticket, James had explained that the he would have to change trains at Nottingham in about twenty minutes, then the next train would arrive at a place called St Pancras Station when the little hand reached the ninth number if everything went well. A bit more than two hours all up. With the dwarf by his side ignoring him, Keeble settled back and waited to change trains.

He was a bit embarrassed a few minutes later when he realized he was back at the station that he had used with Kim and Meledrin. He showed his ticket to a uniformed man on the platform and hurried to the next train. HE found a seat and tried to get some sleep.

When he woke, the sun had climbed much higher and a disembodied voice was telling the passengers that the train had arrived at St Pancras. At least Keeble thought that was what it said. He checked his timekeeper and it seemed about right, so he jumped to his feet and followed the rest of the crowd out onto the platform. He would have liked to stop there for a moment to get his bearings, but the rush carried him onwards and upwards. At a little gate, a dwarf stopped him and Keeble dutifully held up his little piece of paper like everyone else and was allowed to continue on.

Once out on the street, he finally found himself a quiet corner and stopped for a moment to think. He nervously wound his metal fingers in and out, in and out. An endless stream of dwarves went past, young and old, male and female.

He might well have stayed there all day, wedged into the cold brown stone of the corner, but a black cab rolled by, all but silent in the tumult. He grabbed the arm of the dwarf nearest him, a man in a grey suit with a silken leash tied about his throat.

The dwarf shook him off, glared angrily for a moment, and hurried on. Keeble tried a different tack.

"*Hello,*" he said hopefully when he caught the eye of someone else.

The stranger hurried on.

"*Hello.*"

The third stranger smiled thinly and nodded, switching a small black case from one hand to the other like a rugby player protecting the ball. "*Hi.*"

"*Cab?*"

The stranger missed a step then came to a halt. "[You want a cab? They're over there.]" He switched the case back again and, leaning, pointed through the crowd. "[Around that corner there. It's not far. All right?]"

Before Keeble could answer, the dwarf had straightened and was on his way again. He glanced back once before he was lost in the crowd.

Keeble made his way in the direction indicated. Stopping at the edge of the street with everyone else, he watched for a break in the traffic. Then, inexplicably, the rumbling, metal stream suddenly stopped and the people surged across, carrying Keeble with them.

Around the corner was a long line of cars with signs on top. Keeble went to the black one at the front of the queue and climbed in the back seat.

"*Hi there,*" the driver said, adjusting a little mirror so he could see Keeble in the back. "[Where to today, sir?]"

"*American Embassy,*" Keeble said in reply, though he wasn't sure what the driver had asked. He also handed over a little square of cardboard the barman had written on.

"[Not a problem.]"

The driver talked continuously as he drove. Keeble listened, though he understood little and his attention was divided between the world outside and the little handle that rolled the beautiful glass window up and down, up and down.

"[You speak English?]" the driver asked after a while.

Up and down.

"[My wife is pregnant again. Haven't had much luck with the first one. Little terror she is, so we thought we'd try again.]"

Up and down. And the talking continued.

It wasn't long before they arrived at their destination, the large building with an eagle mounted on the top. Masses of people were still crowded around the front as if they hadn't moved since the previous night when Keeble had seen them on television.

Keeble held out his money to the driver and let him take a few of the notes.

"[Don't mind if I take a little tip, do you? A few pence is all. Good.]"

Keeble stuffed the rest of the notes into his pocket as he climbed out of the cab and started pushing his way to the door of the building.

Eventually he found himself standing beside a low, wooden barrier. There were more guards standing there, serious looking dwarves in green uniforms. When he tried to shimmy through a gap in the barrier the men barred his way and started to look even more serious. For a moment Keeble thought of using a bit of force but quickly decided that the men looked like they knew a bit about the use of force themselves.

"Meledrin?" he said, hoping they recognized the name.

"[Sorry, sir, I don't understand.]"

"Meledrin and Kim?" He fluttered his hands in the air. "*Big bats.*"

"[Sorry, Sir. Please step away from the barrier.]"

But the dwarf stopped when his nearest companion touched him on the shoulder. The second dwarf spoke into one of the talking boxes, and a moment later someone came quickly from the building.

Keeble was allowed to pass through, though this action was met with a round of boos from the gathered crowd. He waved merrily to them all and set off a multitude of flashing lights. He wanted to go back and see what had happened but didn't get the chance. He wondered if he was going to be on TV.

"[Hello, sir. I am Damien Roderick.]" He held out his hand.

Keeble held out his hand to be shaken.

"[I assume you're Keeble?]"

Keeble smiled and nodded. "Keeble. *Yes.*"

"[I'm sure Meledrin will be surprised to see you, but not too pleased. And Kim will pleased and not too surprised.]"

Keeble shrugged and shook his head. "I didn't understand most of that."

The man shook his head in turn. "[Well, please, come in. The ladies aren't here. They stayed in a hotel last night and have gone to the airport this morning. I don't know if we can hold the plane, but I'm sure something can be arranged.]"

"*Plane?*"

"[You know about planes?]"

"Not really." Keeble shrugged. "But if I get a chance I will." He smiled and followed the man inside.

21: New Paths

TUKI'S KNEE WAS BADLY SWOLLEN and throbbed in time with his heart. He had fallen two days after leaving Danyon Ford and run almost nonstop in the five days since. The knee hadn't had a chance to recover and was not likely to get the chance anytime soon.

He crouched in the shade at the edge of the village. It was the sixth in line from Danyon Ford. It was the one to which Keala, taking instructions from the 'book', had directed him.

After running so far, Tuki was surprised to find that his resolve was not as strong as he had previously thought. Keala said that the mo'min was the rightful holder of a skyglass. Did *finding* a skyglass make you the rightful holder?

He didn't know. And until he found one, it didn't really matter. He wore two cloth bags tied to his belt. One held his tattooing inks and needles in case he thought of something to put on the back of his hand, and the other was for carrying the 'glass back to Keala.

"What chance that I will find one anyway?" he said quietly.

It was unlikely any mo'min would have forgotten something as important as a skyglass when abandoning the village centuries earlier. He didn't think it was even worth the effort of looking. *But what will happen if I return to Danyon Ford empty handed? It will take a month of extra duties for the mo'shi to be happy with my state of mind.* But would his mind ever be tuned in to the well being of the village when all he could think of was Keala?

While he had crouched, the night had gathered like a wolf pack, silent but palpably watching. Tuki looked up at the sky, catching glimpses of stars and moons through the branches. He offered a silent prayer to the Mother Blower.

When the stillness continued undisturbed, Tuki shook his head and rose painfully to his feet. The memory of Keala's smile, the *taste* of her smile, pushed him forward. He moved as stealthily as his knee allowed, from one shadow to another, as if the creatures of the night might run back to Danyon Ford and report on his activities. As if he could hide from those creatures at all.

He skirted the main plaza and paused for a moment before the line of rubble that had once been the low dividing wall. His heart beat loudly in his chest, and he turned to look skywards again. The moons and stars continued their stately dance across the heavens.

With a deep, calming breath, he stepped into the northern half of the village, circled around the tumbled down remains of a building, and followed a wide, bare path towards the house where the mo'min had once lived.

Hardly any of the buildings were standing. Most were nothing more than a patch of broken stone flooring amidst the tangle of weeds. Even the glassblowing workshop, sturdiest of all buildings, had been reduced to a low-walled pool of wildflowers. Further back, separated from the rest of the village by a line of eight tall, straight trees, was the home of the mo'min.

"Under the floor, to the left of the fire," Tuki said softly as he crept through the remains of the doorway, stealthy as a thief.

I am not stealing anything. Nobody lives here. Nobody owns the skyglass. He didn't think he'd convince himself.

At the rear of the main room was a low hump, now covered with moss and lichen, that might have once been the fireplace. But the pavers to the left had been well laid, as was to be expected, and time had taken away any edges he might grip. Grass had locked silky tendrils into tiny cracks, but that was all. On the other side of the fire, a small tree had sent questing roots to crack apart the cobbles.

Tuki started there, levering up the first paver, digging his fingers down into the dirt and prizing it free. That allowed him to work the next one loose, and the one after that, until he had sixteen of them leading from one side of the room to the other.

He found nothing.

She said it was to the left of the fire. Tuki had no reason to disbelieve Keala. Why would she lie? So he lifted five pavers in another row, bloodying the tips of his fingers as he fought against the stones and the clinging grip of the earth. Then he disinterred another row, becoming more feverish with each fruitless effort.

After the fourth row, he sat back on his heels, sweat coating his brow, soil and blood turning to clay on his hands. He would have stopped there, but the thought of Keala's kiss set him to work again, tearing row after row of pavers from the ground.

Finally, as the third moon dipped out of sight to the west and darkness was almost complete, he pulled up a paver and revealed the edge of another flat stone beneath. He had another three pavers out in a moment to reveal the rest. The stone was old and cracked, with a ring in the center like a handle.

"Oh." He wasn't sure that he wanted to go any further. For a while he stayed where he was, on his hands and knees, as if praying to Poti. The night drifted on around him.

"Keala."

With her in his thoughts, warm to the touch, Tuki reached out gingerly and lifted the stone clear. A small box was revealed with a skyglass within.

He had seen a skyglass previously, when he had attended the Mid-Summer Festival many years earlier, but to be so close, to see the stars reflected in the surface, was another thing entirely. It was about the size of a child's head, smooth and clear and gleaming. He reached forth and touched a shaking finger to the polished surface.

With that slight touch the glass started to change. Darkening, warming. Tuki recoiled in surprise, and in moments the skyglass was nothing more than a perfect glass ball.

Rising to his feet Tuki paced away from the hole. He turned at the remains of the fireplace and strode back again. "I should not be here," he said, looking down at the 'glass. He was prying into women's business, thinking that he could touch the very object that let the mo'min speak with the Mother Blower. "But Keala."

Tuki stooped down and, closing his eyes, took the skyglass in his hands, determined to hold on to it no matter what. When he was standing at his full height, he dared to open his eyes. The 'glass had come to life again, and it was as if he held the night sky in his hands. He had thought that words were needed, but apparently not.

In the center of the globe was a tiny blue dot with a square floating beside it. In the square was a line of numbers and another array of tiny symbols that surely meant something. Were they secret numbers that only the mo'min could know?

Around those were a multitude of stars. Tuki examined the patterns that he knew so well. "The Skeleton constellation," he said out loud, when the six familiar stars caught his eye.

Suddenly the globe was filled with the constellation. Beside each of the stars floated more boxes filled with numbers and symbols. Mikusa, the brightest star in the Skeleton constellation, was so close to Tuki's thumb that he almost thought he could touch it.

On a hunch, Tuki spoke again. "Kiva." His heart pounded.

The Skeleton constellation disappeared and was replaced by a blue half globe that could only be his home world. It took up only a small section on the side of the 'glass, leaving room to show the three moons, brothers of the sky. They were in exactly the right position. Mata and Ki'te were in conjunction. The third, tiny Rangi, was out on his own, almost touching the surface of the 'glass.

Tuki opened his mouth to speak the name of another star when something new appeared on the globe. One moment there was nothing, and the next a tiny point of yellow light appeared and flashed close to the planet.

Looking up, Tuki saw a shooting star staining the sky with its orange glow. His breath quickened. It was the same one he had seen on his pilgrimage, he was sure. And this time he knew it was true. The skyglass confirmed it.

The meteor passed across the night sky in front of him. He watched as it turned, changed direction, and flew away from him along the line of Dry River. Tuki gaped, watching the darkness after the comet had disappeared over the horizon.

When he thought to look at the 'glass he held in his hands, he discovered that the comet had stopped. He checked the sky again, but it wasn't there. In the 'glass it was accompanied by its own little square.

"What do I do?" Tuki asked, for obviously the shooting star was a message from Poti. How could it be anything but? Was he meant to follow it? Or was the message more cryptic than that? Would he need the mo'min to interpret it? He shook his head. If he needed the mo'min to tell him what it all meant, then he would never know, for he would not ask and nobody would believe him anyway. That just left his own interpretation, and Tuki was sure he was supposed to follow. He was supposed to go beyond the horizon, into the lands of man.

Tuki looked at the skyglass again, as if it might change and let him return to Danyon Ford and be married to Keala. But nothing changed. The yellow dot waited just around the curve of the world, and the three brothers progressed infinitesimally through their stately dance.

He rose to his feet and looked back along the River towards his home. Sighing, he turned to limp in the other direction, on the tail of the shooting star.

His hands were shaking, but the Mother Blower was calling him, and he could do naught but follow.

-oOo-

Tuki followed Dry River as it curved north into the hills. He woke with the sun each morning and walked or ran until it had long since sunk into the west, collecting food and water from between its banks as he went. He constantly glanced back over his shoulder, watching the desert grow behind him as the horizon retreated. It was a wonderful place, a universe all of its own, beautiful and vast and unknowable. Golden sand stretched for uncounted kilometers, broken by occasional islands of ancient stone. Poti was letting him see it all, but only as She led him away.

Dawn and noon and dusk he would stop to stare to the south, bowing deeply and thanking the Mother Blower for what She had given him, and for what She was about to give. Then he would walk and look back as he went, making sure he did not miss any detail as it materialized. It was his home, and each new addition to the vista increased his longing. He thought his heart would break when the time came to top the highest rise and the dunes behind would be lost from sight.

That was until he reached the top of the highest rise.

The day before, Dry River had spread out to fill a wide shallow valley and gone no further. Tuki had searched all morning but found only dry, rocky slopes beyond. With much trepidation he had continued on with only the Poti to guide him. All that afternoon and tthrough the bulk of the next day, he had walked or run, all the while waiting for the cooling trees of Dry River to come back to him.

The sun was leaning in over his shoulder as he trudged up what he thought was just another hill in a long line of hills. Each was rockier than the one before, each a little higher, but that was all. The novelty had quickly worn off, and it was just a slope he had to haul his aching legs up. The skyglass was an annoying weight in the sack at his belt. It thumped against his leg with every step until he thought he was ready to rip it away and hurl it back toward the desert. And his mouth was dry, for water had become hard to find.

When he truly thought he could stand it no more, when he was telling himself that the skyglass didn't *really* want to leave the desert, he topped that final hill that marked the edge of the world, and stopped to stare. Just ahead, the land dropped almost directly down, and a new world of color and life called for his attention.

To the left, a golden crop of grain waved to him, a million little hands moving in unison. To the right, thousands of trees beckoned him forward with ancient, nodding heads. He wanted to count them but, closer by, a field of wild flowers danced for him in scattered groups. In another spot a fallow field of rich brown waited to see if he might rather the cool, clean earth beneath his feet.

Tuki didn't know what he wanted. He stood in silence, looking at it all. When the sun dipped its head below the horizon and darkness claimed the world, Tuki was still standing at the top of the hill, mouth open, eyes glazed and staring.

When he could move once more, Tuki reached into the pouch on his belt and brought forth the skyglass with shaking hands. Holding it up to the moonlight, he spoke the word that brought it to life. He had accidentally snuffed the lights a few days earlier and spent a day trying to find it again. Now, he spoke to the 'glass often, wanting to learn all that Poti was willing to teach, but he always returned to the same view in the end. Kiva.

The world was in the middle. Two of the brother moons were hanging close by, but Ki'te, which should have been around the other side of the world, was not displayed, as if the skyglass couldn't see it. Inside the orbit of the brothers was the meteor. The fact that it was completely still worried Tuki. He was not sure, but he felt that it should always be moving, like a toddler who would stumble if momentum were lost. But there were no women to tell him the ways of shooting stars, so all he could do was follow as the Mother Blower decreed.

Marking the direction in his mind, Tuki slipped the skyglass back into the pouch and started down the trail that led across the face of the cliff to the valley below.

With moonlight painting the world monochrome, he could concentrate on walking once he reached level ground. He skirted along the side of a gully, dodging between trees. He didn't stop to stare at each wonder the new world had to offer. Still, he looked left and right, and back over his shoulder as he went, watching here as a bird settled down to roost, there as a small furry creature twitched its whiskers at the night air.

It wasn't long before Tuki found what could only be a road. It was a trail wider than any he had ever seen, and rutted with the passing of many feet. He stopped, looking one way and then the next along this wonder, giving no thought to which direction he might choose, but simply following it with his eyes as it curved through the trees and grass.

Eventually he chose, following the road in the general direction of the meteor, where it hung over the horizon. He jogged all night and into the day, without growing tired of his surroundings. Each new type of tree was a marvel to him, each lizard, bird, and animal a wonder of creation. He stopped for more than an hour in the morning to watch a family of small animals scampering from tree to tree. When the sun was on high, he paused to listen to a chorus of blue-breasted birds.

It was not until fifteen days after he had found the skyglass, with the sun starting its slow descent, that he saw another person. The little boy, holding a curved, knobbly stick, stopped his game and stared. His skin was very pale compared to Tuki's, his hair white and straight.

"Hello," Tuki said.

The boy stared for a moment longer before turning to flee. His screams could be heard long after he had rounded the next bend in the road and was gone from sight.

Tuki looked at the place where he had last seen the boy, then shrugged and followed.

He went slowly along the road, around two bends, and found himself at the edge of a small, rough village. The child was standing in the street waiting for him, surrounded by what must have been every man from the region, or so it seemed to Tuki. The men were holding farming implements or rusting knives as long as their arms.

"Hello," Tuki said again, smiling at the men and nodding. No individual spoke in reply, but the group rumbled ominously. "My name is Tuki."

"Get away from here. We don't want no trolls here," a man at the front of the group shouted.

"Biggest damn troll I've ever seen," another muttered.

"Trolls?" Tuki looked about. He was right on the edge of the village. Trees crowded in on either side, but he could see no threat there. The town itself was as still as death.

"Go." The man who spoke waved a rake, jabbing it at the air.

"What is a troll?" Tuki examined his surroundings again and took a step towards the protection of the buildings. The group of men took a step forward to meet him. Then another.

Almost too late, Tuki realized that they were threatening him. He stepped back quickly, raising his hands.

Before he could say anything the villagers surged forward. He turned and fled back the way he had come.

A kilometer from the village the men had fallen behind and could not be seen. Their shouts were ragged and sparse. Around the next bend, Tuki turned away from the road and jogged along a twisting game trail, calming his racing heart and trying to decide what had happened.

Why would they threaten me? I did nothing to them.

Try though he might to find an answer, Tuki was left to wonder. Trolls were not to be trusted, perhaps, but he was not a troll.

He licked his lips and looked fearfully around. He wiped sweat from his face with a shaking hand and walked quickly up the hill.

It wasn't long before the path started to curve back towards the desert, and Tuki was forced to abandon it. He rested, leaning against a tall, rough barked tree, ever fearful of being found.

When darkness descended, he was jogging slowly again, cutting across the slope in a generally northerly direction. He still knew nothing more than he had earlier. The humans had threatened him for no reason.

"Maybe they were sick!" Tuki had heard of a sickness that made people behave irrationally. Keala said that men often suffered from such an affliction, but he never thought to see such a thing.

The forest didn't seem as welcoming and wonderful as it had been earlier. Dark shapes loomed, shadows offered hiding places for any number of unknown creatures. And trolls as well, for all Tuki knew. He found himself searching the darkness for wild animals and humans, expecting either one to leap into view with every half-heard sound.

He slept for a while, but every sound disturbed him. So he was walking again well before the Mother Blower rose. He tracked the position of the meteor in his mind as the trails he followed wandered lazy courses. He counted his steps so he wouldn't think of other things. He passed a cabin after the sun had set once more, creeping around the edge of the clearing it occupied and quickly picking up the trail again on the other side. He was so nervous that he lost his count and had to start again.

He moved silently among the trees, adjusting his rhythm to the dipping and rising of the trail as he had never had to do in the desert. Counting each step.

Before the first touch of dawn stained the eastern horizon, Tuki paused, listening to a new sound that had intruded on his thoughts of humans and shooting stars. It was a drumming above his head, as if an army of invisible creatures ran across the tops of the trees. He cocked his head, then jumped slightly as water dripped down from above to land among the tattooed ants on his arm.

He stood where he was for several moments, listening and watching as more and more drops splashed around him. All those tiny footsteps?

Is that the sound of water striking the leaves? It can't be!

Tuki searched the semidarkness for somewhere to hide, somewhere to get away from all of the water. He found nowhere, so he started to run.

He didn't know where he was running. After he started to move through the trees, with the water falling quicker every moment, he didn't stop to look for shelter. He simply ran, clutching the skyglass sack in his shaking hand.

After a lifetime of running through the trees, Tuki suddenly broke out into the open and felt the full force of the falling water. The Mother Blower was angry and was wasting all the water the humans would need. It stung his bare skin, pummeling him like pelted stones. Over his head, he could see no stars, nor either of the two brothers who should have been riding high in the sky. The Goddess had closed Her eyes, and now *nobody* could see.

Heart pounding, Tuki ran again, following the path as it crossed the clearing and plunged back under the trees. The protection of the canopy lessened the force of the blows, but still he could hear the Goddess' footsteps as She chased him onwards. And under the trees he was all but blind.

He tripped on a protruding root, splashing down into a pile of mud. He was covered in the cool, sodden mess though he scrambled to his feet instantly and was running again. Moments later the path dipped down through a gully, and he was splashing through an ankle-deep torrent. He gasped at the touch of the water and sprang up and out the other side. He tripped again, rounding another bend as he started to climb. Lying on the ground, water running from his dark curly hair, dripping from the end of his nose, leaving cold tracks across his skin, he saw a huge fallen tree with a sheltered space underneath.

With a sob of despair, he wiped the water from his face and hurried away from the path and into the small dry alcove.

22: New Friends

SCREE ADJUSTED HIS BALANCE, waiting to hit. Then adjusted some more. By the time he realized he was in real trouble it was too late. He fell. Nemucca went with him, pulled through into open air. When the torch breached the doorway, they were both able to see the floor. It was a couple of meters below.

"Scorched kittens." Scree threw his sword away. The pack followed. He adjusted his fall, twisted. He hit the floor and rolled.

His shoulder jarred. He felt his right wrist crack, but he came to his feet a moment later. There was a loud crack when Nemucca landed. The human was flat on his back.

Scree didn't bother to check on him. He knew all about broken backs.

The torch guttered fitfully on a pile of rubble. The weak light it threw showed a large room, half in ruin.

Crouching, Scree listened. Below the ragged, wet scratching of Nemucca's breathing, he could hear nothing. It was an unnatural nothing that sang war cries along the ends of his nerves.

Moving slowly, trying to ignore the screaming pain of his wrist, Scree crossed to his sword but didn't pick it up. "Damns the torch," he muttered. Shadows stood like solid things wherever he looked.

More breathing, somewhere. The short, hurried breaths of fear.

"Cats' piss on thats torch." He peered into the shadows, trying to calm his own racing heart so he could hear more.

Finally he located the room's third occupant. A woman, smaller than just about any human he'd seen, was in a small alcove at the top of some steps. Scree didn't want to scare her. He opened his mouth to speak, though he didn't know what to say. He caught the words forming in his throat, tensed, and examined the wreckage in the room once more.

Who she was hiding from? Was it him, or someone else?

Recent rubble, a hiding woman. The smell of smoke that he'd been too tense to notice. Scree swore under his breath.

The woman was near a doorway, and beyond her...

Scree moved quickly. He took up the sword in his left hand without looking down. A moment later he heard it, the slow clank of armored feet, and a hissing. He thought to move to the door, but was afraid of how the woman might react. She was obviously at the end of whatever courage she possessed.

Then it was too late. The monsters were there.

For a moment he gave thought to flight. His broken arm ached and his head was hardly better. Some food, a bit of sleep, a quick look at his arm before it was beyond help. All he needed was an hour. But he dismissed the thought before it had fully formed. He didn't know what was happening outside so his main concern was to keep the woman alive.

"She's mine," Scree shouted to be sure the monsters' attention stayed fixed on him. Then he swore, wondering if the woman could understand him. "Come and get me, you bastards."

Apparently, the monsters hadn't met any challenge on this world either. Scree watched, amazed, as the first creature started down the stairs, when it should have just stayed where it was and blasted him.

As the gold and blue figure lumbered down towards ground level, Scree dashed forward and went at it. His arm screamed with every movement, though he used the sword in his left hand. He worked furiously, hacking and cutting and thumping at the head, trying to weaken it. Finally, the faceplate cracked slightly. He rammed the point of the blade into the crack and then again, through into creature's face.

When he was done he turned to the second, which was just in the door and swiveling to face him. Scree bolted up the stairs to meet it. Sweat drenched his body, but he kept going, dropping his shoulder and charging forward. When the creature toppled onto its back it struggled like an overturned turtle. It spoke long stings of spitting, grunting gibberish. Scree attacked the face of the helmet with a brick, then the sword, and finally silenced it.

It was all Scree could do to control the blood lust. With the pain in his arm and the shadows dancing in the fitful light of the torch and the woman cowering in the corner...

Woman... It seemed a lifetime since Scree'd been with a woman, though it wasn't that long at all.

He stayed where he was, drawing in one shuddering breath after another. When he was in control he made his way back down to the lower level of the room. The sword slipped from his grasp and he sat on a pile of rubble.

He closed his eyes and breathed.

"Hello," he said in his friendliest voice, when he could speak again. The woman flinched slightly at the sound. "I won't hurts you." Scree held up his shaking hands to show he was unarmed. After a moment, he turned to look at Nemucca, lying on his back where he had first fallen. The pain was etched onto the lad's face. His lips quivered, his eyes pleaded silently.

"I won't hurts you," Scree said, turning his attention back to the woman. She was the only one in the room who could help him. Nemucca was finished.

The pain from his broken wrist throbbed through his body. "I'ms a stranger here. Can you helps me?"

It didn't look like the woman would be much help to herself. She cowered further back into the shadows with every word he spoke.

"I won't hurts you." He finally had to lower his right arm to ease the pain. "Cans you understand me?" he asked, realizing even as he did it that it was a stupid question.

He'd met other trolls that didn't speak his language, but never had trouble working out what they were saying. "At least with thems we had somewheres to start from, eh."

After resting for a few moments, Scree rose and searched about in the shifting torchlight. He found some scraps of furniture and a tattered banner. With grim determination he set about making a splint.

The pain was almost unbearable when he set the bone. He grunted softly, blinking tears from his eyes as splintered ends ground against each other. Then he struggled to hold the arm in place between his legs as he fumbled with the two sticks and long strips of material. While he worked, he talked.

"I thinks I'm from another world," he said. "I gots this book that says there's doors and stuff, between worlds. Hard to believe, I know," he laughed through clenched teeth, "but heres I am, I suppose.

"I'm a troll. You don't know nothing abouts trolls, do you? If you did, you probably wouldn't be stills sitting there, no matter how comfortable you is. Nobody seems to likes trolls too much. But I gotta say, I don't know why. Now, I'm assumin' you can't understand a words of what I'm saying here, so don't takes any of this to heart. So, I mean, yeah, we kills people regular enough, but it's nothing personal the way it always is with humans. Trolls kill peoples for all types of reasons, but at least, with us, you can usually sees it coming. You're in my way, or I needs what you got, or my life would be easier withouts you in it. Know whats I mean. A human? Nows a human will kill you because your ancestor insulted some ancestor of his two hundred years ago. Or maybes cause your skin is the wrong color, or because you lives on the wrong side of a river. How are you supposed to plan for thats? Hows you supposed to expect it? Now, you got a big hunk o' meat and there's a troll nearby who ain't got none... Chances are, he'll want that meat and you knows you gots to look out. See what I means? Don't trust a troll? Huh, never trusts a human is what I say."

Scree finished tying off the splint and stopped to look at his handiwork. It wasn't too bad, considering. Probably better than what he'd managed last time he'd broken his arm. It hurt like hell, but he'd live. That left the decision of what to do next. The doorway back to Kiva was above him, but he didn't know exactly where. There were no fancy columns hanging in the air above his head, just... air.

He didn't want to go back anyway. There was nothing back there to hold him and he had a chance to explore places no other troll had seen. And just maybe he could find a place where he wouldn't have to fight those monsters every day.

"So, I needs your help, woman." He tried to say it in a nice voice, but wasn't sure if he succeeded. "Nemucca ain'ts no use."

Scree moved to kneel by the lad's side. He was slightly surprised to find him still alive. Nemucca's lips moved and Scree leaned in close to try to make out what he was saying. After a moment of listening to the barely audible, wet rasp, Scree looked over to make sure the woman couldn't see.

Satisfied she was still hidden in the shadows of the alcove, Scree reached out and covered Nemucca's nose and mouth with his hand.

The human couldn't even struggle. A pleading looked entered his eyes in the last few moments, but even if Scree had really wanted to help, he knew he was already doing all that he could do. When Nemucca finally died, Scree went through his pockets and slipped the pack off his back before climbing to his feet. With the human's gear, and his own, he went to sit on the top step, near the woman. While he sorted the collected belongings into two groups— wanted in a pile by his side, unwanted tossed out into the room— he started to talk again.

"Friendship's a strange things, don't you think? I means, people talks about doing things for their friends because they likes them or cares for them or whatever, but really, anythings they do they just doing for themselves. They does things to make their friends feel good, because that makes thems feel good. That's all there is to it.

"You wants this bun? It's a bit stale, but..." Scree picked some mould of the corner of the chunk of bread and held it out towards the woman. She didn't move, so he put the food on the top of the steps.

"And family... Don't gets me started abouts family."

From the corner of his eye he saw her leaning forward slightly, eyes locked on the bread.

-oOo-

Scree's arm hurt as if a savage dog was hanging off it constantly. And, though he continued to use the sword left handed, every time he killed another monster the pain became almost unbearable.

He stopped and looked back. The little woman walked three steps behind, silent, eyes drawn to the ground and her sandals like a burning cat to a water trough. One hand was twisted in the stained, torn remains of her dress, as if something worried her, but that was all the emotion she showed even as she passed the burned and broken bodies of her fallen countrymen.

Scree led the way to the side of the street and into the shade of a crumbling wall. An over-turned wagon hid them from view as he sat and once more tried to draw her into a conversation of some kind. He talked and gestured and nudged her. But she had hardly reacted. So he gave up and started to walk again.

Scree wondered if she'd be any help at all. Glancing back over his shoulder, he looked her up and down. She was tiny, hardly bigger than a child. Her tattered dress revealed hints of small, firm tits and slim legs. Scree rubbed his crotch. She could have her uses, but he would wait to see what happened.

The city was quiet. If any residents still lived, they were staying indoors. Scree thought that maybe they spent as much effort hiding from him as they did from the monsters. These people might not know trolls, but they surely knew big, mean looking men with swords, and that was enough.

Most of the monsters seemed to have left too. Perhaps they'd moved on to some other city. Those that remained were solitary figures, lurking at intersections like guards or policemen. Or skulking in shadows like criminals. Scree avoided almost every form of life.

But he couldn't avoid the dead. He'd long ago given up trying. He'd long ago given up looking back to see if the woman was still there after each new crop of corpses. She seemed to ignore them all, stepping over them, or moving around them as if they were sleeping dogs. Scree hardly noticed them either, but was sure it was for different reasons.

He walked almost silently, scanning the surroundings with constant care. A noise erupted from an alley, but Scree ignored it. A dog and cat. He looked back over his shoulder and saw that his companion had stopped. She was dividing her glance between the alley and Scree, as if wondering why he was still there and not dashing off to make another kill.

Scree watched her until the two animals brought their chase into the clear.

"I won't let anything hurts you," he said, and it was true. He needed her alive if he was to have any chance of finding another gate, or even staying alive. There might be other people around somewhere, but the sad case trailing in his wake was the only one he was sure of. "I won't lets you get hurt. All right? You help me and I'll help you. We got a deal?" She didn't react, so he dragged her gently forward. Once she was moving she continued to move, following a few paces behind, so they could continue their slow trek through the city.

At the next corner, one of the monsters was waiting. Scree motioned for his companion to wait where she was as he walked up behind the creature. When he attacked, his sword was a blur of motion. He had struck the creature's neck four times before it even reacted. With the eighth powerful blow, he had success. The green and maroon armor cracked slightly where helmet and body met. The next strike widened the hole enough for him to get the sword through and skewer the creature inside. It crashed to the ground with a hiss and a crackle.

After a quick scan of the area, Scree went back to the little woman. He slung his pack over his back, then took her by the shoulder to start her moving.

He moved on carefully, starting to cross the street heading ever westwards. Though why west and not some other direction, he didn't know. When he looked back, the woman had stopped again. She was standing right beside the body of the monster.

"Great lots of help you'll be I reckons. Come on." Making his way back, he looked at the armor on the ground and gave it a kick before taking her arm yet again. But she resisted his gentle tug. There wasn't a lot of resistance, but it was enough to notice. The woman continued to stare at the body and Scree knew he'd made a mistake. She'd seen the corpses of her own people but it was the first time she'd gotten close to one of the monsters. She seemed to have slipped further away from the world of the living. She stared and stared and Scree didn't know what to do.

Did he leave her for a moment, to vent some grief? Or did he take her away? The woman's slanted eyes were glued to the partially severed neck and the thick, dark blood pulsing out. When she gagged Scree started to draw her away.

"[Wait.]"

Scree almost fell over. He didn't know what she'd said, but she'd spoken, and that was more than anything previously. "Hello?"

"[Look. Look at this.]" She pointed to the hole in the armor.

"What?"

She looked up for a moment and Scree saw a hint of life sparking in her eyes. "[Look. The shell, it isn't attached to the inner part.]"

Scree shrugged. What else could he do? He was beckoned forward, though he didn't know exactly what he was supposed to be looking at.

"[This shell is like armor. It's...]" She laughed thinly. "[Maybe it *is* armor.]" She scratched at the armor as if testing it. "[It's metal.]" Another laugh.

Scree watched her carefully. He had no idea what she was saying, but if the thing that had caught her interest brought her forth, he was willing to hang around for a while to let it do some more.

The woman crouched down and tapped the bright armor on the monster. "[Armor.]" She touched at her own torn shirt. "[It comes off, like clothes.]"

Scree smiled slightly and nodded. "Yes, it's armor. Only just work that out?" He used her word. "*Armor.*"

"[If this is armor, what about this?]" She pointed to the monster's bulging arm, to Scree's sword, and back to the arm.

Scree stood perfectly still, staring, trying to work out what she was saying. "The outer shell bit is armor," he said. "So, the big bit on the arm... is... part of the armor?" Scree smiled broadly. "Gangrene cats. The weapon is part of the armor. Why didn't I think of that?" He checked their surroundings once and handed the woman his sword, which was taller than she was. Then, with a grunt of effort and pain, he grabbed the monster and dragged it into what had once been a fruit store. The woman dragged the sword along behind, staring at the dark blood marking the blade.

SCREE CROUCHED DOWN by the monster's side and looked at his companion. "I'm Scree," he said. "What's your name?" But of course, she didn't understand. He pointed to himself. "Scree."

The woman smiled slightly, pushed dark brown hair away from her eyes. "Ping."

"Well, then, Ping, what do we do now?" But he didn't wait for an answer. He hunted through his pack and pulled out the knife he'd taken from the dead soldier a lifetime ago. In a moment he was working on the elbow joint with the short, broad blade.

It didn't work. Scree swore at his injured arm, dropped the knife and looked around.

"Wait here." He raced outside and, looking around, found a blacksmiths workshop. He collected a mallet and chisel. Back with the armor, he pounded the chisel into the elbow joint. He wrenched it free and swung again.

Eventually the limb came free and he pulled at it carefully. It resisted for a moment, but then the hard armor started to slide away. There were two ropes attached, running through the inside of the armor.

He started to wrench it apart, but Ping placed a hand on his arm and indicated the cords.

"We needs these?" he asked.

It didn't help all that much when Ping shrugged in reply.

"Why would we need the ropes?" They were strange things, not really rope. Soft, but tough at the same time. Shiny.

When Ping shrugged again, Scree tried to think it through.

"Hold on then." He grabbed his tools and started to work on the other arm. In a couple of minutes he had it free and found only one cord in there. Not a great deal of help there either, though obviously they were significant in some way. He started working on the shoulder joint with more care than he had for the elbow.

"Its like a type of burning, what this thing does, right?" He sat back and looked at the half-dismantled arm. "What if it's like sticking a bit of metal in a fire? You stick one end in, and the other end is nowhere near the heat, but it'll get hot eventually, right?" He didn't even look at his companion. "The heat goes along the rope thingy, maybe. Maybe the heat goes from... somewhere... to the arm and the arm throws it out." He smiled and nodded. It seemed like a strange way to do things, but he'd seen enough strange things in the last couple of days that he wouldn't be surprised.

Eventually the shoulder came away and the cords were there as well, heading towards the lump on the back of the armor. Scree wondered what to do next.

"[How do they get out?]" Ping asked. Scree didn't know what she said, but he knew it was a question, so he turned to look at her. Her last few questions had been good ones. She repeated the sentence as if it'd make any difference.

"Yeah, really?" He smiled.

Ping looked exasperated for a moment, then mimed getting undressed. Scree didn't think she wanted to rut. Which was a bit of a shame.

"Taking off clothes," he said.

Then she reached through the gap in the elbow and pointed at the blue leathery skin beneath. She looked to see if Scree was watching.

"Yeah. Monster guy taking off clothes."

And Ping shrugged her shoulders. "[How?]"

Scree went through the forms of questions and tried to relate it to taking off clothes. "What? Why? Who? How? How does he take off his armor? Right." He smiled. *It's armor. He has to be able to take it off somehow.*

"So, how *does* he takes it off?"

Ping sat down by his side, but didn't offer any suggestions.

"A lever maybes." Scree scratched his bald scalp, eyes narrowing in concentration. *This would be a lot easier if there was someone I could beats the answers out of.* "It has to be somewhere that he can get his hand to it, right? So, on the outside— which would be stupid— or inside the suit, near the hand." Scree nodded and got his chisel.

He looked at the creature for a moment, then at Ping. He reached over and covered her eyes with her hand. When he was sure she couldn't see and wasn't going to look, he swapped his chisel for his sword and cut off the creature's left arm at the elbow.

Then he twisted the forearm at right angles to the rest of the arm and, with some twisting and tugging, pulled it free of the armor. Scree tossed the limb, with a flat, broad, four-fingered hand, into the shadows in a corner where Ping might not see it.

After struggling to get his hand inside the armor, he felt some tiny little levers and some buttons.

Pointing the arm at a wall, Scree shifted the first lever. It clicked and locked into the new position.

Nothing else happened. He moved it back to where it had been.

A button next— the weapon sent out a spurt of energy that burned a dark patch on the wall before Scree thought to let go. He looked at Ping and gave a smile.

With the third, another little lever, there was a hiss of air. The armor split open like a clamshell. Every piece hinged open to reveal the twisted, ugly monster— dressed in bright silken breeches— and the interior of the suit.

Ping gave a giggle of joy and knelt by Scree to look— more animation than she had shown since he'd known her. But what were they looking at?

Scree grabbed the monster by a leg and its remaining arm and hauled it free. He dragged the strange, blue skinned thing to the corner near its arm. Spasms of fire lanced through his own arm, but he ignored the pain, hurrying back to see what he could see.

He didn't know what to do next. He could understand a door handle enough to use it. He could understand a lever and a pulley. But the machines inside the suit? He couldn't begin to understand them. If that's what they were. But Ping just looked for a moment before starting to open panels. There was wire and cords and... Scree didn't know what they were.

Ping started to pull free the rope that went to the arm. She followed it as far as she could, then released a large panel in the back to see what was in there. There was a black box, which she seemed to think was important. She undid some buckles and pulled it free.

"[Do you know about electricity, Scree?]"

"You grabs a live cat by the tail and swings it around your head," Scree said, "you can throws it further than you can throw a dead one. Don't knows why, but there you go." He smiled for a moment and shrugged.

"[Well, I think this works by electricity. If only I knew a bit more about it myself. Hardly anyone knows *anything* about it.]"

There were dozens of ropes attached to the black box. One of the ropes from the arm had been unraveled into a lot of smaller ropes and Scree didn't know how they'd work out what any of them were for. Again, Ping didn't look worried. After thinking for a minute, she disconnected one wire, then pointed from the arm to the burnt patch on the wall. Scree took the clue, and, choosing another wall, pressed the weapon's button. As expected, the weapon bucked in his hand slightly and burned a patch on the wall.

Scree watched as Ping reconnected the rope and disconnected another. She nodded again and Scree pressed the button.

Nothing happened.

Ping smiled. But then she scratched at her head and, after reattaching the cord, took off the other one that went from the arm. At her prompt, Scree tried the weapon again. And again, nothing.

"[Try another button.]"

"Whats?" When he got what she wanted, Scree pressed the first lever again. This time, with the helmet hinged open, they could see that something *was* happening, and Scree immediately recognized it. The helmet gave the monsters something like what he could do naturally with his night-eyes. He laughed.

Scree pressed buttons and looked for reactions in the suit while Ping connected and disconnected cords going to the black box. The little woman even got a pencil and paper from a drawer in the shop and drew diagrams. She crossed and marked and wrote and scribbled with solemn concentration.

There were about ten buttons, and each one brought a different response from the suit. The top of the bulging arm opened up and a strong, two-fingered hand emerged. It could be controlled with a little lever and two buttons. Press the first button again and the hand retracted and disappeared. A bright light lanced away from the shoulder, though Scree couldn't work out why they'd want that when they had night-eyes. Another button and a strange, harsh voice erupted from the helmet.

Scree wondered whose voice it was but he couldn't understand it, so he wasn't really worried.

But when Scree turned off the switch that caused the voices, he could still hear them. He looked around to see if anyone had crept up on him while he was occupied. There was nobody there.

The voices were in his head. *In his head.*

Scree held his hands to his ears but that couldn't keep out what was already in.

The strange voices whispered.

He rose to his feet and stormed about the room. He crashed into a wall and the whole building shook with the force of it. He kicked the counter and stomped on the exposed head of the strange monster. But the blow was so weak that Ping didn't even look away. Scree could see his companion watching with barely concealed horror.

The voices continued to bounce around in Scree's mind, strange voices he couldn't understand.

Eventually the fear wore him down. He slumped back to the ground, curling up in a corner with his hands still pressed firmly over his ears. He'd never much liked the idea of magic, but hadn't often been affected by it as far as he knew.

"Go away," he said softly. "Leaves me alone."

But the conversation in is head didn't falter. So he concentrated inwards and said, like a human child who finds a strange troll standing in the kitchen. "<Who are you?>"

As one, the voices stopped.

Scree sat up, surprised. "<Who are you?>" he asked again, though he supposed the voices would understand him no more than he understood them.

"<*[Inken avad,]*>" one of the voices said.

Scree said nothing.

Another voice in his mind, rough and guttural, but certainly different from the first. "<*Acekn jad avenda? Vida?*>"

"<[Osuk.]>"

"<[Dosa?]>"

"<[Osuk.]>"

"<[Figi?]>"

"<[Osuk.]>"

Scree knew a roll call when he heard one.

"<[Gizu?]>"

"<[Osuk.]>"

"<[Sada?]>"

There was a silence that stretched on for long moments. To see what would happen, Scree concentrated on the part of his mind where the voices seemed to commune and said, in his best approximation of the monster's voices, *"<Osuk.>"* Just the one word hurt his throat.

The pause stretched on again after that.

"<[Dinjis Sada. Inken avad]>"

The babble of voices erupted again.

Scree sat in the corner, back against the wall, head down. With the strange voices in his head, he couldn't concentrate. His thoughts flowed along with the words and went nowhere.

Sensing movement in the real world, Scree sprang to his feet, angry that he could be surprised. But it was only Ping, on her hands and knees by his side. She reared back when he moved, fear rearing to life in her eyes, until Scree slid down the wall to the floor again. The tiny woman laid a hand on his arm, but the troll didn't look up. A moment later the slight pressure was gone and, through the voices in his head, Scree knew the woman was examining the armor once more.

She dragged the bulging arm over to the helmet so she could reach the buttons inside and still see what was going on. She carefully avoided the one that controlled the weapon, though Scree knew, vaguely, that she hadn't reattached the cords that gave it power.

Scree returned his gaze to the scuffed tips of his boots as the woman worked. The voices in his head babbled meaninglessly. Then, suddenly, they were coming to him from the helmet too as Ping pressed the button that had started it all. He shrank away from the noise, retreating further into the corner, hands held to his head as if that might stop what was already inside him.

But Ping turned off the voices again without even looking his way. Scree continue to watch her for a moment as she pressed the button that turned on the fake night-eyes...

"Wait a minute," he said. He wasn't talking to Ping, but the woman looked up all the same. "If they have night-eyes in their helmet like I have night-eyes in my head... and they can turn theirs off, and I can turn mine off... And they have the voices in their helmet and can turn it off..."

Scree dug into the corner of his mind where the voices echoed. He spoke to the voices, to be sure he was in the right place. Then he probed with his consciousness like he did when he used his other ability. At first nothing happened, though he felt it should. Then the voices started to slide away, only to be replaced by a scraping noise, like rock on rock. He concentrated some more, leaning the other way. The voices came back, becoming clearer and clearer until he was sure the monsters must be in his head. He worked on another part of his mind, pushing and nudging until... Silence.

He gave a short bark of laughter. He pushed and the voices returned. He nudged and... gone.

Ping was watching him closely and he smiled for her. "These monsters haves all their machines," he said, "but I cans do better in my heads." Nothing the monsters could do with their machines would scare him in the future.

Ping smiled and nodded. He knew she couldn't understand, but the relief must have been plain in his voice and on his face. Taking a deep breath, he spat on the dead monster in the corner and moved to the woman's side as she worked on the armor.

A while later, they pushed the armor out of the way and sat examining the tangle of ropes, attaching the arm and helmet to the black box and a small panel that had been on the top of the bulging back.

"Now what?"

Ping ignored him, or simply didn't react. But after a few heartbeats she collected the troll's pack and removed the small collection of books, his canteen and flint striker. She started trying to arrange the black box inside. Scree used his knife to cut a hole in the side of the bag so the two wires could go to the arm, and a few minutes later it was ready to go. They had the panel tied to the outside, though why that was important, Scree didn't know. He wasn't sure if Ping knew either, but that was the way the monster had organized things so...

Ping examined the books before she started to find places for them in the pack with the box. Scree knew she wouldn't do a very good job so he took them off her. Before he put them away, he took out *The Gates of Hakahei* and found the page that Nemucca had shown him with the map of the worlds.

"Those humans with the noisy weapons comes from Atlantis," the troll said to himself. "And my world was Kiva. So this one has to be..." There were two choices, according to the map. "Harkin?" he said. Ping looked at him, but made no sign of recognition. "Ti..." He struggled over the other strange name. "Tiandi?"

Ping smiled. "Tiandi."

"Tiandi?" Scree repeated and tried to gesture about at the entire world.

"Tiandi."

"So, this is Tiandi." He flipped forward a page and found the place where the locations of the gates were mentioned. Three gates on Tiandi, like there were three gates on most of the worlds. He tapped the floor. "Kansu?"

"[Kansu is that way.]" Ping pointed to the south.

"Shadon?"

She nodded and Scree gave a whoop of delight. "Nows we getting somewheres." He pointed the direction she had and held up three fingers. "Kansu? Three days?"

"What?" Ping said in the troll's language, and he smiled.

So he got up and mimed walking, pointing to the south. "How many days to Kansu?"

"[Oh, ten days.]" And she held up the appropriate number of fingers. "*Ten.*"

"Ten. And what about... Yunnan?"

"Yunnan?" The woman shrugged.

"Shadon. Kansu. Yunnan?"

"[I don't know of any city called Yunnan.]" Ping shook her head and shrugged again.

"No Yunnan? Probably a ruin likes Salisha. Well then, Kansu it is."

Ping mimed walking this time. "Kansu?"

"That's it. South to Kansu."

Scree carefully repacked his pack then rose to his feet and shrugged his way into the shoulder straps. He set the helmet on his head but it didn't fit well.

"Do we need this?"

"What?"

He mimed throwing the helmet away. "Do we need this?"

"[Oh. I don' suppose so.]" She went to the pack, disconnected some ropes and took the helmet away.

With his arm fitted snugly into the sleeve, Scree tested to make sure the weapon still worked. It did. He wasn't willing to risk everything on it though, so he removed the pack once more and attached his sword to the outside, in case he needed it later.

He checked to see that Ping was ready, looking her up and down.

"We gots to find you some decent clothes. And shoes." He stepped back out onto the porch at the front of the store.

The day had slipped by them. A burning building lit the street a little farther to the north. Flames danced against the darkness, but other than that, all was quiet. A few scattered stars were visible through the smoke. Scree wished he could see more of them so he could start to get his bearings.

He turned on the voices in his mind. They nattered away, but didn't give any clues as to what they were planning or where they were or anything at all that might help. He shrugged and started to walk. Ping followed along behind. They kept moving until the moon dipped its head down behind the hills without seeing one building that was undamaged. They didn't see one living creature. Even the monsters in their bright armor seemed to have drifted away with the smoke. The huge bats were nowhere to be seen. Whether they had moved on to some other city or were spending their time roosting amongst the ruins wasn't obvious.

The road they followed angled up the side of the bowl shaped valley, moving past houses and shops all mixed in together. Or at least what was left of those things. And everywhere, at least one every block, were strange buildings with large white circles painted behind the glass windows. There were towers with similar stuff.

Scree stopped in front of one of the windows. A large white circle with two black, metal spokes attached to the front. With most, the metal spokes seemed to be stuck in the same place— both almost pointing to the top of the circle.

"What *are* they?"

"[It is a clock.]"

"They're everywhere. Why?"

"Why?" She shrugged. "[I don't know. It's what we do. It's what the gods tell us to do.]"

Scree shrugged, shifted his grip in the weapon sleeve and turned back to the street. He was almost too late. A monster stood in the mouth of an alley.

With a shove, he sent Ping tumbling down to street level as he dived the other way. While the woman examined her elbow and the wall smoked from the energy weapon, Scree rolled back to his feet in one fluid motion and fired his own weapon. The beam of lightning struck the monster flush on the side of the helmet.

It didn't do anything.

Scree kept the weapon trained on the same area as the monster slowly turned to face him. Still nothing happened.

"Useless cat-pissing thing," he shouted to the weapon. The curses didn't help.

As the monster was about to face him, the muzzle of the weapon zeroing in, Scree moved. He skirted about the creature, staying low. Once behind it, he fired again, concentrating his fire on the creature's bulging back. And after just a few seconds the bulge exploded. Fragments of bright armor flew everywhere. Blue and yellow shards struck Scree, but he didn't care. He kissed the colors of his own weapon and gave a whoop of joy.

"Just gots to shoot thems from behind," he said as he went to see if Ping was all right. "Just shoots them from behinds."

KIM TRIED TO IGNORE MELEDRIN but found she was reading the same paragraph over and over again without having any idea what it said.

"Why will they not tell us the reason for the delay?" Meledrin asked, glaring at the man behind them as if that might make a difference. Kim was pleased to see that the man ignored the elf, not even looking up from the highlighted file he was reading. It was possible he hadn't even heard.

Kim shook her head. "Does it matter?" After spending a couple of years travelling around the world, she was used to all sorts of delays. Normally, when left in peace, the waiting didn't worry her. With Meledrin constantly bringing it to her attention, time seemed to drag.

They were sitting in the main cabin of the plane with about a dozen serious men in serious suits. There were as many empty seats again, all facing a large, flat screen television hanging on the wall. At the rear of the cabin things were arranged in a less formal manner. A horseshoe of chairs around a low table, plus a desk, and a small bar stocked with all manner of drinks.

"Do you think the giant bats are blocking our route?"

Kim gave up and put the book away. "Maybe." It wouldn't have been surprising.

They'd been sitting on the US Air Force Boeing for an hour, though they'd been told they'd be taking off immediately. Kim wasn't particularly worried. She knew there were thousands of things that could be affecting their take off without having anything to do with them. Meledrin wouldn't understand the vast number of people, places, and variables involved. And there was a war on, for Christ's sake.

But in the end, it *was* about them. Kim was just getting serious about ignoring the elf, having started a conversation with a stony faced man in a grey suit, when someone escorted Keeble into the cabin.

The dwarf looked around excitedly and seemed to want to go everywhere at once so he wouldn't miss a single detail. It took him a moment to shift his focus from the location to the people in it. He had a sneer for Meledrin and a smile and a wave for Kim.

"Hello, Keeb'," Kim said. She smiled back.

"Hello." Keeble looked at the seat his escort motioned him towards, then went and took a different one by a window. He allowed himself to be strapped in. "Plane," he said, nodding.

They were moving before everyone else was seated, rolling towards the runway. Keeble strained to see out the window, pressing his face against the glass and muttering to himself. Kim divided her gaze between the elf and dwarf as they started to pick up speed and finally left the ground.

Keeble was smiling like a boy with a new bike, and Kim could almost see the thoughts darting though his head as he tried to see everything at once and work it all out. Meledrin, on the other hand, took one look out the window then stared resolutely forward. Only her hands, gripping the armrests with white-knuckled intensity, showed that she was feeling anything at all.

When, a short while after takeoff, one of the CIA officers rose to his feet and went to get a drink, Keeble quickly unbuckled his own belt and raced to a window that gave a better view of the wing.

There were three fighters flying escort not far away.

"How work?" Keeble asked in horrible English as he grabbed the arm of the closest man. "How work?"

"How does what work?"

"Plane? How work?"

The man glanced at someone else for a moment and received the permission he apparently didn't really want. "Well, the top of a wing is more curved than the bottom, so when air moves past the wing —"

"You do know," Kim said, interrupting the man, "that he doesn't really speak English."

"Oh. Then how do I explain?"

"Try drawing a picture. I think he might understand that better than anything. And Meledrin can translate any bits he doesn't understand."

"Why don't you explain?" But he rose to his feet and motioned for Keeble to follow him to the other end of the cabin. Keeble sat down near the low table while the man collected paper and pen from the desk.

"Coffee?" Keeble asked, pointing to a jar on a shelf.

"You want coffee?"

"Yes, please." The dwarf licked his lips and stared at the jar.

The man sighed but made two cups of coffee.

A few minutes later Keeble and the American were both hunched over the paper as the man drew a rough, profile sketch of a wing. Other men and women wandered over to help or just to watch. The conversation quickly moved from wings to other subjects.

"What are we going to be doing, exactly?" Kim asked when Special Agent Tim O'Donnell, the baby-faced man in charge, broke away from the group gathered around the table. He got himself a scotch before crossing to sit by her side.

"Sorry, I don't know."

"You don't know or you *'don't know'*?"

"I really don't know."

"Ah."

"I'm just your escort. And the only reason I have the job is because I happen to be going your way."

"And everyone else?"

"We were part of a task force working with the British trying to contact the alien mother ships."

"There's more than one mother ship?"

"This is all top secret stuff, you understand. If you tell anyone I'll have to kill you."

He said it with a smile, but Kim had the horrible suspicion he was serious. "I doubt I'll be left unguarded from now until the war ends, so who would I tell?" Her reply was delivered with a smile as well, but she had the horrible suspicion that she would find that *she* was telling the truth.

"Well, there appear to be lots of mother ships, actually." He took a sip of his drink and settled back. "The trouble is, they hardly show up on any of our tracking equipment. There are blobs that may well be one ship or ten."

"So you don't know how many there are? Or how big they are? Or how many of the black bats they each hold? Or how many of the armored monsters?"

"No, to all of those. We can see the ships with telescopes — hell you can see them with an ordinary old pair of binoculars — but they move too much and too quick for us get an accurate count, and without knowing exactly how far away they are, we can't tell how big they are. We're pretty sure they're huge. A few hundred meters long, some of them. How about that? And, as I said, they're quick. There are maybe as many as two hundred of them. We do know for sure that there's normally about forty of the aliens on each bat."

"And how do they get out of orbit? Or back into it, if they even do? The bats are such impossible vehicles."

O'Donnell laughed. "Tell us about it. It took a long time for us to work them out. They do it with a combination of two things." He loosened his tie. "First, antigravity. The aliens have devised a mechanical means of making the bats lighter. That allows them to fly despite the burden of the life support capsules. It also allows them to fly well into the thermosphere. Up to about 300 kilometers. We aren't sure if it's the temperature, the atmosphere, or gravity that stops them going higher. Or maybe the bats just get tired. Anyway, when they reach their limit the mother ships dip down closer to the planet and grab the bats with long tentacles."

"Tentacles?"

"Yes. We think. We think the ships are alive. Creatures that live in space."

"Is that likely?"

"Is any of this likely?"

"Perhaps not."

"And those laser weapon thingies?"

"How do you know about those?"

"I have my sources." Kim smiled. "They haven't told you about how I hooked up with Meledrin and Keeble?"

"No. And hold back payment to that source. The weapons are more like a combination particle beam and Taser."

"Uh huh."

"What they do is align a path of particles in the air then fire a bolt of electricity along the path. I don't understand much more about it than that, but we've had people working on similar stuff for years. Now they're close to getting it figured out."

"Well, don't talk too loud. Keeble might overhear and go out the back to make one for himself."

"Yes, he's amazing, really. I think he's already suggested a couple of things to the flyboys that will jump them forward a couple of decades. He seems to see things once someone's given him a push in the right direction."

The flight from London direct to Washington DC took 10 hours. In that time every one of the CIA agents, plus several of the flight crew, were involved in discussions with Keeble. Somewhere along the way, the subjects veered away from aeronautics into magnetics, and construction, and computers, and a dozen other things. Keeble had an insatiable appetite and seemed to soak up everything, no matter what language it was in. Meledrin did her best to translate, perhaps welcoming the opportunity to think about something other than the distance she was from the ground, but over and over again she was saying that there were no words to say what needed to be said. A computer? Fiber optics? The words were easy to say in most instances, but how do you describe what they mean? A machine that adds. A rope that light travels along.

Often, the questions Keeble asked had the men scratching their heads, arguing with each other, or looking slightly dazed. Sometimes all three at once. Most of the men were merely dilettantes, and it would take a real expert to keep up.

-oOo-

Arriving in Washington DC, Kim stretched and yawned. She'd finished her book earlier and drifted to sleep with Keeble's excited voice in her head, asking question after question.

He'd stopped for a few minutes when half a dozen bats attacked their plane. But the three jets escorting them made short work of the slow, ungainly creatures. It had all been over in minutes. Before the remains had splashed into the Atlantic, Keeble had been asking questions again.

When they started their descent, he'd found a seat by a window and stared out like a little boy. He swung his feet, wound the gears on his hand, and muttered under his breath.

When the plane taxied slowly to a spot that was almost a kilometer from the terminal, the dwarf was the first out the door and down onto the tarmac. He ran to stand beneath an engine as if he could discover how it worked from that alone. Kim wasn't so thrilled. From the top of the stairs she could see another plane waiting for them, not a limousine, or even a jeep. She grunted in disgust.

"What's the matter?" O'Donnell asked, straightening his tie as he waited for Kim to continue forward.

"I was hoping we were here."

"*I'm* here." The agent smiled and nudged her forward.

"Yes, but I'm sure another escort for Keeble, Meledrin, and I will be along in a moment. Or perhaps they're already on the plane."

"They are. I'll walk you to the door though, of course."

"Of course, gentleman that you are."

O'Donnell laughed. Kim liked him. He'd given out more information than expected and chatted for much of the trip.

The second plane was a Lear jet. The escort was made up of Air Force personnel. They mostly wore uniforms, though they did have the same serious expressions as the CIA. Keeble grabbed the first available window seat, ignoring the new men. Meledrin took the first seat on the aisle. Kim just dumped her pack and took the first one she came to. She had no idea where they were going, and hardly cared. The men on the plane, obviously just an escort of convenience like the last lot, watched them as if they were criminals. Kim wondered if perhaps they were, for more reasons than matters of security. Or perhaps people who worked for the United States government were trained to look that way. As she buckled up her belt, she thought that IRS agents probably went around with the same look.

They were airborne in ten minutes and heading west.

"I don't suppose there's a shower on this plane?" Kim asked as soon as the seat belt light went out.

The nearest man looked up from his book and pointed towards the rear of the plane. Kim smiled.

25: Messages

TUKI SAT WITH THE SKYGLASS on his lap, staring beyond the polished surface as if concentration alone could change the message he read within. He'd been looking for a long time. There had been one meteor before, now there were five. They hadn't moved for a while. Seeing the skyglass didn't seem to show anything of the far side of the world, there may have been more there too.

One was right above his location.

That location was on the edge of a clearing halfway down a steep-backed hill. Tuki had topped the rise midmorning and started back down. It wasn't until he entered the clearing, with the uninterrupted view it offered, that he'd seen the human city. If not for that, he would have been right down in the base of the valley and beside the first of the buildings before he realized. As it was, he was closer than he liked.

The city was huge. He had been amazed by the earlier settlement, but the place before him was all but unbelievable. He counted eight hundred and eighty six buildings. One towered above the others, and Tuki wondered if the spire was to assist with the study of the stars.

Humans were everywhere. In a large square on the edge of the city, they dipped beneath cultured awnings and tents like butterflies into flowers. They danced their dance, unaware of the message the Mother Blower was trying to pass on.

The yellow dots in the skyglass hadn't moved.

He wished he could go somewhere else. He wanted to climb back into the mountains and return to the desert. He could follow one of the other meteors shown by the 'glass but he may just go all that way to find himself in the same situation. And Poti had directed him here. He was supposed to go down into the city and talk to the humans of this city first.

But the last humans Tuki had seen tried to hurt him.

With a sigh, Tuki rose and started down the hill. He did not know what the Mother Blower was going to say, either, but maybe he had more chance of finding out than the humans. He had always been told, and had always believed, that Poti was infallible, but surely She had chosen the wrong person for this mission.

"Keala should be here," Tuki said to the skyglass. "Or any of the women."

If he didn't understand anything, how was he to explain it to others? And why would they listen to him, a go'gan? Even the men would laugh, surely. He couldn't help but laugh himself, a go'gan passing on the message of the Mother Blower. He fell silent when he tried to imagine how the women would react to his preaching.

The Goddess *had* chosen him, though, perhaps as a chance to make up for some past indiscretion, or to test if he truly was worthy of marrying someone as special as Keala.

So he would prove himself the best man in Danyon Ford. He would prove to the women who had laughed at him that the Goddess had spoken and he had listened. He slipped the skyglass into the pouch at his belt and marched down the hill. Examining the new meteor tattoo on the back of his hand, he wondered if he should have drawn it on his face.

The first human he saw was sitting on the back of a shaggy, four-legged beast, feet swinging just above the ground. Possessions were slung in sacks across the beast's back. Tuki did not even have the chance to offer a greeting. The man got his feet onto solid ground and fled back the way he had come, leaving the beast standing on the road looking bemused and twitching its long ears.

Tuki knew how both beast and man felt, but he forced his steps onwards. The beast watched him go.

Half a kilometer later, Tuki rounded a bend and looked down a long stretch of road toward the city. He could see lots of people there, milling about. He slowed his pace as the trees thinned and offered him an ever-wider view. There were dozens of wooden-railed yards filled with beasts larger even than the one he had left standing on the road. They surged around, much like the people, as if hearing that there was much to fear but not knowing exactly what the danger was, or what to do about it.

As Tuki drew nearer, the people — if not the animals — seemed to come to a decision. Some went one way, some went the other, but it all seemed to be with a purpose. One man stayed exactly where he was, a monolith in the shifting sands about him. He was still standing and watching when Tuki came to a stop.

"You are not wanted here," the man said, his hand resting on the hilt of a long, curved knife. His accent was strange to Tuki's ears, rugged and clipped, but understandable.

Tuki bowed deeply. He did not know the man's title, could not begin to guess, but the footprints of years traversed his features and the steel in his voice was tempered by authority. "Go'shin," Tuki said after an agonizing moment, praying he would not offend. "Why am I not wanted?"

"Why?" He gave a bark of laughter. "Why are trolls ever *not wanted*? Leave now, or suffer the consequences." His voice was sure and steady, but he checked back over his shoulder. The crowd was surging and muttering. Those at the front were struggling to hold their ground against the press behind.

"But, go'shin, I have been sent by the Mother Blower to speak with your mo'min." Was he supposed to speak with the mo'min? Tuki had been told no such thing.

"Well, troll, the *mo'min* doesn't want to talk with you." Some of the tension leaked from the man's face when he saw others, dressed similarly to himself, pushing their way through the crowd, cursing and shouting and using force when people in the mob did not move quickly enough for their liking.

Tuki moved nervously from foot to foot. "Go'shin, perhaps if you were to ask."

"I'm Kuwisa, Keyman of the Payota City Guard, and I have all the authority needed to send the likes of you on your way." He drew his long knife and stepped forward.

There were now a dozen men standing between the Keyman and the main crowd. They were all dressed in brown breeches and striped, tasseled shirts. Long knives were gripped in their hands. They all stepped forward as well.

"Go, troll. You can't win here, not even you."

Someone from the mob shouted: "If you don't think he can win, Keyman, what are you waiting for?"

This comment was greeted with peels of laughter. Keyman Kuwisa didn't look around, but Tuki saw the look of anger cross his face. Kuwisa stepped forward again. "Last warning, troll. Go, and don't bother us again."

"I am not a troll."

But the Keyman was not listening. He raced forward, knife raised. The other knife wielding men came behind. Tuki turned and ran.

Panicking, he saw that he wasn't moving toward the freedom of the hills. His hasty retreat had taken him among the animal pens, between the high timber fences. The beasts bawled at him and stampeded. They kicked up dust and fear.

Tuki dodged and turned. Left and right. Right and left. Past this turning, through that intersection. Sweat trickled down his face, wasting valuable water. The skyglass thumped against his leg. He didn't know where he went. He didn't look up. He didn't look behind for fear that his pursuers would be right *there*. His heart raced, stampeding with the beasts.

Tuki didn't know how long he ran. It felt like he'd been all night in the desert.

Suddenly he was out in the open again. The dust under his sandals turned to neat, square cobbles. The wooden fences on left and right changed to people.

Tuki stopped.

The people were staring at him.

Tuki's heart raced faster but everything else seemed to slow down. The people were motionless, like startled birds caught balancing on the edge of flight. Then a shout went up. The mob rushed forward.

Tuki turned to run, but they were behind him as well. He could do nothing. When the first man buckled his knees with a solid kick, he tumbled to the ground. With the cool stone against his side, he curled into a ball around the skyglass and screamed.

Tears streamed down his face. The blows continued to fall, boots and fists, savage shouts hurled like stones. Pain blossomed. Tuki covered his face with his arms and prayed for assistance. He curled himself even tighter.

And screamed and screamed.

After a lifetime of pain, Tuki was shocked when it suddenly stopped. He stayed where he was, eyes closed, the cool stones anchoring him to consciousness. He waited for the next blow, the final one that would push him over the edge, and wondered why the Mother Blower had abandoned him? Why had she even sent him here in the first place?

Eventually, a voice reached through the haze.

"Step away. Go on. Away with you."

Mutters and curses greeted the commands, but sunlight suddenly struck Tuki. The Mother Blower's gaze was as painful as any blow. He had failed her in some way, he was sure.

"Move back you fools."

Tuki felt a hand on his shoulder. He flinched again, curled tighter. But the hand didn't hurt. It rested against his burning skin.

"Keyman, get control of this mob, for Anas's sake."

"Why, Sha Yukima? The troll is getting nothing less than he deserves."

"I'm not sure he is a troll, Keyman. And what he deserves, either way, is to be treated as a man."

"Not a troll? Who do you think you're kidding, Sha? Look at him."

"I *am* looking. And what I see is a large man who was passively taking a beating from unarmed commoners. How many trolls have you met that would do that?"

"He's a troll. No other men are that big."

"No men you have met, perhaps, Keyman. But I believe this lad is a moai."

"Never heard of them."

"The moai are men of legend. They are huge it is said, larger than a troll, and come from the desert."

Tuki opened his eyes. Keyman Kuwisa was standing over him, the huge knife still drawn. The other man, far older, was crouching down, a worried expression creasing his gaunt features. He had a long plaited beard and a hat decorated with a long white feather.

"So are they legends, Sha Yukima? Or are they real?" The Keyman's voice clearly held his disdain for all to hear.

Tuki moved his hand to touch at the Moon Gate tattooed on his chest, as if that might keep him safe from the Keyman's anger or let him enter Heaven if all else failed.

"How am I to know, Keyman?" Yukima said. "I am a priest, not a historian."

"Priest or historian, both know the danger of trolls."

"Yes, and I know the danger of this lad," Sha Yukima retorted.

The two men stared at each other.

The Keyman grunted. "Well, what are we going to do then?"

"The lad has made no threats, he was doing nothing wrong. All he has done is come to Payota on market day along with hundreds more of Anas's sons."

"I can *not* let him roam the streets."

"Roam the streets? You think he is capable of roaming anywhere?"

"If he was a troll —"

"If he was a troll we would not be having this conversation. Correct?"

The Keyman grunted once more and Tuki watched, slightly fearful, as Sha Yukima rose to his feet. But the man was not leaving him. He dusted off his long blue robes as he looked around.

"Get some of your men to find a wagon. We will take him to the Municipy."

"If we must."

For several minutes, men rushed about, clearing a path through the crowd and bringing up what was apparently a wagon. Tuki, still curled in a ball, examined it closely as two shaggy, large-eared animals like the one he had seen on the road brought it to a stop by his side.

"Are you able to stand, lad?"

Tuki turned for a moment to look at Sha Yukima, then back at the wagon. The movement made his head pound. His neck ached terribly.

"Perhaps he's stupid," Keyman Kuwisa suggested.

Sha Yukima crouched back by his side. "We just want to get you into the wagon. Are you able to stand?"

"In there?" Tuki asked.

"Yes. We want to take you to some place safe. It would be easiest for you in the wagon. We can take you somewhere out of the sun, where it is cooler."

"I don't mind the sun," Tuki said softly, looking up to the sky to confirm that the Mother Blower was still at work, that she had not really deserted him.

"Of course you don't. You are from the desert, aren't you?" Yukima smiled some more. "Well, how about some food and water? You must be hungry."

"A little. Yes." Tuki slowly uncurled and sat up. Each movement brought screams of pain from his limbs. He glanced over his shoulder. People still surrounded him, but were apparently not going to attack again.

A few painful moments later, Tuki had climbed awkwardly to his feet. His left knee hardly supported his weight as he limped to the back of the wagon. His shoulder grated when he tried to climb up onto the wooden planks. He looked around from his new vantage and saw hundreds of people watching him.

The uniformed men moved in to form a cordon around the wagon, and the animal handler spoke an order. The parade started to move slowly along the road into the city. The priest sat on the boards beside Tuki, legs dangling over the side.

"What is your name, lad?"

"Tuki." Tuki was dividing his glance between the rumbling progress of the wagon and the brightly painted, conical roofed buildings along the way. Most had doorways decorated with feathers and fetishes, weavings and painted balls.

"I'm Sha Yukima. Sha is my title. I'm a priest, a man who talks with God."

Tuki smiled at the ludicrous thought; a *man* who talks with God. But the smile slipped from his face, and he touched the skyglass through the cloth of his waist-sack.

"I am a go'gan, Sha."

"And what is that? What are your duties?"

"A go'gan is a man for whom the Mother Blower has not yet chosen a wife." Tuki paused for a moment, thinking of Keala. She would be waiting for him to take the skyglass back to Danyon Ford. "My duties are to do what I am told."

"What do your tattoos mean? Do they tell a story?"

Tuki shook his head. "They each mean something on their own. This is the Moon Gate. It is the gate to the stars, to where the Mother Blower watches over us." As he spoke, he watched the circular pieces of timber that the wagon moved on.

"And the leaves?" Yukima asked.

"They are leaves from the Tree of Life. Each branch on the Tree is a universe, each leaf is a world that grows with the Mother's warmth."

The old man was nodding but said nothing. Tuki was going to continue explaining the meaning of his tattoos but asked about the circular timber instead.

"What are these called, Sha?"

"They are wheels." Sha Yukima smiled. "You've never seen wheels? I suppose there's not much use for wheels in the desert."

"And the animals?"

"The animals that pull the wagon are called donkeys."

"Donkeys?" Tuki wiped at his chin and brought his hand away covered in blood. His jaw ached terribly.

"I'm sorry. Here." The priest pulled a frilly white cloth from his sleeve and handed it to Tuki. "One donkey, many donkeys. How old are you, Tuki?"

"I have seen nineteen New Year Festivals."

Sha Yukima nodded his head slowly. "Why are you here?"

"I said, Sha. I am here to bring the words of the Mother Blower." He wiped at his chin, and then held the cloth against the corner of his mouth.

"Yes, I know you said that, but you were not sent by your leader?"

Tuki lowered his head, glancing at the meteor on his hand. Sha Yukima was a smart man. "No, Sha. The mo'min did not send me. Poti Herself did."

"Poti is your Goddess? She told you to come and spread Her word?"

Tuki shrugged, embarrassed. "Perhaps. She told me to come here, to your city, but I do not know why."

As they went further into the city, noisy crowds gathered. People hung from windows, or looked down from high balconies. They lined the streets, muttering under their breath and staring hatred. All the people. It was more people than Tuki had seen before.

"So many people, Sha."

Sha Yukima laughed. "About three thousand people live in Payota, Tuki. But it is market day today, so people have come from all about."

There were as many men as women in the crowd, and they were the more vocal by far.

"Do the women allow men positions of power in your city, Sha?"

The priest laughed. "Something like that, Tuki. Something like that."

Tuki didn't know what to make of that. "I would like to talk to your mo'min," he said.

"Don't worry, we are on our way to meet with the city's leaders."

"Thank you."

Even more people had gathered at a spot where the road divided. There was a long narrow stretch of parkland down the middle where people stood and shouted and pumped their fists in the air. They kept moving so Tuki couldn't count them properly. One of them, a man with hair on his face, stooped to a wooden pail by his feet as Tuki and his entourage passed by. When he straightened he had a tomato in each hand. Tuki watched, unable to do anything, as the stranger hurled the fruit his way. The first piece struck his shoulder and the second sailed past his head and landed in the crowd beyond. Then more fruit came, and more, until it seemed to fall out of the sky like the water had.

Tuki ducked his head and tried to ignore everything. Much of the fruit was rotten, but it would not harm him as the fists and feet had earlier. Though it was such a waste. He wondered if he should collect the better missiles to take back to the desert.

The uniformed men about him shouted at the crowd. Sha Yukima held up his hand to try to forestall further action. But it was all to no avail. Within moments, the whole group was dripping with the remains of fruit and vegetables as they moved forward at the donkeys' slow, steady pace.

Eventually, the wagon stopped in front of a squat, stone building that was so large it had two cone roofs. A mass of clamoring humans pushed in from every side, shouting abuse and threats. As Tuki gingerly hopped to the ground, they surged forward. Keyman Kuwisa and his patrol held them back, but Tuki wasn't sure if they were protecting him, or themselves.

The Keyman cleared a path so they could reach the entrance of the building.

Inside was another crowd. This one was quite a bit smaller, but it seemed almost as loud. They finally fell silent when they realized Tuki and his escort had arrived. Within moments only the noise of the crowd outside could be heard.

Sha Yukima cleared his throat and spoke. "This young man is Tuki. He has agreed to stay here until we can work out what we are going to do."

Tuki touched at his lip to be sure that it was not still bleeding, then scrunched the bloodstained cloth into a ball and stood with his head bowed.

"A troll has agreed to stay here?" The man who spoke seemed older than the others. His facial hair was mostly grey, and his hair was receding like a forest giving in to an encroaching desert.

"I do not believe that Tuki is a troll, Nasinwa. I think he may be a moai, come from the desert to visit with us."

"A moai?" The man named Nasinwa laughed and Tuki noticed others hurrying to join in. "The moai are from children's stories, Sha Yukima. You don't expect *us* to believe in them do you?"

"Yes, I do."

The laughter stopped.

"What makes you think he is a troll?" Sha Yukima asked.

"Well, look at the size of him," Nasinwa said.

Yukima nodded. "I've never seen a troll that big. Have you? But I *have* seen many men the size of trolls. Men like you or I. Men like the one you have tending to your garden every week, Councilor. We do not stone him because he is the size of a troll, do we?"

Tuki was stunned. Nasinwa was on some sort of council? What women would allow such a thing? Tuki was uncomfortable and wondered about his decision to place himself in the care of these men. He needed to speak with one of the women so he could tell his story. Surely the women would know of the existence of his people.

"My gardener is obviously not a troll," Nasinwa said.

Sha Yukima raised one eyebrow. "Why is that?"

"You would never meet a gentler man. And he is intelligent, with knowledge of more than death and destruction, that is."

Sha Yukima grunted and shook his head. "And Tuki here is obviously such a violent fellow. We could hardly control him on the way here. He was throwing fruit at all of those meek, intelligent humans crowding along the sides of the road. And he attacked them back in the markets."

The Councilor sneered. "Lock him in the most secure cell, Keyman. And have him guarded at all times."

Sha Yukima shook his head and sighed. "If you will excuse me, I'm going to get cleaned up. Perhaps you would like to join me, Tuki."

"I said, *lock him up.*"

"Kuwisa and his men can watch while we cleanse ourselves and I take a moment to tend to his wounds. The bathing room is quite secure enough. I don't think Tuki will fit through the window."

The Councilor shook his head but relented a moment later with small grace. "Very well. Just don't be all day about it."

"Thank you, Councilor Nasinwa," Tuki said with a slight bow of his head. "Thank you, Sha."

He ducked through a door behind the priest and followed him to a small room with a washtub. The tub was filled to overflowing with clear water.

"All this water," Tuki said, still standing in the doorway. But in the lands of man, water fell from the sky; he shouldn't have been surprised. "It is strange that Poti led me here."

"Why is that?"

"Well, you are so different from the moai. It is a surprise that we even speak the same language. How are we to tell each other anything at all?"

"And if we were the same, would it be worth saying anything?" Sha Yukima washed his hands and splashed water over his face, letting precious drops fall to the floor. "I can speak to my neighbor any day, Tuki."

"Perhaps, but do you?"

The priest finished washing in silence. The rumble of the crowd could still be heard out the window.

Tuki hoped he had not offended.

When Yukima stepped aside, Tuki stepped forward reverently, to take his turn at the trough.

A few minutes later Tuki smiled like a go'gan after his first Seeing. He was totally unconcerned about the water he was wasting, splashing it onto his face, watching as it ran along the joins in the floor tiles, flicking it from his fingers and examining the patterns it created on the walls. He tried to wash his robe and met with some success. He also filled his water bottle.

Tuki smiled at Sha Yukima a few minutes later, watching him bring forth a small sack filled with salves and ointments and elixirs.

The old man spoke while he started to work. "So how, exactly, did the Mother Blower lead you here?"

Tuki was caught in a moment of indecision. Three of Keyman Kuwisa's men were crowded about the door, shifting nervously from foot to foot. Should they, mere men, be allowed to see the skyglass? Should Sha Yukima really be allowed to see it, religious man though he apparently was? But there were no women present, and he needed help in this strange world.

"I will show you." Tuki said. He pulled the skyglass out of the pouch and held it up for the other man to see. The world of Kiva was shown in great detail. "See the blue dot? That is us."

"That is our world? Amazing. I have seen globes before but not like that. And we are the blue dot, you say?"

"Yes."

"And who painted the blue dot on there? Was it the Goddess?"

"It must be. The blue dot follows the skyglass everywhere."

"The dot moves?"

"Yes, I came from down here, and the dot followed me. And you see the yellow dots?" There were still five in the air above the blue dot. Others were still spaced randomly around the part of the world the 'glass showed.

"Of course."

"Well, I followed one of them here."

"What do they represent?"

"Meteors," Tuki said.

"Pardon?"

"A shooting star."

"Yes. Yes, there was a shooting star a couple of days past, right above the city. But do shooting stars normally," He wiggled his fingers towards the yellow dot, "do they normally stop like that?"

"I am sorry, I do not know. Perhaps they are up in the sky all the time but we cannot see them unless they are moving. The mo'min would know for sure."

"Perhaps, but that seems awfully strange. And the shooting star from the other day was so much brighter than any I have ever seen. I almost felt that I could reach out and touch it."

"I know. When I first saw, it I was very surprised." Tuki fell silent as more shooting stars appeared in the globe. Then more still. Soon, there were a dozen yellow dots right above Payota and dozens more all around the world.

"What's happening?"

"I do not know." They watched silently. After a little while, Tuki started to count the yellow spots. Occasionally he looked out the window but could see nothing other than a narrow strip of sky. He reached seventy-five when, outside, the noise of the crowd suddenly died away. He kept counting. One hundred and twenty meteors in all.

The noise of the crowd burst forth once more. This time the people were screaming.

26: Other Gods

TUKI RUSHED TO THE WINDOW so he might see better. Sha Yukima climbed up onto a bench so he could look as well. The guards stayed in position by the door but shifted from side to side in an effort to catch a glimpse. Outside, the crowd was scattering. Tuki had never seen anything like it. Nobody had any thought for anyone else. They pushed and shoved and cursed.

Great black bats circled in the sky. Tuki did not have to watch to know what happened next. This was not his vision from the desert, he knew, but the bats were the same and they were sure to have the same fiery eggs.

"We must go, Sha Yukima."

"What? Why? You are safest in here."

"We must hurry." But where would they go? Tuki did not know what to do. Even as he urged the priest to hurry, he stayed where he was and turned his gaze back to stare up to the sky. "Where can we hide from the fire?" he asked of himself.

"What fire?"

"The bats, Sha. They will drop eggs of fire onto the city."

"Eggs of fire? What are you talking about?"

"Poti showed me, Sha. Fire."

"Fire? She showed you in the skyglass?"

Tuki thought of telling the truth, 'No, she told me in a bottle,' but decided that an admission like that could cause problems. He said nothing.

"Well quickly then, come with me."

Tuki was aware of the priest hurrying from the room, but he could not take his eyes away from the bats above. The first of them were coming straight for him now, gliding down the side of the hills.

He felt a tug on his arm and looked down to see the priest back by his side.

"If there is fire, we must go."

"Yes," Tuki allowed himself to be led from the room. He followed Sha Yukima, glancing over his shoulder as the soldiers came along behind. Back in the room where the officials were gathered, Tuki stepped amidst a sea of angry faces.

"What is going on?" one of them shouted when he saw Tuki. "Did the troll lead these giant bats to us?"

Tuki would have stopped to explain to the man, but the little priest still had hold of his arm and did not slow down. The soldiers were behind him with their big knives. Yukima turned a corner and went out through the room's third door. Tuki ducked through behind him with the officials at his heels.

"What is going on, Yukima?"

"Where are you taking the troll?"

"I am not a troll."

"Make him stop the bats."

"Shut up you fool."

At the end of the hall, Sha Yukima, now at the head of a long line, pushed open a large stone door and ushered Tuki through. "If the rest of you are coming in here," he said, "then you will have to shut up."

Everyone fell silent for a moment. Tuki went carefully down some stairs and waited in darkness.

"This is not your church, Yukima. This is a building belonging to the Council."

"And how long do you think the Council would last without the support of the Church of Anas? Thank you. Now everyone stay calm, and Keyman, please shut the door before you leave. Tuki seems to think there will be fire."

"I will be staying with the Councilors, Sha," Kuwisa said.

"The Priman will need all the men he can get to protect the city, Keyman".

"Then I will stay here with two men and send the rest to the barracks," Kuwisa replied. "The Council is too important to leave unprotected in the company of a troll."

It looked as if the Sha would say something else, but outside a thunderous sound ripped through the continuing sounds of panicked people.

Someone shouted: "Fire!"

Tuki watched as people started to rush down the stairs towards him. The little bit of light that had been coming from the floor above was blocked by their progress. He felt somebody brush past him. He flinched, fearing more pain. But whoever it was must have known the location of flint and a torch, for moments later light sprang into being.

The room was long and low. Luckily, Tuki had not straightened his back, for his head almost brushed the ceiling in his stooped position. Wooden boxes lined two walls, running from either side of the door all the way to the back of the room. Stone columns stood like sentinels along the way, forming deep shadows in the flickering torchlight.

"If he did not bring the bats, how does he know about the fire, Sha?" Nasinwa asked.

"His Goddess showed him."

"His Goddess?" Kuwisa said. "You mean he has gods other than Anas?"

"I believe so."

"And you believe in these gods?" Councilor Nasinwa asked, a smile touching the corners of his mouth.

"It is a Goddess. And I don't see that I have any choice, Councilor. I have seen proof of Her power with my own eyes."

"And where did you see this?"

"Tuki has a crystal ball."

"A crystal ball? Like some hedge witch telling futures?" The Councilor marched over to Tuki who still held the skyglass in his hand. "Let me see this ball. Here, give it to me."

Tuki was reluctant to hand it over. He took a step away from the human who stood with his arm out stretched. "I cannot, go'shin. The Goddess gave it to me, and it cannot be given to another." He could see the look of veiled threat in the other man's eyes, and it scared him.

"You think I will break your sacred ball? Of course I won't. I just want a look."

Tuki examined the skyglass, turning it over in his large, rough hand. The Mother Blower had said nothing to him about the 'glass and who should hold it and who should not. Truth be told, She had not told him he could touch it himself. Councilor Nasinwa was a man of standing, as much as any man could be.

Tuki held the 'glass out hesitantly, and the other man took it with a sudden show of disinterest. Nasinwa weighed it in his hand, as if wondering if he should toss it away. He flinched when the image of Kiva started to fade.

With an uncertain look, Nasinwa quickly gave the skyglass to the Keyman. "Have a look at that," he said. "Talk to Sha Yukima if you have to," he glanced at Tuki, "just don't give it back to him."

"But —"

Nasinwa interrupted Tuki. "You'll get it back when I'm sure."

"Sure of what?" Tuki asked boldly.

The Councilor glared.

"That is not fair, Nasinwa," Sha Yukima said. "You would steal from a young man come to visit our city?"

"I would, if I thought that young man was a danger."

"If he was a danger we'd all be dead by now. If he didn't care, we'd all have been killed because we'd be up above."

"Kuwisa will keep the crystal ball until I say otherwise."

Tuki examined the Keyman and his long, curved knife. He did not think that a blade such as that would be used for peeling tubers. The other man did not look like he wanted the skyglass, given the way he held it out before him on the tips of his fingers, but he was not about to hand it back either. Tuki was sure he could not take it. Seeing there were only three soldiers remaining, he wondered if one of the much-feared trolls would have hesitated.

Councilor Nasinwa continued. "What is in those sacks at his waist?"

"This one is for holding the skyglass," Tuki said, indicating the empty sack. "The other holds inks and needles for tattooing, and my water bottle."

"You can keep those. We will keep the ball for a while."

Sighing, Tuki moved away to sit in the semidarkness with his back against the wall at the far end of the room. Sha Yukima flipped open the lid of one of the boxes and rummaged inside. After a moment he sat on the floor as well.

"You were hungry?"

"Yes."

"Have this." The priest handed him a long red strip that was tough and salty. It was like nothing Tuki had ever tasted.

"What is it Sha?"

"Salted pork."

"Pork? What is pork?"

"Pig. Pork is swine."

Tuki stopped chewing, his eyes widening in horror. After long moments in which he examined the priest to see if he was joking, he spat the food out onto the floor. He spat and spat and wiped his mouth on the back of his hand. Fumbling for his water bottle he raised his eyes to the heavens in prayer, but the heavens were not there. Above him was only rock. No stars, no sky, and no chance of quickly getting to a place where he could see either. As he drank he cast his glance to the far end of the room. The Keyman was examining the skyglass, but it was dull and lifeless in his hand. He had no use for it, could do nothing with it, and Tuki needed it desperately. He spat some more and looked at the cracked stone ceiling. Prayers tumbled from his lips.

"What is it, Tuki?"

Conscious of being polite, as always, Tuki paused for a moment to answer. "I ate a living creature. I cannot eat a living creature."

He started to pray again. When he married Keala he would get her to draw some stars or the sun somewhere on his skin so he could always see it. The taste would not leave his mouth.

"It was not alive. It was long dead, Tuki."

Tuki swallowed and drew in a deep breath. "Once alive, always alive, Sha. Do your gods not teach this?"

"Our gods say that the physical self dies and the spiritual self goes on to another existence. The bodies of the dead are just husks." The priest climbed quickly to his feet and went to search through another box. He returned a short time later with something that was quite obviously a vegetable. "An apple. It has no soul."

Tuki took a bite of the apple. The cool juices cleansed his mouth like the prayers and the water had not been able.

"What does your Goddess tell you of the body, lad?"

"Poti says that the spirit remains in the body until the body is no more," Tuki replied, dribbling juices down his chin. "And when the body is gone, returned to the world from whence it came, then the spirit is set free to join the stars in the heavens."

"A strange thought."

"No stranger than the teachings of your gods. How can a spirit not be attached to the body in every hair and organ and muscle?" He wondered where the thoughts had come from. Should he compare gods with Sha Yukima? The priest was obviously an intelligent man, far smarter than Tuki, so would he believe in gods that didn't exist? Did all the gods live side by side? Or were some people fooled into believing in false gods? And if false gods existed, who was to say which were false and which were real?

Tuki continued to chew on his apple. It was a wonderful fruit, juicy and crisp and clean. He prayed silently and thought about the existence of the gods.

-o◯o-

Tuki watched Keyman Kuwisa suspiciously in the shifting light of the torches. The man examined the skyglass for a long time, twisting it this way and that in his hand as if it would make a difference, twisting it as if it might catch the light at a different angle and spring into life. Not once had the human tried to speak to it. How could he expect to get any results at all?

After several more minutes, Tuki rose painfully to his feet and made his way toward the Keyman. It was a slow journey conducted under the gaze of everyone in the long, low, narrow room. He tried to ignore them: they were only men after all. He stopped when the two other soldiers surged to their feet, long knives in hand.

Tuki stared at the floor. "You must speak to it," he said to Kuwisa between the tense forms of the other men. "Ask questions, and it will answer."

"Answer?"

"Not in words, but you will receive an answer."

"Show me."

Tuki looked at the man before drawing a breath and walking forward. The soldiers parted to let him through.

After sitting down on the cold stone floor, Tuki reached out a shaking hand to take the skyglass. He could not cover the last fraction of the distance, and his hand hovered there. He concentrated on breathing once more as he shifted his gaze to the Keyman's face. He turned his hand over, so the skyglass could be given to him.

As soon as he touched it, the 'glass started to warm and Kiva materialized.

Perhaps talking is not enough, he thought. *Perhaps you have to believe.*

Tuki polished the surface for a moment, enjoying the smooth, solid feel of it in his hands.

The blue dot representing the skyglass was clearly visible with no yellow comet-dots nearby, though there were still many all around the world.

"It is safe to go outside," he said, though the thought of all of those monsters just out of sight over the horizon scared him immensely.

"How do you know?"

Tuki kept his eyes on the ball, though he felt the tension in Kuwisa as the other man considered rising.

"How do you know?" An angry spitting of words, as if he did not want to admit the lack of knowledge in himself.

"Because all the comets have gone. Moved on to somewhere else." He showed him the dots.

"But does that mean the bats and monsters have gone as well?"

"Poti would not lie." But, in truth, he wasn't sure. "We cannot stay in here forever," he added, as if that might make up for the lie.

"*You* can, as far as I'm concerned."

Tuki didn't look up from the 'glass. He didn't know why the humans hated him. Only Sha Yukima spoke to him as if he were a man. "I did not ask to be given the skyglass, Keyman Kuwisa," Tuki said. "I would rather it were the mo'min who was here. But the Mother Blower chose me."

"I don't care about your Goddess, boy," Kuwisa said.

"And yet She sent me to help you."

"Sure She did."

"Are we to stay here? Or do we go back outside?"

"You're staying here." The Keyman took the skyglass. It died in his hand. He swore as he rose to his feet and went to speak with the Councilor.

Tuki couldn't hear what the two men were saying, and he didn't care. He was battered and bruised. His face ached. It was swollen and tender. He almost thought he could feel the blood throbbing beneath the skin. The Mother Blower had sent him to the humans, and he'd done nothing to repay Her faith. He didn't know what to do. He hadn't even had the chance to talk to any women. All he could do was sit and wait, so that was what he did.

After a few minutes of hushed discussion, Keyman Kuwisa spoke to the group at large. "It has been decided that we will stay here for a while longer and then go and see what has happened."

Sha Yukima gave a bark of laughter in response.

"What's so amusing, Sha?"

"Keyman, it is your duty to protect the citizens of Payota. It is what you are paid for, and yet you argue with Councilor Nasinwa to stay safely locked down here while the citizens are above ground."

"You led the way down here, Sha."

"And today is the day you start listening to a priest?"

"In times of crisis, we turn to Anas, Sha. It has always been so."

"Yes, and you turn away as quickly afterwards."

Tuki was shocked. "Keyman, you do not pay homage to even your own gods?"

Kuwisa turned to look at him coldly. "Praying doesn't save lives. In the end, it is always strong doors or strong arms that do that."

"Perhaps," Tuki agreed, "but it is always the Goddess, or gods, who make sure life is *worth* living."

Councilor Nasinwa smiled. "There are three strong sets of arms here that could have been helping above ground, Kuwisa, instead of guarding some old men. And, if the threat has now passed, then the Council should be up there to lead the way."

"Very well, then. If you insist." Kuwisa broke away from the rest of the group and made his way to the stairs. He paused there and looked back over his shoulder.

"We can't stay here forever, Keyman," Nasinwa said. He had the skyglass again but was paying it no mind, tossing it absently from hand to hand as he spoke. He was going to steal it. Though the human couldn't use it, and probably would not know how to read the messages of the Goddess if he *could* use it, Nasinwa would keep the 'glass anyway.

"We could wait until morning," Kuwisa said. "Just to be sure."

The Councilor didn't say anything, merely glared, and the other man climbed the stairs to the stone door. A moment later, the humans were all making their way back to ground level, nervously following the soldiers into the daylight. Tuki tried to follow as well but the door was slammed in his face. The closing cut off angry words from Sha Yukima.

Tuki stayed where he was, listening as the bolts were slipped into place. He sat on the bottom step to wait.

The skyglass was gone.

TUKI SAT ON THE STEP for a long time, examining the comet tattoo on the back of his hand, before thinking to try the door above him. He discovered that, with a little bit of effort, he could make it move. It was not a door designed for keeping people in.

It may have taken only a moment for him to realize that he could leave at any time, but it took considerably longer to decide if he should.

Did the human men have the right to lock him up without so much as a nod from the women? And if they had the earthly authority in general, did they have the right in his case? He'd done nothing wrong. He went through the events of the last few days just to be sure, but they had said as much themselves: he was being kept on the suspicion that he was a troll.

Eventually it was not a question of the rights of the humans, or even his own rights, that decided him. It was the skyglass. Councilor Nasinwa didn't know how to use the 'glass. He didn't understand its importance. As far as Tuki knew there were but two skyglasses in the entire world — he could not let one of those be lost through his own inaction. He gripped the edge of the stone door and pulled. It protested, resisting, but only for a moment.

Outside, the wall of the hallway sagged dangerously, ready to fall at any minute. The rest of the building was no better. It leaned at a crazy angle. Stone blocks were scattered everywhere. Half the tiles from the roof had slipped down to the ground.

The rest of the city was much the same. On either side of the street a line of rubble, both timber and stone, had taken the place of the buildings. They all looked the same now, but it was hardly harmonious. Close to where he was, Tuki could only see three structures still whole. Bodies lay everywhere, strange cold worlds in the expanse of the street. Tuki tried not to look.

Farther away, upright structures were more regular and signs of life could be seen. A thin man dragged a sack out of one house and into the next. A child ran behind a dog. Or perhaps he was *with* the animal.

Tuki couldn't move. It seemed that while he was underground another world had replaced the one he'd left just hours before. The pain and humiliation that had been inflicted upon him by the humans was completely understandable compared to the destruction wrought by the strangers from the sky. Or perhaps it was exactly the same thing — fear, confusion, misunderstanding — on a much larger scale.

He stood where he was for a long time, eyes turned to the sky so he could pray for the Mother Blower to bring back the world he knew.

He eventually moved away from the tilting, half collapsed remains that had sheltered him. There was not a lot of difference between street and buildings, but at the next corner Tuki went left and at the first standing wall, a hundred and twelve meters from his starting position, paused to get his bearings. He needed to find the skyglass but had no idea where he might start to look. Councilor Nasinwa probably had it in his possession, but where was the Councilor?

Away to the west was a river. A real river filled with an unbelievable amount of water. And nearby, a large group of people were congregating beside a small platform and a tree. They milled about as if they had no idea why they were there, beyond the fact that everyone else was there.

Tuki started down towards the river, because everyone else was there.

Perhaps the Councilor has found a woman to set things right. He hoped so, for he didn't want to be caught with only the men in charge.

There were indeed women in the crowd, but they appeared to be as confused as the men. They cried and shuffled and waited for somebody else to tell them what needed to be done.

Tuki watched from inside a huge wrecked building. One of the planks had fallen away from a wall, leaving a gap through which he could watch without being seen. His heart was racing. He set his hands against the old, grey timber to steady their shaking.

Near the edges of the group, guards watched silently. They had their big knives out and seemed eager to use them. They prodded at anyone, women or men, who caused even the slightest stir. They elicited startled shrieks and smiled amongst themselves.

Just when Tuki was ready to move his search to other areas, glad of any excuse to be on his way, the Councilor stepped up onto the platform at the very edge of the river and held up his hands for silence. He held his position for a long time before he was satisfied.

"My good people, quiet, please."

Beside the platform were other elderly, serious looking men and women. The Council, Tuki assumed, though there were many more men than women and one wore similar clothes to those worn by the soldiers.

"Some quiet, please."

The rumbling of the crowed died further.

"Thank you." Nasinwa lowered his arms. "We have suffered grievously today. It has been terrible for all of us, and we know not how any other cities in the area have faired. The Priman has sent runners out to Assinabon and Sarsin and through Salisha

Valley to Klamoth, but they will probably not return for a week at best. So we must assume we are on our own. We must work together to make sure we have food and shelter. If we all put in and help, we will make it through this."

A disbelieving grumble ran through the gathering, but Nasinwa ignored it.

"There is food aplenty in the market yards. Some of the livestock have escaped, but they will not go far. And several of the warehouses remain untouched. This is a black day for Payota, but we will go on."

Tuki continued to listen as the Councilor organized the running of the city. He ordered men to prepare suitable shelter and others to see to the livestock. Women were directed to the warehouses to collect what they could. Children were to scavenge, finding anything they thought might be useful and passing it on to those older than they.

Some looked as if they might do as they had been told, but the majority of people continued grumbling. Someone shouted for Nasinwa to make shelters himself. Another said that if anyone were hungry they could slaughter their own food.

The group surged towards the nervous council members. A dozen guards were close by, but they weren't going to last long against the mob. Tuki saw the look of fear on Nasinwa's face before the old man lurched backwards and fell to the ground. It wouldn't be long before his protective cordon was overrun. Knowing what the old man was going through, Tuki rose from his hiding place and ran a few steps into the clear. He went all the way to the back of the crowd.

He hesitated, but before he could think of what to do, someone nearby turned and saw him. Tuki and the human stared at each other. The human was a little man with a missing tooth and crooked nose. His eyes were wide with shock and fear, but he reacted quickly, setting up a new shout that instantly spread through the crowd. The nearest people stepped back, crowding those behind.

Within moments the focus of the angry crowd had shifted from Nasinwa and his companions to Tuki.

Tuki suddenly wished he had stayed hidden. All eyes were on him, staring. He didn't know what to do. He might have run, but the skyglass had to be reclaimed. He took a hesitant step forward, heart thundering in his chest.

The crowd edged away. Tuki took another step, and another. A path cleared, and he walked all the way to the river without coming within two meters of a human.

The Councilors watched him come. Nasinwa appeared angry, as if he would rather be attacked than saved by a *troll*. The others were fearful but stood their ground. Sha Yukima was there as well, looking unsure.

When he reached the base of the platform, staring at the ground while the humans stared at him, Tuki didn't know what to do next. There were women present so he thought he should wait for instructions, but nobody seemed about to offer them. So Tuki did nothing more than turn to look towards the crowd.

Nasinwa, straightening his robes, held up his hand for silence again though nobody was saying anything. "The strangers from the sky are still out there somewhere," he said. For a moment the crowd shifted their focus from Tuki to the Councilor, but only for a moment.

"What's the troll doing?" someone in the crowd shouted.

"Yeah. Is he with us?"

"Are more trolls coming?"

"Yes," Nasinwa said after a moment. "Umm... Yes. The troll lost his village to the sky-men a week ago and came to warn us. More will come when they have seen to their own."

"Trolls don't have villages."

Nasinwa opened his mouth to speak but was obviously at a loss for words. Still nobody looked at him. Tuki became more nervous under the steady gaze of all those strangers. He turned for a moment to look at one of the councilwomen. She smiled to him and nodded.

Tuki took a small step forward. "We..." It came out as barely more than a whisper. He cleared his throat and looked to the woman for more encouragement. "We do not have villages," he said. The lie was burning on his tongue, but the woman was telling him to go on. "But we, ummm, we have permanent camps that we call villages." He was sure that only those at the very front of the crowd could hear his words, but they were whispered away from him on other tongues.

"Trolls don't have permanent anything," someone shouted in response.

"It's, ummm, a permanent camp, but the population comes and goes." He would have gone on, but he knew less of trolls than these people did and was afraid that his lies would be discovered. He clamped his mouth shut against a babble of explanations. The crowd stared. Tuki felt like running for cover, but the people blocked any escape route except into the water. He doubted they would melt away like before, and he could never walk into water. He stared at the ground instead, and waited for someone else to take up his lie.

Councilor Nasinwa did. "The trolls come to offer us their strength against an enemy worse than any either of our people have ever seen, but we must have something to give them in return: shelter, food, stability. Please. I need a hundred volunteers to see to the rounding up of livestock and the repair of the market yards. We need to search the city for foodstuffs. Some buildings still stand, but not enough to shelter everyone for the night."

This time when a rumbling went through the mob they were organizing themselves into work parties, galvanized by the thought of allies to help win the fight.

Tuki followed the Councilor when he walked away along the river a while later. A dozen or so others followed as well. They crowded around behind the old man, all talking, and all trying to bring his attention to some important matter or other. Soldiers followed behind them, knives drawn but no longer held with any threat.

Night fell soon after, but it didn't lessen the frenetic activity. A camp had been set up on the banks of the river. Rough lean-tos and tilting shacks had been erected, and more still were going up. Dozens of fires burned, eating through what had once been buildings or furniture. Beasts had been put to death so their flesh could be cooked and eaten. Tuki's protests had no effect in this regard, and he had listened to the animals' bawling and, even worse, to the moments of silence that punctuated. He tried not to watch. He tried not to hear. But he could as easily hold back the desert. Nobody else seemed to care.

Piles of food were growing. The beasts were being treated with salt and herbs that were supposed to make them last, but Tuki felt they would have lasted longer had they been left alive. Fruit and vegetables were being collected in baskets from wrecked houses. Bread and cakes and bisca, too.

Tuki, sitting still and quiet, was near one such pile. There was some bread: a fine, white loaf. There was fruit, rich and ripe, and he could smell porridge. There were things he couldn't recognize to which he attached all description of wondrous taste.

Sitting on the other side of the fire, not excluding him but not inviting him into the talks, were the members of the Council. Nasinwa was there with the skyglass resting in his lap, as if he cared for its safety. The old, uniformed man was there as well. Apparently he was the Priman, the leader of the guards. There were half a dozen women in the group, but they didn't add their voices to the proceedings. They sat and listened with the same tired expressions as Tuki. Perhaps they had already talked amongst themselves, or would later. One by one they drifted away while the men continued. Sha Yukima was nowhere to be seen. He had sat close by earlier, taking part in the discussions, before saying there were important things he could be doing and going away.

Tuki sat with the Council well into the night as they talked themselves into knots. He said nothing, was asked nothing. There were some women grouped about a fire nearby that Tuki could have spoken to, but Nasinwa had the skyglass and he was loath to go anywhere with out it.

The men talked of food and shelter, labor and costs, things that Tuki didn't understand. What cost was there to cut down trees to rebuild the city? The trees were right there, and the men to do the cutting. What cost to distribute the gathered food? And who would take little golden disks as payment?

Apparently anyone would take the disks, and in fact, many refused to do anything if the payment was not made.

When the elder brother moons had departed the sky and only little Rangi remained, the Priman turned his gaze across the fire.

"Troll," he said, an edge of disdain in his voice, "will others come to fight with us if you ask?"

Tuki stared at the man. Surely Nasinwa had told his companions the truth!

"I am not a troll," Tuki said slowly, his eyes darting from one face to the next as all the men turned to hear him speak. "I do not know what a troll is."

"But you said..."

Tuki swallowed. "I lied."

Councilor Nasinwa grunted. "You persist with that story when it makes no difference now."

"I persist with the story because it is the truth." Tuki paused to think for a moment. "For all I know I may be a troll, but that is not what my people call ourselves. We live in the desert to the south, far from the world of man. We have done no harm to any of your kind."

Sha Yukima returned just then, walking wearily into the circle of firelight. "And why did you come among us now, after staying hidden away for so long?" He lowered himself carefully to the ground near another old man.

"I told you, Sha. The skyglass led me." He motioned to the glass ball on the ground by Nasinwa's side, and all the men turned to look.

Nasinwa laughed. "The ball is a pretty bauble only. Hedge wizards use similar to tell your fortune."

"I saw patterns on the ball moving," Sha Yukima put in. "You saw something, too, Nasinwa. If it's a hedge wizard's trick, it's the best I have ever seen."

"Well, all I saw was a globe like any that could be made by a skilled glass blower. Here, boy, show us again how it works."

Tuki watched eagerly as the Councilor collected the skyglass and threw it across the fire. Tuki's heart was in his mouth as he watched it sail above the flames, catching the light like a new moon. Only when Tuki had the globe in his hands did he speak.

"In truth, I do not know much in the use of the 'glass, Councilor Nasinwa. Only the mo'min is allowed to use it normally, and only the mo'shi may otherwise see it."

"Oh, so it's a secret that you may not share with us?" Nasinwa said, and his companions laughed with him. "How surprising is that?"

But Tuki didn't hear them. The skyglass was warming in his hands. As the sphere started to glow, the humans fell silent. Kiva soon appeared, filling about a quarter of the glass.

"We are here," Tuki said, pointing to the soft blue spot hovering just below the surface of the glass. "The blue follows the 'glass wherever it goes. I came from down here."

"And what are the yellow dots?" the Priman asked.

Sha Yukima moved from the other side of the fire to sit at Tuki's side. "They mark the bats, correct?"

216

Tuki sighed. "I don't know for sure Sha, but I don't think so."

"So you know nothing then?" Nasinwa asked.

Tuki examined the 'glass.

"Tell us what you are thinking, lad."

"I think the yellow dots are bats, perhaps, but ones that are still high up in the sky. When they come close to the ground, close enough to see, they disappear from the 'glass."

"Why do you think that?"

Tuki shrugged.

Nasinwa grunted again. "You know nothing. You have a toy that you don't understand, and you play with it, wanting us to be jealous." The Councilor reached out his hand. "Give it back to me."

Tuki held the glass out to be taken; he would not throw it as Nasinwa had. Nasinwa sighed and motioned for one of his fellows to collect it. But before the other man could do as he was bid, Keyman Kuwisa strode into the circle of firelight.

"Councilor," the Keyman said loudly, and Nasinwa nodded. "Priman." The other old man nodded as well. Kuwisa glanced back over his shoulder. Two men followed behind, dragging another between them. "We found this man sneaking away with a sack full of food."

"It was my food," the man protested. "Took it from my own larder." The captive changed tactics then with hardly a pause for breath. "I wasn't going nowhere. Just to the stockpiles to add my bit."

"The stockpiles in which town?" Kuwisa asked.

Nasinwa levered himself to his feet, grunting with the effort. "The food belongs to Payota now, and if we allow one man to take a bit, soon every man will be taking a bit and there will be none left to share. We cannot allow that."

"I doubt you'd be taking a bit. None of you Councilors have moved all day."

Captain Kuwisa hit the man in the face, a solid blow that made Tuki wince. He turned away as a long rope of blood extended down from the man's mouth. The prisoner was unconscious.

Nasinwa shook his head. "We cannot allow this. He must be made an example of, Priman. In the morning we will tie him to the oak tree by the river and administer ten lashes."

"Very well," the Priman replied. "Kuwisa will see to it."

"Is that not a bit harsh, Nasinwa?" Sha Yukima asked. "Have we the right to stop a man from eating the food that he owned?"

"We have every right. We are looking after the needs of the many here, Yukima."

"There are other ways this might be done."

"I do not think a mild scolding will do in this case," the Priman said, supporting the Councilor.

"So again we humans prove how meek and mild and *humane* we are, while a *troll* watches on passively?"

Tuki thought of pointing out that he was not a troll but decided Sha Yukima might be trying to make some kind of point with the lie. He remained silent while the two men continued to argue.

Eventually, the priest rose angrily to his feet and stormed away. Some time later Tuki found that he still had the skyglass cupped in his hands. Nobody else seemed to have noticed. Slowly, so the other might not notice, he laid down with the globe clutched against his body protectively.

PING STOPPED WALKING. For a few seconds she thought Scree would continue slogging through the rain without her. But the big man stopped and looked back.

"I'll get sick. Do you understand? If you make me walk all day in this weather, I'll get sick."

The big man shrugged as he walked back. "[Don't understand.]"

"Sick." Ping feigned sneezing. "We won't go anywhere for days if I get sick." He obviously didn't understand, so she walked to the edge of the road and sat under a tree. It offered some protection from the rain— though not as much as she would've liked— and there were no bodies nearby. She shuddered. She'd been stepping around dead zorigami for so long now she hardly noticed any more. She normally waved away the flies and kept walking. It wasn't something she was proud of. It wasn't something she wanted to think about at all.

Trying to massage her aching legs, Ping wondered if the big man had taken 'Ten days' as a challenge. They'd walked until just after eleven o'clock on the first day, climbing up out of the valley that sheltered the centre of Shadon and then down the other side. To the south, the ruins of the city spread well beyond the hills and they'd not stopped to rest until they were a kilometer clear of the last houses.

The day after that, they walked from dawn until dusk, sometimes trudging along the road, at other times in the trees to the west. Ping thought Scree might have walked through the night as well had it not been for her. She was sure she had blisters the size of eggs on her feet but her companion wouldn't allow her to remove her scavenged boots. She might have complained, or taken them off to examine her feet when he wasn't looking. But he never removed his boots either, and seemed to see everything, whether he was looking or not.

"Where are you from?" Ping asked when Scree crouched down by her side.

He didn't reply. The colored armor on his arm hissed open and he laid it on the ground, flexing his fingers. The splint that covered his other arm was barely holding on. The pain from the break must have been terrible.

"Tell me about where you come from." She thought he was from a different world, though there was much of Tiandi she knew nothing about— that *nobody* knew

28: Challenges

anything about, perhaps. But she doubted his people would hide themselves away, and he *had* fallen out of the air under the Great Clock. He'd also asked her for the name of the world. "Are you from a different world?" If he was, how did the people there know of Tiandi?

He looked at her but didn't speak. Ping saw him move the fingers in his right arm and grit his teeth against the pain, so she moved to his side and started to work at the untidy knot that held the splint together.

"[What's you doing?]"

"I'll retie this. I might be able to do it tighter with two hands." Though that was debatable. Possibly the man could have done it tighter with *two* broken arms, though the pain would have been terrible. Two minutes and thirty-seven seconds later she finally got the knot undone and started to unwrap the binding. "What is your world like?"

"[What?]"

"Me," she paused for a moment to point to herself, then around at the world. "Tiandi. You..." And she shrugged.

"Kiva."

Ping waited, but for six seconds he said nothing more.

"[A world,]" he added, shrugging.

"So it is like Tiandi? Your world? Kiva?"

He shrugged again.

Ping knew he understood the question— he wasn't stupid— but simply couldn't be bothered answering. He saw everything, she already knew, and heard everything, but she doubted he bothered much to express what he knew. He did what he did and worried naught for the rest.

They remained silent while Ping finished the retying of the splint and Scree held the arm in place. It seemed to be setting straight, despite what it had gone through. She smiled slightly when Scree nodded his approval but the big man winced with the pain when he tried to move his fingers.

"[Let's goes,]" he said. "Kansu."

"But it's still raining." She gestured at the sky and flicked rain from her fingers. They'd been resting for barely twelve minutes.

Scree waved vaguely at the sky himself. "[And monsters still flying. And burning.]"

Ping got the point. She rose to her feet as Scree donned the weapon once more. They set out at a steady pace that Ping knew would tire her before long. She didn't say anything, merely watched the troll's heels and tried to keep up.

Kansu had never seemed so far away.

-oOo-

Ten days turned into twelve, and Scree wasn't happy with the delay. Ping could see it in the set of his shoulders. She could hear it in his voice. She had tried, crying herself to sleep at night with the pain. She had risen exhausted each morning and walked without complaint. Well, *not much* complaint.

She didn't know why Scree stayed. It had become more obvious as the days passed that he didn't like her any more than she liked him. He obviously though her weak and soft. She thought him heartless and cold. Perhaps they were both right. But she had stayed, and he had stayed. Ping knew where her chances lay, and perhaps he felt the same way, though she couldn't imagine how she might help.

Ping didn't really like the man he was, but she respected him. She watched him walking along ahead of her with an alert calmness that was astounding. He didn't miss a thing. He seemed tireless, was courageous to a fault and intelligent in a methodical way. But he didn't suffer people who were not all of those things as well. She tried to keep up. She tried to be thankful with the little food he gave her each night from his pack; he ate no more, though surely he must need it. But it was hard when she was sore to the bones and tired to the soul.

She just wanted to sit for a week and cry.

The city of Kansu, barely a city at all compared to Shadon, spread about the plain where a wide, brown river met the ocean. The monsters were there, though there didn't seem to be very many of them. The whole place was ablaze.

At the top of a long slope to the north of the city, Ping decided she could go no further. She sank to the ground beside a tree and closed her eyes to cry.

It was all too much.

The monsters. The smoke. The giant bats circling incessantly. The days of walking. The thought that, without Scree, she'd be dead in days, possibly killed by her own people.

They'd seen it in several villages; families at war with each other for the only scraps of food left, attacking anyone who came near. Scree looked competent enough to keep all of them away.

Ping saw Scree stop to look back.

They'd slept longer the previous night, sheltering from the chill of early morning in an abandoned farmhouse that crouched down in a gully by the edge of the road. But she needed more than a few hours of sleep. She needed days. Weeks.

Ping shook her head. She doubted she could walk another step. Her feet didn't ache any more— she couldn't feel them at all. She was hungry and tired and there were knots in her hair that she would need scissors to remove. Her clothes... Though she'd collected what she could along the way, her clothes were hardly decent. She knew Scree had noticed *that*.

So Ping sat under the tree and decided that she wouldn't go down into the city. Scree could find whatever he was after on his own.

"What are you looking for down there, Scree?" Though the monsters were down there, killing any person who moved, he was just going to march down in to the streets.

"[Whats?]"

She tried to order her thoughts. "*Why Kansu?*" she said in his language. She'd learned a surprising amount of it in the last few days.

He eyed her suspiciously. "[Another gate,]" he said after a moment.

Apparently she hadn't learnt that much. "What does mean?"

"[Gate. Doorway.]" He mimed opening a door.

"A door?"

He shrugged.

"*Why door want? Many doors Shadon.*" There had to be more to it than that but Ping couldn't think straight.

Scree sighed. "Kiva, Tiandi," he said. "Tiandi..."

"A door to a new world?" Even the thought of stepping through to another world could not rouse Ping's interest. She ignored Scree as he tried to coax her into motion. There were still several kilometers to go to the outskirts of the city and that was a few hours of painful walking in her current state.

"[Come on.]" He motioned her forward. "[Rest whens there.]"

"But where are we going? What are you looking for?"

"*Whats?*"

Ping sighed and repeated the question, as well as she could, in Scree's language.

"*I'm lookings for a big building,*" he said.

"*A big building?*"

"[A church.]"

"*No understand.*"

He grabbed an imaginary rope and swung it. "*Ding dong. Ding dong.* [A church.] *Maybes. Something likes that.*"

"You want to go to the clock? But you don't even know what a clock is, do you?"

Well, if he was after the clock, he could see it from where he was. She pointed... But the tower that had once stood on the top of the hill at the center of the city was no longer there.

He grabbed her hand in his and dragged her down the hill towards the city.

A few kilometers to the first building, and then another kilometer beyond that, at least, to the center of town— Ping started to cry again, digging in her heels, little that it did.

She didn't notice that one of the bats had stopped circling. The first she knew of it was when Scree fired his weapon into the air. It was right there, just fifty meters up. Hurt by Scree's attack, the creature screeched horribly, banked to the left and dipped towards the ground.

A little over a minute later it had landed and armored figures were climbing from the barrels strapped to its belly. Scree swore and quickened the pace, firing as he went. Ping struggled to keep up now, calling on the last of her strength. When she fell, he dragged her through the grass for four seconds before letting go of her hand and racing forward on his own.

A monster exploded. Two of its fellows were caught in the blast. The troll turned his fire on another as he took cover behind a fallen tree. Ping stayed where she was, hidden by the grass, crying softly, trying to remain unseen.

While she watched, Scree killed half a dozen of the attackers. Another bat came in to land four minutes later and more monsters spilled forth. Scree continued to fire, concentrating on the bulging backs each time. But, even with her amateur's eye, Ping could see that he'd soon be overwhelmed. She watched as he rose into a crouch, cast a glance in her direction, then shot from cover like a broken watch-spring. He raced through the rain towards Kansu, leaving Ping on her own in the grass.

She wanted to follow him— she would die without him— but could not make her legs obey her commands.

29: Better Offers

WHEN PING STOPPED CRYING, she raised her head and peered through the gently waving grass. No living creature remained close by. The last of the monsters had climbed back onto their bats more than twenty-three minutes ago and left for the sky. Some still lurked down in the city. Fires burned out of control. Zorigami ran as if running would make a difference. Scree was down there somewhere as well, though she didn't know where. He was probably looking for the clock tower, or the remains of it. Or he'd found another zorigami and was long gone.

Lying in the grass on the side of the hill, Kansu burning below, Ping knew her best chance of survival lay with Scree. Her own people had proven unable to protect themselves at all. She'd seen hardly any dead monsters other than those that Scree was responsible for. She'd seen no bands of resistance. She'd seen no zorigami who looked to be on her side of sanity. And she couldn't blame them. She'd been with them until Scree brought her back.

He was down in the city looking for a door to another world. Possibly he'd already passed through and was forever out of reach. Even if that were so, there was every chance the other world would be better than Tiandi.

Ping sat up and wiped her eyes. She was caked in mud. Grass clung to her like tassels and ribbons. Her legs still ached. She felt no better now than when she had collapsed an hour and a half earlier. But now she had no choice, and perhaps if she'd been thinking clearly earlier, she would have realized that she didn't have a choice then either.

With a deep breath, Ping stood and started following a trail as it wound away from the trees and down toward the river. The main road was not a hundred meters to the left, but she assumed Scree knew what he was doing and stayed away.

Limping and crying, Ping neared the first of the buildings two hours and twelve minutes later. She stopped to lean against the side of a small, timber house that had somehow remained intact when all those about it were nothing more than piles of charred wreckage.

She stood and leaned and breathed deeply. She wiped at her face and sniffed. Over all of the other smells, Ping could suddenly, as if it was a normal restday morning at home, smell bread. It made her feel instantly better.

She looked about, trying to locate the scent from heaven, before realizing it could only come from the building behind her. Unable to take her mind off the bread for long enough to check her surroundings, Ping made her way to the front door and peered inside. Of course there was nobody there but, on the kitchen table, where it would have been left to air, sat a plump, golden loaf of bread. Flies had gathered, clustering about it like zorigami around a master clockmaker. Ping leaned against the soot-blackened door for a minute and twenty seconds before hobbling forward to chase the flies and tear into the bread. Had she not been so hungry she might have thought to search the cupboard for jam or butter. But the bread, starting to go stale, was a meal fit for a king.

Hunger satisfied for the first time in days, Ping dropped the last small morsel of crust onto the floor and went in search of a drink. In a small, dark cupboard beneath the stairs, she found a dozen bottles of wine. Some were ten years old, while others came with a vintage of the previous year.

"Is anyone there?" Ping called. Outside fires crackled, and in the distance, other sounds. But inside the house, with the flies gone, all was quiet. "Is anyone there?" When no answer came, Ping selected one of the older wines and uncorked it. "I'm drinking your wine."

She might have drunk the whole thing, standing there in the hall, but with the wine half gone, Ping again felt the need to find Scree. Every moment she wasted, the troll was getting further away. And every moment he may be moving in a direction she would never be able to follow. With a sigh of regret, Ping decided it was probably best to leave the bottle behind completely. She took one last swig, closing her eyes when the smooth liquid slid down to her stomach, then dropped the bottle and headed for the front door. If nothing else, the wine had lessened the ache of her feet and legs and gave her renewed confidence.

On the steps, Ping paused to examine her surroundings. She had been to Kansu just a few months earlier— sourcing a special part for the clock in Elephant Tower— and visited the clock. *Rep's Register* had been near the center of town, to the southeast of her position. With the sinking sun at her back, she set out at a steady-if-somewhat-slow pace.

Zorigami littered the ground like drifts of autumn leaves. For the most part she tried to ignore the scenes around her, keeping her eyes peeled for movement, for signs of life. They were few and far between.

When she saw a live monster, Ping was so surprised she stood in the middle of the street for five seconds. It didn't see her though, so when her wine addled senses told her to move, she dashed for the cover of a shadowed doorway and waited for her heart to slow. Her legs were aching again, but she gave them no thought. She leaned slowly towards the corner to peek out. The monster was gone. It had moved on, possibly following some prescribed patrol route.

"I have to be sensible," Ping said to herself. She admitted that the wine might have gone to her head as well as her legs. She knew Scree had helped her because she could help him. That was the only reason. So, if she wanted his help again, she would have to have something to give in return.

When she peeked out again the monster had returned. It stood, swiveling back and forth, in the middle of the intersection. She leaned back and tried to think.

"So what have I got to offer Scree?" She did not want to think of the way he'd looked at her at night. "I'm smarter than he is." Though that was debatable, if she was honest. "I can cook. I can watch his back. I can keep guard at night so he can sleep." But he watched his own back better than she ever could and probably slept with one eye open anyway. Ping didn't know what she could offer the troll that would be of any use but she decided she'd go and find him anyway and worry about payment when the subject came up.

When she looked, the monster was still there and standing like it was going to be at it for the rest of the day. "The first thing I have to do is start being smart." She opened the door behind her and slipped into the house.

In the rear courtyard, breakfast had been laid out on a table as if the owners had just gone back inside for the teapot. Ping took some fruit and a slice of buttered bread before moving quickly out through the gate into the lane beyond. There, the fantasy was destroyed. From where she stood she could see five dead zorigami, bodies black with buzzing flies, limbs twisted in the final brief moment of agony. Maybe it was the family whose breakfast she was eating. She choked on the bread and spat it into the road. After standing for a second with her eyes closed, Ping crossed the lane and hurried into the next courtyard.

What was left of the house let out onto a main road. From the fire-blackened porch, Ping could see a pile of bright monster armor at the corner and headed in that direction; Scree had left his mark. She moved towards the middle of town, careful now to avoid detection, pausing in shadows when they were available to rest and examine her surroundings. Always there were the sounds of the monsters nearby, just a street or two away but none ever came close enough to threaten her. She hurried on, trying not to think.

Finally, with the sun long gone below the horizon, she arrived at the top of a low hill. The smoking remains of *Rep's Register* made a high mound at the crown. Hardly a thing was left standing, just a single stone arch with a single ribbed column in front. Another column had tumbled to the ground nearby. Ping had seen the arch before, just recently in real life and dozens of times in pictures— she was sure it should have been filled in with a carving-decorated slab of black stone.

Was that Scree's gateway? Right in the middle of the city all this time?

There were three monsters lying dead on the ground but another had come to replace them, leaning against the column and watching the street.

Ping ducked behind the cover of what had once been a pergola and watched the guard. Torchlight flickered on its blue and white armor. It was badly dented and... She noticed a hole in the dark material of the faceplate. And she had never seen one *lean* against anything. She dared to stand up and walk slowly forward.

The monster didn't move.

When she had halved the distance between herself and the arch, creeping forward slowly, Ping could see that the monster was dead. Ping looked nervously around, but could see no immediate threat so she mounted the stairs and climbed over the toppled column. Her feet crunched on shards of black stone. The space locked within the arch was painted a faint, shifting, silvery color. She thought she could see something through it but couldn't be sure. Perhaps a hill? Some trees?

Standing in front of the door, Ping once more wondered what she had to offer Scree. She couldn't fight the monsters when they had their armor and their weapons. She couldn't even carry the weapon as Scree could. She...

Ping turned to examine the blue and white armor leaning nearby. She moved close and stood in front of the monster. The armor was much taller than she was but the monsters themselves weren't all that big at all. "I wonder..." But of course, that left the problem of how to get the armor off the monster without wrecking it. She spun about, found a clock makers shop nearby, as was only to be expected, and hurried through the rubble to the building.

Beyond the facade, the shop had tumbled to the ground but Ping slipped through a narrow gap where a cabinet was holding up the ceiling and poked around in some drawers. It only took her three and a half minutes of searching to find a small leather pouch containing a range of tools. She returned to the monster.

It took almost five and a quarter minutes to get the panel off the top of the bulging back— she counted every second, fearful of being seen. She had to use a small hammer to jamb a screwdriver into the join and lever it up. Then she repeated the process a dozen times until it finally popped free. Once it was done, she removed the top of the black box and used a screwdriver to create a link between the power cable and the one that controlled the opening of the armor. With a hiss of escaping air, the suit split open.

Ping gave a shout of joy before realizing where she was and checking her surroundings. Nobody seemed to have heard. At least, no monsters appeared in the time she watched. So, with a small clap, she moved back to look in the front of the armor. The monster, face ruined and bloody, slouched forward as if ready to fall out at the slightest touch. Cringing, Ping obliged and watched the ugly thing tumble to the ground. Before she had time to give it thought she tied her new tool pouch to her waist and she cleaned thick, dark blood from inside the helmet with a scrap of cloth torn from the alien's breeches. She climbed inside and arranged herself as comfortably as she could amongst the bumpy padding. She half stood, half sat, her feet resting on pedals nearly twenty centimeters off the ground. There was a metal strap that went over the top. She could barely reach the controls in the hand.

But she *could* reach. It might work.

"Now or never." She pressed the appropriate button and held her breath as the suit hissed closed. After a moment, she took a small breath, tasting the air. It was a little stale, slightly strange, but seemed to be fine.

"So, I can get in and out but, unless I 'm looking for a new home, it's no good to me if I can't move it." The armor looked very heavy, but she suspected some type of machinery was involved in the movement. There was only one way to find out.

"Now..." The suit was still leaning against the arch, so she reached carefully backwards with her right arm and pushed against the stone. The suit straightened. It started to topple forward so Ping instinctively stepped forward to compensate and almost fell anyway. With the weight of the suit around her she reacted savagely and, when mechanical assistance arrived, found she was taking a huge step. With a bit of thought and care she got herself standing upright.

She did a little jump of excitement and the suit didn't even attempt the movement.

After walking around the top of the hill and testing the various functions of the suit, Ping decided, once again, *Now or never.*

She turned to face the arch and the silvery air. She took a deep breath and walked slowly through.

It wasn't like she expected. She felt there should be a thunderclap or fireworks if she'd just stepped onto another world. There was nothing at all, though there was no doubting she was no longer on Tiandi. Or at least no part of Tiandi she'd heard of. Her heart was racing.

A harsh sun beat down on her, though she couldn't feel it in the suit. She was standing half way up the side of a steep rocky slope. The 'door' was just silvery light on a cliff face at her back with a wind-smoothed column on either side. There were freshly broken stones on the ground around her, as if the cliff had recently been remodeled. Left and right, the slope continued, curving slightly as if, out beyond the horizon, the two arms would meet once more to tell their stories. A hundred meters below her, the ground suddenly flattened out. Piles of stone, most higher than five meters, dotted the slope and the grassy plain beyond. There were bats on the ground a few kilometers distant.

And closer, Scree was sheltering near one of the huge cairns. He'd seen her entrance, of course, and watched warily. His weapon was on the ground by his side.

Ping wondered what to do next. She hadn't considered the fact that the troll's first instinct would be to kill her. She lowered her left arm slowly, wishing she could wipe the sweat from her face.

Scree rose to his feet.

SCREE ROSE SLOWLY TO HIS FEET, never taking his eyes off the monster. He threw the remains of the disgusting fruit he was eating onto the ground and wiped the juice from his fingers.

The weapon was on the ground. He could get to it before the monster could do him any damage, but last time he'd tried the weapon it hadn't worked. The monster wasn't attacking anyway. It was standing there, both arms pointing at the ground. Just when Scree decided to make the first move, the armor gave a hiss of releasing air and started to crack open.

That a good things? Scree wondered as the panels hinged aside.

About the last thing he expected was to see Ping climbing free of the strange contours of the internal padding.

"Hello, Scree."

Scree grunted and gave a slight smile. He'd taken a weapon from a monster, but hadn't even considered the idea of going further. Not that he would have fitted himself.

"Not bad," he said, going to look into the suit, as if it might somehow be different to the one he'd already seen.

Ping ignored him, fiddling with the faceplate, plucking out shards of broken glass.

She was still working, wiggling pieces loose, when Scree went back and sat down behind the pile of rocks. He wasn't sure if Ping had noticed, but about a kilometer away, down on the floor of the valley, there were at least half a dozen of the giant bats, towering over the few pathetic trees amongst the spiky blue-green grass. He could only assume there were monsters with them and that they'd kill any person they happened to see— troll, zorigami or whatever else.

That just left the question of why they were there, with no city or town in sight and, if Ping got behind cover, no people in sight either.

Scree picked up 'The Gates of Hakahei' and resumed reading. It was a long, slow process.

Ping finally gave up her inspection and moved the armor, hissing and clanking, down into the shade. Scree watched her clump over bushes and grass tussocks like they weren't there. She left a path like a landslide.

30: Untold Landscapes

When she was back out in the daylight again she crouched down by Scree's side. "[Where are we?]" she asked. "Where?"

Scree looked at her and then at the suit of armor. "The gate from Kansu leads to a world called... Nexis."

"Nexis?"

"Yep. And this map thing says thats there are five other gates on this worlds." He didn't know how much she understood, though she seemed to be learning the language quickly enough.

He tried to think and thankfully Ping remained silent.

"It mights be impossible to finds any other gates, no matter how manys there is."

"Found others."

"Yeah, but I had locals to help."

"Find people here."

Scree shook his head. "Have you evens looked at this place? Or did youse just march onto a new world to shows off your new armor?"

The woman did look around then, even rising to her feet as if that might make a difference.

"There's bats out theres in the valley. There's scrub grass in the valley. And arounds the edge, over the tops of that hill, there's forest that I reckon a burning cat couldn't find a way through." He had heard animals in there though— lots of them— he just hadn't found a way of moving more than a few meters down the slope. He'd used his sword to hack his way into the scrub but it just seemed to get thicker the further he went.

"Yes, but..."

Scree sighed and went back to reading his book. He was struggling over each of the words, but knew that the only hope lay somewhere among them.

He read more than an entire, head-pounding page, before he found what he needed.

"'There are six Ohoga Gates on the world of Nexis,'" Scree read, "'and unlike the gates of other worlds, they seem to be located with some sort of thought in the mind of whichever god was in charge. The gates all lie with in the boundaries of Tiringil, a large, circular valley almost fifty kilometers across.'"

Scree laughed. He'd narrowed down the search already. He was within fifty kilometers of all the gates on the world— surely he could find one of them. But... he thought about the area he'd have to cover. It was a lot of area, even without being able to do the math, but he figured he'd start by going around the edge of the valley and worry about more after that.

Ping was watching him, sitting silently with her back against the pile of rocks that may once have been a building— a tower, perhaps. Though if that was the case then why there was no sign of outbuildings, and why it had collapsed inwards was beyond understanding.

"All the gates is somewhere in this valley," Scree said.

"Why looked another world? What wrong this?" Ping fumble through in Scree's language.

"You stills haven't looked?" Neither the monsters nor the landscape bothered him in the short term. They hadn't really bothered him on the other worlds either, really. But he figured that if he couldn't find a place without them, he'd have to kill them. He could keep killing them one at a time, but they'd probably get him eventually. So he needed help. Nobody he'd met so far was going to help, although if Ping could use the armor...

Those strange humans would be able to help, he decided. But when he'd met them he hadn't known he needed a new pack. And after he fell out of the sky into Ping's world there was no going back.

So he'd find more worlds, and maybe the people who built the star-ships would be on one of them.

Scree looked up at the searing blue of the sky wondering what other worlds were out there. Was each star of the night sky a world? Or perhaps they were suns circled by any number of worlds.

"Let's go then, if youse coming."

"You going let me come?"

"You knows how to use that suit?"

Ping nodded but didn't look sure.

"There are enough bats down in the valley to bring a lots of monsters. Too many. Just remembers, you have to shoot the back pack things to make the monsters explode."

"What?" Ping was staring to understand so much that Scree was surprised when she *didn't* understand.

He got his weapon onto his arm, then went and pointed it at the armor's back. "Kaboom." Then he pointed it at the front and shook his head. "Nothing."

She didn't sound very confident, but there was nothing Scree could do about that. He'd just hope she did whatever needed to be done. If she didn't, she was no use to him at all. "You just listen to me and do what I say without complaining and without asking questions and I'll try to keep us both alive."

"Yes."

"Right, let's go. Leave the armor for now."

"But..."

"That's a question."

Ping nodded. "Where we go?"

"We's got to go back to get another weapon. This one don't work any more."

He would've done it himself before coming through the gate but he didn't understand half of what Ping had done.

When Scree returned to the strange desolate world a while later with the new weapon on his arm he looked in one direction, then the other. In the distance, barely visibly through the heat haze, there seemed to be a mountain. That was the only difference he could see that was worth noting, and that was as good a reason as anything else.

"What now?" Ping asked.

Scree went to her armor, turned on the 'voices button' and changed one of the settings. He turned the knob that... well, he didn't know exactly what it did. But if the voices of the monsters were in the basement of his mind, he changed the setting so Ping would be in the attic.

"This way."

"What about bats?"

"How long does you wants to sit there? And there's trees up here anyways. Half a kilometer and we'lls be under cover." He looked at her and realized she hadn't understood. He pointed to the trees. She seemed to get the point and rushed to get into her armor.

When the suit hissed shut, Scree started talking and nudged the buttons in his mind. Eventually, he heard a surprised response from his companion.

"<Scree?>"

<Yeps.> He was pretty sure nobody else could hear them.

"<How?>"

Scree shrugged. <Come on.>

Scree wondered if the valley had ever been much different to its present state. Rocks and gravel littered the ground for the most part. Tough, twisted bushes clung to the hard, dry soil between and up ahead, trees had managed to find a foothold. Unlike with Salisha, there was nothing to show that a city might once have thrived here. The strange piles of stone probably hadn't been buildings— where they'd come from was anybody's guess. Out on the valley floor nothing was any different. Gravel, rocks, scrub, and dark, crooked trees. It all might have been there for millennia.

Scree strode across the slope and Ping, the slight tilt giving her a limp, struggled to keep up.

"Hows you learn my language?" Scree asked her, speaking out loud to fill the silence, though it was his mind she would hear.

No animals added background noise to the day. Not even a breeze to scrape at the vegetation and stir the dust into whispering life.

"<Don't know. Just seem... right. Had friend spoke another language I never learn.>"

He didn't understand much of what she was saying— she probably didn't know the proper words so she just used her own— but he could understand enough to work out what she meant. "I heard lots a languages. Never learned none of thems." He gave a grunt of laughter. "Suppose I never spent much time listening though." Ping probably wouldn't find that funny at all if she gave it some thought.

"<Well, I listen you and...>"

So Scree continued to talk. He didn't say anything important. He didn't talk about himself. He spoke of the places he'd seen in his travels. Cities and deserts. Mountains and oceans. Untold landscapes, and none of them had resembled the valley he now found himself in.

When they reached the trees, the thin shade offered was a small respite from the sun. Scree still saw no animals, though this was where they should be, if anywhere. He'd have loved to squash a little stinging bug, just to know there was some life about, other than he and Ping and their enemies out on the plain. The ground between the trees was bare and hard, but there were no paths. Nothing to say they were heading in the right direction, or in any *significant* direction at all.

The slope continued to curve eastwards. The hills steadily grew upwards to meet the mountain. Thirty kilometers, he guessed. A lifetime at Ping's pace. So he trudged and he talked, and the one was as tedious as the other.

Well before noon the talking and the slow pace became too much. Scree grunted in disgust. "Keeps going this way," he said. "Calls if you see anything strange."

Ping protested, saying it'd be safer if they stayed together. He ignored her. Probably *would* be safer for her, but not for him, he guessed.

<I could a beens there by now.> Though that was far from true.

He'd been talking out loud for so long that he'd forgotten Ping was in his mind, listening to his thoughts if he didn't guard them.

The zorigami mumbled an apology. "<Going fast as can. I leave the suit behind if want.>"

But Scree knew she wouldn't leave the armor behind. And at this stage he wouldn't ask her to. He swore to himself, making sure it stayed private this time, and surged away.

<Just keep going this way. I won't be far.> He didn't think there'd be much point in going too far, not unless he intended to continue on his own. He'd only have to come back for Ping, and he doubted there was much to see beyond what he'd already seen.

Might finds a cat I can stomps on. But if there were no bugs to torture, he had slim hope of finding a cat.

31: The Doorway

THE MORNING DAWNED clear and cool, and Tuki discovered he was alone. Back up the river though, a large crowd had gathered. Nasinwa was there, standing on the little stage again with his hand in the air. The breeze was blowing into the old man's face, so when he finally started to talk, Tuki could not hear his words. He did hear the boos of the crowd, however, then watched as the captive man from the previous night was tied to the rough bark of the old, leaning oak tree.

He rose to his feet to watch, but a moment later turned away in horror as Keyman Kuwisa pulled forth a little stick with tails and started to beat the man's bare back.

Tuki turned to look again, as if drawn, and saw the blood striping the man's skin. The Keyman hit him again, and again. Ten lashes, the Councilor had said, but to Tuki the beating seemed to last forever.

If they would do this to one of their own, he thought, *what would they have done to me if Sha Yukima had not intervened?*

He did not want to stay with these people. The previous evening he had thought the only thing keeping him in the city was that Nasinwa had the skyglass. But now he had the 'glass himself and was still there.

Now it was only the will of Poti that held him. *Can I ignore the wishes of the Goddess?* Tuki ran his fingers over the smooth surface of the skyglass, gazing into it as he thought.

Remembering some of the things he had learned about the skyglass, Tuki centered the view on Kiva and shifted back slightly. Almost immediately, he smiled. *I followed the meteor to get here,* he thought, though he no longer believed that it was truly a shooting star, *but there are no meteors here now.* A hundred and nine yellow comets were clustered at various points around the world, but the sky above Payota was clear. If the Goddess had led him to this spot, then She was now leading him on to somewhere else. *And if She did not lead me here?* Then it did not matter.

Without another thought he turned on his heel and started away from the river, the cool, smooth globe back in the sack at his waist.

Once he found a main road, Tuki checked the skyglass, holding it up to the bright, angled light. He wanted to go south, back to the desert, but there were no bats at all in that direction. If he was doing the Goddess' work he had to keep going. If he was not doing the Goddess' work then he was all alone in the world of man. Sighing, he decided to continue in the general direction he had been travelling before being waylaid in Payota. He set off towards the north, happy to be running again. To be under the sky and moving. He smiled as he ran.

Apparently the drawing of blood was great entertainment for humans, for he saw none of them as he made his way between what remained of the buildings. Beyond the city, farmers worked their fields as if nothing had changed. An old man tied sacks of grain before someone younger heaved them into the back of a wagon. A boy sat on a rock watching over a herd of docile beasts. A woman was stuffing straw into to the breeches of a straw man on a stick. On the hill, the city still smoldered.

Tuki passed by all these people and none made comment. They continued about their work as if they saw giants every day or trolls did not scare them. Or perhaps they merely did not care anymore. Their lives had been hard before and were set to get all the harder now.

Sometime later, after trotting for several kilometers without sight of another living creature besides roving beasts from the town, Tuki started to run quicker. Councilor Nasinwa and Keyman Kuwisa would have noticed his absence, and he doubted they would be pleased. The thought of the tailed stick lashing his back pushed him to speeds he would have thought unwise at any other time. The beauty of the landscape meant nothing to him now. Just more fields to run past, more hills to run over, more lakes to run around. Tuki saw nothing except the road beneath his sandals and the tails in his mind.

Tuki was exhausted when night finally came. He stumbled to a halt where the main road curved away to the east and a lesser way continued north.

As he hunched over, breathing deeply, he examined the two paths, wondering which way to go. In the end he decided that it did not matter: one way was as unlikely as the other. So he went north again.

Almost immediately the lesser path started to rise, and over the top of the hill a forest cast its protective shadow in the gathering gloom. He walked down the slope and into the darkness. His feet and legs were hurting. He was more used to running on the shifting sands of the desert than unforgiving solid ground. He stopped to rest again. Sitting in the middle of the path, he rubbed his feet and waited for his eyes to adjust. Soon he could see the outline of the trees but not much more.

He pulled the skyglass out into the open. In the soft radiance of the Goddess's attention he could make out the packed earth of the road and the grassy edges. He stood with a grunt and strode forward with renewed confidence but little energy.

Before long, the road turned abruptly and dipped down into a small hollow where a farmer's hovel crouched beside a narrow, frothing stream. Tuki stood where the road ended and bare earth started. He could see a candle burning within the shack, and movement. He dared not go closer. The beast herder and the sack sewer could inform everyone that they had indeed seen the *troll*, but their testimony would not help as much as that of the owner of the hovel.

Tuki climbed back out of the hollow and turned away from the road. A narrow path led up the side of the hill and through a narrow gap between hills. Beyond, true darkness gathered in a long narrow valley. Tuki sighed as he started forward and held the skyglass aloft to light his way.

"[Stop where you are.]"

Tuki continued for several steps before he even realized that he had heard a voice in the darkness. He did not know the words, but the tone was similar to that of Keyman Kuwisa. He stopped.

"[Jesus, he's bloody huge,]" somebody whispered.

"[Shut up, private. And stay down.]"

"[Sorry, sir.]"

Tuki looked back over his shoulder, wondering if he should run. Wondering if he *could* run. Wondering how far he would get. His legs ached, and he felt ready to fall asleep where he stood.

"[Can you understand me?]"

Tuki still held the skyglass above his head. It seemed he could see everything apart from the men who spoke. The meaning of their words eluded him.

"[Where's Dongoske? He's in the thick of the action, isn't he?]"

The sound of someone approaching, quickly but quietly.

"[Here, sir.]"

"[See if you can talk to this guy.]"

"[Big dude, isn't he! Looks a bit Polynesian with those tattoos.]"

"[Airman!]"

"[Sorry, sir.]" A pause. "Can you understand me?"

Tuki nodded his head slowly. "Yes."

"What is your name? What are you doing here?"

"My name is Tuki. I am running." He did not understand every word the stranger said but he understood enough.

"[He speaks... well, it is a mixture of several languages, sir. Mainly Shoshone, I think, with a lot of other stuff thrown in.]"

"[Don't talk to me, Airman. Talk to him.]"

"[Yes, sir. Of course.]" The unseen stranger cleared his throat. "Why are you running, brother? Where do you run to?"

"I run because it is quicker than walking, and I do not know where I run to."

"[What did he say, Airman?]"

Tuki heard the man sigh before speaking to the other, unseen man.

"[He says he is running to a place he doesn't know, sir.]"

"[Shit, that's all we need. Forest bloody Gump.]"

"[At least we haven't shot him yet, sir.]"

"[Shut up, Dongoske.]"

"[Sir.]"

"[Ask him if he'll follow us.]"

"Tuki, I am called Ben Dongoske. I am a Senior Airman in my nation's army. Will you come with me to our camp?"

"Where is your camp? And why would I want to go there?"

"It is down in the valley, in a cave. We have food and water there. You can rest."

"I can rest here."

"We can't let you. You must come down into our camp, or you must turn around and go back the way you came."

Tuki looked over his shoulder, as if Keyman Kuwisa and his men might rush out of the darkness at that very moment to take the skyglass away. The bruises on his face and body still throbbed.

"You have food and water?"

"We do."

"Do you eat the flesh of beasts?"

"We do, but we have fruit as well, if you would prefer."

"And I can continue on my way tomorrow after I have rested?"

The man paused. "If you wish it, we will take you to the other end of the valley."

Tuki looked behind again. He thought he was safe from the people of Payota, but he was not sure. These strangers hadn't accused him of being a troll or threatened him in any way. Or perhaps they were the fearsome trolls, themselves, and not so fearsome after all. Perhaps these were the people the Mother Blower was leading him to.

"I will come."

"Good. Good." The man stepped into the soft light of the skyglass. He was dark skinned and dressed from head to toe in multihued green clothes, allowing him to blend with the forest and the night. He wore a glass screen over his eyes. His mouth was covered as well. "Come on then. Let's get you some food, hey."

Tuki followed the man down into the valley. He did not see anyone else beside the trail.

-oOo-

Tuki didn't move. He examined the doorway then turned his attention to the room.

The small chamber had humans carved on the walls in relief. Bright lights stood on tall poles.

A dozen men, all clothed in strange noisy white suits and with clear screens covering their faces, worked around him. He couldn't begin to guess what they were doing. Glowing windows looked onto nothing, but showed rows of little symbols. They reminded him of the squares in the skyglass. There were boxes that talked with voices that crackled and hissed, and other boxes that steamed when they were opened. Men adjusted knobs and stared through tubes. Some babbled to each other, or muttered under their breath.

Standing on his own, Tuki watched as everyone cast furtive glances in his direction. Every time he turned their way, the men turned back to continue with their work. It seemed a long time before anyone spoke to him again. A man, large for a human, came through the silvery doorway, shifting uncomfortably in his white suit. Ben Dongoske was with him.

"This is General Hilliard," Dongoske said. "He is our leader here."

"[Hello,]" General Hilliard held out his hand, and Tuki looked at it until it was lowered again. "[We'll be able to let you through the door in about five minutes, and after that we will have to do some tests. Medical stuff.]"

Dongoske translated, but it made little difference to Tuki. *Medical tests?* He shrugged his shoulders and waited. General Hilliard moved purposefully away to speak to a man holding a talking box.

"Where do you live, Tuki? Close by?"

"No. I live many days to the south. It is many years since any moai has visited the lands of man. It is much different than what I expected."

Dongoske laughed. "I'm sure the lands of man on your world are not normally like this," he said.

A third person joined them. Though clad head to toe like everyone else, the newcomer was unmistakably female behind the helmet's transparent faceplate.

"[We're ready for him now.]"

"Okay then. Tuki, we're going through."

"Very well." He followed his companions. "What is that?" he asked as he stepped through the silver sheen. "What is it for?"

"We don't really know the answer to either of those questions, Tuki. Maybe the two worlds need to be divided, or something."

"The two worlds?"

"I'm sorry, you don't even know that, do you? This door leads between worlds. Between your world and the world of my people."

Tuki gasped. "You come from another world?" Beyond the shimmering doorway was a tiny room with reflective walls made mainly from wonderful glass. Beyond that, a large room with stone shelters in the corners. They went quickly through another door and entered a room with polished walls and a big bed in the middle. More of the windowed boxes lined the walls.

I am on another world? He tried to look at everything, as if something in the cave would reveal to him his new location. But of course it was just stone, and a dozen more strangers gathered around a dozen more strange objects. "What is your world called?" He took a little step forward and quickly turned his eyes to the skyglass.

"Earth."

Tuki raised the skyglass. It was still glowing softly.

General Hilliard, nearby once more, took an involuntary step backward. Another man, larger than any other but still not as large as Tuki, stepped forward. Somebody gasped. Everyone was watching.

"[Is it a weapon, Airman?]"

"[I don't think so... How the hell should I know? Jesus... Watch him.]"

Tuki ignored them. "Earth," he said.

Nothing happened.

"Your world has no other name?"

Dongoske shook his head.

So Tuki said the word that would center the view on his location. In the glass the colors shifted, transformed, until a new globe was showing. Huge oceans dominated strange landmasses.

"[Oh my God.]"

Tuki spared a glance for Dongoske before looking at the skyglass again. "Back. Back." And the world was just a small sphere in the center of the 'glass with a single moon showing and the yellow spots of meteors.

"You have many meteors here." Over two hundred. "The Goddess' voice is loud."

"They are not meteors, Tuki. They are starships. They are vehicles, like wagons, that fly between the stars."

Tuki nodded slowly. "I thought they might be something like that, but was not sure. Could it still be a warning from the Mother Blower, do you think, even though they are not shooting stars? The Goddess works in mysterious ways."

"A warning of what?"

"Of the giant bats. They attacked Payota with eggs of fire and hatched dozens of hard shelled babies."

"The gods do work in mysterious ways, Tuki. We can never hope to understand all that they tell us."

Tuki smiled at the human, but Dongoske had already turned to General Hilliard.

"[Sir, the other world is being attacked by the bats as well. Tuki saw the mother ships in his 'skyglass'.]"

"[The first thing we do is get that damn thing off him so we can work out what the hell it is.]"

"[I don't think he'll let us have it, sir. It has some serious religious significance.]"

"[Isn't everything that's religious serious?]" Hilliard grunted. "[All right then, let's just see if we can get him unconscious, and then we can do what we need to do.]"

"[As ever, sir.]" Dongoske turned back to Tuki. "Tuki we have to let our doctors see you, to make sure we don't have any illnesses that can harm you. And to make sure you don't have any that can harm us."

"I am fit and healthy, Airman Dongoske."

"I'm sure, but it's like the monsters invading. Because the humans of... Payota, was it? Because they've never seen the monsters before, they can't beat them. I may have a disease that does not harm me, but because you have never seen it before, your body will not know how to fight it."

Tuki watched the other man carefully, but it was hard to see his face properly because of the coverings he wore. Tuki suddenly wondered if the monsters he'd seen in his vision, the ones riding the bats, did not have hard colorful skins after all. Perhaps, like these humans, they dressed in protective clothing. And if that was the case, who was to say what the creatures inside looked like? Perhaps they were just humans after all.

Tuki shook his head. "No." If he'd been thinking properly earlier and not letting his fear control him, he would not have entered the valley in the first place. If he'd been thinking, he would have run south after leaving Payota, towards Danyon Ford.

"Pardon?"

"No. Your doctors cannot touch me."

"But..."

"I wish to go back to my world."

Dongoske turned to look at his leader. "[General, Tuki wishes to go home.]"

"[What the hell did you say to him?]"

"[Nothing, sir. Perhaps he just knows humans too well.]"

"[Well, tell him he can't go. We need to study him and that crystal ball of his and, if we must, we'll use force to get what we want.]"

"[Sir, we shot the last aliens we saw here. Do we really want to do that again? Do you think we'll be able to overpower this guy?]"

"[We have technology on our side, Airman.]"

"[And he has the right on his.]"

General Hilliard sighed. "[Don't you think I know that, Airman? Do you think I want to do it?]"

"[Sir, I —]"

"[We are talking about the survival of the human race here, Airman. The bat-aliens seem pretty stupid at the moment, but if they ever start to think we could be in real trouble.]"

Tuki could not understand a word the two men were saying but thought he understood well enough anyway. He started backing towards the door, and his suspicions were confirmed when two men moved to block his route.

"[Airman Dongoske, tell him we won't attempt to take the ball from him, but he must allow us to conduct tests on him.]"

"[Tests, sir?]"

The General sighed. "[We aren't talking lab-rat tests here, Airman. We're talking medical tests to make sure that neither he nor we will be harmed by our interaction.]"

"[Very well, sir.]"

"[I wasn't asking, Airman.]"

Airman Dongoske spoke again, and Tuki stood silently while he listened. "Do I have your word? And the word of the General?" Tuki did not think that the word of these humans would hold them to anything, but still he asked. "Do you swear on the moons and the stars?"

"[Sir, he's asking us to give our word.]"

"[So give it.]"

"[I think he'd take it very seriously and, if we broke our word, would basically never trust us again. In any situation. Ever. He's friendly at the moment, and he has knowledge that we don't have and may never acquire on our own.]"

"[Give it, Airman. Swear on whatever he asks.]"

Tuki watched as Dongoske sighed and turned back to face him. He knew that the Airman would swear, and he knew that General Hilliard would break the trust. But there was nothing he could do except as they asked.

"Tuki, you have my word. And the word of the General."

Tuki sighed, himself, then. Only days amongst humans and he knew them already. "Very well. What must I do?"

"Just lie down on this bed. It will be a little small, but that should be okay."

Tuki moved to the bed indicated by the Airman and lay down. His legs hung over the end, and it was too narrow by far, but he said nothing. He stared at the red stone of the ceiling and clutched the skyglass in his hand.

"Now, we're going to give you a needle so we can take some blood and study it. It may hurt a little bit, but only a very little. And it won't last long."

"They wish to stick that in me?"

"If you like, we can stick a needle in somebody else, first, on the other side of that window, to show that it will do you no harm."

"That would be good." Though he knew it would make no difference. With a last look at the skyglass, he muttered the word that switched it off then handed it to Airman Dongoske.

32: The Same World

PING PAUSED HALFWAY UP THE SLOPE, sweating in the confines of the armor. Three full days in there and she was starting to forget what fresh air tasted like. Even with the clear face plate missing it was stuffy and claustrophobic inside. Her hips ached, her bones rattled with every step.

Scree was out of sight, around the corner of the pile of rocks and probably already settled into that half-conscious state he called sleeping. The moon had risen hours ago, but he had insisted on continuing in darkness.

Ping twiddled with the control on the armor's voice throwing unit and listened as Scree told her that he had indeed decided to stop for the night. The troll had been talking almost constantly since turning on the voice machine, using gestures to help make things understood. Now, the two of them could hold sensible conversations on almost any subject, though she doubted it sounded pretty.

At the top of the slope Ping paused again before carefully making her way to the leeward side of the rocks. With a sigh of relief she opened the suit and stepped out into the cool night breeze.

"How much food we have?" she asked.

"Some." Scree was already hunting through his pack. After four seconds he produced a hunk of meat rolled in drying leaves and threw it down on the ground for Ping to get when she was ready. He also found a piece of yellow fruit and offered it in the same manner.

"Is meat still right?"

"Don't knows. But it can't be any worse than the fruits."

"I still think fruit be poisonous." They'd found the fruit the day before, growing on a ground-hugging bush along the edges of a shallow stream. The water in the stream had been salty and brackish, and had only gotten worse after a day in the troll's canteen. The fruit was tart and mushy.

"It ain't poisoned."

"How know?"

"It ain't. Horrible don't means bad." Scree bit into some fruit, through the leathery skin and into the juicy centre. By the way he acted, it might almost have been his food of choice. And, as with so many other times, he seemed to read Ping's thoughts. "You gots to eat any food you can gets, Ping. Yeah, this stuffs is horrible, but it might be better than what you gets tomorrow."

Ping finished her nightly stretch and lowered herself gingerly to the ground. She took up the fruit and, closing her eyes, took a timid bite from the skin. Normally, she would not have gone past the first bite on the first occasion she had tried the fruit, but she trusted Scree more than she had ever trusted another person in her life. And that was the strangest thing of all.

Long ago Ping came to the opinion that her companion was a thief and a murderer and lacked almost any moral graces. He would have sold his own mother if he thought there was some advantage to be gained. But, since he didn't care what anyone else thought of him, since he was almost completely fearless, since he felt that he had nothing to lose, the troll was completely honest.

Above all else, Ping considered herself to be a clockmaker. In her heart, in her soul, that was her life. In *his* soul Scree was a survivor. So, though he might sell his mother for an apple, he would not sell her for an *orchard*, because an orchard was worthless to him.

But she remembered him once saying that he'd never known his mother.

Ping discovered that she'd finished her piece of fruit and almost wished for some more. The meat Scree had given to her would not go close to filling the hole that was left in her stomach.

"Do know what look for?" she asked.

Scree didn't answer straight away. Ping saw him watching as she unwrapped her meat. She had seen that look before. She started to tear away little morsels, fingers shaking, suddenly not hungry at all. But she continued to eat, for she did not know what she would get tomorrow.

The suit of monster armor had kept Scree by her side, for she could be useful, but those thoughts were starting to fade. The monsters' bats had circled over the center of the valley since they'd crossed from Tiandi, occasionally settled in groups out on the valley floor. But they never came within a couple of kilometers of Ping and Scree, so all Ping and her armor did now was slow him down.

"I've got no ideas what I'm looking for," he said eventually. "But I'll know it whens I see it. You probably wills too." Scree leaned back against the rocks, his splinted arm resting on his lap, and closed his eyes. "Your watch first. I need to get some real sleep." And with that, he fell asleep.

Ping watched her companion. His breathing was even, his face relaxed. She had never seen him completely at rest before, but decided that if she were to whisper the words 'look out' he would be awake in an instant. There were no grey areas in the troll's life. Black or white or not worth seeing.

For a moment, Ping thought of finding a comfortable spot on the ground, but was worried she'd fall asleep as quickly as her companion. And the change in the rhythm of her breathing was likely to wake him. So instead she carefully climbed the side of the rock pile. Near the top, she stopped and found a smooth seat from where she could look out over the valley, but would not be silhouetted against the strange stars.

She could see nothing. She could hear nothing beyond the moaning of the wind.

She was still sitting in that spot watching the night when Scree rose several hours later and stretched his broad, bare shoulders.

"Sleep nows. I'll watch."

But as Ping climbed down from her eyrie Scree sank to the ground and fell back to sleep in an instant. She settled down not far from him and prepared to watch the coming of he dawn.

-o◯o-

Ping woke with a start, as was usual these days, and stretched, moving slightly as she became acutely aware of her uncomfortable position. With a grunt of effort, she sat up, shading her eyes against the early morning sun. Then she remained still for a moment, clinging to the edge of her sleep, before climbing to her feet.

Scree was not where she'd last seen him, and for a moment she panicked. But a quick survey of the area found him crouching on top of the rocks, monster gun in hand.

Ping opened her mouth to call to him. Before she could draw breath, Scree raised his weapon, suddenly tense. He swore and rose to his feet. His shoulder bucked as the weapon let out a long stream of crackling energy.

On the edge of decision, Ping did not move. She stood silently, looking at her companion as he cursed and fired his weapon. Then, making up her mind, she headed for her armor. In moments she was in and stumping around to get the view she desired.

When Ping finally saw what the troll was firing at she froze again. A huge black bat had alighted on the ground not far away and armored monsters were stepping down from the outer two of the three metal canisters. Scree's concern stemmed from the fact that he could not easily take aim at his enemies' bulging backs. He fired maniacally, to little effect. Slowly, more monsters were coming into view, making their way towards the rocks, raising weapons as they went.

Ping looked at her own left arm, but she was hardly in a better position than Scree was and...

"Well, I had better move then." She didn't know if she meant it until she took the first step.

Ping turned and started to make her way around the front of the bat, keeping her distance as much as the terrain and her urgency allowed. The great beast watched her with a huge, dark eye, but made no threatening movement.

It seemed to be a lifetime before Ping found herself in a position that allowed her to fire upon the enemies' backs, but not many more of them had descended to the ground. All of those that were outside were firing towards the top of the boulders. Some were making their way carefully around to the high side to get a better view. It would not be long. While he was being fired upon, all Scree could do was hide.

Biting her lip, Ping raised her arm and pointed towards the back of the nearest monster. She took a deep breath and pressed the button to work the weapon. The suit jolted slightly with the power and her aim went awry. It took a few seconds to concentrate her shot in the right place and long agonizing seconds after that before the suit erupted into flames.

With a short laugh of triumph, Ping quickly turned to attack another enemy. She shouted again as the second went up. It was not until she was attacking the third, and the others were turning in her direction, that she realized she was crying. She did not cheer any more. She bit her lip and tried to keep her concentration.

On the top of the rock pile, Scree surged into view the moment the monsters turned their backs to him, firing with cold, deadly accuracy. Ping turned her attention to the monsters still making their way toward the top of the slope while the troll picked off those heading for her. The monsters' arms were raised and the bolts of energy sizzled through the air. Ping flinched as the first attacks rocked her backwards but, like her enemies, she was safe as long as she faced the threat head on. She just hoped that Scree could kill them before they came too close. She took a few steps back.

Tears streaming down her face, lip bleeding, Ping finished off the last of the monsters moving to attack her companion and turned her weapon against those that were still making their way down to the ground. She hoped not many more of the monsters were inside the canisters.

Some of her attackers realized they were being attacked from behind and turned. Ping brought them down before they could raise their weapons high enough to attack Scree in his unprotected position.

The monsters did not stand a chance.

When finally the last of them was dead and the bat had surged back into the air with a storm of wings, Ping lowered her arm and stayed where she was. On the rock pile, Scree gave a whoop of joy and brandished his weapon in the air. His voice crackled in her ear. Ping didn't really listen to what he said, but she got the point.

After a few minutes, Scree rushed down from the rocks. He stalked around, grunting and shouting at the morning sky.

Eventually Ping started to feel some of his pleasure as well. She had finally struck back at the monsters herself. They had killed her friends and countrymen while she'd watched. Without a large amount of luck she would have been amongst the dead herself. Now she had shown them that the zorigami were not all going to wait to die. She tried a small smile, but tears still welled in her eyes.

She pushed the button to open the suit and stepped out into the morning. After the confines of the armor the sun and warm breeze were a welcome reprieve.

Scree rushed towards her, talking quickly. A few meters away he stopped and stared.

For the first time Ping noticed that her clothes were soaked with sweat, clinging to her body. Scree had noticed. That was obvious enough.

Suddenly, Ping was afraid. The way the troll was looking at her. His face was flushed, possibly from the excitement of the fight, possibly not. His breathing was still erratic. The armored arm hissed and he tossed it away as he shrugged out of his pack.

Ping took a step backwards, shaking. The suit was not far away. She turned and ran. She only had to take three steps but they seemed to take a lifetime. She could hear Scree behind her.

With a sob of fear she almost threw herself into the armor. She flicked the switch that closed the panels. Her hands were shaking uncontrollably.

The troll reached the suit before it closed, but even with his strength he could do nothing to stop it.

Ping stared into his wild eyes as he wrenched at the slowly closing panels.

The troll had to snatch his fingers away at the last moment lest they be crushed. He glanced around and quickly went to collect his sword. Ping took an involuntary step back.

"You knows that armor can't stop me."

Ping nodded weakly. "But you're supposed to protect me," Ping said, watching Scree through the broken faceplate.

"Who says?" he growled in reply. He was staring at her, teeth grinding, hand flexing on the hilt of the sword. "Nobody ever said that."

"It's the way it works, Scree." She wanted to wipe the sweat and tears from her face but could not do so in the armor. She worried about accidentally pressing buttons with her shaking hands. "I do things for you and you do things for me."

"Maybe that's how it works in your world, but not in mine."

"But we're in the same world, Scree. I help you and you help me. That's the deal."

Then again, she realized, he had protected her for a long time and what had she done for him in return? She'd slowed him down and eaten his food. He would have found the next door by now if he'd been on his own. He would've been sitting on a new world with fresh fruit and clean water.

I should have splinted his arm properly. I should have cooked his meat. I should have been useful.

As Ping watched, holding her breath, she saw the fire receding from his eyes. She licked her lips as the point of the troll's sword lowered. He muttered something about a deal. Then he snatched up his pack and his monster gun and strode away along the side of the hill.

Ping stayed where she was, breathing deeply and wondering what to do. She was crying harder than ever. She couldn't stop.

KEEBLE RACED DOWN THE STAIRS of the plane and onto the floor of the huge shed.

The men on the second flight hadn't spoken to him at all. They weren't nearly as friendly as the others. Normally, being stuck in his seat with minimal talk would have driven Keeble to distraction, but with all the information swirling through his mind he'd had more than enough to keep occupied.

On the ground again, he took the chance to examine the wing to see if it was the same shape as the last one. What a marvel that such a simple idea could be the secret to flight. He ran his hand along the flaps, felt the heat radiating from the engine. He was left on his own for several minutes before one of the men came to collect him. Then he was led across to where Kim and Meledrin waited near a normal sized door that looked out of place amidst the otherwise huge scale of the shed.

"[Where are we?]" Kim asked a stony faced dwarf.

Keeble couldn't understand her, so he touched the door to see if he could work out what type of metal it was.

"[Groom Lake,]" the dwarf replied.

"[Yeah? Great.]"

"[Area 51.]"

"[Oh.]" Kim looked around as if some startling revelation had suddenly made everything clear. Keeble looked around the shed as well, but everything still looked the same as it had a moment ago. Three small planes, smaller even than the one they had arrived in, were partly stripped down. Keeble wanted to go and look, but he knew he wouldn't be allowed. A little room hung suspended from the wall at the back. Fields of green canvas had been pushed up into mountains by piles of unseen items beneath.

A talking box crackled, and one of the agents opened the door to usher Keeble and his companions through. Keeble went last hoping to examine their surroundings. There wasn't a lot of point. The heat of a desert hit him, and he saw Meledrin wilt at the onslaught, but that was about as interesting as it got. There were a couple of dun-colored sheds nearby to match the one he had just exited, and an up thrust of dun-colored hills beyond them. Between the two was a large, flat expanse of nothing. Dun-colored. Inside had been better.

Nearby, there was a big, black car with a sliding door on the side. He was bustled into the vehicle and felt it starting to move, though the windows had been blanked out and he couldn't see through. The soldiers were suddenly fierce looking and serious behind their dark spectacles.

Keeble was uncomfortable.

He glanced across to Kim and noticed that she didn't seem her usual self either. Meledrin looked as she always did, calm and serious. Keeble spared a moment to sneer at her and then went back to worrying. Normally he would've talked to lessen his unease, but who was he to talk to? Meledrin? The dwife stared straight ahead, her copper-colored hair a stark contrast to everything else in the car. Keeble sneered again and turned to face the front.

When the car finally stopped, Keeble was ready to jump out, but nobody else moved. He tried to look as calm as Meledrin, but as the minutes dragged by he began to worry.

"What's happening?" he asked. He couldn't imagine a set of the colored lights out in the middle of the desert to hold up the traffic.

Finally, the van started to move again.

"[What were we waiting for?]" Kim asked.

"[The van was hit by about three dozen different forms of waves to kill any bacteria we were carrying. We're now in a totally secure, totally clean area. If we don't want something getting into or out of this place, then there's no way that it'll happen.]"

"[Supposedly. How do you know all of your waving can kill the germs those two are carrying?]"

"[You don't know anything about the measures we take.]"

"[Do you think Keeble couldn't break any of your mechanical security systems?]"

"[That little medieval rustic?]"

Whatever Kim and the dwarf were talking about was apparently funny, to the dwarf at least. But Keeble sat glumly. He knew they were now underground, he could feel it in his bones, but he couldn't *see*. He was sure he could hear the hum of electricity. There was also the lower pitched hum of the rubber tires on concrete, with a tap-tap, every now and then when they crossed a join. And the rumble of the engine, spitting out oil fumes like they would last forever. The caves were slipping past without him seeing a single piece of stone.

With everything else he knew of these dwarves, he guessed that any caves would be amazing.

Just when Keeble could stand it no longer, the car came to a stop and the door slid open. A big, black-skinned dwarf stood outside, muscles bulging out of a green shirt with no sleeves. His small, dark eyes watched Keeble for a moment, before he looked both directions along the side of the car and motioned for everyone to come out.

"[General Hilliard is waiting for you down in Room 34,]" the big dwarf said.

One of the dwarves from the car nodded and led the way through a metal door that slid open automatically at their approach. Keeble stopped without going through.

It was a long time since he had been near natural, solid stone, and he felt its presence dancing along his nerve endings. He hadn't realized that he had missed it so much.

The walls of the tunnel were as smooth as the blade of an axe. He ran his fingers along a vein of quartz running though the pale red of the stone. He could hardly feel that the quartz was there.

"Can these dwarves Sing?" Keeble asked Meledrin. She ignored him. "Ask Kim if her people have any knowledge of Rock Singing." He could feel his own Song, like the sound made by the magical gate, building in his mind, unbidden and uncontrollable.

"I have a Song!" It was a shocking thought. He leaned against the wall. "I have a Song."

But Meledrin asked Kim something then said, "Kim says that her people do indeed have knowledge of rock singing."

That explained it then. But the cave must be ancient, for only a whisper of magic still clung to the stone. No dwarf from Sherindel would ever have let magic do the bulk of the labor, needing the feel of tools in their hands to feel that true work was being done, but the strength of the Earth's Singers could not be denied. Keeble laid his hand flat on the wall. With the Song in his mind, he could feel the very presence of the stone.

"Ask her if we will get to meet a Hummer. Or even a Singer."

"Kim says that it is not likely that any singers will be in this area."

"Oh."

The big, black dwarf took Keeble by the arm and drew him beyond the door. But once there, there was nowhere to go anyway. The room was tiny, with just a single button for decoration.

Keeble tried to go back out to examine the wall some more, but the big dwarf grabbed his arm and held him still. A moment later, someone pressed the button and the doors slid closed.

After the room lurched slightly, Keeble smiled. "Hey, we're going down." He pulled free of the restraining hand and pushed his way across to press the button again. Nothing changed. He pressed a second time. Still the little room dropped deeper into the ground. Then it stopped and the door opened.

Keeble's smile grew. "That's amazing." He stabbed at the button again. One of the soldiers reached for his arm, but too late. The doors started to close immediately, and the big black dwarf reached forward to hold them back. Keeble nodded, impressed that he could seemingly hold back hydraulics without any effort at all.

The corridor beyond the door was still bare stone, a beauty to behold. Wonderful stone. Ripples of color flowed in random patterns. Pale blue and yellow. Black and brown. All dancing the red of the wall like the notes of a Song. Keeble moved forward, running his fingers along the stone. There were still small touches of magic, but they were ancient workings. Further down, near the first branching of tunnels, a frieze had been carved. Two dwarves, one of them huge, walking side by side, deep in conversation while over their heads a full moon dominated. The natural colors of the wall had flowed to color the figures as if they'd been painted. On another wall someone knelt by a pool of still blue water, and over there a little dwife stared at the stars high above.

Keeble stopped to examine the work. He didn't get much of a chance, though. The big dwarf nudged him forward and he hurried to catch up with his companions. Kim was looking more nervous with each step she took. She fiddled with the collar of her shirt, twisting it this way and that in her long fingers. Meledrin moved calmly, as ever, not looking to either side, seeming to listen to the idle conversation of the escort. Keeble wished he could understand them as well. He could understand some, when they spoke slowly.

"What are they saying?" he asked Meledrin.

"They speak of others."

"Other whats?"

"Other people. A group of soldiers. They are not sure, themselves. And one other in particular. They refer to her as 'the other'."

"Her? Another bloody dwife?"

Meledrin shrugged. "I merely assume it is a woman as the 'other' appears to have some religious capacity."

"Well, have you noticed that with these dwarves the women aren't in charge? Your people will learn one day."

Meledrin didn't answer, and Keeble smiled. Kim studied the back of the big black dwarf, as if a map to their destination might be sewn into the fabric on his broad back.

"[Where are we going?]" she asked.

One of the dwarves from the car answered. "[We're going to meet General Hilliard. He's in charge.]"

"[And Room 32?]"

"[It's a conference room off the General's office.]"

"[Sure it is.]"

"[Have I given you any reason to doubt me?]"

"[You've hardly said a word. But you work for the US government, and we're walking through a tunnel under Area 51. Should I believe you?]"

The dwarf shrugged. "[Perhaps not. But it makes no difference to my life either way.]"

Keeble looked at the wall and touched the smooth stone while he walked. He could feel it dancing under his fingertips.

Eventually, after a dozen turnings and several short flights of stairs, they stopped in front of a plain, deep-set metal door. They'd seen nobody in all of their travels, no hint of activity. All of the hallways had been empty and featureless, apart from the swirling patterns on the walls that occasionally coalesced into striking pictures. Keeble was surprised to realize that they were apparently at their destination. He went inside when the door was opened.

The room beyond was four meters to a side with a metal locker to the right of the door and a table and four chairs in the middle. A second door, flanked by two beds, was directly opposite the entrance. The biggest dwarf Keeble had ever seen was lying on one of the beds. He was fast asleep and hanging over the edges. The door closed and Keeble turned to discover that he, Kim, and Meledrin were alone with the stranger.

"[Looks more like a cell than a conference room,]" Kim said, taking a chair as she examined the stranger on the bed. "[Who's he, do you think?]"

Meledrin and Kim babbled for a few minutes as Keeble circled the room. He opened the second door and discovered a bathroom with a shower, toilet, and sink. The locker contained some books and cardboard boxes. He closed the door and continued circling.

"This looks like a cell," he said after completing his third lap. "Are we prisoners? What did you tell them?"

But Kim paid him no mind, and neither did Meledrin.

The walls were only about a meter thick. He could feel the resonances. They were perfect, not a fault, not a weak point. Without a Rock Song, even with the proper tools, it would take him the best part of a couple of days to tunnel through. Wonderful stone. He stood for a long time, feeling the Song slowly building in his mind. It wasn't until he sounded the first note out loud that he got control of himself.

With a shudder, he clamped his mouth shut and went to sit down on the vacant bed. Meledrin and Kim were talking quietly.

He wished he had something to do. He unstrapped his arm and examined the rusting gears but, having no tools, that just made him more frustrated than when he'd started.

He was relieved when the big, sleeping dwarf stirred and started to sit up.

"Find out who he is," Keeble said to Meledrin before the stranger had even swung his legs over the side of the bed. "Find out what's going on. See if he can get us out."

"Give him a chance, Keeble," the dwife replied.

Keeble grunted and turned to the stranger. "Hello," he said with a smile. "I'm Keeble." He pointed to himself. "Keeble." There was no reply. "Do you know the way out? Do they have coffee here? And who made this place? It's wonderful stone." He had to fight to keep his attention from wandering.

The big dwarf just turned to look at him for a moment and then lowered his head to his hands. He had strange tattoos on his left arm and shoulder.

"[I think he's been drugged,]" Kim said softly, and that started off another lengthy conversation.

Keeble looked at the wall behind the big dwarf. It was smooth and shiny, though old beyond thinking. Such amazing stone. His Song was singing.

"ASK HIM HIS NAME," Kim said to Meledrin.

Meledrin gave a slight shake of her head. "It does not work like that, Kim."

"Then how does it work?"

The big man, hardly more than a boy, really, had been babbling to himself for five minutes, cowering in the corner like somebody was going to hit him.

"I can learn a language from listening to someone speaking it, but without some context from which to work, it is difficult to even begin."

"Okay. Great." Kim rose to her feet and paced the room before slapping herself in the forehead for being such a fool. She crossed to the giant and crouched down nearby. "Kim," she said, pointing to herself. The lad seemed to ignore her. "Kim." Still no response. He just looked at her and continued to babble. "Keeble, come here." She beckoned the dwarf over. It took awhile for him to react, but eventually he turned away from the wall and introduced himself to the giant again. Meledrin watched silently, apparently not thinking it worth her while to speak to a mere boy.

"Kim," Kim said again. "Keeble."

The giant stopped his muttering but didn't reply. So Kim just started to talk, describing her travels over the past few years. She tried to keep her voice steady and even, and kept a smile on her face. Still, he made no reply.

After ten minutes of this, Kim returned to her seat and sat down. Keeble filled the silence with his own ramblings. Kim understood several words: car, plane, electricity. The giant seemed to listen more intently, though obviously he couldn't understand even as much as she.

"Do you know any legends about giants, Meledrin?" Kim asked as she watched the one-sided conversation between the dwarf and the stranger.

"Not really. No full tales because it has been millennia since the last giant was seen."

"Until today."

"Possibly."

"So what do you know, then, if there are no complete tales?"

34: Lost Ones

"It is said that the gods spoke to them directly, guiding them with voices in the stars. They were called the Navigators, because they guided all people through the shoals of the gods' wishes."

"Very poetic."

Meledrin gave Kim the condescending look that she was getting used to. In the corner, the stranger finally spoke in reply to Keeble's babbling. Kim smiled at the thought that he was probably telling the dwarf to shut up. Meledrin glanced across to the corner as Kim went over and introduced herself again. Keeble slowed down long enough to followed suit. Then, with a sneer, he introduced Meledrin.

Finally the lad pointed to himself and said, "Tuki."

"Hello, Tuki." Kim then proceeded to introduce the table. "Table," she said, pointing and indicating that she would like him to say his word for the item. Eventually he seemed to get the picture, for he said a single word. Kim then went right around the room naming everything in turn and getting his words in response. Then she started pointing to parts of herself. He seemed unusually shy about that, but gave his words with a lowered head and rosy blush. Clothes were next.

"What else can we do?" Kim asked. Keeble had grown bored of the game and had returned his attention to the walls.

"Concepts, perhaps," Meledrin suggested. "Large and small. Hard and soft. Colors. Anything, so long as he knows what we mean and is able tell us his own words."

So Kim set to work again with Meledrin silently watching. Half an hour later, she thought she had exhausted all of the possibilities and told the elf so. Meledrin nodded.

"I think that is enough to get started. It seems an absurdly simple language." She turned to face the lad. "[Are you well?]" she said.

Tuki's eyes widened in surprise.

"[I am not sick or injured, but the humans have taken the skyglass. Thank you for asking, mo'shi.]"

Kim was slightly shocked herself. She could almost understand what the lad was saying. She was sure that she was just a few moments from understanding and listened for when the moment came.

"[The skyglass? What is it?]"

Tuki looked surprised again; whether by the question or something else wasn't entirely clear.

"[It is a glass ball, about the size of your head, mo'shi. The Goddess speaks through it.]"

"[Voices come from the glass?]"

"[No. They speak in the stars, which are shown in the 'glass.]"

"*How long you here?*" Kim asked. She'd finished the question before she realized she was speaking Tuki's language. She'd learned Spanish as a teenager, but it hadn't felt anything like this.

"[I do not know, mo'shi. They stuck something in my arm, and I slept. I awoke for the first time when you were here.]"

Kim only got half of that, which was more than she should have, but it was enough.

"[And where is it that you came from?]" Meledrin again, looking annoyed.

"[My world is called Kiva.]"

"[And what are your people called?]"

"[We are moai, mo'shi.]"

Kim interrupted and made the elf repeat the conversation back. She discovered that she needn't have bothered; she'd understood enough. While she pondered the mysteries of language, Meledrin started talking to the lad once more.

"Now what?" Kim asked when they had gone through all manner of questions and answers.

Meledrin shrugged. "He says he came here by choice, but I think he had as much choice in the matter as we did in the end."

"Yes, I heard what he said."

Kim watched as Meledrin went back to grilling the moai. Keeble was examining the lock on the door, bending down to look in the keyhole and fiddling with the handle. He seemed to lose interest when it didn't magically pop open, and went to look at the stone walls instead, as if they might offer a better option for escape. He ran his fingers along the smooth stone and tried to scratch it with his metal hand. Nothing magical happened there either, but he stayed where he was, staring and mumbling to himself. He kept his hand on the wall, fingers spread, face intense with concentration.

Kim drifted away to sleep as she listened to Meledrin and Tuki and watched Keeble. The words swam through her dreams, in murky water at first, but becoming clearer by the moment.

-oOo-

Kim divided her attention between the television and Meledrin and Tuki. The former was tuned to CNN, while her companions spoke of religion, culture, and agriculture, and everything in between. People were being killed by falling bat-things in most places, but central South America was being decimated. They didn't have the resources of a lot of places and were under almost constant attack. Normally both the news and the conversation might have been interesting, but Kim couldn't concentrate. All she could think about was that she could understand what Tuki was saying. Meledrin picking up a language like a child picked up a lollypop was all well and good, she was an alien after all, but Kim was just a human.

The little that had been said about the skyglass had aroused Kim's interest, but the lad seemed reluctant to talk about it, or didn't have much to say. The skyglass told the moai when to plant crops. It told them when sand storms were coming. It told them when there would be eclipses. And it had told Tuki when the aliens were coming. However, when Meledrin pressed him on the subject, he'd invariably apologize and shake his head.

As far as Kim could tell, Keeble paid no attention to the conversation at all. He had slowly become more distant since entering the caves. He wandered around, muttering and pressing his good hand against the wall. He seemed to be arguing with himself and was having a hard time getting his point across.

"Excuse me, Meledrin?"

"Yes, Kim?" The elf broke off her conversation and turned her cool gaze to Kim.

"What's Keeble saying?"

"'But I failed the test,' he says. 'I have no right. But we are stuck in this room and who knows what these Americans intend. They didn't make these tunnels themselves, that's for sure, so where are the builders now? Who says they didn't make the tunnels? But what if I fail? I think I failed before.'"

Keeble stopped his pacing and stared at the metal contraption on his arm, winding the gears that adjusted its angles.

"What does he mean?"

"I mentioned previously about Keeble failing the test. It relates in some way to the method by which dwarves find their leaders. His failure resulted in him being cast out. I do not know the details."

"Ask him."

"I will not. I am talking to Tuki." She turned back to the moai to resume her conversation.

Snooty bitch, Kim thought. Meledrin didn't care for Tuki at all, in any way, but it was obvious that the youngster treated the elf with great respect and deference, and that seemed to get her attention. It also seemed to reinforce her view that she was so much more wonderful than anyone else and Keeble was little more than a savage.

From what Kim could gather, Tuki had been brought up in a culture where women ruled without dispute. She would have to cure him of that notion at the first opportunity, especially with Meledrin around.

Kim turned back to the television. As far as she could tell, there was no way to change the channel. Of course, the aliens were getting the most coverage, especially since they were starting to meet with some success. They were attacking from higher up, apparently, dropping their crude bombs from altitudes greater than most human planes could fly.

I thought of that days ago.

The experts on the news didn't know how the bats could fly around in space. They couldn't even hazard a guess as to how they could land on the earth and get back up *into* space. Kim was pleased to know that she had a bit more information than they did, but taking her position into account, she thought she didn't know anywhere near as much as she should.

So with the aliens finally learning from their mistakes and anything that even resembled a working satellite long ago shot down, the major powers were having problems coming up with answers. They'd tried firing shrapnel into orbital routes, but the ships, or creatures if that's what they were, seemed to be infinitely maneuverable. They tried bombarding them with radiation, but seeing they lived in space they'd most likely be immune to such things. There were probably a few dozen other things the authorities had tried but weren't telling the media.

Kim wondered how she could change the channel. She didn't want to hear about the war any more. Not today.

As if someone were reading her thoughts, which wouldn't have surprised Kim in this place, the television went dark and the door opened.

Three men, one in an expensive suit and the others in blue uniforms, marched in. The middle man was obviously in charge. He was older than the others, calmer. The look in his eyes would've given his position away, even without the other clues. His bearing was military, his demeanor harsh.

The other two were obviously *not* hired for their non-threatening appearance. The smaller of these two men, a Native American, held a glass ball a little smaller than a human head. The skyglass, Kim guessed. The man held it as if ready to ward off attack, and his eyes danced from Kim to Meledrin to Keeble to Tuki and back again.

The leader took a chair and sat at the table. "We'd like to ask some questions."

"Such as?"

"Such as, how does the elf know Shoshone?"

Kim looked at Meledrin for a moment. "Who's Shoshone?"

The leader sighed. "It would go easier for everyone if you'd drop the smart-ass attitude, Miss McLean."

"And it'd go a lot easier if you'd ask a sensible question. The only people that Meledrin knows with more than a passing acquaintance are in this room, and the Palsamon guy in London."

"Miss McLean, Shoshone isn't a person, it's a language. It's the language spoken by several Native American tribes from around this region. Senior Airman Dongoske here is from one of those tribes." He motioned to the man with the skyglass.

Kim looked at the man again and had to revise her opinion. He wasn't there for his winning personality, for sure, but he wasn't just there for his muscles either. He was there because he could speak to Tuki.

"So, Tuki comes from another world, and yet he speaks a language used by Native Americans?"

Dongoske, perhaps a little overeager, interrupted his superior. "It is not *exactly* Shoshone, Miss McLean, but a lot of it is. I can work out a lot of things Tuki's saying by context. It's surprisingly easy, actually." He finally looked at the other man and fell into an embarrassed silence.

The leader wore a look Meledrin would have been proud of. "But none of this tells us exactly how Meledrin came to know the language."

Kim didn't feel like pointing out that she knew the language as well. That was one advantage she was not yet willing to give up.

"I did not know the language," Meledrin said, and Kim smiled slightly. The tone of the elf's voice showed that she hadn't really learned much at all about humans. "I learned it."

"Excuse me? When?"

"Just now."

"You've been in here for about two hours. Are you telling me you learned the language in two hours?"

"Well, obviously there is still much to learn, but yes."

"Bull*shit*."

Kim laughed. "We have aliens attacking earth from the backs of giant space-going bats. We have gateways to other worlds. We have crystal balls, or whatever the hell it is. And you can't believe in someone's ability to learn a language?"

"It isn't possible to learn a language in a couple of hours."

"Whatever. You're the expert, I'm sure. But remember, Mel's only been on Earth for a couple of days. What's more likely? They speak English on Sherindel, or she's a quick learner?"

"There you go with that attitude again, Miss McLean."

"Well, I'm being held prisoner, but I haven't been read my rights and I haven't been allowed to speak to a lawyer."

"You aren't a prisoner."

"Great." Kim smiled and rose to her feet. "I'm off then." She didn't even bother stepping towards the still-open door. Before she had finished the sentence, two uniformed men stepped into view. "Oh, I get it. I'm not a prisoner, I'm being held for my own safety. Sorry, how could I not see that?"

Kim looked at the man in charge and knew she was about to get the smart-ass allegation thrown at her again. "You ask questions and we'll answer them. Don't blame us if you don't like the answers."

"I'll ask questions, and you'll tell the truth."

"Obviously you'll only accept a version of the truth that suits your ends."

"Miss McLean, you came to us, remember?"

"I do remember, but apparently the significance of that means nothing to you. We won't run away if we're treated with a bit of understanding and respect. All this stuff going on now is just pissing me off, and the more I get pissed off, the more I'll dig my heels in."

"We have ways to make you talk."

Kim sat down, eyebrows raised. "Excuse me? You have ways to make me talk? Perhaps you should try that with a Nazi accent."

The leader sighed. "I apologize, Miss McLean. It has been a tiring few days, though that doesn't really excuse my behavior. But please give some thought to our circumstances." He cleared his throat. "We will leave you alone for a while, and hopefully, when we return you'll be ready to talk."

"I have an idea," Kim said in reply, "why don't you lot go away for a while, and hopefully, when you return you'll be ready to listen." The three men filed out, and Kim gave them the finger. She also turned a complete circle to be sure the cameras captured the image.

"Kim, what are you doing?"

"Shut up, Mel."

The elf sniffed and returned her attention to Tuki. But the moai was in no condition to be continuing their conversation. He alternated between staring at the door through which the men had left and gazing in despair at his hands. Kim guessed he was thinking about the skyglass. He made no reply to anything Meledrin asked him.

A few minutes later, Keeble was searching through the locker in the corner of the room. Pulling out boxes and books and shoving them back in.

"Keeble, why don't you and Tuki have a game of chess?" Kim reached past him and pulled a wooden chessboard from the top shelf.

When she turned to look at Meledrin, the elf sighed and translated. "He states that he is unaware of the rules," she said after he replied.

"Well, I'll show him."

She beckoned Tuki over to a table. He was reluctant to rise from his brooding but did as he was asked. Kim set the board up between the two of them. For the next half hour, with Meledrin's help, she ran through the rules and even played a game to let them get the idea. Then she watched while the two of them played against each other. It was slow going, but they both seemed to remember the rules enough to get by. What one didn't know, the other did.

"Keeble wishes to know who made this game," Meledrin said after a while, sounding bored. "He is enjoying its exact nature."

"You like exact, Keeble? You like things to be black and white?"

"[Well, yes. I think so.]" His forehead wrinkled in thought. "[But I like Rugby as well, you know the game where they stomp on each other and jump on each other. That isn't very exact, is it?]"

Kim laughed when she heard the translation. "That makes it a bit more like real life than chess, doesn't it? Nothing in real life is exact. There are always different ways to look at things. And life wouldn't be much fun if everyone agreed on everything." Kim looked at Meledrin as she continued. "On the other hand, it wouldn't be much fun if people couldn't politely acknowledge another person's point of view even though they don't agree with it."

Keeble cursed under his breath as Tuki took a pawn.

-oOo-

Several hours later, after four meals of hospital grade food had been brought, Airman Dongoske returned to the room. He didn't have the 'glass with him but was obviously intending to stay for a while.

"Have you come to resume the farce of questioning?"

Dongoske smiled. "Well, I've come to talk."

Kim raised her eyebrows.

"Just talk." Dongoske included the others in his gaze. "We sit here and see where conversations about current events take us."

"Well, that should be fun."

"Miss McLean, you really pissed the brass off around here. You could be smarter about things."

"And where's the fun in that?"

"For starters, you'd get out of here quicker."

"We won't be out of here before the war finishes, if your bosses have their way. And by then, they'll be on a number of planets and they can have all sorts of wars and excuses to keep us a while longer."

"You really believe that?"

"Yes. Look at Tuki. I don't believe he's capable of harming anyone, and yet he's in here with us. He had one possession of any value, I bet, and you didn't even have the decency to steal it while he was awake."

"He needed to be tested for diseases. He needed to be tested for resistance to our diseases."

"And then he needed to be robbed."

Dongoske sighed. "Kim —"

"Miss Mclean to you."

"Miss McLean, the skyglass needs to be tested."

"And how have you done so far?"

The Airman blushed. "We can't even turn it on. We've been through just about the entire vocabulary of Shoshone using a computer with no result."

"Did you think of asking Tuki? But no, that's silly: you stole the glass from him, so why would he tell you anything?"

"Kim. Miss McLean. I just —"

"Do what you're told? Don't all soldiers?"

"We're under attack from aliens. We didn't provoke this, so we must simply do what we can to get safely through."

"Have any been captured alive?"

There was a momentary pause, a slight hesitation that told Kim everything she needed to know. "Not that I know of."

"Has anyone tried talking to them?"

"The aliens? There's no evidence they understand us, and besides, they attacked us for no reason."

Kim leaned forward in her chair. "I saw one spare an old woman, Dongoske. I saw one point its weapon at her and choose to turn away." She sighed and sat back, scratching at the table top with a fingernail. "We may not know what reason they have for attacking us, it may not be a reason we think is good enough, but they have a reason. They aren't monsters."

"Anyone who attacks us like they did deserves to be treated as such."

"We can't understand the motives of people on the other side of our own world, and you expect me to believe we can understand the motives of aliens?" Kim held up a stalling hand. "Airman, we could go around in circles with this all night. Why don't you tell us all something interesting?"

"Okay. Well, the giant statues on Easter Island? You know the ones?"

Kim pulled her thoughts away from the aliens and nodded. "Yeah. In general."

"Well, they're called 'moai'."

"Tuki's people are called moai, right?"

Dongoske nodded. "But wait, there's more. My people, the Hopi Indians, who were based to the southeast of here, have legends about our ancestors arriving from other worlds by climbing up through holes in the ground. Our traditional religion is based around that idea with most ceremonies carried out in an underground chamber called a Kiva."

"Kiva is the name of Tuki's world," Meledrin said.

"Correct. So, suddenly, ancient legends take on a whole new light. Here we are, within a few meters of an underground gateway to a world called Kiva."

"But the Indian cultures aren't that old, are they?"

"They're a few thousand years old, but no, nowhere near the kind of timespans we're talking about here. We aren't saying that the Hopi really crossed from another world, but their legends had to start somewhere, and the coincidences are starting to build up. The predecessors of the Hopi were called the Anasazi, a word that means 'ancient ones' or 'lost ones' depending on who you ask."

"What about Roswell? That's around here somewhere, isn't it?"

Dongoske laughed. "Roswell is in New Mexico, not that close to here, but still within the Hopi and Anasazi regions. But, a spaceship did *not* crash there in 1954. A weather balloon crashed." He smiled at the look of disappointment on Kim's face. "However, when the Air Force went to investigate the claims of a spaceship crashing, they did come across something."

"A spaceship?"

Dongoske smiled some more. "Yes. It was made from an amazing material, some type of metal we've never seen. At least we think it's metal. It still looks brand new today. The bodies weren't inside the ship, but they were all protected in an almost airtight hangar. Those famous pictures of the creatures were real, but most of the public misunderstanding revolved around the fact that they thought the ship had just crashed. The bodies were dated at around fifty thousand years."

"Fifty thousand?"

"Yes. And who knows what that amount of time will do to a corpse in those conditions? Certainly no one around here. It wasn't until recently that we were able to discover for sure that they are — were — human."

"You're kidding?"

"Nope. DNA testing and other stuff says they're human. In fact, they're probably more human than we are."

"How can you be more human than a human?"

"Two cars coming off a production line one after the other won't be *exactly* the same. They both look perfect, they both run perfect, but they're still different. Neither of them will match the plan, but one'll be closer than the other. We still don't know what the whole plan looks like with humans, but we know enough to know that nobody matches it perfectly."

"And those creatures were human?"

Dongoske pointed at Keeble. "About his size, actually. And we already know that Keeble, Meledrin, and Tuki are human as well. Though Tuki does have an extra layer in his skull but we'd need to examine it before we know anything for sure."

"I wouldn't even bother asking for permission if I was you. He won't mind." Kim smiled, and Dongoske ignored her.

"The others are also human."

"The others?"

Dongoske looked uncomfortable. "Some others from Tuki's world. We had a bit of a confrontation. It wasn't our fault though."

"Of course not."

"The point is, they're all human."

Kim turned to look at Keeble. "And what does that tell us?"

Dongoske shrugged. "I have no idea."

"Fair enough. But if there were people around fifty thousand years ago, wouldn't we have found more evidence?"

"Perhaps. But we now know that there are other habitable worlds out there. Who says these people lived here and not out there?" He gestured vaguely. "Maybe they just visited."

"So the earth was just one huge camping ground."

Dongoske laughed. "Perhaps. Perhaps. Or maybe they had only just discovered Earth and hadn't gotten around to settling it yet. There could be any number of reasons. They found those hobbit, halfling skeleton things in Indonesia a few years back. Who knows what else is just lying around waiting to be discovered.

"We have no idea if the portal here is natural or man made, but we have reason to believe there are others that aren't as stable."

"Reason to believe?"

"Back in the nineties a sheriff was standing by the side of a road, out in the middle of nowhere. He was looking up for some reason and swore that he saw a piece of paper appear about ten yards above his head and float down to the ground."

Kim raised an eyebrow.

"Exactly. And it wasn't really paper, as such. More like parchment. It was a note, supposedly from a vet who had disappeared with a teenage boy about a year earlier a few hundred miles away. It talked about portals to other worlds and stuff that sounds crazy unless you're in possession of other information. The sheriff probably wouldn't have said anything, except his brother-in-law worked for the FBI. Then we wouldn't have heard about it and added it to the puzzle." Dongoske shrugged. "I guess the point is, the world is a stranger place than most of us can comprehend. We have magical portals and spaceships and… Who are we to say what is real and what isn't anymore."

Kim nodded. "I suppose." She pursed her lips and looked at the soldier. "Is the Roswell ship here? Can I see it?"

Dongoske laughed. "Not a chance. I've never seen it. Very few people are allowed down there. Probably no more than a hundred people have seen it since it arrived."

"Awww, come on. What harm could it do? I wouldn't try to steal it or anything."

"Not while anyone was looking, anyway."

"Exactly."

"Maybe Meledrin or Tuki or Keeble can work out something about it. Well, Tuki or Keeble." She looked at the moai. "Maybe Keeble can work something out."

"We haven't been able to get into it, so unless he has the keys? Or maybe he can pick the lock? I think *we* could pick the lock if we could find it." He shook his head. "You aren't going to see the ship, Kim. Change the subject."

35: Long Day

"OKAY. WHAT'S HAPPENING ON SHERINDEL?" Kim said. "Are you helping the elves?"

"How would I know, Miss McLean? You know it's unlikely my superiors will tell me anything, even if the British army is passing on intelligence. For all I know the elves and dwarves are fighting on their own."

At the mention of the word 'dwarves', amongst all the other babble, Kim saw Keeble pause in his mumbling and look at Dongoske. When the soldier said nothing more, the dwarf returned to his inspection of the wall.

"So," Kim said, trying to rein in her thoughts, "how long are we going to be kept here? I've no doubt you have no qualms about keeping enemies locked away without trial, but what about people who came to you and offered their help?" Kim didn't blame the Americans for what they were doing, but that didn't mean she had to like it. And it didn't mean she thought it was the absolute best course of action.

Dongoske returned Kim's gaze. "My superiors will lock up anyone, friend or foe, if they think it'll gain them an advantage in war. And we *are* at war, Kim, though it may not look like it most of the time."

"And the enemy is learning, Airman, aren't they?"

"Yes. Those bats of theirs can survive in a void, for hours at a time apparently. So now they just stay up in space and attack from there. They took out a lot of our satellites early on and now there isn't a lot we can do to retaliate, to tell you the truth. Not a lot that's having any success anyway."

"To tell me the truth? Surely you don't want to do that!"

"Kim, we are just doing what we have to do to survive."

"Yes, but the American definition of survival is different from that of any other people."

"You don't like us much, do you?"

"Nothing against Americans as individuals, a lot of great people — hell, I'm one myself half the time — but as a group, as a nation..." She left the thought unfinished.

"Do you want to know what Americans think of Australians?"

"Not a lot, I imagine. Too busy thinking of themselves." Kim smiled slightly. "Do you know why I left the army?"

Dongoske paused for a moment, as if unsure whether to answer. "I haven't read the reports in detail."

"I jumped before I was pushed. I have a problem with authority, Airman. I had a few confrontations with superior officers over the years. They generally started with me telling them they were idiots in one way or another. And to this day, I'm sure I was right every time." She paused and held up her hand. "Okay, not every time, but most of them. So, don't get me wrong, it isn't just America I have a problem with. Australia's as bad. As a group, Australians are a hypocritical self-centered mob, and the government is about as pathetic as they get, and we all know they can get pretty pathetic. It's just that the American government has my attention at the moment."

"We're saving the world here, Kim. Isn't that worth something?"

"Of course it is. It's worth a damn lot and a lot of people, including myself, would be willing to thank you for it. But how would you feel in my situation, Airman? How about I tell you. You'd be scared, tired, and pissed off. I went to your government to offer assistance, but nobody believes me." Kim paused for a moment and gestured to the others in the room. "You have three aliens in this room, Airman. Three people, humans apparently, that have so much to offer, and yet the first thing you do is lock them up. Did you ever think that they might do everything they can to help of their own free will? That all of us would? Keeble is probably over there trying to work out if he'd rather be ruled by us or the aliens."

Meledrin spoke. "Actually, he is trying to work out whether he should stay in this room or go somewhere else. It is quite a heated discussion he is having."

Dongoske smiled, seeming to relish this interruption. "And where would he go?"

"Anywhere, I would think. He loves caves, Airman, but has decided that your people did not make these ones and that they have tainted them."

"He really says that?"

"Yes."

"And how does he know?"

"These are caves, Airman. Stone. And Keeble is a dwarf. More than that I cannot explain. More than that does not need to be explained."

-oOo-

Kim knew it probably wasn't a good idea to fight with Airman Dongoske. She quite liked the man, but he was working for her captors. And she *was* tired and scared and pissed off. She had every right to be. If the Australian or British governments were holding her, she'd feel exactly the same way and would shout just as loudly. She could see how the situation might look to them — the world was being attacked, and they couldn't risk any resource being wasted — but it didn't make her feel better.

Dongoske had hung around and chatted for an hour. When it became obvious he wasn't going to get a lot of useful information, he left. Perhaps she was supposed to think there was no reason to hide anything and that Dongoske was her friend.

When Dongoske and his superiors returned early the next morning, Kim had just about had enough. Tuki rose from his position on the floor and walked over to one of the beds, the only seat large enough to accommodate him comfortably. Meledrin reluctantly made room, moving slightly to let him sit in the corner. But Kim wasn't going to let this continue.

"Meledrin, tell Tuki that, no matter what question's asked, he's to answer with the words 'I won't say anything else until I speak with my lawyer'."

"Why?"

"Just tell him to do that. And you do the same thing."

"'I will not say anything else until I speak with my lawyer'?"

"That's right."

"I know what a lawyer is, Kim, but Tuki does not have a word to match."

"Legal representative? Law makers' conduit, maybe. I don't know. Use the word 'lawyer'. I don't care, just think of something."

"Very well. And who is our lawyer? Do we have a lawyer?"

"I have a lawyer friend in Seattle. Well, he's not a friend yet, but if I got him involved in this case he would be my friend for life." There was no such person, but nobody else knew that. Or perhaps they did know — she was dealing with the government of the United States, after all.

General Hilliard shook his head. "Miss McLean, a Washington State lawyer is not allowed to practice in Nevada without the proper papers."

"Yeah, well, I'm sure he knows enough to advise us. And he'll probably know some other lawyer we can use." Kim smiled. "I assume this is going to be a long day," she said, making a great show of getting comfortable.

"All right," the General held up a placating hand. "As a show of faith, we'll return the Skyglass to Tuki."

Kim laughed. "So, you've had absolutely no luck with the thing and hope Tuki will use it and show you what you're doing wrong? My goodness, you're so *tricky*, General."

"What would you like me to do, Miss McLean? I have the feeling you'll twist anything we do to your own advantage."

"Well, General, I have to take every advantage I can get."

"Think what you like, Miss McLean." He left the room with Dongoske and the other man close behind. A soldier brought the glass ball in a moment later and carefully set it on the table on a little polished brass stand. Tuki had the ball in hand before the man exited.

Kim hurried over and laid a restraining hand on his.

She glanced around, as if she'd be able to see those who were watching, or pick out the listening devices. "How does the ball work, Tuki?" she asked in the moai's language. Even though she whispered she was pretty sure the Americans would hear. But she figured that speed and clarity might be more useful than keeping her language abilities secret. The Americans probably wouldn't believe she could really speak Shoshone anyway. She could hardly believe it herself, but it almost felt as natural as speaking English.

"You ask it questions, and the Mother Blower speaks back through it."

The skyglass was growing warm. Kim quickly took her hand away. "You have to physically speak to it?"

"Yes. Well, I think so."

Kim looked around the room again then quickly dragged one bed closer to the other and lined them up. It scraped and juddered across the stone floor.

I hope that was deafening in somebody's earphones. That thought made her think of checking under the beds for bugs. She probably wouldn't know one if she saw it anyway. That done, she had Tuki lift the table up onto the beds.

"You sit here, Tuki," Kim said, indicating a spot on the floor between the beds and under the table, then positioned the moai so his back was to the rest of the room. His head almost brushed the table. Kim and Meledrin then sat on each of the beds.

"What are we doing?" Meledrin asked.

"They have cameras in here," Kim explained. "Little windows that they can look through. Normally the cameras will be in the corners of the room, up near the ceiling, because it's the spot that gives best coverage with the least cameras. I'm just trying to make it so they can't see the skyglass thingy. And if we talk quietly enough, maybe they won't be able to hear, either. Hopefully."

Kim looked around but there was not a lot more she could do. "Wait a sec'. Lift up this end of the table, Tuki." The lad reached up above his head and easily lifted the table, allowing Kim to remove the sheet and blankets from one of the beds. She used them as curtains to hide their activities completely from the room. Keeble crept into the protected area with them, like a little boy when a castle was being built. Meledrin scowled at the dwarf, but Kim patted a spot on the bed beside her and he sat down there.

"Show us what it does, Tuki."

The young man nodded. "On."

Kim watched as the globe started to glow softly. After a few moments, a detailed image of the Earth appeared. Kim examined it closely. There wasn't a lot to see that she didn't expect to see. Continents and oceans. Transparent, moving cloud formations. But there *was* something: three blue crosses. One in the southern United States, which was right beside a blue dot, one in England, and one in South America, somewhere along the western coast.

Tuki said, "Back," and the image shrank to include a large area of space and a few dozen yellow dots.

Tuki nodded. "Airman Dongoske said that the yellow dots are 'alien mother ships'. The blue dot is the skyglass. I do not know what the crosses are."

"Tuki, can you show us your own world?"

He could and he did. "Kiva," he said. Yellow dots swarmed around the other world as well.

Meledrin then asked him to show Sherindel, and he obliged, bringing it up in the 'glass.

"Show us a solar system, Tuki."

"Pardon?"

Kim spoke directly to the skyglass. "Sol," she said, trying to sound authoritative. Nothing happened. "A solar system is one star surrounded by a group of planets. Ours here is called Sol. So say Sol."

Again Tuki obliged, but nothing happened.

"Shit. Earth." Kim said. Nothing.

"I think that perhaps your world was not always called Earth," Tuki said. "I could not get it to work." Then he said, "Centre," and Earth was visible again.

Kim tried again. She touched the glass lightly and said, "Back." Nothing. Tuki repeated the word.

Kim shook her head as she tried to gather her thoughts. "Perhaps knowing the words isn't enough," she said quietly. *Maybe it's that extra layer in his skull.* "I don't know. No wonder our hosts aren't having any luck." She smiled slightly. *Small consolation.*

Tuki said back two more times until the 'glass was showing a tiny yellow pinprick in the center that could only be a sun and eight other tiny spots that could only be planets minus Pluto. Maybe. Each of the planets had a list of data beside it, as did the star, but Kim couldn't read any of it. Apparently Tuki could read numbers there, but letters were beyond him. Kim tried to explain her thoughts.

Nobody could disagree. They just stared at her blankly. Tuki was the only one who really understood the nature of stars and planets. So Kim tried to explain a bit about that as well, whispering in Tuki's language. And she tried to explain a bit about the universe. The other two were still back in the dark ages, but Keeble, obviously understanding every word, nodded and wrinkled his brow in concentration. Kim still didn't know a lot of the words she wanted to use.

When she was done talking, Kim turned her attention back to the skyglass.

"Go outwards," Kim said to Tuki. "Show us more. Show us lots of stars."

The moai spoke and the planets disappeared to be replaced by a cluster of stars.

Kim was completely lost. She couldn't even find the sun. There were dozens of them, but they all had lists beside them, and Kim surmised that there was only so much relevant information about stars that somebody might list.

Kim asked Tuki to find the Earth's sun and read out the numbers listed beside it.

He somehow found it amongst the spread of stars. Ignoring the letters he said: "8, 2, 2, 5."

Kim made a guess. "There are eight worlds in our solar system. Well, that depends on who you're asking, but anyway. I think that first number is telling us how many worlds there are." She found another star with the same symbol on the first line. "That one will have eight worlds as well," she said.

Tuki knew the name of the star, so he quickly zoomed in for a closer look. Kim gave a little cheer. She was right. They tried ten more times to be sure and met with success on every occasion.

That was the last victory. They moved back to the Sol system where Kim had more information to work from, but she could decipher nothing. If the skyglass had been made tens of thousand of years ago like Tuki suggested, then anything she knew would be so far out of date anyway. The numbers could mean a dozen things, each as plausible as the other. Or as implausible.

It wasn't until a meal was brought in on trays an hour later that Kim realized the Americans must've been following their conversation. They wouldn't have been allowed to hide for that long otherwise. She swore to herself as she chewed on a salad sandwich.

When the meal was done, Kim led the others back into the fort, though she was sure it wouldn't do any good. She leaned over and whispered in Meledrin's ear, hardly more than a breath. "We have to get out of here."

"Are they not going to help us?"

That depended on your definition of 'help'. Kim didn't answer.

"And how are we to get out?"

Kim sat back and shrugged. She hadn't thought things through. Then she whispered again. "I suppose all we can do is jump whoever comes in here next."

"And the men they leave outside the door?"

"Okay. Well, we will have to jump the person who comes in *as they come in*, so the door is still open. Then we have a hostage."

Meledrin just raised a long, thin eyebrow.

"Have you got a better idea?"

"I do not think Tuki would be any use in this plan of yours. His people do not even kill base animals."

"There are still three of us."

"Against trained fighting men with weapons?"

"We can't stay here, Meledrin. We'll never be let out."

"Well, perhaps these Americans have a right to do what is best for the many."

"Of course they do. And we have the right to try to get out of here. We can still give them information if we're in Canada or Mexico or something."

"Perhaps."

Kim grunted in disgust. "You think they're worried about Sherindel, do you? They'll forget about your world until it's convenient for them to do something about it. And then it won't be long before humans own your world as well. It's not just the Americans who are like this, most of the world is." Kim didn't believe the first half of what she was saying. The Americans would help Sherindel as much as they could, as would the Brits and anyone else. But the second part she didn't doubt at all. Humans from all around the world would soon be rushing to get their hands on real estate and resources on the newly discovered worlds. But she was pissed off and really wanted to get out. She'd say whatever she had to. Just like the Americans. *Shit*

"Very well, then. Let us try." But the elf still didn't seem convinced.

Kim didn't care. She whispered the plan, such as it was, to Tuki and Keeble. Tuki looked shocked, almost dropping the skyglass. Keeble smiled and nodded.

-o〇o-

Nobody returned before the lights went out.

Kim swore and lay down on a bed. She was still lying there a few hours later, a lifetime away from sleep and staring into the darkness, when something happened.

She stilled her breathing and tried to slow her racing heart. The darkness was all but complete, so she strained to hear.

"What?" A strong hand clamped over her mouth. She was ready to fight in an instant, but the cold press of a blade against her throat stopped her.

Her heart pounded in her chest. Her clothes were soaked with sweat in an instant. Instincts were still telling her to fight, but she remained motionless.

"Miss McLean, you must be quiet." The man released his grip.

"Dongoske?" she said around ragged breaths.

"Of course. Who else did you expect? I've come to get you out of here."

"What?" Kim sat up slowly. Though Dongoske was barely a meter from her, she couldn't see anything.

"My ancestors would not want you to be kept here. I have ignored the spirits of the Hopi long enough to know when I should listen."

Kim thought it was a pretty corny as far as excuses went. She doubted the Hopi had much to do with this at all, but she'd play along, for the moment. "Ok. Let's get going then. I'll wake the others."

But they were already awake. Meledrin explained what was happening to the two men, and they all made their way silently to the door. Kim collected her pack and adjusted the shoulder straps so Tuki could carry it.

"I'd carry it myself, but I may need to act quickly."

The lad nodded as if that was only to be expected.

Outside, a soft light filled the corridor. Dongoske checked their surroundings before turning to speak. "Follow in single file. First person about two meters behind me. Kim, you last."

"Why?"

"Because I can understand you well enough to know what you're thinking. And you can keep an eye on them."

Kim didn't trust Dongoske at all but figured, one way or the other, he was their best chance of getting out. She would follow until an opportunity arose.

36: Different Types

SCREE EXAMINED THE DOORS.

Well, I think it's doors, he said to himself. Two big, shining pieces of metal were set upright in the side of the mountain. They fitted together perfectly, with no chance of getting even the sharpest dagger into the crack between. There were no hinges or handles to be seen either.

Buildings had filled the small expanse of land out the front at some stage, though all but a few faint signs were long gone. Scree kept going along the side of the mountain for a hundred meters to see if there was anything else to see. He found nothing and went back to the door, going to the metal to have another look. He saw nothing he hadn't seen the first time.

No idea hows to open the things.

He examined the stone around the door, wondering if he could break it. But the surface was almost as smooth as the metal. It wasn't about to fall apart without more of an argument than he could offer.

Scree sat down in the shade. He put his weapon and pack on the ground by his side and took off his boots for the first time in weeks. As expected, his feet were swollen and he'd have trouble getting the boots back on, but the warm air against his toes felt good. He massaged his ankles and the soles of his feet to get the blood moving freely. It hurt like hell and he smiled.

When he could feel nothing more than a tingle in his toes, Scree climbed the cliff to the side of the door. The splint on his arm slowed him down. The break seemed to be healing cleanly, though the arm ached, so he pulled the material and wood away as he went.

Five meters up, the ground leveled out and offered a view back out across the valley. The bats had long ago moved on, flying with their masters out over the wilds beyond the valley walls. Scree had attempted a similar sortie himself, and wasn't about to try it again any time soon.

Scree made his way deeper into the mountains. He wasn't sure what he might find, but he was willing to look for as long as was needed. The ground was nice and hot under his bare feet, the sun warm overhead, and he was back in the mountains. It almost felt like he was back at home. He wished he'd brought his horrible bone flute so he could dance trollish tunes in the air of the strange world. A worn trail snaked between natural walls. For a while the walls were waist high, but started to grow until the sun was blocked out and he could see nothing more than the trail, the stone and a narrow strip of pale sky. He trotted along for a couple of minutes before the pathway ended at the base of another cliff. He was about to head back the way he'd come but decided the wall would be easy enough to climb. He found some handholds and hauled himself upwards.

Another five meters up Scree found a metal grate. He stared. Eventually, steadying himself as best he could, he gripped the grate and pulled. It came away easily, the screws holding it in place having rusted away to nothing long ago. The grate itself still shone like it was brand new: the same as the door down below, and the same as the sides of the tunnel behind the grate.

But Scree would never fit inside. Who ever had used this passageway was tiny, or could fold themselves into very strange shapes.

Ping would fit, Scree thought. *She could shimmy down there like a rat down a drainpipe.* But the little woman was hardly likely to help him. She might shoot him on sight.

He climbed some more. The cliff kept going up a long way but the canyon walls ended. Scree stepped onto flat ground and walked, one hand running across the stone. Half a kilometer around the side of the mountain he found another hole exactly like the first. It was half way up a cliff, covered with a grille that fell off in his hands, and too small.

Scree hung on the side of the mountain for a long time before starting to retrace his steps. He wondered where Ping was, and if she really *would* shoot him. If she didn't shoot him, would she help, or did she just want to go home? He wondered if it was even worth the effort of going to ask.

"Gots no choice," he said when he had finally climbed back down to stand in front of the original door.

His pack and weapon were where he had left them. His whole life was sitting on the ground there for anyone to come and take. He swore, though he was pretty sure he was the only thief around. He checked to make sure everything was in his pack. He straightened out the books and the black weapon box then shrugged into the pack and inserted his arm into the weapon. Then, carrying his boots, he made his way back to where he'd left Ping.

-oOo-

Scree saw Ping sitting on the ground near her suit of armor. He could have snuck up on her easy enough but decided not to. He stopped where he was and waited until she spotted him. She climbed quickly into the armor and closed the panels as he went closer. The woman raised her weapon.

"Stinking cats."

Scree thought of returning to the door in the side of the mountain to see if he could find some other way of getting past. But before he'd even completed the thought he knew it would be pointless. The door would never budge if it was locked. He didn't know if unlocking the door would be possible, inside or out, but it was the only chance. There might be other doors, but they'd probably all be the same.

That left the little tunnels. And Ping.

Scree kept walking, slow and steady. He kept his weapon pointing at the ground. He stopped and sat on a rock when he was five meters away. He didn't say anything. Ping remained silent as well.

Shadows lengthened. The day crawled across the valley, settling towards night.

Scree knew about apologies, but he'd never needed to try one out for himself. He didn't think one would be a whole heap of use now either.

Night descended. In the darkness they continued to watch.

Hours later, with the strange moons high overhead, Scree wondered if all the silence was really a good idea. It didn't worry *him*, but he didn't think it would be helping.

Ping was watching warily through the broken faceplate of the helmet

Scree opened his pack and pulled forth his crappy bone flute. He doubted it would ever play a proper note in its life, but the sounds it made were still recognizably music and had to help. Scree knew it would make him feel better anyway. He had no idea how Ping would react.

And she didn't reacted at all.

Scree danced merry tunes all through the night, hardly stopping between. Ping was still awake and watching when the sun peeked over the horizon and he finally lowered his flute and took a deep breath. "It's strange, you knows, but I've never really needed help. I mean, yeah, sure, there were times whens a bit of help made things easier, but I didn't *needs* it. Because the only helps I've ever been offered was with things I cans already do myself." Except the monk. There was always the monk.

Scree examined the valley to see if any of the bats had come back during the night. A few kilometers away, settled into a tight group, were half a dozen of the creatures.

"You knows, other trolls came along and helped me bash things and break things and kill things. But, really, I could've dones all that on me own. You see what I means?"

Ping still didn't react.

"Being big was never a problems before. Being big was always a good thing."

Ping watched silently.

"Burning kittens, woman, how was I supposed to know I was going to need your help?"

That was the whole problem, Scree realized. He didn't know anything any more. Back on Kiva he could do what he wanted, because there was nothing else to do. If he killed one human then... Well, who cared? If he killed a troll, there'd be another to take his place. So he did what the moment needed and worried about the next moment when it arrived. And in most cases it was pretty similar to the one just gone.

Scree looked around. The bats, the circular valley, and the large, hot sun. Not far away was the door into the mountain. How was he supposed to tell what was going to happen next? He surged to his feet and, taking his knife from his pack, headed up out of the valley to find some food. Ping swiveled to watch him go.

Hows am I supposed to knows? Scree stalked along the edge of the trees a few minutes later. *Do I have to keeps everything that might ever be useful? Do I have to collect peoples that mights be useful?* He laughed a moment, before suddenly falling silent.

Wasn't that what humans did? They ended up with a house to keep all their useful things and a town to keep all their useful people. Scree swore and dived into the bushes after a thing that looked a bit like a rabbit. He missed and swore again.

"Cat piss."

He was scratched and bleeding but hardly noticed.

-oOo-

"I gots to wonder whys these monsters is here, you know. I means, there ain't nothing here that I can tell. They just hangs around out there in the middle of the valley and... I don't knows what they does, really. And you'd think, seeing as we seems to be the only peoples around here, that theys would notice whens a whole bat-load of guys go missing. With just some rabbits and insects, it ain't likely they was attacked by wild animals." He spat. "Theys terrible soldiers. Don't seem to have any ideas at all, really."

The monsters still milled about a few kilometers away, not bothering to check the disappearance of their companions. The bodies of the dead monsters still littered the ground for all the world to see, if the world cared to look. Apparently the world didn't care.

"I gots a book here," Scree said when the silence stretched on. He reached into his pack and pulled out the *Gates of Hakahei*. He opened it up at random and started to read. "'Ancient records show that the six people of Hakahei are one people. There are giants and imps, warriors and poets, but at heart, beyond the skin, they are the same.

"'Millennia past, before those we erroneously call the first men, there were just men who worshipped the older gods. But these gods reshaped the minds and bodies of men in new molds; stronger molds, more useful molds; and flung them out into space.'"

All the reading was giving Scree a headache so he put the book down and looked at the little woman, standing in the armor as if she was willing to do it for the rest of the year. She was ignoring him.

By the time night fell, Ping was still there and Scree was hoarse from talking. He'd exhausted the topic of the bats and the monsters long ago. He'd read sections from different books— there had been a story about a fire breathing lizard, and something describing a land Scree had never visited. He'd talked about fighting and food and magic and carefully avoided the topic of sex or anything like it. So what else was there he could say?

"The place wheres I grew up is kind of like this," he said eventually, taking a moment to glance around. "Lots of mountains and not a lots of anything else. The caves, now theys was something worth hanging around for. Natural, they was. Well they'd have to be— you wouldn't catch no troll digging holes to live in. And theres was kilometers of 'em. All through the mountains, more thans the trolls is ever likely to use. I haven't been there since abouts me twelfth summer, I think."

This place wasn't a lot like Mount Cardenze at all, when he thought about it. Sure, they both had mountains and not a lot of anything else, but there were mountains and there were *mountains*. "See how these mountain is all cold and grey?" he said. "Well, backs home the mountains are red. The dust, the stones, sometimes the air. Theys were all red.

"And the caves. There are too many to describe. Somes of them is just bare rock, like most people think caves is— with stalactites and stalagmites and all dank and dark and stuffs, but others..." Scree leaned back against the rock and stared upwards. The two moons had cleared the horizon. Neither were very large, but they were bright. "There was one cave wheres the light got in, but nobody could works out where or how. The whole cavern just glowed golden, days and nights. Another one had a waterfall that was green likes an emerald in the morning and blue likes a sapphire at night. And another where the walls was covered in all types of gems and it was like youse was standing outside looking up at the stars."

Scree could see Ping watching him like she hadn't done all day. He returned his gaze on the sky and tried to think of something else he could say about the Star Chamber. He'd spent most of the rare idle moments there when he was a troddler.

"Me and... my friend... used to sits in that cavern whens we were boys and name constellations." He smiled at the thought. A friend? "There was the Dog Constellation and the Fire. Nobody else could see the pictures thats we saw."

Ping stirred. "In Shadon," she said softly, "there's a place like that. Old crazy man build a huge dome and put holes so light shine through. Different times of day and different times of year constellations painted on floor with light." She fell silent again.

"Now that woulds be something to see. Real constellations, was they? Or make believe ones likes I had? It's amazing whats some people think of doing, isn't it? The crazy guy... was he really crazy? Or did people just say he was crazy because of thats one strange thing he did?"

The little woman may have shrugged then but Scree couldn't tell. When she spoke again, Scree had to lean forward to hear. "I thought he nice old man. He gave all children cookies when visit and look at the stars."

"Well, thats ain't so crazy. I could have dones with some cookies whens I was a boy."

"Why?" Ping said loudly. "Would it made difference?" She stared, jaw set, waiting for an answer.

"I needs your help, Ping," Scree said. He stared back at her for a moment then looked away to examine his hands. "I reckons I won't go any further if you don't helps me. There's a door inside that mountain I reckons, somewhere, but I can't gets in there without you. And you don't likes me about now, I reckons, and maybe I don't blame you. But that's the same as it always was. You didn't likes me, you just thought that I could helps you. You was using me."

"You right, Scree, I not like you. But did have some respect."

Scree laughed, until he realized Ping was serious. "You respected me? Ain't nobody never done thats before."

"I not respect everything about you. But strength and courage and fighting ability. None of those are thing endear a person to me, but they things I can respect. But attitude towards life and towards others make you beast."

Scree grunted. Normally he would have killed a person for that. He took a deep breath. "And hows is that?"

"Beast lives for moment with no thought for future. Beast has no concern for others."

"Well, you knows that ain't true. Squirrels and ants store things for the winter months. And wolves live in packs that will fight for each other. And ants again, looks like they lives in communities to me."

"So you less than animal?"

Scree clenched his fist, cords of muscle standing out on his forearm. "No. I'm saying that theres different types of animals and theres are different types of men. I will admit thats I put myself above all else, but whats else should I do when for the last... I don't knows how long... humans have hunted my people for sport?" He rose to his feet and paced. Ping took a clanking, hissing step back. "Theys attack from afar with bows and arrows. Or they rides into the mountains and chase troddlers with maces. Only when we's outnumbered, of course. Is that the type of man you wants me to be? And most men, no matter the race, looks out for themselves above all else. It's just that for most of thems the greatest advantages lay in numbers and finding other peoples who will fight and die in their place." But he remembered what he had thought earlier, about gathering all the people that might be useful and keeping them close.

"That not true."

"Was you expected to fight whens those monsters attacked? No. You expected others to go and die for you."

"Right, but other expected me to mend clothes and clean their houses. Those men was paid and most time they sat in barracks or broke petty squabbles."

"And as theys lay dying I'm sure theys were glad you had mended the holes in their clothes and thats they had been well paid."

"They choose join Guard, choose to risk violence."

"That's right, buts I didn't choose to be a troll. I didn't choose to watch my friends get killed whens I was a troddler. I dids *not* choose. But sometimes things don't always goes the way we plans, or the way we wants. And when that happens? You decide the best way out of the hole, you decide the best way forward, and you forget the past and go." He sat down again, picking at a tuft of grass. "You forgets and go. You thinks about the next moment and live that. Sometimes there ain't no other choice."

PING CLIMBED SLOWLY. It wasn't a difficult wall to scale, but the drop below was distracting and she ached all over. Scree had offered to help, but she shuddered at the thought. She couldn't stand the thought of the troll being too near, so she clung to the side of the mountain testing each hand and foot hold as she went. At the same time, she dreaded the thought of entering the little tunnel on her own.

It is strange, she thought, *hating somebody, fearing them, and yet wanting to keep them in sight, if not near.*

Scree stood below, watching.

He is probably worried I'll fall and force him to go back to Tiandi. She was afraid he'd leave her behind if she didn't do what he asked. Or that he'd go somewhere else and she'd be forced to go home on her own.

Ping took a moment to glance down, checking to see he was still there. She immediately regretted the action and lay against the stone, closing her eyes until she had calmed her heart.

After two minutes and ten seconds of climbing, she found the little metal tunnel Scree had mentioned. Crawling into the long, narrow space seemed less dangerous than the climbing of the wall, but she was suddenly unsure she could go on.

"What's you waiting for?"

Ping flinched. She started to look down but stopped herself in time. She took a deep breath. "I just wonder if should go head first or feet."

"Obviously you gots to go head first."

She stayed where she was until the sound of Scree scrambling up the cliff forced her into motion. Pulling herself up a little higher she slithered into the opening.

A short way down the slight slope, Ping stopped to wait, craning her neck to look back over her shoulder. A moment later, Scree poked his head into view.

"What happens if can't find door?" she asked, voice hollow and echoing. "Or I can't open?" She moved a little further down, getting further from the troll and his steady gaze.

"Ummm..." Scree passed in two hastily made torches and the flint-striker from his pack, sliding them along the shining metal. "I suppose you'll just haves to come back out this ways."

37: Take the Sky

"And what if I lost?" Ping struck a spark after several attempts and got a flame burning.

"If you tooks a bit of string you could follows it back?"

"Do have string?"

"No."

She sighed. "Probably silly plan then."

She could see the flare of anger in his eyes and almost thought her heart would stop, but he gritted his teeth and gave the matter a bit more thought.

Ping didn't think there was a solution to the problem, so she would just have to see what happened. That seemed to be Scree's method for getting through life, and he'd done pretty well so far, if being alive was proof of that.

"How long you wait by door?" she asked quietly, as if afraid of the answer.

Scree shrugged. "As long as I'm willing."

That didn't help, though Ping didn't really know what sort of answer she was after. She started to move away from him before he said anything more.

It wasn't long before Ping came to a cross tunnel. She peered to the left and to the right but there was nothing to suggest which way was best. For ten seconds she stayed where she was, trying to picture the position of the locked door in her mind as she worked out where she should go.

"Left," she said, changing the burning torch to her left hand and extending her arm into the tunnel on that side as if it might make a difference. Metal walls shone in the flickering light. She could see nothing else. She started to crawl.

After fourteen seconds of clanging and clattering along, banging her head and her knuckles where she held the torch, Ping looked back over her shoulder. It felt as if she was lost already though she could still see the faint glow of light coming from outside the mountain. She considered going back— after all, what was the chance she would find a door and then be able to get it open? But going back now would mean that she was no help to Scree. And if she was no help to Scree...

Taking a deep breath Ping looked down the new passage and kept going. She resisted the urge to turn back every second to see if the glow was still visible.

And nine seconds later she found another passage. It was smaller than the one she was currently in and joined at right angles. It didn't look like it was anything special. It didn't look as if it would lead her out. So she decided to keep crawling. But with her torch held out before in the original passage, with the glare partially shielded by the wall, she thought she could see a soft glow coming from the new passage. She changed her mind in an instant and turned aside. And around a bend was a little louvered trap door leading down into a wide hallway. Ping gave a little smile.

The door fell away when she pushed and it was not until she had dropped the torches through and was hanging from the edge, feet dangling a meter above the ground, that she truly noticed that there was light, clear and still. She dropped to the smooth floor. Her knee jarred, one more pain to go with all of her others.

Nervously, she looked about.

There wasn't much to see. The passage, painted with a thick layer of dust, continued for ten meters in either direction. One way was a dead end. The other ended in a T-intersection. Three doors broke the smooth perfection of the walls. The air was alive with subtle sounds that eluded careful listening. It tasted musty and dry.

Ping sat down in the dust. She was safe. Scree could not get to her no matter how hard he tried. She wanted to rest, and sleep, and bathe. She hugged her knees and wondered what to do.

Sounds drifted down the corridors, insubstantial whispers and dull thuds. Above her head, a red light pulsed beside the large, steady white of the lighting. Ping suddenly felt naked without her monster armor. She picked up the torches and moved quickly to the nearest door.

At least I won't get lost, she thought, kicking up an eddy of dust with each movement. She left a clear path to follow.

There was no handle evident on the door, but when she touched her hand to the cool shining metal, it gave a slight hiss. With a groan of protest it started to slide open.

Ping turned and fled down the passage. She took the first corner without thought and stopped at the next. The remains of a pile of furniture blocked the passageway. There was a bed frame and some chairs and a couple of large metal cabinets. She paused to listen, breathing heavily, gripping her two torches in sweating hands and examining the blockade nervously. All she could hear were the background noises that had been with her all along.

After a tense minute and a half Ping lowered her torches slightly and, heart racing, sidled closer to the upturned furniture and glanced over the top. She didn't know what she expected to see, but she was relieved when she saw nothing at all beyond what was also behind her. She took a deep breath and wiped at her face with shaking hands.

"Course there nothing," she said softly. "Nobody been here long time." She looked around again just to be sure.

There was another door nearby. Again, there was no handle. Just the smooth, bare metal and the smooth, painted walls. Approaching this door with caution, she reached out a trembling hand and was running back the way she'd come almost before she had made contact. This door opened as well, grinding and hissing.

Around the first bend she stopped and peered back. The door stood open, though from her angle she could see nothing but a thin, vertical strip of white wall in the room beyond. The door remained like that for three seconds and then sighed quietly closed.

Ping continued to watch. Eventually she crept forward, this time holding her position when the door started to open. There was nobody there. The room was slightly cleaner than the corridor, the dust just a thin coating. It was completely empty. *Most of the furniture is outside, I suppose,* she thought looking at the blockade. The door closed, startling her.

At the next door, the whole process was repeated. The door hissed open, grinding horribly, paused, and started to close. Only it could not close all the way. It stuck halfway, leaving a narrow gap. The view beyond was not much different to the last one offered. One of the cabinets was lying on the floor, that was all. Ping was about to try one more time when another noise drifted to her. She stopped, cocking her head to listen. It came again.

She moved towards the beeping and scraping before thinking better of it. Going the other way, she ducked through the half-closed door and waited.

Her hands were shaking again and she pushed them against the wall. He heart was not so easy to control.

Four minutes and thirty-seven seconds later Ping watched, amazed, as a metal box came around the corner. It stopped where she'd been standing. She licked her dry lips and the box let out another series of beeps and spun about.

After a second of stillness, it exploded.

Sparks of red and blue and white spat outwards and smoke filled the hall. The box continued to beep occasionally. Finally, it went bang. The noises died away to nothing.

Ping peered around the door and, when the smoke had cleared, took a tentative step forward. The box didn't move. She took another step. It still didn't move. Metal panels covered most of the outside. Three glass panels protected other pieces of glass. Bits of colored string were in there as well, like she had found in the monster armor, only smaller.

Using one of her torches, Ping pushed the machine onto its side. Underneath there was nothing to see besides three wheels. She almost pulled the tool pouch from her belt to examine the box. But she didn't. What she wanted to do most was find the door and be out under the sky again. She felt as if she was being watched in the echoing, dusty passages. Anything could attack her and she wouldn't be able to do anything about it. She felt naked without her armor but felt Scree's absence even more keenly. Scree would help if he were there.

Ping wiped tears from her eyes. Scree or the sky. Either would make her more comfortable. She shook her head. *But I cannot take the sky with me, and I do not want to take Scree.* Looking one way and then the other, trying to get her bearings, she retraced her route in her mind to work out which direction she was facing. She set off once more.

For ten minutes, Ping wandered through the halls, looking back every now and then to be sure that the trail of her footprints was visible. Without Scree's innate sense of direction she was soon lost. But she kept going, running her fingers trough the dust on the walls, and with each step, her unease grew. She passed more blockades. There were places where furniture was scattered on the floor, as if more protective piles had been breached and pulled down.

When she heard the familiar beeping sound again she continued to walk, listening as the metal box slowly caught up. Was it a different box or the same one? She thought the first one had been broken but she didn't know for sure. Ping stopped to look when the box rounded a corner, veering from one side of the hallway to the other. The beeping seemed to grow more insistent. When it finally stopped a few meters away the box was beeping maniacally.

Ping smiled slightly. Then a ray of light shot from the box. It burned a hole in the leg of her breeches. She gasped and backed away a step. The light came again, scorching the wall to her left. With her second step the box beeped shrilly, fired and then started spitting sparks, as the other had.

Heart racing, Ping examined her breeches and the wall. It wasn't the same weapon as that used by the monsters, but it was close enough to scare her.

"I need to get out of here." But there was nothing to tell her which way to go. She might wander all day without success. The only things that broke the regularity of her surroundings were the metal boxes. She looked at the trail the box had made, as clear as her own.

She swallowed noisily. *I have no idea where it will lead,* she thought, *but I cannot get lost.* There might well be a thousand boxes at the end of the trail, but that didn't change the facts.

"What would Scree do?" Ping shuddered and examined the hall again. She followed the trail left by the box before she could change her mind. She resisted the urge to run.

Occasionally she opened one of the doors to see what was beyond. Not all of the doors opened. Some merely groaned or jammed halfway. Those that hissed aside showed the same bed and the same chair and the same cabinet, or just empty spaces where they should be. She thought she might be returning to the same doors again and again, but the dust on the floor in front of her was marked only by the passage of little wheels.

Once, she thought she heard a beeping, but it stopped as suddenly as it had started. Around two corners, through a snowdrift of furniture, she found a box with smoke spewing from between the joints. And three corners after that the trails of three boxes disappeared through a small hatch beside yet another door. Neither the little door nor the big door opened for her. Ping wondered what to do. There was still no handle or bell. Just a metal door with a film of dust. Beside it, she saw a plaque with words carved into the surface. She traced the indentations with her fingers but they were in a strange language and meant nothing to her. Below the plaque was a button.

Reaching out to press the button, Ping paused as the *little* door slid open. A beeping box trundled out and spun in her direction. In a panic, she skipped forward and pushed the contraption onto its side. Then she quickly pushed the button on the wall and darted inside the room. It might have been full of boxes, but she didn't have time to think.

But there were no boxes inside. She breathed a sigh off relief. There was no bed or chair or cabinet either.

Finally, a room that was different. Along one of the walls a long row of panels displayed a series of flashing lights and glowing windows that seemed to somehow look into the hallways outside. The images flickered, and she thought that they might be looking at a different passage each time. She saw the remains of one of the boxes on one screen. A minute later she saw it again. And then again.

After she'd seen the box for the third time a light started to flash amidst a row of buttons on a bench. Thirty seconds later, she heard a hiss. The door behind her was opening. A box was coming through.

Before Ping could reach the box a bolt of energy struck the wall behind her. Another sent a flash of searing pain along the side of her knee. Heart racing, she limped forward and up-ended the box. She sent it tumbling backwards into the hall just as the door closed.

The wound on her leg screamed at her. A long line had been burned along the skin and blood oozed out, but it wasn't as serious as it felt. She wiped the tears from her eyes.

Scree wouldn't have noticed. He notices his own pain as little as he notices others'. She tore the bottom of her breeches and wrapped the cloth tightly around her knee, biting her lip as she tightened the knot. But that was all she had time for. She was worried about more boxes coming for every second she delayed.

"Now what?"

Hitting the button by the door with shaking hands, Ping hurried to examine the two fallen boxes and the little door through which they'd come. Both machines were sending out streams of acrid smoke, apparently having succumbed to whatever had disabled the others. The only way she could think to stop the next ones was to block the door. She slid the boxes into place then waited to see if the plan would work. And she waited.

Finally the door opened and she could see movement beyond. But nothing emerged or even attempted to push out into the clear.

With a sigh of relief, she returned to her search. She opened drawers in metal cabinets, but whatever had once been inside had long disintegrated. The windows continued to switch from one view to another, with writing in the corner of each, but did not show anything that resembled the door that led outside. She examined the buttons and switches on the bench but they meant nothing to her. She pushed some but nothing seemed to happen.

For eleven minutes and forty-two seconds she searched the room but found nothing that would help. She gave up and slumped into one of the metal chairs at the bench, head in hear hands, fighting back tears. Here was her chance to help Scree, to prove her worth, and she couldn't even find the door, let alone open it. She looked around the room one more time, desperate, hoping there was something she'd missed. And she saw a streak of color on the wall where she had leaned to rest earlier. Every other wall she had seen had been the same mustard color hidden behind a layer of dirt.

Rising quickly to her feet, Ping crossed the room and wiped at the dust. She found a map hidden behind. When she wiped some more she found another map. And another. In all, fifteen maps had been painted onto the wall.

But Ping had no idea where she was, so how was she to work out where she wanted to go? She had seen her friends killed. She had crossed between worlds—surely she could find her way through some passages when she had maps to help.

She examined the maps for a long time with no luck. With their geometric patterns of halls and rooms, they all looked much alike. There were words on the maps, but without knowing....

Ping rushed outside to examine the sign on the wall near the door. She tried to memorize the symbols, then went back in and wrote them on the dust of another wall. She examined the maps for more than twenty-three minutes. She felt each second.

Finally, after looking at the words several times, she found [LEVEL C HABITAT] written several times on one of the maps. And after that it was a simple enough exercise to find [SECURITY].

"I'm here," she said, pointing at the spot. She wondered whether she was right, but decided to trust her judgment. What else could she do? She checked her writing on the wall once more, comparing it to the map, and shrugged. All she had to do now was decide where it was that she wanted to go. At least she felt she had made some progress. She breathed a long sigh and tried to think.

The map she was on did not look promising. A passage ran all the way around the outside with no doorways or small passages leading away. But she found what had to be some stairs leading down and followed the symbols to the correct map. There she found what she thought she wanted: several short passages with a labeled doorway on the end and nothing beyond.

Ping had no idea which direction she was facing. She had no idea which of her suspected doors Scree might be waiting at, if any. So she traced her route to the top of the stairs, and, swapping maps, to the nearest door. She ran through the directions three times, chanting each turn and each intersection.

"Scree would not hesitate." *Scree does not hesitate to do many things.* With a deep breath and a shrug, she was off.

After descending the stairs, Ping was confronted by another of the boxes on wheels. She ignored it as best she could and hurried on. They were obviously faulty in some way and she outpaced it easily.

"Miss one. Left."

But there was another blockage and she scrambled over as quickly as she could then paused for a moment to gather her thoughts. A deep breath and walking again. "Miss two. Right." Weaving past more furniture. "Left... Miss..." She was almost there but couldn't remember. "Scree would do it with his eyes closed." And Ping closed her eyes for a few seconds. It didn't help. She chose a direction at random. It was the wrong way. She went back to try again. The second passage proved to be correct. She made just one more turn and found a large, double door. It was unlike any of the others she'd seen.

There was beeping behind her, as if a half dozen of the boxes were in pursuit. They were slow, but it would not take them long to catch up.

Heart racing, Ping examined the door. This one also had a button nearby. Holding her breath, she pushed it.

Nothing happened.

She hit the button again. Nothing. Nothing. Nothing.

The beeping came closer.

"And if I do get the door open," she said, trying to think, "then what's to stop it from closing again?"

There was a bang as one of the pursuing boxes exploded. Ping jumped. Another bang came soon after, as if one had set off the other. But the beeps kept coming.

Quickly removing the tool pouch from her belt Ping took out a screwdriver and used it to pry at the button. The red outer casing popped away and clattered to the floor. A mess of the colorful cords were revealed. But what did she do with them? For seven second she stood looking, trying to ignore the sounds behind, before sticking her screwdriver in amongst the cords.

A spark arced from a piece of metal sending a shock up her arm. The door groaned horribly. It moved slightly... then stopped.

Ping glanced over her shoulder. The first box rolled around the corner.

Bracing herself she inserted her driver amongst the cords a second time. She ignored the energy biting at her fingers and cramping her arm. She watched through tears as the door slid open a little more.

A bolt of energy struck the wall near where she stood. She jumped again and dropped her screwdriver. The box that had fired buzzed to a halt, whining and screeching. The next was coming closer. It sounded like a dozen of them were just around the corner.

Ping searched the ground for her screwdriver, found it, picked it up with shaking fingers. One last time she jabbed it into the wires, gritting her teeth against the pain. Then the door was open just enough. She slipped through the narrow gap. Her tool pouch caught, holding her in place for two seconds that seemed a lifetime. Then she slipped out into the sunlight.

A box stopped just inside the door, twirling out of control and smoking. After four seconds another appeared. It stopped, beeping quietly. It did not try to pass through after her. Soon there were a half dozen of them there, watching like a pack of wild dogs but not attacking.

Ping collapsed to the ground, breathing heavily and trying to shake the last of the tingling pain from her fingers.

Eventually she looked around. Scree was nowhere to be seen. She did not know where she was. She did not know whether to be relieved or afraid, but laid down where she was to rest.

38: Escape

MELEDRIN FOLLOWED KIM and Airman Dongoske into the hallway. She was pleased to be moving again, though she wished it were Kim leading the way instead of the saveigni. She commenced a *Beginning* but changed her mind and wove a *Greater Beginning* instead.

Meledrin longed to see trees and sky once more. She longed to hear something other than the hum of mankind. Keeble added to the hum himself, mumbling, running his fingers along the swirling pattern of the walls. Tuki was as quiet as always. He knew what was proper.

"Where are we going?" Keeble whispered in Tuki's language as they waited near an intersection several minutes after leaving the cell.

Meledrin had been surprised earlier when she discovered Kim had been able to quickly learn Tuki's language. To then discover that Keeble could understand it as well had been truly shocking. She shook her head in displeasure.

Kim shrugged. "I don't know. We're just following Dongoske."

"Do you think he'll lead us out of here? Or into a trap."

Tuki watched it all as if nothing surprised him.

"He'll lead us out."

"What the hell?"

Meledrin turned to examine Airman Dongoske. He was standing in the middle of the hall, mouth hanging open like a saveigni who had found himself present at a bathing ritual.

"What?" Kim asked in reply. A small smile was playing at the edges of her mouth.

"You both speak Shoshone?"

"You should talk to your superiors a bit more often."

"You've spoken it all along and said nothing?"

Kim shook her head. "Nope. I don't know about Keeble, but I learned it after talking with Tuki."

"That's impossible."

"You keep saying that, Dongoske," Kim said with another smile, this one in Keeble's direction, "despite evidence to the contrary."

"You can't just learn a language like that," Dongoske insisted.

"Once I started listening, and concentrating, I found it was impossible not to learn. It was like a missing part of my mind fell back into place and everything was as it should have been. Perhaps it's a *genetic* thing."

"'*Genetic* thing'?" Dongoske shook his head. "If it was a genetic thing, everyone would be able to learn the language as easily as you have."

"Perhaps they can."

"Then why don't they?"

"Perhaps they don't really want to. Perhaps they haven't concentrated. You can't tell me General Hilliard has made any attempt at all to learn? You speak the language, so what more does he need, right?"

Meledrin joined the conversation then, clearing her throat as she looked between the two humans. "This is all extremely interesting, I am sure, but should we not discuss it at some later time, in some other location?"

Kim agreed. "Let's get out of here."

Dongoske grunted and nodded.

Kim looked around. "So, where are we going?"

That worried Meledrin, Kim not even knowing where they were going. The surrounding stone was weighing on her mind, and she wanted someone she trusted to know what was happening. The soldier did not answer. He merely beckoned for them to follow and moved down the next passage.

As far as Meledrin could tell, there was no pattern to the route Airman Dongoske followed, but they traversed the hallways silently for a long time before coming into contact with anyone else. Rounding a corner, they discovered two men standing guard on either side of a closed door. Meledrin felt herself shoved aside as Kim charged at the two men. With a curse, Dongoske attacked as well. The guards stood still for a moment, shocked. By the time they thought to reach for the weapons at their belts, it was too late.

Slightly bemused, Meledrin watched as Kim kicked one man in the groin and struck the other in the throat. Airman Dongoske didn't even take part in the action.

"Jesus! Are they all right?" Dongoske asked when Kim had finished.

"Are *they* all right? I thought you wanted us to get out of here?" Kim wrung her hand and grimaced in pain. "Shit; that hurt."

Meledrin felt like pointing out that she could quite easily let the men handle the sweaty hand-to-hand violence and save herself the embarrassment. But the two humans were talking, so she remained silent.

"Well, yes." Dongoske looked guiltily at the two fallen men. "You know, I'd rather not kill anyone."

"They aren't dead, Airman. I know what I'm doing."

"I find that hard to believe."

"And I find it hard to believe we're still standing here. Either lead the way or piss off."

"Come on then."

Meledrin sniffed her displeasure, but everyone ignored her so she was forced to follow the man again.

She weaved an *Action*.

Dongoske watched the two downed men as he went past. Kim watched Dongoske.

From that point, the journey became more difficult. The sounds of humans became louder and more frequent. Before, everything had been softly lit, now bright lights cut through the dimness from under doors or through windows.

Near one side passage Airman Dongoske grabbed Meledrin by the arm. She squealed slightly, unable to control her shock, but the man pulled her through an open doorway before Meledrin could shake loose his strong grip.

"How dare you touch me."

"What? Shut up, there's someone there."

"I will not shut up. If you lay hands on me again, I will have no choice but to —"

Another hand grabbed her arm. Meledrin spun about to see Kim standing with a finger pressed to her lips. "If you don't shut up," Kim whispered, "*none* of us will have any choices."

The sound of the footsteps slowed, then paused. The voices of two men trailed away. Meledrin held her breath. A moment later the two humans in the passageway moved on again.

"If you touch me again," Meledrin said quietly, "I will kill you."

Airman Dongoske flapped his jaw wordlessly, then shook his head and went back out into the hall. Kim said nothing, but as Meledrin straightened her clothes and muttered a *Changing* to calm her nerves, she could feel the woman's stare. She brushed the memory of the man's touch from her arm and followed him through the door.

They continued on, darting across brightly lit or open spaces like thieves. For all their caution, pausing at each corner to listen, waiting in shadows, they didn't go far before finding trouble once more.

Meledrin walked quickly around a corner and found herself staring at the hairless chest of a heavily muscled, shirtless man. He was not much taller than she was, but he *seemed* much larger. They both stood staring for a moment before Keeble blundered around the corner and almost knocked Meledrin into the stranger's arms. The human broke eye contact as Keeble swore.

"Whistler's wart, woman, what's the holdup?"

Kim rounded the corner and did not hesitate at all. Her cocked shoulder struck the stranger in the solar plexus as she charged forward. They both grunted with the impact, but the man was driven back into the wall. A moment later he lay on the ground groaning, and Kim finished the fight with a short sharp blow. Before she had even straightened, trying to shake the pain from her fist, she was speaking.

"Come on, let's keep moving."

They continued down the hall, running now, still in single file. Dongoske glanced up at the ceiling at one point, as they crouched in the shadows and waited for a human to pass. Meledrin wondered if he was seeking the help of his gods or if it was some human trait that she had not yet experienced. She thought to ask Kim what the action meant, but did not have the chance. They were moving forwards again.

They dashed across the passage then stopped outside a door, and Dongoske held a cautionary finger to his lips.

"Through here," he whispered, "is a guardroom. Two men. Armed, but not expecting anything. We'll have to take them quickly, but we should be safe. You sure you want to do this? They'll kill you, they'll kill us, if they get the chance."

Kim nodded. "Do it."

"Me first. You in ten, nine, eight..." Dongoske opened the door and strolled in like he was supposed to be there. He left the door open behind him.

Meledrin counted down slowly in her head, as seemed to be expected, but did not follow Kim into the conflict when the time counted down. She followed slowly and saw the woman kick a man in the stomach twice in quick succession. Dongoske had the other man against a wall with a weapon pointed at his face.

"Kim, stop. Roger, step back with your hands on top of your head or I shoot."

"You won't shoot." The man stepped away from Kim with his hands up.

"Try me."

Meledrin sat down in a cold metal chair, straightening her dress. *Changing*. It was a small room with lockers around the walls and a pair of metal doors almost completely filled the far wall of the room. There were two buttons nearby.

Meledrin watched Tuki standing in the corner, clutching the skyglass protectively. Keeble started talking to himself again. He was examining the wall. His fingers touched at the stone delicately.

"I could Sing a Song and walk out of here," he said softly in his own language. "A moment, and I would be away from here, on my own. I could tunnel as far as I wanted in a moment, and just walk away."

Meledrin listened as Keeble started to hum tunelessly. He slowly built a wall of sounds, clicking and tapping and making other strange noises. As the sound grew, Meledrin thought she could feel a pressure in her head, a tingle down her spine.

Meledrin watched, spellbound, as Keeble raised his left arm. But when the metal of his mechanical hand touched the stone, he shuddered, convulsed, and took a step back. The wall of sound he had been building collapsed. He looked at the stump of his hand. "No," he said eventually, shaking his head. "There is nothing I can do."

Meledrin shuddered as well, shaking off the feeling of power. "I know I have been in bad company too long when I start to imagine dwarfish magic."

Kim and Airman Dongoske had been talking, but when Meledrin spoke, Kim turned to face her.

"What was that?"

"Pardon?"

"What did you say?"

"I merely stated that I need to rest, because I am suddenly imagining strange things."

"You noticed it too?"

"What?"

"I'm not sure. I didn't really notice it until it was gone. It was like a cool breeze on my consciousness."

"We both need to rest, it would seem."

"Or maybe we both really felt something. What was it, do you think?"

Meledrin was reluctant to voice her opinion on the matter. It was ridiculous. But Kim seemed to like ridiculous ideas. "I was under the impression that whatever was happening was caused by Keeble."

"Keeble?"

"That is correct."

Meledrin watched as Kim called to the dwarf. He did not reply. He seemed to take no notice at all, continuing to talk to himself in his own language.

"Mel, what's he saying?"

"In the first instance, he said that he could construct a tunnel in but a moment and be away from here. But most recently he stated that there is no action that he is able to take. Since then, it seems that he has been arguing with himself."

"Ask him?"

"You are capable of asking. He speaks the language of the moai."

"But he doesn't appear to be listening. Ask him in his own language."

"Question him of what?"

"About how the hell he was going to dig a tunnel in a couple of seconds."

When she turned, Meledrin discovered that Keeble had sat on another metal chair. He was examining his mechanical hand, winding the gears. He adjusted the leather straps that held the contraption to his arm.

"Keeble cannot be trusted," Meledrin told Kim. "It would be a more sensible course of action if we followed Airman Dongoske."

"Ask him."

Meledrin sniffed. She did not appreciate being spoken to like a saveigni. *"Keeble, are you able to get us out of this place?"*

He looked up for a moment. *"Maybe."* He wound the gears on his hand. *"But..."*

"Our world is being attacked, Keeble, and these Americans worry only about themselves."

"And why shouldn't they worry about themselves? Dwarves have never been too worried about helping other people, either. Nor elves, from what I know of them."

"You can facilitate our escape if you wish, and yet you refuse to do so?"

"Well, maybe I was just going to do it later when you weren't around."

Kim interrupted. "Well?"

"The breeze on your consciousness was not Keeble. Merely coincidence. He can do nothing."

Kim turned to glare at the dwarf. "Keeble, can you get us out of here?"

"No."

Kim sighed. "Well then, we'll just have to follow the good Airman here. He says that when we get off the lift, we'll be about fifty meters from the surface, but there's another guard station in the way."

"Will we be able to make our way past?"

"Without being seen?" Kim said. "No. Wouldn't be a very helpful guard post otherwise. But we have guns, so we are just going to run out there and threaten to kill somebody."

"Will that prove to be successful?"

"In most circumstances it wouldn't, but in this one it will."

Dongoske had finished tying the two guards with sticking tape and turned to join the conversation. "Why is that? Why will it work?"

It was a moment before Kim answered. "Because we're coming at them from behind. They won't be expecting an attack from *inside* the complex."

Meledrin could tell she was lying, but Dongoske nodded grudgingly. "Of course," he said. He picked up a weapon and handed it to Kim, who did something to it, releasing a small section and snapping it back into place. The American continued. "Let's go then. When the lift doors open at the top, you all stay out of sight. Well, just stay by the door and watch silently. All right?"

"Wait," Kim said. "I have a better idea."

"What?" Dongoske asked.

Kim stepped smoothly forward and pointed her weapon at the American's head. "For a start, you put down the gun."

"What? What the hell are you doing?"

"I want to thank you and General Hilliard for your help, but I'll be able to take it from here."

Meledrin tried to work out what was going on. Was Kim suggesting that General Hilliard knew of the escape and approved?

"I have no idea what you're talking about," Airman Dongoske said.

"Don't bother." Kim motioned with her chin. "Mel, get the tape for his hands."

"You won't shoot me."

Kim did something and the weapon made a loud click.

"Is that supposed to scare me?"

Meledrin didn't think he looked scared at all, but he was slowly crouching down to discard his weapon. Except that was not what he was going to do. Meledrin saw the movement a moment before Dongoske lashed out with the handle of his weapon. She called out, softly, but Kim was already moving. The woman twisted away from the blow aimed at the top edge of her hipbone. She grunted with pain, but struck back, attacking Airman's Dongoske's jaw with the heel of her hand. Neither of them was willing to use their weapons in the intended method. Kim used the handle, as her opponent had, and he fell limply to the floor.

Meledrin smoothed out her dress as if she'd been the one involved in the combat. "The escape was a ruse?" Meledrin said.

Kim nodded. She was breathing heavily and sweating.

She collected the tape that Meledrin had ignored earlier and used it to bind Airman Dongoske's feet. He started to struggle before his hands were secure as well, but Meledrin stepped in to assist, even going down on her knees to grab his flailing fists. She grabbed one of his wrists in both her hands and twisted. Not too much, but just enough. He went suddenly still, grimacing with pain but not willing to react lest she decide to complete the maneuver.

"You do not lay your hands on a woman without her permission," Meledrin hissed in his face. "Under any circumstances."

Kim bound his wrists while Meledrin spoke an *Ending*.

"How stupid do you think I am, Dongoske? Jesus, did you and the General really think I'd fall for it? And do you really think I'd go around attacking elite American soldiers if I thought they'd be serious about fighting back?"

Airman Dongoske grunted and laid his head on the floor. "You're just making it hard for yourself, Kim, and you know it. How far do you think you'll get?"

Kim shrugged. "I guess we're about to find out. Come on you lot, let's get out of here." She taped the mouths of the three soldiers and pressed one of the buttons on the wall.

The two big doors slid open and they entered the lift. Kim was swearing before the doors had even closed.

"What is the matter?"

Kim sighed. "We want to go down, but we need a key for that."

"Down?"

"Yes."

"But are we not trying to escape from this complex. Going down will merely take us further from the surface."

"Yeah, well apparently I have a problem with authority even when it's making me do exactly what I wanted to do." She hit the wall. "Stupid damn lift. Up it is then."

But as she was reaching out to press one of the buttons on the wall, Keeble reached past and pressed a different one. The doors opened, and Keeble marched back out into the room.

"Keeble, where are you going?" Meledrin asked. She wanted to be away from this place. She wanted to see the sky. She wanted to breathe fresh air.

"Come on, Keeble," Kim said, stabbing at a button to keep the doors open. "I want to go down, but up is the second best option."

The dwarf stepped over airman Dongoske, who rolled onto his back to watch, and started going through some cupboards. He didn't find what he was after, apparently, for he went out the door into the hallway. Meledrin noticed that Kim was staring after him stupidly. Apparently chasing him was not part of her plans, but she had just started to do so when he returned with a small plastic box in his hands.

"There's a utility closet just down the hall," he explained. He returned to the elevator, set the box down, and opened it up. There were all manner of tools inside. He selected one, waited for Kim to release the button she was still holding, and went to work on a small panel close by. "I think we are going to have some company very soon." He was seemingly more lucid than he had been for a long time. Perhaps the prospect of manual labor had calmed him.

Meledrin waved her fingers in a *Greater Changing* as Kim swore again.

39: Deeper

KIM WATCHED FOR A COUPLE OF MINUTES as Keeble worked on the elevator. "Do you have any idea what you're doing?" she asked. She could imagine half the personnel in the complex gathering in the small room outside.

The dwarf had a screwdriver in his mouth but answered anyway. "This is just like a computer. I pulled one of them apart in Colin's office. And I talked about them on the plane."

Kim shook her head. "I could pull the thing apart too, doesn't mean it would do anything after I put it back together."

But Keeble snapped the panel closed and pushed the down button. The lift started to move. Kim smiled and stopped herself just before she ruffled his hair. "Way to go."

"So why do you wish to go down?" Meledrin asked from her spot in the corner.

"Three reasons. A spaceship, a captured alien, and because Hilliard didn't want me to."

Meledrin sniffed and Kim shrugged in reply.

The journey down didn't take long. When the doors opened, Kim expected to be confronted by a dozen armed men. There was only one, and he looked slightly surprised. Hadn't they worked out what she was doing?

"Ahhh, hi," Kim said. "Don't move." The problem was, she said it in Tuki's language. She said everything in Tuki's language unless she thought about it first. While she raised the gun, she gave the instructions again in English. *"Don't move."*

It didn't look as if the young man was about to disobey.

"Take me to your alien," Kim said.

He swallowed. *"I can't."*

"Why not?"

"I've only been beyond this room a couple of times. I don't know where the alien is, exactly, but I know there are more guards and more security systems to get through before you can get to it."

Kim shrugged. *"Well, this next door will have to do for now."*

The guard nodded before using a key and scanning his hand on a panel beside the door. Kim took the key and led the others through into the hall beyond. Still no people. Tuki didn't say anything but nervously adjusted the pack on his back while he gazed into the gloom. Kim knew how he felt.

Keeble was still carrying his toolbox, gripping it in the metal prongs of his left hand. "Where is everyone?" he asked.

Kim looked over her shoulder at the guard and asked the question in English.

"*They have better things to do than stand around in hallways, I suppose,*" he said.

"*But that's what guards are made for,*" Kim said.

He shrugged. "*If you can get through everything above, a couple more down here won't make all that much difference.*"

"*How long until some arrive?*"

"*A couple of minutes.*" He looked over his shoulder as the elevator doors closed and the lift started to go back up. "*Or less.*"

Kim let the door close. "*Right.*" She looked back down the hall and hefted her gun. Surely this wasn't part of Hilliard's plan. How was she supposed to tell? "Damn it. Can you fix this door, Keeble?"

The dwarf immediately set to work, awkwardly working his hand loose so he could put the tools down. He undid four screws on a panel beside the door and carefully placed everything in a pile on the floor. He scratched his head and muttered to himself as he looked carefully amongst the wires and circuits in the wall. Then he took up some pliers, reached carefully into the hole, and ripped out and cut everything he could grab in one go. For good measure he smashed a circuit board as well.

"Huh." Kim was so hyped up and expecting everything to be nearly impossible that she wouldn't have thought of something so simple. "Will that work?"

Keeble shrugged. He didn't look particularly happy. "Can't see why not." He looked into the hole as if thinking maybe he *could* have found the one correct wire to do the job. "I'm not an expert on that type of thing."

"You fixed the elevator."

"Yeah, but it took me a few minutes. I didn't have time for fiddling here."

Meledrin sniffed, though Kim thought it was probably more out of habit than anything else.

"Right," Kim said. "Of course. Come on then."

Heart pounding, she led the way quickly down the hallway, stalking through the soft light. Tuki and Keeble, tool box in hand again, crept along behind like boys playing hide and seek while Meledrin came at a leisurely stroll. Colors and patterns swirled through the walls, and there was a slight rut along the center of the floor. The air was heavy and still. There were no people.

"There should be more people," Kim muttered.

"Is it night time?" Tuki asked softly, looking around as if he expected the missing people to magically appear at any moment.

According to Kim's watch it was just after midnight, but she would've expected this place to be buzzing with activity at all hours. With the war going on above there was no time for resting.

There were Tuki-sized brown metal doors off either side of the passage, and Kim checked a couple at random. She didn't expect to find anything significant in such a nondescript location and wasn't disappointed. Quiet, dark offices. Neat storage rooms. A kitchen.

Before she closed the door on this last room, Kim called Tuki forward. She took the pack off his back, tossed out most of the clothes and filled the newly created space with tins of nonperishable food and bottled water. The odds of them needing the supplies were slim but it was no use getting onto the spaceship if they just had to let Hilliard in tomorrow when they got thirsty.

Kim could hardly lift the pack, but the moai had no trouble.

When they finally saw someone else, they found the spaceship. A tired looking woman with wisps of loose hair and a crumpled white coat stepped out through a door. She was examining papers on an overloaded clipboard and didn't see them as Kim ducked down a branching passage with her companions close behind. And when footsteps came in their direction, they opened another door and slipped into the room beyond.

Holding her breath, Kim listened at the door. "I don't think she's coming this way," she whispered. For a moment, nobody replied.

Eventually, Meledrin said, "I am wondering if that is the ship for which we are searching."

Kim turned to look around her. There was no spaceship. "Pardon?" The room was long and narrow, barely two meters across and almost completely filled by a gallery of chairs that looked out through a window. Tuki had taken off the pack and was sitting, but Keeble and Meledrin were both standing beyond that.

"I have never seen a spaceship," Meledrin said, "unless those bats count. But I believe that could well be one." The elf pointed out through the window.

"I think she could be right. It's a bit like a plane, but not really."

But by that stage Kim could already see. She leaned against the window as if every centimeter could make the difference. Tuki went to stand a small distance away, looking silently down into the room. The ship was about the size of a small bus and shaped something like an egg sliced length wise, small end forward. There were two stubby wings and a tall pointed tail. It squatted low to the ground on four articulated legs. Spotlights and scaffolding tied it in a web of shadows.

Kim thought it would have people crawling all over it, but the room was empty of life.

"It isn't very big, is it?" Keeble said.

"No, not really."

Meledrin sniffed. "It is large enough."

"Are we going to steal it?" Keeble wound the gears on his hand.

"Steal it? How the hell would we get out?"

"Well, they got it in there," Keeble said.

"I do not believe it is a good idea to give her any ideas, Keeble."

Kim followed the dwarf's gaze upwards. Far above, probably at ground level, she guessed, was what looked like a trapdoor. She smiled.

"Come on. We can spring the alien, then steal the ship." *Why not?* She smiled and clapped Keeble on the back.

The dwarf was nodding as if it were all a foregone conclusion. He collected his tool box from near his feet and headed for the door.

"I do not think it is worth the risk."

"What are they going to do?" Kim asked. "Kill us?"

"Perhaps."

Maybe they would. Kim wasn't sure, but she was going to find out. She licked her lips.

"So why do we need the alien?" Keeble asked. "I thought Dongoske said it was a human ship."

"He did, but I want to talk to the alien and find out what the hell is going on."

Tuki followed Kim out of the room without complaint or question. He'd probably been following women without question all his life and wasn't about to change now. Kim didn't really care if Meledrin followed at this stage, though she doubted the elf would go off on her own.

"We need some stairs or a lift," Kim said once she was back out in the main passage. There were no doors leading directly into the hangar from this level, but there were several others on the other side of the hall. The second door contained a stairwell.

Keeble started through. "No. We should look for the alien up here first. Come on."

But it was just more offices and more utility rooms, so a few minutes later they made their way down to the next level. Straight away there was more activity. When Kim opened the door, she found herself face to face with the same harried woman who had almost caught them earlier. They both stared stupidly for a moment.

Kim reacted first, grabbing her and dragging her through the door. Keeble slammed it shut behind them, hopefully cutting off her shout.

"Shut up," Kim said, centimeters from her face. She said it in Tuki's language first then again a moment later in English, but the woman kept shouting. Kim slapped her. That did the job. Kim didn't know what she would have done next. Punching her didn't seem right. "You got any tape in that box of tricks, Keeble?"

He did, and he put it to use binding the woman's hands and feet. Kim apologized before gagging her as well.

Out in the hall she checked both ways then picked a direction at random. More offices. A mess hall with a tired looking soldier.

Kim faltered, swallowed. "Ahh, was Brian here?"

The soldier shook his head and Kim got out of there as quickly as she could.

"Who is Brian?" Meledrin asked.

"Don't worry about it."

Sleeping quarters next, with the sounds of snoring. Then a blank wall.

Back the other way, well past the end of the hangar, Kim checked another door, opening it up and poking her head through. More soldiers. And she knew immediately that she wasn't talking her way out of this one. The guards here, closer to the important stuff, were more experienced and more alert. They were on their feet in an instant, weapons drawn.

"*Put down your weapon,*" one of them shouted as his three companions spread out.

It took Kim a moment to sort through the English words and work out what he was actually saying. She got the point anyway.

"*Put it down now.*"

Keeble was ready to fight but Kim held him back. The guards looked serious. One of them had an edgy look that made Kim's heart pound even faster. Her finger was well away from the trigger and the safety was on. But they weren't to know that, so she slowly, carefully, did as she was asked.

She cleared her throat. "I don't think General Hilliard is going to be very happy with us."

"Was he ever happy?" the dwarf asked vaguely.

"Good point," Kim replied. "It was fun while it lasted though."

She shifted her focus past the guards to examine the rest of the room. It was big — twenty meters to a side, at least — and was full of a lot of busy looking people. There were a dozen or more scientists of one kind or another working at computers and consoles plus a couple of dozen soldiers who, until a moment ago, had been checking their equipment. Now all those serious looking men and women were starting to relax after realizing the excitement by the door was under control.

"Brian may be amongst these people," Meledrin said softly, "but I am not sure she will be able to assist us, whoever she is."

Kim took a moment to start thinking in English again so she could talk to the Americans. "*I should probably let you know there's some lady tied up in the stairwell.*"

"*Jack, go and check it out. All of you, shut up and get into the corner.*" They shifted so Jack could slip out.

"*So what happens now?*" Kim asked the Americans while trying to keep an eye on Keeble.

Apparently that wasn't immediately obvious.

Keeble was muttering to himself. "There's another gate through there," he said.

"You mean the gate to the other world?" Kim said, shocked out of her nervousness. "How do you know it's there?" There were five other doors in the room, and Keeble was looking at the largest of them, on the wall opposite the hangar. It didn't look very special, apart from its size.

"I can hear it. I can feel it." He muttered and wound the gears on his hand. "It isn't right there, there are five or six walls between us and it, but it's close."

"*You two shut up.*"

"*We'll put them in a cell until the General gets here. Somehow I don't think this was part of his plan.*"

The leader shanghaied another couple of soldiers into his detail and led the way across the room, past a lot of curious people, to a small, metal door with a glowing green hand scanner. Beyond was a short passage, then another guardroom.

From there, they went through another door and Kim muttered, "Great, we broke into jail."

But, one of the three small cells held the alien prisoner.

Kim stopped in her tracks. Keeble ran into her back. A moment later the guard was swearing. He pushed roughly, and Kim stumbled into an empty cell. She couldn't take her eyes off the alien. It was an ugly bipedal thing that was actually closer to Keeble's height than Meledrin's though the size of the armor they wore has suggested otherwise. It had rough, tough looking, leathery blue-tinged skin, a flat nose, and two large brown eyes. Wearing only a pair of trousers, it stood silently in the corner of its cell, staring at the floor. "Bad science fiction," she muttered. "A humanoid alien." She'd called it ugly, but maybe it was considered gorgeous by others of its kind.

Kim jumped when the door clanged shut. There was a hint of finality about the sound. The soldiers left them alone.

"What do we do now?" Keeble asked. He was looking at the alien as if it were nothing more than a puzzle to be solved. Maybe it was, for now.

Kim looked around. There wasn't much to see. One long, uncomfortable looking bench, three barred walls, and the alien. No pinball machine. No spa bath.

Meledrin was sitting on the bench, as if preparing for a long wait. Tuki crouched on the floor by the pack, skyglass in hand. Kim tested the bars near the door. She tested the bars to the adjoining cell. They were as solid as they looked.

She stood by the bars, looking at the alien. "Now we wait for General Hilliard."

"But I want to go in the spaceship." Keeble looked over his shoulder. "Or see the other gate." But the gate was obviously a poor second choice.

"Well, unless you can get us out of here in the next few minutes it isn't going to happen."

The dwarf pursed his lips and turned to look at the stone wall. "I *might* be able to."

Kim turned to look at him. "You were saying something about that before." Her mind kept twitching back to the alien, making it hard to concentrate. She wanted to talk to it. She wanted to grab it and shake it and ask it what the hell was going on.

"I failed the Rock Singing Test. I shouldn't Sing at all."

"What is this singing?"

He wound the gears on his hand. "I shouldn't Sing at all."

Kim went and stood before him. "Keeble, if you want to go in that spaceship we have to do it now. If General Hilliard comes down here we won't get another chance. We'll all be put in a more secure cell than this one, with guards there to watch us all the time."

"But if I get it wrong, someone could get hurt, or die."

"Meledrin can talk to the alien." Could she? Kim didn't stop to think about it. No time. She licked her lips. "We may be the only people who can stop this war anytime soon, but the American's won't let us. Not because they don't want to stop the war, but because they don't understand." Kim couldn't blame them for that. She wasn't sure she understood. "We need to get out of here, Keeble."

He looked at her, but Kim wasn't sure he really saw.

"I shouldn't Sing at all." He wound the gears on his hand in and out, in and out, until Kim grabbed his twitching fingers.

"I trust you, Keeble."

Meledrin shook her head. "It is pointless. Even if we could get out of here we still must get into the space ship."

She was right of course, but Kim didn't care. The ship was their one chance to stop the war anytime soon. And if they couldn't get into it, if there was no chance, she could at least see it. She could touch it before Hilliard turned up with his handcuffs and his questions. That would be pretty cool if nothing else. Kim held up her hand to silence the elf, but she kept going anyway.

"The Americans have been trying to breach the hull for more than fifty years, and you think we might be able to do it in a matter of moments?"

Kim kept her eyes locked on the dwarf's face.

SCREE HAD BEEN STARING at the door for a long time, but it didn't make any difference. Night came, a storm rolled in. The giant bats on the plain had gone and come and gone again. Ping still hadn't come back.

"Probably sitting downs with food and ale," Scree said bitterly. "Should never have trusted her." But he hadn't had any choice then, and he had no choice now. He had to sit and wait. The thing was, he did trust her.

Eventually he started worrying, thinking something might have happened. He'd gone back to anger by the time she came along the path from the north. Scree rose and ran out into the rain when she walked slowly into the area in front of the door.

"What are you doings coming that ways?" he asked.

"That was first door I found and didn't have time to look for *right* door. If don't like it can go and find your own door." They were brave words, but Scree could see her watching him carefully.

"There's more thans one door?"

"Obviously."

"Where is it?"

"Five kilometers that way about."

"So, what took you so long?" Scree asked, the anger creeping into his voice.

Ping took a step back, her hands twisting in the stained material of her shirt. Scree took a deep breath. It could take all day to find the door without her.

"Sorry." Scree almost laughed until he realized he meant it. He just didn't know whether he was sorry for himself or her. He didn't know if there was a difference.

Ping watched him, as if she too was trying to decide. She took another step back. "Took long, because there's whole city under mountain. Took while to get out, especially since I chased by... things. And there barricades across passages as if people fighting. Once did get out, had no idea where you were. I went other direction before deciding it was wrong way."

Scree stared at her. "Fighting? When?"

"Not recent."

"Well, let's go then."

"No, I rest. Going to sleep here, and go in morning."

Scree grunted in disgust and returned to the shelter offered by the doorway. He saw Ping staring at him after he'd settled. He grunted again, swore under his breath, and found a spot out in the open. He wondered if he should just find the door on his own. But she'd said something about being chased, so he might need all the help he could get.

Scree knew that the little woman didn't sleep, even with the best spot. She stayed awake the whole night, staring at him. Before dawn, she rose quietly, as if to avoid waking someone, and climbed into her armor. Scree stayed where he was, lying silently. If she started to raise the weapon, he'd have plenty of time to move. He waited with his night-eyes painting the darkness, watching her face through the broken helmet.

He could see in her eyes that she thought about it. It was a strange feeling, having someone stare at him like that and not react. To lie still and silent while someone thought about his death. It made him wonder how others felt when he looked at them in the same way.

When she started to cry, Scree stirred, as if waking. "You up early," he said, stretching.

She cleared her throat. "Couldn't sleep," she replied eventually.

He thought of saying that he couldn't sleep either. "Thinking about the underground city?" he said eventually

She nodded slightly.

"What's down there?"

She seemed reluctant to talk about it, so Scree got ready. A couple of minutes later they were following the path around a huge boulder and continuing along the side of the mountain.

With Ping in her armor it was a slow journey and Scree silently complained at every pause for rough ground. He could've covered five kilometers quicker than his companion ate breakfast in the mornings, but he didn't say anything.

Around the mountain, Scree finally saw another metal door. This one was jammed halfway open. He gave a whoop of joy and raced to take a closer look.

A dozen little metal boxes were hanging about just inside. A handful more weren't moving at all. Others had smoke pouring from various holes. A sound echoed from nearby, blaring in time to a flashing red light.

"What's all this thens," Scree asked Ping when she finally caught up.

"Those little boxes like guard dogs. They fire..." she raised her weapon arm "...fire like monsters."

"You still alive."

"Because they don't fire straight. Think they're broken."

"Broke?"

"Think they machines, like the armor, except without creature inside. Kind of clockwork guard dog."

"So why isn't theys shooting now?"

"Don't know. Perhaps we're outside."

"Maybe."

Scree watched the boxes as they spun about and bumped into each other near the doorway. After a while he wondered what he was doing. Raising his weapon, he fired at them one by one. They sizzled and popped and threw out sparks before grinding to a halt or exploding completely.

Soon, smoking remains blocked the door. Scree smiled at Ping. It was a while longer before they could get inside. The opening may have been wide enough for Ping to pass through, but neither Scree nor the armor were close to fitting. He lent his strength against one door and Ping set the strength of the armor against the other. Long, straining minutes later, Scree was able to slip inside. While Ping worked for just a bit more room, he made his way to the first intersection. There, he stopped.

He looked one way, then the next. There were pale, dust covered walls, a couple of doors and not much else. There were footprints in the dust on the floor that could only belong to Ping, but he didn't want to just retrace her path unless she'd found the next gateway. He was still standing, lost in thought, when the woman clanked up beside him. She waited for him to keep going.

"Which ways?" he asked, but she didn't say anything. He could imagine her shrugging her slim shoulders inside the armor. "How did you find your ways to the door?"

"Was a map." She raised an arm slowly to point. "That way. Up stairs."

"Let's go thens. See whats we can find."

"There were more of the guard boxes up there."

The little boxes weren't going to worry Scree. He started to follow the path of footprints in the dust.

They walked slowly through the corridors. Ping could not climb the blockades, so she simply walked through them, pushing aside beds and cabinets with the inexorable plodding strength of the monster armor. They climbed a set of wide stairs. Then there were more of the same. At the end of the trail, two of the clockwork dogs had been toppled to block a small door.

"You do that?" Scree asked Ping when she eventually caught up.

"Yes."

He grunted in admiration.

"The maps in there. Have to press button to open door."

Scree pressed the button and the door slid noisily aside. Inside, Ping had wiped dust from a wall to show the maps. Scree was impressed again, surprised she'd found them and was able to work out what they were.

He studied the images. He retraced their journey in his mind. It wasn't until he'd worked out where they were that he thought he should tell Ping she'd done well.

He took some time to think about how he might do that. He cleared his throat. "You done good," he said eventually. He glanced at her. She was looking at him, eyes wide, but looked away almost immediately.

"Umm... We on third level from top," she said.

"Yeah, I knows."

The passages were amazing and, according to the painted lines on the wall, there were fifteen levels of them all up with the middle ones being the largest. Scree looked at the maps for little more than a minute then turned to his companion.

"You ready?"

"No. Need paper and something write with."

"What fors?"

"For the maps."

"I got the maps," he said, shaking his head and wondering why she'd want to draw the maps on something as temporary as paper. Scree wasn't exactly sure where he was going, but all the interesting stuff seemed to start at about level 7. There were lots more places marked and labeled from that point, but the couple of words he could read meant nothing to him. He'd just have to go and look for himself, starting at the top and working down. He set off and Ping clanked into motion behind.

-o⭘o-

Scree pushed the button to open the door to the seventh level from the top, four below where they'd originally entered, and immediately knew something was different. The blockade across the door was more impressive than any that had come before. Along with desks and chairs there were heavy, strange machines and odd pieces of metal. And the air was fresher. Scree could feel it moving against his skin. The sounds he'd heard all the way down were clearer, sharper. He cocked his head to listen.

<Wait,> he whispered in his mind and Ping paused on the steps above.

"<*What is it?*>" She whispered as well.

<Don't knows.>

He climbed over into a T-intersection, pointing his weapon down one direction, looking the other— covering his own back. He heard Ping start downwards again and moved away from the doorway as she got close.

<Go right whens you comes through,> he said.

She muscled through the barricade and did as she was told, marching away from him towards the corner. Scree followed, walking backwards and concentrating on the shifting air around him.

<T-intersection,> Ping said quietly as she kept moving forward.

<You look right.>

Scree quickened his pace so that he went to the left at the same time that she went right.

<Two boxes,> she said. Scree had three as well.

These were bigger than on the previous levels though, sixty centimeters high instead of twenty. They moved with none of their fellows' uncertainty. Scree fired his weapon and heard Ping doing the same. He kept moving from side to side, dancing left to right, not allowing the boxes to aim. He could hear Ping talking in his mind, though she was only talking to herself. She was being fired upon constantly, but the weapons had no effect against the monster armor. The monster weapons were not affecting the boxes either.

<Isn't working, Scree.>

<I knows.> The machines attacking Scree were starting to compensate for his movement, learning, for they started to fire spasmodically and it was all he could do to keep clear. He was breathing heavily, sweating. <Back around the corner so they're only in front of us.>

When they were together, Scree stood behind Ping and they were able to concentrate their fire and get results. The first machine moved steadily towards them, firing constantly. It wasn't long before the metal of its outer casing warped and buckled. The softer materials melted. The colored cords beneath were open to attack. Ping fired into the hole while Scree shifted his attack to the next box in line.

The last box finally stopped moving.

<Cannot keep doing that, Scree. Not if as many as there were the smaller ones.>

<Right. Let's see if we can finds where they's coming from then.>

<But came from both directions.>

<Let's go... left.>

Scree led the way, moving far ahead of Ping, following the trails in the dust, leaping scattered furniture, quickly climbing barricades, weaving through the dust. One of the boxes found him. He didn't stop moving as he fired at the little clear window on the front. Finally, the window melted and then so did the cords behind. The box ground to a halt, crackling and spitting sparks. Wasn't so hard one on one, and when you knew the weak spot.

He moved on again and found a map room like the one right up the top and the little door beside it.

He arrived just as another box started to come out. He raced down the hallway and hit the box with his shoulder, driving the contraption back into its den. The heat of the weapon scorched his hip but he stayed where he was, wondering what to do next. He was too close to use his weapon. Half in the den as he was, though, he could see about ten more of the boxes waiting. He had to do something.

When Ping arrived she didn't offer any help.

Scree dropped his weapon and punched the clear window. He pounded against it until his knuckles bled and then pounded some more. Just when he thought it would never happen, the window cracked. One more punch and he was through. He ripped at the cords beneath, sparks of energy biting at his fingers.

"Howling cats." But the lights on the box went out and it fell silent. <Now what do we do?>

<*Lay it down so others can't get past.*>

Sweating with the effort, Scree toppled the box onto its side and backed carefully out into the open. "What's to stop thems from just pushing past?"

<*Don't know but last ones didn't.*>

Scree grunted.

<*Do you think there another of rooms somewhere?*>

He grunted again. <How am I to knows?> But he went to the maps painted on the wall of the nearby room and worked out where they were. Then he looked for another spot marked 'SECURITY'. He found one on the next level— he'd know where to go next time without waiting to be attacked.

<Come on. Let's go.>

<*Where going?*>

<Next level. Looks at all of those markings. There's important things everywheres down there. A gate will haves to be there somewhere.>

<*Right.*>

-oOo-

Eighth level from the top, seventh from the bottom. It was almost double the area of the floor above and reached by more than a hundred stairs. Scree stopped a moment, listening to Ping coming along behind him one slow step at a time. It'd be a while before she arrived, so he set off to find the clockwork-dog den.

Racing through the corridors he realized there weren't any signs of fighting. He didn't know what that meant. When he found the SECURITY room a short while later, the door to the den was closed. He stood staring, waiting. He continued to wait.

Eventually he gave up and hit the button to open the human sized door beside it. He looked around the room to see if there was anything to see, but everything seemed to be the same as it had been at the top of the warren of caves.

A soft shrill noise suddenly filled the room and a red light on a desk started flashing. There was a wheeze of escaping air and a metallic scraping from the corridor. The den door was opening.

Too much of a coincidence, he thought, going to look at the flashing light. There was a small red button beside it. *Does I press it, I wonders?* He shrugged and pressed.

The beeping stopped. Scree went outside to discover that the little door in the wall, already half open, was sliding closed with grinding difficulty. He didn't know if that would stop the door opening permanently.

<*Where are you Scree?*> Ping asked in his mind.

There was no point bringing her here, so Scree examined the map in his mind. There were several huge rooms in the middle of the level and, as he gave Ping directions to the nearest one, he headed there himself. Around two corners, through a door that opened automatically as he approached, around a bend.

Then he was there.

The room was huge, larger in reality than it had seemed on the map. Whole villages could fit in it with room to spare. Scree had come down a whole heap of stairs to reach this point but was still only halfway down to floor level. He could descend another fifty meters, at least. There was an open doorway at one end of the room. It was huge, taking up most of one of the room's shorter walls.

And scattered across the floor were dozens of... Scree didn't know what they were, but he thought maybe they were something like the clockwork dogs. Only much, much larger. A group away in the northern corner were each the size of a house, and they were the smallest, crouched on three feet as if ready to spring at any moment. The largest of them all was a sphere that went most of the way from floor to ceiling. Each of the contraptions had four metal spikes sticking from one side, like a family of battering rams.

Scree heard Ping clumping closer, but didn't turn to look until she halted by his side and stepped free of the armor.

"Looks at it," Scree said. "It looks like... Well, it don't looks like anythings I know. But whats if it was a suit of armor, like your armor? Look at the clear bit on the top there where a monster could look out." He pointed to a clear dome on the very top of the closest sphere. "And look at..." But that was where the similarity to the armor ended really. Most of the larger ones were the same general design.

"What if they were..." It seemed that Ping didn't know what it might be either.

But Scree remembered his book and what Nemucca had said in the cave on Kiva. He'd read the passages himself a couple of times since. "A ship to fly between the stars." There were gaping mouths all around the sphere that could be used to spit out fire like the book described. "Come on, let's go have a look."

Down on the main floor, Scree stopped to stare.

Like the room, the ships— for Scree was positive that's what they were— were larger than could be imagined from afar. He stood near the largest one, craning his neck at the black curve of the hull. The foot was taller than he was, though if he wanted he could have stood under the belly of the ship and touched it without stretching.

"How do we get in, do you think?" he asked as Ping stepped out beside him. Before she answered, he crossed to a foot and leapt up to grab the top. He pulled himself up as Ping watched silently.

Scree scaled the giant leg, going from nut to bolt to join to joint. He climbed all of the way up into the body of the machine. But there was nowhere else to go. He found himself in a separate compartment, sealed off from anything else. With a curse, he made his way back down. Ping was no longer there. He could hear her clanking away behind a pile of boxes and went to see what she was up to.

<Find anything?> Scree asked.

<*Parts?*>

<Parts of what?>

<*Parts of the...*>

<Ship.>

"I think. It's like whole thing runs on clockwork. Gears and pulleys and springs and cords that in the armor as well."

Scree looked around and saw a metal tower about a hundred meters away with stairs leading to the top. It was standing beside one of the medium sized ships, a sphere about fifty meters across. He jogged across and made his way to the top. He needn't have bothered. There was nothing there except the cool, dusty curve of the hull and a join in the surface. Two of the large funnels were on either side of his position, and he could look down into the mouth of a third. There was nothing to see there either. A metal grille a couple of meters in covered any workings and denied access. He grunted in disgust and climbed back down.

<*Are staying here or we looking for the gateway?*>" Ping asked, back in the armor again. She was on the other side of the room.

<No use staying here.> There were only a couple of other rooms on this level and Scree doubted any of them were important. <Come on.>

PING FOLLOWED SCREE'S DIRECTIONS as he moved ahead. He led the way through an arch into a second huge room filled with the amazing ships. Then they went through the next, smaller arch and into a long, wide corridor. Scree was fifty meters away, working on a barricade. He was tossing aside furniture and other flotsam of the battles long gone. She arrived as he finally made it to the door and slipped his arm back into the monster weapon. When she stumped to his side he hit the button and readied for what might lie beyond.

Except the door didn't open.

Ping watched as he glared at the door, perhaps daring it to defy him again. Then he hit the button and got the same result.

"Stinking cats."

As Scree looked around, Ping took a couple of steps back and waited for the explosion. Shedding the monster weapon once more, the troll found a nice, solid piece of metal and used it to attack the door.

Four minutes later and he might as well have been beating at it with a feather duster. There was not a mark. Not a scratch.

"Stinking, rotten cats."

Ping cleared her throat. "Perhaps there another door," she said.

Scree turned his glare on her and she took another step back.

"There isn't. This is its."

"Well..."

"Well nothing. We ain't getting through there."

"Well..." Ping watched as Scree snatched up his weapon and stormed away from her. After a moment she hurried to follow.

When she finally made it back to the first of the huge rooms Scree was next to one of the smaller ship, shooting it with his weapon and having as much luck as previously. She was surprised that he seemed to stay calm.

After five more seconds she opened the suit and stepped out into the fresh air. She stretched and scratched an itch that had bugging her for what seemed like a lifetime. She was covered in sweat. She wiped her face on her sleeve. "We know where all other doors are, Scree. Well, we know approximately where are. We can find another."

Without replying, the troll turned and stalked away. Ping followed him out through the huge doors and stopped on a stone platform that reached out into the dense, dark forest with a long range of saw toothed mountains opposite. The circular valley was behind them.

"Stinking cats," Scree repeated.

"The book said all doors were close by, Scree."

Scree swore and pulled his pack from his back. He searched through the contents until he finally pulled free the book in question. "This book?"

Ping nodded.

"This has been nothing but trouble."

"If not for the book, we wouldn't be here."

The troll nodded, as if that was his point. He examined the leather cover of *The Gates of Hakahei* then looked out at the valley again. Ping followed his gaze to a flight of stairs that led down to a game trail. And with a sudden surge he was moving again, down the stairs. At the bottom he dropped the book into the dust.

"Scree?" Ping said. She stood watching as Scree disappeared into the trees. She wanted to get her armor but knew that, in his current mood, the troll was unlikely to wait for her slow pursuit. With a final glance over her shoulder, Ping hurried down the stairs.

Left on his own, Scree walked almost as fast as Ping could run and was already lost from sight. Stillness remained in his wake as if the forest held its breath waiting for him to pass. After two and a half minutes she stopped, breathing deeply and starting to worry.

"Scree," she called. "Where are you? There's a fork in path." She looked down one branching and then the next. If she had her armor she'd be able to talk to the troll in his head. She used one of Scree's swear words then blushed and glanced around as if someone might be watching. Finally, she looked down at the ground and saw scuffed dirt on one of the paths. It wasn't much, and might have been made by an animal, but it was all she had. Wiping sweat from her face she started to run again.

The forest seemed to be crowding closer, reaching for her with clinging, twiggy fingers, catching at her clothes, scratching her face. She started to panic. What if Scree had gone the other direction? What if she was stuck here on her own? After four minutes Ping was ready to turn around and go back, positive she'd made the wrong choice. Positive she'd made so many wrong choices that if she could just go back to the fork in the path that everything would be all right, that she would find herself watching the Jugglers of Jilin as the Great Clock chimed the noon chorus.

The path divided again and she came to a sudden, knee jarring halt. She wiped her face, this time to remove tears. Sitting down in the dirt of the path she looked back at all the choices she had made since Scree had fallen out of the air in the Great Clock. And she knew she would not have changed any of them if she had the chance. Even the last decision she had made at the fork in the path. So here she was, with one more decision and this time there was no disturbed dirt on the path to offer her any hints.

"He go that way," she said after moment of thought, pointing to the path that angled up the slope. "He want to stick to the higher ground." The higher path would also keep him in contact with the circular valley that held the six Ohoga Gates.

Decision made, Ping climbed to her feet and started to walk. She had barely taken two steps when Scree came into sight, striding down the path towards her.

"That's a dead end," he said as if he had not all but abandoned her a few minutes earlier. "Got a good view thought. There's a tower looking thing a few miles in that direction." He pointed further around the side of the mountain.

"So..."

"Come on, let's see what we can see." He turned onto the second path and this time Ping followed immediately. She was pleased that her instincts had been correct, but did not want to be forced to trust them a second time if it could be helped.

-oOo-

The tower Scree had seen was just a broken stub. There were a lot more broken concrete blocks littering the ground suggesting the original structure had been massive.

Ping watched Scree lever open the door. While the troll gave the ground floor a cursory inspection she climbed the stone stairs up to the first level and beyond. Most of the floor on the second level was still in tact— just one small section had disappeared— but the roof and walls were all but gone. First she looked out over the valley and could see nothing but trees and a wide river down at the base and the mountains beyond. In the other direction, the trees were much thinner and the crumbling outlines of a vast complex of buildings could be seen climbing to the top of the ridge. There was another circular building further up the hill that might have been the base of another tower but only a meter of wall showed above the ground on the down hill side. The other side had been dug into the hill and a door seemed to lead underground.

Scree came up the stairs to look around as well. "Not much down there," he said as if he had been expecting otherwise.

Ping had another look around. "Not much here either, except..." She pointed towards the door in the other tower but Scree had already seen it. "Do you think it's Ohoga Gate?" But that was unlikely. It probably led into another underground complex that would house the gate.

Scree shook his head. Then he stared at the doorway and didn't move.

"What we looking for, Scree? Where we going?"

Looking at all the ruined buildings clinging to the side of the hill, Ping wondered if that was what Shadon would look like in a hundred years time. Would someone be standing on the remains of a clock tower wondering what secrets the ruins might reveal. She didn't want that to happen. She wanted the city to be saved, to be rebuilt. And the zorigami would never be in a position to do that without help. "Scree, if monsters win, all that will be left will be fighting. You won't have choices. It will be fight or hide. If we can find a way to stop them..."

"We can't stop them."

"Someone can. We need machines like the ones back at the other complex— if they really are ships that can fly to other worlds— and we need someone who knows how to use them."

"There's no people here. We won't ever find someone who can help." But he moved back down to the ground and headed for the second tower. "I'm going to find a place where I can eat some real food then sleep for a week."

Ping stayed where she was for five seconds then made her way slowly back down as well. By the time she caught up, Scree had broken down the door in the back of the second tower.

"The lights are working here as well. Do you think the clockwork dogs will be in here?"

Ping peered into the passage. It was lit with the same steady glow as the last place. If the lights were working who was to say about the rest? She shrugged. "One way to find out." Except last time she'd been wearing the monster armor. She wouldn't be able to help Scree at all.

The troll seemed to realize the same thing. He looked her up and down for a moment then glanced into the doorway. "I'll go in and haves a quick look first."

Ping put her back to the wall and looked out over the ruined walls, tracing the lines in her mind, imagining the people who had once lived and worked there. Possibly there would have been zorigami and trolls working alongside them, working towards goals that were beyond her understanding.

The shadow of a tree marched across the small patch of cleared ground in front of her as the afternoon wandered towards night. Ping waited in silence for more than half an hour, every now and then edging closer to the glow of light from the doorway.

"No clockwork dogs in there."

Ping jumped and turned to see Scree smiling at her. "Don't do that."

"Don't falls asleep in dangerous places."

"Wasn't sleeping."

"Close enough." He beckoned her into the passage. "Come on, let's go."

"Do you know where we going."

Scree didn't answer. Ping knew that if he didn't know where he was going he'd find out quick enough.

The hallways were bright and dusty and quiet. The walls were the same as those in the previous complex. Most of the lights glowed the same steady glow, with only an occasional dark patch on the ceiling showing where one was no longer working. Scree was following his own footprints and Ping trailed along behind, watching his broad back.

Eventually, the footprints stopped at a door that, judging by the marks in the dust, had been closed until very recently.

"Up or down?" Scree asked.

Ping poked her head through the door and found stairs leading in both directions. She shrugged. "Down I suppose. Can't be much up left." The top of the hill had not been far away at all.

They explored three levels, roaming from room to room, traipsing along passageways that always looked the same. Sometimes they had to turn around and go back when they came to a dead end. There were other times when Ping wanted to stop so she could examine machines that dominated rooms or tiny, dust caked contraptions on tables or on benches. But Scree was always moving on, looking for something else— something that he could not name or describe. His need was palpable and Ping was not about to argue. When they found another Gate, lit by bright white spotlights, Scree finally stopped. Ping stood just inside the doorway waiting to see what he would do.

"Well," Scree said, looking back over his shoulder.

"Are you looking help? Or looking ale and food?"

He looked back at the door. "Don't knows. Tell you when I get there. You comings?"

Ping didn't want to follow him but knew she had no choice. He may not have needed her any more, but apparently he was willing to suffer her presence, so she was going to stay with him. She nodded. And without another word the troll stuck his head through the doorway. A moment later he stepped through as if it was the easiest thing in the world— or two worlds. Ping didn't know how he did it but she followed. A few weeks earlier she would have felt more trepidation stepping in to see the workings of the Great Clock in Shadon.

On the far side the dust was a little bit deeper and a little bit heavier— it puffed out from Pip's stolen boots and quickly settled back down again. They could have been in the same building. Maybe they were. Maybe all this talk of different worlds was a lie. There were places on Tiandi— some were even close to Shadon— where a river or a steep rocky hill seemed to divide landscapes that were worlds apart.

They found a set of narrow winding stairs that led upwards for a long time. It was as if the building was carved amidst a system of natural caves. Or perhaps the builders here had been as much concerned with form as with functionality.

One level above the door and Ping was following Scree mechanically. It was unlikely she would see or hear or do anything that would help in his search. He would notice anything before she did and she didn't really know what he was looking for anyway.

The troll stopped and Ping ran into his back. She instinctively cowered back against the wall but couldn't decided if she was cowering away from Scree or whatever had made him stop. The troll's back was tense, but his monster weapon remained pointing at the ground. Eventually he strode forward again, out of the passage and into a large room.

Ping could finally see past him. There was a room full of more of the strange metal ships though the largest one here would have been dwarfed by most in the last place. There was one that was hardly larger than a wagon. The largest, four times that size, had an open door at the back. Scree was already inside by the time Ping got there. For a long while Ping stood near the door, looking at a cargo area, empty except for a couple of small boxes. But the troll was muttering to himself and Ping was sure he would damage something if left to his own devices. So she climbed up into the ship and went carefully forward to see what he was doing.

"Doesn't work," Scree said as Ping came near. He was sitting in a big chair with a strange array of buttons and switches, levers and dials in front of him. "Stupid thing." He pressed another button.

"You can't just press buttons randomly," Ping said. She shrank back slightly when he rounded on her. She stayed where she was, hand shaking where it rested on the back of his seat.

"Why not?"

She licked her lips. "Because even if something happens you won't know what you did."

Scree stared at her for a moment, jaw tense as he gave her words thought. "What do we do then?"

Ping didn't want to do anything. The ship wasn't like the armor. It was huge. There was nothing at all recognizable about it. But Scree would just keep pressing buttons and get angrier by the minute. "We do as we did with the armor. We test each switch in turn and..." Ping looked around. *And hope nothing works.*

But of course it worked.

They had only been pressing buttons for six minutes, waiting in a tense silence after each one. When something happened. The ship began to shake. It hummed and rattled and shook some more.

Scree gave a whoop of joy. Ping shrank back in her chair and wondered what she could possibly say to convince the troll to quit while he was ahead.

"What do we do now?" Scree asked when he had calmed down.

Ping sighed and sat up to look at the controls.

KEEBLE LOOKED AT KIM. He saw hope and fear in her eyes, but he didn't see any doubt. Meledrin didn't believe he could do anything, but Kim did. She believed he could do something to help, simply because he said he could. So he nodded once and started to construct the Song in the air. He hummed the foundations carefully, making sure everything was right, before building it up with a wordless, dancing cadence, and sealing the joints with a series of clicks. When it was all there, he kept it going perfectly, all of the sounds combining like the stones of the mountains, or the water of a stream. He could feel the power washing through him.

After he had been Singing the completed Song for a few seconds, Keeble started to change it again, condensing it, whittling away the edges, honing it until it was focused tightly at one small section of wall.

He stepped forward. He reached out towards the focus of his Song. And paused.

Keeble looked at his metal hand. He could feel the power of his Song, but still he doubted. He glanced towards the others. They probably couldn't feel anything, but they watched him and trusted that he would do *something*. Kim and Tuki trusted.

Keeble returned to the rhythm of his Song, making sure all the elements were still in place, making sure he was still focusing on the stone in front of him. He reached forward, and his mechanical hand passed into the wall. Then his arm, up to the elbow. He could feel the stone there, mist on his skin, and the Song was like a mountain in his mind.

But he remembered how he'd lost his hand. He'd been in the Testing Chamber, Singing. He'd felt his Song, like he did now, but still he had faltered and the Song had died. It had died with his hand still in the wall.

Keeble tried to calm himself with another deep breath. He had lost his hand *inside the wall*. That proved he could Sing, didn't it? His hand was in the stone now, and still the Song continued.

"Holy shit."

He turned to see Kim staring.

"Holy shit."

42: Song of Being

"I've passed through one gate," he said, shaping the Song around his words, "and I can still hear that other one. They've helped make my Song stronger."

Kim snapped her mouth shut and blinked. "Right. Ummm. So we can just walk through, can we?"

He changed the rhythm slightly then nodded.

"I cannot just walk through stone," Meledrin said, aghast. Keeble had almost forgotten she was there. "It is not possible."

And Tuki, too. He was standing on the far side of the room, clutching his crystal ball like it might somehow save him. This was not quite the escape he had expected.

Keeble turned back to Meledrin. "It is possible," he said, and he stepped through the wall to prove it. Even as he did it, his heart raced, but the Song remained strong. He was in a small office with two desks and bookshelves that covered most of one wall.

A few seconds later, Kim pushed him aside as she stepped through, dragging Tuki by the arm. Meledrin came through a moment later but didn't look pleased.

"We need to get the alien," Kim said.

"Are you sure?"

"Positive."

So Keeble shifted the focus of his Song to the left and entered the alien's cell. He didn't even consider how the creature might react to his reappearance. The Song made extraneous thoughts difficult.

The alien held up its hands to cover its eyes and cowered away.

"Hello," Keeble said around his Song.

The only response was more cowering. Keeble, though reluctant to ask a dwife for help, was about to call out to Kim when he noticed she was already standing by his side. She didn't waste any time with talk. Crossing the room she grabbed the alien by the arm and tried to pull it towards the hole in the wall. But, apparently, if the alien didn't want to go somewhere it was going to take more than one dwife to make it.

Kim swore. "Mel, get in here and tell it what we're trying to do."

"It is not that easy," Meledrin replied from the other room.

"Yeah, I know. Without a context it's difficult to even start." Kim looked around the cell as if for inspiration. She grabbed the alien again and tried to pull its hand away from its face. "Keeble, help me."

"I need to concentrate."

"Right. Tuki."

The moai, looking very nervous, poked his head through the wall, as if being half in was safer than going all the way through. "Yes, mo'shi?"

"Move this guy's hands away from his face for me."

Tuki didn't look comfortable with that idea either, but stepped forward to do as asked. He towered over the creature but struggled, teeth gritted, to make it move at all. For ten seconds it looked as if it had turned to stone. Finally, Kim smiled at the alien and beckoned it after her.

"[Hey, what the hell is going on?]" There was an American standing outside the cell. He didn't look happy.

Keeble looked from the guard, to the alien, to the hole in the wall, which couldn't really be seen anyway. He knew he should be worried but merely stayed where he was and sang his Song.

Fumbling with his keys, the dwarf outside called for help. At that moment, the alien seemed to decide who its friends were. Showing as much emotion as an elf, it followed Kim and Tuki through the gap into the next room. The American, keys forgotten, was staring with his mouth open. Keeble smiled around his Song, waved, and went through as well.

Back in the office, Kim already had the door open and was looking out into the hall. "We've got to find the door to the hangar," she said. "We've got a couple of minutes at most."

"Why can't we just go through the wall?" Keeble asked. "The ship is in the next room."

"Are you sure?"

He nodded. Of course he was sure. He'd seen the room so he knew the dimensions perfectly. He also knew exactly how far they had walked since leaving the viewing room. Since starting to Sing his Song, he was thinking much clearer than he had in a long time. "The wall is one meter thick, and the ship is ten meters beyond that."

"Well, tell us when you're right."

"Move the shelf. I can't sing through metal and books."

"Right."

The alien was as bad as Tuki, standing by passively while Kim spent a second trying to move a shelf before giving up and simply toppling it onto the floor.

Keeble punched his Song at the wall as he heard the door opening. He went through the hole with the others on his heels. The moment they were all safe, he shut off the Song with a snap that was almost painful. He didn't notice though, because the ship was right there. It was bigger up close than it looked from the room above but was still a bit disappointing if it was meant to fly between the stars. Dwarves had made steam trains that were bigger. He started to do a lap around it, examining the hull, running his fingers over the rough surface.

"What is the next course of action?" Meledrin asked. "As was previously pointed out, the Americans have been trying to gain entry to the vessel for some years. You can not expect to succeed in the next few minutes where they have failed."

"That bit there is stone," Keeble said. He knew it as soon as he saw it, though the small square section didn't look any different to the rest. It was on the side of the ship right next to another recessed panel, 2.6 meters to a side. "It's the densest, toughest stone I've ever seen, but it's stone."

"Which bit," Kim asked.

As Keeble pointed it out, he started his Song again, building it quickly. By the time Kim arrived at his side it was filling his mind. He climbed up on the scaffolding and slipped his hand into the stone.

"It's an access panel like they have in planes and elevators." She probably didn't know what he was talking about. He'd have to explain. "They let you get to equipment and machinery in the walls."

"I get it, Keeble."

"There's a handle." He turned the handle and the large panel slid silently upwards.

Kim's mouth was hanging open again. Meledrin and Tuki had come to see. The alien was hanging back near the wall.

"That was easy," Keeble said.

A pile of metal crates blocked half the doorway.

"Easy for someone who can stick his hand in solid stone, maybe."

Keeble saw Kim take a deep breath before sticking her head inside to have a look. It seemed she had walked through the stone with less trepidation. Either way, he decided, she did show a remarkable amount of courage and decisiveness for a dwife. She was almost like a dwarf. Almost.

"Alrighty then. All aboard, I guess, before somebody else turns up."

Keeble nodded and went inside while Kim went to talk to the alien, as if that was going to do any good. The crates occupied a storage compartment 2.8 meters high and three meters square. It was neat and tidy and everything was secure. Keeble gave a nod of satisfaction.

"Are you able to move further, Keeble?" Meledrin asked from close behind. "If not, then all our struggles will have been for naught."

Keeble grunted but walked into the room. Meledrin followed close behind, and when Tuki came in as well, the room seemed to halve in size.

There were a dozen access panels to the rear of the ship and another door leading forward. After a moment of hesitation Keeble headed for the door and found himself in the driver's cabin, the cockpit. There were two chairs and hundreds of screens and controls. He reached out and pressed some buttons at random and gripped the edge of the panel, choosing the next button while he waited for something to happen. Nothing happened. Inside the ship, anyway.

Out in the hangar, a door opened and General Hilliard marched through with a dozen soldiers at his back. On the other side of the ship, Kim was still trying to coax the alien forward.

"[You continue to amaze me, Miss McLean,]" the general said loudly. Keeble found speaking Tuki's language so natural that he was surprised each time he heard a different one. Meledrin muttered a translation. The general would soon be in a position to see the open door on the ship and would probably be quite a bit more amazed then. "[I don't know what you hoped to achieve.]"

The threat of soldiers seemed to do it again — the alien stumped towards the ship with Kim urging it on.

"There's nowhere to hide in here," Meledrin translated when the General spoke again.

That's what you think, Keeble silently replied. And what made him think they couldn't just walk through the wall like last time if they couldn't hide? Maybe nobody had believed the guard from the cells when he told the story.

Keeble heard someone clambering into the ship and wondered if they knew how to close the hatch. Hurrying back, he wondered if *he* knew. Kim was still between the crates.

"Out of the way, dwife" Keeble said, but when Kim looked around the panel was already sliding closed. "Oh." He checked it had been done properly.

Tuki was sitting with his back against the rear access panels with Kim's pack by his side. He looked like he would be quite happy to stay there for a while. "What do we do now, mo'shi?"

Meledrin nodded. "Yes. It is unlikely this vehicle is still operational after all this time."

"That's it Mel, optimistic as usual."

"I am merely pointing out the facts."

"Well, I don't know. It was unlikely we'd get this far."

Keeble shook his head. "Pointing out that we escaped the first million to one chance doesn't help us with the next one."

"That wasn't my point."

"You had a point, did you?"

The sound of voices coming from outside the ship increased as the soldiers discovered their quarry had escaped again.

Kim smiled. "The day's going well, whatever happens from here. Now, the sooner we get to work, the sooner we can get out of here."

"Sounds easy," Keeble muttered as he led the way back to the cockpit and sat down in a chair. "Do you always just make things up as you go?"

Kim sat by his side, looking at the controls. But they didn't get any further. A shout went up out in the hangar and a soldier pointed into the ship. All sorts of stuff started happening. More men rushed to surround the ship, weapons raised though they must've hit the ship with a lot more than those without any luck in the last fifty years. General Hilliard stormed back into the room and stood shouting in front of the ship. Kim waited while he blustered and threatened. She smiled the whole time as if she was having a great time.

"What are you so happy about?" Keeble grumbled. "We may just have to open the door eventually and let them in."

She shrugged as if she didn't really care. "A bit of a head start on working out how to use this thing would have been nice, but we still have all the power for the moment. And we've shown that it would be better if they tried to work with us a bit more. Or at least with you, Mel, and Tuki. I'm probably excess baggage about now."

"I'm surprised you were brought along at all." Keeble sat back and listened to the General as well. He couldn't understand a word of it, but he got the idea. "Well why are we just sitting here now instead of working?" he said eventually. He was almost as bad as an elf, sitting around listening to someone talk when there was work to be done.

KIM TURNED TO LOOK at Keeble. His whole manner had changed since he sang his song and got them out of the cell. It was as if he had suddenly grown up and become an arsehole all at once. He obviously wasn't a big fan of women. In this case, however, he was right.

"Of course. No time to waste," Kim said, turning her attention to the controls. Unfortunately there was no big red button with 'Start' written on it. Or maybe there was, but she couldn't read the label.

There were what looked like three main controls, which were centered between the two seats. A wheel, half buried in the console, a huge foot pedal that pivoted in the middle, and a little joystick with a ball on the end. Kim fiddled with the joystick and discovered that it actually went up and down and no other direction.

"Okay," she said, nodding to herself, "that's a start."

"What's a start?" Keeble asked. "You can't know anything yet."

"Just because *you* haven't worked anything out doesn't mean *I* haven't. This wheel steers us, like a car, the pedal is forward and back, and the knob is up and down."

"You *do* just make things up."

"Maybe I did, but I think they're reasonable guesses. Anyway, none of it does us any good if we can't get the thing started."

There was a harsh, guttural sound behind Kim, and she turned to see the alien standing in the door. It was talking, pointing to the controls, and waving its arms about. She couldn't understand a word of it, and Meledrin couldn't either, judging by the look on her face.

Outside, the General had finally started to calm down. With an effort, Kim shifted gear into English and listened.

"*Miss McLean,*" he said, "*are you going to let us in?*"

"*No, thank you, General. Don't worry though, we've already started to make some progress.*"

"*What do you hope to achieve?*"

"*Besides lift off? Well, how about getting you to use your resources more wisely? That would be a start. Now, if you'll excuse me, I have some buttons to press.*"

She turned her attention to the controls but didn't press anything. It had been more than five years since she'd sat in a cockpit, and that hadn't looked much like this one at all.

"We really need power, Keeble."

"Obviously. If it's even possible."

"Just see what you can find."

Kim started working her way across her half of the control panel. She hit each button quickly, paued, then pressed and held before releasing. Each time she waited for a response without joy. She flicked switches and turned dials backwards and forwards. Keeble watched for a moment before setting to work on his side.

"How long will this process take?"

Kim almost jumped out of her seat. She turned to look at Meledrin, who was looking over the alien's shoulder.

"I inquire because we have only a small amount of food and water."

"I *know* that. Can you speak to the alien yet?"

"It isn't that simple."

"For Christ's sake, Mel, use your brain." Kim sighed and rubbed at her eyes. She thought she could feel a headache coming on. "Sorry. Look, this isn't Sherindel. You can't just sit back and let things happen, otherwise a few hundred years will go by and you'll still be complaining about Chinese table manners."

"I do not understand."

"Don't worry about it. But we learned to speak Tuki's language, right. Do the same thing with the alien."

Meledrin sniffed but tapped the creature on the shoulder and beckoned it back into the hold where Tuki waited silently. The moai was probably going to be in charge of the charades seeing the elf wouldn't want to demean herself like that.

"Back to work, Keeble." But he was still pressing buttons. They worked their way to the center reaching what looked like half a skyglass at about the same time. "Well, I guess that's it then." Kim sat back in the seat and sighed.

Keeble was still examining the console as if they might have missed a button or switch in their methodical fiddling. "Maybe we need to do things in combination. Like turning the key and pushing the accelerator."

"Well, there are a lot of possible combinations. We could go at that all day." The only thing they hadn't touched was the skyglass thing. She poked at it angrily with as much reaction as she expected.

"That won't do any good."

"Well, thanks for pointing that out."

Outside the Americans had brought in some heavy drilling equipment. Kim doubted it was a new approach.

"I mean," Keeble said, "it looks like a skyglass."

"Yes."

"Well, Tuki is the only one who can use the other skyglass. What makes you think this one would be any different."

"Right."

Keeble drummed his fingers on the edge of the console. He looked at her and shook his head. "So let's see if he can do anything."

"Right. Good idea." She called Tuki, but it was Meledrin who answered.

"Tuki is assisting me."

"Well you can do that on your own for a minute."

The moai ducked in through the door. "You want me to do something, mo'shi."

"Can you get that skyglass working?"

"I do not know."

Kim tried to keep her impatience in check. "Why don't you give it a go?"

"Very well." He sidled between the two seats and touched his finger to the crystal. "It is not turned on," he said. He muttered the word that turned it on before Kim had a chance to say anything.

"It is working." The ball started to glow softly, but nothing else happened. Kim waited. She waited some more.

"Now what?" Keeble asked.

Kim sighed and started pressing buttons again, working her way across the panel. Keeble grunted and set to work as well.

"Should I go back to helping Meledrin?" Tuki asked.

"Yes, Tuki. If you want."

He hesitated — Kim couldn't blame him for that — then made his way back.

She kept pressing buttons, and when there were only a couple left...

All her frustration and fear was washed away, for a moment at least, amid the whir and beep of machines starting up. There was a deep, gentle rumbling that could only be an engine.

Kim sat stunned for a moment, before doing a jig in her seat. Suddenly there was a lot of movement out in the hangar. Men were racing everywhere, though it didn't look as if anything particularly dangerous were happening. Not that she was in the best position to tell. But, looking around at the flashing lights and strange symbols which were becoming visible, she decided that, in general, she *was* in the best position.

General Hilliard had made his cautious way to a position in front of the ship. "*What now, Miss McLean?*" he shouted. "*You don't imagine we'll open the doors, do you?*"

"What did he say?" Keeble asked.

Kim told him.

"You really haven't thought this out, have you?" the dwarf said.

"Shut up." Kim had liked him more when he was crazy. "*You* didn't mention the door earlier."

"Well, you're the one who's supposed to know everything."

"Who said that? An hour ago I was in a cell with no realistic chance of getting out. I think I've done pretty damn well to get us this far."

"Yes. Wonderful. Now we're in a *hangar* with no realistic chance of getting out."

Kim took a deep breath and tried to get her thoughts in order. "Arguing about it won't help. We'll just have to think of something."

Keeble grunted.

For a long time after that, Kim and Keeble sat in silence staring at the controls and switches in front of them.

"Let's just try it," Keeble said eventually.

"What?"

"You think you know how the main controls work, right? But it's no use worrying about the door unless you're right."

"Right." Kim nodded.

"So I'll see if I can at least get us to fly."

For a moment, Kim didn't know what to say. "Okay, some parts of your plan have merit, but there's no way in hell *you're* going to drive this thing." At that moment she thought she'd rather just open the door and let Hilliard in.

"Then who? You? Women aren't allowed to use machines."

"Let's get this straight right now, buddy — this is Earth, not some cave on Sherindel. People who can do things, do them. Gender doesn't come in to it." She took a deep breath. "A few days ago you thought a steam engine was the height of technology. I can drive *cars* and fly *planes* and *helicopters*, Keeble. You can't even program a *VCR*."

"You've never flown anything like this before."

"I've been closer than you. So don't touch a damn thing." Kim sat forward and examined the controls. Most still meant nothing to her so she decided to ignore them and concentrate on the main three. Outside, the Americans were creeping closer again, so Kim shouted a warning and waited for them to scuttle back to the walls. Then she sat, staring at the controls.

"So," Keeble said, "you control the ship with the power of your mind, do you?"

Kim glared at him for a moment then gently pulled the knob she thought controlled the elevation. And it worked. Kim smiled as the ship rose steadily into the air. She could see General Hilliard, and he wasn't pleased with the way things were going.

Keeble didn't look all that thrilled either. "Now what? We just break through the doors do we? I'm sure if you concentrate hard enough, you can actually open them."

She wasn't going to let the dwarf ruin her mood. When the ship was about ten meters above the ground she released the knob, and they stopped almost instantly. The ship hovered with barely a tremor. Backwards and forwards probably wasn't a good idea so she turned the steering wheel instead. When the ship spun, she did a little happy-dance.

"Huh," she said to Keeble. "Just like riding a *bike*." If the bike was a space-age penny-farthing.

"Right. Does the door open if we spin really quickly?"

"Shut up, Keeble. One step at a time."

"Well, tell me when we're ready for the next step." He sat back as if preparing to wait for a while.

The ship continued to rotate slowly. On the fifth revolution, Kim spotted what was probably their only chance. "I've got a plan," she said. It wasn't so much a plan as an idea.

For the next five minutes Kim moved randomly around the room. Forward and backwards were as easy to control as everything else, but she made sure she ran into walls occasionally and even bumped into the ceiling and touched down on the floor.

Keeble's anger grew by the moment. "Yes," he said eventually. "Great idea. Let's let you drive."

"See that there," Kim said. High up in the wall, opposite the gallery room they'd been in earlier, was another window. It was only a few meters long and leaned out over the hangar.

"What about it?"

"I think that's the control room, or something similar."

"What's it do?"

"That's where the person who opens and closes the door sits."

Keeble leaned forward to look. "How do you know that?"

"I don't, but if I'm wrong then we've got no hope, so let's just pretend." Kim could see by the look on Keeble's face that he didn't like the idea of going into a situation without having detailed schematics and a sound plan already formulated. Well, if he was going to stick around, he'd just have to get used to it.

"So fly up there and see what we can see."

"I intend to." In all her 'random' flying, she had ended up with a wingtip almost touching the wall. If she went directly up, it would be lined up with the window. "If I'd done it straight away, they would've worked out something was going on in about two seconds. This way, hopefully, they think it's just more random madness, and we'll get a bit of a head start."

"So someone has to walk out on the wing and go through the window?"

"Yep."

"Who?"

"That's a good question." Kim looked back into the hold.

Tuki was sitting on the floor, knees pulled up to his chest as he listened to the alien talk. He already looked like he was in way over his head and getting him to climb on wings and jump through windows wouldn't be a good idea. Meledrin? Kim almost laughed. Even if she were desperate enough to ask, the elf would never agree. That left two choices.

"Here's what we'll do." She took a deep breath and wondered how she kept getting into these situations. "You go in the back, find something hard and heavy to throw at the window, then wait by the door." Kim said. "When you're ready, I'll fly us up there then you open the door. We'll try to break the window, then I go across to the room. Hopefully I can open the door and get back in quickly. Then we get the hell out of *Dodge*."

Keeble opened his mouth and Kim knew he was going to say something about 'Dodge'.

"You know what I mean."

He gave a grunt.

"Off you go, then. Let me know."

It wasn't long before the dwarf called that he was ready.

"All right, then. Here goes."

Kim went forward slightly. Then back. And, with no idea if all her posing was doing any good, she pulled the knob that would move the ship up the wall. When they were in position she jumped out of the seat and dashed into the cargo area. The door was already open, and Keeble had his head out.

"All clear," the dwarf said.

Kim didn't really listen. Heart pounding, mouth dry, she stooped down to grab what looked like two book-sized metal cogs from a pile on the floor and jumped the short distance down onto the wing. Easy. "What the hell am I doing?"

She threw one of the cogs. It bounced off the window. And fell down to clatter on the floor.

"Shit."

But the glass was cracked.

She threw the second one, and the same thing happened. Keeble threw a third and a fourth from the ship, and finally the glass shattered.

Kim kept low as long as possible and then, careful of glass shards, vaulted over the wall into the room. She found herself on top of a console with about a hundred controls. Before she'd even climbed down to the floor, she was scanning the strange symbols that went with them.

A minute later Keeble called to her. "Something's happening," he said, and at almost the same moment she heard the sound of booted feet approaching. She looked at the door for the first time. There was a square, green button set into the stone wall. Crossing the small room, she tried the button and the door hissed shut. But she couldn't see any way of locking it.

"Shit." She grabbed a dirty, recently used, coffee cup from a small table in the corner and used it to smash the switch. She ripped out some of the wires behind, electricity biting at her fingers.

"Come on, Kim. We need to get out of here."

"You don't say," Kim muttered. She returned to the console and started hitting buttons at random.

Men were pounding at the metal door. There were curses and shouted warnings from outside.

"*You can't get out, Miss McLean,*" Hilliard shouted from below.

Kim hit a few more buttons, stabbing at them with shaking fingers, and was rewarded with a clunk from out in the hangar. She leaned out the window and saw the two huge doors that made up the entire roof sliding back out of the way. "That's what *you* think, General," she said, though not loud enough for him to hear. She didn't want to get ahead of herself.

After checking the console again to see if there was something she'd missed, she climbed back out the window. The wing was as solid as rock when she dropped onto it and slipped back into the ship. Tuki and the alien looked like they wanted to be somewhere else, though with the alien it was a bit hard to tell. It waved its arms about and said something in its deep, throaty voice. Meledrin started to say something as well, but Kim ignored them all. She was back in the cockpit before Keeble had closed the door, and the ship was climbing a moment later.

Soldiers had gained access to the control room. The doors were starting to close once more.

"Damn it."

Bullets clattered against the hull, and Kim ducked instinctively though she knew the Americans were probably in more danger from ricochets.

Trying to ignore what was happening outside, Kim maneuvered the ship towards the narrowing gap overhead. It handled like a hovercraft. The only way to steer was to point the nose in another direction, which changed the angle of the thrust but generally left them travelling sideways as much as forwards. Maybe it wasn't a spaceship at all. Maybe it was a hovercraft that could hover slightly further from the ground than expected.

They bumped against the closing doors. "Shit. Concentrate."

With the elevation knob still slightly raised, Kim turned the ship then nudged the throttle. They scraped along the doors. Back to neutral. Bullets pinged off the hull. Turn again. More throttle. Turn, nudge. And they popped out through the narrow opening.

"Yes." Kim started another happy-dance before realizing they weren't in the clear yet. They had emerged inside a huge modern hangar. By the time she gathered her thoughts and released the elevation knob, it was too late. They crashed into the ceiling and stopped half in, half out of the building. When the scraps of metal fell away, there was blue sky above.

"Huh. Told you we'd make it."

Keeble didn't look happy to have been proven wrong. Tuki, eyes closed, was hanging onto a crate as if his life depended on it. Meledrin leaned over and looked through the door. Her face was pale. She opened her mouth to say something but changed her mind. She pointed out the front window instead.

Kim swore. She seemed to be doing that a lot recently. It was better than screaming or crying.

There were a few fighter jets close to the ground, loud and fast. Higher up, there were about a dozen more weaving a net of contrails. They were keeping away what looked like a whole fleet of bats. The remains of both bats and planes could be seen close by, smoke drifting skywards. Men swarmed on the ground, manning weapons, fighting fires.

And Kim knew the spaceship was quickly becoming the focus of a lot of attention as well. Helicopters were taking off. Teams of men were turning in her direction.

She was starting to worry but tried to control her racing thoughts. Panicking wouldn't help now. She licked her lips and took a deep breath. "So where are we going?"

"I don't even know where we are," Keeble replied.

"Tuki, there were three blue crosses on your skyglass, weren't there?"

"Yes, mo'shi."

"Come and show me."

While Kim waited for Tuki to uncurl himself, a line of green lights flickered on the console and a voice erupted from somewhere in the cockpit.

"*Can you here me?*" It was an American.

There was a stalk next to the lights that might have been a microphone. Kim found a likely button and pressed it. "Hello," she said. She shook her head and changed to English. "*Are you there?*" No response. Another button. "*Hello?*"

The unseen speakers crackled. "*Kim McLean, you are to land the craft immediately or you will be considered hostile.*"

"*You wouldn't shoot us down, even if you could.*"

General Hilliard came on. "*What makes you think that?*"

"*This ship thing contains the things most likely to end this war quickly.*"

"*And what things are they?*"

"*My wonder bra and the amazingly powerful super weapon we found sitting on the seat.*"

"*Miss McLean —*"

"*You're right, my attitude is much more powerful than any super weapon.*"

"We cannot let that craft leave this base, Miss McLean. We will shoot you down."

"Mel is learning the alien's language as we speak, Keeble stuck his hand through solid stone to get us on this ship, and Tuki can use the skyglass. You'd probably happily kill me about now, but you need them alive. And anyway, if you could damage this thing you would've found a way inside years ago."

Tuki was standing in the door, skyglass in hand. One cross over England. The second in the southwest United States. And the third somewhere in central South America. "Of course." That was where she'd seen all the fighting on CNN.

"What?"

"Nothing, General."

But did they want to go there? Kim didn't really have a plan, it was more an idea. The last idea had worked out pretty well, though. First of all she wanted to talk to the alien and find out the reason for the war. Why had they attacked out of the blue? They weren't just a mad, megalomaniacal race hell bent on taking over the universe. Maybe. And then she wanted to talk to the aliens in general and get them to stop. That could be done here as easily as anywhere else. Except the Americans wouldn't give her any peace. Though that argument didn't work because they probably wouldn't give her any peace no matter where she went.

With her current resources, she probably wouldn't have much luck anyway. She needed a way of talking to the aliens without any interference. To do that, she needed to get into space or find a quieter place. A quiet planet. Looking around the ship, she decided she'd only try to take it into space as a last resort. Even if it could get there, and she had her doubts, the aliens were unlikely to listen to her, even if she could already talk to them.

"Okay," she decided, "we're going to South America. We'll go through the gate there and see what we can see." Kim was glad she didn't have much time to think. Her life was crazy, and if she had time to think she might just go crazy with it.

She hit the microphone button. *"We'll leave you to it, General. Good luck. Seriously."*

"Where are you going?"

A jet raced by, a hundred meters overhead and heading south.

"We've got a war to stop." Kim spun the steering wheel and pointed the ship southwards as well. She hit the thrust lever as a helicopter flew into position about fifty meters away. There was a moment as g-forces rushed up and hit her in the chest, then the sensations slipped away. The landscape flashed by below as they caught and left behind the jet with startling ease. It was out of sight before she really had a chance to think. "Holy shit." She'd barely touched the pedal.

After staring for a moment, she swallowed, increased altitude, and wondered if there was anything else she should do. Besides panic.

Kim took a deep breath and tried to calm down. She'd made it this far. She was doing a great job. She *was*.

44: Worlds Away

"WHAT IS OUR DESTINATION?" Meledrin asked, looking through the doorway. "How long will our journey take?" The motion of the ship was hardly noticeable, but it made her nauseous nonetheless. Just as the plane and cars had done. She did not think she would ever become used to it. She hoped she would be back at home, among her own people, before she had the opportunity.

Kim shook her head. "I have no idea." She stood up to look down at the ground as if she had done it a dozen times before. Shaking her head, she slumped back into her seat. "And, not very long at all."

"Do you wish to converse with Cuto? Is there sufficient time?"

"Who? What?"

"Cuto. The hurgon. The alien. There will be much that I don't understand but will be able to infer through context."

"You're ready to talk? And he's ready."

Meledrin nodded. She had been talking to the alien for more than an hour but thought she had learnt more about Kim's language in ten minutes. "Though I am unsure that Cuto is a male. As far as I can ascertain no mention of gender specific pronouns has been made. I do not think the hurgon use any pronouns at all."

"Right. Okay." Kim peered out the window again then across at Keeble. "Can you keep an eye on things up here, Keeble?"

The dwarf smiled and nodded. "Of course."

Meledrin turned to leave, but Kim stayed where she was. "You can't just sit there and fiddle with the controls. No fiddling with the controls at all, actually. You're smart enough to know when things should be left alone, right? So, you watch out the window and see if we're heading towards any battles or mountains or anything else that looks unusual."

"I can do that." He did not seem as excited by the prospect as he had a moment ago.

"Tuki, do you want to sit up here, too?"

Tuki shrugged, then nodded. Finally, Kim exited the cockpit and let the young moai pass.

"On which subjects do you wish to converse?" Meledrin asked.

"None in particular at this stage, I think. Let's just make conversation."

"Very well. And you wish me to translate everything for you?"

"No. Just tell me what you think I need to know for now. You can tell me the rest later."

Meledrin nodded, though she was not sure if she would know what Kim needed to know. The woman had a lot of strange ideas and seemed to reach conclusions from the strangest pieces of information. With a deep breath Meledrin started speaking to the alien.

"*Cuto stated the American food was mostly unpalatable?*" Just those few words hurt her throat. The aliens used a sign language in concert with the spoken words, a strange chorus of sound and vision, that Meledrin was slowly learning. She hoped to soon be able to dispense with the talk entirely.

The alien grunted. "*Cuto is sick.*" The hand signals added nothing at all to the conversation, as far as Meledrin was able to ascertain. "*Hakans do not eat proper food at all.*"

"*The Americans were not intentionally making Cuto sick, Meledrin is sure. Unfortunately, it is unlikely these hakans will be able to offer anything more suitable at this moment.*"

"*Hakans really eat that karakca?*" There was a tilt to the hand signals that Meledrin interpreted as disbelief, but she was unsure that she would ever fully grasp the finer details of the language. "*It is only three more hakan days before Cuto needs to eat again. Will these hakans be sending Cuto back to the T'loop before then?*"

"*Meledrin does not know, Cuto. Communication between hakans and hurgon has been impossible until this point in time.*"

The alien grunted.

"*What sort of food does Cuto customarily eat?*" Meledrin asked.

"*Vegetables and fruit.*"

"*What sort of vegetables and fruit?*" She listened as the alien gave a long list. "*Meledrin knows none of these things, describe some of them.*"

"*Haackhir is a soft yellow fruit that grows on a tree. It has large green seeds.*"

The alien described others, but none of the descriptions informed her in any useful way.

"*Meledrin knows none of these,*" she said when Cuto finished. "*Do all grow in the one region of Cuto's world? During which part of the year do they grow?*"

"*None grow on Hulgorn anymore. Not for hundreds of suns. They grow on several other worlds, all year round.*"

"*Surely the fruits cannot grow in both the colder and warmer times of the year.*"

"*On worlds with krikhavk, farming is done near the vakakal. Other industries are located in the seasonal areas.*"

Meledrin turned to Kim and tried to explain what the alien had said. It was not easy, as the two words she had no understanding of seemed to be the most important.

"Seasonal areas? Maybe he's talking about axial tilt. So Hulgorn has no axial tilt? What does that tell us?" Kim nodded slowly, chewing on her bottom lip. "If nothing else, the hurgon are probably slow to adapt, slow to pick up new ideas."

"Pardon? What is axial tilt, and how does its lack lead you to that conclusion?"

Kim explained the concept. It seemed strange but may well have been the truth. Meledrin had never before given thought to what caused the seasons. That they existed and had to be dealt with was enough for her and, indeed, for every elf she had ever known.

Kim continued. "So, humans, as a race, have evolved with the idea of adapting and changing every year. Summer, winter, droughts, floods. Different animals, different plants. It's those sorts of things that have led to a lot of advances in our society. To the hurgon, every year must be exactly like the one before, so why would they change?"

With a slight nod, though she wasn't sure she really agreed, Meledrin turned back to the alien. "*How long since there was contact between hurgon and hakans?*"

"*It was almost six hundred Hulgorn years ago. In hakan years? Cuto does not know.*"

She informed Kim.

"Good, we might be able to find their home planet. We can work out how long their year is compared to ours, so that'll narrow things down. Find out about their ships."

"We already know what the world is called."

"It probably won't have the same name in the skyglass."

Meledrin conceded the point without saying anything. She turned back to Cuto. "*What of hurgon ships, Cuto? Are they native to Hulgorn?*"

Cuto gave a soft grunt that might have been a laugh at the absurdity of the suggestion. "*Kil'ini are natural to no world. Kil'ini have lived in space for all of time. If Kil'ini could fly down to worlds, would hurgon ride the kidol to attack hakan worlds?*"

"*Kil'ini are the creatures that fly between stars? And kidol are the giant* bats?"

"*Yes, though Cuto does not know the final word?*"

Meledrin nodded. "*So, how did hurgon meet with kil'ini? How did the relationship start?*"

"*When hakans ships departed from Hulgorn, hurgon watched and waited, wondering when the hakans would return. With eyes turned to the sky, hurgon saw the kidol. Some wondered if it was possible to ride kidol, like the hakans rode their shining metal birds. It was possible.*" Cuto's hand signals had become slow and smooth, like it was singing, almost, or reciting a poem. Meledrin guessed that the story held great importance for all hurgon. She studied the hand signals closely, trying to learn.

"*From the backs of the kidol, hurgon could see further still — to kil'ini flying even higher above. Kidol were urged higher and higher, right to the upper edge of the sky. Hurgon and kidol could not fly all the way to Kil'ini, and Kil'ini do not have the ability to hear, but communication was possible with signals and gestures.*

"Never could hurgon fly high enough, but one day a kidol, Lapenti — with Zorta riding — was injured in flight and in danger of falling to the ground. A kil'ini reached down to help.

"The kil'ini, Ila'nidri, sheltered Lapenti and Zorta until the injuries healed and a return to the world was possible. While waiting, Zorta and Ila'nidri spoke of many things. Ila'nidri offered to take hurgon between the stars if that was wanted. Soon other Kil'ini were making the same offer."

When Cuto was done, Meledrin began translating.

"Wait a second, we attacked them?" Kim interrupted when Meledrin reached that part of the story. She had barely begun at all. "They hadn't yet gotten into space and humans were attacking them?"

"That is what Cuto says."

"Ask again."

Meledrin sighed. *"Kim wishes confirmation of the fact that hakans attacked Hulgorn before hurgon had a knowledge of flight and the stars."*

"That is correct. The hakan is trying to blame the hurgon for this war?"

"Cuto, modern hakan society knows nothing of these attacks. Our societies have come and gone and come again since then."

"Do not lie. No time at all has passed since the Great Sun Wars began. Do not pretend this is a bygone war."

"Ages have come and gone for our people Cuto. Truly we knew nothing of hurgon or the war until hurgon attacked the hakan worlds."

Meledrin could hear Kim fidgeting and turned to the woman.

"Make sure Cuto understands that we want peace with the hurgon, Mel," Kim said in response to the translation.

Meledrin sighed. *What else did she expect me to say?* *"Cuto, hakans desire peace with your people."*

Cuto was not convinced. *"How is Cuto to believe? Millions of hurgon died at the hands of hakans."*

"Meledrin does not know what can be done to convince Cuto, beyond treat Cuto as well as can be, which is being done already."

"Hakans could let Cuto go."

"Where, Cuto? Do the hakans just drop Cuto off somewhere and hope Cuto is found by hurgon?"

"Let Cuto talk to them."

"How?"

"Cuto is a communications technician. If tools are available, Cuto can fix the hakan radio so it can hear hurgon radio."

"Meledrin will pass this information on to Kim and complete the telling of Lapenti and Zorta's tale."

When Meledrin had finished the translation, Kim laughed.

"Shit. They fluked it. Talk about *deus ex machina*. A superior being reached down from heaven and helped them. No wonder Cuto is so in awe of the ships."

"I beg your pardon?"

"Don't worry. But what now, do you think?"

"Cuto suggests that if tools are available, our radio might be modified to hear hurgon radio."

"Really?"

Meledrin glanced at Kim, thinking that perhaps the woman was accusing her of lying.

Keeble's voice emerging from the cockpit delayed any opportunity to inquire. "Ahhh, Kim. I think you should come in here."

Meledrin felt a strange shifting in her weight, like she had felt when they first moved away from the American base, and Kim dashed back into the cockpit to lean on the backs of the two chairs to look. "I thought I told you..."

Meledrin followed at a more sedate pace and discovered that they were motionless in a sky full of planes and kidol. The alien bats, much more maneuverable than the planes, were no match for the human weapons. They dodged and weaved, retaliating with missiles of their own and dropping their bombs onto the world below.

"I thought it was a good idea to slow down," Keeble said. "The way we were going before, we'd run into stuff before we saw it, just about."

A plane turned and skimmed past a ponderous alien missile. The missile exploded anyway, engulfing the aircraft in a huge ball of flame and sound. Kim swore. Meledrin's heart was racing, but she schooled her face to calmness in case someone should observe her.

"Christ. We need a radar." Kim scanned the controls, eyes darting back and forth, as if the use of each one would suddenly become obvious now that she thought the need was real.

"What is a radar?"

"It lets us see things like missiles from a long way away, even if they're behind us."

Meledrin shook her head before remembering the way Tuki had used the skyglass at the American base. She mentioned the idea to Kim.

"You're a bloody genius, Mel. Tuki shift the focus, would you? Shift it in close so we can see what's around us."

The moai did as he was asked. In the meantime Kim moved up to the main controls in the middle of the panel and dropped the ship down near the ground. They advanced along a shallow river valley. The skyglass was soon showing the ship and a few kilometers all around. There were so many dots, they almost became one large smudge of yellow. Tuki touched the crystal and spoke a single word. Suddenly there were fewer dots, further apart. One seemed to be directly over the ship and descending rapidly.

A moment later Meledrin jumped, despite her best intentions, as a kidol plummeted past the front of their craft. It seemed to be just meters away, almost close enough to touch. She could hear the creature's panicked shrieking as it went by. The metal cylinders strapped to its belly were ablaze.

Cuto was standing just behind her. *"That was a Ma'sosa Family kidol."*

"How can Cuto tell?"

"The colors painted on the side. The Ma'sosa are a small family."

Meledrin watched as Kim increased their speed. They slewed from one side to the other as she struggled to keep them from colliding with the mountains.

"Do the hakans want Cuto to fix the radio?"

Meledrin translated for Kim, though she was almost certain what the answer would be. She could tell what the woman was thinking by just looking at her face.

"Now isn't the best time," Kim replied while still working at the controls. And to Tuki: "Where the hell is this gate?"

Tuki worked at the skyglass again. He chewed on his lip as if unsure. "I think it is five hundred and twenty seven kilometers directly south of us."

"Right."

There was a sound like rain against the hull of the ship moments before a jet streaked past. Meledrin jumped and held her hand to her racing heart as if someone might otherwise see. And again a few seconds later, when a sound like thunder washed over them.

"They shot us," Kim said.

They had already established that human weapons had no effect on the craft, through both overburdened logic and practical tests, so Meledrin was uncertain what the fuss was about.

"Hakan weapons have not improved since the start of the war," Cuto said. *"In fact they have gone backwards. Hurgon have made many advances but, still, Cuto thinks there is no chance."*

Meledrin did not know much about reading the alien's body language, but there seemed to be a resigned tilt to his sign language.

"All the more reason for Cuto to help us stop the war."

After a couple of minutes struggling along near the bottom of the valley, Kim sighed and took them up. Then she pointed the ship towards what looked like a clear section of sky and accelerated.

Meledrin closed her eyes for a moment and held her breath.

45: One Small Step

KIM FLINCHED WHEN A JET PASSED BY, no more than eighty meters ahead. According to the skyglass, there were another couple coming from the other direction. Or maybe they were kidol. It didn't matter. Both sides were likely to have a shot at her if they could.

A warning alarm sounded. Luckily, Kim had her hand on the elevation knob, and she held on as she flinched. A missile, definitely of human design, passed below as they shot upwards like a cork from a champagne bottle. Her heart was racing. When she thought to release the knob, they were almost eye-to-eye with a couple of kidol. A moment later a missile dropped from the central cylinder of one creature. It fell a few meters then powered up and darted forward. Kim sent her ship up again. This time, when they stopped, they seemed to be above the main battle. For now.

They'd climbed a few hundred meters in a couple of seconds. There had been the momentary thump of g-forces when they first moved, then nothing at all. Amazing.

She breathed and looked around at her companions.

"That was close." She stood up on shaking legs and looked at the battle below. The sun was rising was painting hundreds, maybe thousands of aircraft with golden light. There were so many of them, filling the sky like a plague of locusts.

The skyglass was indicating they'd have company again very soon.

Kim looked back out the window then back at the controls. It was possible the ship had all sorts of defensive equipment, but she was forced to jump around like a startled rabbit every time someone came close. Or maybe the ship was for doing the shopping, and the only thing it could defend against was wild shopping trollies. Looking around, she decided the final option was the most likely. There was so much she wanted to find out, but she wasn't likely to get an opportunity in the near future. She wondered how Keeble was doing. He was constantly reviewing the control panel, as if all the action outside was of no consequence, and doing an admirable job of controlling himself. His fingers were twitching with suppressed need to be doing *something*.

"South, right, Tuki?" She pushed at the thrust pedal. "Let's get the hell out of here."

There were battles for much of the five hundred kilometers, seemingly from the ground all the way up. The death and destruction was horrible. Kidol and jets were falling from the sky like ducks in hunting season. There were more kidol than planes, and that was where their only real advantage lay. For every one of the creatures shot down another three were waiting to take its place. Smoke was rising from wrecks and towns and forest fires. Kim did her best to ignore them all, finding open air and heading for it, passing by before anyone had a chance to react.

Half an hour later Tuki, watching his skyglass in the cargo cabin, started to fidget quietly.

Kim looked back at him. "What is it, Tuki?"

"We are in the right area. I think. The gate is close by."

"You're sure?"

"I think so."

"You think you're sure?" Kim muttered.

There were more than a dozen kidol high up to the west and a few dozen more scattered around the area. There were a few planes flying around the perimeters, but the humans seemed to be content to leave them alone for the most part.

Kim stood up and examined the mountains below them. There didn't seem to be anything there.

"Are you sure, Tuki?" Kim probably would have let the aliens have the area as well.

Tuki checked the skyglass again. He shifted the focus. "I think so."

He probably hadn't been sure of much in his life.

"That way, I think. The cross is very large, though, so it is hard to be sure."

"Okay." Kim sighed. "Let's find this thing." It could take forever.

After nearly an hour of searching, Kim brought the ship to a halt, hovering a few miles away from their destination. She slumped back in her seat and looked at the ruins clinging to the ridge.

"Where are we?" Keeble asked.

Kim could tell he wouldn't be able to control himself for much longer. "Machu Picchu," she said. She'd never been there, but it wasn't hard to recognize. "It's an ancient city that nobody really understands."

"What is it that you mean?" Meledrin asked.

"Well, there's no real reason for the city to be where it is. It's not on a major road, it probably wouldn't have been self sufficient, which was strange at the time, and it's in a really out of the way place. Nobody has ever been able to think of a sensible reason why anyone would build a city there."

"How old is this city?"

"Not overly, in the scheme of things. A few thousand years, maybe. Maybe they didn't know about the gate, they just knew the site was important."

"But where's the gate?" Keeble asked.

"I don't know. Exactly. You know as much as me. Tuki? How about you?"

"Pardon, mo'shi."

"Can you narrow down the location on the skyglass any more?"

"I do not know. I do not know how to use the skyglass very well. I am just a go'gan."

"Don't say stuff like that. You're getting better at using it all the time, Tuki. Just keep working on it."

"Yes, mo'shi."

"Right, then. Let's just land and we'll see what we can see."

Keeble grunted, and Kim knew exactly what he was going to say. "Great plan. The gate has been hidden for fifty thousand years or something, but we'll find it in the next half an hour."

"Well, we'd better. The Americans have a base in Peru. It can't be more than a couple of hours from here."

A crashing plane had taken the tops off a few walls and cut a long furrow in the earth. It had eventually come to rest, tail in the air, against a terrace wall. It had exploded sometime during the process. There were half a dozen dead kidol as well, plus another that writhed and kicked feebly. Smoke rose from the canisters on all of them.

Kim carefully guided the ship down towards a large open area in the center of the ruins. The plane had passed that way and a kidol was sprawled awkwardly, wing and neck at odd angles, but there was still plenty of room to land. She was going to need it. She'd forgotten how hard it was to actually steer towards somewhere in particular without stopping and starting and wavering backwards and forwards. She probably could have done it if she'd been willing to waste ten minutes or if she could see straight down.

There was one consolation. At this time of the day, there should have been tourists everywhere, but the war had kept them away. *Yay for the war.*

Getting close to the ground, Kim panicked and searched desperately for the switch that controlled the landing gear. It was a couple of seconds before she realized she hadn't done anything to raise it back in Nevada. They thumped down heavily, and Kim let out a breath she didn't realize she'd been holding.

"Mind the step, and no smoking until you have cleared the terminal building."

"What?"

"Never mind. Come on." She had to keep moving. No time for thought, or she would collapse in a blubbering heap.

Kim opened the back door and jumped down to the grass. Despite what she'd said to Keeble, she looked around for some obvious sign of the gate. The dwarf, toolbox clamped in his hand, clattered to the ground, and Meledrin landed lightly a moment later. The elf crossed to her side.

Cuto, following close behind the only person who could understand him, said something and pointed at the sky. Kim was waiting for a translation when she worked out for herself what the alien had said. Three Chinook helicopters emerged from behind a cloud, heading straight for Machu Picchu. Where else would they be going?

"General Hilliard isn't stupid." If the spaceship had been tracked then, once they had stopped to search, their destination must have been obvious to anyone with a map.

"I believe time is running short," Meledrin said, shading her eyes to watch the helicopters as well.

"Yeah, great, Mel. Well deducted."

"How do we go about this search," the elf asked, either ignoring or completely missing the sarcasm. "Do you have a plan?"

Kim turned to look when Keeble grunted behind her. She expected him to follow up with a smartarse comment, but he was staring off into the ruins. "How about we just follow Keeble," she said.

"I beg your pardon? Keeble has not previously been at this location, as you well know."

"You know where the gate is, Keeble, don't you?" She hadn't thought of the possibility before. It was obvious, really.

The dwarf nodded and pointed. "It's that way," he said absently. "I can hear it as plain as day"

"Well, don't just stand there. Lead on."

It didn't look as if Keeble even heard her, but he headed down the long slope. Kim wanted to tell him to hurry but didn't think it would do any good. He was in a daze. They moved into the shade of a building-topped cliff then climbed a low wall onto a path.

"How far, Keeble?" Kim checked the sky.

"Not far," Keeble said. He might have been talking about the helicopters. They were a couple of minutes away, at most, and the pilots would land them a lot quicker than Kim had landed the spaceship. But he pointed through a gap between two tall walls. "Just through here."

The dwarf ran his fingers over the stone as he passed through, as if wanting to stop for a closer look at the workmanship, but apparently the song called him on. Beyond the walls was a small square with what looked like a ceremonial stone in the middle and a spectacular view out over terraces and a steep-sided valley. The dwarf ignored both of these. On the northern side of the square was a small lawn enclosed on three sides by tall walls, some of them looking as if they couldn't decide whether to topple over in the next few minutes or stay where they were for another few thousand years.

The sound of the helicopters was growing.

"It's there," Keeble said, pointing at the rear wall.

"Where?" Kim went and touched the stone. It looked and felt like normal stone.

Keeble shook his head even as he went to put his good hand gently against the wall as well. "It's on the far side."

"Do not waste our time, Keeble," Meledrin said, starting back the way they'd come. "If we have to go around the wall why did you not lead us there immediately?"

Keeble shook his head again and sneered. "It is right against the stone," he said, "and we can only go through from one side. This side."

"So our journey was pointless then. These stones have been in place for millennia, and we will not change that in the next few moments."

Kim shook her head and looked at Keeble. "He can sing, Meledrin. And if he's going to, he'd better do it quick."

Helicopters were landing out near the spaceship. Kim thought it was all of them until one of them came over the wall and hovered barely twenty meters away. If the pilot got desperate, he could probably land in the square. Kim shielded her eyes against the dust and wind before turning to see that there *was* something that could distract Keeble from the gate.

"Don't just stand there, Keeble," Kim shouted over the noise. "Sing."

The dwarf wrenched his eyes away from the Chinook and turned his attention to the wall. His song was audible over the thump of the helicopter rotors, but Kim could feel it building anyway.

"NOBODY MOVE." The voice on the loud speaker was easy enough to hear. The side door of the helicopter was open and a few soldiers were visible. One had a microphone, one had a heavy caliber machine gun bolted to the floor, and the others were preparing to rappel down to the ground.

"How's it going, Keeble?" Kim shouted.

"Ready."

"Ready?"

"Yes."

Kim went to the wall, taking a deep breath to steady her nerves. The others were watching her. She'd passed through to Sherindel, but that had only been for a moment and she hadn't really believed she'd be passing through to another world at that time. She'd had time to think about it since then, and the idea scared her as much as it excited her.

She might have stood there all day, staring at the misty stone, but one glance over her shoulder and she saw that the first American soldier had just reached the ground.

"Come on. Quick." She took another deep breath, nodded, and stepped into the stone. Then she took another step. Nothing happened. She was in a big, dusty room —

fifteen meters long and ten wide — that most definitely wasn't in Peru, but nothing had *happened*. She stepped through the door like she would have stepped though any other door.

"That's it?" she said. "I expected... I don't know. Something."

"Thunder?" Keeble asked, pushing her out of the way. The dwarf let his song slip away after the others crowded through behind.

Kim nodded. "Yeah. Maybe. Just something." She almost wanted to turn around and go back through, just to see if she'd missed something. It wasn't as if the destination was all that amazing either. It might well have been on Earth. There were ancient, fading frescoes on the walls. The subjects looked boringly human and were holding some very mundane items. Electrical lighting, or something similar, cast a pale glow. Did the air taste strange? Kim laughed. It probably did taste different, but that didn't mean anything at all. On Earth the air could be different from one street to the next. From one minute to the next, as well.

In some ways Kim was disappointed. If she were on another world, surely things should be different. At the same time she was comforted. Maybe *her* people didn't know this world, but humans had at some stage. "One small step," she said softly. One small step, and it had taken her from one world to another.

"I reckon we should close these."

Kim looked. There were two slabs of stone that looked like doors folded back out of the way of the doorway they'd just used. There didn't seem to be a lock or catch of any kind. Columns stood on either side of the door, though it wasn't likely they had anything to do with holding up the roof.

"I don't think it'd be much use. I think they're more ornamental than anything else. Besides, it'll take them a while to pull down that wall on Earth. They probably have to get council permission — destroying one of the wonders of the world and all."

"If you're sure. It'll only take a moment."

Kim thought about it then shook her head. "We want them to get through. We don't want to be doing this on our own."

"I am still unaware of what it is we are attempting to achieve," Meledrin said. "You have not made it clear."

She hadn't made it clear because she wasn't exactly sure. Get away from the Americans, first. Done, for the moment. Talk to the hurgon and end the war. She'd certainly made progress in that direction but wasn't sure how being on this new world would help, beyond evening out the playing field with the Americans. She knew as much about this place as they did.

"We see if we can find people on this world and see if they are technologically advanced." The dusty room they were in did nothing more than muddy those waters. "And we try to contact the hurgon and see what the hell we can do about this war. They don't want this any more than we do. Not really."

"You are basing this assessment on the fact that one hurgon failed to kill one elderly human?"

"Yes. And this hurgon right here is friendly enough. He's obviously someone we can get along with."

"So," Keeble said, "we need to find a radio so Cuto can fix it and we can talk to the rest of them."

"Yes."

"Right. Well it won't get done standing here." He shifted his toolbox to his good hand and stumped from the room. Though Cuto could not have understood a word of what was said, the alien followed. Tuki waited until first Kim and then Meledrin followed as well.

"This world may be in worse condition than the others we have seen," Meledrin said. "The hurgon may already have been victorious and moved on."

Hurrying after Keeble, Kim sucked in a deep breath as she started to catch up with reality. She was on another world. Another world. Her companions were all primitive people who still believed in magic. Hell, Keeble could *do* magic. Crossing between worlds was probably not such an impossible thought for them. They also wouldn't understand the odds of finding a group of worlds that were so alike.

It was all so unlikely. So impossible. Ending a war should be easy in comparison.

As far as Kim could tell, they were in some type of military installation. On the first level was a mess hall with a huge kitchen. There was what looked like a first aid room and a laundry. There was an office with twenty desks lined up with regimental precision. There was what could have been a rec' or torture room. Or something else entirely.

Every surface was covered in a few centimeters of dust and looked to have been that way for centuries. They left a storm of it in their wake.

At the end of a long hall, with a utility room and workshops that Keeble had to be pulled away from, they found a door that opened at the push of a button, and a set of stairs. Up was the only option. Kim went slowly, pausing at the next level, ear against the door to listen.

"What do you hear?" Keeble whispered.

"Nothing. Come on."

Beyond was more hallway and more quiet, dusty rooms. Kim didn't know what half of them were for, and she wasn't interested in the ones whose purpose she could guess. There wasn't anything that looked like machinery.

More stairs at the end of the hall, and more rooms above. Then the same again. They hadn't even found a door leading outside, or a window. Just fifty meters of straight, dusty blandness with stairs at either end. Keeble and Tuki checked every door as they went past, long after Kim had given up hope. They could have passed a dozen radios already, without realizing. Cuto didn't look particularly interested, though it was probably all very strange to it.

At the end of the hallway on the fifth level, Kim leaned against the door. "We might as well go back," she said.

Keeble shook his head. "The Americans are probably through by now."

"Right. Of course. We might as well wait here, then. They'll catch up soon enough."

"They will not return us to prison?" Meledrin asked as she straightened her hair.

"Of course they will. One made entirely of metal."

"And you desire this."

Kim sighed. "No."

"Then perhaps we should continue on."

"Come on, then." Kim levered herself off the door so Keeble could open it and followed him up the inevitable stairs beyond. And there was another door at the next landing.

"Do we look at this floor or choose floors at random or go straight to the top?" Kim said before the dwarf had a chance to open the door. But she knew what his answer would be. Skipping floors would be leaving the job half done, and that wasn't right.

"No shirking, dwife. There may be a radio right through here."

There wasn't. There was a hallway. But the hallway was wider, higher, and shorter than usual. And it was filled with all types of furniture and rubbish scattered around like a fall of autumn leaves. Kim didn't know what the mess might mean, so she gave it no thought. The one door that marred the right hand wall was three meters wide and went all the way from floor to ceiling. There was no door at the far end, just an opening that took up the entire wall.

"Well," Kim said, striding down the hall as if her plan was finally coming together. Keeble stopped halfway to open the door, but Kim didn't slow. She went all the way to the end and through the opening. On the other side, she stopped so suddenly Meledrin almost ran into her.

"The door won't open," Keeble was saying as he caught up. "I think it's hydraulic. There's a panel near it but Cuto climbed up to have a look through the window and said there wasn't anything worth seeing."

"Cuto told you?" Meledrin asked.

But Keeble didn't answer. Kim decided he was probably staring at the same thing she was. The room was the size of a football field and filled with row upon row of spaceships. It was a pretty amazing sight, even if Meledrin didn't think so. Most of them were not much larger than the one they had already flown, but some were the size of a house, and there was an arch that led through to some even larger ships.

Keeble went to run his hand along the nearest hull, but Kim headed for the other hangar. Meledrin wandered along behind as if she didn't care either way. Tuki followed because that was what he did, and Cuto said something but followed before Meledrin had a chance to answer. The next room was five times the size of the first, and it needed to be. The smallest ship was a vaguely plane shaped thing about the size of a jumbo jet. The largest was a sphere more than a hundred meters across. It was massive. She couldn't believe something that size could ever move, let alone get all the way into space. Maybe it was just another plane. Maybe it was a building. Maybe it was a moon. No vehicle could be that big.

Kim was still staring, with the others gathered behind, when Keeble caught up again.

"Don't just stand there blocking the door," he said, pushing his way through. "Trust women to just stand around looking." But he stopped to stare as well. He went for a closer look a minute later. Kim watched as he went to rub his hand along a hull nearby.

Cuto broke the silence, and Kim jumped. Meledrin and the alien spoke and waved their arms for a few seconds before the elf translated.

"Cuto is adamant that someone is on the level below us. Cuto suggests we might want to either move on or make our way into one of these ships."

"There'll probably be a radio in the ships," Kim said.

"In that case, which one shall we enter?"

"How would I know? Ummm... a medium sized one."

"For which reason?"

"Because..." Yes, why? "Well, a little one might not carry us all properly, and a big one might be too hard to fly." It sounded good. Kim looked around and saw a fifty-meter sphere halfway across the huge hangar. It was probably larger than she wanted, but steps led up through a network of scaffolding that stood by its side. "That one there?" Examining it, she felt like one of the Amish trying to fool a used car salesman into thinking she knew what she was talking about.

Keeble had apparently heard the conversation, or liked the look of the scaffolding, for he was already making his way in that direction. He didn't climb the stairs though. He wandered slowly around, looking up at the curve of the hull and the huge funnels, like intake vents, that were all over the ship. There were also thousands of other holes, a few centimeters across, spread all over the ship.

Kim started to follow, but her shadow stretching out before her caught her attention. She turned and discovered that the hangar door was open. The door was huge, obviously, and offered up a view of a strange world. Kim went closer. There was a platform outside, then the land fell away into an enormous, densely forested river valley. On the far side, ten miles away or maybe twenty, sharp-edged mountains bit at a faintly purple sky.

Kim stood in the doorway, staring. The air seemed so much clearer than on Earth. The forest so much greener. It was like some primordial world that was untouched by the destructive hands of advanced creatures. Except there was a hangar full of spaceships and... Kim looked at the ground.

She looked back into the hangar and saw all her companions. Meledrin had hardly moved at all. Keeble and Cuto were examining the ships, and Tuki was not far away from Kim, also examining the valley. She took a step backwards.

The untouched valley. Except there was the hangar and a strange set of footprints in the dust. Boot prints, to be more precise. Actually, there were two sets. Who ever made the first set was big, either that or had stolen boots off someone big. Kim didn't want to try to steal shoes off somebody that big. She licked her lips and looked around. The other prints might have belonged to a child.

Heart racing, Kim followed the prints to the end of the platform where they went down a flight of worn stairs and disappeared into the forest.

"What is it, mo'shi?" Tuki asked. He was still standing by the door, as if afraid to venture any further.

Kim glanced back. She wiped her hands on her jeans, chewed her bottom lip. "Nothing." But she saw something just beyond the bottom of the stairs. It looked like a book. "Wait there." She didn't think he was likely to follow anyway.

She glanced around then hurried down. Then she hesitated before actually stepping down onto the hard, dusty ground. A small puff of dust kicked up when her foot touched. *Just like Neil Armstrong,* she thought. She looked around at the forest. It crowded in close, dense and shadowed, except for a narrow path that snaked away along the side of the hill. Another sign of life, one that seemed a lot more real, a lot more permanent than the boot prints or even the hangar. Kim felt as if she were being watched. She snatched up the book and raced back up the stairs. Tuki watched, wide-eyed, as Kim approached. He took a step back.

"What is it, mo'shi?"

"A book."

"That is a book?"

As if it were some mystical talisman. Perhaps it was. Kim nodded. The red leather cover was worn and cracked, stamped with strange, indecipherable symbols. The pages were brittle with age.

"What does it do, mo'shi?"

"Nothing." There were pictures and lists and what might have been maps. It didn't matter what it was if nobody could read it. "Come on. Let's go look at the ship." *Keep moving. Don't lose momentum.* She made her way quickly to the scaffolding, trying not to notice that she was backtracking along the trail of footprints. She almost ran up the steep stairs. They ended above the ship's equator, but a platform reached out the side to touch the ship.

The hull was rough and pitted. There was an inset, round-cornered rectangle, about three meters to a side. "It looks like a door." Kim looked for a hidden handle or a panel that would reveal a handle, without really expecting to see anything. She ran her hands around the outside edge of the door. Then around the inside edge. She felt nothing unusual.

She laughed. *Nothing unusual? My hand is on the side of a spaceship and I can't feel anything unusual?*

She poked a finger into one of the holes on the hull and leant out over the rail to look inside. She couldn't see or feel anything.

She followed Keeble back down to the ground.

"What do you reckon, Keeble?"

"That panel there, between those two funnels," the dwarf pointed. "It's stone."

Kim examined the patch of hull. She could see a slight difference in color, but she thought it was just a trick of the light. "Are you sure?"

"Yes."

Kim narrowed her eyes as if concentrating would help. Eventually she shook her head. "If you say so. So you can sing us in then?"

KEEBLE FOUND A SMALLER SCAFFOLD and dragged it over so he could climb up to look at the panel. First Kim, then Tuki and the alien helped. When it was in place, they all climbed the steep stairs.

Cuto said something but Meledrin didn't bother to translate for everyone else. The alien spoke again, and Keeble turned to see it glaring at Meledrin. The elf sighed. "Cuto is not surprised that our civilizations failed if we are somehow able to lose two whole rooms full of huge ships such as these."

Keeble gave a small grunt and smiled, but quickly turned back to the ship. "I'm not sure if I can do it," he said, reaching out with his good hand. The stone was like nothing he'd ever felt. It was even stronger than the stone on the ship they'd flown from America and would withstand as much, if not more, than the metal sections of the hull. It was so dense and compact that it was a wonder it didn't collapse under its own weight.

"What do you mean?" Kim asked. "Why not?"

"The stone is amazing. It's so strong."

"Well, give it a go. Just don't hurt yourself."

Cuto spoke and Meledrin translated. "Cuto wishes to know how your singing works."

But Keeble was already building his Song. It was even stronger now. He'd passed through another gate and could add the knowledge he'd gained to his Song. He hummed the foundations carefully, making sure everything was right, before building up the Song with a wordless, dancing cadence, and sealing the joints with a series of clicks. When it was all there, he kept it going perfectly, all of the sounds combining like the stones of the mountains, or the water of a stream. He could feel the power washing through him.

After he'd been Singing the completed Song for more than a minute, Keeble started to change it again, condensing it, whittling away the edges, honing it until it was focused tightly at one small section of the stone panel on the hull.

He stepped forward. He reached out towards the focus of his Song. And paused.

46: Rugby

Whistler's Mother, Meledrin is an elf. He wondered how he hadn't known. He wondered how he'd gone all this time with a woman and an elf as a companion. He felt his Song falter but clung to the rhythms tenaciously.

"Meledrin's an elf," he said, working the words into his Song. "She's an elf. And Kim is a human." The Song carried on, even with the revelations. He took a deep breath and concentrated. "Chess is an amazing game. Exact. Proper. But rugby is fun as well."

And even if Meledrin was an elf, she was part of his work gang. *A work gang is like family.* Keeble took a deep breath. *She'd argued with that other elf at Grovely to let me stay. If not for her, I would not be here.*

He looked at the elf, gave a small nod, and changed the Song again, spreading the focus until he had created a hole large enough to climb through. He put his head inside the ship, pulling himself up to get all the way through the wall.

Inside, everything was dark.

"It's dark," he said when he was back out in the open. "Like, can't-see-my-nose dark."

"Doesn't light get through the sung stone?"

"A bit, but the hull's about a meter thick."

"Shit." Kim looked around as if a torch might suddenly appear. It sort of did. "In my pack. There's a torch in my pack. Quick, Tuki."

The moai removed the pack and looked at it in confusion. "How do you open it?"

"It's a zipper," Kim said. As if that would help.

Keeble shook his head. "You realize he has no idea what a torch looks like, don't you?"

Kim grabbed the pack and rifled through it until she found a small torch. Keeble took it, found the switch, and stuck his head inside the ship again. After a moment he climbed in completely, surveyed his surroundings, then spun around and poked his head out to talk to Kim. The woman was waiting impatiently, chewing her lip, shuffling her feet, and glancing towards the door the Americans would enter by.

"It's just a box," he told her. "It's sixty centimeters square and runs 2.3 meters directly into the ship. The inner end's made of stone."

"What?"

"It's just a box."

"But that's crazy."

Keeble recognized the moment Kim came up with the idea.

"It's an airlock."

"Why does it need an airlock?"

"Because there's no air in space."

"There isn't?"

"No. Look, I think you're in a maintenance hatch. If you sing through that inner wall, you'll be in passageways or something."

"How do you know?"

"Just trust me"

Keeble wasn't so sure. Apparently it showed on his face.

"Just get in there and sing, and we'll follow you."

"There's no way Tuki or Cuto will fit."

"Oh. Right. Damn it." Kim chewed her lip some more. "Here's the plan, then. We'll go and wait by the door up there, and you open it from the inside."

Keeble nodded, "Right," and went back into the ship. "Go open the door," he muttered. "Sounds easy." He stopped, stuck his head out and looked at Kim. "Somebody bring my tools." It wouldn't surprise him if they couldn't even manage that between them.

Back inside the ship, he adjusted his mechanical hand to hold the torch and crawled along the passage. He Sang his way through the next wall and entered an intersection. He grunted and muttered as if Kim might hear him if he swore out loud.

After a moment he picked a direction at random, left, and crawled. Then a turn to the right. When he reached the end of the passage, if his calculations were correct, he was nine point seven meters from the outside of the ship. There was no reason why his calculations wouldn't be correct.

A ladder led upwards.

Keeble rose to his feet and climbed. His metal hand, still gripping the torch, clanked against the rungs, his good hand was slippery with sweat. At the top, he climbed out into another low passage.

"This is almost like home," he said to himself. He had spent a good part of his work gang apprenticeship crawling through the ventilation ducts of Tab Cavern.

Making his way slowly forward, Keeble emerged into a full sized room. He was looking at the biggest engine he'd ever seen. Not that he'd seen many true engines. Rising to his feet, he craned his neck to look at the top of the monstrosity and took a moment to wonder at the size of the engines in the larger starships.

He wondered about the room for a minute, shining his light into nooks and crannies, trying to match what he saw with parts he knew from planes and cars. Many of them were made from stone, strong and perfect. He may well have stayed longer, but the need to talk to someone, to bounce ideas off them and hear theirs in return, reminded him of his companions waiting outside. He doubted any of them would have worthwhile ideas, but they'd be better than nobody at all. With one last, quick look around and a pause to clean the dust away from a small, blank screen, Keeble found a door and continued on.

But he discovered that the next room was a workshop of some kind, with blank screens and tools and cabinets filled with parts. It was all he could do to drag himself away. He hurried through the nearest door and paused at the base of a set of narrow stairs. He didn't know where to go. He tried to orient himself in his mind.

"I came up that way," he said, "and turned that way." He spun about in the hallway as he spoke, gesturing to push his thoughts in the right direction. "So that means that the others are this way." He started to climb, trying to calculate distances in his mind. If he added the height of the ladder he'd climbed, to the distance between each floor... He climbed three levels higher.

He stopped on a landing and shone his torch through an open hatch and out into a hallway. After a moment of thought, he went out for a better look. Keeble shone his light around and examined everything for a moment before reining his curiosity in once more. To his right, a passage led to a large window. The window certainly hadn't been visible from outside. He hurried along the passage and looked down into the hangar.

The first thing he saw was a human.

Keeble gasped as the man darted behind the cover of a much smaller ship one hundred and seventeen meters away. Another ran across the narrow strip of bare floor and hid. About two dozen men were quartering the hangar, looking for any signs of life. It wouldn't be long before they reached the larger ships and found what they were after.

When he drew his attention away, Keeble saw the scaffolding and his companions not far away in the opposite direction. The window stopped right near them with the wall taken up by what could only be a door. There was a wall blocking the passage just beyond. There was a vehicle of some kind clamped to the floor along the end wall and a row of cabinets, some of them opened, lined the other.

When he went closer, Keeble could see three buttons near the door. He tried them all, though he knew they wouldn't work.

"No power."

Next, he examined the wall nearby. There was an access panel. He pulled it open and was rewarded with the sight of a metal wheel.

With a little smile, he gripped the wheel with his good hand and turned.

Nothing happened. It didn't move. He grunted and tried again. Putting all of his strength into it. It moved slightly, but hardly enough to even measure.

If only he'd brought his tools, instead of leaving them with Kim. He took a deep breath and tried again, calculating the progress of the Americans across the hangar outside.

He gritted his teeth with the effort and finally the wheel started to turn. He kept working as quickly as possible, sweaty hend slipping on the wheel. The Americans had to be getting close.

"I'll feel like a fool if this doesn't open the door."

But even as he spoke, the door started to slide open, half one way and half the other. When there were ten centimeters between the two edges, big moai hands gripped from the outside to help. Not long after, Meledrin slipped through sideways, followed by Kim and Cuto when the gap had widened a little more.

But there was still a long way to go before Tuki would be through. Keeble continued to work at the grinding wheel. Kim lent her strength to the task.

Shouts came from outside.

"[Stop where you are.]"

"[Stop or we'll shoot.]"

They continued to work, and Tuki squeezed through a few seconds later.

Keeble started to work the wheel in the other direction, but Cuto pushed him out of the way. The alien worked quickly, big hands not slowing.

Gunshots rang out, bullets pinging off the hull.

Keeble didn't know if they were warning shots or not, but he willed Cuto to work faster, feeling each moment as if it was a lifetime.

Outside, the scaffolding started to rattle and shake, but the wheel had been loosened by its journey in the other direction, and the door was soon closed.

Keeble collapsed to the floor next to Kim. He gave no thought to who he was sitting beside as he struggled for air. He unstrapped his mechanical arm and threw it into a corner, rubbing at his wrist as he tried to calm his heart.

Cuto, Tuki, and Meledrin were standing silently, eyes closed.

"I don't know how much time that'll give us," Kim said between gasps. Her face was flushed though she had done little of the work. "There's all types of equipment out there. They might be able to find something that will help."

"Nothing in *here* works, though," Keeble motioned vaguely. "Don't see why anything out there would. Besides, the stuff is ancient, so they probably won't know how to use it."

"And if this vessel does not function, then what is the purpose of all that we have done? And *it* is ancient too, so even if it remains functional, who is to say Kim is capable of operating it?"

Keeble hadn't thought of that. He figured he could get it working anyway.

"I found the engine. I think there might be more than one, actually."

Kim sighed. "Well, any ideas? The torch batteries won't last forever. An hour, if we're extremely lucky. What happens if we don't get the lights working?" She looked at everyone.

Tuki cleared his throat. "The skyglass can be used to see, though it is not very bright." To demonstrate, he looked at the crystal ball and mumbled quietly.

Keeble watched as the ball started to glow, giving off a soft radiance. It wasn't bright, but better than nothing.

"Can you get the 'glass to just show a star, Tuki? And zoom right in?"

"Possibly." He muttered again, and a moment later the glass was filled with a bright yellow fire. Tuki smiled.

"Well, you lot will just have to stay near the windows," Keeble said. "I'll take the lights and see if I can fix the engine."

"We can still help," Kim said.

Keeble grunted but knew better than to argue.

FOR A WHILE, Scree stared at all the controls in bewilderment. It would take forever to work out what they all did. Then he decided that he didn't really care what most of them did. All he wanted to do was fly. Forward and backwards, up and down and turning around— it couldn't be that hard. He examined the ones that looked the most important.

"I'm going to trys this ones," he told Ping eventually.

"What? No, can't just—"

"If we don't do somethings we'll sit here forever." So he spun the wheel before she could argue and the ship spun around on the spot. "Huh, told you."

That left a lever and a knob. Scree tried the lever without even warning Ping and ran into the next ship.

"Scree!"

"What? We knows what that one does now." And that just left one more control. Scree tried the knob, spinning it and pushing it and pulling it until the ship rose a little bit higher. "Huh, easy as skinning as cat." Skinning cats wasn't that easy if the cat was still alive, but it was just a saying. He pushed back down and the ship sank back to its original position.

"We're ready to go then." It wasn't a question and Ping didn't look like she wanted to answer anyway. So Scree spun the wheel to get them facing the big door and nudged the control to get them moving. The ship pushed between two smaller craft, screeching complaints as it shouldered them aside. Then it broke into the clear and darted out into the open air.

Scree managed to stop the ship and turned to grin at Ping. "Easy." And it was. It seemed stupidly easy. He wasn't sure if this was a ship that traveled to the stars— the thought of that seemed a bit like crossing an ocean in a rowboat— but either way, it felt as if he had been doing it all his life.

"Now what?" Ping asked nervously. She obviously wasn't excited about the prospect of flying.

Scree was starting to feel confident again. He didn't know if he'd find someone who could fight the monsters, but flying the ship made him think he might be able to do something himself if needed. He definitely wouldn't have to spend the rest of his life hiding. "Maybe this is a worlds where we can fight back. Maybe this is the one

where we have a chance of winning. So we looks for people and see where theys at."
He turned his attention to the outside world again. They were hovering just above a
wide ledge half way up the side of a basalt cliff looking out over what might have
been an endless desert. Waves of sand rolled away as far as the eye could see.

It wasn't a promising start. There were no signs that civilization had ever
clustered round the gate like it had everywhere else. It seemed to have washed away
long ago, taken by desert and years. He swore and pulled the knob that would give
them more height. With the cliff below them he spun the ship to face the other way.
The ancient complex had been carved into a nub of stone barely two hundred meters
across and on the far side the desert took up its eternal march once more,
shouldering up to the sinking sun.

Scree swore.

"Should we go back?" Ping asked.

Scree shook his head. "The desert ain't the problem. I don't likes the look of the
sun is all."

"What you mean?"

"We'll wait for dark. We got any of that horrible fruit left anywhere?"

"In your pack?" Ping went to have a look. "Maybe you should land. The ship
might stop working like your monster gun did."

Scree did as she suggested and sat to stare at the sun.

Half an hour later his suspicions were confirmed. He wiped juice from his chin
and craned his neck to check the position of the emerging stars. He spun the ship in
the other direction.

"What?"

"We're on Kiva."

"Your home world?"

He nodded. For a moment he felt like kicking something, then realized the
situation wasn't all bad. "Good news though." He smiled. "I know how to find some
humans with a chance of killing them monsters." He checked the stars again. The
place he'd found his sword was somewhere to the north. He guessed it would take a
couple of months if he was walking but he had no idea how long it would take in the
ship. He squared his shoulders and pushed the lever to send the ship forward.

"So we fly out into desert?"

"What else you think we should do?"

Ping didn't say anything and Scree pushed the lever further. Soon they were
racing forward, covering more ground than he would have thought possible. "We'll
be there in no time."

The news didn't seem to comfort Ping at all.

-oOo-

"You sure it's real?" Ping asked.

Scree shook his head and squinted into the distance. The line out near the edge of the horizon seemed to be solid and getting closer, but it was hard to tell in the star speckled night. It was the only thing that had broken the monotony of the desert for the last two hours. He wasn't really worried, he knew where he was going, but the emptiness obviously made Ping nervous.

He was about to say there was nothing to worry about when the ship shuddered. Scree sat back and looked at the controls. A red light was flashing, which didn't look good, but there was no way he could tell what it really meant. The ship shuddered again and Scree swore. He dropped closer to the ground and slowed the ship down while he tried to work out what was going on.

He gave a grunt of laughter.

"What's funny?"

"I'm trying to work out what's wrong when all I knows is what three of the control does."

"Not funny at all."

The ship lurched this time and Scree slowed to walking pace before it stopped working completely. It dropped to the ground like a stone. Scree braced himself and threw out an arm to keep Ping in her seat as well. The ship hit the ground and stopped almost instantly. Clouds of sand sprayed up into the night and rained back down into the desert. The silence that followed was unsettling.

"Told you should have waited," Ping said eventually.

Scree grunted. "No you didn't." He looked in Ping's direction and didn't say anything more. He could see that she was close to the edge. He cleared his throat and turned his attention to the world outside. There was nothing to see. "Come on." He headed for the door.

"Should wait until morning? I need some sleep."

"You're jokings, right? We only gots a little bit of food and water and in the morning we'll fry in about ten minutes."

"Oh." In the cargo area of the ship, Scree checked to make sure the contents of his pack were neatly arranged and fitted the monster gun onto his arm. He stepped out into the cool of the night and turned to face north once more. Ping took so long to join him he was about to go and see what was going on. But she emerged from the ship, turned and started walking without saying a word. Scree gave a grunt of admiration. She had done nothing but complain about the effort of walking from Shadon to Kansu. Now she conserved her energy and got on with what needed to be done.

They walked in silence for a long time, slogging up the side of dune and down into the hollow beyond.

"How far, Scree?"

Scree shrugged. He really didn't want to say.

"I'm going to find out sooner or later."

"Thirty kilometers. Forty maybe."

Ping sighed. "So we won't make it anyway? Not before dawn?"

He shrugged again. "Maybes." It depended on how far it really was, and the height of the dunes and how hard the sand was and how well Ping would keep up. He shifted his pack and kept walking.

-oOo-

The dune looked the same as the one before and the one before that. The sand was no different to what it had been when they left the ship but each step was a struggle. Scree urged Ping onwards though he hardly had the energy for the climb himself. The sun beat down like a troll with a war hammer.

"I need a drink," Ping said, hardly audible.

Scree stopped halfway to the top and turned to look at her. They had maybe one mouthful of water left and Scree needed that himself— he hadn't had anything to drink since shortly after dawn. "Not yets," he said.

The woman didn't complain. She walked up to his side but didn't even pause, as if once standing still she'd never get her legs moving again. Head down, hands on knees, she kept walking, up the dune as sand slithered back the way they'd come. Scree watched her go. He had set a tough pace but she still hadn't complained, walking through the night, because he told her she had to. They both needed water badly and the chances of finding it soon were slim, but Scree had always thought he would die on the day he gave up, and he wasn't giving up today. As he walked up the dune behind Ping he wondered why he'd given her any water at all. He would have had a chance if he'd left her behind at the ship and took the food and water for himself. He could have made it five or ten kilometers further, at least.

But he'd made a deal with her. You help me and I'll help you. She hadn't understood at the time, but that didn't matter. And she *had* helped. Without her he wouldn't have gotten into the underground city. Of course, if he hadn't gotten into that city he wouldn't be here in the damn desert. But that didn't matter either. He'd collected a useful person, and she'd collected one as well. And that seemed like a whole nother deal in itself. He grunted at his own stupidity and continued to climb.

"Can't stop now," Scree said to Ping, barely more than a harsh, grating whisper. "Keep goings?"

"I can't, Scree." She had stopped at the top of the dune and stood wavering. "I can't go any further."

"Yes, you can."

"No."

Scree had been expecting this conversation for the last few hours.

"You going to die here, or at the top of the next dune?"

Ping sank to her knees. "I can't walk any further."

A simple enough statement. Looking around at the sand and the sky, Scree took out his canteen and removed the lid. Maybe one mouthful left. "Dead kittens." *This is no way to die.* He looked at Ping and considered his options. Then he tipped back his head and drank the last of the water. Two mouthfuls. Huh. Never in his life had he been so grateful for two mouthfuls of water. He didn't waste energy with words.

He picked Ping up and slung her over his shoulder. She didn't complain. If she had, Scree wouldn't have had the breath to argue back.

Scree didn't like deserts. He never had. And now he knew why. He'd seen a few of them but had always had the sense to stay near the edge or follow well-known, well-marked trading routes. Oases were nice enough places, in their way, but all they really did was show how harsh and horrible the rest of the desert really was.

And big.

When you were tired and thirsty, when you were dying, harsh and horrible really started to look insignificant compared to 'big'. Scree thought a lot about the size of deserts as he half stumbled down the back of the dune then started to slog up the face of the next. He could hardly raise his eyes above his feet and from that perspective the sand seemed to go on forever. At the top of the dune he did look up, and all he saw was another dune. Silently swearing at all the cats in the world he lowered his gaze again and kept going.

One more dune, and another after that until he didn't know how many impossible hills he'd carried the woman up and down. The sand always slithering downwards like a whisper of death, fighting his every step, no matter if he was going up or down.

One slow painful step after another. Ping seemed to weigh as much as a bag full of useless, tainted gold and he wondered if all that weight on one shoulder was making him walk around in circles. So, as he reached the top of the next dune he turned around to find the position of the sun. And shading his eyes he compared the position of the sun to the quickly disappearing trail of his footprints. But all the comparing in the world wouldn't help seeing he couldn't remember which direction he was supposed to be traveling. And was it morning or afternoon? Did the sun rise in the east or in the north? For all he could tell the sun had always been there, beating down on him for a life time, draining the energy from his legs and the moisture from his skin.

"Scree," Ping croaked.

He blinked. Ping. Yes, Ping. On his shoulder like a parrot from the pirate tales he'd read during the eternal night he'd waited for the little woman to talk to him. "What?"

"Trees."

Scree gave the word some thought. *Interesting.* "Where?" If they weren't at the bottom of the dune they were standing on, then they were probably too far away.

"Bottom."

Scree turned slowly around again and stood blinking in the light. He'd heard of mirages but... Not a hundred meters away, a narrow strip of trees marched through the desert, a river of green amongst the sand. He stared for a long time.

"Trees," he said. "At the bottoms of the dune." He grunted in disbelief. "Come on thens. It won't walk to us." But Ping was over his shoulder and facing the wrong direction now. So he forced himself into motion.

When he dipped in under the first of the spreading branches, Scree thought the shade might almost be better than a drink of water. Without the sun on his shoulders and head he felt as if he had a new lease on life, as if the energy that had been used to keep him cool was now flowing back into his tired muscles.

The feeling didn't last. He trudged all the way to the other side of the strange river and didn't see any water at all. Cursing his luck he sank to the ground and decided he'd stay right where he was. What was the use of a river without water?

He felt a gentle pressure against his side and turned to see Ping looking at him.

"Hello," he said softly.

"Need water," Ping said. At least he thought that was what she said. He couldn't really hear and didn't care enough to ask.

The little woman crawled away from him to a small hollow near the base of a tree. She paused for a moment then started to dig.

Scree wondered if she was digging a grave. Was it for her? Or was it for him? He didn't know if he wanted to be buried.

But if it was for him, maybe he should help. So Scree crawled over to look.

As he got close, Ping moved aside and he saw a small puddle of water in the bottom of the hole. More was seeping in by the moment. Of course. He knew that. If only he'd had enough energy to think.

He reached down and scooped out some of the water. It was dirty and held the tang of unknown minerals but seemed as cool and fresh as the wine the crazy monk had given him while his legs healed. Ping drank as well, smacking her lips and sighing with pleasure. She sat back and leaned against a tree while Scree took another drink and tried to work out how to fill his canteen without doing any more work. In the end he gave up and made the hole bigger.

When he was done, Scree was about to suggest they find a spot to wait out the hottest part of the day when he noticed Ping was already asleep.

KIM HIT ONE OF THE BUTTONS by the chair. "Engage," she said. "Make it so." Nothing happened.

The bridge was slightly more than half a circle and housed in a dome at the very top of the ship. The seat in which she sat was located at the very center of the complete circle and raised above the others. It faced forward out toward a huge, curving window and could only have been the pilot's chair. Knowing that didn't help much.

There was another seat nearby, three steps down and also facing forward. Other than that, there were three other consoles and seats. Plus another seat encased in what was almost a complete sphere. Only an empty doorway broke the perfection of the single piece of clear, plastic-like material. The seat was beside one of the consoles. So, six control stations all together, in sets of two. She couldn't decipher any of those controls either.

Between them all was a small amphitheater with two rows of tiered seats set in a horseshoe.

Kim sighed and watched the American serviceman who was standing on the ship's hull, looking like a giant space bug splattered on the windscreen. "There's no wind in space," Kim said. "That's a view port."

The soldier had been pounding on the view port with a sledgehammer for the better part of ten minutes without any sign of damage. As if he or his superior officers could have expected otherwise. Keeble had wandered through the bridge a few minutes earlier, taking a break from his exploring perhaps, and laughed when he saw the man outside.

Kim was still watching half an hour later when the Americans moved on to gas cutting equipment. The futility was it all was very obvious, really. It had to be obvious to the Americans as well.

"This ship came down from space, you moron," she said to the man on the view port as if it was all his idea. "It can withstand more heat than your little oxy-torch."

But the man continued with his oxy and another came along to take up the challenge of the sledge. When Kim went closer to the view port, she could see others working with similar tools.

48: Illumination

"Oxy-morons." But she couldn't hear all the pounding, so they certainly weren't going to hear her lame jokes.

Of course, the officers probably thought the exercise needed to be done anyway, just in case. And they were probably right.

"There are two each of three different types of engines."

Kim spun to look at Keeble.

"What?"

Keeble nodded his head in satisfaction as if he'd put the engines there himself. "Well, one of the pairs may be clocks. I can't really tell without investigating a bit more."

"What?" Kim said again.

Keeble carried on as if she hadn't said anything at all. Perhaps the dwarf didn't really care if she was there. "The matching ones can run at the same time, or separately. The different sets are linked together, but only loosely. Two pairs near the middle, along with a pair of huge batteries. Then there is another pair of engines at the front, linked to those four antenna things on the outside of the ship. Like the man said, backups for everything."

"Which man? Do any of them work?"

Keeble shrugged. "I don't even know how to try to start them to test. If you don't either, I'll need to keep looking." He looked like he wanted to leave but was not going to give up that quickly.

Kim sighed. "Shit." For a while, she'd been down with the others trying to help, but when it came to fixing things her expertise ended just after she opened the toolbox and before she selected a tool. The lack of progress had started to make her mad. "What else is down there?"

"You could go and look for yourself."

Kim couldn't argue with that. "It'd be quicker if you told me now."

"There's a hold."

"Yeah? Anything in it?"

"Lots. Don't know what, though. Only just managed to get the door open. Back up was broken."

"Excellent." There was something Kim could handle. She was a backpacker by trade, so she could find useful things almost anywhere. But that didn't help with the real problem.

"So, can you work out how the engines work? You said you learned about cars just by pulling them apart."

Keeble shook his head as if Kim didn't understand anything. "I had books there, as well, that showed how things were linked. No books here. And the engines are nothing like a car engine. I can't find anything I recognize."

Kim sat up straighter. "There *will* be books, but they'll be on computer. The first thing we need to do is find the power switch for this stupid machine."

"Power switch?"

"Yeah. There's got to be something like a standby mode, or something." It sounded reasonable. "There are two huge batteries, right? We need to find what they're linked to."

"They don't help. They're linked to thousands of things. Without power I can't check anything to see what's useful."

"Oh. I guess I'd better stop moping and help then."

Keeble grunted. "Don't need help."

"Rubbish."

The only way down from the bridge with no power was a spiral staircase. It ran round the side of a lift shaft that was in the very center of the dome of the bridge, directly beneath the captain's chair. And once she got to the floor below, where there were a couple of offices, a boardroom, and a storeroom, she followed Keeble and his torch to the next set of stairs. Level two seemed to be exclusively sleeping quarters. On the third level, they went to the dining area. There were rows of metallic tables bolted to the floor and cabinets around the walls, all of which had been opened and ransacked.

Tuki was watching his crystal ball as if its light would tell him something. Meledrin was reading. At least, she was looking at the book Kim had found out on the world. There were another couple of books on the table.

Turning off the torch, Keeble stopped in the center of the room, looking around as if disgusted by the mess the search of the lockers had created. Despite its age, a lot of the clutter seemed to be in remarkably good condition.

There was a lot of general, mixed stuff, plus about a dozen strange looking yellow contraptions.

"What are those things?" Kim asked. They were cylindrical, with hinged carrying handles and levers on the side.

Keeble answered with a shrug. "Don't know. They're everywhere though."

Kim picked one up and examined it. "Have you tried the lever?"

Keeble hadn't, which Kim found surprising. Perhaps he just had more important things on his mind.

"Well then."

"You can't just..."

Kim moved the lever, and a few seconds later the top half of the cylinder started to glow. After about thirty seconds there was enough light to reach all but the furthest corners of the room.

Kim smiled. "Huh. Well, there you go." But there were heaps of the things. Were blackouts common occurrences on starships? The light continued to grow until it was blindingly bright.

"That's a bit bloody bright," Keeble said, as if that was the reason he hadn't been using them.

"Who cares? It's better than what we had." Kim shrugged, squinting against the glare. "How are you going, Mel? Did you find anything interesting?"

"There is a library, but all the books seem to be written in the same language as this one you found."

"So it came from the library, do you think?"

Meledrin shook her head. "The one you found is handwritten on rudimentary paper. The others are printed on high quality paper such as I saw on your world."

"So can you read them?"

"There are many with pictures which I have been attempting to cross reference. There are signs on the walls outside many of the rooms, as well, that I have noted down." She indicated a piece of paper on the table. She nodded. "I am making progress."

"Well, keep going." Kim sat silently for a moment, watching her stark, sharp-edged shadow on the wall. "Keeble thinks two of the engine things might be clocks."

"Clocks?"

"Yep." She gave the clocks some thought. "They're mechanical clocks. Why have those when a digital clock would take up a lot less room and be a whole heap more accurate?"

Meledrin shook her head. "I do not know."

"Does it matter?" Keeble shrugged.

"It must. They're huge, so they must be important. Vitally important. They'd hardly make huge clocks just to wake people up in the morning. But if nothing else it narrows down what do we need to fix in order to get this thing moving. We can worry about the clocks later."

Keeble muttered something under his breath.

"Pardon?"

"I can't fix the clocks." The dwarf scuffed his boot on the floor. "Clocks are very specialized. If one little thing is out, nothing works properly. And these ones look more complicated than any I've ever seen."

"Well, let's worry about that when the time comes."

Kim knew she had to get Keeble doing something or he'd get grumpy. "Keeble, you go look at the engines to see what you can learn. I'll think of something useful to do."

Sneering, Keeble nodded, took a lamp, and made his way out the door. Cuto watched the dwarf for a moment then collected a lamp of its own and followed.

Kim pointed to the book. "So, what can you read so far, Mel?" It could be the answer to their prayers or a recipe book — which might not be so bad either. Kim had a feeling it was important, though. It appeared to be out of place in this world. With the ships and the printing and everything else, an old leather book was not something that would be just lying around.

The elf shook her head. "Nothing, really." She shook her head again. "It is as it was when we were learning Tuki's language. I am understanding more than I should at this juncture, but it is all very strange."

"So, what have you got?"

Mel took up one of the books from the ship and started flicking through the pages. "Using these pictures I was —"

"Don't bother telling me how you worked it out. I trust you."

"Very well." Mel paused for a moment then took up the book Kim had found. "This part seems to say something about the stars being a gift from the gods to man."

"Ummm, okay. It's some type of religious text?"

"I do not believe so, though it does go on to say that the power of the stars and the glare of the gods' gaze overwhelmed any man who reached out to take the gift." Meledrin's brow was wrinkled as she attempted to tease meanings out of the strange symbols scrawled on the page. "So the gods bestowed another gift, reshaping men into six different tribes that could form a 'great all mind' so they would not be overburdened by the gift of the stars.

"That is if I have the translation correct. I am unsure that it means anything at all."

Kim wasn't so sure. In Area51 she'd discovered that what might be considered fanciful, impossible legends could have a basis in reality. This talk of six tribes and reshaping people struck too close to home. Keeble, Mel, and Tuki were all human, apparently, just slightly different from those on earth. Reshaped by the gods, perhaps?

Tuki shifted slightly in his chair, and Kim knew enough to know that was significant. He had something he wanted to say but was too nervous to say it.

"What is it, Tuki? Don't be afraid to speak up."

"It is just that the moai say we came from the stars and that one day five 'greater beings' will come and lead us back there."

"Five and a moai make six, right? The six tribes."

He nodded for a moment, stopped and shrugged.

A moment later, Kim surged to her feet, and grabbing a lantern, rushed to the stairs then to the flight deck above. Once there, she stopped to stare. The chair near the door and the one in the clear sphere were large by human standards. The two on the other side of the room were smaller than the others, though situated on a platform so the controls were all the same height.

Kim heard a noise and spun to see Meledrin and Tuki watching her.

"What is the matter, Kim?"

She went up to the captain's chair, as if the different angle might change what she saw, change the significance of what she was seeing. "We need to go get Keeble up here."

"I will get him, mo'shi." Tuki disappeared down the stairs, but the light of his lamp seemed to linger for a long time.

"Mel, you might as well take a seat. Up here."

The elf sniffed but made her way to the second central seat. The others arrived a few minutes later.

"Will the two of you please sit down over there," Kim said, pointing to the side of the ship with the larger chairs.

While Cuto loitered by the door, Tuki did as he was asked, selecting the seat in the sphere, perhaps because it reminded him of the skyglass.

Keeble stayed near the alien. "Why should I? What's going on?"

"I think I've worked something out." Though it was crazy.

"So? What's it got to do with me?"

Kim sighed. "Everything, Keeble. Just sit down."

He grumbled, but stumped across to the seat. "Dwarves have known about chairs for centuries. I could have told you about them and saved you the strain of thinking." He sat down and looked at the seat. He wiggled a bit and swung his feet. They were well off the floor. "It's a bit big."

"Yes. Isn't it?" Kim chewed on her thumbnail for a moment. "Okay. Now, both of you swap to the chairs over the other side, please."

"For Whistler's sake, woman, make up your mind."

But Keeble and Tuki walked across to the other side of the bridge and stepped up onto the platform.

The dwarf sat down and nodded. "That's much better."

But Tuki couldn't even get his knees under the console.

Keeble noticed straight away. "That's interesting."

Kim nodded. "Isn't it?"

"But what does it mean?"

"It means this ship was made for us."

"How could they know we were coming?" Tuki asked.

"No, not us in particular, but people like us. We're from four of the six tribes. A long time ago humans were genetically engineered, or changed by the gods or whatever, so we could help fly this ship." She slumped back into the pilot's chair. Was she supposed to be sitting there? She didn't know what the controls in front of Meledrin's chair were for, exactly, but seeing she wasn't about to let the elf drive she gave no thought to switching.

"Does this assist us in any useful manner?"

Kim looked about, as if knowing the secret of the seats might get the ship to start on its own. Nothing happened, so she went to stand near Keeble. She chewed on her lip as she thought.

"It tells us that these controls are for engineering." She hoped she was right, otherwise they were back to square one and going nowhere. "When they're working, Keeble, you can keep track of all of the systems on the ship. Do you understand? In a car there is the oil gauge and the temperature gauge and fuel gauge. This is where all those things will be for this ship." Keeble was nodding his head and studying the layout, as if it would mean anything without power.

"Tuki, your seat is one of those two back over there."

Unlike the seats for Keeble and his missing partner, the seats on the opposite side were obviously at two different sets of controls. Kim looked from one to the other but was unsure where Tuki should sit.

Tuki was in the sphere chair again, studying the dozen or so controls on the armrests as if each would bring on a different, equally hideous form of torture. Among all the buttons there was what appeared to be a trackball on each side, and two pedals. The other seat faced three monitors. There was a clear space right in the middle, as if somebody had forgotten to install a very large keyboard or, perhaps, forgotten to install another trackball. There was a large depression in the console where such a thing might have fitted. To either side of that were a few buttons and a joystick.

Kim looked from one set of controls to the next, looking for some clue as to what they were for. Finally, she saw it.

With an excited laugh, she crossed to Tuki and took hold of the skyglass. He was reluctant to let it go, but Kim smiled. "It's okay, Tuki. You're in the wrong seat, though, and I'll need this for just a moment."

He let the ball go and Kim took a deep breath, gave a small prayer, and slotted the skyglass into the depression on the console. It fitted perfectly and clicked satisfyingly into place. Kim took another deep breath and smiled to herself. Three quarters of the ball was visible above the counter.

The console beeped. A single light flashed.

Kim almost cheered. She gripped the console so tight her fingers hurt.

Cuto said something and finally moved away from the stairs to look.

"I hope this thing doesn't run on Windows," Kim said, voice quavering. The joke was lost on everyone else.

"What did you do?" Keeble raced across the room.

"I think I found the key." *It's a strange sort of key,* she thought, *but perhaps there were other ways to get it started as well.*

All around, systems were coming to life. Light flooded the room.

Kim smiled fully now, more relieved than she thought completely necessary. She felt like doing a jig but didn't think it was appropriate — she was in charge, after all. Apparently. She tried to sound businesslike. "Alrighty then. Let's see what we've got."

She looked up and discovered Keeble standing by Tuki's seat, examining the skyglass and its new home. The image shown in the 'glass was also hanging in the air above it in all its 3D glory.

"Why are you standing here, Keeble? I'm pretty sure you'll have a computer over at your console that tells you how everything works."

The dwarf glanced over to the other side of the flight deck, then back at Kim. A broad smile split his face, and he ran back to his seat. Kim followed at a more leisurely, dignified pace, to see if she could help get him started.

When she got there, crouching down so she didn't feel like a teacher looking down at a preschooler, Kim found herself looking at a screen full of meaningless writing and what looked like iconic buttons. None of it meant anything to her.

"So, how do we start the engines then, woman?"

Kim chose to ignore Keeble's tone. "No idea. It might not even be done from this console." Kim made her way back up the stairs to the pilot's seat and examined the brightly lit array of controls while Meledrin puzzled her way through menus on Keeble's computer. She listened vaguely as she chose a button at random and pressed it. She was fairly relieved when nothing happened.

She chose another button, and when she pressed it a buzzer sounded from various speakers. It sounded more like a paging system than an alarm and came from speakers at all the consoles and probably all around the ship. She spoke into what might have been a microphone. "Hello." She wondered if she could be heard from outside.

After that, she decided to quit while she was ahead. She didn't want to start the engines then find out the ship was in gear.

Over at the engineering console, Keeble was making progress with Meledrin's assistance.

"Propulsion," Keeble said, and hit the button himself.

Meledrin struggled with the next list, spending a long time with her eyes closed and talking silently to herself. "Clocks, *Gravitic* Field generators, Ohoga Engines..."

"What does *Gravitic* mean?" Kim wandered back over to look, as if it would make a difference.

"I am unsure. But the tree on Sherindel where the gate is located is called the Ohoga tree."

Kim wanted to say something enlightening, but nothing came to her.

Meledrin shrugged.

"Maybe the guy who invented the engine found the gates?" Kim suggested.

She shrugged again.

"Try 'Ohoga Engines,' then."

They did, and Keeble spent the next five minutes examining what appeared to be a wiring diagram.

"Not very detailed," he complained.

Kim had to agree. If there were ten wires in the 'Ohoga Engines,' then being able to point out the Big Dipper would make her an astrophysicist. "This is probably a simplified version. All the good stuff will be in the engineering bay. Or in some other section."

"Good. But this won't let me start anything. The Ohoga Engines are those two bits at the front connected to the batteries and the antennae." He looked closer. "They are connected to the clocks, as well, and one button."

"Really?" Kim said. "Well, these clocks just keep getting more interesting, don't they? What about the other one? What does *Gravitic* mean, Mel?"

"I told you, I am unaware of the meaning."

"Doesn't help a lot, really. And 'clocks' is in the propulsion section?" That didn't mean a lot either, without more information to go with it. "Try the gravitic thing then."

49: Alignment

KEEBLE FUMBLED THROUGH SOME MENUS with Meledrin looking over his shoulder and carefully reading each heading in her self-important voice. He knew he wouldn't have made any progress without the elf's help, but that didn't mean she was any less annoying. Eventually they made their way to a diagram that told Keeble what he wanted to know. After examining the screen for a moment, he got out of his chair, crossed to the pilot's console and counted buttons. It was Kim watching over his shoulder this time.

When he found the right button he pushed. The whole ship hummed quietly for a moment. Then it shuddered violently. Lights dimmed and an alarm sounded. Keeble quickly hit the button again and stillness returned.

"What just happened?" Kim asked.

Keeble shrugged. "I think something's wrong."

"You don't say."

Keeble looked at Kim. It looked as if she wanted to solve all their problems in a moment.

She gave a decisive nod. "Okay then, here's what we need to do. Keeble, you need to get to the engineering bay and see if you can find out what's wrong with the engines. For that, you'll need Meledrin to help with the reading."

"I don't need her help. I think I'm starting to understand the writing already."

"Maybe, but Meledrin will make it quicker and easier." Kim laughed. "She's our communications expert. So bloody obvious."

"You learned to speak this language in a matter of hours yourself, Kim," Meledrin pointed out. "As did Keeble."

"Yeah, I know, but you're still the expert. You seem to be able to learn *any* language. Maybe when the gods redesigned man, they wanted to make sure we'd always be able to understand each other enough to get by, so they hardwired a language into us. And into elves, they hardwired the ability to learn *any* language."

Keeble thought it sounded a bit ridiculous, but then so did so many other things that were happening.

"Very well."

"Well, let's all get down to engineering then, shall we?" Kim said with a smile. "Let's see about getting the engine started. I'll be your assistant, Keeb'."

"I don't need an assistant." *How could she assist? She'd do nothing more than get in the way.*

"Yes, you do, and we need to learn as well, just in case."

"Do you even know what the Gravitic Field Generator is?"

"No. Do you? Maybe 'Gravitic' has something to do with gravity. Or antigravity?"

"Antigravity isn't possible." But Keeble wasn't willing to bet what might be possible any more.

"The CIA seems to think the aliens use antigravity."

Keeble wanted to know more but wasn't about to show that. "And what is Tuki going to do during all of this? If you knew anything about leading, you'd know that it isn't good to have one person just sitting around doing nothing. It's bad for morale."

"Tuki can continue doing what he's doing. It may be the most important job on the ship."

Keeble looked across at the moai. It didn't look like he was doing much at all. Ever since his silly globe had clicked into place, he had stared at the projected image that hung in the air above it.

Kim seemed to suddenly think the same thing, for she went over and encouraged Tuki to play and experiment.

"But what if I do something wrong?" he asked. "What if I break something?"

Kim smiled for him. "I doubt it's possible to do either. Just play with the controls and see what happens."

As if to demonstrate, Kim did something and the suspended image changed, scrolling to the left.

"There you go, see?"

Tuki's eyes lit up. He smiled and nodded and hesitantly reached out to do something himself.

Meledrin was talking with Cuto, waving her arms about as she did. "Cuto wishes to assist with the repairs," the elf said eventually.

"Great," Keeble muttered.

Kim said it as well, but she sounded as if she meant it. "Maybe you should start teaching us Cuto's language as well."

"The spoken words may be beyond all of us, in the end. Just a minute of conversation hurts my throat tremendously. But the hand signs will perhaps be easier."

"Just as long as we can start to understand each other. Which will mean the hurgon leaders will understand us as well."

Meledrin nodded. "In the future, I will talk in this language and do the hurgon signs. I shall, for a while, try to use the signs as much as possible when others are speaking." She was already suiting words to actions, waving her hands as she spoke.

Keeble tried to match them up. The alien interrupted her, and she stopped to listen. "Cuto says the hand signals are called ini rituals. The kil'ini are unable to hear, so the rituals were designed to make it possible to communicate with them."

"Cool. Be prepared for lots of questions, too," Kim said, and the elf waved her hands.

Sick of waiting, Keeble headed for the engineering department. The others, except for Tuki, hurried to catch up. Now that there was power, the elevators were working so the trip was quite a bit quicker than it had been previously. One elevator from under the captain's chair down to level one. Then another to level 7.

Down in engineering, Keeble immediately took charge. He took a seat at the computer, Meledrin and Kim towering over him as he started to go through the menus.

Like Kim had said, the computers up on the flight deck showed only the bare essentials. It would have taken him a lifetime to discover anything important on them. But in engineering he was able to power forward. The computers told him everything, slow process though it was.

Cuto watched as well, occasionally offering suggestions, but hanging back for the most part. When a dull boom reverberated throughout the ship the alien hardly seemed to even notice. The lights dimmed, then came back to life.

Meledrin stopped reading for a moment. "What was that?" She forgot the ini rituals but corrected her mistake a moment later.

"The Americans, probably," Kim said, "still trying to get in."

Keeble grunted. "Not much we can do about it."

But Kim had other ideas. "Maybe not, but the computer will probably tell us if they're doing anything we need to worry about."

"Really?"

"Yep. Somewhere."

They went back to the start of the menus and, in 'Maintenance', found 'Hull'. According to the diagrams, the hull was slightly damaged, but whether that was recent or fifty thousand years old was impossible to tell.

The muffled thud a few seconds later helped.

"Looks good," Kim said.

"How?" Meledrin asked, waving her arms and flicking her fingers. She looked slightly shocked, which was a lot for her. "Surely this graphic indicates that the vessel is damaged." She obviously didn't understand.

"Yes, we're damaged," Keeble said with a sigh. "But nothing changed with that last explosion, so the Americans didn't cause it."

"If you are sure?" Meledrin looked to Kim, as if Keeble's explanation wasn't enough. She remembered the ini rituals after a moment of hesitation, and Keeble tried to follow.

"I think we're safe for now."

"Right, but we should still get out of here," Keeble said. "What does this say?"

"Let me know what you come up with," Kim said. "I'm going down to the hold to see what I can find."

Cuto said something.

"You were going to help with the repairs," Meledrin translated.

Kim looked at the computer. "Yeah, but I guess I know my limits. If Cuto is a radio technician, he should be able to help more than me."

"Cuto is not a male," Meledrin pointed out, again.

"Whatever. Look, I'm going. Let me know if you do actually need me."

Keeble was back at work before she had left the room.

Another half an hour in the 'Maintenance' program, and he discovered that the Gravitic Field Generators were out of alignment by 9.67 percent. He didn't quite know what that meant. But he thought he knew how to fix it.

Another explosion shook the ship as Keeble got up from his chair and went to find Kim. He found her talking to herself in a huge metal packing container.

"How desperately do we want to fly?" he asked poking his head through the door.

She nearly brained him with a metal bar.

Recovering her composure, she wiped sweat from her brow and sat down. "What do you mean?"

"I think I could have us flying in a couple of hours, but not in optimum circumstances."

"Meaning?"

He sighed. "Meaning, the two Gravitic Field Generators are out of alignment. If I disconnect them and we run off only one, that should solve the problem. I think. But then we're left with the question of which generator is aligned correctly, and can I realign them once we're flying." Keeble knew what he'd choose. He'd be flying as soon as possible and worry about the rest later.

But he had to admit that Kim was in charge and probably the best person for the job. It wasn't something he *wanted* to admit. It wasn't something that he should have to admit. It wasn't right. But Kim had managed to get them all to this point. She was the only one who understood something of all the areas they might happen to need. She could fly a plane, and she'd worked out other things.

But there was more to leading than knowing things. There was also acting, making a decision and running with it, and Keeble had never known any woman who could do that when it was really needed.

"Worse case scenario if we go with the one generator?" Kim asked.

She knew as much as he did, but he answered. "You can't fly with any sort of control at all because the alignment is out, and we crash." He didn't know what a single unaligned field generator could do, if anything, but it sounded reasonable. Or perhaps the two Gravitic fields just had to be aligned with each other and nothing else. "Or we get into space and have to stop to do repairs and get attacked. Or the generator fails when we really need it."

"Do you really have any idea, or are you guessing?"

"Does it matter?"

"No, but I'd like to know anyway."

Another thing he didn't want to admit. "I'm guessing." No dwarf liked to guess.

"Okay, well, a couple of hours to disconnect the generators and get us flying that way. How long to align them?"

Keeble shrugged.

"Guess."

He shifted uncomfortably. "I really don't know."

"The computer doesn't tell you?"

"Probably, but I didn't get that far."

"Right. Well, I say let's fly. Disconnect the things, and let's worry about the rest later. People are dying as we speak."

Keeble nodded. *You have to know when to stop thinking and start doing.* He smiled slightly. *And when you decide to do things, you have to decide with conviction.*

"Give me a couple of hours."

"Great. Can I help?"

"No. It's just a case of finding the right panels and disconnecting the right wires. I think."

"Okay. Then let me know when you're done."

At least she didn't pretend to know how to fix anything.

"Keeble."

"What?"

"See if you can talk to Cuto about making those adjustments to the radio."

"What adjustments?"

"So we can talk to the hurgon."

"Oh. Right."

Keeble returned to the engineering department and the computers. Three quarters of an hour later, his eyes were starting to ache and his head was spinning with all the words and diagrams. He hoped Meledrin was feeling at least a little bit of what he was feeling. If she was, she didn't show it. He scowled at her and switched the machine off. He knew all he needed to know. All he had to do now was find where he needed to go and find out what he needed to do, exactly.

There was a stone panel in the corner that led to the first of the engines. He touched the wall. The first sounds of his Song sprang into his mind, and he started to Sing them. He didn't need to concentrate like he had not so long ago. It was like he was breathing, thoughtless and easy. While he Sang, he turned away from the panel and started to search for tools in the cabinets around the walls. After a moment, Cuto searched as well.

A few minutes later, the alien said something.

"Cuto has found some tools," Meledrin said.

Keeble went to look. "Good. Just what we need." He tried a hand signal that he'd seen Meledrin use several times. Cuto tilted its head to the left in reply.

"What did I just say?"

"You said 'Good.' The tilting of Cuto's head to the left is equivalent to a smile"

"Good." He took the large box down from the cabinet and carried it across the room. It was full of all manner of tools. Keeble recognized some of them.

Cuto followed and poked through the tools for a moment. Keeble scowled again. He couldn't work out if Cuto was male or female. Should the alien be allowed to work? Or should it be made to keep out of the way? No decent dwife would consider trying to work. Except Ari. Ari had wanted to work. He remembered that she'd mended his socks while he worked in the tunnels. She'd cleaned her own room in the bunker, despite him saying she wasn't allowed. Meledrin wouldn't try to do any real work, but everyone knew that elves were lazy.

The alien picked up something and examined it, turning it from side to side. Then another one. A wave of hand signals.

"Cuto recognizes some of the tools," Meledrin translated, "but not all."

Keeble returned his attention to his Song, which he'd continued during the search, and started to build the higher layers. With the toolbox in hand, he stepped up to the wall and through it into a small recessed area. Cuto followed.

Keeble reigned in his thoughts. *Hope this is the best engine to disconnect.* There may have been something in the computer to tell him, but he didn't know how to find it. He shrugged and got to work. He was starting to work like an elf, no concrete plans. Almost making it up as he went along. If Milo could see him now.

He used a wonderful, automatic, star-shaped screwdriver to undo a set of four screws and carefully laid aside the panel they'd been holding. With the panel removed, he could see the part he thought he was after, two and a half meters beyond. He crawled awkwardly into the hole, dragging the tools with him.

Cuto grunted and scratched out some words.

Keeble started, hitting his head on something hard and unforgiving. The alien was right behind him, squeezed in amongst the machinery. It was motioning towards the toolbox.

Keeble nodded and, free of his burden, moved quickly into a more open space and sat up to look. Cuto did the same.

"Let's see what we have here, then," he said to himself. He identified what was called the coupling block and set to work.

The instructions for disconnecting the generator were inscribed on Keeble's mind, but he didn't blindly follow. He found the first control panel that needed to be modified. It was only a minor operation, but he wanted to do everything right. He sorted through the wires, identified the terminals.

"Give me some..." But Cuto didn't understand, so he turned and pointed. The alien found the right tools and offered a simple, one-handed signal as it handed them over.

With each task he needed to complete, Keeble checked to see the results of what he intended to do, following pipes and electrical wires and circuits from here to there and back again. Every time he disconnected something, he connected it again to make sure it could be done.

Every time he needed a tool, Cuto found it, held it out, and translated into sign language or gave the alien version of a shrug. More than once the alien was there to lend a hand, working with solid concentration and a steady grip. Its big hands, with three fingers and a thumb and too many knuckles by far, were as strong as clamps but also surprisingly dexterous.

In an hour the job was done, or at least Keeble thought it was. He turned to look at Cuto. The alien shrugged an alien shrug.

"I guess we'll find out." He packed away the tools and followed Cuto back out into the engineering bay. And now for the next job. He shook his head and asked Meledrin, who was studying the computer, to ask Cuto about the radio.

KIM DIDN'T GO STRAIGHT TO THE HOLD. For a while she just wandered around the ship, shining her lantern in through doors and into corners that hadn't seen light for about fifty thousand years. There was a hangar with a couple of strange looking craft parked untidily about. There was a cup sitting on a desk in a small office near there. Kim stared at it for five minutes, imagining the man or woman who had once sat in the chair, drinking and talking. Working on some small problem that had come up. Or playing solitaire on the computer while the boss wasn't looking. Shivering, she hurried on.

In the hold she found a crate with a partially opened door. Putting the lantern on the floor, Kim gripped the handle and pulled. At first she thought nothing at all was going to happen, then it creaked open further. A sliver of light made it through the gap and revealed smaller boxes full of shiny silvery bags and square black containers. There were labels, but Kim couldn't decipher anything. In the end, she bit the bullet and tore open one of the bags. It contained what might have been food. The dry block crumbled to dust in her fingers. Then she fiddled with one of the square containers for five minutes before the lid came off. Inside was a gloopy mess that actually smelled pretty good. Maybe it *was* food. Maybe it was still edible. She hadn't really given any thought to what they'd all eat. She had the tins of baked beans, or whatever it was they'd stolen from Area 51, but that wasn't going to last very long at all.

She dipped her finger into the slop, raised it to her mouth, then thought better of it. She would wait until she was a bit hungrier yet.

The dull boom of another explosion echoed slightly around the hold. It all seemed so far away, like someone else's life, or a bad movie on TV in another room. Kim tried to forget about it.

There were no other open containers that she could see, so Kim grabbed a door handle at random and pulled. Nothing happened. The handle was stuck. She tried another with the same result and decided she'd need a tool. A big, heavy, bashing tool.

She found a metal bar in a corner and used it first to pound, then to lever. Eventually the handle gave up and did as she wanted. And inside the container was machinery of some kind. It was beyond her to even come up with a sensible guess as

50: Fly

to the purpose of anything. Can openers, which might be handy for getting to the baked beans, or planet destroying weapons.

She made her way through half a dozen more containers, wrestling with every door but one. Standing in the most recent container, lantern throwing her shadow across more piles of the unknown, Kim wiped sweat from her face and wondered if there was anything to drink. Preferably alcoholic. Great rebel leader she'd turned out to be. She'd stolen a spaceship that wasn't going anywhere and a cargo load of nothing useful. At least, as far as she knew. Meledrin would be handy to help with some translation but was busy doing more important things.

"Shit." Fixing the engines wasn't a lot of point if they couldn't talk to the aliens.

Kim jumped when another shadow joined hers. She spun, metal bar ready, and saw Keeble poking his head in through the door. Perfect timing.

"How desperately do we want to fly?" he asked.

Kim didn't want to sit around in the dark — lantern lit or not — for any longer than was necessary. They needed to fly, to talk to the aliens, to end the war. She thought of telling the dwarf that outright but thought he might appreciate a bit more thought going in to the matter. It all came down to the same answer in the end, though. She also mentioned the radio and received the expected scowl in response. *Priorities, woman.*

When the dwarf stumped away, grumbling to himself but obviously pleased with the idea of fiddling with the ship, Kim made her way back out into the hold. She looked around. There were containers everywhere. Some were piled neatly while others looked as if they'd been dumped, ready to organize later. The point was, there were hundreds of them, plus a whole extra level down below. She could search all day and still miss all the good stuff.

"Well then, I guess I could go work out how to fly this thing."

But she needed to eat first. They'd all gone too long without food already.

Collecting her lantern she made her way to the lift and up to the mess. She organized a meal of tinned spaghetti in tomato sauce and not much else. She took some down to the engineering department. Cuto sniffed at some then gave the hand signal for 'no' and said something.

"Cuto does not need to eat yet. And even if there was need, Cuto is unsure of what you are offering." Meledrin poked at hers with her spoon and raised her eyebrows. Apparently she wasn't sure either.

"If you don't want it," Kim said, "just let me know. There'll just be more for the rest of us."

Keeble was already eating. Kim divided Cuto's portion between the other bowls, skipping Meledrin's when the elf gave a small shake of her head.

On the bridge Tuki was still playing with the skyglass, hardly even noticing when she arrived. He only looked up when Kim offered the food, accepting it with a slight smile. When another explosion thundered in the hangar outside, he quickly turned back to his study. It was as if he was using it as a distraction. Kim didn't have any encouraging words for him. She didn't think the ship was being damaged, Keeble would have said something otherwise, but the constant battering wasn't doing much for her state of mind either.

She climbed up to the pilot's chair and examined the controls as she ate. They'd worked out which button started the engines. Other than that, she decided, she could work from what she knew of the controls in the ship they'd stolen from the Americans. Except there was no steering wheel. It seemed to have been replaced with a ball, which sat on a pedestal directly in front of the seat. The pedestal wouldn't move, so it wasn't a joystick, but the ball rotated in all directions. "Perhaps in a life without gravity you needed steering wheels that could point up and down, and all the points between, as easily as left or right." Which would mean that the thing they stole from Area 51 had only been a plane after all.

The ball was colored a pleasant, pastel green and decorated with a pattern of concentric circles. On one side, the circles were so close together that they were almost indistinguishable from each other. In the center of the smallest was a red spot. The further you went from that spot, the further the lines were apart. The effect meant that, no matter which direction the ball was facing, you could always tell exactly where the red spot was. There was a blue spot directly opposite, in the middle of a smooth, blank area.

There was what looked like an altitude knob but it could also be moved like a regular joystick. And there were three pedals instead of just the one that was in the plane they'd stolen. Added to the mix was a lever, currently set in what appeared to be the neutral position, halfway along its range.

They seemed to be the main controls, but there were dozens of buttons and switches besides. There were another two little levers side by side. Switches and knobs, gauges and screens and dials.

So, the ball for steering. The knob for lift and something else. The lever for something, and the pedals for...

"Shit."

When Keeble, Meledrin, and Cuto stepped into view an hour later she hadn't made any further progress.

"Do you know how to fly yet?" the dwarf asked.

"No. But I wasn't game to try anything until everyone was in here and strapped in."

"Well, I don't think Cuto sits down, but Meledrin and I can." He made his way to his chair.

Kim's mouth dropped open. "You mean we're ready to go?" *She* wasn't ready.

"Yes. Well, maybe." As usual, Keeble didn't seem pleased with not knowing for sure.

"The Gravitic Field Generators are separated?"

"Yes."

"Well, do you think we should go now? Or get some sleep first?"

"The hull is still holding together, but who knows for how long? Those American's don't quit, do they?"

"But..."

"Let's fly."

"Okay. I'll try."

Keeble gave a whoop of joy and hurried to strap himself in. Meledrin followed suit, though she didn't look quite as excited. Cuto crouched down behind the horseshoe of seats and locked meaty hands around a backrest.

Kim looked at the controls in front of her and then at her companions. She couldn't blame them for their nervousness. "Should we name the ship first?" she asked, trying to delay the moment as much as possible.

Keeble had a sour look on his face but was nodding. "It's traditional, I suppose."

Her first idea was Kittyhawk, but she was sure the Americans would already have taken that one. "How about *The Hakahei?*"

"What the hell is that?"

"It's what the Hurgon call our worlds."

Meledrin looked as if she didn't care. Possibly she was staying silent in case she started jabbering like a normal person. Tuki was still staring at the skyglass, fiddling with the controls.

Keeble was over it as well. "Whatever."

"Right. *Hakahei* it is, then." It wasn't quite the reaction Kim was after, though she didn't really know what she'd been expecting. She took a deep breath and, out of excuses, turned her attention to the controls once more. "So, what do I do now?"

Keeble grunted. "Don't lose your nerve now, woman."

"What?"

"Start the engine. You know the button."

Kim pressed the button. Her heart was racing like a jazz drum solo.

On a small screen to her left, an iconic, profile view of the ship appeared. The two legs shown on the bottom of the craft flashed a few times then disappeared. Down in the corner of the screen a small picture of the legs appeared colored in red.

"Umm..."

"What is it?"

"I think we're flying."

"But we aren't moving."

"Well, no." The Americans certainly were, scurrying like cockroaches caught in the light. From her vantage point, Kim could see soldiers out in the hanger, all making for the limited protection of the far wall, pulling out their weapons like those cockroaches shaking their fists at a passing car. Or like pretend knights pointing cannons at space bats.

Only one thing seemed to have changed on the panel. There were now three indicating lines near the altitude knob. Two of them showed all red, but the final line had one bar of green.

"Well," Keeble said, "start with a control that doesn't look very important. See what happens."

"All right then." She picked a dial and, with a deep breath and one eye closed, slowly spun it. "The ship's spinning," she said with a laugh, watching as a wall came into view outside. So much for the green ball being the steering wheel.

"I'm not so sure," Keeble said. He unbuckled himself from his seat and went to the view port for a closer look.

"What do you mean? I saw it."

"Do it again."

Kim spun the dial in the other direction, hoping to get them facing the door once more.

Keeble gave a grunt. "The dome is spinning, but the ship itself isn't moving."

"Are you sure?"

The dwarf looked back over his shoulder.

As the bridge continued to turn, Kim noticed something. "Hey, the ball doesn't move." She indicated the pastel ball she'd thought was the steering wheel.

"What?" Keeble came closer.

Kim turned the dial. The bridge spun, but the ball stayed in exactly the same position, as if the whole structure was spinning about the pedestal.

"Keeble, how does the engine work?"

The dwarf didn't have anything to say.

"You understand the concept of gravity, right."

He gave her a look that spoke volumes.

"Well, just because you're controlled by gravity doesn't mean your people have given it any real thought. Or that you know how it works. But anyway, let's assume that the Gravitic Field Generators somehow create gravity. Or antigravity."

"Well, all those big holes or funnels or whatever they are on the outside of the ship seem to do *two* things. Something goes out of them, and something comes in."

Kim ignored that. "First of all, for the sake of convenience, let's say that the funnel surrounded by those four antennas is at the front. No, let's call it north. Okay."

"All right."

The look on Keeble's face showed what he thought of that idea, but Kim knew it would be best because she was sure she knew how it worked. She was *pretty* sure she knew how it worked. She smiled and did a little jig in her seat.

"Here's how it is," she said. "Gravity can be funneled out any of those funnel things and that obviously dictates the direction you travel. Right? Right. So, what you do is, you use this ball to point the gravity in the right direction."

"So, where is the gravity now, then?" Keeble asked. "How do we make it funnel?"

Kim examined the main controls. "We use this lever for thrust," Kim said. "Forward and backward."

"And why does this room spin around? And when the room spins, why doesn't the ball?"

"Only the room spins and the ball doesn't because there isn't really any forward or backward for this ship. We can go in whatever direction we want without actually turning the ship around. So, if the room didn't spin we'd sometimes be looking in the wrong direction. And the ball doesn't turn with the room because we want to be able to *look* in all directions without actually *changing* directions."

"But the lever? You said it was to make us go forward and backwards, then you said there is no forward or backward."

That was obvious as well. There was a blue dot on the top side of the range and a red one at the bottom. "This way means we move towards the red dot." Or was it away? Kim pushed the lever a fraction of a centimeter away from the neutral position. She'd forgotten the engine was running, until the *Hakahei* started to move.

"Shit. Shit. Shit." It took a moment for Kim to gather her wits and shift the lever back to neutral. Luckily, she hadn't moved the lever far and luckily the dot was directing them away from the wall. Momentum carried the ship forward, and it wasn't until they scraped along the side of another vessel that they finally stopped.

"Okay," she muttered, "we move away from the dot. I hope someone remembered to renew the insurance."

The others all looked at her.

"Give me a break."

"So, are we going to sit here until the Americans work out how to shoot us, or are we going to leave?"

Kim looked at the others.

"I'd rather crash out there than get shot in here," Keeble said. The others didn't look so sure.

"But they can't get us," Kim said. "They can't get in. Otherwise they would have gotten into the ship at Area 51. In fact, this one is probably tougher, because I think the other one is only a plane."

"So we just sit here until we starve, then?"

"I found food in the hold. Maybe. Dried, sealed, in tins. All sorts of long-life stuff."

"Long life? 50,000 years?"

"Maybe."

"So what was the point of all this if we're just going to sit here?"

"The point was to talk to the hurgon and stop this war."

"Right. How will we do that sitting here?"

"Does the radio work? The hurgon might be able to hear us from here."

Keeble sighed. "Try it then."

"Right. Meledrin."

"Yes, Kim?"

"See if you can get the hurgon on the radio for me."

"I am not aware of the method for doing that. Is it accomplished from this work station?"

"Yes. I think so."

Cuto interrupted and Meledrin turned to listen "Cuto says that the hangar doors are closing."

"What? Shit."

The two huge hangar doors were starting to slide closed like twin glaciers. Kim froze for a moment and totally forgot the little she knew about flying the ship.

"Don't just sit there," Keeble said. "We're quickly losing one of our only two options."

Kim took a deep breath. She fiddled with the steering ball — all forward, no up or down, and watched the doors close some more.

"Move, woman."

Kim closed one eye and nudged the thrust lever.

"Go straight, for Whistler's sake."

"I'm pointing at the door but it isn't going that way." They pushed amidst a flotilla of smaller ships until she adjusted slightly and had them going in generally the right direction.

"Of course it isn't your fault. Never is."

"Keeble," Meledrin said, "is it not true that the engines were incorrectly aligned?"

Keeble grunted. "Maybe the engines aren't aligned with the steering ball," he admitted.

Kim didn't care. "Whatever," she snapped. "It wasn't going straight." She tried to calm down.

"Well, we're going the right way now, I suppose." Keeble gestured towards the doors. "A bit faster would be good, though."

They weren't going to make it, was what he meant. Kim nudged the thrust lever a bit further. It was hardly above neutral at all, but the ship lurched forward, picking up speed. The Americans were either scattering again or firing their weapons, as if each hoped their bullet would be the one that broke the camel's back.

"Are we going to make it?" Kim asked. The doors seemed to be closing very quickly now, although they probably hadn't changed speed at all.

"I don't think so."

Cuto said something as well, but Meledrin didn't bother translating. The elf was staring at the doors as if indignation alone would keep them open. Apparently it wouldn't.

Kim adjusted her aim slightly, increasing thrust again. They scraped along the side of a smaller ship and slewed slightly. Before she could work out how to fix the problem they crashed into the edge of one of the still closing doors. The ship nearly stopped. It spun, pushing against the door, until they were almost facing back the way they'd come. The other door was approaching. Amidst her panic, Kim had a moment of inspiration. She reversed the thrust and the ship hesitated for a moment before popping out onto the exterior platform while Kim spun the bridge.

The ship quickly gained speed. It dropped serenely over the edge and out over the forest. It slid down towards the bottom of the valley, nudging trees out of the way as it went.

"More up would be nice," Keeble said. He was holding on tightly.

Meledrin had her eyes closed. Tuki was staring out the window like a man watching a train rush towards him.

Kim nodded, trying to think. There was the steering ball and the altitude knob. She tried the knob first. The ship certainly got further from the ground, but not much. It seemed to max out at about a hundred meters.

Keeble shook his head. "Space looks more like a planet than I thought it would."

"Shut up, Keeble." Biting her lip as they continued towards the bottom of the valley Kim examined the steering ball. She reached out for it. So many things could go wrong. Was she missing something? "What have we missed?"

"Certainly not any trees. We hit every one, I think."

"Well what about... Have you checked on life support?"

"What?"

"Life support. I told you there's no air in space, remember? So something on this ship makes air. And the ship has to be airtight so it doesn't all escape."

"How am I supposed to check that?'

Meledrin, much put upon, sighed and went to look. It didn't take long.

"Everything is green," Keeble said. "That's good, right?"

"I think it is. What color were the displays when the Americans were shooting at us before? Green is good on Earth today, but how am I supposed to know. Shit. What about fuel?"

"Checked it earlier. According to the computers we have 87% fuel."

"Right. Okay. Are we ready then, folks?"

Nobody said they weren't. Kim still wasn't ready. She didn't know if she would ever be, but she decreased the thrust slightly and spun the steering ball so the dot was facing almost directly down. She felt the heavy hand of G-forces for a moment as the ship started to climb.

51: You Are Here

TUKI STARED AS THE SHIP SURGED UPWARDS. All he could see was sky, but he could not take his eyes off it.

I am closer to the Goddess than any moai has been for millennia, he thought.

He offered a silent prayer to Poti. He would have looked to the four points of the compass to offer his thanks, but he was strapped in his chair, and with no ground on which to locate himself, the idea of directions seemed meaningless.

The world was nowhere to be seen, and suddenly, though it was surely still day below, an endless array of stars sprang into view.

"Batteries are charging," Keeble said. "The ship is taking something in through the funnels that aren't being used and converting it to power."

The dwarf sounded a lot more vague than he had recently, and Tuki wondered if he was slipping back into wherever he had been before. He stole a worried glance at his friend. Immediately he knew nothing was wrong. Keeble could hardly concentrate on his monitor. He stole glances at it every now and then, but otherwise the scene outside trapped his gaze.

"Don't worry about the batteries, Keeb'. What about life support? Check that again." Kim was obviously trying to keep her mind on the matters at hand, as well, but not having much more success than Keeble. Tuki saw her craning her neck to try and see everything at once. "Wow."

Meledrin did not look like she had been affected at all. She continued to translate into Cuto's sign language as she calmly surveyed the view, as if she had seen something as magnificent every day of her life.

"We're still moving," Tuki said after a moment. He thought it might be a good idea if they stopped, for a short while at least, so they could get their bearings. He watched Meledrin, trying to decipher her signals, but it wasn't easy.

"Shit, shit, shit. We aren't just moving, we're accelerating."

Tuki watched the view. He didn't see what Kim did to halt their progress but could feel when it happened. He thought he could tell when they stopped completely.

"Tuki, can you show us a view of where we are?"

Tuki looked at Kim for a moment, his heart racing. She wanted him to show her on the skyglass. But no, not just that, she wanted to see from her own seat.

This is what I am here for, Tuki thought. *Keeble is here to fix the engines. Kim is here to drive, and Meledrin to talk to people. I am here to show them all the way.* Which was a horrible thought. He was merely a go'gan. Did they not realize? He should not be telling them anything. He should wait and watch and do as he was told.

"Tuki?"

"Yes, mo'min?"

"Show us."

Tuki had been practicing with the controls earlier, but suddenly he could remember nothing at all. He decided to work on the skyglass first and worry about the rest later.

Touching his finger to the cool, smooth glass, he spoke the word that made the 'glass the center of the view. Then he made the view step back slightly, so more could be seen. And again. Soon, the world below was in view — or was there no below, now — and the moon halfway around the far side. Plus fifty-three yellow dots that could only be other ships like their own, except driven by the hurgon. Not meteors as he had once thought.

"One thing I don't understand," Keeble said from across the other side of the room. Tuki tried to block the sounds out as he concentrated. "I understand how we were all shaped this way by the gods so we could all do our work on these starships. Well, not how, but why. Dwarves are small so we can climb around in all the little nooks and crannies to fix things. Meledrin looks all calm and controlled and important or something, maybe, so we look good to strangers. And Kim, you... Well, I don't know about you. Maybe flying the ship doesn't need anything special. But Tuki? If he's just here to be a map-reader, why is he so big? I mean, he could do that if he was my size, couldn't he?"

Tuki did look up then. The whole conversation was really about him. He listened as he worked.

Kim was nodding. "I've been thinking about that, and I think I know the answer. There's a book on Earth called *The Hitchhiker's Guide to the Galaxy.* It's a comedy book, but still. In it, the author describes a form of torture. People are taken into a room and shown a map of the entire universe, the whole thing, with a little sign saying 'you are here' pointing to where they are in the universe. And it doesn't just show them, it makes them *understand.*"

"So?"

"Well, most individuals in the book go crazy when they see that, because they realize just how totally insignificant they really are."

"That's just stupid."

"Not really. You don't know how big the universe is, Keeble. I'll tell you."

"Are you sure I won't go crazy?" Keeble said with a smile.

"No, because you won't really *understand*. You won't be able to picture this. Okay, light travels at about 300,000 kilometers per second, I think. More or less. Do you understand that much? Light isn't an instantaneous thing – it has to travel."

"Like sound?"

"Exactly. Only much, much, quicker."

"300,000 kilometers per second?"

"Yep. Now, a light-year isn't a measure of time, but a measure of distance. It's the distance light will travel in a standard year of Earth time. Still with me?"

"Yes."

Tuki didn't think he sounded sure.

"You know how long a second is?"

"Yes."

"Right, well an Earth year is..." Kim squinted and cocked her head to one side. "Shit. Sixty seconds in a minute, 3600 seconds in an hour, twenty four hours in a day..."

Tuki worked it out easily. "86,400 seconds in a day," he said.

And Kim turned to look at him. Tuki looked back down at the skyglass and blushed.

"Okay." Kim was nodding her head slowly and still looking at Tuki when he stole a glance a few seconds later. "86,400 seconds in a day. And 365 days in a year, Tuki?"

"31,536,000 seconds in a year."

"So, this light travelling at 300,000 kilometers per second will travel how many kilometers in a year, Tuki?"

He juggled the numbers in his head. He started to sweat. "Do you want exactly?"

"No, close will do."

"Well, I do not know how to say the number. In the decimal system that humans seem to use, it is a bit more than nine with twelve zeros after it."

"Nine trillion? Do you know the decimal system, Keeble?"

"Yes."

"So you understand a nine with twelve zeros after it?"

"Of course."

"Big number isn't it?"

"Yes."

"That many kilometers in a light year. Right?"

"Yes, but I don't see the point. Who uses numbers that big?"

"That's the thing, bud'. From the star the Earth orbits to the next closest star is about four light years. Or five light years. Four or five light years."

"Four of those light years in distance?" Keeble gaped.

Tuki looked back to his work so as not to stare at the dwarf. He noticed that the dots that showed the alien ships were starting to move. The picture Tuki was looking at was still only in the skyglass.

Kim continued. "That's right. Now, I'm sure you're sitting there thinking, 'Wow, what a big number that is'. And intellectually, I'm sure you realize that completely. But to realize and to truly *understand* are two different things. I don't understand. I think that if I did, I may well just curl up and whimper for the rest of my life. Especially since I now think I can fly between those stars, and it's not just an interesting notion any more. But I think Tuki really has to understand.

"And, I think, because he has to carry all those huge ideas of numbers and space around in his head, the gods had to add that extra layer to his brain. Airman Dongoske said he had an extra bit in there." Kim got a thoughtful look. "Or maybe that's the bit that let's him control the skyglass."

"Umm... mo'min..." Tuki said.

"So? Why make his body bigger?"

Kim sighed. "Because they had to make his head bigger. He'd look really stupid with a huge head and normal sized body."

"Oh."

Tuki didn't want to interrupt, but thought he really should tell Kim about what was happening. "Mo'min." He finally remembered the combination of buttons he had to press and worked up the nerve to try them. He stabbed at the moai-sized buttons with shaking fingers, and the scene shown in the skyglass flickered into existence in the top of the dome. He knew he could press another button to label the different aspects of the scene, but seeing nobody would know what the labels meant, he didn't bother. "I think the alien ships are coming towards us."

"What? Alien ships? What alien ships?"

Tuki divided his glance between the display above and the window of amazing glass. "There are fifty-three alien ships coming towards us."

"Christ. Turn the radio on. Get Cuto talking to them."

Keeble made his way up to Meledrin's console. He counted controls, flicked switches, and pushed buttons.

"The radio is on," he said, "but there's nothing to hear."

"Have you tried all frequencies?"

"We rerouted one of the controls."

Cuto said something.

"Cuto asks if you have the radio on shower or beam?" Meledrin translated.

Tuki had no idea what either of those things were, but apparently Keeble did.

The dwarf swore under his breath. "It's on beam and aimed at nobody," he said, hitting some buttons with needless force. Whatever he did fixed the problem, for the harsh alien language burst into the air like a flock of startled crows.

"Does Cuto need to come up here to speak with the hurgon," Meledrin asked.

"Probably not," Kim replied, with Meledrin translating, "but for now it will probably be easier."

Cuto went up to stand near Meledrin's chair and scanned the controls. It was Keeble who pressed the buttons though and pointed to a flexible stick that poked up above everything else. The alien started to speak.

Meledrin cocked her head to one side to listen. "I believe Cuto is speaking codes at the moment, offering greetings from an ally, verifying identity. Grandson Cuto — though 'grandson' is not right. It is merely the closest approximation I can make. It seems particularly complicated and convoluted, but I believe it is something like a rank. Grandson Cuto of the T'loop Family, Lo'anen Branch, As'elda Sub-branch — he has mentioned these previously — on board the human hakan construct." She tilted her head the other way. "Then a long string of numbers."

While Meledrin spoke, Tuki tried to watch her hand signals, but the image in the dome held his attention. The hurgon ships continued to get closer. They were a few thousand kilometers away, but that did not seem to be very far at all. Tuki divided the image into segments, counted seconds in his mind, and worked out that the aliens would only take a few minutes to arrive if they continued at their current speed. They did not appear to be listening to Cuto at all for the babble on the radio continued unchanged. According to Meledrin, Cuto was repeating his greeting and trying to talk to a 'Mother'. Any mother.

Remembering something he had tried earlier, Tuki pressed some buttons and an image of space appeared on the wall behind Kim's chair. Another button, and the focus shifted. From there he used a little lever and was quite proud when an image of the closest alien ship came into focus.

"It is as Cuto said," Tuki said softly. "The ship is alive." It was seven hundred meters long, green and lumpy, smudged and pulsing with life. It had four eyes on stalks and three tentacles reaching out kilometers behind it.

"What?" Kim asked. She was so busy concentrating on Cuto and the translation that she hadn't even noticed the image behind her.

Tuki pointed.

"Jesus." She sat silently for a minute. "It isn't at all like what I expected."

Tuki had not known what to expect at all when Cuto described the kil'ini. It was a strange and magnificent creature, but it and its fellows might kill them if Cuto was not successful very soon.

An alarm shrieked out of the strange ball-chair near Tuki, making him jump. His heart started to pound. He examined the chair for a moment, wondering what it meant, before looking back at his own controls. A red light was flashing. Words were scrolling across one of the screens. He couldn't read them, but he didn't think he needed to. There was a new dot on the image made by the skyglass. It was colored orange and was racing towards them from the closest kil'ini.

"Mo'min. I think they have fired a weapon at us." He didn't say it very loud. Even had he been certain, he didn't know if he could have spoken any louder.

"Pardon?"

Tuki cleared his throat. "I think they have fired a weapon at us." His fingers were trembling on the edge of the console.

Cuto stopped talking for a moment as Meledrin translated.

Keeble was working at his console, lips moving silently as he read. He stabbed at some buttons, and the alarm cut off as suddenly as it had started. The silence was eerie.

Eventually Cuto started talking again. There was an unmistakable note of urgency now.

Kim stared at the image. Her mouth was open, eyes wide. "Should we run?" she asked.

Tuki turned to look as well. His heart was still racing. His mouth was dry. Did Kim say there wasn't much water?

"Cuto says that hurgon weapons carried by the kil'ini are stronger than those carried by the kidol, but is unaware how successful they will be against this construct. Seeing it is the only one known to be flying, nobody can know."

"Right." Kim turned her attention to her controls. "Here goes then." She spun the ball and pushed the thrust lever.

The pressure of acceleration disappeared after a moment.

The dot was gaining on them.

"We will have to go faster, mo'min."

"What? That's all we've got." She pushed at the lever again, as if hoping she was somehow mistaken.

Tuki examined the moving images above him. He tried to calculate. *Fifteen seconds*, he thought. *We will be caught in fifteen seconds.* Should he tell Kim? He wasn't sure that he was right, so he remained silent and counted down in his head. The computer would probably tell him how long they had, but he couldn't even read as well as Keeble yet. Nobody had shown him how.

Three, two...

The ship was rocked by an explosion, then another, and it was set to spinning wildly. Tuki grabbed at the console in front of him, expecting to fall on his head. The ship tumbled through space, stars flashing past the window. Another explosion knocked them the other way. Though the ship somehow made it feel that they weren't spinning at all, Tuki felt he was going to be sick. He closed his eyes and held on.

"Hull breach in sector 178, level seven," Keeble shouted over the thunder of another hit. "That's something to do with fuel. I think." He seemed to be keeping calm through a sheer act of will, as if concentrating on his screens and controls, doing the tasks he had been assigned, would make the reality go away.

Tuki swallowed and forced his eyes open. Kim would know what to do. She had gotten them so far already.

He watched the kil'ini in the image in the dome. They were still catching up, spreading out as if to trap the ship in a net. He thought of telling Kim, but it didn't seem relevant. And he didn't know if he could make his voice work anyway.

"Shields are at 100%," Keeble added.

"Shields? What shields? How do we turn them on?"

"I don't know."

"No use then, Keeble." Kim was gripping her console, staring at the steering ball. It seemed to be spinning wildly, when really it was perfectly still and the ship was spinning. "Talk to them Cuto. What the hell are you doing?"

MELEDRIN GLANCED AT KIM. "I will not translate that literally," she said. In fact she didn't say anything at all to Cuto. Though the alien seemed calm on the surface, it was obviously trying desperately to get through to their attackers. To suggest otherwise might be seen as an insult. Kim had no sense about how to deal with people.

"Cuto and the hakans have not attacked," the alien was saying. *"The hakans will not attack. Cuto has information that could bring immense profit."*

And finally, whether it was something that was said or how it was said, the chatter on the radio stopped and, after ten more seconds, the explosions stopped as well. A lone voice issued from the radio.

"This is Mother Konu of the F'nago Family with Re'angadano'a," Meledrin translated. *"Is Cuto a prisoner?* I believe that the failure to mention a family branch is significant. Re'angadano'a is the kil'ini." The elf cocked her head to listen again as Cuto replied. *"Cuto is not a prisoner. The hakans aboard this construct rescued Cuto from a prison on Target World Three 3."*

"Why? Why should Mother Konu believe that Cuto is not under duress?"

"Have these hakans fired upon Re'angadano'a or any other kil'ini? Have the hakans made any threatening move at all?"

There was a moment of silence. *"No. That does not mean this is not a trick or a trap."*

The alien ships now completely surrounded the *Hakahei*. It would all be over very quickly if Cuto failed to convince Mother Konu.

"If that was the case, Cuto would have used the proper codes."

Another stretch of silence. *"Are these hakans important? Can the hakans be ransomed?"*

"No."

"Then where is this profit Cuto speaks of?"

"The profit would come with the end of the war."

Other hurgon, mothers and fathers from other kil'ini, joined the conversation. Meledrin listened as they discussed contract law and other subjects she did not understand. She did not translate all that was said, explaining to her companions that much of the detail was irrelevant.

52: The Enemy

"Do you think it worked?" Kim asked. "Have we stopped the war?"

Meledrin was unsure and said as much. "None of the hurgon here can make such a decision, but they can speak to their superiors. They can make recommendations." She paused to listen to Cuto. "Mother Konu wishes to speak with the Mother on our ship. I believe that would be you, Kim. It is akin to a captain."

Kim suddenly looked very nervous. "Are you sure?" She took a deep breath but did not look any calmer when she was done. "Of course you are. Okay then. Pass on my greetings and thank what's-her-name for listening."

Meledrin raised an eyebrow. "What's-her-name?"

"You know who I mean. Konu."

Meledrin shook her head in disgust. "Some respect would not be out of place."

"I respect them, I just can't pronounce their names properly."

Meledrin sighed and waved her hands in the ini rituals. Cuto translated into the microphone then paused to listen to the reply.

"*Mother Konu says the F'nago Family are pleased to have the opportunity to speak with the hakans about a possible end to the war. Kuno says if agreements can be reached it will bring much esteem and wealth to the F'nago and to Cuto's T'loop Family. Furthermore, lasting peace would —*"

Meledrin paused in her translation as Kuno commenced speaking again. She could not understand all the words, but it was immediately obvious that the alien was not pleased. Cuto interrupted Kuno's interruption. Neither raised their voice or seemed overly agitated at all.

Meledrin was unable to believe what she was hearing. She realized her mouth was hanging open and snapped it closed. She gathered her thoughts and wove a *Changing*. "Kuno says Cuto's deception has bought dishonor upon all the T'loop."

"What?" Kim said, almost shouting. "No. Come on, damn it."

Meledrin almost felt like shouting herself. She cleared her throat. "*The F'nago and the other families holding Target World 1 will not let the action go unpunished. The Greater Council will hear of the deception. Sanctions will be enforced. Matters will —*"

Four missiles struck the ship in quick succession, and Meledrin lost the thread of the conversation. Possibly the details didn't matter all that much in any case.

"What's going on?" Kim shouted.

It seemed obvious enough to Meledrin. She closed her eyes and hung on as the ship tumbled under a barrage of missiles. "Kuno has ceased trusting us for some reason," she said into a moment of silence as she attempted to loosen her grip on the arms of her chair. "Cuto is currently discussing the matter with Kuno."

"No shit?" Kim was staring at Cuto as if force of will could change the outcome of the conversation.

Meledrin did not understand the term, so made no reply.

"How many moons were there before?" Keeble asked.

She turned to examine the image in the dome overhead, which now also included the world they had fled. Something was different, though she could not quite grasp what it was.

"I'm not sure," Kim replied vaguely, glancing at the three-dimensional image located in the center of the room. "As long as I wasn't going to run into it, I didn't really care."

Meledrin had not taken particular notice, either. She had never considered the fact that there might be other than two.

"There was only one," Tuki said quietly.

Meledrin watched as well as the smaller of the two moons moved. She shifted nervously on her chair, weaving a *Greater Beginning* with shaking hands. It was an unseemly display but appeared to go unnoticed.

Meanwhile, Kim gasped and Keeble muttered under his breath.

"It is a ship," Tuki added hesitantly. He zoomed in but could not get close enough to see it clearly. "It is a cylinder, twenty point four kilometers long and three point three in diameter."

"Jesus."

Meledrin shifted again. She examined the ship but could not truly grasp the implications of the dimensions Tuki was listing.

"It's killing the aliens," Keeble said.

The small yellow dots of the aliens were disappearing from the view overhead. Those closest to the strange ship went first. The others were scattering.

"Are you sure they're being killed?" Kim asked, almost as quietly as Tuki. She was leaning forward in her chair as if wishing to go to help the hurgon. "Or are they just disappearing?"

"Some were shot," Tuki confirmed.

"Are you sure?"

Tuki suddenly looked as if he was *not* sure. He glanced at Kim for a moment, then back at his screens. "Some are leaving of their own accord now. Others are dying."

Meledrin was unsure if a young saveigni such as Tuki could be trusted to make such a judgment but was not about to argue. The yellow dots were disappearing by the handful. Those that chose to remain were moving randomly, dodging towards the newcomer as they fired their weapons, if she was interpreting all the dots correctly. But all their maneuvering seemed to do nothing more than delay the inevitable for scant seconds.

"Mother Kuno obviously believes this recent arrival fights at our behest," Meledrin said. She sat back in her seat and smoothed down her dress to disguise the shaking of her hands. The rapid beating of her heart could not be controlled so easily.

To have come so far and fail now.

Cuto was the first to notice that the image on the back wall had changed. Shifting away, the alien pointed and Meledrin turned to look. Where previously there had been a view of the stars outside, now there was a perfectly white, reflective, humanoid face. It was perfectly symmetrical, perfectly formed. Too perfect to be real.

The cold, dark eyes flickered. The mouth moved rapidly as if the androgynous being were mumbling. Symbols came and went at the bottom of the screen. They slowed. Slowed. Slowed. Stopped. Meledrin could read the word. It said 'Rongo', the language of Kiva.

"*Where are you running?*" the creature inquired a moment later. Its voice, like its face, was expressionless. It was a dull monotone. "*Like ninth level beings leaving a stricken vessel, you scurry for safety. You cannot run fast enough.*"

On the screen, the creature smiled, but merely as if it had seen a smile somewhere else and wanted to see how the gesture tasted. "*Multeese will kill these hurgon,*" it said, "*and then chase you at our leisure.*"

Meledrin could understand passion, any type of passion, but the face of the creature did not suggest it would gain anything at all from killing them. Thinking of its vessel, she did not doubt that it *would* kill them. In an instant. The ease with which it was destroying the kil'ini suggested it would be no effort at all.

"*Run all you like. It makes no difference to us. Multeese superiority is unchallenged, though even fifth and six level creatures, all claiming some form of intelligence, never admit that before their deaths.*"

Kim nodded, a cold look in her eyes. "Well, let us get to our running then."

The figure on the screen paused, as if attempting to drag another expression from its memory and failing. "*We* will *kill you.*"

"We'll be expecting you."

"*You will not escape.*"

"Not much of a conversationalist, are you," Kim said. She turned to Meledrin. "Switch that damn thing off, would you."

Meledrin had not turned the image on in the first instance, but the expression on Kim's face made her withhold any comments. After a moment of hesitation as she attempted to remember, Meledrin selected a button and pressed. The screen did not go blank, but the cold, white face froze.

Tuki looked terrified.

Keeble was shaking his head. "So, you were trying to get us killed?" he said to Kim. "There are easier ways of committing suicide."

Kim shrugged.

Keeble was hitting buttons. "We have to get back to the planet."

"We aren't going down there."

"It's our only chance, woman."

Kim was staring at the screen, as if trying to memorize the face of the alien. "Us going down there will kill *everyone*, one way or the other. Even if that guy doesn't kill us, then the hurgon will."

"You don't want to be friends with this new alien?" Keeble asked with a sneer.

"There was always a spark of compassion in the hurgon."

Meledrin slowly sat back in her seat. She felt the need to wave a ceremony but was unsure which might be most suitable. *Greater Beginning? Greater Ending? Greater Changing?* Perhaps an 'ini ritual would be better. In the end, she did none. "Then what is it you are proposing?" She did not wish to admit to agreeing with Keeble.

"We run."

"Why?" Tuki asked quietly. "It was killing the kil'ini easily."

Kim sighed. "I haven't come all this way to give up now. I haven't come all this way to die without a fight."

Meledrin had seen Kim like this on one another occasion. At Sherwood Forest, her determination had been partially obscured by her uncertainty, but here it was burning fiercely. *Greater Beginning.*

"So, that's your plan then? We run?"

"Part of it. Meledrin has to get on her radio and warn the Americans, give them time to prepare for an attack as well. And we have to run faster, because the longer we last, the longer they have. Right?"

Keeble depressed some buttons and checked his console. He still read slowly, but seemed to be improving remarkably quickly for a dwarf. "We *were* going two kilometers a second under our own power. The hurgon bombs gave us a push along though, so now we're doing double that."

"Good." Kim appeared slightly stunned by the figures. She checked her safety belt. "Meledrin, you're just sitting there? Find the Americans. I need to talk to them."

Meledrin did not like Kim's tone but was accustomed to it by now. She sighed and turned to do as she had been asked.

"They appeared out of nowhere," the dwarf pointed out. "Can we really outrun them?"

Kim shrugged. "Who knows? But leading them to the hangar down there will be a very bad idea. Those ships are the only real hope we have at the moment. So, we have to warn the Americans and draw the bad guy away."

"We don't even know how to fly this thing properly," Keeble added. "And we're running on one engine."

"Well then, we'd better all learn and get things working." Kim examined her controls. "I'd better start by stopping all this spinning."

Meledrin studied her companions.

Keeble shook his head but turned his attention to his screens. Tuki strapped himself in and examined the skyglass, as if answers to all their problems lay within.

Cuto was crouching adjacent to the center of the bridge, gripping the back of a chair. The strangest group of allies an elf had ever known. Was this truly the group that could save all the hakan people? Or would they merely be the first to go?

Probably they would be killed, but perhaps Kim was correct. Perhaps their own deaths were insignificant compared to the thousands of deaths that might well occur. Delfrana had scorned her desire to help Keeble because he was merely a dwarf. Meledrin had done it anyway. And she felt the same obligation now. Neither her companions nor their peoples deserved to die, no matter that they were not elves.

The frozen image of the alien looked down from the screen on the rear wall with cold dark eyes. Meledrin felt a shiver run down her spine. She was afraid. More afraid than she had ever been.

With a glance around to be sure nobody was looking, Meledrin licked her lips and turned her attention to the controls.

There was work to do and only herself to do it.

ALL KIM COULD SEE OUT THE MAIN VIEWPORT was a sky full of unknown stars and for a moment she forgot about the aliens who were trying to kill her. For a moment.

But Cuto was standing not far away, huge meaty hands locked around the back of a seat, watching as Meledrin translated all the conversations into the arm waving 'ini rituals. The alien had the patience of a mountain— he would wait for as long as required. The rest of his people were apparently the same, planning their revenge over fifty thousand years.

But the hurgon didn't scare her. They might kill her, given the chance, but they were still just people fighting a war. Short, ugly, leathery people with no genetic relationship to humans, but people all the same. The other alien was a different matter entirely. The multeese would swat them from existence and not even consider the fact that it should feel some sort of emotion during the process. The memory of the cold face on the monitors— humanoid but obviously not human— still made her shake.

Kim took a quick look at the rest of her companions. Keeble, Tuki and Meledrin *were* genetically human but vastly different, though each had traces of earth in their appearance. Kim took a deep breath and tried to concentrate. She needed to find a way to keep them all alive.

They'd been traveling at two kilometers per second when the thrust had cut out, leaving them coasting. She wanted more thrust, lots more thrust. The ship was a sphere and the controls allowed it to travel in every direction equally. "But there are antennas— or whatever the hell they are— to the north," she said softly. She'd called it 'north' for ease of orientation— she could call it the bow, but seeing it might not always actually be the front... "The antennas prove that one direction isn't the same as every other." They meant she had to be able to turn the entire thing around to face somewhere else.

Back on Nexis— was it only half an hour ago?— Kim had decided the three main controls were the steering ball, the power lever and three pedals. The pedals were the only things she hadn't been game to try. With a shrug, she pushed the left-hand pedal gently. It was a bit stiff, as was to be expected after 50,000 years, and didn't seem to do anything at all.

53: A Damaged Ship

"Keeble, what happened?"

Down on the left hand side of the bridge, the dwarf hit some buttons on his console. He didn't come from earth but probably wouldn't have looked out of place in South America. He had dark skin, a broad nose and full mouth. "Do it again," Keeble said, scratching at his short, beard with the mechanical hand strapped to his left arm.

The pedal had pivoted in the middle, along the top-bottom axis, so Kim pressed the opposite side.

Keeble hit some more buttons. "Huh. The ship turned and the *bridge* stayed still this time."

There was a dial that worked the other way, spinning the bridge atop the ship.

"Are you sure?"

Keeble looked up over his console, eyes narrowing as if he was being accused of murder. He was sure.

To change the subject, Kim indicated the steering ball— it didn't change the direction the *Hakahei* faced, but controlled the direction of the thrust. "But that thing didn't move again."

Kim tried the other two pedals, rotating the ship every which way possible. She gripped the edge of her seat, expecting to fall on her head at any moment. And the ball stayed still in relation to the universe outside— as if that was the point around which the entire ship spun.

"No matter where we spin," Keeble said, as if reading her mind, "we keep traveling in the same direction. We aren't under thrust now, but if we were, the ship would automatically transfer the thrust to different funnels to keep us moving in a constant direction. There's a button near the bridge-spinning dial?"

There was. A large button decorated with a strange symbol. *Everything* was decorated with strange symbols. "Yep."

"That button locks the bridge in place on the top of the ship, so when the ship spins on the top-bottom axis, so does the bridge. It won't affect the ball either."

"Right." They made things too *complicated*. What was wrong with a plane that flew in space? Kim could fly a plane.

Kim fiddled until they were looking at the planet they'd recently vacated. It was an amazing sight, one half basking in the light of the star, the other half in shadow. It took up most of the view-port— clean and pure and colorful.

"Is anyone following us, Tuki?" It was a sensible question— one that should have been asked earlier. After examining the space around the planet for a moment, Kim looked across at the young man seated behind a console on the right-hand side of the room. "Can you show us the aliens? The new ones in the big ship..."

"Perhaps, mo'min." If Keeble was from South America, then Tuki was from somewhere in the middle of the Pacific Ocean. He too had dark skin but was about two meters tall and had tattoos all down one arm.

Kim turned to look as an image appeared in the depression in the middle of the room. It showed the planet, it's moon and a whole heap of aliens. The living ships of the hurgon were like flies buzzing around the huge multeese ship.

"Nobody seems to be following us," Meledrin said from her seat just below Kim's, still waving her arms so Cuto could understand. Tall, slim and pale, like some red headed Nordic ice-queen, the elf sat with calm dignity, as if she'd been sailing between the stars all her life and not just for the last half an hour.

Kim considered the fact that she may appear calm and rational as well, but at least she hadn't been living in a 'timber-age' society a week earlier. Still, she was finding it hard to ignore the immensity of what was happening and concentrate on the moment-to-moment details. "Do you have the Americans on the radio yet?"

"In a manner of speaking. They are able to hear me— and I am able hear them— but they are not responding."

"Well, switch them over to my console. I'll get them to respond."

Meledrin just looked at her.

"You don't know how?"

"Not at this point in time." Apparently that didn't need translating for Cuto.

Kim sighed again. Things weren't looking promising. She went down to where the elf sat.

They had escaped from military custody and sprung Cuto from prison as well. Then they'd led the American Air force on a merry chase across two planets. And now they didn't even want to talk?

"Hey there," she said into the microphone, before remembering to speak English. Like everyone else, she'd learned Tuki's language of Rongo in just a few hours, and now English felt unwieldy.

She tried again. "I need to speak to General Hilliard, right now."

"Kim, do you not think that a modicum of manners would be—" Meledrin stopped mid-sentence as an American accented voice erupted from the speaker. Kim smiled.

"General Hilliard is not in control on the ground here."

"Then who the hell is?"

"Who are you?"

"I'm Kim McLean— one of the people you're trying to catch."

"Oh. Major Williams is in charge."

"Well, in about five minutes he won't be, so go get him right now."

"Is that a threat?"

"Just get him. Are you saying he doesn't want to talk to me?"

"I'll see what I can do. He busy at—"

"Bullshit. I was in the army, I know what being in charge means."

The American didn't reply.

Kim stared out at the stars while she waited.

Eventually, a new voice erupted from the speakers.

"This is Major Harrison Williams. Have you called us to gloat, Miss McLean? I wouldn't bother. We'll catch you soon enough."

"You had one of the spacecraft at Area 51 for fifty years and didn't get inside, Major, and you expect me to believe you're going to get into one that's not even on the same planet as you?" Kim sighed. "But no, anyway, I'm not here to gloat. I'm here to warn you."

"Warn me?"

"That's right. The usual aliens, they call themselves hurgon, are in space above your position." The usual aliens? Kim almost laughed. "There's nineteen of them— but when we entered orbit there were fifty or sixty of them."

"They're leaving? I'd have thought that was a good thing."

"They aren't leaving. There's another ship up here Major, and it's killing the hurgon like it's shooting fish in a barrel."

"Again, Miss McLean, I'd have thought that was a good thing."

"We talked with this newcomer, Major. He isn't doing it to help us. He isn't going to stop with the hurgon."

"And while we hide down here you'll be getting further away. How convenient."

"Major, close that hangar door if you can and get back though the gate to Peru on the double. If you can't close the door, then forget it and get back to Peru anyway." Kim doubted anything she said would make a difference. "The new alien didn't just drop subtle hints about what was going to happen."

"Why should I believe you, Miss McLean?"

"Well, just step out the door and have a look, for God's sake. The alien ship is huge— about twenty kilometers long. You should be able to see it clearly enough."

"Miss McLean—"

"That's all the warning you get, Major. You need to get the hangar closed and hopefully save the ships. We have enough problems of our own."

"Look, we—"

"We're going to have to co-operate if we want to live through this Major. I hope you can work that out quicker than General Hilliard. Now, you do what you think's best, I have to concentrate."

"Miss McLean, we—"

"Turn it off, Mel." But she did it herself, hitting a few buttons until she found the right one. She returned to her seat.

All the movies made flying a ship and getting away from hordes of ravening aliens look relatively easy. The thing was, the pilots of those ships never faced that threat forty-five minutes after first getting into space in a ship they'd never before seen... A *damaged* ship they'd never before seen.

She breathed deeply and tried to think. She couldn't remember a calm moment since watching Keeble and Meledrin step out of the Major Oak in Sherwood Forest a few days earlier. It wasn't even calm she wanted. Just a few minutes where she wasn't thinking she was about to die. Just a moment for her heart to stop racing.

But if she wanted any calm or peaceful moments in the future, she'd have to work for them.

"Keeble." Kim sat up and turned to look at the dwarf. He'd been quiet for a while but Kim doubted he'd been idle.

"What?"

"We need to get out of here."

"You don't say."

Kim ignored his tone. He didn't like women all that much, but at least he was *trying* to be civil. "There must be a hyperspace drive or something."

"A what?"

"Something that allows us to travel faster than the speed of light."

"Why must there?"

"Because I don't intend to spend five years traveling to the nearest star."

Tuki cleared his throat. "The nearest star is over six light-years away."

"Thank you, Tuki."

"According to the charts there are no planets there."

"So, what does this thing look like?" Keeble asked. "What will it do?"

"How should I know?"

Keeble grunted in disgust but apparently gave the matter some thought. "We know what the batteries, Gravitic Field Generators and clocks do... basically..."

Kim nodded and smiled. "Yes, we do." The Gravitic thingies made something like gravity and threw it around in space to move the ship. The two clocks... well, they kept time, but why there were two *mechanical* clocks— with geared wheels and pistons and springs— was anyone's guess. "That only leaves one thing. Or two things. Those bits at the front, connected to the aerials."

"The Ohoga Drive."

"Yes." Kim drummed her index finger on the edge of the consol. "What if they open a Ohoga Gate?"

Keeble shook his head, paused, nodded. "Could be... But the power involved in those gates is amazing. I doubt we have enough power on this ship to make one."

"Well, maybe we don't make one as powerful as the gates. Maybe they don't let us travel that far. Tuki, how far between the gates?"

The lad ducked his head again, hiding from the unwanted attention, even as he gently worked at the buttons on his navigation consol. "Nexis to Earth is... 53.74 light years, Earth to Kiva 70.09, Nexis to Tiandi 59.22. I can tell you the others..."

"No, that's fine. So, maybe we only go ten light years at a time." Kim was glad she couldn't grasp just how far a light-year really was, though she knew intellectually. Just saying the words, she could ignore the ramifications of the single step that had taken her from Earth to Nexis through the 'magical' gate. "Let's just assume for now and see where that line of reasoning takes us."

Keeble nodded slowly. "But we have no idea about... anything."

"That isn't what I want to hear."

"It isn't what I want to say."

Kim knew how Keeble liked everything to be sure and perfect. Everything had an ideal state and it was Keeble's mission in life to make sure everything was in that state. It made him ideal for the role of ship's engineer. But of course he was— tens of thousands of years ago his ancestors had been engineered for the role. All the races had been shaped in some way to better be able to live and work in space. And it was Kim's job to lead, to find solutions to problems and keep everyone alive and well. *I'm not off to a good start.* Though they weren't dead yet.

They continued to race away from the planet and the aliens while Kim tried to think.

Tuki shifted in his seat.

"Yes, Tuki?"

"Eight hurgon ships remaining, mo'min."

"Thank you. Tell us again at five."

"Yes."

Kim drummed her fingers on the side of her seat. "All right, Keeble, how do I turn on the Ohoga engines?"

"We don't know—"

"I *know* we don't know. Christ." Kim closed her eyes and pinched the bridge of her nose. Did humans get headaches 50 thousand years ago? And if so, did they have any painkillers on the ship? "We have to do something or we'll be dead in about five minutes." Five minutes? That was probably a bit generous. She avoided looking at the image below her so she wouldn't have to witness the fates of the hurgon ships.

"All right then."

A couple of hours earlier, Keeble hadn't been able to read at all but he seemed to find his way among the touch screen menus easy enough. He was probably following a trail of pictures, tracing schematics as much as anything, but Kim didn't think it would be long before he was reading. She suspected the language had been hard-wired into their brains— it seemed the writing had as well.

Keeble grunted. "You were right, I think. We make a gate and go through it..."

Kim needed to get up and walk around. She thought better on her feet, on solid ground, and with a ceiling of sky above her. How could she think when there were no limits to the universe? She gripped the edge of her console and stayed where she was.

"Four buttons to your right," Keeble said eventually, just when Kim thought she could no longer stand the waiting.

"Yes. A group of three, then one below them. There's a readout beside the top ones."

"Press the first of the three."

Kim did as suggested. She was rewarded with a chiming noise and a series of symbols appeared on the display. "It looks like..." What it looked like was a series of symbols.

"They're numbers. Are they flashing?"

"Yes."

"Well, that means it won't work. It's connected to the clocks and they aren't turned on."

"Five life forms left, mo'min," Tuki said softly, scratching nervously at the meteor tattooed on the back of his left hand.

Kim hardly took any notice. "Thanks, Tuki. So, the flashing lights are a clock?"

"No, they're *connected* to the mechanical clocks." The dwarf examined his screen some more. "The first three buttons turn the time on and adjust it up and down. When you press the last button, the clocks start to count down from the set time. And when the countdown reaches zero... the Ohoga engines work."

"The gateway opens after whatever amount of time is shown on this display?"

"Yes."

"But what about *now*? Surely we don't have to plan to use the gate an hour in the future or something."

"The time's adjustable," Keeble said. "From one hour all the way to... 140,000 seconds."

Kim looked at Tuki and the lad answered almost immediately. He hardly looked up and spoke softly. "Approximately 40 hours."

But that didn't really answer the question. "But what about *now*?"

Keeble's brow wrinkled as he tried to read. "The Ohoga Gate opens when the time reaches zero, but pressing the button also opens a gate immediately."

"Two gates?"

"Yes, though..."

"Though what?"

He worked furiously at his console, cursing whenever he tried to use his mechanical arm in his haste. "The Ohoga Gates make a noise like a symphony or, more accurately, they are created by the symphony, or they... Anyway, the symphony of the timed gate is different to the one that opens immediately."

"How do you know?"

He poked a metal prong at his monitor. "It says here, once you know what you're looking at."

"Okay. So... Does that help?"

"Well, obviously the first gate takes us somewhere, and the second one brings us back."

Tuki broke the ensuing silence on the bridge. "Two life forms remaining, mo'min."

Kim examined the controls in front of her as if a new one, with a big helpful label, might have appeared while she wasn't looking. "Shit. We have to open a gate and go through. How do we turn on the clocks?"

Cuto said something in his harsh, rasping language and Kim turned to Meledrin. She tried to decipher the 'ini rituals but knew it would be a while before she understood much at all. She waited for a translation.

The elf paused for a moment, obviously sorting the words in her head. "Cuto says it madness to use a gate in these circumstances."

"These circumstances? We're about to die."

Meledrin spoke with the alien and eventually translated. "Cuto say that to go blindly into such a dangerous situation is bad enough. To rush the process is even worse."

"What does he suggest then?"

"Cuto is not a he— the hurgon have no gender specific pronouns."

"I know," Kim said. "Whatever."

Kim stared at Meledrin until the elf sniffed and spoke to Cuto for a moment.

"Cuto suggests that we cut all power and hope the alien can not detect our whereabouts."

"SO WE LITERALLY DO NOTHING?" Kim said. "That may well be the stupidest plan I've ever heard." She shook her head. If not the stupidest it was certainly tied for the honor— with her own plan.

Keeble grunted in agreement. "The level of technology the alien's shown so far suggests it's unlikely it won't see us."

"I am merely translating what Cuto has said."

Kim sighed and sat back in her seat.

"One life form remaining," Tuki said softly.

Kim turned to look at the lad. "What do you think, Tuki?"

Tuki still looked startled every time someone asked for his opinion. "You know more about this than me, mo'min. I will do whatever you think is best."

"Right. Great. Thanks for your help." But after a moment, Kim realized it did help. She knew more about the situation than Tuki, but Cuto knew more than anyone on the ship. "Cut the power, Keeble," she said.

"It won't work."

"How do you feel about using a machine that you don't understand?"

"It's never a good idea."

"Right. We don't even know if it still works. Cut the power."

"What about life support?"

"There's enough air in here to last us a while. That won't be what kills us."

Keeble obviously wasn't sure he liked the way that was worded, but he nodded, checked his screens one last time, and cut the power.

Throughout the ship various things were making noises— fans slowing inexorably, motors approaching stillness. And then...

Silence.

Not a sound.

Kim took a breath.

The silence stretched on.

"How long do we wait?" Meledrin asked eventually, hardly louder than a whisper.

Kim didn't know. And she found the passing of time impossible to measure anyway. Had they been sitting in the dark for five minutes or twenty? "We wait a while yet."

54: The Time Comes

They drifted onwards.

Kim thought she was getting cold, but then thought it was her imagination. A noise, but if she could hear something it was coming from inside the ship, not out. She waited for the missiles to hit. She waited for the explosion that would end everything. With the ship's power turned off they couldn't even know what was happening. It would be over before they found out.

Perhaps they were about to die and didn't even know.

All they could do was wait.

Kim drifted off to sleep. She woke with an aching back and cramp in her arm. Five minutes or an hour? Silence hung heavy on the bridge like it had been there for eons, gathering dust and mass as it waited.

"How long?" Kim asked. She sat up, loosening her grip on the arms of her chair and scrubbing at her face.

Keeble shifted in his seat, a glacier of thought propelling him along. He shrugged. "An hour, maybe. If you hadn't fallen asleep you'd know."

"Bite me."

The dwarf narrowed his eyes as if giving the idea some thought. He was probably just trying to work out what she meant.

Kim sighed and wiped her face again. "All right. Let's go."

"Are you sure?"

"No."

The dwarf looked at her some more but pushed the relevant button. Systems started coming back online one by one. Machines beeped. Light flooded the bridge. Kim was holding her breath.

Tuki sat perfectly still.

"Can you see anything, Tuki?" Kim asked.

Kim watched as the moai looked out the window before realizing he had to use the skyglass. He worked silently for a minute. "The alien is not here, mo'min. It has gone."

"Are you sure?"

He pressed some more buttons. "Yes, mo'min." He didn't *sound* sure.

Across the other side of the bridge Keeble, brow furrowed, was talking to himself as he worked at his console.

"What's going on, Keeble?"

The dwarf continued to mutter. Eventually he spoke out loud, eyes still on his read-outs. "I was checking on damage. It doesn't look like we've sustained any serious damage," he said eventually. "There's a crack in the hull. Plus lots of little things. Possibly it was there before the hurgon started shooting at us. I didn't really know how to look before. One of the fuel tanks is empty though."

Kim cleared her throat. "What fuel tanks? I thought we had the batteries and they were recharged when we flew? You never said anything about fuel tanks."

Keeble grunted in disgust. "Of course there has to be fuel, otherwise we'd have a perpetual motion machine, which all dwarves know is impossible."

"So, how much fuel do we have?" Kim asked. The need for fuel was obvious, really, but she hadn't thought. *Shit. Concentrate, woman.* The rush to leave the surface of the planet and then the rush to escape the aliens had short-circuited everyone's common sense. Little things like that could kill them as quickly as the multeese.

Keeble grunted again. "We have a total of eight tanks totaling 1164 cubic meters and overall they are 86 percent full, but what does that tell you unless you know how much fuel we *use?* And who says the readings are correct anyway, after all this time."

"Well..."

"Well, indeed. So, what do we do now, *Captain?*" he said it with a sneer that Kim ignored.

She sat back in her chair and tried to sort through the options. There weren't all that many of them. Except for the hundreds that she and her earth-bound mind couldn't think of. "Right... How much of a problem is this minor damage that we've sustained?"

Keeble shrugged. "No really sure. The trouble is there are a hundred little things and it would take me a week to find anything out on my own. I'm not totally sure what half the stuff mentioned actually does so I don't know where to start."

"Okay, start with the clocks and we'll see after that."

"Clocks are very specialized— I don't have any training."

"You'll figure out more than the rest of us." *Next. What next?* "Meledrin is going to see if she can get a hold of the Americans on the radio. And other than that... We'll worry about that when the time comes." *Great plan. Sit around and do not much until the time comes,* then *think of something.*

But Keeble didn't seem to mind, for once— he was already working, tapping his metal hand against the console while he hit buttons with the other.

"Kim, Major Williams is waiting to speak with you."

"Thanks, Mel. I'll..."

"I believe I have the ability to transfer it through to your seat."

"Cool." Kim took a moment to get herself thinking in English before she spoke. "Major Williams, how are you?"

The delay was noticeable.

"*Annoyed.*"

"And why's that?"

"*Because nothing happened. We evacuated almost everyone, like you said— just a couple of people here to man the radio— and* nothing happened."

"For now, Major. The aliens seem to have gone but I'm sure they'll be back."

"*Do you ever have any doubts, Miss McLean?*"

Kim rubbed at her eyes. She didn't have time for doubts. If she slowed down for a moment to think of all the wrong decisions she might be making she curl up and cry. "Look, right now we need to get another skyglass. A dozen of them would be even better."

"*Why's that?*"

"Mainly, it's a navigation computer, Major. We also used it to start the ship. Like a key."

"*And to fly it?*"

"At this stage we haven't used it for anything specific, though it still may be needed. If we want to go interstellar, we'll need it for sure."

"*Maybe there are ships in the hangar that already have a skyglass. Did you think of that?*"

Damn. That was the type of comment Kim normally came up with; it was really annoying. "Well... No, I didn't think of that, actually." But she could call his imaginary bluff. "If you can get inside a ship and get it started then good for you. Let us know if you need our help with something else."

There was a moment of silence from the other end— longer than the usual delay— before Williams decided to ignore the digression. "*I don't imagine you'll give up your skyglass, so how do we get one?*"

"Just a second." Kim released the microphone button and sat back to the creak of ancient something-like-leather. *How to get another skyglass?* It was a few seconds before she thought to ask Tuki.

The lad shrugged. "I only know of one other, mo'min. It is in Danyon Ford, but I doubt the mo'min there would give it up."

"There are only two of them?"

"There used to be hundreds, but they have been lost for centuries. There may be some on other worlds as well, but I do not know."

"Would you be able to see them in our skyglass?"

"I doubt it. The mo'min would have collected the others already, if they could be seen."

Keeble grunted. "Maybe she didn't know what she was looking at."

Tuki shrugged again.

That didn't leave a lot of options. Which was good in a way— it made Kim's decision easy. "Then I guess we just have to go and get the one we know about."

"I do not think the mo'min will give it to you, mo'min."

"It's a religious thing, right?" Kim gave a small smile. "I'm pretty sure she'd give it up if your goddess turned up."

Meledrin cleared her throat. "It may be a religious artifact, Kim but my understanding is that it is also used for studying the weather and seasons, so they know the best times for planting crops and similar actions important to the life in the village."

Kim laughed and shook her head. "I'm not much of a gardener, but I think after a couple of years I could work most of the stuff out. The skyglass might have been more at one stage, but now it's just a symbol that gives the women power."

"Perhaps..."

"Think of it this way, Mel— the multeese will kill everyone if they aren't stopped. Are we going to stop them on our own?"

A voice crackled from the radio. "*Are you there, Miss McLean?*"

Kim stabbed at the button... "One minute..." And turned to Keeble. "Keeble, what sort of fuel does this thing use?"

"You told me to look at the clocks."

Prioritize, she thought. But the damage should have been the first priority. "Yes, I'm sorry, but things change."

"Right, but only around women." Keeble worked for a minute. "The ingredients seem to be kept separately. The main thing is a gas called... well that won't help much, really. I don't know your word for it, or Tuki's, and you don't know mine. On the scale of elements it is number one."

"Atomic number one? That's... hydrogen. Huh, there's heaps of that everywhere. We can pull up near just about any star and get hydrogen."

"There's whole tanks for it but there's other stuff in there as well."

"Like what?"

"Number 12. It's a type of metal."

"Right." She didn't know *that* much about the periodic table, though apparently Keeble did.

"And number 11. That's the main ingredient in salt."

"Sodium."

"And... 8— a liquid metal..."

"Mercury?" Was there more than one liquid metal?

Keeble shrugged. "They are all mixed in a special way to get it all to work."

"Well..."

"*Miss McLean—*"

She hit the button so hard her finger hurt. She just needed half an hour on her own to get her head straight. Or maybe just half a carton of beer on her own... "You think this is easy up here, Major? Shut up and let me think."

Meledrin had been translating for Cuto and the alien offered. "Very little fuel will be used in traveling between stars. Starting and stopping and entering or leaving gravity wells is all fuel will really be needed for."

"Right." Kim nodded. "And we have 86 percent, right?"

Keeble nodded.

"So, at most, we've used fourteen percent to leave the planet. That's not much. Keeble, if we had the ingredients, could you make the fuel here on the ship?"

"If we have the ingredients then the ship should do it itself. A hundred liters, or whatever, of each should last a long time. Hydrogen is the main thing."

"Right." Kim took a deep breath and returned her attention to the microphone. "Here's the deal, Major. We'll get you a skyglass, and in return, you get us three elements. Numbers 11, 12 and 8. 100 liters or kilos of each will do us."

"And coffee," Keeble said. "We need coffee."

Kim sighed. "And some coffee, Major. And food. Lots of food. Pallets of food."

"*You're selling us the skyglass? I thought you were helping.*"

"Just get us the stuff. We'll be back as soon as possible."

"*How long?*"

Kim shrugged, though it wouldn't help. "No idea. Have to work out how to drive this thing. And have to travel..."

"Just over sixty light years each way," Tuki offered.

Kim relayed the information. "We're going to Tuki's world."

"*Wouldn't it be quicker to go through the gates, Miss McLean?*"

"Maybe, but we still need to work out how to drive, so this'll be good practice. And besides, I think it's a long way from the gate on earth to where we're going."

"*Very well, Miss McLean—*"

"I wasn't asking for your permission, Major. Now, I suggest you keep that door closed and keep everyone under cover." Kim sat back and looked around, annoying people in authority made her feel better. It made her calmer. Or... well, it made her calmer about the things she really needed to be calm about.

She thought of something else. "Major, we'd also like Palsamon to be brought to us..."

"*I don't know that he's fit enough to travel, Miss McLean.*"

"Major..."

"*I'll see what I can do, but I can't promise anything.*"

"Well, we'll see what we can do about the skyglass, but we can't promise anything."

"*Right.*"

"We'll be in touch." Kim sat back again. "Keeble, we need the clocks up and running."

"Right. I'm going to the Engineering Bay." He got out of his seat and headed for the lift.

But how did Kim find out about the Ohoga engines? She turned to Cuto. The alien was the only real source of information they had, though it wasn't likely to know much at all. Kim asked and watched the hand signals while Meledrin and the alien spoke. She was starting to get some of the signals, but was a long way from understanding an entire sentence.

"As far as the hurgon have been able to ascertain, from talking with hakans at the time when the war began, the gates lead to a parallel universe," Meledrin translated. "This other universe is linked closely with our own, but is quite a bit smaller. So, for every kilometer we travel over there, we will have traveled quite a few more here when we return."

"That's it? What's the catch?"

"The difficulty lies in the fact that no complicated machinery will work in this other universe for more than a moment. We are unable to undertake powered flight. We are unable to steer. We are unable to stop."

"So, how do we get back?" But she already knew— the timer. So, you set the huge mechanical clocks to open a gate for you at a certain time, then sailed through and back into the real world at the end. What worried her more than anything else was the fact that none of this information surprised her. Another universe? Was she going insane? But she'd stepped between worlds. She was in space. Perhaps nothing was ever going to surprise her again. "So is there atmosphere in the other universe or something? What slows us down?"

Meledrin asked Cuto then explained. "Cuto says it is unsure though something exists to slow our progress."

"How much will it slow us?"

"Cuto is unsure. The hurgon use a similar method of travel but go to a different universe entirely."

Kim nodded vaguely, trying to sort through the facts. "Are there any planets or anything that we might run into after we go through a gate?"

"Cuto does not believe so, though the hurgon have not explored it in full."

"Is there anything else Cuto thinks we should know?"

"Cuto believes it has given us all known information that may assist in this matter."

"'No' would've done, Mel."

Meledrin straightened her skirt and didn't reply.

-oOo-

"How did we go?" Kim asked when Keeble returned to the bridge an hour later. She was bored and also petrified that the multeese would return at any moment.

"One of the clocks is completely buggered. I've disconnected it. The other one works but it's losing time in relation to the electronic clocks. I had a look around but..." He shrugged. "Like I said, clocks are very specialized."

"How much time is it losing?"

"About a minute since we turned it on."

One minute over an hour was a lot but as long as they didn't try to cut anything too close... "Well, it will have to do because Cuto has explained how the gates work."

Keeble was suddenly interested. "How?"

He'd obviously gotten the wrong impression. "Well, not how they *work*, but what they allow us to do."

"Oh... And what's that?"

Kim explained while she went through a checklist of her controls, preparing to get the ship moving.

"That's it?" Keeble asked when she'd finished speaking.

"Well, there *is* a catch. Nothing really works in this other universe. That's why there are the stairs between levels." And it also explained the couple of hundred gas lanterns scattered around the ship.

"So, after we pass through, the ship starts slowing immediately and all we can do is sit and watch?" Keeble asked. "Then the timer uses the stored power in the batteries to open another gate so we can pass back to our universe?"

"That sounds about right."

"And if we *aren't* moving?"

He wasn't supposed to pick up on that so quickly. "Then we sit in the dark until we die, basically." Kim cleared her throat. "So, are we ready then? How much power do we have in the batteries?"

"One is nowhere near full."

"Then we need to get moving." Kim hesitantly nudged the ship into motion then, once she was sure they were heading in the direction she intended, she pushed the thrust lever to it's limit. Like last time, they reached 2 kilometers a second before the thrust cut out and they were coasting. She looked out the view-port, and at the controls, and back out at the stars again.

"It will be about an hour and a half at this speed."

"An hour and a half? Jeeze."

"At this speed. We can go faster, you know."

"No, I don't know. How would I know?"

Keeble explained which switch was needed and when Kim flicked it over she immediately felt the power kick in. She had a small smile for her companions. Eighteen minutes later, their speed had increased to 20 kilometers a second.

"Batteries are charging quicker. Another forty minutes until full."

"Right-i-o then, forget that and concentrate on matters at hand. Tuki, which direction do we want to go."

The young moai looked nervous again, suddenly called upon to make a decision for everyone. "Ummm..."

"You know this stuff, Tuki. Just tell us."

"We want to turn fifty degrees to the east, mo'min." He checked the map, which he had displayed in the dome overhead. "And half a degree up."

"Right. Tell me when to stop." Kim spun the body of the ship around without changing the direction of the thrust. When Tuki told her to stop, she did, but it took several fine adjustments before he was completely happy that the aerials were pointing in the right direction. Then she had to get the ship moving in that direction as well.

"This is bloody impossible." She set the thrust from the side and turned their line of travel too far. Then she over corrected.

"Next time I'll get us pointing in the right direction before we start to move," Kim muttered.

"I'm sure the aliens will wait for you to get everything just right."

"Shut up, Keeble," Kim snapped. "Have you fixed the clocks yet?"

The dwarf glowered but fell silent and Kim tried to concentrate.

"How's that?" she asked eventually. It had taken more than thirty-five minutes and a great deal of frustration. Keeble took the opportunity to once more let her know what he thought of the exercise.

"It is not exact," Tuki replied, "but exact will not help."

That didn't sound good. "Why not?"

"Because we do not know if we will be effected by gravity in the other universe the same way as we are effected in this one."

"Huh?"

"You explained to me that in a journey from Nexis to Kiva we would be effected by the gravity of many stars and planets even if they are a long way away..." He made it sound as if it was his fault... "Does that happen in the other universe?"

"Ummm... I don't know." Kim tapped on the edge of her consol. "Well, how about we just go for an hour first and then maybe you can do some calculations and work out how quickly we slow down and how far our aim is out."

"Yes, mo'min."

"Tuki."

"Yes."

"Call me Kim, remember?"

"Yes, mo—"

"Don't worry about it."

There was no reason they couldn't go. The batteries were charged, they were pointing in the right direction, or near enough, and... Kim still didn't press the button.

"We're going top speed," Kim said eventually. "The timer goes up to about forty hours, so we should be able to easily travel in the other universe for an hour, right? We aren't going to stop in an hour." Kim looked to Keeble.

The dwarf shrugged. "Sounds logical."

"Right." She held her breath as she turned the Ohoga engines on, then took a moment to think some more.

Is there anything I've overlooked? I wonder what my mother would think if she could see me now. Shit, focus.

She held her breath while she adjusted the electronic readout to one hour, the smallest time possible. When she was ready, she looked around the bridge. "Are we ready?"

Nobody said anything.

"Tuki, you know our exact position so you can work out exactly how far we go?"

"Yes, mo'min."

"Right. Anybody want to say anything?" Apparently they didn't. "Well, what are we waiting for then?"

Kim's finger hovered over the button that would open the gate and start the timer all in one. Her heart was racing. She'd stepped between worlds— this was going to be a piece of cake.

"Mo'min?"

"Yes." Any excuse to delay.

"Something on the scanners."

"The alien returning, do you think?"

"Perhaps."

"Can you tell which direction it's coming from? Can you tell anything?"

"Maybe, mo'min, but without something to compare it to..."

"Yes, without a context—"

Meledrin cleared her throat. "If it is the alien then do we really wish to remain here?"

"Right. Let's do it." Her hands were sweating. She closed her eyes and hit the button. She opened one eye in time to see a shifting silvery sheen materialize in the crisp darkness in front of the ship. She opened the other eye just as they went through.

There was no flash and no bang. There was no indication at all that something momentous had just happened except every system on the ship suddenly shut down and the stars disappeared— that was no small thing.

They were in another universe.

And again, all throughout the ship machines hummed and whirred towards stillness. It was much scarier than last time because there was no switch to turn everything back on.

And then...

Silence.

"Is this what's supposed to happen, do you think?" Tuki asked, barely above a whisper.

Meledrin was finally overawed by something. She whispered a reply. "Cuto did inform us that nothing would operate."

"So what are we supposed to do?" Keeble asked. "Sit here for an hour and do nothing?"

Kim shifted in her seat wondering how her voice would sound. She cleared her throat. "Ummm... I guess so."

The strange universe outside offered a small amount of light, though not really enough to actually *see*. They were racing though a colored, softly glowing mist. There were streams of lavender and puce and other sickly colors she couldn't name, all swirling wildly. The ship's speed was much more obvious with something to compare it to. *With a context...* Kim laughed softly and shook her head.

"I fail to see what is so amusing."

55: Engineering

GETTING TO HIS FEET, Keeble made his way carefully to the lockers located in the wall beneath Kim's seat. Inside he found lanterns, as expected, and he fiddled with one until it finally burst into life. He stared at the contraption for so long that Kim eventually asked him what was wrong.

Keeble grunted. "You have to ask? In our universe the lanterns are so bright they almost blind us. Here they burn at a comfortable level."

"Oh right. What does that mean?"

"I'm not completely sure. I'll look into it when I get time." He made his way back to his seat and sat down. "So now we wait?" He asked again, hoping the answer might be different. If he knew more about the ship he might be able to do some repairs, even without power, but anything he did now could cause as many problems as it fixed.

Kim shrugged.

"There must be some means of amusing oneself," Meledrin said, "if being powerless like this is a regular occurrence."

"You must be right," Kim agreed. "Chess, maybe, or something like that. Cards. Books."

After a moment of silent contemplation of the universe outside, Keeble collected another lantern from the locker. When he had it going he headed for the lower levels. "I can't sit here for an hour. Do you want to see if we can find a chess board, Tuki?"

"No, thank you, Keeble. I think I will sit here."

Kim had descended from her seat to take up another lantern. "Why don't you teach Cuto how to play, Keeble?"

Keeble looked at the alien and decided nothing could be worse than doing nothing at all for an hour. He wondered if Meledrin would come as well so they could talk— he was learning more of the sign language all the time, but it was not yet enough. He sighed. There was only one way to find out.

-o○o-

When the time finally came there was a moment of humming from the ship, hardly noticeable, then suddenly the silver sheen of the gate was racing at them out of the gloom. The next moment they were back amongst the stars of their own universe and power returned to the ship's systems one by one. Keeble let out his breath before realizing he'd been holding it. He liked to know something about the machines he was using. Trusting them blindly seemed too much like religion.

He started checking systems as they came back on line and hoped Tuki was doing something similar. Meledrin was scanning the radio frequencies for signs of activity.

"Batteries charging," Keeble said. "They should be fully charged in... two hours at this speed. And all systems should running again in... three minutes. At the moment all we have is basic functions on each console and life support is trying to catch up."

"Two hours 'till we can jump again?" Kim asked. "And three minutes until I can accelerate? Right." She sat back and looked around. "Tuki, what can you tell us?"

"I am still looking, mo'min. Without the computer to do the adding..." He worked silently for what seemed a long time. "Mo'min, we have traveled 22.893 trillion kilometers in the hour. That is 2.42 light years."

"2.42 light years an hour? Jeeze, that's pretty quick. I think."

"We would not be able to travel that speed over longer times though, mo'min."

"What? Why not?"

"Because we decelerate. The longer we remain in the other universe, the slower our average speed."

"Right, I knew that. By how much?"

Tuki shrugged then said, "We slowed by 1/2 a kilometer a second over the hour. We would need to do another journey to see if that rate of decline is steady."

"Right. But we are now about..." Kim added with one eye closed... "58.5 light years from Kiva? So how long would we need the next jump to be?"

"Without more information..."

"Guess, Tuki. Just make sure you drop us short and don't over shoot."

"Well... We would not make it in one trip."

"What? It's more than forty hours?" Kim didn't sound pleased by the prospect. Keeble knew how she felt. Teaching Cuto how to play chess, even with Meledrin watching on, had been painful.

But Tuki shook his head. He had that look on his face that meant he was adding again.

When Keeble said, "We have power to all systems," Tuki immediately started working on his computer.

"In the thirty-nine hours allowed by the timer we would, if we started at 20 kilometers a second and our rate of deceleration was constant, travel 48.5 light years. Then we would need to go back in for another four hours." Tuki said.

"Plus two hours for the batteries to charge in the middle," Keeble added.

Tuki glanced up but didn't stop talking. "But we could do two journeys of 14 hours forty-five minutes, approximately, plus the charging time in the middle. So, less than thirty-two hours."

"So, what if we do three trips?"

Tuki added again. "That would be... three trips of just over nine hours each, mo'min. With four hours for charging this time."

"Christ. Which moron invented the universe?" Kim shook her head. "Let's just stick with the two fourteens."

Fourteen hours of the nothing, of the darkness? Twice. Keeble could imagine himself being bored stupid. Two hours until that happened though. He could fix as many problems as possible in the mean time. And find some solutions to work on while in the other universe as well.

-oOo-

The computers told him everything about the ship. It was a Taranev Scout Schooner, Class 1. Weighing 4576 ton when empty. Top speed in Real-space was 20 kilometers per second. The information was never ending.

The ship had a cargo capacity of 7300 cubic meters in the standard form or 4200 with the garden option installed.

"Garden option? What the hell are they talking about?"

The *Hakahei* was designed for a maximum crew of 85 and could, with the garden, go without an atmosphere or water purge for up to six months in deep space. It had a weapons compliment equal to that of a FSN (whatever that was) Ketch plus a compliment of support craft, which meant that it could survive on its own indefinitely— depending on the availability of food— even in hostile territory.

And... Keeble felt his mouth drop open... 98 percent of the ship's structure was made of stone.

"It can't be."

Cuto said something, unintelligible as ever, but Meledrin translated. Keeble didn't know why either of them were there but he tried to sort through the arm sign language that went with the words.

"I can't feel it," he replied eventually. "I can't sense it. How can it be stone?"

He went to the wall and put his hand against it but still couldn't feel anything. He hummed the first level of his Song of Being, but found nothing in the wall that he could recognize as stone.

"It can't be stone." But the computer said it was. "But it is."

"What does that mean?" Meledrin asked.

"It means I know how to fix the hole, but can't do it. My song is a Song of Being— I can make stone insubstantial. You need a Song of Doing to make the stone into clay so it can be shaped and molded and joined."

"So if you knew a Song of Doing?"

"No, I can't feel the stone, so I couldn't do anything either way."

"But you went through the wall to get in."

He sighed and shook his head. "Yes, but obviously the bit I went through to get into the ship was different."

"Cuto wishes to know what we will do in that case."

"I'll just have to patch it as best I can until I can work something else out." He didn't like the idea— a job should be done right the first time— but didn't have much choice.

Level 8, where the hole was, was all fuel and water tanks. Access was through the Gravitic field ducts. He would need something to help him breathe, but as long as he found the right access door and didn't let out any of the gaseous fuel, he shouldn't have any problems having a look at the damage.

The Engineering Bay was in the very center of the ship. It had batteries to the east and west, Gravitic field generators north and south and clocks above and below. According to the computers, Ohoga engines, plus water and air-recycling systems took up the remainder of the level. There were two of each thing as usual. Everything had a backup. There was also a bathroom, an office and six sleeping cabins, presumably for engineering workers. Keeble knew where he'd be sleeping.

He searched amongst the lockers and storage compartments and found a lamp. He also found a row of white rubberised suites with masks. He assumed they would keep him safe. He looked Cuto up and down.

"One of these might fit Cuto," he said after a moment, holding out one the same size as his own.

But the alien shook his head and spoke a few short bursts to Meledrin.

"Cuto will not need any protective clothing. The hurgon can apparently survive for some time without it."

It made no difference to Keeble. He shrugged and made his way to a room to change.

The room he found was plenty big enough. It was four point two meters square. There was a bed big enough for two people, a table with three chairs, and a few cabinets. The mess of millennia was everywhere, some of it still in one piece.

After moving everything into one pile so he could investigate it later, Keeble removed his heavy boots, tough cotton breeches and shirt. He laid them neatly on the bed. After a moment of thought he removed his mechanical arm as well and set it down on the table. Finally, he pulled the new suit on, stretching it over his stocky frame and testing the breather. He examined the empty left arm, wondering what to do with it. And the glove for the right hand...

When he made his way back out into the passage, Cuto and Meledrin were waiting.

Keeble cleared his throat and stood where he was, examining the ground.

"What's is the matter? Meledrin asked.

"I need your help," Keeble told her quietly.

"Pardon?"

In reply, he held up the glove for his right hand. "I can't get this on by myself. I probably don't need it though..."

Before Meledrin could move— perhaps she had no intention of helping— Cuto stepped forward. The alien took the glove, opening the end so he could stuff his hand inside then tied a knot in the other arm.

Keeble nodded his thanks. "Come on then."

There was a staircase, just a meter wide and book-ended by lifts 1 and 2, that ran all the way down from the Administration level to Level 7. A second set of stairs on the eastern side of the ship led past Level 8 to the cargo holds below. Halfway down these stairs, Keeble found an access door. A large red sign said, 'Warning: Access to Gravitic Field ducts'.

"Kim isn't intending to go anywhere just yet, is she?" Keeble asked. But Cuto couldn't understand him and Meledrin had stayed behind in the Engineering Bay.

Keeble had no idea what Kim intended to do— she was a woman, after all. He pulled the hood up over his head then fitted the mask and breather. He switched on his lamp and looked to see that Cuto was ready.

When the door opened, they found themselves looking out into a Gravitic field duct, a meter wide and the same high. There was a warren of ducts around the lower clock with the dark passages leading to every outlet vent from both Gravitic field generators. If one of the generators broke down, the other could be used on its own with no loss of control. There was not a lot to see— black walls, floor and ceiling, and doors leading away in all directions allowing access to other ducts and other tanks.

"Section 130— somewhere in the south east." Keeble said to himself. He crawled— awkward with only one hand— through a half dozen passages and doors, making his way to the correct part of the ship. A readout by a door showed the tank beyond was empty of atmosphere. Keeble spun the handle and felt a breeze pick up as the air in the duct moved to fill the void. He went through with it and closed the door behind Cuto.

The damage, when they found it, was hardly visible. It was a faint line on the dark hull, down in the lower corner of the tank. If the material really was stone, and he could sense it, and he had a Song of Doing, Keeble could have fixed the problem.

It wouldn't have been hard, just time consuming, digging all the way to the outer edge of the hull and then rejoining the stone as he worked his way back in.

He crouched down, but could see nothing new. He tried to *feel* something with his mind, but there was nothing. He might as well have been looking at a piece of wood.

On the way back out, Keeble wondered if they really had to fix it. The crack was so small. But he shook his head, disgusted at his attitude. Of course it had to be fixed, if for no other reason than it was damaged and nothing should be left that way. "If we enter a planet's atmosphere, the heat created will be immense," he said to Cuto, as if the alien was the one who'd suggested leaving the damage the way it was. "That could make the problem worse. Secondly, there will probably still be fumes in the tank— that heat could make something explode."

But how was he supposed to fix it? "Short term," he said, half to himself, but remembering to do the sign language for Cuto, "we could just put a metal plate over it and glue it in place, but the pressure..." He stepped into the Engineering Bay and sat down in front of one of the five computers.

Meledrin was waiting and translated when Cuto replied. "What if we just pumped air into the tank, that way the internal pressure would help hold the seal in place."

Keeble had thought of the idea just a moment before Cuto had spoken. It was simple but effective and he couldn't think of an alternative. They couldn't weld. They couldn't brace it because anything long enough to reach across the room wouldn't fit down through the ducts.

"That should work," he said eventually, "depending on the expansion and contraction of the hull, of course..." Which would be a problem in any case. "See if you can find some adhesive and sealant and I'll find a piece of metal."

But where to start looking? He pulled up a map of the ship and scrolled through the floors one by one. Throughout the top and mid levels there were four elevators forming the four corners of a square around the center of the ship. On Levels 4, 5, 7 and 8, the ship's huge clocks filled the space between. A hangar took up a large part of Level 4 and near that was a workshop and a storeroom. Keeble surmised that if there were vehicles in the hangar that were fixed in the workshop, then there was likely to be sheets of metal in the storeroom.

"I'm going to Level 4."

Cuto said something but was already working at a computer with Meledrin.

Keeble made his way to a lift and stood silently inside while it rose, resisting the urge to remove the ceiling panels to see how it worked.

When he stepped out into the workshop a moment later, he had to work even harder to keep his mind on the task at hand. Ten meters away, at the far end of the long room, two vehicles were half dismantled. One appeared to be a Loader and the other a flying machine with a funnel at the front and an almost irresistible array of machinery on the back. A door into the storeroom was close by and he had no excuse to go near the vehicles.

The storeroom was almost as interesting as the workshop. There were thousands of different parts lined up neatly on shelves or thrown into boxes. There were tiny things that might have been used to fix a reluctant door and huge metal contraptions that could have been the part needed to fix the misaligned Gravitic field generators. And there was everything in between.

Once he had his mind on the job, it didn't take Keeble long to find a container of scrap metal and a circular piece of boiler plate that was exactly what he needed.

Cuto was waiting for him in Engineering, gun-like contraption in hand. "There's glue in that machine," Meledrin translated for the alien. "Or, there was several thousand years ago, but it's still sealed so..."

"It'll have to do. Where did you find it?"

"It was in a storage room on the next floor. We also investigated a means for pumping the tank below full of air."

"How?"

Meledrin explained but she obviously didn't really understand. Keeble would just assume Cuto knew and find out the details from the alien when it was relevant. "The computer shows you how," the elf finished.

"Come on then, Cuto, let's see if this will work." Then there were other problems to solve.

FOURTEEN HOURS WASN'T THE END OF IT.

"Three minutes until systems are back on line," Keeble informed them. "Fuel is fine."

Tuki was staring at the ceiling while he added. Eventually he looked up and spoke. "We are 470,000 kilometers from Kiva. At top speed, that will be just over six and a half hours... Sorry, mo'min, we should be closer."

Keeble grunted. Another six and a half hours?

It seemed to take a moment for Kim to realize that Tuki was apologizing. "Tuki, you did great. You should be proud you got us so close."

"Thank you, mo'min." He didn't look convinced.

Keeble grunted. "And it will give me a chance to look at the Ohoga engines."

He started working in the computer and Cuto came to watch over his shoulder.

-oOo-

Keeble looked at the planet. It was a colored disk in the centre of the port and, after almost a day and a half with not much at all to look at it was the most beautiful thing he'd ever seen.

According to Tuki there were a dozen alien life forms in orbit. Meledrin scanned radio frequencies until their guttural babble erupted from a speaker.

Kim took a deep breath. "Are they talking about us?"

"Yes, they are."

"Well, tell them we mean them no harm. We wish to land on the planet for a short time and then leave again."

Meledrin spoke gibberish for a few minutes, seeming to repeat herself several times. She occasionally waved her arms in the strange sign language as well, as if that might help.

"They say they do not trust us. They say that this time we may merely land and then leave again but what of next time?"

"Get Cuto to talk to them."

56: Dry River

"What is it that you wish Cuto to say?"

"He can work it out."

"Very well. But Cuto is not—" Meledrin fell silent when Kim turned to glare at her.

Cuto spoke for several minutes and Meledrin didn't bother to translate. Keeble kept one eye on his console and the other on the planet outside.

"I do not think it is working," the elf eventually said. "Cuto is not trusted."

"Just get Cuto to keep talking. Hopefully that will distract them a bit while we get closer. Does anyone happen to know the best angle for re-entry?"

Keeble had no idea. It probably wouldn't even say in the computers.

"No? Well, we will just have to go straight down then, I suppose, as slow as the aliens will allow." Kim took a deep breath. "Tuki, where's your village?"

The moai spent some time examining his displays. "It must be around the far side, mo'min."

"Right. Tell me when we're over the top of it." Kim changed the angle of the *Hakahei*'s movement to take them around the back before they reached the orbiting kil'ini. The aliens remained watchful but didn't attack.

"We are close, mo'min. I cannot tell exactly."

Kim spun the ship so the bridge was facing away from the world and started almost directly towards it. Soon, it would be down. There were hardly any aliens at all in the area, but they were coming quickly.

In the end, re-entry wasn't all that hard, as far as Keeble could tell. Kim slowed the ship as much as she dared with the aliens approaching and kept them heading straight down.

Tuki used the skyglass to fill the viewing well with an image of the world below.

Keeble didn't know how far up they were, though it seemed to be a long way, but desert stretched across most of the enormous continent below. There was green to the north and west, distilled through the wide reaching smoke of war, but in every other direction...

A ribbon of green divided the desert in two ragged, uneven parts.

"That is Dry River, mo'min. You can see where it curves south at the hills... Danyon Ford is three hundred and twenty five kilometers this side of that point."

"Hokey-dokey then."

When they got closer Keeble discovered that Dry River was just that, a riverbed that no longer held water between its banks. Instead it contained vegetation— trees and shrubs attracted by the ground water and given their one chance at life in the desert. When they were closer still, smoke was visible as well. It was not the smoke of war, though. It was the smoke of life.

"We'll slow down a bit and give them a chance to think."

"Do we want them to think?" Meledrin asked, squinting at the image in the well.

"Yes."

Tuki adjusted the view, focusing on the village and making it larger.

At that point Dry River ran more or less east-west. The village, Danyon Ford, sat close to the northern bank with a scattering of small buildings to the north of a shin high stone wall. A handful of older women were gathered there, watching the sky. To the south of the wall a few larger buildings were centered on a square. The square was full of young women and girls who'd all stopped their work to watch the sky as well. Men were streaming in from surrounding vegetable patches and work sites.

"I think they're thinking," Keeble said.

The ground seemed to be coming up very quick. Keeble wondered if Kim had any idea what she was doing. It was a bit late to be asking that now though. He gritted his teeth and wondered if there was anything he could do to help. He almost laughed at that. He really didn't know anything more than she did. He was in deep water and struggling to keep his head dry but he wasn't going to let anyone else know that if he could help it.

He saw Kim grimace as she slowed the ship and thumped it down onto the ground amidst a storm of sand. They were about fifty meters from the river.

"Come on. Let's go."

"Everyone?" Keeble asked. He didn't think it was a good idea to leave the ship unattended, even if the locals were unlikely to do any damage in the also unlikely event they got inside.

Kim hesitated and shook her head. "No. You and Cuto stay here to keep an eye on things. And think of something dramatic you can do in case it's needed."

"Dramatic? In case it's needed?"

"Yes. I'm going to be telling them I'm their goddess, remember. They might need convincing."

"Right, easy." He shook his head but didn't say anything else as the two women left the bridge with Tuki slinking along behind, looking remarkably small for someone his size.

While he waited, Keeble tried to think of something dramatic and godlike. He assumed that was what Kim had meant. There was probably a speaker outside. He could just turn that up to full volume and shout at the moai. Or, if he knew how to use some of the weapons he could blow up a tree or something, although that sounded a bit risky. It annoyed him that Kim, a woman, was in charge, but he didn't like his chances of surviving long if he landed a tree on her head. She might not know much but she was in the habit of making good guesses.

A crowd of moai, led by a relatively small woman that was still taller than Meledrin, waited in the sun at the edge of the river. The woman out front looked calm, the rest looked as if they wanted to be somewhere else.

"Can you hear me, Keeble?"

He looked around for the intercom. There would be one at his console somewhere. He eventually found something that looked about right and hit the button. "Of course I can. Why wouldn't I be able to?"

"Because I found some things before that I thought were radios, but I wasn't sure."

"Right, well yes, I can hear you. What's happening?"

"I'm just trying to work out how to fly one of these Lander things. Keep an eye out and let me know if you see anything interesting. And don't get distracted by anything."

"Why would I get distracted? I've got a job to do."

"Shit, you heard that?"

"I just told you—"

"Yes, but I didn't say the bit about distractions out loud. I just thought it."

"Well, keep your thoughts to yourself." It wasn't until he spoke that Keeble realized what Kim had actually said.

"I'll try. Let us know if you see anything, remember."

"You spoke in your mind and my radio heard it?"

"Apparently. Now keep an eye out."

Keeble didn't like being treated like and apprentice. "I'll do my job, you do yours."

He thought about going to Tuki's chair to adjust the cameras but Cuto could probably do that as well as he. So with a lot of arm waving and frustration he eventually got the alien to understand. A few minutes later it was playing with the controls, trying to get them working. Finally, the image in the well showed a group of moai women, all huge like Tuki, standing close together as if that alone might protect them from attack if that was what was to come. Other women were standing nearer the bank of Dry River. They all looked extremely nervous.

The only men in evidence were hiding amongst the trees.

Kim didn't sound all that confident herself. Her muttering and cursing came over the radio as she tried to work out how to fly the Lander.

A few minutes later the little craft moved into the camera's range. It wobbled, dipped, lifted slightly, then settled. *"Much more touchy than the ship on earth."*

"I wonder what the moai would think if their goddess crashed at their feet," Keeble said. Cuto looked at him and he tried to say it again in the sign language. Either he didn't get it right or the alien had no sense of humor, for Cuto just stared blankly for a moment then turned back to the task it had been assigned.

The Lander slowly drifted to the ground and touched down with a slight thump and a spray of sand. Keeble let out his breath, slightly disappointed.

"Right," Kim said. *"Let's do this. Meledrin, you first. We need to hit them with a woman straight away. Tuki, you next... Ummm... A couple of steps behind. Carry the skyglass in front of you. Don't bow your head or anything like that. Look confident and proud. You're a servant, but an honored one. Right?"*

"*Yes, mo'min.*"

Apparently Tuki had a radio as well. That probably meant Meledrin did, too. Keeble was surprised he hadn't heard her offering all sorts of instructions for the last ten minutes.

"*You can't call me that, Tuki. The mo'min's out there, remember. I'm better than that. I'm Poti.*"

"*Yes... mo'ma.*"

"*Right. Whatever. I'll wait a few seconds then come out as well. I'll speak English at first. Mel, you translate.*"

There was a moment of silence.

"*How do you do that?*"

Another silence.

"*Talk so it doesn't come over the radio. I only just realized you were doing it.*"

Pause.

"*Well, you could have let me know before. But talk so Keeble can hear you anyway— he needs to know what's going on.*"

"*Very well, though I don't know what difference it will make. Do you really think it is wise for you to speak a different language? You are their goddess...*"

"*Yes, I know, but I don't want to be too familiar at first. I'll speak properly later.*"

"*Very well.*"

"*Let's go then.*"

When the holy party moved out into the sunlight, Keeble thought he saw Meledrin wilt under the ferocity of it. If anything, Tuki seemed to welcome it, and Kim looked like she didn't care at all. Keeble had never been in a real desert but he'd heard dwarves describe it like standing in front of a furnace. The effort of appearing unaffected by the heat must have been difficult for Kim. Keeble grunted and turned his attention back to the engineering computers— there were some things that only a man could do.

57: Bigger Problems

SCREE PULLED PING DOWN BEHIND A FALLEN LOG a hundred meters from the outermost building, took off his pack and monster arm and settled down to watch.

The remains of villages dotted the river, some large, some barely more than a few houses clustered around a central square. None had more than a few walls standing amidst the creeping hands of nature. There'd been a well in the first one, choked with weeds but still collecting water. Clusters of feral vegetables surrounded the next. After scavenging for wild berries and fruits for days the selection was overwhelming. Carrots and radishes, corn and tubas. The third was covered in a dusting of tiny white flowers. The forth erupted in a blur of red and green as hundreds of parrots took flight. And the fifth was full of people.

"Who are they?" Ping asked after a while. She was peeking through a hole in the rotting trunk and not likely to see anything that wasn't right in front of her.

"They're moai, I reckons," Scree replied, but that wasn't the information she was really after and he couldn't help her with that.

"What are they doing here?"

And that was a stupid question. "Living."

They didn't do anything interesting. The women sat around in the square talking and preparing food and handcrafts while the men worked in gardens and repairing things around the village. Scree was about to get up and walk into the village to ask for some real food— though he knew that moai didn't eat meat— when things started to get interesting.

The first thing he noticed was something in the sky. He knew straight away it wasn't one of the monster's bats, but he didn't know what it *was*. It took him a few minutes of staring, watching as the thing got closer, to work out it was a ship. It was like the big ones he had seen in the hanger.

Very interesting.

It was a sphere about fifty meters across and looked about as graceful and as likely to fly as a bumblebee. It was an amazing thing to see.

A short while after that the ship was settling down in the desert on the far side of the village. It made a deep humming sound, like a stampede of cattle, and kicked up a storm of sand but wasn't nearly as dramatic as Scree expected.

Apparently the moai thought it was dramatic. They were leaving the village, streaming through the trees towards the ship like they wanted to be doing anything else.

Scree grabbed Ping's arm and hurried that way as well. He wasn't worried about being seen.

At the edge of the desert he lay down under the last of the trees and looked at the ship. Nothing he hadn't seen before. And then a smaller ship, about the size of the one he'd driven himself, came out through a door, wobbled for a moment, then dropped down to land. When the sand had rained back down a moai and a tall thin woman emerged. They moved to stand silently in front of a group of local women.

"Interestings," Scree muttered.

Then a voice crackled in his head.

<It's all right, Tuki. You're doing great.> And a moment later another woman stepped out of the small ship.

"What's happening?" Ping asked.

Scree shook his head and tried to follow the conversation. He couldn't hear half of the conversation in the real world and the speakers were blocking half of what was being said in his head. He was confused by just about everything he *could* hear. He whispered the conversation to Ping, hoping she could work out what was going on. He was sure of one thing though. The woman talking wasn't any type of goddess no matter what she said. Her name was Kim, and she was just an ordinary human. The other two weren't all that special either, as far as he could tell.

And then things got even more interesting. Scree smiled.

At least a dozen trolls were slinking through the trees towards the village. Scree took Ping's hand and dragged her, as quietly as possible, under the spreading leaves of a lakatil bush.

The trolls stopped just out of the village to see what was what. They must have heard the ship arrive, and felt it reverberating through the ground, but they were coming out of the trees and might not have seen it.

"Are we going to help them?" Ping whispered.

"They don't need our help. They'll mangle that village in no time."

"Not the trolls," Ping said. "The other ones."

Scree hadn't thought of that. He turned back to look at the ship. *Interesting.*

<You got trouble, woman,> he said in his head.

<Who the hell are you? What's going on?>

<I'm Scree and you got a pack of hungry trolls ready to mangle that village and everyone in it.>

There was a pause before the woman replied and she sounded flustered. *<What?>*

<Don't know whats you're up to but you'd better hurrys up about it.>

Another pause. *<Can you stop them?>* Kim asked in his mind.

<Why should I? Likely get myself killed if I try.>

<But... The trolls are going to kill the moai?>

<Usually what happens.>

<But...>

<You don't want the moai killed?>

<Of course not.>

<You're as bad as Ping. Waits.>

Scree checked the trolls again and sat down to think while the broken conversation continued in his mind. Finally, he decided that here was what he had been searching for all along. Someone who could fight back against more than one monster at a time.

<You in charge of that ship, woman?>

<Yes.>

<You fly to the stars?>

<Yes.>

<You can fight the monsters? The ones that ride the bird things?>

<If we have to, but we don't want to. They aren't the real problem.>

<They aren't the real problem? You got bigger problems than them monsters?>

<There are always bigger problems.>

<Well, right now I reckon these trolls is your biggest problem. If I stop them will you let me and Ping go with you?>

Kim hesitated. *<Well...>*

<We got a deal?>

<Yes. Try not to kill them though.>

Try not to kill them? Scree laughed. Try not to *die*. He made sure the monster weapon was working and took a deep breath. "Stay down," he said to Ping as he stood up.

He was spotted almost instantly and one of the trollops rose to her feet. She was huge, almost as large as the moai. Some time during the last few days she'd dispensed with her clothes and her scarred skin was burnt red by the sun. "Who's you?"

"I'm Scree."

"Pumice."

Scree had known lots of Pumice's in his life, male and female. Trolls didn't spend too much time thinking of names.

"You wanna join?" she asked. "We just about to smack some humans."

He took a breath, at least he was going to get a chance to talk. "They ain't humans."

"What is they then?" She twirled a large club in her hand.

He looked her up and down. It seemed a lifetime since he'd had sex. "They's moai."

"Moai? Giants?"

"Yep. Deadly buggers."

"Deadly? More deadly than us?"

"Beat up their babies to see if they's tough."

Another troll rose to his feet. "You don't look worried."

"I can runs fast."

The pack laughed until Pumice cut them off. "They's not tough. I heard of moai. They stand there and watches you while you does it."

Scree grimaced and didn't say anything.

"Why you protecting them?"

"Not protecting them. Protecting my pack."

"You got a pack? You ain't protecting them then, you just stopping us from getting the loot."

"No, my pack's different. They needs protecting."

"But I want the best loot. You ain't getting it."

Scree sighed, shifted his grip in his monster gun and wondered if he could kill them all before he was overwhelmed. But they were trolls. While he and Pumice talked they'd been spreading out until they almost encircled him. Twelve trolls, nine trollops. Plus Pumice. Lots. They stood, silent and watchful, ready for anything.

"Well, you ain't getting it, so how 'bout I just kills you now."

"Youse gunna kill me? I don't think so."

"I can kills you without moving."

"Lets see you do it then."

So Scree killed her, letting off a long sizzle of energy that cooked the trollop where she stood. The others watched, open mouthed and stunned— not quite as ready as they thought. If they'd attacked straight away he was finished, but that hesitation gave him a chance. He could see the anger and blood lust growing in all of them and spoke before it got out of control.

"Who's in charge now?"

For a moment nobody moved, then a big troll stepped forward.

"Bluff."

The name suited. Bluff was tall and broad.

"You sure you's in charge, Bluff?"

"Well, I know that you ain't."

So, one demonstration of the weapon wasn't enough to convince them. Scree didn't think he'd live long after a second demonstration. He listened in his mind, trying to work out how the human was going with whatever it was she was doing. It was hard to tell. "How abouts if I wrings your neck. Is I in charge thens?"

Bluff laughed. "Don't ask me. Ask them."

"Yeah," one of them said. "You's in charge then, hey." Others agreed, as if they didn't think it'd make any difference.

"Right then." He removed the monster gun from his arm and got ready. "You can keep you club, if you wants."

"Oh, I want. You don't expect me to help you, do you?"

Scree shrugged and attacked.

Bluff responded a fraction of a moment too late and Scree was inside the arc of the club, too close for the weapon to do any damage. He blocked easily with his forearm, punched twice in quick succession. Bluff rocked back, stumbled, righted himself as Scree moved back.

"You don't think I needs your help, does you?" Scree said. He saw the blood lust rising in Bluff's eyes and was surprised when he didn't respond likewise. And he was surprised how much more effective that made him. Had his time with Ping changed him that much?

He stepped inside again, went down low. He struck his opponent's knee with the heel of his hand. Bluff grunted, but nothing broke. Scree rolled away. He came to his feet in the clear. His opponent was already coming at him, yelling wordlessly and swinging his club.

Scree blocked again, lashing out with his arm and glancing the club past his shoulder. He punched Bluff in the throat.

The big troll gasped for air. He clutched at his throat, wheezing. While he struggled, Scree broke his neck.

With a deep breath, Scree glanced at the log where Ping was still hiding and wondered how she was reacting. Then looked around at his new pack. They looked as mean as ever, but didn't move against him. He decided to get the monster gun back on his arm just in case.

"What now, boss?"

"Who you?"

"I'm Stone."

"Well, Stone, now we waits for a few minutes, then I goes, and you does whatever you wants."

"You was serious?"

He remembered what the woman had asked him. "Well, it'd be nice if you didn't kills any of them moai. Or even hurt thems."

They didn't look too happy about that.

"Just maybe take some food and move on?"

"So you goes goes," a trollop said, "but still expects us to do something something like that 'cause you asked?"

Scree shrugged. "Don't expect it. But that's what the boss wants so I's asking."

"You ain't in charge?"

"Nope."

Stone gestured to the gun, now on Scree's arm. "You ain't running with them monsters, is you?"

"Nope. I's just got me a new pack a couple of minutes ago. They was hunting the monsters, in the sky, but they after something bigger nows."

"Bigger than them monsters?" Stone raised his eyebrows and whistled softly. "And how do you know your boss don't want us in the pack?"

Scree thought about that for a moment and shrugged. "Don't knows, really."

"Why don't you ask? I think you should ask," a younger troll said. "He should ask, shouldn't he? Sounds like fun, I reckon, so he should find out what the boss thinks."

Scree thought about that as well. "Why you want to come?"

Stone laughed. "Why you going with them? Fighting something worse than them monsters? Where else would we go?"

Scree nodded but he knew trolls. And he knew what the woman had said and he knew that so far humans were about the only people he'd seen with any idea about machines. "One thing youse gotta understand," he said eventually. "Ain't no choice of boss. The human is it. And she don't like killings. And she don't even likes maiming unless it's needed."

"What?"

"Yeps. And what she says goes, cause without her we ain't getting nowheres."

"You serious, hey?"

"Yeps. That's the way it is. If she says stand still, that's what we does. If she says no killing, then no killings."

"And if we don't wanna do what she says, hey?"

"Then I'll kills ya."

"She won't like that, aye," another trollop said with a wicked smile.

"Nope," and he remembered something Kim had said to the other woman in his head, "but she's smart enough to know that sometimes the need arises."

Scree knew they wouldn't change their minds now. He also knew that a lot would change their minds some time soon. And they knew he knew. Scree decided to ask Kim what she thought anyway. He eyed up a tasty young trollop while he spoke, smiling and licking his lips. She gave a toothy smile in reply. Flaming cats, it was a long time since he'd had a rut.

<You don't wants some trolls, does you?> Scree asked in his head.

<*What?*>

<I gots me a pack.>

<*Well, what would I do with a pack of trolls?*>

<So you wants me to just leave them here near the village?>

<What will they do?>

<Told you already.>

<And what's to stop them from mangling my ship?>

<Me.>

The woman didn't reply.

<Trolls is good at fighting,> Scree continued, <and if you got bigger problems then I may need some help.>

<Will they do what they're told? Will you do what you're told?>

<If you gives orders worth following.>

<Well, okay then. I suppose. Shit.>

<Good. Meets you at the little ship.>

"Right, you lot are in," Scree said.

"I thought you was asking the boss?"

"Already asked." He looked at the trollop. "Got a couple of minutes before we gots to be there though."

TUKI HELD THE SKYGLASS like he had been instructed and walked silently behind Meledrin. When the elf stopped a few meters short of the nervous group from Danyon Ford, Tuki stopped as well. But after that he did not know what to do. Kim had told him to hold his head high, to be proud, but Ko'uka, a mo'shi, was watching him with harsh concentration. He could not return her gaze for that would be disrespectful, but he could not look away, for Kim had said...

After a moment of nervously looking at the silently watching moai, perhaps hoping for a distraction amongst them, Tuki stared resolutely at the tops of the trees behind. He wanted to look out at the desert. Though his time away could be measured in days it felt as if he had been gone for much longer. It felt as if he had slipped into some other life in the intervening time. He held the skyglass and wiggled his feet in the sand and stared at the trees.

<It's all right, Tuki. You're doing great.>

Tuki jumped slightly and glanced back over his shoulder— it was as if Kim was whispering in his ear, or in his mind, when she was still out of sight in the Lander. <The leader here is Ko'uka.> He said in his mind, touching at the band that wrapped around his head as if that might somehow help carry his voice to Kim. Perhaps it might— he had no idea how the machine worked.

For long moments nobody said anything. In moai communities it was proper for visitors to speak first, asking for the blessing of the hosts and permission to enter. But Kim had not yet left the Lander and Meledrin was not likely to speak before she arrived. Tuki longed to look back over his shoulder again to see what was happening, but this time he held himself still.

Finally, Kim arrived, stepping lightly across the sand in her 'dressing-gown'. As she approached, Meledrin stepped aside, went down onto her knees and bowed her head. After a moment of hesitation, Tuki did the same, skyglass held before him. That position was preferable to looking at the women from the village, so he stayed that way, even when he noticed Meledrin raise her head.

Kim stood nearby, not saying anything.

Finally Ko'uka spoke, breaking the silence with words harsher than was proper. "Who are you? What do you want?"

From the corner of his eye, Tuki could see go'gan hiding amongst the greenery of Dry River. He did not know what they intended to do should harm befall the women.

Kim replied in her native tongue. Tuki could understand none of it but Meledrin translated into Rongo a moment later.

"Poti— the Mother Blower— wishes to be shown the respect that She deserves. She wishes for you to abase yourselves, as is proper."

"This woman— this human— claims she is Poti?"

A quick exchange, Kim staring straight ahead as she spoke, Meledrin paying close attention.

"Poti is aggrieved that belief and humility have gone from the moai. All people are equal to Poti, humans and moai alike. Men and women alike."

Tuki heard a gasp from the trees. A go'gan stepped into the clear for a moment, before slipping back under cover.

"Tell *Poti* that women and men are not equal. They never have been."

And Kim spoke in Rongo, though Tuki thought that perhaps it was earlier than she wanted. "Ko'uka, show me where it is said that women are better than men?"

"It is shown every day, in all of our lives."

"Tell me how."

"Men cannot speak to the skyglass."

Kim laughed. "They can not use the skyglass because women will not let them. There is no other reason." She made a gesture and Tuki heard Meledrin in his ear.

<Stand up, Tuki. Turn on the skyglass and do something with it.>

<No, Tuki. Just stand. Don't do anything else. You stand too, Mel.> Kim took a step forward. "But I wish to know why I talk with you, Ko'uka. Where is the mo'min? Respect has joined humility and belief, thrown into the furnace of the moai."

"The mo'min has much to do. She has remained in the village."

"Mel, lead on. Tuki, tell her if she goes the wrong way."

But it was not hard to find the way. The well-worn path led directly to the village, skirting along the edge of an irrigation drain for much of the way. Moai, female and male, streamed through the trees on either side, racing to reach the village before 'Poti'.

Tuki followed Meledrin between the first of the buildings, past his friends from another life. The men watched as if he and the skyglass together were a miracle happening before their eyes, more amazing than the ship coming down from the sky.

As he followed Meledrin across the square beyond the building, Tuki saw Keala.

He almost stopped. The last time he had seen Keala he had promised that he would return with a skyglass. And he had. But he was not sure the skyglass could ever really be his to give and knew he would not hand it over anyway. He saw her watching, as beautiful as ever, with her dark eyes and long, thick plait. He wanted to explain to her what had happened, why he had taken so long, why he would keep the 'glass for himself. But Kim was in his ear urging him forward.

<Where will the mo'min be, Tuki?>

<In her house, I think, at the very north of the village.>

<Let's go then, Mel.>

<But mo'min... Kim... I cannot pass the wall.> The wall that divided the village in two, that kept the unmarried moai and the married moai separate, was just a few meters away. Tuki was walking towards it as if he did not intend to stop, but he did not know if he could force himself through the narrow gap near the tree.

<Which wall? That wall? Of course you can pass it, Tuki. Don't even slow. Don't look aside. You have every right to go wherever the hell you please— you have a skyglass, remember.>

Tuki swallowed and nodded, though it was not until he had taken that step through the opening, from one side of the wall to the other, that he knew he could do it. It felt like a greater step than stepping between worlds. Kim seemed to sense his unease.

<Your people think women are superior, Tuki. The elves agree. But Keeble thinks men are better. I think they're all as useless and wonderful as each other. Somebody has to be wrong.>

<You are right, mo'min, but what if it is Keeble who is wrong?>

<Then we change the answer.>

With all the talking, Tuki had not noticed the commotion his progress had caused. In the square behind him, women were shouting, calling on somebody to halt the outrage. The men stood in shocked, thoughtful silence.

Tuki took a moment to wonder who the women were imploring into action. Surely they could not be asking the go'gan, for that would mean they too would step beyond the wall. If anyone was to stop Tuki's sacrilegious march, it would need to be the women or the go'shin, though obviously they thought the men better suited to the task. Tuki smiled slightly at the thought.

"*<To the left, Meledrin,>*" he muttered. "*<The house in the trees.>*"

Apparently word had preceded them for, as they got nearer, the mo'min emerged from the house to stand between two trees that acted like a gateway in front. She was an old moai but still with a straight back and steady gaze.

"Who are you? What do you want?"

"Mo'min, Ko'uka greeted me in exactly the same manner. It annoyed me greatly then, and annoys me even more now."

"Well, I do not care to know your thoughts. You claim to be Poti? What proof do you have?"

"Faith requires no proof, mo'min."

"Well, I do."

"Show me proof that says I am not Poti. Or do people come from the sky every day?"

Tuki had an idea though... he swallowed and spoke quietly to Kim. <Ask her of the meteors that have foretold your coming. Ask her why I was not believed. I told Ko'uka that I saw a meteor change direction.>

"For weeks," Kim said, "meteors have warned of my coming. Have you not seen them?"

"Meteors are common things, for those who—"

Kim gestured briefly at the skyglass Tuki carried. "I know how to look, mo'min."

<*You got trouble, woman.*>

Tuki almost dropped the skyglass. The voice in his ear, delivered by the radio, was not one that he knew. Unable to stop himself, he turned to look around. All he could see was Danyon Ford and the moai who had always been there.

Kim was obviously as shocked as he was. <*Who the hell are you? What's going on?*> The unease in her voice was obvious but she avoided looking around and somehow managed to concentrate on her conversation with the mo'min. "I sent my faithful servant, Tuki, a message but you ridiculed him when he passed it on. Why?"

"He is but a go'gan—"

"I watch over all moai, mo'min. Is he, or any man, less worthy of my protection than you? Is he less worthy of my attention than you? I sent a message that you ignored."

The mo'min glared for a moment. "The message that Tuki passed on was not ignored. I just thought it better to consult the heavens before acting."

The other voice returned again. <*I'm Scree and you got a pack of hungry trolls ready to mangle that village and everyone in it.*>

<*What?*>

<*Don't know whats you're up to but you'd better hurrys up about it.*>

Tuki swallowed. <*Trolls? Kim all the humans I met on Kiva were terrified of trolls. They are fearsome men.*> And now there were some ready to attack Danyon Ford? He spoke to the mo'min then, giving Kim a chance to speak with the stranger. He hoped he was doing the right thing. "Ko'uka told me standing by the wall," he said, blushing despite himself. "She did not ask you anything, mo'min, or consult the skyglass. She said I would probably never be married."

<*Can you stop them?*> Kim asked the stranger.

<*Why should I? Likely get myself killed if I try.*>

<*But... The trolls are going to kill the moai?*>

<*Usually what happens.*>

<*But...*>

<*You don't want the moai killed?*>

<*Of course not.*>

<*You're as bad as Ping. Waits.*>

The stranger fell silent and Tuki watched as Kim gathered herself. "That is true, mo'min. Did the skyglass show you the future so you could pass these instructions to Ko'uka before Tuki even brought the matter to her attention? When did you tell her it was a matter best investigated in private? When did you tell her that Tuki should be publicly ridiculed?"

The mo'min sniffed. "I did not tell her."

"So was Ko'uka punished?"

"There was no punishment."

Tuki saw Kim raise an eyebrow. "Perhaps there should have been."

"The skyglass did not—"

"Perhaps I should have Tuki consult his skyglass to discover what punishment he sees there."

"Tuki cannot use the skyglass. He is just a go'gan."

"Tuki can, mo'min. Tuki does. He has been with me to the heavens and knows more of them and the skyglass than you ever will."

"A go'gan cannot—"

"Mo'min, collect Danyon Ford's skyglass."

"I will not."

<Mel, go in and get it. Hopefully it's in the open or we'll look like complete idiots.>

<And if the mo'min attempts to stop me?>

<Don't let her. You can handle yourself, can't you?>

<If the need arises, but...>

<We'll if it arises, then handle yourself. We don't have time for this.>

<Very well.>

59: Skyglasses

TUKI WATCHED AS MELEDRIN STRODE FORWARD and the mo'min moved slightly to bar her path. Tuki hid a smile at the thought of Meledrin being cowed by anything as insignificant as size. The two women stared at each other. The set of the elf's shoulders was calm and relaxed. Fury was rising in the mo'min's eyes but it was she who looked away first. Meledrin could have stepped past the larger woman then, but she did not. She stayed where she was, staring, until the mo'min stepped aside.

<You in charge of that ship, woman?>

Tuki listened as Kim and Scree spoke for a minute until it seemed the *Hakahei* had two new crewmembers. Tuki wasn't sure if he liked that at all, but before he could even decide if he should say something Meledrin returned from the cabin, the skyglass held carefully before her.

"Let us go to the square, mo'min," Kim said.

When Meledrin did not slow, Tuki fell into step a couple of meters behind, and Kim walked behind him. The mo'min and a dozen mo'shi, the only people who'd gone beyond the wall, bought up the rear.

Back at the square, the entire village had gathered. Meledrin stopped just beyond the gateway, amidst the closest of the moai. Tuki found that he was still in the northern half of the village. Perhaps Meledrin had deliberately left him there to prove a point. He stepped aside to let Kim pass.

"I am Poti," Kim said softly. People at the back of the crowd strained to hear. "And today marks a new beginning for the moai." She went forward and took the 'glass from Meledrin, holding it up for all to see. *<Is this thing on, Tuki?>*

When Kim stepped close Tuki reached out and touched a finger to the skyglass she held. He muttered the word that turned it on.

Kim made her way to the nearest go'gan and took his hand. Tuki doubted Kim knew that the moai was unmarried but male was all that mattered, he was sure.

<That is Inaki,> Tuki said silently. *<He is a go'gan— unmarried. By touching him you have given him great honor.>*

"Inaki, you have never touched the skyglass?"

The young go'gan shook his head. "No, mo'ma."

"Why is that?"

"It is not allowed, mo'ma. Only the mo'min and mo'shi can touch the 'glass and read the messages from the... from you."

"Who told you this, Inaki?"

"I do not know, mo'ma. It has always been so."

"It has not. You all know Tuki." She gestured and Tuki tried not to lower his eyes. "He thought the same as you, but now he is responsible for the care of my skyglass."

The crowd gasped, as if they had not noticed Tuki with the 'glass.

"The moai are on many worlds, Inaki, but it is only here that the mo'shi deny the rights of all male moai. Here, take the 'glass."

Another gasp. Tuki watched as Inaki took a step back. He was Tuki's age, but they had had little to do with each other. Tuki realized that he had not had much to do with any of the others. But he could think of a few go'gan who would have been better choices.

"I cannot, mo'ma. It would not be proper."

"Who says?"

"The mo'min. The mo'shi." Inaki lowered his eyes and put his hands behind his back, as if wanting to avoid temptation. Kim continued to hold the 'glass out in front.

"I have my own skyglass, Inaki." Kim gestured towards Tuki. "By all the laws set out by your leaders, I am a mo'min. Is that not correct?"

"Yes, mo'min. Mo'ma."

"Then it is permissible for me to make new laws. Take this skyglass, it is allowed."

Kim offered Inaki the skyglass and he reached out a tentative hand. The glass started to glow the moment his fingers made contact and the go'gan withdrew his hand quickly. He looked from Kim to the mo'min as if wondering whose word he should believe.

"Would that happen if it were not allowed?" Kim asked.

"No, mo'ma. I don't think so."

"Take the skyglass, Inaki."

Tuki watched Inaki reach forward again and wondered if his own face had worn the same expression when he had first dared to touch the 'glass. Tuki searched the faces of the people around him. The men all wore much the same expression, as if they were the ones reaching out. The women... The women looked afraid. Except Keala... Keala was staring at him, fury stark and plain in her eyes.

Tuki quickly turned away.

He knew the skyglass was not magical, but made by men, to be used and controlled. If the women were wrong about that, what else might they be wrong about?

Meledrin thought women were better than men and said so on many occasions. But Keeble was as competent as any woman could hope to be.

He looked up at the sky for a moment. *Perhaps women are more suited to life in the desert,* he said to himself, *but I now know that the desert is not everything.*

When he returned his attention to the square and to Inaki, he saw that the go'gan was speaking the names of different constellations and watching as they appeared in the polished surface of the skyglass. The watchers gasped with each change, crowding closer and straining to see all the better.

"Men and women must live as equals, side by side," Kim said, retrieving the skyglass from Inaki. <*Tuki, do you think you can knock down part of that wall?*>

<Ummm... I think so.>

<*Yes or no?*>

<Yes.>

<*Good, when you're right then.*> And to the crowd, "Marriage is a holy union, but those who remain unmarried are no less loved by me than those who are married."

Tuki bent forward and, straining slightly, removed a rock from the wall, right near the gate. For a moment he wondered what to do with it, before passing out into the square. The crowd divided before him. In the centre of the square he placed the stone carefully on the ground. He started to return to his position behind Meledrin but, after a moment of indecision, stopped by her side instead.

"The skyglass was never supposed to be used to control the moai. It was a gift for all to share. But now you must all go forward together, without the skyglass."

One final gasp from the crowd as Kim handed the second glass ball to Tuki. Tuki quickly turned it off.

"But the skyglass tells us—"

"It tells you nothing you do not already know..."

<Dosa,> Tuki whispered quickly.

"Dosa."

"Poti, we—"

"I must return to the sky. And you must look to yourselves, to see how you will live your lives in the future." Kim started to leave and Tuki and Meledrin followed close behind. <*How are those trolls going?*> Kim asked.

<*You don't wants some trolls, does you?*> the stranger replied.

<*What?*>

<*I gots me a pack.*> Whoever he was seemed amused by the idea.

<*Well, what would I do with a pack of trolls?*>

Tuki didn't like the idea of Scree and his friend joining the crew when nobody really knew who they were. But a whole pack of trolls as well... But all he knew about trolls was what the humans at Payota had said and he knew that they had been wrong about a lot of other things.

Kim and Scree spoke a bit more before the troll said, <*Trolls is good at fighting and if you got bigger problems then I may need some help.*>

Tuki nodded slightly— that was a good point. The ship was built to carry many people— surely it must be that way for a reason. He adjusted the strap around his head.

And then the Hakahei had a whole pack of trolls for crew as well. He would trust Kim's decision and hope she was right.

As he walked behind Meledrin, Tuki looked back and saw that the moai gathered in the square had divided into two groups. One group was staying put, watching as some of their number, all men, started to tear down the wall to make a pile of stones where Tuki had left his own stone. The others were following Kim.

The procession made its way through the trees and out into the sun beside the Lander. The ship had thrown much of the area surrounding the Lander into shadow and many moai were already gathered there waiting. The stranger was nowhere in sight. Tuki half hoped he was lost somewhere.

"Poti? Mo'ma?"

"Yes, Inaki, what is it?"

"What is heaven like, mo'ma?"

"It is... Tuki?"

Tuki looked at Kim, who was looking at him, and realized she wanted him to answer the question. He looked upwards. "Mo'ma. Inaki. Heaven is the most amazing place. The desert no longer feels like home for me, though I have only known heaven for a few hours."

Inaki nodded as he stared upwards too. "Thank you, Tuki. Mo'ma, is there room in heaven for more moai?"

"There is room in heaven for every moai, Inaki. But that is not what you mean, is it? You mean is there room in heaven for you, right now."

Tuki saw Kim examining the skyglasses and knew what she was thinking. Two glasses, two moai. She was possibly also thinking of the stranger and the trolls.

<Anyone can use the glass once it is plugged in, mo'min. Kim,> Tuki said softly.

<*But still, the moai were made for the task. You can show Inaki how to work the controls while we return...*> She took a deep breath, "Inaki, what Tuki says is correct. Heaven is the most amazing place there is, and there is room there for you now. But it would not be like you expect. It is not perfect—"

"How can heaven not be perfect, mo'ma?"

Kim paused for a moment more and seemed to give it some thought. "Because perfection for humans and moai and all the other races in heaven has nothing to do with a lack of flaws. Heaven for all of those people is a place where they can try to be better."

"Yes, mo'ma. I understand."

Tuki, with a skyglass in each hand and Keala somewhere at his back, understood. He doubted Inaki really did. Not yet.

"I would like to go, mo'ma, if you would take me."

"Inaki, I—"

"I would like to go as well, mo'ma." Another go'gan stepped forward, trying to keep his gaze above the ground.

And a third moai raced forward. Okalani, a mo'by— an unmarried woman. "Aka'mu!" she said, coming to a halt by the go'gan's side.

As he watched the two of them, Tuki wondered how he would react if Keala was to rush to him in the same manner. He looked around, but could not see her in the growing crowd.

"You can both come, if you want. But you must make up your minds quickly."

The two of them looked at each other, and it seemed the decision was made.

"We are leaving now," Kim said to the crowd. "But we will return. If you do not all live as one by that time, men and women, married and unmarried, I cannot say how I will react. But you do not want to see it happen."

With that she moved quickly, without hurrying, around to the rear of the Lander. Tuki followed. When he looked inside the large back door and saw the trolls he stopped. Even though he was expecting to see them, he was still shocked. There were seven on each side of the little craft and five packed in the aisle. They all looked fierce. There were several semi-naked women among them and Tuki blushed furiously. When he discovered that he would be forced to sit in a vacant seat beside one of those women...

He clenched the two skyglasses tighter, but they were about the same size as... as... That just made him blush all the more. The trolls squashed up and Meledrin took her seat as if the dirty, hulking figures were nothing more than she expected. Kim shook her head and sidled through to the front, cursing all the while about her burnt feet and something called deodorant. The two seats in the driver's section were taken.

"You're Scree?"

Scree was a troll? He certainly looked similar to those sitting in the back.

"Yeah. This is Ping."

Tuki could only just see a tiny woman, barley half Scree's size, squeezed beside the troll's seat.

"Well Scree, you're in my seat," Kim said.

"I saw you fly out of the big ship."

"You think you can do better?"

The troll didn't answer. "We all in?" he asked. "Bloody moai holding us up."

The three newest recruits stood near the door, on the outside, and it looked like that was as far as they would go.

"There are all types in heaven," Tuki told them, surprised he could even speak. He stole a glance at the troll woman by his side. "All types."

The moai finally, nervously, climbed aboard and stood in the aisle, gripping handles above their heads.

Tuki watched as the troll maneuvered the Lander with much more confidence than Kim had earlier.

PING TRAILED BEHIND THE CROWD as it surged up the stairs. The four moai hung back as well, seemingly as nervous about the raucous, muscled mob as she was herself.

"You're name is Ping?"

Ping looked at the moai named Tuki and nodded.

"It might be best if you came up to the bridge so you can strap yourself in. Kim has not..." Tuki blushed slightly and looked at his silent companions. "There are monsters in the sky above us and it might be difficult to reach orbit."

Ping nodded though she didn't really understand what the moai had said. She understood most of the words but... "Very well."

Tuki did not go to the stairs. Instead, he went to a small room close by and, when everyone was inside, pushed a button on the wall. The doors closed and Ping felt a lurch of motion.

"What's happening?"

"This room is called a lift. It carries us up and down so we don't have to climb the stairs."

"Why didn't..." Ping remembered the two parallel conversations Scree had translated for her. She glanced at the other moai. "Why didn't Poti use it?"

Tuki shrugged. "I do not understand half the things she does."

Ping nodded. She knew what it was like to have a companion like that. She glanced at the two skyglasses held by Tuki and then at the other moai again. "So all that she did in the village was to get that?"

Tuki nodded though he too glanced at Inaki, Aka'mu and Okalani.

The bridge, at the very top of the ship, was seemingly filled with trolls. They were a loud, ever shifting mob that Scree was trying to get into some seats arranged around the front of the room. He was shouting. It looked as if Kim had been shouting just a short while ago though she was now sitting quietly in a chair raised up above all the others. She seemed relieved when Tuki arrived.

"Where have you been," she said, as if he'd been gone an hour. "We need a skyglass to get out of here."

Tuki blushed again and headed for a chair near the entrance. He placed one of the skyglasses into a depression on the desk before him. A moment later, Ping felt the ship start to vibrate slightly, then she felt her stomach lurch as it had when the lift had started to rise not long before. And they were flying, heading straight upward, racing towards the clouds. The trolls finally fell silent.

"I suggest you sit down," Kim said into the stillness. "Things could get hairy very soon."

Ping saw Tuki fastening a strap around his waist and decided that it might be wise to do as Kim suggested. 'As long as you give orders worth following,' Scree had said. As she hurried to a seat as far as possible from everyone else, Ping looked at the troll. She found it hard to believe that he would so easily give his life into the hands of a stranger. But she had long ago decided that Scree was no fool and also that trolls did whatever was best for themselves. Perhaps in this case that meant relinquishing control.

Ping was struggling with the strap, trying to work out the buckle, when two huge hands, each with three fingers and a thumb, reached past her to assist. She jumped, shied away, but could go nowhere. She looked over her shoulder and saw a monster, flat ugly face devoid of emotion, close to her ear.

She screamed and the little noise that had remained in the room stopped completely.

The monster jumped back, hands raised, and scurried across to the nearest wall.

"What is that... What is that doing here?" Ping asked. She stared up at Kim, now struggling to unclip the buckle she had been struggling to do up a moment earlier.

"That is Cuto," the slim, tall woman sitting down from Kim said.

Ping turned to look at the alien for a moment. "It has a name?" Ping tried to remember the name of the woman— she had been down in the village with Kim earlier. Meledrin.

Meledrin nodded. "Yes. Cuto is not an exact pronunciation— the exact pronunciation is painful— but is close enough." She waved her arms elaborately as she spoke.

Ping ceased her battle with the buckle. Everyone was looking at her. "Scree?"

"Whats?"

"Are you just going to sit there?"

The troll's eyes narrowed as he gave the question some thought. "What do you want me to do?"

"Well..."

"Kim knows Cuto is here and she ain't worried. Why should I be worried? I don't know nothing about anything, so I'm gunna do what I was told— sit down and hold on."

Ping shrank back in her seat and looked at the monster again. It looked strange and ugly, but she had to admit that without the armor it did not appear all that threatening. Neither that, nor Scree's lack of concern, made her feel any better. Keeping one eye on the creature, she tried to relax.

"So what do trolls *normally* do, exactly?"

Ping looked around to see who had spoken. A little man, with a beard and mechanical hand, was sitting at a seat on the far side of the room. He didn't look up from his desk as he spoke.

"What does you mean?" Scree was watching the sky as he spoke. Ping watched as well. They plunged into a cloud. For a moment all that could be seen was a blanket of white, then they broke through into the clear again.

"What's your specialty?"

"Ummm..." Scree looked around at the other trolls for a moment. Then he glanced towards Ping. "I don't know."

Ping didn't know what the little man really meant by the question, but she thought she knew the answer.

Kim joined the conversation then, though she kept her concentration on her task. "You said trolls were best at fighting, Scree. Back in Danyon Ford."

"Maybe."

The little man grunted. "So maybe we should get one of them to sit at the weapons' console."

"You've got to be kidding, Keeble."

Keeble shook his head. "The trolls must be a part of the six tribes, or whatever they were."

"What? Why's that?" Kim finally looked down.

"They must be. They were on one of the Hakahei worlds and they are too similar to us to be unrelated, surely."

"We don't know that."

"Of course we don't. When has that stopped us?"

"Be that as it may," Kim continued, "we can't just shove one of the trolls in the seat and let them loose. They come from a primitive world and—"

"Scree can drive— I think he does it better than you— so he obviously knows something."

"Not now, Keeb'. We don't want to kill anyone anyway, remember."

"What we want and what might get us through the next few minutes aren't necessarily the same thing."

The ship and its occupants were not quite what Ping had been expecting. She didn't know exactly what she had been expecting, but it wasn't this. It seemed they were fighting amongst themselves as much as they were fighting the monsters. And they had one of the monsters roaming free around the ship. And Scree had told the other trolls that there were worse enemies than the monsters anyway. She didn't know what to think so she decided not to think at all. Ping turned away from the conversation to look out the huge window at the front of the ship again. The sky was starting to peel way, blue becoming purple becoming black. And stars were starting to shine, far brighter than they had been from the surface of the planet during the night.

Ping looked up at Kim. "Are all the stars worlds?" she asked.

It was Tuki who answered. "Some of them. Some of them are suns with more than one world."

"But there are thousands of stars."

Tuki nodded. "Not all suns have worlds. Not all worlds have life. And there are more than thousands of stars. There are many that are too far away to see."

Ping swallowed and looked out at the stars. They were beautiful, a tapestry of light the Jugglers of Jilin could stand on to juggle the worlds. But when she had a moment to think, when she wasn't running along in Scree's wake, the worlds she had seen were more than enough. She was scared by the thought of thousands more, with any number of unknown creatures. How many would be like the zorigami and how many like trolls? And how many would not be people at all? How many would be monsters with colorful skin and the wrong number of fingers?

"The kil'ini are coming, Kim," Tuki said. "They are coming quickly."

Kim and Tuki were both working again. The ship spun around so it was facing back the way they had come. At the same time an image appeared up near the curved ceiling. The image wobbled for a moment, one way then the next, then a small, indistinct spot in the middle suddenly grew to fill the dome. It was shaped something like a fish though it was rough and lumpy and finished in a four-finned tail. The surface was green and rubbery looking and covered with dozens more fins that rippled with movement. And between the fins were muscled holes. Three big red eyes followed the Hakahei's progress and three tentacles trailed out behind.

Another creature came up beside the first though it didn't look the same. It was smaller and darker in color. The holes and fins seemed to be scattered randomly.

"That's a kil'ini?" Ping asked. "But... What is it?" And how had the picture appeared? Ping wasn't sure if it was machines or magic that made all the strange things possible.

The monster, still against the wall behind Ping, said something in a rough, growling voice. He waved his hands as well.

Meledrin spoke a moment later. "Cuto has answered you, Ping. Cuto states that the kil'ini are creatures who have chosen to carry the hurgon between the stars."

"The monsters ride inside them?"

Meledrin sniffed. "I do not think monster is an appropriate term, Ping. The hurgon are alien to us, but that does not make them monsters."

"But they attacked us for no reason."

"They did not. They are merely continuing a war we started with them many thousands of years ago."

"The zorigami do not know how to fly between the stars."

"If the zorigami were attacked as the rest of our peoples were then it is possible they flew between the stars long ago."

Ping sat back to watch the image. Other kil'ini were appearing. And there was one, hardly more than an indistinct spot, visible out the window as well. Then five were visible, racing closer.

"We're at ten kilometers per second," Kim said and Ping gaped at her. Ten kilometers a second? It hardly felt like they were moving at all. "How are the batteries going, Keeble?"

"Two hours at this speed."

"Right."

Cuto said something and Meledrin translated. "Kim, Cuto states that the kil'ini will be unable to keep up in this universe but will catch us easily if they skim."

"What's skimming?"

Meledrin asked the monster. Cuto.

"Cuto states that there are actually gaps between all the universes. The kil'ini can enter these gaps using almost no energy at all, but can stay only seconds before the energy bounces them out again closer to their destination. Then they merely go back in immediately and repeat the process."

"Right. Great. Batteries, Keeble?"

"An hour at this speed."

"Well, we're at 20 kilometers a second, so this is all the speed we've got."

Twenty kilometers a second? Ping swallowed.

"The kil'ini will catch us in fifteen minutes, Kim," Tuki said, working at the buttons on his console.

"Cuto states that it may not be a concern. The kil'ini have been tasked with guarding the planet and may choose not to follow."

But they did follow, appearing and disappearing, again and again. And each time they reappeared they were considerably closer.

It was a terrible feeling, watching as the creatures came closer and not being able to do anything other than sit and wait.

"Where's this weapon chair?" Scree asked as he watched as well. Ping thought it strange that he might also be growing more tense as the kil'ini approached.

Ping looked up and saw Kim looking at the troll, as if trying to decide if she should tell him. Eventually she reached a decision and gave a slight nod. "It's that big ball behind you. You can have a play and see what you can learn, but don't shoot at any kil'ini unless I say."

Scree looked back at her as if giving her orders some consideration. He nodded as well then unbuckled his belt and moved to the ball beside Tuki. There was a seat inside and a moment later he was strapping himself in.

After thirty seconds of quiet concentration, Scree picked a switch and the dome around the chair darkened. Small points of light, like stars, sprang into being on the surface as the gap left for the door closed. Then he sat and stared again before starting to play with the controls. Eventually he did something to make his chair inside the sphere rotated.

"Why the hell does the chair do that?" Kim asked nobody in particular.

Tuki answered quietly. "Enemies can come from all directions, Kim. Whoever is firing the weapons must be able to see all directions as well, no matter which direction the ship is facing."

Though he knew how to see, it took some time for the troll to work out what to do next. Ping saw the moment when he realized. If his hands were busy with all of the controls, then he must fire the weapons with his feet...

And he did, firing out into empty space.

"Don't, Scree." Kim said.

"I'm not hitting anything," he complained.

"I know but they might think you're trying to."

Ping wasn't sure what she wanted. The hurgon had killed all her friends. They had destroyed the Great Clock. No matter what Kim said, she could not help but think of them as the enemy, and she doubted she would ever think otherwise. In some ways she wanted Scree to fire at the kil'ini and kill them all. But at the same time, they were magnificent creatures, like none she had ever seen or imagined before. She sighed when Scree spun the seat and fired away from the planet, where there was no risk of hitting anything at all.

It wasn't long before he moved on to other controls.

Ping turned away and watched the three dimensional image above her with growing dread as the kil'ini caught up.

"The kil'ini has fired a weapon at us," Tuki said.

Ping didn't know how he knew. She had not seen anything change.

"Is it like the monster..." She looked back at Cuto, then at Meledrin. "Is it like the hurgon guns."

Kim replied with a shake of her head. But by then Ping could see it in the image as well, a metal ball coming towards them, racing ahead of the kil'ini.

"Five more have fired."

"Are they like the things the bats drop?" She remembered the balls of fire engulfing Shadon, destroying her life and the lives of her people. Nobody answered. There was no need. She clung to the arm of her seat.

"Scree you can turn the shields on," Keeble said. "I think we'll need them."

"Where? Hows?"

Out the window, a blue sheen appeared, like a mist that clung close to the ship. Ping didn't understand how it could possibly work— more magic for all she knew—

and watched out the window with her heart in her mouth as she waited to see the bomb approach. But before anything was visible at all, Kim spun the bridge away from the planet, protecting it behind the bulk of the ship, and all the eyes in the room transferred to the image above.

The bomb exploded when it hit the shields, a flare of brightness that was gone in a moment. A tracery of blue veins flickered around the outside of the ship like lightning then they were gone too.

"That didn't seem so bad," Ping said softly, looking around to see how everyone else was reacting.

"Shield integrity dropped," Keeble said, working at his controls.

"What?" Kim asked.

Another three bombs impacted before he could answer.

"Down to 75% integrity," he said into the silence that followed.

"With just four bombs?"

"You didn't think this was a real military ship, remember," Keeble said. "Maybe we're supposed to run away before we get hit. Or maybe the shields are faulty."

"Stinking lot of good that does."

"More missiles coming," Tuki said softly. "Ten of them. Twelve. Fifteen. The missiles are different, I think. They are a different color, though I don't know what that means."

"Shit."

"Sorry Kim, another five have fired. Twenty missiles heading towards us. Twenty-five. We..." He paused and looked up from his screens for the first time. For the first time, Ping realized that the moai was actually younger than she was. He suddenly looked like a boy, hoping his mother would solve all his problems. "What should we do?"

Apparently Kim didn't know. She looked at the image and said nothing. But if mother could not fix it, perhaps father could. Scree's seat came alive again, spinning to face the bottom of the ship, where the aliens were positioned. He started firing, but like the armored hurgon, the creatures didn't die easily. He used two guns, firing constantly, and the seat spun one way and the next. It made Ping sick just to watch.

"Scree what are you doing?"

"You want to die here because you think the people trying to kill us ain't our enemy?"

Twenty seconds later the closest ship exploded and a few seconds after that green blood sent energy sparking along the shields. Chunks of meat sizzled and fried. Scree had already shifted aim and kept firing. His seat shifted and twisted and spun. When the second creature exploded, the others retreated a little, but not very far. They continued firing.

The new missiles did not seem to be constructed at all. Green globules came from various parts of the kil'ini bodies, all heading directly for the *Hakahei* without fail.

"Them spitting at us," one of the trolls said.

The first of the green missiles hit.

"Shields at 50 percent," Keeble said.

Cuto spoke, startling Ping, and Meledrin translated. "Cuto states that the second, lesser missiles are used to weaken the shields. They are not as powerful, but plentiful. The constructed missiles will be used again once we are without protection."

"Thirty missiles approaching."

More struck in quick succession and Ping was sure she felt the ship lurch one way and then the next. Or perhaps it was just her heart.

"30 percent."

Another kil'ini exploded. And after that, Scree changed tactics. He continued to fire at the creatures with one gun, but used the other to hit the missiles. Five splattered a long way out from the ship leaving behind a quickly dispersing green mist. But the troll was not quick enough.

"There are four more weapons chairs down stairs," Keeble said.

"Where?" Six trolls jumped to their feet.

Keeble was working furiously. "Take the first set of stairs. Go through the door on your right, then right again."

"Do you know how to use them?" Kim asked. But the trolls were already gone.

Another flicker of blue outside. And another.

"I've transferred all the power I can into the shields," Keeble said. "They're at 40 percent. Two hours until full charge on the batteries."

More missiles and Keeble swore. "Twenty percent."

Then the trolls who had raced down stairs were firing as well. It did not surprise Ping that they could work the weapons. Even as they watched the approach of the kil'ini earlier, they had probably been watching Scree as well, taking in everything like he did himself.

But even when all five weapons were working in unison there were too many aliens and too many missiles.

"Shields 10 percent."

Ping looked from Keeble to Kim. It was obvious the woman was only just keeping control of herself.

"There's too many," Scree said fiercely. "Can't you dodge or something?"

Kim didn't reply immediately. "No. Not really."

"Flayed kittens."

There was a beeping noise. It didn't stop and outside the blue mist of the shields faded away to nothing.

"Shields are gone," Keeble said.

Ping didn't really think that needed to be said.

"What happens now?" Scree asked.

Nobody answered.

More and more of the green globules were hitting the hull though they didn't seem to do much. Ping thought she could hear them sizzling like acid. She was probably imagining it.

Scree cheered as another alien died spectacularly.

"They are firing the constructed missiles again," Tuki said.

Ping couldn't believe he sounded so calm. She turned to look.

"We're screwed," Kim said. "Shit. We're screwed."

The trolls didn't think so. They kept firing constantly, knocking out missiles and, occasionally, kil'ini as well. Hardly anything was getting through, but Ping didn't know how long they could keep it up.

But the hurgon and the ships weren't stupid.

Another two dozen missiles exploded, all well away from the ship.

Then the aliens started spitting again.

The green globules escorted the larger, deadlier missiles toward the *Hakahei*. It took the trolls four or five shots to blast the spit out of the way, and by that time it often too late.

Scree grunted as he continued to fire.

A missile struck. And another.

"Hull split in two places but not breached," Keeble said. "How do I turn off these warning lights?"

Another missiles struck and the ship started to spin, like the errant balls of the Jugglers of Jilin. Scree didn't stop firing at the kil'ini as his seat automatically adjusted to the ship's movement.

But in the next few moments Ping noticed the focus of the kil'ini changing.

So did Scree. "Hey, what's going on?" he asked as the kil'ini he was targeting turned and disappeared.

Everyone else was examining the image in the dome overhead as Tuki changed the image to include the world they'd fled.

"The multeese," Tuki said.

Ping had no idea what Tuki meant, but apparently Kim did.

"What? Where?"

But that seemed obvious enough to Ping. There was a ship— it seemed to be a long way away but if that was the case it was huge.

"It's killing the hurgon," Scree said. "Look at that. It's like they swatting flies."

"Yeah," Kim replied. "It does that."

"These the ones you was talking about?"

Kim nodded. "The multeese."

"Batteries charged in half an hour," Keeble said.

"Keeble, do the batteries charge when the power is off?"

"Yes."

Kim took a deep breath. "Right, I'm cutting the power then. Hopefully they haven't noticed us. Or they forget about us?"

Ping couldn't believe what she was hearing. "Hopefully they forget about us?" she said.

Kim shrugged. "They did last time. They seem to have a short attention span."

Ping shook her head.

"If they chase us we're dead, Ping. Let's hope they forget us."

So when Kim turned off the power, Ping sat silently in the dark and waited. It seemed like a crazy way to fight.

TUKI DID NOT KNOW WHY *HE* HAD TO EXPLAIN. He was not the one who lied to them. But Kim had bestowed the rank of Lieutenant upon him, whatever that meant, and told him that his first task was to tell Inaki, Aka'mu and Okalani the truth. And to make them understand.

"When Kim... the mo'ma... said that heaven would not be what you expected she... Well, there is no heaven." But before he even finished the sentence he knew that was the wrong thing to say. And he did not believe it was true. The others started to voice their disapproval at his words and he held up a forestalling hand. "Sorry, of course there is a heaven, but we are not from there. We are not going there now."

"But..."

"And the mo'ma... is not Poti. She is just a human."

"What do you mean, Tuki?"

Tuki did not know how to explain. He looked across at Meledrin, but the elf was sitting in the too bright light of a lamp reading one of the old books while she waited for the battery to charge. She paid him no mind.

When Kim wandered in, Tuki shifted his attention to her but she shook her head before he could even ask.

"The mo'ma is just a human, like Ko'uka said. And this is not a magical..." He had no word for vehicle that they would understand. "This is not a magical... vessel... we are in. It is a machine." But they did not understand 'machine' either.

"What are you trying to tell us?"

If he could explain that... "The globe we are in is made by men, it allows us to travel between the stars." Obvious, really. "But that is all it does. It allows us to travel very quickly. And the stars are worlds and suns."

"We know all of this, Tuki."

"Yes, but... The worlds and stars are not messages from the Mother Blower. They are controlled by gravity, and nothing more."

"But the skyglass..."

"They were made by men as well, many thousands of years ago. They let us point the sphere in the right direction, so we can travel to the other stars."

He knew they understood all the words.

"So we can read the Mother Blower's message more clearly?" Okalani smiled and nodded to her bewildered companions. The two go'gan were willing to latch on to anything at that point and a lifetime of experience meant a woman's suggestions were even more welcome.

Tuki shook his head and sighed. "In the world of humans the villages are spread out everywhere, not just along one line like the Dry River. Go one way and you will get to one village, go a different way and you can go straight to another village, without going through the first village."

"Like the ruins in the desert?"

"Yes. The villages can be anywhere. So the humans draw pictures of the land and mark on it the villages and the hills and the paths. So even if you have never been to a village, you will be able to find it."

"Can you not just get somebody to tell you which direction it is in?" Inaki asked, scratching at the back of his tattooed hand.

Tuki sighed again. "Yes, but what if the villages moved?"

"But they can not."

"What if they could, Inaki?"

"Then a picture would not help."

Tuki held up the skyglass. "What if the picture could move as well?"

The three moai looked at the glass ball. It was Aka'mu who spoke first. "So... the stars are villages? And the skyglass is a picture that shows you how to get there?"

"Yes. The picture is called a map and this is a star map." Finally, he thought they understood.

"How does it work?"

Tuki shrugged slightly. "We do not really know for sure."

"And the mo'ma?"

"Her name is Kim. She comes from a world called Earth." Tuki called up the Sol system in the skyglass and pointed to Earth. "It is many kilometers from Kiva."

"How many?"

He calculated in his head. "Nearly 663 trillion kilometers."

"Trillion?"

"In base ten, a trillion had twelve zeros after it."

"That is many kilometers," Okalani said. Inaki and Aka'mu just stared.

"Yes. It is many."

Okalani examined the 'glass, reaching out hesitantly to take it when Tuki offered it to her. "The skyglass is a map and Kim is not the Mother Blower... But are you sure that the Mother Blower, the *real* Mother Blower, did not give us the map?"

"She did not. Humans and moai all come from the same people and the same place, and it was that original people who made the skyglass. Speak the name of a star or a constellation, Okalani."

The mo'by did as she was instructed and gasped in delight when the image changed to the Archer constellation. "The mo'ma lied to you, Tuki."

"Kim lied, yes, but only because she—"

"No, her world is not called Earth. It is called Atlantis. What other lies might she have told?"

"How do you know what it is called?"

"All the stars and worlds are named." She pointed to the little boxes near each star of the constellation.

Tuki struggled to read the writing, sounding out each little symbol. The mo'by was right. "So?"

"So I read the words beside the world you pointed to and it said 'Atlantis'. I did not know what it meant at the time."

"Kim did not lie about that," Tuki replied eventually. "All the people on the world call it Earth. The name must have changed since the skyglass was made."

"I do not know Tuki. Perhaps you should—"

"She did not lie, Okalani." The mo'by was angry when Tuki cut her off. A week ago he would never have done such a thing. He swallowed and quickly tried to turn her attention to other matters. "You can move in closer on the skyglass, or further out, without naming a constellation," he said. He gave Okalani the commands that would increase and decrease the scale, and scroll in the various directions.

Okalani would have kept the 'glass to herself, but Tuki made her pass it to the two go'gan. The three of them played for half an hour, passing the ball back and forth, changing images, moving them. Tuki was still as much in awe of the 'glass as they were, but tried not to show it. And he found that he felt a little bit jealous watching them play, but contented himself with the fact that his own skyglass was in place on the bridge.

"So, what Kim said to the mo'min was not true?" Okalani asked angrily, falling back into the role of female amongst males.

"What she said is correct, Okalani. I am able to use the skyglass. So can Aka'mu and Inaki. According to the mo'min, that should not be possible. And during my pilgrimage I *did* see something in the sky that changed direction. It was not a meteor, but one of the kil'ini, and the mo'min denied its presence."

"The mo'min must watch over all the moai of Danyon Ford. Perhaps she had her reasons for saying what she did. Perhaps she was unsure what the message meant and needed time to think and consult the skyglass."

Tuki shook his head. "Perhaps if she asked the men for help occasionally she would not have to do that."

Kim entered the mess hall again, looking around to see who was present.

"We're ready to jump, Tuki. Keeble and Cuto have gotten the Ohoga engines aligned."

"So we are returning to Nexis?"

Kim shook her head. "Slight detour. We're going to Sherindel— Keeble and Mel's world."

"But why? I thought we needed to..."

"Yes, I know. We need to get the Americans flying so they can help us, but they won't be able to do anything without a dwarf or two to look after things. And like the troll said, we need more people ourselves."

"How far is it to Sherindel? How long will that take us?"

Kim shrugged. "You're the expert, you tell me."

Tuki turned back to the skyglass, held tightly in Aka'mu's hand. While Okalani was still pouting, Aka'mu and Inaki were watching him with undisguised wonder. A woman, Poti or not, admitting that a man knew more. And not just any man— a go'gan, hardly a man at all.

Tuki gave a small smile. *I am the expert.*

He took the skyglass and found Sherindel. But that on its own told him nothing. He needed to go to the bridge to use the ship's computer.

"We are going now?"

"Yes. As soon as you're ready."

"Very well." Tuki turned back to his companions. "The power will be coming on for a short while, but after that it will be dark again."

"How long for?" Inaki asked.

"I do not know, yet. It depends on how far we must jump— it will be many hours though. After we have started, I will come back and tell you."

"Very well." They all knew where the lamps were and had seen them started.

Tuki nodded to them, wondering if there was anything else he should say. A couple of weeks ago his main responsibilities were gardening and doing whatever a mo'shi asked of him. Now he was making decisions for everyone and teaching others as well. It was hard to get used to.

With a shrug he made his way to the stairs and all the way up to Level 1. Then up to the bridge.

Tuki nodded to Kim as he settled in his seat and worked out what he needed to do.

"Are we ready?" Kim asked. "Once I turn the power on the multeese will be able to see us if they're still around." She took a deep breath. "If that's the case I'll be trying to organize a jump as quickly as possible."

Tuki swallowed and nodded but when Kim turned on the ship there was no sign of the huge alien ship.

Tuki breathed a sigh of relief.

"Let's not waste any time though," Kim said. "Just in case."

So Tuki started to work. He brought up their current location, and then made the computer show both that and the world of Sherindel at the same time. There was a lot of space between. Forty-five light-years. And in the wrong direction— they would be traveling further from Nexis. That was not for him to worry about; Kim wanted to go to Sherindel.

While he worked, Kim brought the ship to a complete halt so she could more easily point it in the right direction.

Tuki wanted to do the calculations in his head. The computer could do them easily, but he liked doing the difficult sums and then using the computer to see how close he was. But Kim was rightly keen to leave the area a quickly as possible so he pressed the buttons that would do all the work. A moment later he told Kim which direction to turn and she started her part of the process.

When the ship was pointing the right direction there was a beep. "That is it, mo'min. Kim."

Kim started to accelerate. "Right. And how far is it?"

"It is 45.14 light-years."

"Well, not as bad as last time, I suppose. "

"The trip back to Nexis will be approximately seventy-five."

"Seventy-five? Damn. Well, what am I setting the timer for now?"

"That depends, mo'min."

"What are our options?"

"Well, one jump of 29 hours fifteen minutes if we start at twenty kilometers a second. Or two jumps of approximately ten hours forty-one minutes, plus two hours. Or three jumps of 6 and a half hours plus four hours."

"So, two jumps then..."

"Well, doing three jumps will also allow us to get closer to Sherindel with the final jump, so we will spend less time traveling once we get there. Also, we will have an extra two hours in the middle in which we can do things."

"Hmmm... Three jumps it is then. Let's do it."

Tuki looked at her. "You are the one with the timer, mo'min."

"Right. Of course."

Tuki strapped himself into his seat and watched out the view port a minute later as the shifting silvery sheen of the gate appeared. Five seconds later darkness descended.

For a while, he waited. Everyone waited.

"If something goes wrong…" Scree said.

Kim nodded distractedly. "If something goes wrong, there will be absolutely nothing we can do. So there really isn't any point waiting here." She sighed. "In fact, if there's an emergency, I think I'd rather die in ignorance." But she didn't get up to leave.

Tuki sat for a while longer but, while he doubted Kim's desire for ignorance, he decided he quite liked idea himself. So after a couple of minutes, he unclipped his belt and took the stairs down from the bridge. At the mess hall, he stood at the door without saying anything. The three moai sitting at the table did not notice him and continued to talk quietly.

"Tuki said it would be dark, Okalani, there is nothing to worry about," Inaki said. But he did not look completely calm himself.

"It could be dark for many reasons." Tuki could only see the back of the mo'by's head— her black hair moved as she divided her glance between her two companions. "Tuki is..."

"Tuki is a go'gan? Not any more, Okalani. He is something else now. We all are. We do not have to listen to what you say any more."

Tuki did not think that sounded very good. Everyone was supposed to be equal— men and women. Inaki was acting as if he was suddenly *better* than Okalani, or had more rights than she. Tuki cleared his throat and the three of them turned to look at him.

"Nobody said you do not have to listen to what Okalani says, Inaki," Tuki said, walking into the room and taking a seat at the table. "You have to listen, but you do not have to do as she says simply because she is a woman."

Aka'mu nodded his head, seemingly happy to forego the difficult task of choosing sides and sticking in the middle. But apparently that was not a simple option either. "But how do we know what is right?" he asked. "Before..."

"Before we could just ask a woman and she would tell us what was right?"

Aka'mu nodded.

And Tuki didn't know. Just because Kim said men and women were equal, did that make it so?

"The mo'min was in charge in Danyon ford," Okalani said, sitting up taller and straightening her robe. "And Kim is in charge here. It is obvious women are better."

For a moment, Tuki thought she was right. What proof did he have otherwise? But Okalani was using Kim in her equation to prove that women were right and women were better. "If women are better," he said, "then who are we to argue with Kim? She says we are equal."

"But—"

"I can use the skyglass, Okalani." She had not like being interrupted the first time and did not like it any more the second. Tuki hurried on. "Inaki and Aka'mu can use the skyglass. Would we be able to do that if what Kim said is wrong?"

Okalani did not reply. She studied her hands where they lay on the table. Aka'mu was studying her. He shifted slightly in his chair, as if suddenly re-examining their relationship. Would she like him as much if he could disagree with her?

"You said you would tell us how long it would be dark, Tuki," Okalani said eventually.

"Yes. It will be for nearly six and a half hours."

"Is there somewhere I can sleep?"

"Yes, I will show you."

"Very well." She rose and went to the door. Tuki collected a lamp and hurried to catch up.

When he had shown Okalani to a room where she could sleep, and made sure she had a lantern of her own, Tuki sat in a hallway and leaned back against the wall. He looked at the tattooed ants crawling on his forearm. If they were to win the battle they were fighting, against the hurgon and the multeese, all the different races on the ship would need to work together. And they were heading to Sherindel to find even more people for to crew the ship. They would need to make their differences into a strength, as the ancients intended, but Tuki found it hard to believe they could succeed at such a task when just the moai seemed to be divided by the whole desert.

Tuki closed his eyes. Not so long ago, his entire world had been the desert. It had filled his days from horizon to horizon. Now his world was endless, but the danger he faced made him feel like walls were closing in about him. It made breathing difficult. It made him wish he could go back to Danyon Ford to dig for tubers and simply do as the mo-min told him. But his task was here now. He had to help the village by staying on the *Hakahei* and doing as *Kim* told him.

Tuki took a deep breath and rose to his feet. "I have travelled far," he said, "but there is still a long way to go."

-oOo-

Other Books
By Scott J Robinson

The Bygone Wars: Book 2
All the Wars of Heaven

Kim's plans are starting to come together (well, there wasn't a lot of planning involved), but as usual things start falling apart quicker than she can pull them back together. When the crew of the *Hakahei* travel to the hurgon homeworld they find themselves in the middle of a civil war that could bring an end to everything they are fighting to save.

The hurgon might be aliens, but they are just a different type of people, and Kim can see an end to the war with them. But the Multeese are the real enemy, hanging over all her plans like a battleship over a Combi van. She doesn't know how to beat them, but if she doesn't work it out soon then all the contracts and treaties in the world aren't going to help.

And just when she thought she's at least bought herself some time, the multeese brings the fight to her. And this time, there won't be any running away.

The Last Great Hero:
The Age of Heroes
A History of Magic
An Army of Heroes

Rawk is one of the great Heroes. He has travelled the world for forty years, hunting exotic creatures, battling magic and fighting evil wherever he found it. But he has been fighting mostly mundane battles since Prince Weaver outlawed magic. And with no great deeds left to be done, Rawk is afraid he'll soon be the old man in the corner of the tavern, dreaming of the good old days and telling tales for anyone who will buy him a drink.

But when a huge wolden wolf is spied from the walls of Katamood it signals a return to a time when magic and monsters prevailed. And, as always, the city turns to Rawk to save them.

Rawk will fight to ensure the Age of Heroes doesn't slip away into history, but what if the good old days aren't quite as good as he remembers?

The Brightest Light

Kade was once the up and coming star of The Skyway Men, a ruthless criminal organization. Then he made one mistake. The another. Then one too many. Lucky to be left alive, he was banished to a backwoods skyland that flew the quietest wind-lanes.

When he's finally offered another chance Kade can't believe his luck. But ten years working a smithy and fixing crystal engines is a long time, and with a weapon like none other up for grabs, the stakes are higher than ever.

In a world of death and corruption, shady deals and dirty deeds Kade doesn't know who to trust. He doesn't know who's on which side. He doesn't even know which side *he's* on any more.

All he knows is that murder and mayhem aren't what they used to be.

About the Author

Scott J. Robinson has been writing fantasy and Science Fiction for as long as he can remember. He's had short stories and poetry published in various publications over the last 25 years.

When he isn't writing, Scott wastes too much time on Facebook. He also likes photography and recently retired from a very mediocre cricket career.

Scott lives in Woodford, a small town near Brisbane in Queensland, Australia with his wife and 3 children.

For more information visit www.tengama.com